ROBIN COOK

THREE COMPLETE NOVELS

ROBIN COOK

THREE COMPLETE NOVELS

OUTBREAK

MORTAL FEAR

MUTATION

G. P. PUTNAM'S SONS   NEW YORK

G. P. Putnam's Sons
Publishers Since 1838
200 Madison Avenue
New York, NY 10016

Library of Congress Cataloging-in-Publication Data

Cook, Robin, date
Three complete novels / Robin Cook.
p. cm.
Contents: Outbreak—Mortal fear—Mutation.
ISBN 0-399-13876-5
I. Title.
PS3553.O5545A6 1993
823'.914—dc20   93-3230 CIP

Printed in the United States of America
1 2 3 4 5 6 7 8 9 10

CONTENTS

—

OUTBREAK

*For my mother, Audrey,
who ultimately is responsible
for all this.*

PROLOGUE

ZAIRE, AFRICA
SEPTEMBER 7, 1976

A twenty-one-year-old Yale biology student by the name of John Nordyke woke up at dawn at the edge of a village north of Bumba, Zaire. Rolling over in his sweat-drenched sleeping bag, he stared out through the mesh flap of his nylon mountain tent, hearing the sounds of the tropical rain forest mixed with the noises of the awakening village. A slight breeze brought the warm, pungent odor of cow dung permeated with the acrid aroma of cooking fires. High above him he caught glimpses of monkeys skittering through the lush vegetation that shielded the sky from his view.

He had slept fitfully, and as he pulled himself upright, he was unsteady and weak. He felt distinctly worse than he had the night before, when he'd been hit by chills and fever an hour or so after dinner. He guessed he had malaria even though he'd been careful to take his chloroquine phosphate as prophylaxis against it. The problem was that it had been impossible to avoid the clouds of mosquitoes that emanated each evening from the hidden pools in the swampy jungle.

With a hesitant gait, he made his way into the village and inquired about the nearest clinic. An itinerant priest told him that there was a Belgian mission hospital in Yambuku, a small town located a few kilo-

13

meters to the east. Sick and frightened, John quickly broke camp, stuffed his tent and sleeping bag into his backpack and set out for Yambuku.

John had taken a six-month leave from college to photograph African animals, such as the highland gorilla, which were threatened by extinction. It had been his boyhood dream to emulate the famous nineteenth-century explorers who had originally opened the Dark Continent.

Yambuku was scarcely larger than the village he'd just left, and the mission hospital did not inspire confidence. It was no more than a meager collection of cinder-block buildings, all in dire need of repair. The roofs were either rusting corrugated metal or thatched like the native huts, and there seemed no signs of electricity.

After checking in with a nun, swathed in traditional attire, who spoke only French, John was sent to wait among a throng of natives in all states of debility and disease. Looking at the other patients, he wondered if he wasn't likely to catch something worse than what he already had. Finally he was seen by a harried Belgian doctor who could speak a little English, though not much. The examination was rapid, and as John had already surmised, the diagnosis was a "touch" of malaria. The doctor ordered an injection of chloroquine and advised John to return if he didn't feel better within the next day or so.

The examination over, John was sent into the treatment room to wait in line for his injection. It was at that point that he noticed the lack of aseptic technique. The nurse did not have disposable needles but merely rotated one of three syringes. John was certain that their short stay in the sterilizing solution was not nearly long enough to render them germ-free. Besides, the nurse fished them out of the fluid with her fingers. When it became his turn, he was tempted to say something, but his French was not fluent enough, and he knew he needed the medicine.

During the next few days, John was glad that he'd been silent since he soon was feeling better. He stayed in the Yambuku area, occupying himself by photographing the Budza tribesmen. They were avid hunters and eager to demonstrate their prowess to the blond foreigner. By the third day John was preparing to recommence his journey up the Zaire River, following Henry Stanley's footsteps, when his health took a rapid turn for the worse. The first thing he noticed was a violent headache, followed in rapid succession by chills, fever, nausea and diarrhea. Hoping it would pass, he took to his tent and shivered through the night, dreaming of home with clean sheets and a bathroom down the hall. By morning he felt weak and dehydrated, having vomited several times in the darkness. With great difficulty, he got his things together and made his way slowly to the mission hospital. When he arrived in the compound, he vomited bright red blood and collapsed on the clinic floor.

An hour later he woke in a room occupied by two other patients, both suffering from drug-resistant malaria.

The doctor, the same man who'd examined John on his previous visit, was alarmed by the severity of John's condition and noted some curious additional symptoms: a strange rash over his chest and small surface hemorrhages in his eyes. Although the doctor's diagnosis was still malaria, he was troubled. It was not a typical case. As an added precaution, he decided to include a course of chloramphenicol in case the boy had typhoid fever.

SEPTEMBER 16, 1976

Dr. Lugasa, District Health Commissioner for the Bumba region, glanced out the open window of his office at the expanse of the Zaire River as it shimmered in the morning sunlight. He wished it was still called the Congo with all the mystery and excitement that name invoked. Then, forcing his mind back to work, he looked again at the letter he'd just received from the Yambuku Mission Hospital concerning the deaths of an American male, one John Nordyke, and of a visiting farmer from a plantation near the Ebola River. The mission doctor claimed that their deaths had been caused by an unknown infection that spread rapidly; two patients housed with the American, four members of the planter's household who'd been caring for the farmer, and ten of the clinic's outpatients had come down with severe cases of the same illness.

Dr. Lugasa knew that he had two choices. First, he could do nothing, which was undoubtedly the wisest choice. God knew what kind of rampant endemic diseases there were out there in the bush. His second option was to fill out the bewildering array of official forms reporting the incident to Kinshasa where someone like himself, but higher on the bureaucratic ladder, would probably decide it was prudent to do nothing. Of course Dr. Lugasa knew that if he elected to fill out the forms, he would then be obligated to journey up to Yambuku, an idea that was particularly odious to him at that particularly damp, hot time of year.

With a twinge of guilt, Dr. Lugasa let the onionskin letter slip into the wastebasket.

SEPTEMBER 23, 1976

A week later Dr. Lugasa was nervously shifting his weight from one foot to the other as he watched the aged DC-3 aircraft land at the Bumba airport. First out was Dr. Bouchard, Dr. Lugasa's superior from Kinshasa. The day before, Dr. Lugasa had telephoned Dr. Bouchard to inform him that he'd just received word that a serious outbreak of an unknown disease was in progress in the area around the Yambuku Mission Hospital. It was affecting not only the local inhabitants, but the hospital staff as well. He had not mentioned the letter he'd received some seven days before.

The two doctors greeted each other on the tarmac and then climbed into Dr. Lugasa's Toyota Corolla. Dr. Bouchard asked if there was any more news from Yambuku. Dr. Lugasa cleared his throat, still upset about what he'd learned that morning from the wireless. Apparently eleven of the medical staff of seventeen were already dead, along with one hundred and fourteen villagers. The hospital was closed since there was no one well enough to run it.

Dr. Bouchard decided that the entire Bumba region had to be quarantined. He quickly made the necessary calls to Kinshasa and then told the reluctant Dr. Lugasa to arrange transportation for the next morning so they could visit Yambuku and assess the situation firsthand.

SEPTEMBER 24, 1976

The following day when the two doctors pulled into the deserted courtyard of the Yambuku Mission Hospital they were greeted by an eerie stillness. A rat scampered along the balustrade of an empty porch, and a putrid odor assaulted their senses. Holding cotton handkerchiefs over their noses, they reluctantly got out of the Land-Rover and gingerly looked into the nearest building. It contained two corpses, both beginning to decay in the heat. It wasn't until they'd peered into the third building that they found someone still alive, a nurse delirious with fever. The doctors went into the deserted operating room and put on gloves, gowns and masks in a belated attempt to protect themselves.

Still fearful for their own health, they tended to the sick nurse and then searched for more of the staff. Among nearly thirty dead, they found four other patients barely clinging to life.

Dr. Bouchard radioed Kinshasa and requested emergency aid from the Zairean Air Force to airlift several patients from the mission hospital back to the capital. But by the time the infectious disease department at the university hospital was consulted about how to isolate the patients during transport, only the nurse still lived. Isolation techniques would have to be excellent, Bouchard pointed out, because they were obviously dealing with a highly contagious and very deadly disease.

SEPTEMBER 30, 1976

The Belgian nurse airlifted to Kinshasa died at 3:00 A.M. despite six days of massive supportive therapy. No diagnosis was made, but after the autopsy, samples of her blood, liver, spleen and brain were sent to the Institut de Médicine Tropical in Antwerp, Belgium; to the Centers for Disease Control in Atlanta, U.S.A.; and to the Microbiological Research Establishment in Porton Down, England. In the Yambuku area there were now two hundred ninety-four known cases of the illness, with a fatality rate of approximately ninety percent.

OCTOBER 13, 1976

The Yambuku virus was isolated almost simultaneously at the three international laboratories. It was noted to be structurally similar to the Marburg virus, first seen in 1967 in a fatal outbreak in laboratory workers handling green monkeys from Uganda. The new virus, considerably more virulent than Marburg, was named Ebola after the Ebola River north of Bumba. It was thought to be the most deadly microorganism seen since the bubonic plague.

NOVEMBER 16, 1976

Two months after the initial outbreak, the unknown disease in Yambuku was considered successfully contained since no new cases had been reported in the area for several weeks.

DECEMBER 3, 1976

The quarantine of the Bumba region was lifted and air service reinstated. The Ebola virus had evidently returned to its original source. Where that source was remained a complete mystery. An international team of professionals, including Dr. Cyrill Dubchek of the Centers for Disease Control who had played a big role in localizing the Lassa Fever virus, had scoured the area, searching for a reservoir for the Ebola virus within mammals, birds, and insects. The virologists had no success whatsoever. Not even a clue.

LOS ANGELES, CALIFORNIA
JANUARY 14
PRESENT DAY

Dr. Rudolph Richter, a tall, dignified ophthalmologist originally from West Germany, and cofounder of the Richter Clinic in Los Angeles, adjusted his glasses and looked over the advertising proofs laid out on the circular table in the clinic's conference room. To his right was his brother and partner, William, a business-school graduate, who was examining the proofs with equal attention. The material was for the next quarter's drive for new prepaid subscribers to the clinic's health-care plan. It was aimed at young people, who as a group were relatively healthy. That was where the real money was in the prepaid health-care business, William had been quick to point out.

Rudolph liked the proofs. It was the first good thing that had happened to him that day. It was a day that had begun badly with a fender-bender on the entrance to the San Diego freeway, resulting in a nasty dent in his new BMW. Then there was the emergency surgery that had backed up the clinic. Then there was the tragic AIDS patient with some weird complication who'd coughed in his face while he tried to examine the man's retinas. And on top of everything else, he'd been bitten by one of the monkeys used in his ocular herpes project. What a day!

Rudolph picked up an ad scheduled for the L.A. *Times Sunday Magazine*. It was perfect. He nodded at William, who motioned for the ad man to continue. The next part of the presentation was a slick thirty-second TV spot slotted for the evening news. It portrayed carefree bikini-clad girls on a Malibu beach, playing volleyball with some handsome young men. It reminded Rudolph of an expensive Pepsi ad, though it extolled the concept of prepaid health maintenance as delivered by an organization like the Richter Clinic in contrast to conventional fee-for-service medicine.

Along with Rudolph and William were a handful of other staff doctors, including Dr. Navarre, Chief of Medicine. They were all directors of the clinic and held small amounts of stock.

William cleared his throat and asked if there were any questions from the staff. There were none. After the advertising people had departed, the group voiced unanimous approval of what had been presented. Then, after a brief discussion about the construction of a new satellite clinic to deal with the increase in subscribers from the Newport Beach area, the meeting was adjourned.

Dr. Richter returned to his office and cheerfully tossed the advertising proofs into his briefcase. It was a sumptuous room, considering the relatively low professional salary he drew as a physician in the group. But his salary was just incidental remuneration compared to the profits from his percentage of the outstanding stock. Both the Richter Clinic and Dr. Rudolph Richter were in sound financial shape.

After catching up on his calls, Dr. Richter made rounds on his own postoperative inpatients: two retinal detachments with difficult medical histories. Both were doing well. On his way back to his office, he thought about how little surgery he was doing as the sole ophthalmologist of the clinic. It was disturbing, but with all the ophthalmologists in town, he was lucky to have what he did. He was thankful that his brother had talked him into the clinic idea eight years ago.

Changing his white coat for a blue blazer and picking up his briefcase, Dr. Richter left the clinic. It was after 9:00 P.M., and the two-tiered parking garage was almost empty. During the day it was always full, and William was already talking about the need to expand it, not only for the spaces but for the depreciation; issues like that Rudolph didn't truly understand, nor did he want to.

Musing about the economics of the clinic, Dr. Richter was unaware of two men who had been waiting in the shadows of the garage. He remained unaware even after they fell in step behind him. The men were dressed in dark business suits. The taller of the two had an arm

19

that seemed permanently frozen into a flexed position. In his hand was a fat briefcase that he held high due to the immobility of the elbow joint.

Nearing his car, Dr. Richter sensed the footsteps behind him as they quickened in pace. An uncomfortable sensation gripped his throat. He swallowed hard and cast a nervous glance over his shoulder. He caught sight of the two men, who seemed to be coming directly toward him. As they passed beneath an overhead light, Dr. Richter could appreciate that they were carefully dressed, with fresh shirts and silk ties. That made him feel a little better. Even so, he moved more quickly, rounding the back end of his car. Fumbling for the keys, he unlocked the driver's-side door, tossed in his briefcase, and slid into the welcome smell of coach leather. He started to close the door, when a hand stopped him. Dr. Richter reluctantly raised his eyes to what turned out to be the calm, blank face of one of the men who had followed him. The suggestion of a smile crossed the man's countenance as Dr. Richter looked at him inquiringly.

Dr. Richter tried again to pull his door shut, but the man held it firmly from the outside.

"Could you tell me the time, doctor?" asked the man politely.

"Certainly," said Richter, glad to have a safe explanation for the man's presence. He glanced at his watch, but before he had a chance to speak, he felt himself rudely pulled from the car. He made a half-hearted effort to struggle, but he was quickly overwhelmed and stunned by an open-handed blow to the side of his face that knocked him to the ground. Hands roughly searched for his wallet, and he heard fabric tear. One of the men said "businessman," in what sounded like a disparaging tone, while the other said, "Get the briefcase." Dr. Richter felt his watch yanked from his wrist.

It was over as quickly as it had begun. Dr. Richter heard footsteps recede and a car door slam, then the screech of tires on the smooth concrete. For a few moments he lay without moving, glad to be alive. He found his glasses and put them on, noting that the left lens was cracked. As a surgeon, his primary concern was for his hands; they were the first thing he checked, even before he picked himself up off the ground. Getting to his feet, he began to examine the rest of himself. His white shirt and his tie were smeared with grease. A button was missing from the front of his blazer, and in its place was a small horseshoe-shaped tear. His pants were torn from the right front pocket all the way down to his knee.

"God, what a day!" he voiced to himself, thinking that being mugged made the morning's fender-bender seem trivial by comparison. After a moment's hesitation, he recovered his keys and returned to the clinic, going back to his office. He called security, then debated whether to call the L.A. police. The idea of bad publicity for the clinic made him hesitate, and really, what would the police have done? While he argued with himself, he called his wife to explain that he'd be a little later than expected. Then he went into the lavatory to examine his face in the mirror. There was an abrasion over the right cheekbone that was sprinkled with bits of parking-garage grit. As he gingerly blotted it with antiseptic, he tried to estimate how much he had contributed to the muggers' welfare. He guessed he'd had about a hundred dollars in his wallet as well as all his credit cards and identification, including his California medical license. But it was the watch that he most hated to lose; it had been a gift from his wife. Well, he could replace it, he thought, as he heard a knock on his outer door.

The security man was fawningly apologetic, saying that such a problem had never happened before, and that he wished he'd been in the area. He told Dr. Richter that he'd been through the garage only a half-hour before, on his normal rounds. Dr. Richter assured the man that he was not to blame and that his, Richter's, only concern was that steps be taken to make certain that such an incident did not recur. The doctor then explained his reasons for not calling the police.

The following day, Dr. Richter did not feel well but he attributed the symptoms to shock and the fact that he'd slept poorly. By five-thirty, though, he felt ill enough to consider canceling a rendezvous he had with his mistress, a secretary in the medical records department. In the end, he went to her apartment but left early to get some rest, only to spend the night tossing restlessly in his bed.

The next day, Dr. Richter was really ill. When he stood up from the slit lamp, he was light-headed and dizzy. He tried not to think about the monkey bite or being coughed on by the AIDS patient. He was well aware that AIDS was not transmitted by such casual contact: it was the undiagnosed superinfection that worried him. By three-thirty he had a chill and the beginnings of a headache of migraine intensity. Thinking he had developed a fever, he canceled the rest of the afternoon's appointments and left the clinic. By then he was quite certain he had the flu. When he arrived home, his wife took one look at his pale face and red-rimmed eyes, and sent him to bed. By eight o'clock, his headache was so bad that he took a Percodan. By nine, he had violent stomach cramps and diarrhea. His wife wanted to call Dr. Navarre, but Dr. Richter told her that she was being an alarmist and that he'd be fine. He took some Dalmane and fell asleep. At four o'clock he woke up and dragged himself into the bathroom, where he vomited blood. His terrified wife left him long enough to call an ambulance to take him to the clinic. He did not complain. He didn't have the strength to complain. He knew that he was sicker than he'd ever been in his life.

1

JANUARY 20

Something disturbed Marissa Blumenthal. Whether the stimulus came from within her own mind, or from some minor external change, she did not know. Nonetheless her concentration was broken. As she raised her eyes from the book in her lap she realized that the light outside the window had changed from its pale wintery white to inky blackness. She glanced at her watch. No wonder. It was nearly seven.

"Holy Toledo," muttered Marissa, using one of her expressions left over from childhood. She stood up quickly and felt momentarily dizzy. She had been sprawled out on two low-slung vinyl-covered chairs in a corner of the library of the Centers for Disease Control (CDC) in Atlanta for more hours than she cared to think about. She had made a date for that evening and had planned on being home by six-thirty to get ready.

Hefting Fields' ponderous *Virology* textbook, she made her way over to the reserve shelf, stretching her cramped leg muscles en route. She'd run that morning, but had only put in two miles, not her usual four.

"Need help getting that monster on the shelf?" teased Mrs. Campbell, the motherly librarian, buttoning her omnipresent gray cardigan. It was none too warm in the library.

As in all good humor, there was some basis in truth for Mrs. Campbell's whispered comment. The virology textbook weighed ten pounds—one-tenth as much as Marissa's hundred-pound frame. She was only five feet tall, although when people asked, she said she was five-two, though that was only in heels. To return the book, she had to swing it back and then almost toss it into place.

"The kind of help I need with this book," said Marissa, "is to get the contents into my brain."

Mrs. Campbell laughed in her subdued fashion. She was a warm, friendly person, like almost everyone at CDC. As far as Marissa was concerned, the organization had more the feeling of an academic institution than a federal agency, which it had officially become in 1973. There was a pervading atmosphere of dedication and commitment. Although the secretaries and maintenance personnel left at four-thirty, the professional staff invariably stayed on, often working into the wee hours of the morning. People believed in what they were doing.

Marissa walked out of the library, which was hopelessly inadequate in terms of space. Half the Center's books and periodicals were stored haphazardly in rooms all over the complex. In that sense the CDC was very much a federally regulated health agency, forced to scrounge for funding in an atmosphere of budget cutting. Marissa noted it also *looked* like a federal agency. The hall was painted a drab, institutional green, and the floor was covered in a gray vinyl that had been worn thin down the middle. By the elevator was the inevitable photograph of a smiling Ronald Reagan. Just beneath the picture someone had irreverently tacked up an index card that said: "If you don't like this year's appropriation, just wait until next year!"

Marissa took the stairs up one flight. Her office—it was generous to call it that; it was more cubbyhole than office—was on the floor above the library. It was a windowless storage area that might have been a broom closet at one time. The walls were painted cinder block, and there was just enough room for a metal desk, file cabinet, light and swivel chair. But she was lucky to have it. Competition for space at the Center was intense.

Yet despite the handicaps, Marissa was well aware that the CDC worked. It had delivered phenomenal medical service over the years, not only in the U.S., but in foreign countries as well. She remembered vividly how the Center had solved the Legionnaires Disease mystery a number of years back. There had been hundreds of such cases since the organization had been started in 1942 as the Office of Malaria

Control to wipe out that disease in the American South. In 1946 it had been renamed the Communicable Disease Center, with separate labs set up for bacteria, fungi, parasites, viruses and rickettsiae. The following year a lab was added for zoonoses, diseases that are animal ailments but that can be transmitted to man, like plague, rabies and anthrax. In 1970 the organization was renamed again, this time the Centers for Disease Control.

As Marissa arranged some articles in her government-issue briefcase, she thought about the past successes of the CDC, knowing that its history had been one of the prime reasons for her considering coming to the Center. After completing a pediatric residency in Boston, she had applied and had been accepted into the Epidemiology Intelligence Service (EIS) for a two-year hitch as an Epidemiology Intelligence Service Officer. It was like being a medical detective. Only three and a half weeks previously, just before Christmas, she'd completed her introductory course, which supposedly trained her for her new role. The course was in public-health administration, biostatistics and epidemiology—the study and control of health and disease in a given population.

A wry smile appeared on Marissa's face as she pulled on her dark blue overcoat. She'd taken the introductory course, all right, but as had happened so often in her medical training, she felt totally ill-equipped to handle a real emergency. It was going to be an enormous leap from the classroom to the field if and when she was sent out on an assignment. Knowing how to relate to cases of a specific disease in a coherent narrative that would reveal cause, transmission and host factors was a far cry from deciding how to control a real outbreak involving real people and a real disease. Actually, it wasn't a question of "if," it was only a question of "when."

Picking up her briefcase, Marissa turned off the light and headed back down the hall to the elevators. She'd taken the introductory epidemiology course with forty-eight other men and women, most of whom, like herself, were trained physicians. There were a few microbiologists, a few nurses, even one dentist. She wondered if they all shared her current crisis of confidence. In medicine, people generally didn't talk about such things; it was contrary to the "image."

At the completion of the training, she'd been assigned to the Department of Virology, Special Pathogens Branch, her first choice among the positions available. She had been granted her request because she'd

25

ranked number one in the class. Although Marissa had little background in virology, which was the reason she'd been spending so much time in the library, she'd asked to be assigned to the department because the current epidemic of AIDS had catapulted virology into the forefront of research. Previously it had always played second fiddle to bacteriology. Now virology was where the "action" was, and Marissa wanted to be a part of it.

At the elevators, Marissa said hello to the small group of people who were waiting. She'd met some of them, mostly those from the Department of Virology, whose administrative office was just down the hall from her cubicle. Others were strangers, but everyone acknowledged her. She might have been experiencing a crisis of confidence in her professional competence, but at least she felt welcome.

On the main floor Marissa stood in line to sign out, a requirement after 5:00 P.M., then headed to the parking area. Although it was winter, it was nothing like what she'd endured in Boston for the previous four years, and she didn't bother to button her coat. Her sporty red Honda Prelude was as she'd left it that morning: dusty, dirty and neglected. It still had Massachusetts license plates; replacing them was one of the many errands that Marissa had not yet found time to do.

It was a short drive from the CDC to Marissa's rented house. The area around the Center was dominated by Emory University, which had donated the land to the CDC in the early '40s. A number of pleasant residential neighborhoods surrounded the university, running the gamut from lower middle class to conspicuously rich. It was in one of the former neighborhoods, in the Druid Hills section, that Marissa had found a house to rent. It was owned by a couple who'd been transferred to Mali, Africa, to work on an extended birth-control project.

Marissa turned onto Peachtree Place. It seemed to her that everything in Atlanta was named "peachtree." She passed her house on the left. It was a small two-story wood-frame building, reasonably maintained except for the grounds. The architectural style was indeterminant, except for two Ionic columns on the front porch. The windows all had fake shutters, each with a heart-shaped area cut out in the center. Marissa had used the term "cute" to describe it to her parents.

She turned left at the next street and then left again. The property on which the house sat went all the way through the block, and in order for Marissa to get to the garage, she had to approach from the rear. There was a circular drive in front of the house, but it didn't connect with the rear driveway and the garage. Apparently in the past the two driveways had been connected, but someone had built a tennis court, and that had ended the connection. Now, the tennis court was so overgrown with weeds it was barely discernible.

Knowing that she was going out that evening, Marissa did not put her car in the garage, but just swung around and backed it up. As she ran up the back steps, she heard the cocker spaniel, given to her by one of her pediatric colleagues, barking welcome.

Marissa had never planned on having a dog, but six months previously a long-term romantic relationship that she had assumed was leading to marriage had suddenly ended. The man, Roger Shulman, a neurosurgical resident at Mass. General, had shocked Marissa with the news that he had accepted a fellowship at UCLA and that he wanted to go by himself. Up until that time, they had agreed that Marissa would go wherever Roger went to finish his training, and indeed Marissa had applied for pediatric positions in San Francisco and Houston. Roger had never even mentioned UCLA.

As the baby in the family, with three older brothers and a cold and dominating neurosurgeon for a father, Marissa had never had much self-confidence. She took the breakup with Roger very badly and had been barely able to drag herself out of bed each morning to get to the hospital. In the midst of her resultant depression, her friend Nancy had presented her with the dog. At first Marissa had been irritated, but Taffy—the puppy had worn the cloyingly sweet name on a large bow tied around its neck—soon won Marissa's heart, and, as Nancy had judged, it helped Marissa to focus on something besides her hurt. Now Marissa was crazy about the dog, enjoying having "life" in her home, an object to receive and return her love. Coming to the CDC, Marissa's only worry had been what to do with Taffy when she was sent out in the field. The issue weighed heavily on her until the Judsons, her neighbors on the right, fell in love with the dog and offered—no, demanded—to take Taffy anytime Marissa had to go out of town. It was like a godsend.

Opening the door, Marissa had to fend off Taffy's excited jumps until she could turn off the alarm. When the owners had first explained the system to Marissa, she'd listened with only half an ear. But now she was glad she had it. Even though the suburbs were much safer than the city, she felt much more isolated at night than she had in Boston.

She even appreciated the "panic button" that she carried in her coat pocket and which she could use to set off the alarm from the driveway if she saw unexpected lights or movement inside the house.

While Marissa looked over her mail, she let Taffy expend some of her pent-up energy racing in large circles around the blue spruce in the front yard. Without fail, the Judsons let the dog out around noon; still, from then until Marissa got home in the evening was a long time for an eight-month-old puppy to be cooped up in the kitchen.

Unfortunately, Marissa had to cut Taffy's exuberant exercise short. It was already after seven, and she was expected at dinner at eight. Ralph Hempston, a successful ophthalmologist, had taken her out several times, and though she still had not gotten over Roger, she enjoyed Ralph's sophisticated company and the fact that he seemed content to take her to dinner, the theater, a concert without pressuring her to go to bed. In fact, tonight was the first time he'd invited her to his house, and he'd made it clear it was to be a large party, not just the two of them.

He seemed content to let the relationship grow at its own pace, and Marissa was grateful, even if she suspected the reason might be the twenty-two-year difference in their ages; she was thirty-one and he was fifty-three.

Oddly enough the only other man Marissa was dating in Atlanta was four years younger than she. Tad Schockley, a microbiologist Ph.D. who worked in the same department she ultimately had been assigned to, had been smitten by her the moment he'd spied her in the cafeteria during her first week at the Center. He was the exact opposite of Ralph Hempston: socially painfully shy, even when he'd only asked her to a movie. They'd gone out a half dozen times, and thankfully he, like Ralph, had not been pushy in a physical sense.

Showering quickly, Marissa then dried herself off and put on makeup almost automatically. Racing against time, she went through her closet, rapidly dismissing various combinations. She was no fashion plate but liked to look her best. She settled on a silk skirt and a sweater she'd gotten for Christmas. The sweater came down to mid-thigh, and she thought that it made her look taller. Slipping on a pair of black pumps, she eyed herself in the full-length mirror.

Except for her height, Marissa was reasonably happy with her looks. Her features were small but delicate, and her father had actually used the term "exquisite" years ago when she'd asked him if he thought she was pretty. Her eyes were dark brown and thickly lashed, and her thick, wavy hair was the color of expensive sherry. She wore it as she had since she was sixteen: shoulder length, and pulled back from her forehead with a tortoiseshell barrette.

It was only a five-minute drive to Ralph's, but the neighborhood changed significantly for the better. The houses grew larger and were set back on well-manicured lawns. Ralph's house was situated on a large piece of property, with the driveway curving gracefully up from the street. The drive was lined with azaleas and rhododendrons that in the spring had to be seen to be believed, according to Ralph.

The house itself was a three-story Victorian affair with an octagonal tower dominating the right front corner. A large porch, defined by complicated gingerbread trim, started at the tower, extended along the front of the house and swept around the left side. Above the double-doored front entrance and resting on the roof of the porch was a circular balcony roofed with a cone that complemented the one on top of the tower.

The scene looked festive enough. Every window in the house blazed with light. Marissa drove around to the left, following Ralph's instructions. She thought that she was a little late, but there were no other cars.

As she passed the house, she glanced up at the fire escape coming down from the third floor. She'd noticed it one night when Ralph had stopped to pick up his forgotten beeper. He'd explained that the previous owner had made servants' quarters up there, and the city building department had forced him to add the fire escape. The black iron stood out grotesquely against the white wood.

Marissa parked in front of the garage, whose complicated trim matched that of the house. She knocked on the back door, which was in a modern wing that could not be seen from the front. No one seemed to hear her. Looking through the window, she could see a lot of activity in the kitchen. Deciding against trying the door to see if it was unlocked, she walked around to the front of the house and rang the bell. Ralph opened the door immediately and greeted her with a big hug.

"Thanks for coming over early," he said, helping her off with her coat.

"Early? I thought I was late."

"No, not at all," said Ralph. "The guests aren't supposed to be here until eight-thirty." He hung her coat in the hall closet.

Marissa was surprised to see that Ralph was dressed in a tuxedo.

Although she'd acknowledged how handsome he looked, she was disconcerted.

"I hope I'm dressed appropriately," she said. "You didn't mention that this was a formal affair."

"You look stunning, as always. I just like an excuse to wear my tux. Come, let me show you around."

Marissa followed, thinking again that Ralph looked the quintessential physician: strong, sympathetic features and hair graying in just the right places. The two walked into the parlor, Ralph leading the way. The decor was attractive but somewhat sterile. A maid in a black uniform was putting out hors d'oeuvres. "We'll begin in here. The drinks will be made at the bar in the living room," Ralph said.

He opened a pair of sliding-panel doors, and they stepped into the living room. A bar was to the left. A young man in a red vest was busily polishing the glassware. Beyond the living room, through an arch, was the formal dining room. Marissa could see that the table was laid for at least a dozen people.

She followed Ralph through the dining room and out into the new wing, which contained a family room and a large modern kitchen. The dinner party was being catered, and three or four people were busy with the preparations.

After being reassured that everything was under control, Ralph led Marissa back to the parlor and explained that he'd asked her to come over early in hopes that she'd act as hostess. A little surprised—after all, she'd only been out with Ralph five or six times—Marissa agreed.

The doorbell rang. The first guests had arrived.

Unfortunately, Marissa had never been good at keeping track of people's names, but she remembered a Dr. and Mrs. Hayward because of his astonishingly silver hair. Then there was a Dr. and Mrs. Jackson, she sporting a diamond the size of a golf ball. The only other names Marissa recalled afterward were Dr. and Dr. Sandberg, both psychiatrists.

Making an attempt at small talk, Marissa was awed by the furs and jewels. These people were not small-town practitioners.

When almost everyone was standing in the living room with a drink in hand, the doorbell sounded again. Ralph was not in sight, so Marissa opened the door. To her utter surprise she recognized Dr. Cyrill Dubchek, her boss at the Special Pathogens Branch of the Department of Virology.

"Hello, Dr. Blumenthal," said Dubchek comfortably, taking Marissa's presence in stride.

Marissa was visibly flustered. She'd not expected anyone from the CDC. Dubchek handed his coat to the maid, revealing a dark blue Italian-tailored suit. He was a striking man with coal black, intelligent eyes and an olive complexion. His features were sharp and aristocratic. Running a hand through his hair, which was brushed straight back from his forehead, he smiled. "We meet again."

Marissa weakly returned the smile and nodded toward the living room. "The bar is in there."

"Where's Ralph?" asked Dubchek, glancing into the crowded living room.

"Probably in the kitchen," said Marissa.

Dubchek nodded, and moved off as the doorbell rang again. This time Marissa was even more flabbergasted. Standing before her was Tad Schockley!

"Marissa!" said Tad, genuinely surprised.

Marissa recovered and allowed Tad to enter. While she took his coat, she asked, "How do you know Dr. Hempston?"

"Just from meetings. I was surprised when I got an invitation in the mail." Tad smiled. "But who am I to turn down a free meal, on my salary?"

"Did you know that Dubchek was coming?" asked Marissa. Her tone was almost accusing.

Tad shook his head. "But what difference does it make?" He looked into the dining room and then up the main staircase. "Beautiful house. Wow!"

Marissa grinned in spite of herself. Tad, with his short sandy hair and fresh complexion, looked too young to be a Ph.D. He was dressed in a corduroy jacket, a woven tie and gray flannels so worn they might as well have been jeans.

"Hey," he said. "How do you know Dr. Hempston?"

"He's just a friend," said Marissa evasively, gesturing for Tad to head into the living room for a drink.

Once all the guests had arrived, Marissa felt free to move away from the front door. At the bar, she got herself a glass of white wine and tried to mingle. Just before the group was summoned into the dining room, she found herself in a conversation with Dr. Sandberg and Dr. and Mrs. Jackson.

"Welcome to Atlanta, young lady," said Dr. Sandberg.

"Thank you," said Marissa, trying not to gawk at Mrs. Jackson's ring.

"How is it you happened to come to the CDC?" asked Dr. Jackson. His voice was deep and resonant. He not only looked like Charlton Heston; he actually sounded as if he could play Ben Hur.

Looking into the man's deep blue eyes, she wondered how to answer his seemingly sincere question. She certainly wasn't going to mention anything about her former lover's flight to L.A. and her need for a change. That wasn't the kind of commitment people expected at the CDC. "I've always had an interest in public health." That was a little white lie. "I've always been fascinated by stories of medical detective work." She smiled. At least that was the truth. "I guess I got tired of looking up runny noses and into draining ears."

"Trained in pediatrics," said Dr. Sandberg. It was a statement, not a question.

"Children's Hospital in Boston," said Marissa. She always felt a little ill at ease talking with psychiatrists. She couldn't help but wonder if they could analyze her motives better than she could herself. She knew that part of the reason she had gone into medicine was to enable her to compete with her brothers in their relationships with their father.

"How do you feel about clinical medicine?" asked Dr. Jackson. "Were you ever interested in practicing?"

"Well, certainly," replied Marissa.

"How?" continued Dr. Jackson, unknowingly making Marissa feel progressively uneasy. "Did you see yourself solo, in a group, or in a clinic?"

"Dinner is served," called Ralph over the din of conversation.

Marissa felt relieved as Dr. Jackson and Dr. Sandberg turned to find their wives. For a moment she had felt as if she were being interrogated.

In the dining room Marissa discovered that Ralph had seated himself at one end of the table and had placed her at the other. To her immediate right was Dr. Jackson, who thankfully forgot about his questions concerning clinical medicine. To her left was the silver-haired Dr. Hayward.

As the meal progressed, it became even clearer that Marissa was dining with the cream of Atlanta's medical community. These were not just doctors; they were the most successful private practitioners in the city. The only exceptions to this were Cyrill Dubchek, Tad and herself.

After several glasses of good wine, Marissa was more talkative than normal. She felt a twinge of embarrassment when she realized that the entire table was listening to her description of her childhood in Virginia. She told herself to shut up and smile, and she was pleased when the conversation switched to the sorry state of American medicine and how prepaid health-care groups were eroding the foundations of private practice. Remembering the furs and jewels, Marissa didn't feel that those present were suffering too much.

"How about the CDC?" asked Dr. Hayward, looking across at Cyrill. "Have you been experiencing budgetary constraints?"

Cyrill laughed cynically, his smile forming deep creases in his cheeks. "Every year we have to do battle with the Office of Management and Budget as well as the House Appropriations Committee. We've lost five hundred positions due to budgetary cuts."

Dr. Jackson cleared his throat: "What if there were a serious outbreak of influenza like the pandemic of 1917–1918? Assuming your department would be involved, do you have the manpower for such an eventuality?"

Cyrill shrugged. "It depends on a lot of variables. If the strain doesn't mutate its surface antigens and we can grow it readily in tissue culture, we could develop a vaccine quite quickly. How quickly, I'm not sure. Tad?"

"A month or so," said Tad, "if we were lucky. More time to produce enough to make a significant difference."

"Reminds me of the swine flu fiasco a few years ago," interjected Dr. Hayward.

"That wasn't the CDC's fault," said Cyrill defensively. "There was no doubt about the strain that appeared at Fort Dix. Why it didn't spread is anybody's guess."

Marissa felt a hand on her shoulder. Turning, she found herself looking at one of the black-dressed waitresses.

"Dr. Blumenthal?" whispered the girl.

"Yes."

"There is a phone call for you."

Marissa glanced down the table at Ralph, but he was busy talking with Mrs. Jackson. She excused herself and followed the girl to the kitchen. Then it dawned on her, and she felt a stirring of fear, like the first time she had been called at night as an intern: It had to be the CDC. After all, she was on call and she'd dutifully left Ralph's number. No one else knew she was there.

"Dr. Blumenthal?" asked the CDC operator, when Marissa picked up the phone.

The call was switched to the duty officer. "Congratulations," he said jovially. "There has been an epidemic aid request. We had a call from the California State Epidemiologist, who would like CDC help on a problem in L.A. It's an outbreak of unknown but apparently serious illness in a hospital called the Richter Clinic. We've gone ahead and made a reservation for you on Delta's flight to the coast that leaves at 1:10 A.M. We've arranged hotel accommodations at a place called the Tropic Motel. Sounds divine. Anyway, good luck!"

Replacing the receiver, Marissa left her hand on the phone for a moment while she caught her breath. She didn't feel prepared at all. Those poor, unsuspecting people in California had called the CDC expecting to get an epidemiologic expert, and instead, they were going to get her, Marissa Blumenthal. All five feet of her. She made her way back to the dining room to excuse herself and say good-bye.

2

JANUARY 21

By the time Marissa had gotten her suitcase from the baggage carousel, waited for the rent-a-car van, gotten the rent-a-car (the first one wouldn't start) and had somehow managed to find the Tropic Motel, the sky had begun to lighten.

As she signed in, she couldn't help thinking of Roger. But she wouldn't call. She'd promised herself that much several times on the flight.

The motel was depressing, but it didn't matter. Marissa didn't think she'd be spending much time there. She washed her hands and face, combed her hair and replaced her barrette. With no other plausible reason for delay, she returned to the rent-a-car and set out for the Richter Clinic. The palms of her hands were damp against the steering wheel.

The clinic was conveniently situated on a wide thoroughfare. There were few cars at that time of morning. Marissa pulled into a parking garage, took a ticket and found a spot near the entrance. The entire structure was modern, including the garage, the clinic, and what Marissa guessed was the hospital, which appeared to be seven stories tall. Getting out of the car, she stretched, then lifted out her briefcase. In it were her class notes from the epidemiology portion of the introductory course—as if that would be any help—a note pad, pencils, a small

35

textbook on diagnostic virology, an extra lipstick and a pack of chewing gum. What a joke.

Once inside, Marissa noted the familiar hospital odor of disinfectant—a smell that somehow calmed her and made her feel instantly at home. There was an information booth, but it was empty. She asked a maintenance man mopping the floor how to get to the hospital wing, and he pointed to a red stripe on the floor. Marissa followed it to the emergency room. There was little activity there, with few patients in the waiting room and only two nurses behind the main desk. Marissa sought out the on-call doctor and explained who she was.

"Oh, great!" said the ER doctor enthusiastically. "Are we glad you're here! Dr. Navarre has been waiting all night for you. Let me get him."

Marissa absentmindedly played with some paper clips. When she looked up, she realized the two nurses were staring at her. She smiled and they smiled back.

"Can I get you some coffee?" asked the taller of the two.

"That would be nice," said Marissa. In addition to her basic anxiety, she was feeling the effects of only two hours of fitful sleep on the flight from Atlanta.

Sipping the hot liquid, Marissa recalled the Berton Roueché medical detective stories in *The New Yorker*. She wished that she could be involved in a case like the one solved by John Snow, the father of modern epidemiology: A London cholera epidemic was aborted when Snow deductively isolated the problem to a particular London water pump. The real beauty of Snow's work was that he did it before the germ theory of disease was accepted. Wouldn't it be wonderful to be involved in such a clear-cut situation?

The door to the on-call room opened, and a handsome, black-haired man appeared. Blinking in the bright ER light, he came directly toward Marissa. The corners of his mouth pulled up in a big smile. "Dr. Blumenthal, we are so glad to see you. You have no idea."

As they shook hands, Dr. Navarre gazed down at Marissa. Standing next to her, he was momentarily taken aback by her diminutive size and youthful appearance. To be polite, he inquired about her flight and asked if she was hungry.

"I think it would be best to get right down to business," said Marissa.

Dr. Navarre readily agreed. As he led Marissa to the hospital conference room, he introduced himself as chief of the department of medicine. This news didn't help Marissa's confidence. She recognized that Dr. Navarre undoubtedly knew a hundred times more than she about infectious disease.

Motioning for Marissa to sit at the round conference table, Dr. Navarre picked up the phone and dialed. While the call was going through, he explained that Dr. Spenser Cox, the State Epidemiologist, was extremely eager to talk to Marissa the moment she arrived.

Wonderful, thought Marissa, forcing a weak smile.

Dr. Cox sounded equally as happy as Dr. Navarre that Marissa was there. He explained to her that unfortunately he was currently embroiled in a problem in the San Francisco Bay area involving an outbreak of hepatitis B that they thought could be related to AIDS.

"I assume," continued Dr. Cox, "that Dr. Navarre has told you that the problem at the Richter Clinic currently involves only seven patients."

"He hasn't told me anything yet," said Marissa.

"I'm sure he is just about to," said Dr. Cox. "Up here, we have almost five hundred cases of hepatitis B, so you can understand why I can't come down there immediately."

"Of course," said Marissa.

"Good luck," said Dr. Cox. "By the way, how long have you been with the CDC?"

"Not that long," admitted Marissa.

There was a short pause. "Well, keep me informed," said Dr. Cox.

Marissa handed the receiver back to Dr. Navarre, who hung up. "Let me bring you up to date," he said, switching to a standard medical monotone as he pulled some three-by-five cards from his pocket. "We have seven cases of an undiagnosed, but obviously severe, febrile illness characterized by prostration and multi-system involvement. The first patient to be hospitalized happens to be one of the cofounders of the clinic, Dr. Richter himself. The next, a woman from the medical records department." Dr. Navarre began placing his three-by-five cards on the table. Each one represented a patient. He organized them in the order in which the cases had presented themselves.

Discreetly snapping open her briefcase without allowing Dr. Navarre to see what it contained, Marissa extracted her note pad and a pencil. Her mind raced back to the courses she'd recently completed, remembering that she needed to break the information down into understandable categories. First the illness: Was it really something new? Did a problem really exist? That was the province of the simple 2×2 table and some rudimentary statistics. Marissa knew she had to characterize the illness even if she couldn't make a specific diagnosis. The next step would be to determine host factors of the victims, such as age, sex, health, eating habits, hobbies, etc., then to determine time, place and circumstances in which each patient displayed initial symptoms, in order to learn what elements of commonality existed. Then there would be the question of transmission of the illness, which might lead to the infectious agent. Finally, the host or reservoir would have to be irradicated. It sounded so easy, but Marissa knew it would be a difficult problem, even for someone as experienced as Dubchek.

Marissa wiped her moist hand on her skirt, then picked up her pencil once more. "So," she said, staring at the blank page. "Since no diagnosis has been made, what's being considered?"

"Everything," said Dr. Navarre.

"Influenza?" asked Marissa, hoping she wasn't sounding overly simplistic.

"Not likely," said Dr. Navarre. "The patients have respiratory symptoms but they do not predominate. Besides, serological testing has been negative for influenza virus in all seven patients. We don't know what they have, but it is not influenza."

"Any ideas?" asked Marissa.

"Mostly negatives," said Dr. Navarre. "Everything we've tested has been negative: blood cultures, urine cultures, sputum cultures, stool cultures, even cerebrospinal fluid cultures. We thought about malaria and actually treated for it, though the blood smears were negative for the parasites. We even treated for typhoid, with either tetracycline or chloramphenicol, despite the negative cultures. But, just like with the antimalarials, there was no effect whatsoever. The patients are all going downhill no matter what we do."

"You must have some kind of differential diagnosis," said Marissa.

"Of course," responded Dr. Navarre. "We've had a number of infectious disease consults. The consensus is that it is a viral problem, although leptospirosis is still a weak contender." Dr. Navarre searched through his index cards, then held one up. "Ah, here are the current differential diagnoses: leptospirosis, as I mentioned; yellow fever; dengue; mononucleosis; or, just to cover the bases, some other enteroviral, arboviral or adenoviral infection. Needless to say, we've made about as much progress in the diagnostic realm as the therapeutic.''

"How long has Dr. Richter been hospitalized?" asked Marissa.

"This is his fifth day. I think you should see the patients to have an idea of what we are dealing with." Dr. Navarre stood up without waiting for Marissa's response. She found she had to trot to keep up with him. They went through swinging doors and entered the hospital proper. Nervous as she was, Marissa could not help being impressed by the luxurious carpeting and almost hotel-like decor.

She got on the elevator behind Dr. Navarre, who introduced her to an anesthesiologist. Marissa returned the man's greeting, but her thoughts were elsewhere. She was certain that her seeing the patients at that moment was not going to accomplish anything except to make her feel "exposed." This issue had not occurred to her while taking the introductory course back in Atlanta. Suddenly it seemed like a big problem. Yet what could she say?

They arrived at the nurses' station on the fifth floor. Dr. Navarre took the time to introduce Marissa to the night staff, who were making their initial preparations to change shifts.

"All seven patients are on this floor," said Dr. Navarre. "It has some of our most experienced personnel. The two in critical condition are in separate cubicles in the medical intensive-care unit just across the hall. The rest are in private rooms. Here are the charts." With an open palm, he thumped a pile stacked on the corner of the counter top. "I assume you'd like to see Dr. Richter first." Dr. Navarre handed Richter's chart to Marissa.

The first thing she looked at was the "vital-sign" sheet. Beginning his fifth hospital day, she noticed that the doctor's blood pressure was falling and his temperature was rising. Not a good omen. Rapidly she perused the chart. She knew that she'd have to go over it carefully later. But even a cursory glance convinced her that the workup had been superb, better than she could have done herself. The laboratory work had been exhaustive. Again she wondered what in God's name she was doing there pretending to be an authority.

Going back to the beginning of the chart, Marissa read the section entitled "history of the present illness." Something jumped out at her right away. Six weeks previous to the onset of symptoms Dr. Richter had attended an ophthalmological convention in Nairobi, Kenya.

She read on, her interest piqued. One week prior to his illness, Dr.

Richter had attended an eyelid surgery conference in San Diego. Two days prior to admission he'd been bitten by a Cercopithecus aethiops, whatever the hell that was. She showed it to Dr. Navarre.

"It's a type of monkey," said Dr. Navarre. "Dr. Richter always has a few of them on hand for his ocular herpes research."

Marissa nodded. She glanced again at the laboratory values and noted that the patient had a low white count, a low ESR and low thrombocytes. Other lab values indicated liver and kidney malfunction. Even the EKG showed mild abnormalities. This guy was virulently sick.

Marissa laid the chart down on the counter.

"Ready?" questioned Dr. Navarre.

Although Marissa nodded that she was, she would have preferred to put off confronting the patients. She had no delusions of grandeur that she would uncover some heretofore missed, but significant, physical sign, and thereby solve the mystery. Her seeing the patients at that point was pure theater and, unfortunately, risky business. She followed Dr. Navarre reluctantly.

They entered the intensive-care unit, with its familiar backdrop of complicated electronic machinery. The patients were immobile victims, secured with tangles of wires and plastic tubing. There was the smell of alcohol, the sound of respirators and cardiac monitors. There was also the usual high level of nursing activity.

"We've isolated Dr. Richter in this side room," said Dr. Navarre, stopping at the closed doorway. To the left of the door was a window, and inside the room Marissa could make out the patient. Like the others in the unit, he was stretched out beneath a canopy of intravenous bottles. Behind him was a cathode-ray tube with a continuous EKG tracing flashing across its screen.

"I think you'd better put on a mask and gown," said Dr. Navarre. "We're observing isolation precautions on all the patients for obvious reasons."

"By all means," said Marissa, trying not to sound too eager. If she had her way, she'd climb into a plastic bubble. She slipped on the gown and helped herself to a hat, mask, booties, and even rubber gloves. Dr. Navarre did likewise.

Unaware she was doing it, Marissa breathed shallowly as she looked down at the patient, who, in irreverent vernacular, looked as if he was about to "check out." His color was ashen, his eyes sunken, his skin slack. There was a bruise over his right cheekbone; his lips were dry, and dried blood was caked on his front teeth.

As Marissa stared down at the stricken man, she didn't know what to do; yet she self-consciously felt obliged to do something, with Dr. Navarre hanging over her, watching her every move. "How do you feel?" asked Marissa. She knew it was a stupid, self-evident question the moment it escaped from her lips. Nonetheless Richter's eyes fluttered open. Marissa noticed some hemorrhages in the whites.

"Not good," admitted Dr. Richter, his voice a hoarse whisper.

"Is it true you were in Africa a month ago?" she asked. She had to lean over to hear the man, and her heart went out to him.

"Six weeks ago," said Dr. Richter.

"Did you come in contact with any animals?" asked Marissa.

"No," managed Dr. Richter after a pause. "I saw a lot but didn't handle any."

"Did you attend anyone who was ill?"

Dr. Richter shook his head. Speaking was obviously difficult for him.

Marissa straightened up and pointed to the abrasion under the patient's right eye. "Any idea what this is?" she asked Dr. Navarre.

Dr. Navarre nodded. "He was mugged two days before he got sick. He hit his cheek on the pavement."

"Poor guy," said Marissa, wincing at Dr. Richter's misfortune. Then, after a moment, she added, "I think I've seen enough for now."

Just inside the door leading back to the ICU proper, there was a large frame holding a plastic bag. Both Marissa and Dr. Navarre peeled off their isolation apparel and returned to the fifth-floor nurses' station. Compulsively, Marissa washed her hands in the sink.

"What about the monkey that bit Dr. Richter?" she asked.

"We have him quarantined," said Dr. Navarre. "We've also cultured him in every way possible. He appears to be healthy."

They seemed to have thought of everything. Marissa picked up Dr. Richter's chart to see if his conjunctival hemorrhages had been noted. They had.

Marissa took a deep breath and looked over at Dr. Navarre, who was watching her expectantly. "Well," she said vaguely, "I've got a lot of work to do with these charts." Suddenly she remembered reading about a category of disease called "viral hemorrhagic fever." The diseases were extremely rare, but deadly, and a number of them came

41

from Africa. Hoping to add something to the tentative diagnoses already listed by the clinic doctors, she mentioned the possibility.

"VHF was already brought up," said Dr. Navarre. "That was one of the reasons we called the CDC so quickly."

So much for that "zebra" diagnosis, thought Marissa, referring to a medical maxim that when you hear hoof-beats, think of horses, not zebras.

To her great relief, Dr. Navarre was paged for an emergency. "I'm terribly sorry," he said, "but I'm needed in the ER. Is there anything I can do before I go?"

"Well, I think it would be better to improve the isolation of the patients. You've already moved them to the same general area of the hospital. But I think you should place them in a completely isolated wing and begin complete barrier nursing, at least until we have some idea as to the communicability of the disease."

Dr. Navarre stared at Marissa. For a moment she wondered what he was thinking. Then he said, "You're absolutely right."

Marissa took the seven charts into a small room behind the nurses' station. Opening each, she learned that besides Dr. Richter, there were four women and two men who presumably had the same illness. Somehow, they all had to have had direct contact with each other or been exposed to the same source of contamination. Marissa kept reminding herself that her method of attack on a field assignment, particularly her first, was to gather as much information as she could and then relay it to Atlanta. Going back to Dr. Richter's chart, Marissa read everything, including the nurses' notes. On a separate sheet in her notebook, she listed every bit of information that could possibly have significance, including the fact that the man had presented with an episode of hematemesis, vomiting blood. That certainly didn't sound like influenza. The whole time she was working her mind kept returning to the fact that Dr. Richter had been in Africa six weeks previously. That had to be significant even though a month's incubation was unlikely, given the symptomology, unless he had malaria, which apparently he did not. Of course there were viral diseases like AIDS with longer incubation periods, but AIDS was not an acute viral infectious disease. The incubation period for such a disease was usually about a week, give or take a few days. Marissa painstakingly went through all the charts, amassing diverse data on age, sex, life-style, occupation and living environment, and recording her findings on a separate page in her notebook for each of the patients. Rather quickly, she realized that she was dealing with a diverse group of people. In addition to Dr. Richter, there was a secretary, a woman who worked in medical records at the Richter Clinic; two housewives; a plumber; an insurance salesman and a real estate broker. Opportunity for commonality seemed remote with a group this diverse, yet all of them must have been exposed to the same source.

Reading the charts also gave Marissa a better clinical picture of the illness she was dealing with. Apparently it began rather suddenly, with severe headaches, muscle pain and high fever. Then the patients experienced some combination of abdominal pain, diarrhea, vomiting, sore throat, cough and chest pain. A shiver went down Marissa's spine as she thought about having been exposed to the disease.

Marissa rubbed her eyes. They felt gritty from lack of sleep. It was time to visit the rest of the patients whether she wanted to or not. There were a lot of gaps, particularly in activities of each patient in the days directly preceding their illness.

She started with the medical secretary, who was located in a room next to Dr. Richter's in the ICU, and then worked her way through to the last patient to be admitted. Before seeing each case, she carefully dressed in full protective clothing. All the patients were seriously ill, and none felt much like talking. Still, Marissa went through her list of questions, concentrating on whether each patient was acquainted with any of the other people who were ill. The answer was always no, except that each one knew Dr. Richter, and all were members of the Richter Clinic health plan! The answer was so obvious she was surprised that no one seemed to have spotted it. Dr. Richter might have spread the disease himself since he might even have been in contact with the medical secretary. She asked the ward clerk to call for all the patients' clinic outpatient records.

While she was waiting, Dr. Navarre called. "I'm afraid we have another case," he said. "He's one of the lab techs here at the clinic. He's in the emergency room. Do you want to come down?"

"Is he isolated?" asked Marissa.

"As well as we can do it down here," said Dr. Navarre. "We're preparing an isolation wing upstairs on the fifth floor. We will move all the cases there the moment it is ready."

"The sooner the better," said Marissa. "For the time being, I recommend that all nonessential lab work be postponed."

"That's okay by me," said Dr. Navarre. "What about this boy down here? Do you want to see him?"

"I'm on my way," said Marissa.

En route to the ER, Marissa could not shake the feeling that they were on the brink of a major epidemic. Concerning the lab tech, there were two equally disturbing possibilities: the first was that the fellow had contracted the illness in the same fashion as the others, i.e., from some active source of deadly virus in the Richter Clinic; the second, more probable in Marissa's estimation, was that the lab tech had been exposed to the agent from handling infected material from the existing cases.

The ER personnel had placed the new patient in one of the psychiatric cubicles. There was a Do Not Enter sign on the door. Marissa read the technician's chart. He was a twenty-four-year-old male by the name of Alan Moyers. His temperature was 103.4. After donning protective gown, mask, hat, gloves and booties, Marissa entered the tiny room. The patient stared at her with glazed eyes.

"I understand you're not feeling too well," said Marissa.

"I feel like I've been run over by a truck," said Alan. "I've never felt this bad, even when I had the flu last year."

"What was the first thing you noticed?"

"The headache," said Alan. He tapped his fingers against the sides of his forehead. "Right here is where I feel the pain. It's awful. Can you give me something for it?"

"What about chills?"

"Yeah, after the headache began, I started to get them."

"Has anything abnormal happened to you in the lab in the last week or so?"

"Like what?" asked Alan, closing his eyes. "I did win the pool on the last Lakers game."

"I'm more interested in something professional. Were you bitten by any animals?"

"Nope. I never handle any animals. What's wrong with me?"

"How about Dr. Richter? Do you know him?"

"Sure. Everybody knows Dr. Richter. Oh, I remember something. I stuck myself with a vacu-container needle. That never happened to me before."

"Do you remember the patient's name on the vacu-container?"

"No. All I remember is that the guy didn't have AIDS. I was worried about that, so I looked up his diagnosis."

"What was it?"

"Didn't say. But it always says AIDS if it is AIDS. I don't have AIDS, do I?"

"No, Alan, you don't have AIDS," said Marissa.

"Thank God," said Alan. "For a moment there, I was scared."

Marissa went out to find Dr. Navarre, but he was occupied with a cardiac arrest that had just been brought in by ambulance. Marissa asked the nurse to tell him that she was going back to the fifth floor. Returning to the elevators, Marissa began organizing her thoughts to call Dr. Dubchek.

"Excuse me."

Marissa felt a tap on her arm and turned to face a stocky man with a beard and wire-rimmed glasses. "Are you Dr. Blumenthal from the CDC?" asked the man.

Nonplussed at being recognized, Marissa nodded. The man stood blocking her entrance to the elevator. "I'm Clarence Herns, with the L.A. *Times*. My wife works the night shift up in the medical ICU. She told me that you were here to see Dr. Richter. What is it the man has?"

"At this point, no one knows," said Marissa.

"Is it serious?"

"I imagine your wife can answer that as well as I."

"She says the man is dying and that there are six other similar cases, including a secretary from medical records. Sounds to me like the beginnings of an epidemic."

"I'm not sure that 'epidemic' is the right word. There does seem to be one more case today, but that's the only one for two days. I hope it will be the last, but no one knows."

"Sounds scary," said the reporter.

"I agree," said Marissa. "But I can't talk any longer. I'm in a hurry."

Dodging the insistent Mr. Herns, Marissa boarded the next elevator and returned to the cubicle behind the fifth-floor nurses' station and put through a collect call to Dr. Dubchek. It was quarter-to-three in Atlanta, and she got Dubchek immediately.

"So, how's your first field assignment?" he asked.

"It's a bit overwhelming," said Marissa. Then, as succinctly as she could, she described the seven cases she'd seen, admitting that she had not learned anything that the Richter Clinic doctors didn't already know.

"That shouldn't bother you," said Dubchek. "You have to keep in

45

mind that an epidemiologist looks at data differently than a clinician, so the same data can mean different things. The clinician is looking at each case in particular, whereas you are looking at the whole picture. Tell me about the illness.''

Marissa described the clinical syndrome, referring frequently to her note pad. She sensed that Dubchek was particularly interested in the fact that two of the patients had vomited blood, that another had passed bloody diarrhea and that three had conjunctival hemorrhages in their eyes. When Marissa said that Dr. Richter had been to an ophthalmology meeting in Africa, Dubchek exclaimed, "My God, do you know what you are describing?"

"Not exactly," said Marissa. It was an old medical-school ploy: try to stay on neutral ground rather than make a fool of yourself.

"Viral hemorrhagic fever," said Dubchek, "and if it came from Africa, it would be Lassa Fever. Unless it was Marburg or Ebola. Jesus Christ!"

"But Richter's visit was over six weeks ago."

"Darn," said Dubchek, almost angrily. "The longest incubation period for that kind of fulminating illness is about two weeks. Even for quarantine purposes, twenty days is considered adequate."

"The doctor was also bitten by a monkey two days before he became ill," offered Marissa.

"And that's too *short* an incubation period. It should be five or six days. Where's the monkey now?"

"Quarantined," said Marissa.

"Good. Don't let anything happen to that animal, particularly if it dies. We've got to test it for virus. If the animal is involved, we have to consider the Marburg virus. In any case, the illness certainly sounds like a viral hemorrhagic fever, and until proven otherwise, we'd better consider it as such. We've worried about something like this happening for some time; the problem is that there's no vaccine and no treatment."

"What about the mortality rate?" asked Marissa.

"High. Tell me, does Dr. Richter have a skin rash?"

Marissa couldn't remember. "I'll check."

"The first thing I want you to do is draw bloods, obtain urine samples, and do throat swabs for viral culture on all seven cases, and have them rushed to the CDC. Use Delta's small-package service. That will be the fastest way. I want you personally to draw the blood, and for Christ's sake be careful. From the monkey, too, if you can. Pack the samples in dry ice before shipping them."

"I've just seen what might be another case," said Marissa. "One of the clinic's lab techs."

"Include him, too. It sounds increasingly serious. Make sure that all the patients are totally isolated with complete barrier nursing. And tell whoever is in charge not to do any lab work until I get there."

"I have," said Marissa. "You're coming yourself?"

"You bet I am," said Dubchek. "This could be a national emergency. But it is going to take some time to prepare the Vickers Mobile Lab. Meanwhile, start setting up a quarantine for contacts, and try to get in touch with the people who sponsored that eye meeting in Africa and see if any of the other doctors who went are ill. And one other thing: don't say anything to the press. With all the publicity about AIDS, I don't think the public could deal with the threat of another fatal viral disease. There could be widespread panic. And Marissa, I want you to wear full protective clothing, including goggles, when you see the patients. The pathology department should have them if no one else does. I'll be there as soon as possible."

Hanging up, Marissa experienced a rush of anxiety. She wondered if she'd already exposed herself to the virus. Then she worried about having already talked to Clarence Herns from the L.A. *Times*. Well, what was done was done. She was glad that Dubchek was coming. She knew she'd been in over her head from the moment she'd arrived in L.A.

After putting in a call for Dr. Navarre, Marissa had one of the nurses help her get the materials ready to draw blood from the patients. She needed vacu-containers with anticoagulants, plastic bags, and sodium hypochlorite to decontaminate the outside of the bags. She also needed urine containers and throat swabs. Then she phoned the micro lab and asked to have containers of viral transport media sent up, along with shipment containers and dry ice. When Dr. Navarre called, she related what Dubchek had said about complete barrier nursing and about no lab tests until he'd arrived with a special facility. She also mentioned that they had better get together to talk about systematically quarantining all contacts. Dr. Navarre agreed, shocked to hear that Dubchek thought they might be dealing with viral hemorrhagic fever.

Following Dubchek's advice, Marissa got goggles from pathology. She'd never thought about catching an illness through her eyes, but she was aware that their surface was a mucous membrane and was obviously as available to viral assault as her nasal mucosa. When she was fully attired in hood, goggles, mask, gown, gloves and booties, she went to Dr. Richter's cubicle to begin her sampling.

Before she started, she examined him for a skin rash. His arms were clear, but he did have a curious red area about the size of a quarter on his right thigh. Lifting up his hospital gown, Marissa noted a fine, but definite, maculopapular eruption covering most of his trunk. She was impressed that Dubchek had anticipated it.

She drew the blood first, then filled the urine container from the catheter bag. After each was sealed, she washed its exterior with sodium hypochlorite, then put it in a second bag. After the exterior of the second bag was washed in the disinfectant, she allowed it to be removed from the room.

Disposing of the hood, mask, gown, gloves and booties, and then donning new ones, Marissa went on to the next patient, the medical secretary, whose name was Helen Townsend. Marissa repeated the same procedures she'd done on Dr. Richter, including looking for skin eruptions. Helen also had a faint rash on her trunk, but no red circle on her thigh or elsewhere. She seemed less ill than Richter, but none of the patients appeared well enough to question Marissa much as she went about her sampling. Only Alan Moyers could muster the strength to offer some objections. At first he refused to allow Marissa to draw blood unless she told him what his diagnosis was. He was terrified. When Marissa told him the truth, that she did not know what he had and that that was why she needed the samples, he finally gave in.

As for the monkey, Marissa didn't even attempt to get a blood sample. The animal keeper was out for the day, and she had no intention of trying to handle the animal alone. The monkey looked healthy enough, but was not friendly. He threw feces at Marissa through the mesh of his cage.

Once Marissa completed the packing, making certain that all the screw caps were tightly in place so that carbon dioxide from the dry ice could not penetrate the samples, she personally rode out to the airport and sent the boxes on their way to Atlanta. Luckily she got them on a convenient nonstop.

Back at the Richter Clinic, Marissa made a detour to the small clinic library. There were a few standard texts there that included sections on viral diseases. She quickly scanned the entries for Lassa Fever, Marburg and Ebola virus. Then she understood Dubchek's excited reaction on the telephone. These were the most deadly viruses known to man.

Arriving back on the fifth floor, Marissa found that all eight patients had been isolated in a separate wing. She also found that the clinic outpatient records she'd ordered had arrived. After putting in a call for Dr. Navarre, Marissa sat down and began to study the charts.

The first belonged to Harold Stevens, the real estate broker. She started from the back and immediately discovered that the last outpatient entry was a visit to Dr. Richter: Harold Stevens had chronic open-angle glaucoma and saw Dr. Richter on a regular basis. His last checkup had been on January 15, four days before he was admitted to the hospital.

With a sense of growing certainty Marissa looked at the last entry on each chart. There it was. Each patient had seen Dr. Richter on either the fifteenth or the sixteenth of January. All except Helen Townsend, the secretary from medical records, and Alan, the lab tech. The last entry in Ms. Townsend's outpatient file recorded a visit to an OB-GYN man for cystitis. Alan had seen an orthopod the previous year for a sprained ankle he'd suffered in a hospital basketball league. Except for the medical secretary and the lab tech, there was the strong suggestion that Dr. Richter was the source of the illness. The fact that he'd seen five of the patients just before he developed symptoms had to be significant.

Marissa could explain the lab tech getting the illness by his sticking himself with a contaminated needle, but she couldn't immediately explain Helen Townsend. Marissa had to assume that Helen had seen Dr. Richter sometime earlier in the week. She had come down with the illness just forty-eight hours after the doctor. Maybe he had spent a lot of time in medical records earlier that week.

Marissa's musings were interrupted by the ward clerk, who said that Dr. Navarre had called to ask if Marissa would kindly come down to the hospital conference room.

Returning to the room where she'd started the day reminded Marissa of how long she'd been working. She felt bone weary as Dr. Navarre closed the door and introduced the other person who was present. He was William Richter, Dr. Richter's brother.

"I wanted to thank you personally for being here," said William. Although he was impeccably dressed in a pin-striped suit, his haggard face was mute testimony to his lack of sleep. "Dr. Navarre has told me your tentative diagnosis. I want to assure you that we will support your effort to contain this illness to the limits of our resources. But we are also concerned about the negative impact the situation could have on our clinic. I hope that you agree that no publicity would be the best publicity."

Marissa felt mildly outraged, when so many lives were at stake, but Dubchek himself had said essentially the same thing.

"I understand your concern," she said, uncomfortably aware that she had already spoken to a reporter. "But I think we have to initiate further quarantine measures." Marissa went on to explain that they would have to separate the possible contacts into primary and secondary contacts. Primary contacts would be those people who had spoken with or touched one of the current eight patients. Secondary contacts would be anyone who had had contact with a primary contact.

"My God," said Dr. Navarre. "We're talking about thousands of people."

"I'm afraid so," said Marissa. "We're going to need all the manpower the clinic can spare. We'll also tap the resources of the State Health Department."

"We'll provide the manpower," said Mr. Richter. "I'd prefer to keep this 'in-house.' But shouldn't we wait until we actually have a diagnosis?"

"If we wait, it may be too late," said Marissa. "We can always call off the quarantine if it is unnecessary."

"There's no way we'll keep this from the press," moaned Mr. Richter.

"To be truthful," said Marissa, "I think the press can play a positive role by helping us reach all the contacts. Primary contacts must be instructed to stay as isolated as possible for a week and to take their temperatures twice a day. If they run a fever of 101° or over, they'll have to come to the clinic. Secondary contacts can go about their business but should still take their temperatures once a day."

Marissa stood up and stretched. "When Dr. Dubchek arrives he may have some suggestions. But I believe what I've outlined is standard CDC procedure. I'll leave its implementation up to the Richter Clinic. My job is to try to find out where the virus originated."

Leaving two stunned men in her wake, Marissa left the conference room. Passing from the hospital to the clinic building, she approached the clinic information booth, asking directions to Dr. Richter's office. It was on the second floor, and Marissa went directly up.

The door was closed but unlocked. Marissa knocked and entered. Dr. Richter's receptionist was dutifully behind her desk. Apparently she hadn't expected company, because she quickly stubbed out a cigarette and put the ashtray in one of the desk drawers.

"Can I help you?" she asked. She was fiftyish with silver-gray, tightly permed hair. Her name tag said Miss Cavanagh. Reading glasses perched on the very end of her nose, their temple pieces connected by a gold chain that went around her neck.

Marissa explained who she was, adding, "It's important that I try to determine how Dr. Richter contracted his illness. To do that, I want to reconstruct his schedule for a week or two prior to his getting sick. Could you do that for me? I'm going to ask his wife to do the same."

"I suppose I could," said Miss Cavanagh.

"Did anything out of the ordinary happen that you can recall?"

"Like what?" asked Miss Cavanagh, with a blank face.

"Like his being bitten by a monkey or getting mugged in the parking garage!" Marissa's voice had a sharp edge to it.

"Those things did happen," said Miss Cavanagh.

"I realize that," said Marissa. "How about anything else odd or different?"

"I can't think of anything at the moment. Wait, he did dent his car."

"Okay, that's the idea," encouraged Marissa. "Keep thinking. And by the way, did you make the arrangements for his African medical meeting?"

"Yes."

"How about the San Diego meeting?"

"That too."

"I would like to have the phone numbers of the sponsoring organizations. If you could look them up for me, I'd appreciate it. Also I'd like to have a list of all the patients Dr. Richter saw during the two weeks before his illness. And finally: do you know Helen Townsend?"

Miss Cavanagh took her glasses off her nose and let them hang on their chain. She sighed disapprovingly. "Does Helen Townsend have the same illness as Dr. Richter?"

"We believe she does," said Marissa, watching Miss Cavanagh's face. The receptionist knew something about Helen Townsend, but she seemed reluctant to speak, toying with the keys of her typewriter. "Was Helen Townsend a patient of Dr. Richter's?" Marissa prodded.

Miss Cavanagh looked up. "No, she was his mistress. I warned him about her. And there: she gave him some disease. He should have listened to me."

"Do you know if he saw her just before he got sick?"

"Yes, the day before."

Marissa stared at the woman. Helen Townsend didn't give Dr. Richter the disease; it was the other way around. But she didn't say anything. It all fit into place. She could now relate all the known cases to Dr. Richter. Epidemiologically, that was extremely important. It meant that Dr. Richter was an index case and that he, and only he, had been exposed to the unknown reservoir of the virus. Now it was even more important for her to reconstruct the man's schedule in minute detail.

Marissa asked Miss Cavanagh to start working on an outline of Dr. Richter's schedule for the past two weeks. She told the woman that she'd be back, but if needed, she could be paged through the hospital operator.

"Can I ask you a question?" said Miss Cavanagh timidly.

"Of course," said Marissa, with a hand on the door.

"Is there a chance I might get ill?"

Marissa had been suppressing the thought because she didn't want to frighten the woman, but she could not lie. After all, the secretary would have to be considered a primary contact.

"It's possible," said Marissa. "We will be asking you to restrict some of your activities during the next week or so, and I'd advise you to check your temperature twice a day. Personally, however, I think you will be fine since you haven't experienced any symptoms so far."

Back at the hospital, Marissa fought off her own fears and her developing fatigue. She had too much to do. She had to go over the clinic charts in detail. She hoped to find a reason why some of Dr. Richter's patients had gotten the disease and others hadn't. Also Marissa wanted to call Dr. Richter's wife. Between the wife and the secretary, she hoped she could construct a reasonably complete diary of the man's activities during the two weeks before he became ill.

Returning to the fifth floor, Marissa ran into Dr. Navarre. He looked as tired as Marissa felt. "Dr. Richter's condition is deteriorating," he said. "He's bleeding from everywhere: injection sites, gums, GI tract. He's on the brink of kidney failure, and his blood pressure is way down. The interferon we gave him had no effect whatsoever, and none of us knows what else to try."

"What about Helen Townsend?" asked Marissa.

"She's worse, too," said Dr. Navarre. "She's also starting to bleed." He sat down heavily.

Marissa hesitated for a minute and then reached for the phone. She placed another collect call to Atlanta, hoping Dubchek was already on his way. Unfortunately, he wasn't. He came on the line.

"Things are pretty bad here," reported Marissa. "Two patients are experiencing significant hemorrhagic symptoms. Clinically, it is looking more and more like viral hemorrhagic fever, and no one knows what to do for these people."

"There's little that can be done," said Dubchek. "They can try heparinization. Otherwise, supportive therapy—that's about it. When we make a specific diagnosis we may be able to use hyperimmune serum, if it is available. On that track, we've already got your samples, and Tad has begun processing them."

"When will you be coming?" asked Marissa.

"Shortly," said Dubchek. "We've got the Vickers Mobile Isolation Lab all packed."

Marissa woke up with a start. Thankfully, no one had come into the little room behind the nurses' station. She looked at her watch. It was ten-fifteen at night. She'd only been asleep for five or ten minutes.

Getting to her feet, she felt dizzy. Her head ached and she had the beginnings of a sore throat. She prayed that her symptoms were a product of exhaustion and not the beginnings of viral hemorrhagic fever.

It had been a busy evening. Four more cases had presented themselves in the ER, all complaining of severe headache, high fever and vomiting. One already had hemorrhagic signs. The patients were all family members of the previous victims, underlining the need for strict quarantine. The virus was already into the third generation. Marissa had prepared viral samples and had them shipped to Atlanta by an overnight carrier.

Recognizing that she was at the limit of her strength, Marissa decided to go back to her motel. She was just leaving when the floor nurse said Dr. Richter's wife was able to see her. Realizing it would be cruel to put her off, Marissa met her in the visitors' lounge. Anna Richter, a well-dressed, attractive woman in her late thirties, did her best to fill in her husband's schedule over the past two weeks, but she was desperately upset, not just alarmed about her husband but fearful for their two young children as well. Marissa was reluctant to press her for too much detail. Mrs. Richter promised to provide a more complete chronology the next day. Marissa walked her to the doctor's BMW. Then she found her own car and drove to the Tropic Motel where she fell directly into bed.

3

JANUARY 22

Arriving at the clinic the next morning, Marissa was surprised to see a number of TV trucks pulled up to the hospital entrance, with their transmission antennae raised against the morning sky. When she tried to enter through the parking garage, she was stopped by a policeman and had to show her CDC identification.

"Quarantine," the policeman explained, and told her to enter the clinic through the main hospital entrance where the TV trucks were located.

Marissa obeyed, wondering what had been happening during the six-plus hours she'd been away. TV cables snaked their way along the floor to the conference room, and she was amazed at the level of activity in the main corridor. Spotting Dr. Navarre, she asked him what was going on.

"Your people have scheduled a news conference," he explained. His face was haggard and unshaven, and it seemed obvious he had not been to bed. He took a newspaper from under his arm and showed it to Marissa: A NEW AIDS EPIDEMIC, shouted the headline. The article was illustrated with a photo of Marissa talking with Clarence Herns.

"Dr. Dubchek felt that such a misconception could not be allowed to continue," said Dr. Navarre.

Marissa groaned. "The reporter approached me right after I'd arrived. I really didn't tell him anything."

"It doesn't matter," said Dr. Navarre, patting her gently on the shoulder. "Dr. Richter died during the night, and with the four new cases, there was no way this could have been kept from the media."

"When did Dr. Dubchek arrive?" asked Marissa, getting out of the way of a camera crew headed into the conference room.

"A little after midnight," said Dr. Navarre.

"Why the police?" asked Marissa, noticing a second uniformed officer standing by the doors leading to the hospital.

"After Dr. Richter died, patients started signing themselves out of the hospital, until the State Commissioner of Health issued an order placing the whole building under quarantine."

Marissa excused herself and made her way through a throng of press and TV people outside the conference room. She was glad Dubchek had arrived to take charge but wondered why he hadn't gotten in touch with her. When she entered the room, Dubchek was just about to start speaking.

He handled himself well. His calm no-nonsense manner quieted the room immediately. He began by introducing himself and the other doctors from the CDC. There was Dr. Mark Vreeland, Chief of Medical Epidemiology; Dr. Pierce Abbott, Director of the Department of Virology; Dr. Clark Layne, Director of the Hospital Infectious Disease Program; and Dr. Paul Eckenstein, Director of the Center for Infectious Disease.

Dubchek then went on to downplay the incident, saying that the problem was not "A New AIDS Epidemic" by any stretch of the imagination. He said that the California State Epidemiologist had requested help from the CDC to look into a few cases of unexplained illness thought to be of viral origin.

Looking at reporters eager for copy, Marissa could tell they were not buying Dubchek's calm assessment. The idea of a new, unknown and frightening viral illness made for exciting news.

Dubchek continued by saying that there had only been a total of sixteen cases and that he thought the problem was under control. He pointed to Dr. Layne and announced that he would be overseeing the quarantine efforts and added that experience proved this kind of illness could be controlled by strict hospital isolation.

At this, Clarence Herns jumped up, asking, "Did Dr. Richter bring this virus back from his African conference?"

"We don't know," said Dubchek. "It is a possibility, but doubtful.

The incubation period would be too long, since Dr. Richter returned from Africa over a month ago. The incubation period for this kind of illness is usually about a week.''

Another reporter got to her feet: "If the incubation period for AIDS can be five years, how can you limit it here to less than a month?''

"That's exactly the point,'' said Dubchek, his patience wearing thin. "The AIDS virus is totally different from our current problem. It is essential that the media understand this point and communicate it to the public.''

"Have you isolated the new virus?'' asked another reporter.

"Not yet,'' admitted Dubchek. "But we do not expect to have any difficulty. Again, that's because it is a very different virus from AIDS. It should only take a week or so to culture it.''

"If the virus has not been isolated,'' continued the same reporter, "how can you say that it is different from the AIDS virus?''

Dubchek stared at the man. Marissa could sense the doctor's frustration. Calmly he said, "Over the years we've come to realize that totally different clinical syndromes are caused by totally different microorganisms. Now that is all for today, but we will keep you informed. Thank you for coming at this early hour.''

The conference room erupted as each reporter tried to get one more question answered. Dubchek ignored them as he and the other doctors made their exit. Marissa tried to push through the crowd but couldn't. Outside the conference room the uniformed policeman kept the reporters from entering the hospital proper. After showing her CDC identity card, Marissa was allowed to pass. She caught up to Dubchek at the elevators.

"There you are!'' said Dubchek, his dark eyes lighting up. His voice was friendly as he introduced Marissa to the other men.

"I didn't know so many of you were coming,'' she said as they boarded the elevator.

"We didn't have much choice,'' said Dr. Layne.

Dr. Abbott nodded. "Despite Cyrill's comments at the news conference, this outbreak is extraordinarily serious. An appearance of African viral hemorrhagic fever in the developed world has been a nightmare we've lived with since the illness first surfaced.''

"If it proves to be African viral hemorrhagic fever,'' added Dr. Eckenstein.

"I'm convinced,'' said Dr. Vreeland. "And I think the monkey will turn out to be the culprit.''

"I didn't get samples from the monkey," admitted Marissa quickly.

"That's okay," said Dubchek. "We sacrificed the animal last night and sent specimens back to the Center. Liver and spleen sections will be far better than blood."

They arrived on the fifth floor, where two technicians from the CDC were busy running samples in the Vickers Mobile Isolation Lab.

"I'm sorry about that L.A. *Times* article," said Marissa when she could speak to Dubchek alone. "The reporter approached me when I first entered the hospital."

"No matter," said Dubchek. "Just don't let it happen again." He smiled and winked.

Marissa had no idea what the wink meant, nor the smile, for that matter. "Why didn't you call me when you arrived?" she asked.

"I knew you'd be exhausted," explained Dubchek. "There really wasn't any need. We spent most of the night getting the lab set up, autopsying the monkey, and just getting oriented. We also improved the isolation situation by having fans installed. Nonetheless, you are to be congratulated. I think you did a fine job getting this affair underway.

"For the moment, I'm buried in administrative detail," continued Dubchek, "but I do want to hear what you've learned. Maybe you and I could have dinner tonight. I've gotten you a room at the hotel where we are staying. I'm sure it's better than the Tropic Motel."

"There's nothing wrong with the Tropic," said Marissa. She felt an odd twinge of discomfort, as if her intuition were trying to tell her something.

Marissa went back to her small room behind the nurses' station and began to catch up on her own paperwork. First she phoned the sponsoring organizations for the two medical meetings Dr. Richter had attended. She told them that she needed to know if any of the other attendees had become ill with a viral disease. Then, gritting her teeth at the cruelty of her next call, she dialed Dr. Richter's home number and asked if she could pick up the diary Mrs. Richter had promised her the night before.

The neighbor who answered the phone seemed appalled by her request, but, after checking with the widow, told Marissa to come over in half an hour.

Marissa drove up to the beautifully landscaped house and nervously rang the bell. The same neighbor answered and rather angrily directed Marissa to the living room. Anna Richter appeared a few minutes later.

She seemed to have aged ten years overnight. Her face was pale, and her hair, which had been so carefully curled the night before, hung about her face in lank strands.

The neighbor helped her to a chair, and Marissa was amazed to see that she was anxiously folding and unfolding some lined papers that seemed to contain the requested list of her husband's activities over the last weeks. Knowing what a strain the woman must have been under, Marissa didn't know what to say, but Anna simply handed her the sheets saying, "I couldn't sleep last night anyway, and maybe this will help some other poor family." Her eyes filled with tears. "He was such a good man . . . a good father . . . my poor children."

Despite knowing of his affair with Helen Townsend, Marissa decided that Dr. Richter must have been a pretty good husband. Anna's grief seemed real, and Marissa left her as soon as she politely could.

The notes that she read before starting the car were surprisingly detailed. Put together with a further interview with Miss Cavanagh and the doctor's appointment book, Marissa felt they would give her as good a picture of Richter's last few weeks as anyone could get.

Back at the hospital, Marissa made a separate sheet of paper for each day of January and listed Richter's activities. One fact she discovered was that he had complained to Miss Cavanagh about an AIDS patient named Meterko who was suffering from an undiagnosed retinal disorder. It sounded like something Marissa should look into.

In the afternoon, the phone in Marissa's cubicle rang. Picking it up, she was startled to hear Tad Schockley's voice. The connection was so good that for a moment she thought he was there in L.A.

"Nope," said Tad, responding to her question. "I'm still here in Atlanta. But I need to speak to Dubchek. The hospital operator seemed to think that you might know where he was."

"If he's not in the CDC room, then I guess he's gone to his hotel. Apparently they were up all last night."

"Well, I'll try the hotel, but in case I don't get him, could you give him a message?"

"Of course," said Marissa.

"It's not good news."

Straightening up, Marissa pressed the phone to her ear. "Is it personal?"

"No," said Tad with a short laugh. "It's about the virus you people are dealing with. The samples you sent were great, especially Dr.

Richter's. His blood was loaded with virus—more than a billion per milliliter. All I had to do was spin it down, fix it and look at it with the electron microscope.''

"Could you tell what it was?" asked Marissa.

"Absolutely," said Tad excitedly. "There are only two viruses that look like this, and it tested positive with indirect fluorescene antibody for Ebola. Dr. Richter has Ebola Hemorrhagic Fever.''

"Had," said Marissa, mildly offended by Tad's callous enthusiasm.

"Did the man die?" asked Tad.

"Last night," said Marissa.

"It's not surprising. The illness has a ninety-percent-plus fatality rate."

"My God!" exclaimed Marissa. "That must make it the deadliest virus known.''

"Some people might give rabies that dubious honor," said Tad. "But personally I think it is Ebola. One of the problems is that almost nothing is known about this illness because there has been so little experience. Except for a couple of outbreaks in Africa, it's an unknown entity. You're going to have your work cut out for you trying to explain how it popped up in Los Angeles.''

"Maybe not," said Marissa. "Dr. Richter had been bitten just prior to his illness by a monkey that had come from Africa. Dr. Vreeland is pretty sure the monkey was the source.''

"He's probably right," agreed Tad. "Monkeys were responsible for an outbreak of hemorrhagic fever in '67. The virus was named Marburg after the town in Germany where it occurred. The virus looks a lot like Ebola.''

"We'll soon know," said Marissa. "Now it's up to you. Hepatic and splenic sections from the monkey are on the way. I'd appreciate it if you'd check them right away and let me know.''

"My pleasure," said Tad. "Meanwhile, I'm going to start work on the Ebola virus and see how easily I can culture it. I want to figure out what strain it is. Let Dubchek and the others know they're dealing with Ebola. If nothing else, it will make them super careful. I'll talk with you soon. Take care.''

Leaving the cubicle, Marissa stepped across the hall and peered into the CDC room. It was deserted. Going into the neighboring room, she asked the technicians where everyone was. They told her that some of the doctors were down in pathology, since two more of the patients had died, and some were in the ER admitting several new cases. Dr. Dubchek had gone back to the hotel. Marissa told the technicians that they were dealing with Ebola. She left it to them to pass the bad news to the others. Then she went back to her paperwork.

The Beverly Hilton was just as Dubchek had described. It was certainly nicer than the seedy Tropic Motel, and it was closer to the Richter Clinic. But it still seemed like unnecessary effort to Marissa as she plodded after the bellman down the eighth-floor corridor to her room. The bellman turned on all the lights while she waited at the door. She gave him a dollar, and he left.

She'd never unpacked at the Tropic, so the move wasn't difficult. Yet she wouldn't have made it if Dubchek hadn't insisted. He'd called her that afternoon, several hours after she'd talked with Tad. She'd been afraid to call him, thinking that she'd awaken him. As soon as he was on the line, she told him Tad's news about the outbreak being Ebola Hemorrhagic Fever, but he took it in stride, almost as if he'd expected it. He then had given her directions to the hotel and told her that she merely had to pick up the key for 805, since she was already registered. And he had told her that they'd eat at seven-thirty, if that was all right with her, and that she should just come to his room, which was conveniently located a few doors from hers. He said he'd order up so they could go over her notes while they ate.

As she eyed the bed, Marissa's exhaustion cried for attention, but it was already after seven. Getting her cosmetics bag from her suitcase, she went into the bathroom. After washing, brushing out her hair and touching up her makeup, Marissa was ready. From her briefcase, she removed the sheets of information concerning Dr. Richter's activities before he'd become ill. Clutching them to her, she walked down to Dubchek's door and knocked.

He answered her knock and, smiling, motioned for her to come in. He was on the phone, apparently talking to Tad. Marissa sat down and tried to follow the conversation. It seemed the samples from the monkey had arrived and they had tested clear.

"You mean the electron microscopy showed no virus at all?" said Dubchek.

There was a long silence as Tad relayed the details of the outcomes of the various tests. Looking at her watch, Marissa calculated that it was almost eleven in Atlanta. Tad was certainly putting in overtime.

She watched Dubchek, realizing the man had a disturbing effect on her. She recalled how unnerved she'd been when he'd turned up at Ralph's dinner party and was upset to find herself inexplicably attracted to him now. From time to time he looked up, and her glance was trapped by an unexpected glint in his dark eyes. He'd removed his jacket and tie, and a *V* of tanned skin was visible at the base of his neck.

Finally he hung up the phone and walked over to her, gazing down at her. "You're certainly the best-looking thing I've seen today. And I gather your friend Tad would agree. He seemed very concerned that you don't put yourself at risk."

"Certainly I'm in no more danger than anyone else involved in this," she said, vaguely annoyed at the turn the conversation was taking.

Dubchek grinned. "I guess Tad doesn't feel the rest of the staff is as cute."

Trying to turn the talk to professional matters, Marissa asked about the monkey's liver and spleen sections.

"Clean so far," said Dubchek, with a wave of his hand. "But that was only by electron microscopy. Tad has also planted the usual viral cultures. We'll know more in a week."

"In the meantime," said Marissa, "we'd better look elsewhere."

"I suppose so," said Dubchek. He seemed distracted. He ran a hand over his eyes as he sat down across from her.

Leaning forward, Marissa handed over her notes. "I thought that you might be interested in looking at these." Dubchek accepted the papers and glanced through them while Marissa talked.

In a chronological fashion, Marissa described what she'd been doing since her arrival in L.A. She made a convincing argument that Dr. Richter was the index case and that he was the source of the Ebola, spreading the disease to some of his patients. She explained his relationship to Helen Townsend and then described the two medical meetings that Dr. Richter had attended. The sponsoring organizations were sending complete lists of the attendees, with their addresses and phone numbers, she added.

Throughout her monologue Dubchek nodded to indicate that he was listening, but somehow he seemed distracted, concentrating more on her face than on what she was saying. With so little feedback, Marissa trailed off and stopped speaking, wondering if she were making some fundamental professional error. After a sigh, Dubchek smiled. "Good job," he said simply. "It's hard to believe that this is your first field assignment." He stood up at the sound of a knock on the door. "Thank goodness. That must be dinner. I'm starved."

The meal itself was mediocre; the meat and vegetables Dubchek had ordered were lukewarm. Marissa wondered why they couldn't have gone down to the dining room. She'd thought that he'd intended to talk business, but as they ate, the conversation ranged from Ralph's dinner party and how she came to know him, to the CDC and whether or not she was enjoying her assignment. Toward the end of the meal Dubchek suddenly said, "I wanted to tell you that I am a widower."

"I'm sorry to hear that," said Marissa sincerely, wondering why the man was bothering to inform her about his personal life.

"I just thought you should know," he added, as if reading her mind. "My wife died two years ago in an auto accident."

Marissa nodded, once again uncertain how to reply.

"What about you?" asked Dubchek. "Are you seeing anyone?"

Marissa paused, toying with the handle of her coffee cup. She had no intention of discussing her breakup with Roger. "No, not at the moment," she managed to tell him. She wondered if Dubchek knew that she had been dating Tad. It had not been a secret, but it wasn't public knowledge either. Neither of them had told people at the lab. Suddenly Marissa felt even more uncomfortable. Her policy of not mixing her personal and professional lives was being violated, she felt. Looking over at Dubchek, she couldn't help but acknowledge that she found him attractive. Perhaps that was why he made her feel so uncomfortable. But there was no way she was interested in a more personal relationship with him, if that was what this was leading up to. All at once she wanted to get out of his room and return to her work.

Dubchek pushed back his chair and stood up. "If we're going back to the clinic maybe we should be on our way."

That sounded good to Marissa. She stood up and went over to the coffee table to pick up her papers. As she straightened up, she realized that Dubchek had come up behind her. Before she could react, he put his hands on her shoulders and turned her around. The action so surprised her that she stood frozen. For a brief moment their lips met. Then she pulled away, her papers dropping to the floor.

"I'm sorry," he said. "I wasn't planning that at all, but ever since you arrived at CDC I've been tempted to do that. God knows I don't believe in dating anyone I work with, but it's the first time since my wife died that I've really been interested in a woman. You don't look like her at all—Jane was tall and blond—but you have that same enthusiasm for your work. She was a musician, and when she played well, she had the same excited expression I've seen you get."

Marissa was silent. She knew she was being mean, that Dubchek certainly had not been harassing her, but she felt embarrassed and awkward and was unwilling to say something to ease over the incident.

"Marissa," he said gently, "I'm telling you that I'd like to take you out when we get back to Atlanta, but if you're involved with Ralph or just don't want to . . ." His voice trailed off.

Marissa bent down and gathered up her notes. "If we're going back to the hospital, we'd better go now," she said curtly.

He stiffly followed her out the door to the elevator. Later, sitting silently in her rent-a-car, Marissa berated herself. Cyrill was the most attractive man she'd met since Roger. Why had she behaved so unreasonably?

4

FEBRUARY 27

Almost five weeks later, as the taxi bringing her home from the airport turned onto Peachtree Place, Marissa was wondering if she would be able to reestablish a pleasant, professional relationship with Dubchek now that they were both back in Atlanta. He had left a few days after their exchange at the Beverly Hilton, and the few meetings they'd had at the Richter Clinic had been curt and awkward.

Watching the lighted windows as the cab drove down her street, seeing the warm family scenes inside, she was overcome with a wave of loneliness.

After paying the driver and turning off the alarm, Marissa hustled over to the Judsons' and retrieved Taffy and five weeks' worth of mail. The dog was ecstatic to see her, and the Judsons couldn't have been nicer. Rather than making Marissa feel guilty about being gone for so long, they acted truly sad to see Taffy leave.

Back in her own house, Marissa turned up the heat to a comfortable level. Having a puppy there made all the difference in the world. The dog wouldn't leave her side and demanded almost constant attention.

Thinking about supper, she opened the refrigerator only to discover that some food had gone bad. She shut the door, deciding to tackle the job of cleaning it out the next day. She dined on Fig Newtons and Coke as she leafed through her mail. Aside from a card from one of

64

her brothers and a letter from her parents, it was mostly pharmaceutical junk.

Marissa was startled when the phone rang, but when she picked up the receiver, she was pleased to hear Tad's voice welcoming her home to Atlanta. "How about going out for a drink?" he asked. "I can pop over and pick you up."

Marissa's first response was to say that she was exhausted after her trip, but then she remembered on her last call from L.A. he'd told her he had finished his current AIDS project and was hard at work on what he called Marissa's Ebola virus. Suddenly feeling less tired, she asked how those tests were going.

"Fine!" said Tad. "The stuff grows like wildfire in the Vero 98 tissue cultures. The morphology portion of the study is already complete, and I've started the protein analysis."

"I'm really interested in seeing what you're doing," said Marissa.

"I'll be happy to show you what I can," said Tad. "Unfortunately, a majority of the work is done inside the maximum containment lab."

"I'd assumed as much," said Marissa. She knew that the only way such a deadly virus could be handled was in a facility that did just what its name suggested—contained the microorganisms. As far as Marissa knew, there were only four such facilities in the world—one at the CDC, one in England, one in Belgium and one in the Soviet Union. She didn't know if the Pasteur Institute in Paris had one or not. For safety reasons entry was restricted to a few authorized individuals. At that time, Marissa was not one of them. Yet, having witnessed Ebola's devastating potential, she told Tad that she was really eager to see his studies.

"You don't have clearance," said Tad, surprised by what seemed to him her naiveté.

"I know," said Marissa, "but what could be so terrible about showing me what you're doing with the Ebola in the lab right now and then going out for a drink. After all, it's late. No one will know if you take me now."

There was a pause. "But entry is restricted," said Tad plaintively.

Marissa was fully aware that she was being manipulative, but there was certainly no danger to anyone if she were to go in with Tad. "Who's to know?" she asked coaxingly. "Besides, I *am* part of the team."

"I guess so," Tad agreed reluctantly.

It was obvious that he was wavering. The fact that Marissa would only see him if he took her into the lab seemed to force his decision. He told her that he'd pick her up in half an hour and that she wasn't to breathe a word to anyone else.

Marissa readily agreed.

"I'm not so sure about this," admitted Tad, as he and Marissa drove toward the CDC.

"Relax," said Marissa. "I'm an EIS officer assigned to Special Pathogens for goodness sakes." Purposefully, Marissa pretended to be a little irritated.

"But we could ask for your clearance tomorrow," suggested Tad.

Marissa turned toward her friend. "Are you chickening out?" she demanded. It was true that Dubchek was due back from a trip to Washington the next day and that a formal request could be made. But Marissa had her doubts about what his response would be. She felt that Dubchek had been unreasonably cold over the last few weeks, even if her own stupidity had been the cause. Why she hadn't had the nerve to apologize or even say she'd like to see him one evening, she didn't know. But with every day that passed, the coolness between them, particularly on his side, increased.

Tad pulled into the parking lot, and they walked in silence to the main entrance. Marissa mused about men's egos and how much trouble they caused.

They signed in under the watchful eyes of the security guard and dutifully displayed their CDC identity cards. Under the heading "Destination," Marissa wrote "office." They waited for the elevator and went up three floors. After walking the length of the main building, they went through an outside door to a wire-enclosed catwalk that connected the main building to the virology labs. All the buildings of the Center were connected on most floors by similar walkways.

"Security is tight for the maximum containment lab," said Tad as he opened the door to the virology building. "We store every pathological virus known to man."

"All of them?" asked Marissa, obviously awed.

"Just about," said Tad like a proud father.

"What about Ebola?" she asked.

"We have Ebola samples from every one of the previous outbreaks. We've got Marburg; smallpox, which otherwise is extinct; polio; yellow fever; dengue; AIDS. You name it; we've got it."

"God!" exclaimed Marissa. "A menagerie of horrors."

"I guess you could say that."

"How are they stored?" she asked.

"Frozen with liquid nitrogen."

"Are they infective?" asked Marissa.

"Just have to thaw them out."

They were walking down an ordinary hall past a myriad of small, dark offices. Marissa had previously been in this portion of the building when she'd come to Dubchek's office.

Tad stopped in front of a walk-in freezer like the kind seen in a butcher shop.

"You might find this interesting," he said, as he pulled open the heavy door. A light was on inside.

Timidly Marissa stepped over the threshold into the cold, moist air. Tad was behind her. She felt a thrill of fear as the door swung shut and latched with a click.

The interior of the freezer was lined with shelves holding tiny vials, hundreds of thousands of them. "What is this?" asked Marissa.

"Frozen sera," said Tad, picking up one of the vials, which had a number and a date written on it. "Samples from patients all over the world with every known viral disease and a lot of unknown ones. They're here for immunological study and obviously are not infective."

Marissa was still glad when they returned to the hallway.

About fifty feet beyond the walk-in freezer the hall turned sharply to the right, and as they rounded the corner, they were confronted by a massive steel door. Just above the doorknob was a grid of push buttons similar to Marissa's alarm system. Below that was a slot like the opening for a credit card at an automatic bank teller. Tad showed Marissa a card that he had around his neck on a leather thong. He inserted it into the slot.

"The computer is recording the entry," he said. Then he tapped out his code number on the push button plate: 43-23-39. "Good measurements," he quipped.

"Thank you," said Marissa, laughing. Tad joined in. Since the virology building had been deserted, he seemed more relaxed. After a short delay, there was a mechanical click as the bolt released. Tad pulled open the door. Marissa felt as if she had entered another world. Instead of the drab, cluttered hallway in the outer part of the building, she found herself surrounded by a recently constructed complex of color-coded pipes, gauges and other futuristic paraphernalia. The lighting was dim until Tad opened a cabinet door, exposing a row of circuit breakers. He threw them in order. The first turned on the lights in the room in which they were standing. It was almost two stories tall and was filled with all sorts of equipment. There was a slight odor of phenolic disinfectant, a smell that reminded Marissa of the autopsy room at her medical school.

The next circuit breaker lit up a row of portholelike windows that lined the sides of a ten-foot-high cylinder that protruded into the room. At the end of the cylinder was an oval door like the watertight hatch on a submarine.

The final circuit breaker caused a whirring noise as some kind of large electrical machinery went into gear. "Compressors," said Tad in response to Marissa's questioning look. He didn't elaborate. Instead, with a sweep of his hand he said: "This is the control and staging area for the maximum containment lab. From here we can monitor all the fans and filters. Even the gamma-ray generators. Notice all the green lights. That means that everything is working as it is supposed to be. At least hopefully!"

"What do you mean, 'hopefully'?" asked Marissa, somewhat alarmed. Then she saw Tad's smile and knew he was teasing her. Still, she suddenly wasn't one hundred percent sure she wanted to go through with the visit. It had seemed like such a good idea when she'd been in the safety of her home. Now, surrounded by all this alien equipment and knowing what kinds of viruses were inside, she wasn't so certain. But Tad didn't give her time to change her mind. He opened the airtight door and motioned for Marissa to go inside. Marissa had to duck her head slightly while stepping over the six-inch-high threshold. Tad followed her, then closed and bolted the door. A feeling of claustrophobia almost overwhelmed her, especially when she had to swallow to clear her ears due to the pressure change.

The cylinder was lined with the portholelike windows Marissa had seen from the outer room. Along both sides were benches and upright lockers. At the far end were shelves and another oval airtight door.

"Surprise!" said Tad as he tossed Marissa some cotton suits. "No street clothes allowed."

After a moment's hesitation during which time Marissa vainly glanced around for a modicum of privacy, she began unbuttoning her blouse. As embarrassed as she was to be stripping down to her underwear in front of Tad, he seemed more self-conscious than she. He made a big production of facing away from her while she changed.

They then went through a second door. "Each room that we enter as we go into the lab is more negative in terms of pressure than the last. That ensures that the only movement of air will be into the lab, not out."

The second room was about the size of the first but with no windows. The smell of the phenolic disinfectant was more pronounced. A number of large, blue plastic suits hung on pegs. Tad searched until he found one he thought would fit Marissa. She took it from his outstretched hand. It was like a space suit without a backpack or a heavy bubble helmet. Like a space suit, it covered the entire body, complete with gloves and booties. The part that covered the head was faced with clear plastic. The suit sealed with a zipper that ran from the pubic area to the base of the throat. Issuing from the back, like a long tail, was an air hose.

Tad pointed out green piping that ran along the sides of the room at chest height, saying that the entire lab was laced with such pipes. At frequent intervals were rectangular lime green manifolds with adapters to take the air hoses from the suits. Tad explained that the suits were filled with clean, positive-pressure air so that the air in the lab itself was never breathed. He rehearsed with Marissa the process of attaching and detaching the air hose until he was convinced she felt secure.

"Okay, time to suit up," said Tad, as he showed Marissa how to start working her way into the bulky garment. The process was complicated, particularly getting her head inside the closed hood. As she looked out through the clear plastic face mask, it fogged immediately.

Tad told her to attach her air hose, and instantly Marissa felt the fresh air cool her body and clear the face piece. Tad zipped up the front of her suit and with practiced moves, climbed into his own. He inflated his suit, then detached his air hose, and carrying it in his hand, moved down to the far door. Marissa did the same. She had to waddle to walk.

To the right of the door was a panel. "Interior lights for the lab," explained Tad as he threw the switches. His voice was muffled by the suit; it was difficult for her to understand, especially with the hiss of the incoming air in the background. They went through another airtight door, which Tad closed behind them.

The next room was half again smaller than the first two, with walls and piping all covered with a white chalky substance. The floor was covered with a plastic grate.

They attached their air hoses for a moment. Then they moved through a final door into the lab itself. Marissa followed close behind Tad, moving her air hose and connecting it where he did.

Marissa was confronted by a large rectangular room with a central island of lab benches surmounted by protective exhaust hoods. The walls were lined with all sorts of equipment—centrifuges, incubators, various microscopes, computer terminals, and a host of things Marissa did not recognize. To the left there was also a bolted insulated door.

Tad took Marissa directly to one of the incubators and opened up the glass doors. The tissue culture tubes were fitted into a slowly revolving tray. Tad lifted out one and handed it to Marissa. "Here's your Ebola," he said.

In addition to the small amount of fluid the tube contained, it was coated (on one side) with a thin film—a layer of living cells infected with the virus. Inside the cells, the virus was forcing its own replication. As innocent as the contents looked, Marissa understood that there was probably enough infectious virus to kill everyone in Atlanta, perhaps the United States. Marissa shuddered, gripping the glass tube more tightly.

Taking the tube, Tad walked over to one of the microscopes. He positioned the airtight specimen, adjusted the focus, then stepped back so Marissa could look.

"See those darkened clumps in the cytoplasm?" he asked.

Marissa nodded. Even through the plastic face mask, it was easy to see the inclusion bodies Tad described, as well as the irregular cell nuclei.

"That's the first sign of infestation," said Tad. "I just planted these cultures. That virus is unbelievably potent."

After Marissa straightened up from the microscope, Tad returned the tube to the incubator. Then he began to explain his complicated research, pointing out some of the sophisticated equipment he was using and detailing his various experiments. Marissa had trouble concentrating. She hadn't come to the lab that night to discuss Tad's work, but she couldn't tell him that.

Finally he led her down a passageway to a maze of animal cages that reached almost to the ceiling. There were monkeys, rabbits, guinea pigs, rats and mice. Marissa could see hundreds of eyes staring at her: some listless, some with fevered hatred. In a far section of the room, Tad pulled out a tray of what he called Swiss ice mice. He was going to show them to Marissa, but he stopped. "My word!" he said. "I just inoculated these guys this afternoon, and most have already died." He looked at Marissa. "Your Ebola is really deadly—as bad as the Zaire '76 strain."

Marissa reluctantly glanced in at the dead mice. "Is there some way to compare the various strains?"

"Absolutely," said Tad, removing the dead mice. They went back to the main lab where Tad searched for a tray for the tiny corpses. He spoke while he moved, responding to Marissa's question. She found it hard to understand him when he wasn't standing directly in front of her. The plastic suit gave his voice a hollow quality, like Darth Vader's. "Now that I've started to characterize your Ebola," he said, "it will be easy to compare it with the previous strains. In fact I've begun with these mice, but the results will have to wait for a statistical evaluation."

Once he had the mice arranged on a dissecting tray, Tad stopped in front of the bolted insulated door. "I don't think you want to come in here." Without waiting for a response, he opened the door and went inside with the dead mice. A mist drifted out as the door swung back against his air hose.

Marissa eyed the small opening, steeling herself to follow, but before she could act, Tad reappeared, hastily shutting the door behind him. "You know, I'm also planning to compare the structural polypeptides and viral RNA of your virus against the previous Ebola strains," he said.

"That's enough!" laughed Marissa. "You're making me feel dumb. I've got to get back to my virology textbook before making sense of all this. Why don't we call it a night and get that drink you promised me?"

"You're on," said Tad eagerly.

There was one surprise on the way out. When they had returned to the room with chalky walls, they were drenched by a shower of phenolic disinfectant. Looking at Marissa's shocked face, Tad grinned. "Now you know what a toilet bowl feels like."

When they were changing into their street clothes, Marissa asked what was in the room where he'd taken the dead mice.

"Just a large freezer," he said, waving off the question.

Over the next four days, Marissa readjusted to life in Atlanta, enjoying her home and her dog. On the day after her return, she'd tackled all the difficult jobs, like cleaning out the rotten vegetables from the refrigerator and catching up on her overdue bills. At work, she threw herself into the study of viral hemorrhagic fever, Ebola in particular. Making use of the CDC library, she obtained detailed material about the previous outbreaks of Ebola: Zaire '76, Sudan '76, Zaire '77 and Sudan '79. During each outbreak, the virus appeared out of nowhere and then disappeared. A great deal of effort was expended trying to determine what organism served as the reservoir for the virus. Over two hundred separate species of animals and insects were studied as potential hosts. All were negative. The only positive finding was some antibodies in an occasional domestic guinea pig.

Marissa found the description of the first Zairean outbreak particularly interesting. Transmission of the illness had been linked to a health-care facility called the Yambuku Mission Hospital. She wondered what possible points of similarity existed between the Yambuku Mission and the Richter Clinic, or for that matter, between Yambuku and Los Angeles. There couldn't be very many.

She was sitting at a back table in the library, reading again from Fields' *Virology*. She was studying up on tissue cultures as an aid to further practical work in the main virology lab. Tad had been helpful in setting her up with some relatively harmless viruses so that she could familiarize herself with the latest virology equipment.

Marissa checked her watch. It was a little after two. At three-fifteen she had an appointment with Dr. Dubchek. The day before, she'd given his secretary a formal request for permission to use the maximum containment lab, outlining the experimental work she wanted to do on the communicability of the Ebola virus. Marissa was not particularly sanguine about Dubchek's response. He'd all but ignored her since her return from Los Angeles.

A shadow fell across her page, and Marissa automatically glanced up. "Well! Well! She is still alive!" said a familiar voice.

"Ralph," whispered Marissa, shocked both by his unexpected presence in the CDC library and the loudness of his voice. A number of heads turned toward them.

"There were rumors she was alive but I had to see for myself," continued Ralph, oblivious of Mrs. Campbell's glare.

Marissa motioned for Ralph to be silent, then took his hand and led him into the hallway where they could talk. She felt a surge of affection as she looked up at his welcoming smile.

"It's good to see you," said Marissa, giving him a hug. She felt a twinge of guilt for not having contacted him since returning to Atlanta. They'd talked on the phone about once a week during her stay in L.A.

As if reading her mind, Ralph said, "Why haven't you called me? Dubchek told me you've been back for four days."

"I was going to call tonight," she said lamely, upset that Ralph was getting information about her from Dubchek.

They went down to the CDC cafeteria for coffee. At that time of the afternoon the room was almost deserted, and they sat by the window overlooking the courtyard. Ralph said he was en route between the hospital and his office and that he had wanted to catch her before the evening. "How about dinner?" he asked, leaning forward and putting a hand on Marissa's. "I'm dying to hear the details of your triumph over Ebola in L.A."

"I'm not sure that twenty-one deaths can be considered a triumph," said Marissa. "Worse still from an epidemiologic point of view, we failed. We never found out where the virus came from. There's got to be some kind of reservoir. Just imagine the media reaction if the CDC had been unable to trace the Legionnaires bacteria to the air-conditioning system."

"I think you are being hard on yourself," said Ralph.

"But we have no idea if and when Ebola will appear again," said Marissa. "Unfortunately, I have a feeling it will. And it is so unbelievably deadly." Marissa could remember too well its devastating course.

"They couldn't figure out where Ebola came from in Africa either," said Ralph, still trying to make her feel better.

Marissa was impressed that Ralph was aware of the fact and told him so.

"TV," he explained. "Watching the nightly news these days gives one a medical education." He squeezed Marissa's hand. "The reason you should consider your time in L.A. successful is because you were able to contain what could have been an epidemic of horrible proportions."

Marissa smiled. She realized that Ralph was trying to make her feel good and she appreciated the effort. "Thank you," she said. "You're right. The outbreak could have been much worse, and for a time we thought that it would be. Thank God it responded to the quarantine. It's a good thing, because it carried better than a ninety-four percent fatality rate, with only two apparent survivors. Even the Richter Clinic seems to have become a victim. It now has as bad a reputation because of Ebola as the San Francisco bathhouses have because of AIDS.''

Marissa glanced at the clock over the steam table. It was after three. "I have a meeting in a few minutes," she apologized. "You are a dear for stopping by, and dinner tonight sounds wonderful.''

"Dinner it will be," said Ralph, picking up the tray with their empty cups.

Marissa hurried up three flights of stairs and crossed to the virology building. It didn't appear nearly as threatening in the daylight as it had at night. Turning toward Dubchek's office, Marissa knew that just around the bend in the hallway was the steel door that led to the maximum containment lab. It was seventeen after three when she stood in front of Dubchek's secretary.

It was silly for her to have rushed. As she sat across from the secretary, flipping through *Virology Times* with its virus-of-the-month centerfold, Marissa realized that of course Dubchek would keep her waiting. She glanced at her watch again: twenty of four. Beyond the door she could hear Dubchek on the telephone. And from the telephone console on the secretary's desk, she could see the little lights blink when he'd hang up and make another call. It was five of four when the door opened and Dubchek motioned for Marissa to come into his office.

The room was small, and cluttered with reprinted articles stacked on the desk, on the file cabinet and on the floor. Dubchek was in his shirt-sleeves, his tie tucked out of the way between the second and third button of his shirt. There was no apology or explanation of why she'd been kept waiting. In fact there was a suggestion of a grin on his face that particularly galled Marissa.

"I trust that you received my letter," she said, studiously keeping her voice businesslike.

"I did indeed," said Dubchek.

"And . . . ?" said Marissa after a pause.

"A few days' lab experience is not enough to work in the maximum containment lab," said Dubcheck.

"What do you suggest?" asked Marissa.

"Exactly what you are presently doing," said Dubchek. "Continue working with less-pathogenic viruses until you gain sufficient experience.''

"How will I know when I've had enough experience?" Marissa

realized that Cyrill had a point, but she wondered if his answer would have been different had they been dating. It bothered her even more that she didn't have the nerve to withdraw her earlier rebuff. He was a handsome man, one who attracted her far more than Ralph, whom she was happy enough to see for dinner.

"I believe *I* will know when you have had adequate experience," said Dubchek interrupting her thoughts, "or Tad Schockley will."

Marissa felt cheered. If it were up to Tad, she was certain that she would eventually get the necessary authorization.

"Meanwhile," said Dubchek, stepping around his desk and sitting down, "I've got something more important to talk with you about. I've just been on the phone with a number of people, including the Missouri State Epidemiologist. They have a single case of a severe viral illness in St. Louis that they think might be Ebola. I want you to leave immediately, assess the situation clinically, send Tad samples and report back. Here's your flight reservation." He handed Marissa a sheet of paper. On it was written Delta, flight 1083, departure 5:34 P.M., arrival 6:06 P.M.

Marissa was stunned. With rush-hour traffic, it was going to be a near thing. She knew that as an EIS officer she should always have a bag packed, but she didn't, and there was Taffy to think of, too.

"We'll have the mobile lab ready if it is needed," Cyrill was saying, "but let's hope it's not." He extended his hand to wish her good luck, but Marissa was so preoccupied with the thought of possibly facing the deadly Ebola virus in less than four hours, that she walked out without noticing. She felt dazed. She'd gone in hoping for permission to use the maximum containment lab and was leaving with orders to fly to St. Louis! Glancing at her watch, she broke into a run. It was going to be close.

5

MARCH 3

It was only as the plane taxied onto the runway that Marissa remembered her date with Ralph. Well, she should touch down in time to catch him as soon as he got home. Her one small consolation was that she felt more comfortable professionally than she had en route to L.A. At least she had some idea of what would be demanded of her. Personally, however, knowing this time how deadly the virus could be, if indeed it was Ebola, Marissa was more frightened at the thought of her own exposure. Although she hadn't mentioned it to anyone, she still worried about contracting the disease from the first outbreak. Each day that passed without the appearance of suspicious symptoms had been a relief. But the fear had never completely disappeared.

The other thought that troubled Marissa was the idea of another Ebola case appearing so quickly. If it was Ebola, how did it get to St. Louis? Was it a separate outbreak from L.A. or merely an extension of that one? Could a contact have brought it from L.A., or could there be an "Ebola Mary" like the infamous "Typhoid Mary"? There were many questions, none of which made Marissa cheerful.

"Will you want dinner tonight?" asked a cabin attendant, breaking Marissa's train of thought.

"Sure," said Marissa dropping her tray table. She'd better eat, whether she was hungry or not. She knew that once she got to St. Louis she might not get the time.

As Marissa climbed out of the taxi that had taken her from the St. Louis airport to the Greater St. Louis Community Health Plan Hospital, she was thankful for the elaborate concrete porte cochere. It was pouring outside. Even with the overhead protection, she pulled up the lapels of her coat to avoid wind-driven rain as she ran for the revolving door. She was carrying her suitcase as well as her briefcase, since she'd not taken the time to stop in her hotel.

The hospital appeared an impressive affair even on a dark, rainy night. It was constructed in a modern style, with travertine-marble facing, and fronted by a three-stories-tall replica of the Gateway Arch. The interior was mostly blond oak and bright red carpeting. A pert receptionist directed Marissa to the administration offices, located through a pair of swinging doors.

"Dr. Blumenthal!" cried a diminutive oriental man, jumping up from his desk. She took a step backward as the man relieved her of her suitcase and enthusiastically pumped her freed hand. "I'm Dr. Harold Taboso," he said. "I'm the medical director here. And this is Dr. Peter Austin, the Missouri State Epidemiologist. We've been waiting for you."

Marissa shook hands with Dr. Austin, a tall, thin man with a ruddy complexion.

"We are thankful that you could come so quickly," said Dr. Taboso. "Can we get you something to eat or drink?"

Marissa shook her head, thanking him for his hospitality. "I ate on the plane," she explained. "Besides, I'd like to get directly to business."

"Of course, of course," said Dr. Taboso. For a moment he looked confused. Dr. Austin took advantage of his silence to take over.

"We're well aware of what happened in L.A. and we're concerned that we might be dealing with the same problem here. As you know, we admitted one suspicious case this morning, and two more have arrived while you were en route."

Marissa bit her lip. She had been hoping that this would turn out to be a false alarm, but with two more potential cases, it was difficult to sustain such optimism. She sank into the chair that Dr. Taboso proffered and said, "You'd better tell me what you have learned so far."

"Not much, I'm afraid," said Dr. Austin. "There has been little time. The first case was admitted around 4:00 A.M. Dr. Taboso deserves credit for sounding the alarm as soon as he did. The patient was immediately isolated, hopefully minimizing contacts here at the hospital."

Marissa glanced at Dr. Taboso. He smiled nervously, accepting the compliment.

"That was fortunate," said Marissa. "Was any lab work done?"

"Of course," said Dr. Taboso.

"That could be a problem," said Marissa.

"We understand," said Dr. Austin. "But it was ordered immediately on admittance, before we had any suspicion of the diagnosis. The moment my office was alerted we called the CDC."

"Have you been able to make any association with the L.A. outbreak? Did any of the patients come from L.A.?"

"No," said Dr. Austin. "We have inquired about such a possibility, but there has been no connection that we could find."

"Well," said Marissa, reluctantly getting to her feet. "Let's see the patients. I assume that you have full protective gear available."

"Of course," said Dr. Taboso as they filed out of the room.

They crossed the hospital lobby to the elevators. Riding up in the car, Marissa asked, "Have any of the patients been to Africa recently?"

The other two doctors looked at each other. Dr. Taboso spoke: "I don't believe so."

Marissa had not expected a positive answer. That would have been too easy. She watched the floor indicator. The elevator stopped on eight.

As they walked down the corridor, Marissa realized that none of the rooms they were passing were occupied. When she looked closer, she realized that most weren't even fully furnished. And the walls of the hall had only been primed, not painted.

Dr. Taboso noticed Marissa's expression. "Sorry," he said. "I should have explained. When the hospital was built, too many beds were planned. Consequently, the eighth floor was never completed. But we decided to use it for this emergency. Good for isolation, don't you agree?"

They arrived at the nurses' station, which seemed complete except for the cabinetry. Marissa took the first patient's chart. She sat down at the desk and opened the metal cover, noting the man's name: Zabriski. The vital-sign page showed the familiar complex of high fever and low blood pressure. The next page contained the patient's history. As Marissa's eyes ran down the sheet, she caught the man's full name: Dr. Carl M. Zabriski. Raising her eyes to Dr. Taboso, she asked incredulously, "Is the patient a physician?"

"I'm afraid so," answered Taboso. "He's an ophthalmologist here at the hospital."

Turning to Dr. Austin, she asked, "Did you know the index case in L.A. was also a doctor? In fact he was an ophthalmologist!"

"I was aware of the coincidence," said Dr. Austin, frowning.

"Does Dr. Zabriski do any research with monkeys?" asked Marissa.

"Not that I know of," answered Dr. Taboso. "Certainly not here at the hospital."

"No other physicians were involved in the L.A. outbreak that I can recall," said Dr. Austin.

"No," said Marissa. "Just the index case. There were three lab techs and one nurse, but no other doctors."

Redirecting her attention to the chart, Marissa went through it rapidly. The history was not nearly as complete as that done on Dr. Richter at the Richter Clinic. There were no references to recent travel or animal contact. But the lab workup was impressive, and although not all the tests were back, those that were suggested severe liver and kidney involvement. So far everything was consistent with Ebola Hemorrhagic Fever.

After Marissa finished with the chart, she got together the materials necessary for drawing and packing viral samples. When all was ready, she went down the hall with one of the nurses to the isolation area. There she donned hood, mask, gloves, goggles and booties.

Inside Zabriski's room, two other women were similarly attired. One was a nurse, the other a doctor.

"How is the patient doing?" asked Marissa as she moved alongside the bed. It was a rhetorical question. The patient's condition was apparent. The first thing Marissa noticed was the rash over the man's trunk. The second thing was signs of hemorrhage; a nasogastric tube snaked out of the man's nostril and was filled with bright red blood. Dr. Zabriski was conscious, but just barely. He certainly couldn't answer any questions.

A short conversation with the attending physician confirmed Marissa's impressions. The patient had been deteriorating throughout the day, particularly during the last hour, when they began to see a progressive fall in the blood pressure.

Marissa had seen enough. Clinically, the patient resembled Dr. Richter to a horrifying degree. Until proven otherwise, it had to be assumed that Dr. Zabriski and the other two subsequent admissions had Ebola Hemorrhagic Fever.

The nurse helped Marissa obtain a nasal swab as well as blood and urine samples. Marissa handled them as she'd done in L.A., double bagging the material and disinfecting the outsides of the bags with sodium hypochlorite. After removing her protective clothing and washing her hands, she returned to the nurses' station to call Dubchek.

The phone conversation was short and to the point. Marissa said that it was her clinical impression that they were dealing with another Ebola outbreak.

"What about isolation?"

"They've done a good job in that regard," reported Marissa.

"We'll be there as soon as possible," said Dubchek. "Probably tonight. Meanwhile, I want you to stop all further lab work and supervise a thorough disinfection. Also have them set up the same kind of quarantine of contacts that we used in L.A."

Marissa was about to reply when she realized that Dubchek had hung up. She sighed as she replaced the receiver; such a wonderful working relationship!

"Well," said Marissa to Drs. Taboso and Austin, "let's get to work."

They quickly set the quarantine measures in motion, arranging for the sterilization of the lab and assuring Marissa that her samples would be sent overnight to the CDC.

As they left to attend to their tasks, Marissa asked for the charts on the other two patients. The nurse, whose name was Pat, handed them to her, saying, "I don't know if Dr. Taboso mentioned this, but Mrs. Zabriski is downstairs."

"Is she a patient?" asked Marissa with alarm.

"Oh, no," said Pat. "She's just insisting on staying at the hospital. She wanted to be up here, but Dr. Taboso didn't think it was a good idea. He told her to stay in the first-floor lounge."

Marissa put down the two new charts, debating what she should do next. She decided to see Mrs. Zabriski, since she had very few details with regard to the doctor's recent schedule. Besides, she had to stop by the lab to check the sterilization. Asking directions from Pat, Marissa rode down to the second floor on the elevator. En route she looked at the faces of the people next to her and guessed what their responses would be when they heard that there had been an Ebola outbreak in the hospital. When the doors opened on the second floor, she was the only one who got off.

Marissa expected to find the evening shift in the lab and was surprised to see that the director, a pathologist by the name of Dr. Arthur Rand, was still in his office, even though it was after 8:00 P.M. He was a pompous older man, dressed in a plaid vest complete with a gold fob protruding from one of the pockets. He was unimpressed that Marissa had been sent by the CDC, and his facial expression did not change when Marissa said it was her clinical opinion that there was an outbreak of Ebola in his hospital.

"I was aware that was in the differential diagnosis."

"The CDC has requested that no more lab tests be done on the involved patients." Marissa could tell that the man was not going to make it easy for her. "We'll be bringing in an isolation lab sometime tonight."

"I suggest you communicate this to Dr. Taboso," said Dr. Rand.

"I have," said Marissa. "It's also our opinion that the lab here should be disinfected. In the outbreak in L.A. three cases were traced to the lab. I'd be willing to help, if you'd like."

"I believe that we can handle our own cleanup," said Dr. Rand with a look that seemed to say, *Do you think I was born yesterday?*

"I'm available if you need me," said Marissa as she turned and left. She'd done what she could.

On the first floor she made her way to a pleasant lounge with its own connecting chapel. She was unsure how she would recognize Mrs. Zabriski, but it turned out she was the only person in the room.

"Mrs. Zabriski," said Marissa softly. The woman raised her head. She was in her late forties or early fifties, with gray-streaked hair. Her eyes were red rimmed; it was obvious she had been crying.

"I'm Dr. Blumenthal," said Marissa gently. "I'm sorry to bother you, but I need to ask you some questions."

Panic clouded the woman's eyes. "Is Carl dead?"

"No," said Marissa

"He's going to die, isn't he?"

"Mrs. Zabriski," said Marissa, wanting to avoid such a sensitive

81

issue, especially since she believed the woman's intuition was correct. Marissa sat down next to her. "I'm not one of your husband's doctors. I'm here to help find out what kind of illness he has and how he got it. Has he done any traveling over the last—" Marissa was going to say three weeks, but remembering Dr. Richter's trip to Africa, she said instead, "—the last two months?"

"Yes," Mrs. Zabriski said wearily. "He went to a medical meeting in San Diego last month, and about a week ago he went to Boston."

"San Diego" made Marissa sit up straighter. "Was that an eyelid surgery conference in San Diego?"

"I believe so," said Mrs. Zabriski. "But Judith, Carl's secretary, would know for sure."

Marissa's mind whirled. Zabriski had attended the same meeting as Dr. Richter! Another coincidence? The only problem was that the conference in question had been about six weeks previous, about the same interval of time as from Dr. Richter's African trip to the appearance of his symptoms. "Do you know what hotel your husband stayed in while he was in San Diego?" asked Marissa. "Could it have been the Coronado Hotel?"

"I believe it was," said Mrs. Zabriski.

While Marissa's mind was busy recalling the central role played by a certain hotel in Philadelphia during the Legionnaires Disease outbreak, she asked about Dr. Zabriski's trip to Boston. But his wife did not know why he'd gone. Instead, she gave Marissa her husband's secretary's phone number, saying again that Judith would know that kind of thing.

Marissa took the number and asked whether Dr. Zabriski had been bitten by, or had been around, any monkeys recently.

"No, no," said Mrs. Zabriski. At least none that she knew of.

Marissa thanked the woman and apologized for bothering her. Armed with the secretary's home phone number, she went to call Judith.

Marissa had to explain twice who she was and why she was calling so late before the secretary would cooperate. Judith then confirmed what Mrs. Zabriski had told her: namely, that the doctor had stayed at the Coronado Hotel while in San Diego, that Dr. Zabriski had not been bitten recently by any animal, and, as far as she knew, that he'd not been around any monkeys. When Marissa asked if Dr. Zabriski knew Dr. Richter, the answer was that the name had never appeared on any correspondence or on his phone list. Judith said the reason that Dr. Zabriski had gone to Boston was to help plan the Massachusetts Eye and Ear Infirmary's upcoming alumni meeting. She gave Marissa the name and phone number of Dr. Zabriski's colleague there. As Marissa wrote it down, she wondered if Zabriski had unknowingly transferred the virus to the Boston area. She decided that she'd have to discuss that possibility with Dubchek.

As she hung up, Marissa suddenly remembered that she hadn't called Ralph from the airport. He answered sleepily, and Marissa apologized both for waking him and for not getting in touch with him before she left Atlanta. After she explained what had happened, Ralph said that he would forgive her only if she promised to call him every couple of days to let him know what was going on. Marissa agreed.

Returning to the isolation ward, Marissa went back to the charts. The two later admissions were a Carol Montgomery and a Dr. Brian Cester. Both had come down with high fevers, splitting headaches and violent abdominal cramps. Although the symptoms sounded nonspecific, their intensity gave sufficient cause for alarm. There was no reference to travel or animal contact in either chart.

After gathering the material necessary for taking viral samples, Marissa dressed in protective gear and visited Carol Montgomery. The patient was a woman one year older than Marissa. Marissa found it hard not to identify with her. She was a lawyer who worked for one of the city's large corporate firms. Although she was lucid and able to talk, it was apparent that she was gravely ill.

Marissa asked if she had done any recent traveling. The answer was no. Marissa asked if she knew Dr. Zabriski. Carol said that she did. Dr. Zabriski was her ophthalmologist. Had she seen him recently? The answer was yes: she'd gone to him four days ago.

Marissa obtained the viral samples and left the room with a heavy heart. She hated making a diagnosis of a disease with no available treatment. The fact that she'd been able to uncover information that mirrored the earlier outbreak was small compensation. Yet the information reminded her of a question that had troubled her in L.A.: Why did some of Dr. Richter's patients catch the disease and others not?

After changing into fresh protective clothing, Marissa visited Dr. Brian Cester. She asked the same questions and got the same replies, except when she asked if he was one of Dr. Zabriski's patients.

"No," said Dr. Cester after a spasm of abdominal pain subsided. "I've never been to an ophthalmologist."

"Do you work with him?" asked Marissa.

"I occasionally give anesthesia for him," said Dr. Cester. His face contorted again in pain. When he recovered, he said, "I play tennis with him more often than I work with him. In fact I played with him just four days ago."

After obtaining her samples, Marissa left the man, more confused than ever. She had begun to think that fairly close contact—particularly with a mucous membrane—was needed to communicate the disease. Playing tennis with someone did not seem to fit that mold.

After sending off the second set of viral samples, Marissa went back to Dr. Zabriski's chart. She read over the history in minute detail and began the same type of diary she'd drawn up for Dr. Richter. She added what material she'd learned from Mrs. Zabriski and the secretary, knowing that she would have to go back to both of them. Although such work had not resulted in determining the reservoir of the virus in the L.A. outbreak, Marissa had hopes that by following the same procedure with Dr. Zabriski she might find some common element in addition to both doctors having been to the same eye conference in San Diego.

It was after twelve when Dubchek, Vreeland and Layne arrived. Marissa was relieved to see them, particularly because Dr. Zabriski's clinical condition had continued to deteriorate. The doctor taking care of him had demanded some routine blood work be done to determine the state of the patient's hydration, and Marissa had been caught between the conflicting demands of treating the patient and protecting the hospital. She finally allowed those tests that could be done in the patient's room.

After a cursory greeting, the CDC doctors all but ignored Marissa as they struggled to get the mobile isolation laboratory functioning and improve the isolation of the patients. Dr. Layne had some large exhaust fans brought in, while Dr. Vreeland immediately went down to the administration area to discuss improving the quarantine.

Marissa went back to her charts but soon exhausted the information they could supply. Getting up, she wandered to the isolation lab. Dubchek had removed his jacket and had rolled up his sleeves while he labored with the two CDC technicians. Some kind of electrical bug had developed in the automatic chemistry portion of the apparatus.

"Anything I can do?" called Marissa.

"Not that I can think of," said Dubchek without looking up. He immediately began conversing with one of the technicians, suggesting they change the sensing electrodes.

"I would like a minute to go over my findings with you," called Marissa, eager to discuss the fact that Dr. Zabriski had attended the same San Diego medical meeting as Dr. Richter had.

"It will have to wait," said Dubchek coolly. "Getting this lab functioning takes precedence over epidemiologic theories."

Going back to the nurses' station, Marissa seethed. She did not expect or deserve Dubchek's sarcasm. If he'd wanted to minimize her contribution, he had succeeded. Sitting down at the desk, Marissa considered her options. She could stay, hoping he might allow her ten minutes, at his convenience, or she could go and get some sleep. Sleep won out. She put her papers in her briefcase and went down to the first floor to rescue her suitcase.

The operator woke Marissa at seven o'clock. As she showered and dressed, she realized that her anger toward Dubchek had dissipated. After all, he was under a lot of stress. If Ebola raged out of control, it was his neck on the line, not hers.

When she arrived back at the isolation ward, one of the CDC lab techs told her that Dubchek had gone back to the hotel at 5:00 A.M. He didn't know where either Vreeland or Layne was.

At the nurses' station things were a bit chaotic. Five more patients had been admitted during the night with a presumptive diagnosis of Ebola Hemorrhagic Fever. Marissa collected the charts, but as she stacked them in order, she realized that Zabriski's was missing. She asked the day nurse where it was.

"Dr. Zabriski died just after four this morning."

Although she'd expected it, Marissa was still upset. Unconsciously, she had been hoping for a miracle. She sat down and put her face in her hands. After a moment she forced herself to go over the new charts. It was easier to keep busy. Without meaning to, she caught herself touching her neck for swelling. There was an area of tenderness. Could it be a swollen lymph node?

She was pleased to be interrupted by Dr. Layne, the Director of the CDC's Hospital Infectious Disease Program. It was obvious from the dark circles under his eyes, his drawn face and the stubble on his chin that he had pulled an "all-nighter." She smiled, liking his slightly heavyset, rumpled looks. He reminded her of a retired football player. He sat down wearily, massaging his temples.

"Looks like this is going to be just as bad as L.A.," he said. "We have another patient on the way up and another in the ER."

"I've just started looking at the new charts," said Marissa, suddenly feeling guilty for having left the night before.

"Well, I can tell you one thing," said Dr. Layne. "All the new patients seem to have gotten their disease from the hospital. That's what bothers me so much."

"Are they all patients of Dr. Zabriski's?" asked Marissa.

"Those are," said Dr. Layne, pointing at the charts in front of Marissa. "They all saw Zabriski recently. He apparently inoculated them during his examinations. The new cases are both Dr. Cester's patients. He'd been the anesthesiologist when they had surgery during the last ten days."

"What about Dr. Cester?" asked Marissa. "Do you think that he contracted the disease the same way that Dr. Zabriski did?"

Dr. Layne shook his head. "Nope. I talked at length with the man, and I found out that he and Zabriski were tennis partners."

Marissa nodded. "But would such contact count?"

"About three days before Dr. Zabriski became ill, Dr. Cester borrowed his towel between sets. I think that's what did it. Transmission seems to depend on actual contact with body fluids. I think Zabriski is another index case, just like Dr. Richter."

Marissa felt stupid. She had stopped questioning Dr. Cester just one question short of learning a crucial fact. She hoped that she wouldn't make the same mistake again.

"If we only knew how the Ebola got into the hospital in the first place," said Dr. Layne rhetorically.

Dubchek, looking tired but clean-shaven and as carefully dressed as always, arrived at the nurses' station. Marissa was surprised to see him. If he'd left at five, he'd hardly had time to shower and change, much less get any sleep.

Before Dubchek could get involved in a conversation with Layne, Marissa quickly told both doctors that Zabriski had attended the same San Diego medical conference as Richter had and that they had stayed in the same hotel.

"It's too long ago to be significant," Dubchek said dogmatically. "That conference was over six weeks ago."

"But it appears to be the only association between the two doctors," protested Marissa. "I think I should follow up on it."

"Suit yourself," said Dubchek. "Meanwhile, I'd like you to go down to pathology and make sure they take every precaution when they post Zabriski this morning. And tell them that we want quick-frozen samples of liver, heart, brain and spleen for viral isolation."

"What about kidney?" interjected Layne.

"Yeah, kidney, too," said Dubchek.

Marissa went off feeling like an errand girl. She wondered if she would ever regain Dubchek's respect, then remembering why she'd lost it, her depression was wiped out by a surge of anger.

In pathology, a busy place at that time of day, Marissa was directed to the autopsy rooms, where she knew she'd find Dr. Rand. Remembering his pompous, overbearing manner, she was not looking forward to talking with him.

The autopsy rooms were constructed of white tile and gleaming stainless steel. There was a pervading aroma of formalin that made Marissa's eyes water. One of the technicians told her that Zabriski's post was scheduled for room three. "If you intend to go, you have to suit up. It's a dirty case."

With her general fear of catching Ebola, Marissa was more than happy to comply. When she entered the room, she found Dr. Rand just about to begin. He looked up from the table of horrific tools. Dr. Zabriski's body was still enclosed in a large, clear plastic bag. His body was a pasty white on the top, a livid purple on the bottom.

"Hi!" said Marissa brightly. She decided that she might as well be cheerful. Receiving no answer, she conveyed the CDC's requests to the pathologist, who agreed to supply the samples. Marissa then suggested the use of goggles. "A number of cases both here and in L.A. were apparently infected through the conjunctival membrane," she explained.

Dr. Rand grunted, then disappeared. When he returned he was wearing a pair of plastic goggles. Without saying anything he handed a pair to Marissa.

"One other thing," Marissa added. "The CDC recommends avoiding power saws on this kind of case because they cause significant aerosol formation."

"I was not planning to use any power tools," said Dr. Rand. "Although you may find this surprising, I have handled infectious cases during my career."

"Then I suppose I don't have to warn you about not cutting your fingers," said Marissa. "A pathologist died of viral hemorrhagic fever after doing just that."

"I recall," said Dr. Rand. "Lassa Fever. Are you about to favor us with any further suggestions?"

"No," said Marissa. The pathologist cut into the plastic bag and exposed Zabriski's body to the air. Marissa debated whether she should go or stay. Indecision resulted in inaction; she stayed.

Speaking into an overhead microphone activated by a foot pedal, Dr. Rand began his description of the external markings of the body. His voice had assumed that peculiar monotone Marissa remembered from her medical school days. She was startled back to the present when she heard Rand describe a sutured scalp laceration. That was something new. It hadn't been in the chart, nor had the cut on the right elbow or the circular bruise on the right thigh, a bruise about the size of a quarter.

"Did these abrasions happen before or after death?"

"Before," he answered, making no attempt to conceal his irritation at the interruption.

"How old do you think they are?" said Marissa, ignoring his tone. She bent over to look at them more carefully.

"About a week old, I'd say," Dr. Rand replied. "Give or take a couple of days. We'd be able to tell if we did microscopic sections. However, in view of the patient's condition, I hardly think they are important. Now, if you don't mind, I'd like to get back to work."

Forced to step back, Marissa thought about this evidence of trauma. There was probably some simple explanation; perhaps Dr. Zabriski had fallen playing tennis. What bothered Marissa was that the abrasion and the laceration were not mentioned on the man's chart. Where Marissa had trained, every physical finding went into the record.

As soon as Rand had finished and Marissa had seen that the tissue samples were correctly done, she decided to track down the cause of the injuries.

Using the phone in pathology, Marissa tried Zabriski's secretary, Judith. She let the phone ring twenty times. No answer. Reluctant to bother Mrs. Zabriski, Marissa thought about looking for Dr. Taboso, but instead decided to check Dr. Zabriski's office, realizing it had to be right there in the hospital. She walked over and found Judith back at her desk.

Judith was a frail young woman in her mid-twenties. Mascara smudged her cheeks; Marissa could tell that she'd been crying. But she was more than sad; she was also terrified.

"Mrs. Zabriski is sick," she blurted out as soon as Marissa introduced herself. "I talked with her a little while ago. She's downstairs in the emergency room but she is going to be admitted to the hospital. They think she has the same thing that her husband had. My God, am I going to get it too? What are the symptoms?"

With some difficulty, Marissa calmed the woman enough to explain that in the L.A. outbreak the doctor's secretary had not come down with the illness.

"I'm still getting out of here," said Judith, opening a side drawer of her desk and taking out a sweater. She tossed it into a cardboard box. She'd obviously been packing. "And I'm not the only one who wants to go," she added. "I've talked with a number of the staff and they are leaving, too."

"I understand how you feel," said Marissa. She wondered if the entire hospital would have to be quarantined. At the Richter Clinic, it had been a logistical nightmare.

"I came here to ask you a question," said Marissa.

"So ask," said Judith. She continued to empty her desk drawers.

"Dr. Zabriski had some abrasions and a cut on his head, as if he'd fallen. Do you know anything about that?"

"That was nothing," said Judith, making a gesture of dismissal with her hand. "He was mugged about a week ago, in a local mall while he was shopping for a birthday gift for his wife. He lost his wallet and his gold Rolex. I think they hit him on the head."

So much for the mysterious question of trauma, thought Marissa. For a few minutes she stood watching Judith throw her things into the box, trying to think if she had any further questions. She couldn't think of any just then, so she said good-bye, then left, heading for the isolation ward. In many ways she felt as scared as Judith did.

The isolation ward had lost its previous tranquillity. With all the new patients, it was fully staffed with overworked nurses. She found Dr. Layne writing in several of the charts.

"Welcome to Bedlam," he said. "We've got five more admissions, including Mrs. Zabriski."

"So I've heard," said Marissa, sitting down next to Dr. Layne. If only Dubchek would treat her as he did: like a colleague.

"Tad Schockley called earlier. It is Ebola."

A shiver ran down Marissa's spine.

"We're expecting the State Commissioner of Health to arrive any minute to impose quarantine," continued Dr. Layne. "Seems that a number of hospital personnel are abandoning the place: nurses, technicians, even some doctors. Dr. Taboso had a hell of a time staffing this ward. Have you seen the local paper?"

Marissa shook her head, indicating that she had not. She was tempted to say that she didn't want to stay either, if it meant being exposed.

"The headline is 'Plague Returns!' " Dr. Layne made an expression of disgust. "The media can be so goddamned irresponsible. Dubchek doesn't want anyone to talk with the press. He wants all questions directed to him."

The sound of the patient-elevator doors opening caught Marissa's attention. She watched as a gurney emerged, covered by a clear plastic isolation tent. As it went by, Marissa recognized Mrs. Zabriski. She shivered again, wondering if the local paper really had been exaggerating in their headline.

6

APRIL 10

Marissa took another forkful of the kind of dessert that she allowed herself only on rare occasions. It was her second night back in Atlanta, and Ralph had taken her to an intimate French restaurant. After five weeks with little sleep, gulping down meals in a hospital cafeteria, the gourmet meal had been a true delight. She noticed that, not having had a drink since she'd left Atlanta, the wine had gone right to her head. She knew she was being very talkative, but Ralph seemed content to sit back and listen.

Winding down, Marissa apologized for chattering on about her work, pointing to her empty glass as the excuse.

"No need to apologize," Ralph insisted. "I could listen all night. I'm fascinated by what you have accomplished, both in L.A. and in St. Louis."

"But I've filled you in while I was away," protested Marissa, referring to their frequent phone conversations. While she'd been in St. Louis, Marissa had gotten into the habit of calling every few days. Talking with Ralph had provided a sounding board for her theories as well as a way to relieve her frustration at Dubchek's continued insistence on ignoring her. In both cases, Ralph had been understanding and supportive.

"I wish you'd tell me more about the community reaction," he said.

"How did the administrators and medical staff of the hospital try to control the panic, considering that this time there were thirty-seven deaths?"

Taking him at his word, Marissa tried to describe the turmoil at the St. Louis hospital. The staff and patients were furious at the enforced quarantine, and Dr. Taboso had sadly told her he expected the hospital to close when it was lifted.

"You know, I'm still worried about getting sick myself," admitted Marissa with a self-conscious laugh. "Every time I get a headache I think 'this is it.' And though we still have no idea where the virus came from, Dubchek's position is that the virus reservoir is somehow associated with medical personnel, which doesn't make me any more comfortable."

"Do you believe it?" asked Ralph.

Marissa laughed. "I'm supposed to," she said. "And if it is true, then you should consider yourself particularly at risk. Both index cases were ophthalmologists."

"Don't say that," laughed Ralph. "I'm superstitious."

Marissa leaned back as the waiter served a second round of coffee. It tasted wonderful, but she suspected she'd be sorry later on when she tried to sleep.

After the waiter left with the dessert dishes, Marissa continued: "If Dubchek's position is correct, then somehow both eye doctors came into contact with the mysterious reservoir. I've puzzled over this for weeks without coming up with a single explanation. Dr. Richter came in contact with monkeys; in fact he'd been bitten a week before he became ill, and monkeys have been associated with a related virus called Marburg. But Dr. Zabriski had no contact with any animals at all."

"I thought you told me that Dr. Richter had been to Africa," said Ralph. "It seems to me that is the crucial fact. After all, Africa is where this virus is endemic."

"True," said Marissa. "But the time frame is all wrong. His incubation period would have been six weeks, when all the other cases averaged only two to five days. Then consider the problem of relating the two outbreaks. Dr. Zabriski hadn't been to Africa, but the only point of connection was that the two doctors attended the same medical conference in San Diego. And again, that was six weeks before Dr. Zabriski got sick. It's crazy." Marissa waved her hand as if she were giving up.

"At least be happy you controlled the outbreaks as well as you did. I understand that it was worse when this virus appeared in Africa."

"That's true," agreed Marissa. "In the Zaire outbreak in 1976, whose index case may have been an American college student, there were three hundred eighteen cases and two hundred eighty deaths."

"There you go," said Ralph, feeling that the statistics should cheer Marissa. He folded his napkin and put it on the table. "How about stopping at my house for an after-dinner drink?"

Marissa looked at Ralph, amazed at how comfortable she'd become with him. The surprising thing was that the relationship had developed on the telephone. "An after-dinner drink sounds fine," she said with a smile.

On the way out of the restaurant, Marissa took Ralph's arm. When they got to his car, he opened the door for her. She thought that she could get used to such treatment.

Ralph was proud of his car. It was obvious in the loving way he touched the instruments and the steering wheel. The car was a new 300 SDL Mercedes. Marissa appreciated its luxuriousness as she settled back in the leather seat, but cars had never meant much to her. She also couldn't understand why people bought diesels since they had an uncomfortable rattle when they started and idled. "They are economical," said Ralph. Marissa looked around at the appointments. She marveled that someone could delude himself that an expensive Mercedes was economical.

They didn't speak for a while, and Marissa wondered if going to Ralph's house at that time of night was a good idea. But she trusted Ralph and was willing to let their relationship develop a little further. She turned to look at him in the half-light. He had a strong profile, with a prominent nose like her father's.

After they had settled on the couch in the parlor, with brandy snifters in hand, Marissa mentioned something she had been afraid to point out to Dubchek in his current patronizing mood. "There is one thing about the two index cases that I find curious. Both men were mugged just a few days before they got sick." Marissa waited for a response.

"Very suspicious," said Ralph with a wink. "Are you suggesting that there is an 'Ebola Mary' who robs people and spreads the disease?"

Marissa laughed. "I know it sounds stupid. That's why I haven't said anything to anyone else."

"But you have to think of everything," added Ralph. "The old medical-school training that taught you to ask everything, including what the maternal grandfather did for a living in the old country.''

Deliberately, Marissa switched the conversation to Ralph's work and his house, his two favorite subjects. As the time passed, she noted that he did not make any moves toward her. She wondered if it were something about herself, like the fact that she'd been exposed to Ebola. Then, to make matters worse, he invited her to spend the night in the guest room.

Marissa was insulted. Perhaps just as insulted as if he'd tried to drag her dress over her head the moment they walked in the front door. She told him thank you, but she did not want to spend the night in his guest room; she wanted to spend the night in her own house with her dog. The last part was meant to be an affront, but it sailed over Ralph's head. He just kept on talking about redecorating plans he had for the first floor of the house, now that he'd lived there long enough to know what he wanted.

In truth, Marissa did not know what she would have done if Ralph had made any physical advances. He was a good friend, but she still didn't find him romantically attractive. In that respect, she thought Dubchek's looks distinctly more exciting.

Thinking of Cyrill reminded her of something. ''How do you and Dr. Dubchek know each other?''

''I met him when he addressed the ophthalmology residents at the University Hospital,'' said Ralph. ''Some of the rare viruses like Ebola and even the AIDS virus have been localized in tears and the aqueous humor. Some of them even cause anterior uveitis.''

''Oh,'' said Marissa, nodding as if she understood. Actually she had no idea what anterior uveitis was, but she decided it was as good a point as any to ask Ralph to drive her home.

Over the next few days, Marissa adapted to a more normal life, although every time the phone rang, she half expected to be called out for another Ebola disaster. Remembering her resolve, she did pack a suitcase and kept it open in her closet, ready for her to toss in her cosmetics case. She could be out of her house in a matter of minutes, if the need arose.

At work, things were looking up. Tad helped her perfect her viral laboratory skills and worked with her to write up a research proposal on Ebola. Unable to come up with a working hypothesis for a possible reservoir for Ebola, Marissa concentrated instead on the issue of transmission. From the enormous amount of data that she'd amassed in L.A. and St. Louis, she had constructed elaborate case maps to show the spread of the illness from one person to another. At the same time, she'd compiled detailed profiles on the people who had been primary contacts but who had not come down with the disease. As Dr. Layne had suggested, close personal contact was needed, presumably viral contact with a mucous membrane, though, unlike AIDS, sexual transmission had only been a factor between Dr. Richter and the medical secretary and Dr. Zabriski and his wife. Given the fact that hemorrhagic fever could spread between strangers who shared a towel, or by the most casual close touch, Ebola made the AIDS scare seem like a tempest in a teapot.

What Marissa wanted to do was to validate her hypothesis by using guinea pigs. Of course such work required the use of the maximum containment lab, and she still had not obtained permission.

"Amazing!" exclaimed Tad, one afternoon when Marissa demonstrated a technique she'd devised to salvage bacteria-contaminated viral cultures. "I can't imagine Dubchek turning down your proposal now."

"I can," answered Marissa. She debated telling Tad about what had happened in the L.A. hotel, but once again she decided not to do so. It wouldn't accomplish anything and might cause problems in Tad's relationship with Cyrill.

She followed her friend into his office. As they relaxed over coffee, Marissa said, "Tad, you told me when we went into the maximum containment lab that there were all sorts of viruses stored in there, including Ebola."

"We have samples from every outbreak. There are even samples frozen and stored from your two outbreaks."

Marissa wasn't at all sure how she felt about people referring to the recent epidemics as "hers." But she kept that thought to herself, saying instead, "Is there any place else that the Ebola virus is stored, other than here at the CDC?"

Tad thought for a moment. "I'm not sure. Do you mean here in the U.S.?"

Marissa nodded.

"The army probably has some in Ft. Detrick at the Center for Biological Warfare. The fellow that runs the place used to be here at the CDC and he had an interest in viral hemorrhagic fevers."

"Does the army have a maximum containment lab?"

Tad whistled. "Man, they've got everything."

"And you say the man in charge at Ft. Detrick has an interest in viral hemorrhagic fever?"

"He was one of the people along with Dubchek who had been sent out to cover the initial Ebola outbreak in Zaire."

Marissa sipped her coffee, thinking that was an interesting coincidence. She was also beginning to get a germ of an idea, one so unpleasant that she knew she could not consider it a reasonable hypothesis.

"One moment, ma'am," said the uniformed sentry with a heavy Southern accent.

Marissa was stopped at the main gate to Ft. Detrick. Despite several days of trying to argue herself out of the suspicion that the army might have somehow been responsible for Ebola being loosed on an unsuspecting public, she had finally decided to use her day off to investigate for herself. Those two muggings continued to nag at her.

It had only been an hour-and-a-half flight to Maryland and a short drive in a rent-a-car. Marissa had pleaded her field experience with Ebola as an excuse to talk to anyone else familiar with the rare virus, and Colonel Woolbert had responded to her request with enthusiasm.

The sentry returned to Marissa's car. "You are expected at building number eighteen." He handed her a pass that she had to wear on the lapel of her blazer, then startled her with a crisp salute. Ahead of her, the black-and-white gate tipped up, and she drove onto the base.

Building #18 was a windowless concrete structure with a flat roof. A middle-aged man in civilian clothes waved as Marissa got out of her car. It was Colonel Kenneth Woolbert.

To Marissa, he looked more like a university professor than an army officer. He was friendly, even humorous, and was unabashedly pleased about Marissa's visit. He told her right off that she was the prettiest and the smallest EIS officer he'd ever met. Marissa took the good with the bad.

The building felt like a bunker. Entry was obtained through a series of sliding steel doors activated by remote control. Small TV cameras were mounted above each door. The laboratory itself, however, appeared like any other modern hospital facility, complete with the omnipresent coffeepot over the Bunsen burner. The only difference was the lack of windows.

After a quick tour, during which the presence of a maximum containment lab was not mentioned, Colonel Woolbert took Marissa to their snack shop, which was nothing more than a series of vending machines. He got her a donut and Pepsi, and they sat down at a small table.

Without any prompting, Colonel Woolbert explained that he'd started at the CDC as an EIS officer in the late fifties and had become increasingly interested in microbiology and ultimately virology. In the seventies, he'd gone back to school, at government expense, to get a Ph.D.

"It's been a hell of a lot better than looking at sore throats and clogged ears," said the Colonel.

"Don't tell me you were in pediatrics!" exclaimed Marissa.

They laughed when they realized they had both trained at Boston's Children's Hospital. Colonel Woolbert went on to explain how he'd ended up at Ft. Detrick. He told Marissa that there had been a history of movement between Detrick and the CDC and that the army had come to him with an offer he couldn't refuse. He said that the lab and the equipment were superb, and best of all, he didn't have to grovel for funds.

"Doesn't the ultimate goal bother you?" asked Marissa.

"No," said Colonel Woolbert. "You have to understand that three-quarters of the work here involves defending the U.S. against biological attack, so most of my efforts are directed at neutralizing viruses like Ebola."

Marissa nodded. She'd not thought of that.

"Besides," continued Colonel Woolbert, "I'm given complete latitude. I can work on whatever I want to."

"And what is that just now?" asked Marissa innocently. There was a pause. The colonel's light-blue eyes twinkled.

"I suppose I'm not violating the confidentiality of the military by telling you, since I've been publishing a string of articles on my results. For the last three years my interest has been influenza virus."

"Not Ebola?" asked Marissa.

Colonel Woolbert shook his head. "No, my last research on Ebola was years ago."

"Is anyone here at the center working on Ebola?" asked Marissa.

Colonel Woolbert hesitated. Then he said, "I guess I can tell you, since there was a Pentagon policy paper published on it in *Strategic Studies* last year. The answer is no. No one is working on Ebola, including the Soviets, mainly because there is no vaccine or treatment for it. Once started, it was generally felt that Ebola Hemorrhagic Fever would spread like wildfire to both friendly and hostile forces."

"But it hasn't," said Marissa.

"I know," said Colonel Woolbert with a sigh. "I've read with great interest about the last two outbreaks. Someday we'll have to review our assessment of the organism."

"Please, not on my account," said Marissa. The last thing she wanted to do was encourage the army to work with Ebola. At the same time she was relieved to learn that the army was not fooling around with the virus just then.

"I understand you were part of the international team that was sent to Yambuku in 1976," she said.

"Which makes me appreciate what you're doing. I can tell you, when I was in Africa I was scared shitless."

Marissa grinned. She liked and trusted the man. "You are the first person to admit being afraid," she said. "I've been struggling with my fear from the first day I was sent to L.A."

"And for good reason," said Colonel Woolbert. "Ebola's a strange bug. Even though it seems it can be inactivated quite easily, it is extraordinarily infective, meaning that only a couple of organisms have to make entry to produce the disease. That's in marked contrast to something like AIDS, where billions of the virus have to be introduced, and even then there is only a low statistical chance that the individual will be infected."

"What about the reservoir?" asked Marissa. "I know the official position is that no reservoir was discovered in Africa. But did you have an opinion?"

"I think it is an animal disease," said Colonel Woolbert. "I think it will eventually be isolated to some equatorial African monkey and is therefore a zoonosis, or a disease of vertebrate animals that occasionally gets transmitted to man."

"So you agree with the current CDC official position about these recent U.S. outbreaks?" asked Marissa.

"Of course," said Colonel Woolbert. "What other position is there?"

Marissa shrugged. "Do you have any Ebola here?"

"No," said Colonel Woolbert. "But I know where we can get it."

"I know, too," said Marissa. Well, that wasn't quite true, she thought. Tad had said that it was in the maximum containment lab, but exactly where, she did not know. When they'd made their covert visit, she'd forgotten to ask.

7

APRIL 17

The phone must have been ringing for some time before Marissa finally rolled over to pick up the receiver. The CDC operator instantly apologized for waking her from such a deep sleep. As Marissa struggled to sit up, she learned that a call had come through from Phoenix, Arizona, and that the operator wanted permission to patch it through. Marissa agreed immediately.

While she waited for the phone to ring again, she slipped on her robe and glanced at the time. It was 4:00 A.M.; that meant it was 2:00 A.M. in Phoenix. There was little doubt in her mind that someone had discovered another suspected case of Ebola.

The phone jangled again. "Dr. Blumenthal," said Marissa.

The voice on the other end of the wire was anything but calm. The caller introduced himself as Dr. Guy Weaver, the Arizona State Epidemiologist. "I'm terribly sorry to be phoning at such an hour," he said, "but I've been called in on a severe problem at the Medica Hospital in Phoenix. I trust you are familiar with the Medica Hospital."

"Can't say I am."

"It's part of a chain of for-profit hospitals which have contracted with the Medica Medical Group to provide prepaid, comprehensive care in this part of Arizona. We're terrified that the hospital's been hit with Ebola."

"I trust that you've isolated the patient," said Marissa. "We've found that—"

"Dr. Blumenthal," interrupted Dr. Weaver. "It's not one case. It's eighty-four cases."

"Eighty-four!" she exclaimed in disbelief.

"We have forty-two doctors, thirteen RN's, eleven LPN's, four lab techs, six of the administrative staff, six food service personnel and two maintenance men."

"All at once?" asked Marissa.

"All this evening," said the epidemiologist.

At that time of night, there was no convenient service to Phoenix, though Delta promised the most direct flight available. As soon as she dressed, Marissa called the duty officer at the CDC to say that she was leaving for Phoenix immediately and to please brief Dr. Dubchek as soon as he came into the Center.

After writing a note to the Judsons asking them to please collect Taffy and pick up her mail, Marissa drove to the airport. The fact that the new outbreak had started with eighty-four cases overwhelmed her. She hoped Dubchek and his team would arrive by the afternoon.

The flight was uneventful, despite two stops, and was certainly not crowded. When it landed, Marissa was met by a short, round man, who nervously introduced himself as Justin Gardiner, the assistant director of the Medica Hospital.

"Here, let me take your bag," he said. But his hand was shaking so, the bag fell to the floor. Bending down to retrieve it, he apologized, saying that he was a bit upset.

"I can understand," said Marissa. "Have there been any further admissions?"

"Several, and the hospital is in a panic," said Mr. Gardiner, as they started down the concourse. "Patients started checking out—staff were leaving, too—until the State Health Commissioner declared a quarantine. The only reason I could meet you was that I was off yesterday."

Marissa's mouth felt dry with fear as she wondered what she was getting herself into. Pediatrics began to look a lot more attractive than this.

The hospital was another elaborate modern structure. It occurred to Marissa that Ebola favored such contemporary edifices. The clean, almost sterile lines of the building hardly seemed the proper setting for such a deadly outbreak.

Despite the early hour, the street in front of the hospital was crowded with TV trucks and reporters. In front of them stood a line of uniformed police, some of whom were actually wearing surgical masks. In the early light, the whole scene had a surreal look.

Mr. Gardiner pulled up behind one of the TV trucks. "You'll have to go inside and find the director," he said. "My orders are to stay outside to try to control the panic. Good luck!"

As she walked toward the entrance, Marissa got out her identification card. She showed it to one of the policemen, but he had to call over to his sergeant to ask if it was okay to let her pass. A group of the reporters, hearing that she was from the CDC, crowded around and asked for a statement.

"I have no direct knowledge of the situation," protested Marissa, as she felt herself buffeted by the surging journalists. She was grateful for the policeman, who shoved the press aside, then pulled one of the barricades open and allowed her through.

Unfortunately things on the inside of the hospital were even more chaotic. The lobby was jammed with people, and as Marissa entered, she was again mobbed. Apparently she was the first person to pass either in or out of the building for several hours.

A number of the people pressing in on her were patients, dressed in pajamas and robes. They were all simultaneously asking questions and demanding answers.

"Please!" shouted someone to Marissa's right. "Please! Let me through." A heavyset man with bushy eyebrows pushed his way to Marissa's side. "Dr. Blumenthal?"

"Yes," said Marissa with relief.

The heavyset man took her by the arm, ignoring the fact that she was carrying both a suitcase and briefcase. Pushing his way back through the crowd, he led her across the lobby to a door that he locked behind them. They were in a long, narrow hallway.

"I'm terribly sorry about all this turmoil," said the man. "I'm Lloyd Davis, director of the hospital, and we seem to have a bit of a panic on our hands."

Marissa followed Davis to his office. They entered through a side door, and Marissa noticed the main door was barricaded from the inside with a ladder-back chair, making her believe that the "bit of panic" had been an understatement.

"The staff is waiting to talk with you," said Mr. Davis, taking

Marissa's belongings and depositing them next to his desk. He breathed heavily, as if the effort of bending over had exhausted him.

"What about the patients with suspected Ebola?" asked Marissa.

"For the moment they'll have to wait," said the director, motioning Marissa to return to the hallway.

"But our first priority has to be the proper isolation of the patients."

"They are well isolated," Mr. Davis assured her. "Dr. Weaver has taken care of that." He pressed his hand against the small of Marissa's back, propelling her toward the door. "Of course we'll follow any additional suggestions you have, but right now I would like you to talk with the staff before I'm faced with mutiny."

"I hope it's not that bad," said Marissa. It was one thing if the inpatients were upset, quite another if the professional staff was hysterical as well.

Mr. Davis closed his office door and led the way along another corridor. "A lot of people are terrified at being forced to stay in the hospital."

"How many more presumed cases have been diagnosed since you called the CDC?"

"Sixteen. No more staff; all the new cases are Medica Plan subscribers."

That suggested that the virus was already into its second generation, having been spread by the initially infected physicians. At least that was what had happened in the two previous outbreaks. Marissa herself quaked at the idea of being locked up in the same building with such a contagion, making her question how much consolation she would be able to extend to the staff. With so many people infected, she wondered if they would be able to contain the problem as they had in L.A. and St. Louis. The horror of the thought of Ebola passing into the general community was almost beyond comprehension.

"Do you know if any of the initial cases had been mugged recently?" asked Marissa, as much to distract herself as in hope of a positive answer. Davis just glanced at her and raised his eyebrows as if she were crazy. That seemed as much of a response he felt the question merited. So much for that observation, thought Marissa, remembering Ralph's response.

They stopped in front of a locked door. Davis took out his keys, unlocked the door and led Marissa onto the hospital auditorium's stage. It was not a big room: There was seating for approximately one hundred and fifty people. Marissa noticed all the seats were occupied, with still more people standing in the back. There was the buzz of a dozen simultaneous conversations. They trailed off into silence as Marissa nervously walked toward the podium, all eyes upon her. A tall, exceptionally thin man stood up from a chair behind the podium and shook her hand. Mr. Davis introduced him as Dr. Guy Weaver, the man she'd spoken to on the phone.

"Dr. Blumenthal," said Dr. Weaver, his deep voice a sharp contrast to his scrawny frame, "you have no idea how happy I am to see you."

Marissa felt that uncomfortable sense of being an impostor. And it got worse. After tapping the microphone to make certain it was "live," Dr. Weaver proceeded to introduce Marissa.

He did so in such glowing terms that she felt progressively more and more uneasy. From his comments, it was as if she were synonymous with the CDC, and that all the triumphs of the CDC were her triumphs. Then, with a sweep of his long arm, he turned the microphone over to Marissa.

Never feeling comfortable talking to a large group under the best of circumstances, Marissa was totally nonplussed in the current situation. She had no idea of what was expected of her, much less of what to say. She took the few moments required to bend the microphone down to her level, to think.

Glancing out at the audience, Marissa noted that about half were wearing surgical masks. She also noticed that a large portion of the people, both men and women, were ethnic-appearing, with distinctive features and coloring. There was also a wide range of ages, making Marissa realize that what Mr. Davis meant by staff was anybody working for the hospital, not just physicians. They were all watching her expectantly, and she wished she had more confidence in her ability to affect what was happening at the hospital.

"The first thing we will do is ascertain the diagnosis," began Marissa in a hesitant voice several octaves above her normal pitch. As she continued speaking, not sure of which direction she would go, her voice became more normal. She introduced herself in reasonable terms, explaining her real function at the CDC. She also tried to assure the audience, even though she wasn't sure herself, that the outbreak would be controlled by strict isolation of the patients, complete barrier nursing, and reasonable quarantine procedures.

"Will we all get sick?" shouted a woman from the back of the room. A murmur rippled through the audience. This was their major concern.

"I have been involved in two recent outbreaks," said Marissa, "and I have not been infected, though I've come into contact with patients who had." She didn't mention her own continuing fear. "We have determined that close personal contact is necessary to spread Ebola. Airborne spread is apparently not a factor." Marissa noticed that a few of the people in the audience removed their masks. She glanced around at Dr. Weaver, who gave her an encouraging thumbs-up sign.

"Is it really necessary for us to remain within the hospital?" demanded a man in the third row. He was wearing a physician's long white coat.

"For the time being," said Marissa diplomatically. "The quarantine procedure that we followed in the previous outbreaks involved separating the contacts into primary and secondary groups." Marissa went on to describe in detail what they had done in L.A. and St. Louis. She concluded by saying that no one who'd been quarantined had come down with the illness unless they had previously had direct, hands-on contact with someone already ill.

Marissa then fielded a series of questions about the initial symptoms and the clinical course of Ebola Hemorrhagic Fever. The latter either terrified the audience into silence or satisfied their curiosity—Marissa couldn't decide which—but there were no further questions.

While Mr. Davis got up to talk to his staff, Dr. Weaver led Marissa out of the auditorium. As soon as they were in the narrow hallway, she told him that she wanted to see one of the initial cases before she called the CDC. Dr. Weaver said he'd assumed as much and offered to take her himself. En route he explained that they had placed all the cases on two floors of the hospital, moving out the other patients and isolating the ventilation system. He had every reason to believe they'd made it a self-contained area. He also explained that the staff employed to man the floors were all specifically trained by his people, that laboratory work had been restricted to what could be done in a hastily set up unit on one of the isolated floors and that everything used by the patients was being washed with sodium hypochlorite before being directly incinerated.

As for the quarantine situation, he told Marissa that mattresses had been brought in from the outside and the outpatient department had been turned into a huge dormitory, separating primary and secondary contacts. All food and water was also being brought in. It was at that point that Marissa learned that Dr. Weaver had been an EIS officer at the CDC six years previously.

"Why did you introduce me as the expert?" asked Marissa, remembering his embarrassing exaggerations. Obviously he knew as much as or more than she did about quarantine procedures.

"For effect," admitted Dr. Weaver. "The hospital personnel needed something to believe in."

Marissa grunted, upset at being misrepresented, but impressed with Dr. Weaver's efficiency. Before entering the floor, they gowned. Then, before entering one of the rooms, they double-gowned, adding hoods, goggles, masks, gloves and booties.

The patient Dr. Weaver brought Marissa to see was one of the clinic's general surgeons. He was an Indian, originally from Bombay. All Marissa's fears of exposure came back in a rush as she looked down at the patient. The man appeared moribund, even though he'd been sick for only twenty-four hours. The clinical picture mirrored the terminal phase of the cases in L.A. and St. Louis. There was high fever along with low blood pressure, and the typical skin rash with signs of hemorrhage from mucous membranes. Marissa knew the man would not last another twenty-four hours.

To save time, she drew her viral samples immediately, and Dr. Weaver arranged to have them properly packed and shipped overnight to Tad Schockley.

A glance at the man's chart showed the history to be fairly sketchy, but with eighty-four admissions in less than six hours she could hardly have hoped for a textbook writeup. She saw no mention of foreign travel, monkeys, or contact with the L.A. or St. Louis outbreaks.

Leaving the floor, Marissa first requested access to a telephone, then said she wanted to have as many physician volunteers as she could get to help her interview the patients. If many patients were as sick as the Indian doctor, they would have to work quickly if they were going to get any information at all.

Marissa was given the phone in Mr. Davis's office. It was already after eleven in Atlanta, and Marissa reached Dubchek immediately. The trouble was, he was irritated.

"Why didn't you call me as soon as the aid request came in? I didn't know you had gone until I got into my office."

Marissa held her tongue. The truth was that she'd told the CDC

105

operators that she should be called directly if a call came in suggestive of an Ebola outbreak. She assumed Dubchek could have done the same if he'd wanted to be called immediately, but she certainly wasn't going to antagonize him further by pointing out the fact.

"Does it look like Ebola?"

"It does," said Marissa, anticipating Dubchek's reaction to her next bomb. "The chief difference is in number of those infected. This outbreak involves one hundred cases at this point."

"I hope that you have instituted the proper isolation," was Dubchek's only reply.

Marissa felt cheated. She'd expected Dubchek to be overwhelmed. "Aren't you surprised by the number of cases?" she asked.

"Ebola is a relatively unknown entity," said Dubchek. "At this point, nothing would surprise me. I'm more concerned about containment; what about the isolation?"

"The isolation is fine," said Marissa.

"Good," said Dubchek. "The Vickers Lab is ready and we will be leaving within the hour. Make sure you have viral samples for Tad as soon as possible."

Marissa found herself giving assurances to a dead phone. The bastard had hung up. She hadn't even had a chance to warn him that the entire hospital was under quarantine—that if he entered, he'd not be allowed to leave. "It'll serve him right," she said aloud as she got up from the desk.

When she left the office, she discovered that Dr. Weaver had assembled eleven doctors to help take histories: five women and six men. All of them voiced the same motivation: as long as they had to be cooped up in the hospital, they might as well work.

Marissa sat down and explained what she needed: good histories on as many of the initial eighty-four cases as possible. She explained that in both the L.A. and the St. Louis incidents there had been an index case to which all other patients could be traced. Obviously, there in Phoenix it was different. With so many simultaneous cases there was the suggestion of a food- or waterborne disease.

"If it were waterborne, wouldn't more people have been infected?" asked one of the women.

"If the entire hospital supply was involved," said Marissa. "But perhaps a certain water fountain . . ." Her voice trailed off. "Ebola had never been a water- or foodborne infection," she admitted. "It is all very mysterious, and it just underlines the need for complete histories to try to find some area of commonality. Were all the patients on the same shifts? Were they all in the same areas of the hospital? Did they all drink coffee from the same pot, eat the same food, come in contact with the same animal?''

Pushing back her chair, Marissa went to a blackboard and began outlining a sequence of questions that each patient should be asked. The other doctors rose to the challenge and began giving suggestions. When they were done, Marissa added as an afterthought that they might ask if any of the patients had attended the eyelid surgery conference in San Diego that had been held about three months before.

Before the group disbanded, Marissa reminded everyone to adhere carefully to all the isolation techniques. Then she thanked them again and went to review the material that was already available.

As she had done in L.A., Marissa commandeered the chart room behind the nurses' station on one of the isolation floors as her command post. As the other doctors finished their history taking, they brought their notes to Marissa, who had begun the burdensome task of collating them. Nothing jumped out of the data except the fact that all the patients worked at the Medica Hospital, something that was already well known.

By midday, fourteen more cases had been admitted, which made Marissa extremely fearful that they had a full-blown epidemic on their hands. All the new patients, save one, were Medica subscribers who had been treated by one of the original forty-two sick physicians before the physicians developed symptoms. The other new case was a lab tech who had done studies on the first few cases before Ebola was suspected.

Just as the evening shift was coming on duty, Marissa learned that the other CDC physicians had arrived. Relieved, she went to meet them. She found Dubchek helping to set up the Vickers Lab.

"You might have told me the damn hospital was quarantined," he snapped when he caught sight of her.

"You didn't give me a chance," she said, skirting the fact that he had hung up on her. She wished there was something she could do to improve their relationship, which seemed to be getting worse instead of better.

"Well, Paul and Mark are not very happy," said Dubchek. "When they learned all three of us would be trapped for the length of the outbreak, they turned around and went back to Atlanta.''

"What about Dr. Layne?'' asked Marissa guiltily.

"He's already meeting with Weaver and the hospital administration. Then he will see if the State Health Commissioner can modify the quarantine for the CDC.''

"I suppose I can't talk to you until you get the lab going,'' said Marissa.

"At least you have a good memory,'' said Dubchek, bending over to lift a centrifuge from its wooden container. "After I finish here and I've seen Layne about the isolation procedures, I'll go over your findings.''

As Marissa headed back to her room, she mulled over a number of nasty retorts, all of which only would have made things worse. That was why she had said nothing.

After a meal of catered airplane food eaten in an area of the outpatient clinic reserved for staff in direct contact with the presumed Ebola patients, Marissa returned to her chart work. She now had histories on most of the initial eighty-four cases.

She found Dubchek leafing through her notes. He straightened up on seeing her. "I'm not sure it was a good idea to use the regular hospital staff to take these histories.''

Marissa was caught off guard. "There were so many cases,'' she said defensively. "I couldn't possibly interview all of them quickly enough. As it is, seven people were too sick to speak and three have subsequently died.''

"That's still not reason enough to expose doctors who aren't trained epidemiologists. The Arizona State Health Department has trained staff that should have been utilized. If any of these physicians you've drafted become ill, the CDC might be held responsible.''

"But they—'' protested Marissa.

"Enough!'' interrupted Dubchek. "I'm not here to argue. What have you learned?''

Marissa tried to organize her thoughts and control her emotions. It was true that she'd not considered the legal implications, but she was not convinced there was a problem. The quarantined physicians were already considered contacts. She sat down at the desk and searched for the summary page of her findings. When she found it, she began reading in a flat monotone, without glancing up at Dubchek: "One of the initial patients is an ophthalmologist who attended the same San Diego conference as Drs. Richter and Zabriski. Another of the initial cases, an orthopedic surgeon, went on safari to East Africa two months ago. Two of the initial cases have used monkeys in their research but have not suffered recent bites.

"As a group, all eighty-four cases developed symptoms within a six-hour period, suggesting that they all were exposed at the same time. The severity of the initial symptoms suggests that they all received an overwhelming dose of the infective agent. Everyone worked at the Medica Hospital but not in the same area, which suggests the air-conditioning system was probably not the source. It seems to me we are dealing with a food- or waterborne infection, and in that regard, the only commonality that has appeared in the data is that all eighty-four people used the hospital cafeteria. In fact, as nearly as can be determined, all eighty-four people had lunch there three days ago."

Marissa finally looked up at Dubchek, who was staring at the ceiling. When he realized that she had finished speaking, he said, "What about contact with any of the patients in the L.A. or St. Louis episodes?"

"None," said Marissa. "At least none that we can discover."

"Have you sent blood samples to Tad?"

"Yes," said Marissa.

Cyrill headed for the door. "I think you should redouble your efforts to associate this outbreak with one of the other two. There has to be a connection."

"What about the cafeteria?" asked Marissa.

"You're on your own there," said Dubchek. "Ebola has never been spread by food, so I can't see how the cafeteria could be associated. . . ." He pulled open the door. "Still, the coincidence is curious, and I suppose you'll follow your own instincts no matter what I recommend. Just be sure you exhaust the possibilities of a connection with L.A. or St. Louis."

For a moment Marissa stared at the closed door. Then she looked back at her summary sheet and the huge pile of histories. It was depressing.

Almost as if Cyrill's last words had been a challenge, Marissa decided to visit the cafeteria, which had been built as a separate wing over a garden courtyard. The double doors leading to the large room were closed, and on the right one a notice had been tacked up stating:

CLOSED BY ORDER OF STATE HEALTH COMMISSIONER. Marissa tried the door. It was unlocked.

Inside, the room was spotlessly clean and furnished in stainless steel and molded plastic. Directly ahead of Marissa was the steam table, with stacks of trays at one end and a cash register at the other.

A second set of double doors, with little round windows, was located behind the steam table and led to the kitchen. Just as Marissa was deciding whether to go through or not, they opened, and a stout but attractive middle-aged woman appeared and called out to Marissa that the cafeteria was closed. Marissa introduced herself and asked if she could ask the woman a few questions.

"Certainly," replied the woman, who explained with a faint Scandinavian accent that her name was Jana Beronson and that she was the cafeteria manager. Marissa followed her into her office, a windowless cubicle whose walls were filled with schedules and menus.

After some polite conversation, Marissa asked to see the lunch menu for three days ago. Miss Beronson got it out of the file, and Marissa scanned the page. It was a usual cafeteria menu, with three entrées, two soups and a selection of desserts.

"Is this all the food offered?"

"Those are all the specials," answered Miss Beronson. "Of course we always offer a selection of sandwiches and salads and beverages."

Marissa asked if she could have a copy of the menu, and Miss Beronson took the paper and left the office to Xerox it. Marissa decided that she would go back to each of the initial cases and ask what they had eaten for lunch three days ago. She would also question a control group made up of people who ate from the same menu but who did not become ill.

Miss Beronson returned with the copy. As she folded the paper, Marissa said, "One of your employees was stricken, wasn't she?"

"Maria Gonzales," said Miss Beronson.

"What was her job here?"

"She worked either the steam table or the salad bar," answered Miss Beronson.

"Could you tell me what she did on the day in question?" asked Marissa.

Getting up, Miss Beronson went over to one of the large scheduling boards on her wall. "Desserts and salads," she told Marissa.

Marissa wondered if they should test the whole cafeteria staff for

110

Ebola antibodies. Although Ralph had been joking when he'd suggested an "Ebola Mary," perhaps it was possible, although it had not been the case in Africa.

"Would you like to see our facility?" asked Miss Beronson, trying to be helpful.

For the next thirty minutes Marissa was given a grand tour of the cafeteria, including both the kitchen and the dining area. In the kitchen, she saw the walk-in cooler, the food preparation area and the huge gas ranges. In the dining area, she walked along the steam table, peering into silverware bins and lifting the covers of the salad-dressing canisters.

"Would you like to see the stock rooms?" Miss Beronson asked, when they were done.

Marissa declined, deciding it was time to start checking to see what the initial Ebola patients had chosen from the menu in her purse.

Marissa rocked back in the swivel chair and rubbed her eyes. It was 11:00 A.M. of her second day in Phoenix, and she'd only managed four hours of sleep the previous night. She'd been assigned one of the examination alcoves in the OB-GYN clinic, and every time someone went by, she'd been awakened.

Behind her, Marissa heard the door open. She turned and saw Dubchek holding up the front page of a local newspaper. The headline read: CDC Believes Hidden Source of Ebola in U.S.A. Looking at his expression, Marissa guessed that he was, as usual, angry.

"I told you not to talk to the press."

"I haven't."

Dubchek smacked the paper. "It says right here that Dr. Blumenthal of the CDC said that there is a reservoir of Ebola in the U.S.A., and that the outbreak in Phoenix was spread by either contaminated food or water. Marissa, I don't mind telling you that you are in a lot of trouble!"

Marissa took the paper and read the article quickly. It was true that her name was mentioned, but only at second hand. The source of the information was a Bill Freeman, one of the doctors who'd helped take patient histories. She pointed this fact out to Dubchek.

"Whether you talk directly to the press, or to an intermediary who talks to the press, is immaterial. The effect is the same. It suggests that the CDC supports your opinions, which is not the case. We have no evidence of a food-related problem, and the last thing we want to do is cause mass hysteria.''

Marissa bit her lower lip. It seemed that every time the man spoke to her, it was to find fault. If only she'd been able to handle the episode in the hotel room in L.A. in a more diplomatic way, perhaps he wouldn't be so angry. After all, what did he expect—that she wouldn't talk to anyone? Any team effort meant communication.

Controlling her temper, Marissa handed Dubchek a paper. ''I think you should take a look at this.''

''What is it?'' he asked irritably.

''It's the result of a second survey of the initially infected patients. At least those who were able to respond. You'll notice that one fact jumps out. Except for two people who couldn't remember, all the patients had eaten custard in the hospital cafeteria four days ago. You'll remember that in my first survey, lunch in the cafeteria on that day was the only point of commonality. You'll also see that a group of twenty-one people who ate in the cafeteria on the same day but did not eat the custard remained healthy.''

Dubchek put the paper down on the counter top. ''This is a wonderful exercise for you, but you are forgetting one important fact: Ebola is not a food-borne disease.''

''I know that,'' said Marissa. ''But you cannot ignore the fact that this outbreak started with an avalanche of cases, then slowed to a trickle with isolation.''

Dubchek took a deep breath. ''Listen,'' he said condescendingly, ''Dr. Layne has confirmed your finding that one of the initial patients had been to the San Diego conference with Richter and Zabriski. That fact forms the basis of the official position: Richter brought the virus back from its endemic habitat in Africa and spread it to other doctors in San Diego, including the unfortunate ophthalmologist here at the Medica Hospital.''

''But that position ignores the known incubation period for hemorrhagic fever.''

''I know there are problems,'' admitted Dubchek tiredly, ''but at the moment that's our official position. I don't mind you following up the food-borne possibility, but for God's sake stop talking about it. Remember that you are here in an official capacity. I don't want you conveying your personal opinions to anyone, particularly the press. Understood?''

Marissa nodded.

"And there are a few things I'd like you to do," continued Dubchek. "I'd like you to contact the Health Commissioner's Office and ask that they impound the remains of some of the victims. We'll want some gross specimens to be frozen and sent back to Atlanta."

Marissa nodded again. Dubchek started through the door, then hesitated. Looking back he said more kindly, "You might be interested to know that Tad has started to compare the Ebola from the L.A., St. Louis and Phoenix outbreaks. His preliminary work suggests that they are all the same strain. That does support the opinion that it is really one related outbreak." He gave Marissa a brief, self-satisfied expression, then left.

Marissa closed her eyes and thought about what she could do. Unfortunately, no custard had been left over from the fatal lunch. That would have made things too easy. Instead, she decided to draw blood on all the food staff to check for Ebola antibodies. She also decided to send samples of the custard ingredients to Tad to check for viral contamination. Yet something told her that even if the custard were involved she wasn't going to learn anything from the ingredients. The virus was known to be extremely sensitive to heat, so it could only have been introduced into the custard after it had cooled. But how could that be? Marissa stared at her stacks of papers. The missing clue had to be there. If she'd only had a bit more experience, perhaps she'd be able to see it.

8

MAY 16

It was nearly a month later, and Marissa was finally back in Atlanta in her little office at the CDC. The epidemic in Phoenix had finally been contained, and she, Dubchek and the other CDC doctors in the hospital had been allowed to leave, still without any final answers as to what caused the outbreak or whether it could be prevented from recurring.

As the outbreak had wound down, Marissa had become eager to get home and back to work at the Center. Yet now that she was there, she was not happy. With tear-filled eyes, due to a mixture of discouragement and anger, she was staring down at the memo which began, ''I regret to inform you . . .'' Once again Dubchek had turned down her proposal to work with Ebola in the maximum containment lab, despite her continued efforts to develop laboratory skills in relation to handling viruses and tissue cultures. This time she felt truly discouraged. She still felt that the outbreak in Phoenix had been connected to the custard dessert, and she desperately wanted to vindicate her position by utilizing animal systems. She thought that if she could understand the transmission of the virus she might develop an insight into where it came from in the first place.

Marissa glanced at the large sheets of paper that traced the transmission of the Ebola virus from one generation to another in all three U.S. outbreaks. She had also constructed less complete but similar diagrams concerning the transmission of Ebola in the first two outbreaks in 1976. Both had occurred almost simultaneously, one in Yambuku, Zaire, and the other in Nzara, Sudan. She'd gotten the material from raw data stored in the CDC archives.

One thing that interested her particularly about the African experience was that a reservoir had never been found. Even the discovery that the virus causing Lassa Hemorrhagic Fever resided in a particular species of domestic mouse had not helped in locating Ebola's reservoir. Mosquitoes, bedbugs, monkeys, mice, rats—all sorts of creatures were suspected and ultimately ruled out. It was a mystery in Africa just as it was in the United States.

Marissa tossed her pencil onto her desk with a sense of frustration. She had not been surprised by Dubchek's memo, especially since he had progressively distanced her from his work in Phoenix and had sent her back to Atlanta the day the quarantine had been lifted. He seemed determined to maintain the position that the Ebola virus had been brought back from Africa by Dr. Richter, who had then passed it on to his fellow ophthalmologists at the eyelid surgery conference in San Diego. Dubchek was convinced that the long incubation period was an aberration.

Impulsively, Marissa got to her feet and went to find Tad. He'd helped her write up the proposal, and she was confident he'd allow her to cry on his shoulder now that it had been shot down.

After some protest, Marissa managed to drag him away from the virology lab to get an early lunch.

"You'll just have to try again," Tad said when she told him the bad news straight off.

Marissa smiled. She felt better already. Tad's naiveté was so endearing.

They crossed the catwalk to the main building. One benefit of eating early was that the cafeteria line was nonexistent.

As if to further torment Marissa, one of the desserts that day was caramel custard. When they got to a table and began unloading their trays, Marissa asked if Tad had had a chance to check the custard ingredients that she'd sent back from Arizona.

"No Ebola," he said laconically.

Marissa sat down, thinking how simple it would have been to find some hospital food supply company was the culprit. It would have explained why the virus repeatedly appeared in medical settings.

"What about the blood from the food service personnel?"

"No antibodies to Ebola," Tad said. "But I should warn you: Dubchek came across the work and he was pissed. Marissa, what's going on between you two? Did something happen in Phoenix?"

Marissa was tempted to tell Tad the whole story, but again she decided it would only make a bad situation worse. To answer his question, she explained that she'd been the inadvertent source of a news story that differed from the official CDC position.

Tad took a bite of his sandwich. "Was that the story that said there was a hidden reservoir of Ebola in the U.S.?"

Marissa nodded. "I'm certain the Ebola was in the custard. And I'm convinced that we're going to face further outbreaks."

Tad shrugged. "My work seems to back up Dubchek's position. I've been isolating the RNA and the capsid proteins of the virus from all three outbreaks, and astonishingly enough, they are all identical. It means that the exact same strain of virus is involved, which in turn means that what we are experiencing is one outbreak. Normally, Ebola mutates to some degree. Even the two original African outbreaks, in Yambuku and Nzara, which were eight hundred fifty kilometers apart, involved slightly different strains."

"But what about the incubation period?" protested Marissa. "During each outbreak, the incubation period of new cases was always two to four days. There were three months between the conference in San Diego and the problem in Phoenix."

"Okay," said Tad, "but that is no bigger a stumbling block than figuring out how the virus could have been introduced into the custard, and in such numbers."

"That's why I sent you the ingredients."

"But Marissa," said Tad, "Ebola is inactivated even at sixty degrees centigrade. Even if it had been in the ingredients, the cooking process would have made it noninfective."

"The lady serving the dessert got sick herself. Perhaps she contaminated the custard."

"Fine," said Tad, rolling his pale blue eyes. "But how did she get a virus that lives only in darkest Africa."

"I don't know," admitted Marissa. "But I'm sure she didn't attend the San Diego eye meeting."

They ate in exasperated silence for a few minutes.

"There is only one place I know the dessert server could have gotten the virus," said Marissa at last.

116

"And where's that?"

"Here at the CDC."

Tad put down the remains of his sandwich and looked at Marissa with wide eyes. "Good God, do you know what you're suggesting?"

"I'm not suggesting anything," said Marissa. "I'm merely stating a fact. The only known reservoir for Ebola is in our own maximum containment lab."

Tad shook his head in disbelief.

"Tad," said Marissa in a determined tone, "I'd like to ask you for a favor. Would you get a printout from the Office of Biosafety of all the people going in and out of the maximum containment lab for the last year?"

"I don't like this," said Tad, leaning back in his seat.

"Oh, come on," said Marissa. "Asking for a printout won't hurt anyone. I'm sure you can think up a reason to justify such a request."

"The printout is no problem," said Tad. "I've done that in the past. What I don't like is encouraging your paranoid theory, much less getting between you and the administration, particularly Dubchek."

"Fiddlesticks," said Marissa. "Getting a printout hardly puts you between me and Dubchek. Anyway, how will he know? How will anybody know?"

"True," said Tad reluctantly. "Provided you don't show it to anybody."

"Good," said Marissa, as if the matter had been decided. "I'll stop over at your apartment this evening to pick it up. How's that?"

"Okay, I guess."

Marissa smiled at Tad. He was a wonderful friend, and she had the comfortable feeling that he'd do almost anything for her, which was reassuring, because she had yet another favor to ask him. She wanted to get back into the maximum containment lab.

After giving the emergency brake a good yank, Marissa alighted from her red Honda. The incline of the street was steep, and she'd taken the precaution of turning the wheels against the curb. Although she and Tad had gone out any number of times, Marissa had never been to his apartment. She climbed the front steps and struggled to make out the appropriate buzzer. It was almost 9:00 P.M. and was already dark.

The moment she saw Tad, Marissa knew that he had gotten what she wanted. It was the way he smiled when he opened the door.

Marissa plopped herself into an overstuffed sofa and waited expectantly as Tad's big tabby rubbed sensuously against her leg.

With a self-satisfied grin, Tad produced the computer printout. "I told them that we were doing an internal audit of frequency of entry," said Tad. "They didn't raise an eyebrow."

Turning back the first page, Marissa noted that there was an entry for each visit to the maximum containment lab, with name, time in and time out all duly noted. She traced down the list with her index finger, recognizing only a few of the names. The one that appeared most often was Tad's.

"Everybody knows I'm the only one who works at the CDC," he said with a laugh.

"I never expected the list to be so long," complained Marissa, flipping through the pages. "Does everyone on here still have access?"

Tad leaned against Marissa's shoulder and scanned the pages. "Go back to the beginning."

"That guy," said Tad, pointing to the name, "Gaston Dubois, no longer has access. He was from the World Health Organization and was in town only for a short visit. And this fellow"—Tad pointed to an entry for one Harry Longford—"was a graduate student from Harvard, and he had access only for a specific project."

Marissa noticed Colonel Woolbert's name listed a number of times, as well as that of a man called Heberling, who seemed to have visited fairly regularly until September. Then his name disappeared. Marissa asked about him.

"Heberling used to work here," explained Tad. "He took another job six months ago. There's been a bit of mobility in academic virology of late because of the huge grants generated by the AIDS scare."

"Where'd he go?" asked Marissa, going on to the next page.

Tad shrugged. "Darned if I know. I think he wanted to go to Ft. Detrick, but he and Woolbert never hit it off. Heberling's smart but not the easiest guy in the world to get along with. There was a rumor he wanted the job Dubchek got. I'm glad he didn't get it. He could have made my life miserable."

Marissa flipped through the list to January and pointed at a name that appeared several times over a two-week period: Gloria French. "Who's she?" asked Marissa.

"Gloria's from Parasitic Diseases. She uses the lab on occasion for work on vector-borne viral problems."

118

Marissa rolled up the list.

"Satisfied?" asked Tad.

"It's a little more than I expected," admitted Marissa. "But I appreciate your effort. There is another thing, though."

"Oh, no," said Tad.

"Relax," said Marissa. "You told me that the Ebola in L.A., St. Louis and Phoenix were all the identical strains. I'd sure like to see exactly how you determined that."

"But all that data is in the maximum containment lab," said Tad weakly.

"So?" said Marissa.

"But you haven't gotten clearance," Tad reminded her. He knew what was coming.

"I don't have clearance to do a study," said Marissa. "That means I can't go in by myself. But it's different if I'm with you, especially if there is no one else there. There wasn't any problem after my last visit, was there?"

Tad had to agree. There hadn't been any trouble, so why *not* do it again? He'd never been specifically told that he could not take other staff members into the lab, so he could always plead ignorance. Although he knew he was being manipulated, it was hard to withstand Marissa's charm. Besides, he was proud of his work and wanted to show it off. He was confident she'd be impressed.

"All right," he said. "When do you want to go?"

"How about right now?" said Marissa.

Tad looked at his watch. "I suppose it's as good a time as any."

"Afterwards we can go for a drink," said Marissa. "It'll be my treat."

Marissa retrieved her purse, noting that Tad's keys and his access card were on the same shelf by the door.

En route to the lab in Marissa's car, Tad began a complicated description of his latest work. Marissa listened, but just barely. She had other interests in the lab.

As before, they signed in at the front entrance of the CDC and took the main elevators as if they were going up to Marissa's office. They got off on her floor, descended a flight of stairs, then crossed the catwalk to the virology building. Before Tad had a chance to open the huge steel door, Marissa repeated his code number: 43-23-39.

Tad looked at her with respect. "God, what a memory!"

"You forget," said Marissa. "Those are my measurements."

Tad snorted.

When he switched on the lights and the compressors in the outer staging area, Marissa felt the same disquiet she'd felt on her first visit. There was something frightening about the lab. It was like something out of a science-fiction movie. Entering the dressing rooms, they changed in silence, first donning the cotton scrub suits, then the bulky plastic ones. Following Tad's lead, Marissa attached her air hose to the manifold.

"You're acting like an old pro," said Tad as he turned on the interior lights in the lab, then motioned for Marissa to detach her air hose and step into the next chamber.

As Marissa waited for Tad in the small room where they would get their phenolic-disinfectant shower on the way out, she experienced an uncomfortable rush of claustrophobia. She fought against it, and it lessened as they entered the more spacious main lab. Her practical work with viruses helped since a lot of the equipment was more familiar. She now recognized the tissue culture incubators and even the chromatography units.

"Over here," called Tad, after they'd both hooked up to an appropriate manifold. He took her to one of the lab benches, where there was a complicated setup of exotic glassware, and began explaining how he was separating out the RNA and the capsid proteins from the Ebola virus.

Marissa's mind wandered. What she really wanted to see was where they stored the Ebola. She eyed the bolted insulated door. If she had to guess, she'd guess some place in there. As soon as Tad paused, she asked if he would show her where they kept it.

He hesitated for a moment. "Over there," he said, pointing toward the insulated door.

"Can I see?" asked Marissa.

Tad shrugged. Then he motioned for her to follow him. He waddled over to the side of the room and pointed out an appliance next to one of the tissue-culture incubators. He wasn't pointing at the insulated door.

"In there?" questioned Marissa with surprise and disappointment. She'd expected a more appropriate container, one that would be safely locked away behind a bolted door.

"It looks just like my parents' freezer."

"It is," said Tad. "We just modified it to take liquid-nitrogen coolant." He pointed to the intake and exhaust hoses. "We keep the temperature at minus seventy degrees centigrade."

Around the freezer and through the handle was a link chain secured by a combination lock. Tad lifted the lock and twirled the dial. "Whoever set this had a sense of humor. The magic sequence is 6-6-6."

"It doesn't seem very secure," said Marissa.

Tad shrugged. "Who's going to go in here, the cleaning lady?"

"I'm serious," said Marissa.

"No one can get in the lab without an access card," said Tad, opening the lock and pulling off the chain.

Big deal, thought Marissa.

Tad lifted the top of the freezer, and Marissa peered within, half expecting something to jump out at her. What she saw through a frozen mist were thousands upon thousands of tiny plastic-capped vials in metal trays.

With his plastic-covered hand, Tad wiped the frost off the inside of the freezer's lid, revealing a chart locating the various viruses. He found the tray number for Ebola, then rummaged in the freezer like a shopper looking for frozen fish.

"Here's your Ebola," he said, selecting a vial and pretending to toss it at Marissa.

In a panic, she threw her hands out to catch the vial. She heard Tad's laughter, which sounded hollow and distant coming from within his suit. Marissa felt a stab of irritation. This was hardly the place for such antics.

Holding the vial at arm's length, Tad told Marissa to take it, but she shook her head no. An irrational fear gripped her.

"Doesn't look like much," he said, pointing at the bit of frozen material, "but there's about a billion viruses in there."

"Well, now that I've seen it, I guess you may as well put it away." She didn't talk as he replaced the vial in the metal tray, closed the freezer and redid the bicycle lock. Marissa then glanced around the lab. It was an alien environment, but the individual pieces of equipment seemed relatively commonplace.

"Is there anything here that's not in any regular lab?"

"Regular labs don't have air locks and a negative pressure system," he said.

"No, I meant actual scientific equipment."

Tad looked around the room. His eyes rested on the protective hoods over the workbenches in the center island. "Those are unique," he said, pointing. "They're called type 3 HEPA filter systems. Is that what you mean?"

"Are they only used for maximum containment labs?" asked Marissa.

"Absolutely. They have to be custom-constructed."

Marissa walked over to the hood in place over Tad's setup. It was like a giant exhaust fan over a stove. "Who makes them?" she asked.

"You can look," said Tad, touching a metal label affixed to the side. It said: Lab Engineering, South Bend, Indiana. Marissa wondered if anyone had ordered similar hoods lately. She knew the idea in the back of her mind was crazy, but ever since she'd decided that the Phoenix episode had been related to the custard, she hadn't been able to stop wondering if any of the outbreaks had been deliberately caused. Or, if not, whether any physician had been doing some research which had gotten out of control.

"Hey, I thought you were interested in my work," said Tad suddenly.

"I am," insisted Marissa. "I'm just a little overwhelmed by this place."

After a hesitation for Tad to remember where he was in his lecture, he recommenced. Marissa's mind wandered. She made a mental note to write to Lab Engineering.

"So what do you think?" asked Tad when he finally finished.

"I'm impressed," said Marissa, "and very thirsty. Now let's go get those drinks."

On the way out, Tad took her into his tiny office and showed her how closely all his final results matched one another, suggesting that all the outbreaks were really one and the same.

"Have you compared the American strain with the African ones?" she asked him.

"Not yet," admitted Tad.

"Do you have the same kind of charts or maps for them?"

"Sure do," said Tad. He stepped over to his file cabinet and pulled out the lower drawer. It was so full that he had trouble extracting several manila folders. "Here's the one for Sudan and here's Zaire." He stacked them on the desk and sat back down.

Marissa opened the first folder. The maps looked similar to her, but Tad pointed out significant differences in almost all of the six Ebola proteins. Then Marissa opened the second folder. Tad leaned forward and picked up one of the Zaire maps and placed it next to the ones he'd just completed.

"I don't believe this." He grabbed several other maps and placed them in a row on his desk.

"What?" asked Marissa.

"I'm going to have to run all these through a spectrophotometer tomorrow just to be sure."

"Sure of what?"

"There's almost complete structural homology here," said Tad.

"Please," said Marissa. "Speak English! What are you saying?"

"The Zaire '76 strain is exactly the same as the strain from your three outbreaks."

Marissa and Tad stared at one another for a few moments. Finally Marissa spoke. "That means there's been just one outbreak from Zaire 1976 through Phoenix 1987."

"That's impossible," said Tad, looking back at the maps.

"But that's what you're saying," said Marissa.

"I know," said Tad. "I guess it's just a statistical freak." He shook his head, his pale blue eyes returning to Marissa. "It's amazing, that's all I can say."

After they crossed the catwalk to the main building, Marissa made Tad wait in her office while she sat and typed a short letter.

"Who's so important that you have to write him tonight?" asked Tad.

"I just wanted to do it while it was on my mind," said Marissa. She pulled the letter out of the machine and put it in an envelope. "There. It didn't take too long, did it?" She searched her purse for a stamp. The addressee was Lab Engineering in South Bend, Indiana.

"Why on earth are you writing to them?" Tad asked.

"I want some information about a type 3 HEPA filtration system."

Tad stopped. "Why?" he asked with a glimmer of concern. He knew Marissa was impulsive. He wondered if taking her back into the maximum containment lab had been a mistake.

"Come on!" laughed Marissa. "If Dubchek continues to refuse me authorization to use the maximum containment lab, I'll just have to build my own."

Tad started to say something, but Marissa grabbed his arm and pulled him toward the elevators.

123

9

MAY 17

Marissa got up early with a sense of purpose. It was a glorious spring morning, and she took full advantage of it by going jogging with Taffy. Even the dog seemed to revel in the fine weather, running circles about Marissa as they crisscrossed the neighborhood.

Back home again, Marissa showered, watched a portion of the *Today Show* while she dressed, and was on her way to the Center by eight-thirty. Entering her office, she deposited her purse in her file cabinet and sat down at her desk. She wanted to see if there was enough information available on Ebola viruses for her to calculate the statistical probability of the U.S. strain being the same as the 1976 Zairean strain. If the chances were as infinitesimally small as she guessed, then she'd have a scientific basis for her growing suspicions.

But Marissa did not get far. Centered on her green blotter was an interoffice memo. Opening it, she found a terse message telling her to come to Dr. Dubchek's office immediately.

She crossed to the virology building. At night the enclosed catwalk made Marissa feel safe, but in the bright sun the wire mesh made her feel imprisoned. Dubchek's secretary had not come in yet, so Marissa knocked on the open door.

The doctor was at his desk, hunched over correspondence. When he looked up he told her to close the door and sit down. Marissa did as she was told, conscious the whole time of Dubchek's onyx eyes following her every move.

The office was as disorganized as ever, with stacks of reprinted scientific articles on every surface. Clutter was obviously Dubchek's style even though he personally was always impeccably dressed.

"Dr. Blumenthal," he began, his voice low and controlled. "I understand that you were in the maximum containment lab last night."

Marissa said nothing. Dubchek wasn't asking her a question; he was stating fact.

"I thought I made it clear that you were not allowed in there until you'd been given clearance. I find your disregard for my orders upsetting, to say the least, especially after getting Tad to do unauthorized studies on food samples from Medica Hospital."

"I'm trying to do my job as best I can," said Marissa. Her anxiety was fast changing to anger. It seemed Dubchek never intended to forget that she'd snubbed him in L.A.

"Then your best is clearly not good enough," snapped Dubchek. "And I don't think you recognize the extent of the responsibility that the CDC has to the public, especially given the current hysteria over AIDS."

"Well, I think you are wrong," said Marissa, returning Dubchek's glare. "I take our responsibility to the public very seriously, and I believe that minimizing the threat of Ebola is a disservice. There is no scientific reason to believe that we've seen the end of the Ebola outbreaks, and I'm doing my best to trace the source before we face another."

"Dr. Blumenthal, you are not in charge here!"

"I'm well aware of that fact, Dr. Dubchek. If I were, I surely wouldn't subscribe to the official position that Dr. Richter brought Ebola back from Africa and then experienced an unheard of six-week incubation period. And if Dr. Richter didn't bring back the virus, the only known source of it is here at the CDC!"

"It is just this sort of irresponsible conjecture that I will not tolerate."

"You can call it conjecture," said Marissa, rising to her feet. "I call it fact. Even Ft. Detrick doesn't have any Ebola. Only the CDC has the virus, and it is stored in a freezer closed with an ordinary bicycle lock. Some security for the deadliest virus known to man! And if you think the maximum containment lab is secure, just remember that even I was able to get into it."

125

* * *

Marissa was still trembling when she entered the University Hospital a few hours later and asked directions to the cafeteria. As she walked down the hallway she marveled at herself, wondering where she'd gotten the strength. She'd never been able to stand up to any authority as she'd just done. Yet she felt terrible, remembering Dubchek's face as he'd ordered her out of his office. Uncertain what to do and sure that her EIS career had come to an end, Marissa had left the Center and driven aimlessly around until she remembered Ralph and decided to ask his advice. She'd caught him between surgical cases, and he'd agreed to meet her for lunch.

The cafeteria at the University Hospital was a pleasant affair with yellow-topped tables and white tiled floor. Marissa saw Ralph waving from a corner table.

In typical style, Ralph stood as Marissa approached, and pulled out her chair. Although close to tears, Marissa smiled. His gallant manners seemed at odds with his scrub clothes.

"Thanks for finding time to see me," she said. "I know how busy you are."

"Nonsense," said Ralph. "I always have time for you. Tell me what's wrong. You sounded really upset on the phone."

"Let's get our food first," said Marissa.

The interruption helped; Marissa was in better control of her emotions when they returned with the trays. "I'm having some trouble at the CDC," she confessed. She told Ralph about Dubchek's behavior in Los Angeles and the incident in the hotel room. "From then on things have been difficult. Maybe I didn't handle things as well as I could have, but I don't think it was all my responsibility. After all, it was a type of sexual harassment."

"That doesn't sound like Dubchek," said Ralph with a frown.

"You do believe me, don't you?" asked Marissa.

"Absolutely," Ralph assured her. "But I'm still not sure you can blame all your problems on that unfortunate episode. You have to remember that the CDC is a government agency even if people try to ignore the fact." Ralph paused to take a bite of his sandwich. Then he said, "Let me ask you a question."

"Certainly," said Marissa.

"Do you believe that I am your friend and have your best interests at heart?"

Marissa nodded, wondering what was coming.

"Then I can speak frankly," said Ralph. "I have heard through the grapevine that certain people at the CDC are not happy with you because you've not been 'toeing the official line.' I know you're not asking my advice, but I'm giving it anyway. In a bureaucratic system, you have to keep your own opinions to yourself until the right time. To put it baldly, you have to learn to shut up. I know, because I spent some time in the military."

"Obviously you are referring to my stand on Ebola," said Marissa defensively. Even though she knew Ralph was right, what he'd just said hurt. She'd thought that in general she'd been doing a good job.

"Your stand on Ebola is only part of the problem. You simply haven't been acting as a team player."

"Who told you this?" asked Marissa challengingly.

"Telling you isn't going to solve anything," Ralph said.

"Nor is my staying silent. I cannot accept the CDC's position on Ebola. There are too many inconsistencies and unanswered questions, one of which I learned only last night during my unauthorized visit to the maximum containment lab."

"And what was that?"

"It's known that Ebola mutates constantly. Yet we are faced with the fact that the three U.S. strains are identical, and more astounding, they are the same as the strain in an outbreak in Zaire, in 1976. To me, it doesn't sound as if the disease is spreading naturally."

"You may be right," said Ralph. "But you are in a political situation and you have to act accordingly. And even if there is another outbreak, which I hope there won't be, I have full confidence that the CDC will be capable of controlling it."

"That is a big question mark," said Marissa. "The statistics from Phoenix were not encouraging. Do you realize there were three hundred forty-seven deaths and only thirteen survivors?"

"I know the stats," said Ralph. "But with eighty-four initial cases, I think you people did a superb job."

"I'm not sure you'd think it was so superb if the outbreak had been in your hospital," said Marissa.

"I suppose you're right," said Ralph. "The idea of further Ebola outbreaks terrifies me. Maybe that's why I want to believe in the official position myself. If it's correct, the threat may be over."

"Damn," said Marissa with sudden vehemence. "I've been so

concerned about myself, I completely forgot about Tad. Dubchek must know it was Tad who took me into the maximum containment lab. I'd better get back and check on him.''

"I'll let you go on one condition," said Ralph. "Tomorrow's Saturday. Let me take you to dinner.''

"You are a dear. Dinner tomorrow night would be a treat.''

Marissa leaned forward and kissed Ralph's forehead. He was so kind. She wished she found him more attractive.

As Marissa drove back to the CDC she realized her anger at Dubchek had been replaced by fear for her job and guilt about her behavior. Ralph was undoubtedly correct: She'd not been acting as a team player.

She found Tad in the virology lab, back at work on a new AIDS project. AIDS was still the Center's highest priority. When he caught sight of Marissa he shielded his face with his arms in mock defensiveness.

"Was it that bad?" asked Marissa.

"Worse," said Tad.

"I'm sorry," said Marissa. "How did he find out?"

"He asked me," said Tad.

"And you told him?"

"Sure. I wasn't about to lie. He also asked if I was dating you.''

"And you told him that, too?" asked Marissa, mortified.

"Why not?" said Tad. "At least it reassured him that I don't take just anybody off the street into the maximum containment lab.''

Marissa took a deep breath. Maybe it was best to have everything out in the open. She put her hand on Tad's shoulder. "I'm really sorry I've caused you trouble. Can I try to make it up to you by fixing supper tonight?"

Tad's face brightened. "Sounds good to me.''

At six o'clock Tad came by Marissa's office and then followed her in his car to the supermarket. Tad voted for double loin lamb chops for their meal and waited while the butcher cut them, leaving Marissa to pick up potatoes and salad greens.

When the groceries were stashed in Marissa's trunk, Tad insisted that he stop and pick up some wine. He said he'd meet her back at her house, giving her a chance to get the preparations going.

It had begun to rain, but as Marissa listened to the rhythm of the windshield wipers, she felt more hopeful than she had all day. It was definitely better to have everything out in the open, and she'd talk to Dubchek first thing Monday and apologize. As two adults, they surely could straighten things out.

She stopped at a local bakery and picked up two napoleons. Then, pulling in behind her house, she backed up toward the kitchen door to have the least distance to carry the groceries. She was pleased that she'd beat Tad. The sun had not set yet, but it was as dark as if it had. Marissa had to fumble with her keys to put the proper one in the lock. She turned on the kitchen light with her elbow before dumping the two large brown bags on the kitchen table. As she deactivated the alarm, she wondered why Taffy hadn't rushed to greet her. She called out for the dog, wondering if the Judsons had taken her for some reason. She called again, but the house remained unnaturally still.

Walking down the short hall to the living room, she snapped on the light next to the couch. "Ta-a-a-affy," she called, drawing out the dog's name. She started for the stairs in case the dog had inadvertently shut herself into one of the upstairs bedrooms as she sometimes did. Then she saw Taffy lying on the floor near the window, her head bent at a strange and alarming angle.

"Taffy!" cried Marissa desperately, as she ran to the dog and sank to her knees. But before she could touch the animal she was grabbed from behind, her head jerked upright with such force that the room spun. Instinctively, she reached up and gripped the arm, noticing that it felt like wood under the cloth of the suit. Even with all her strength she could not so much as budge the man's grip on her neck. There was a ripping sound as her dress tore. She tried to twist around to see her attacker, but she couldn't.

The panic button for the alarm system was in her jacket pocket. She reached in and juggled it in her fingers, desperately trying to depress the plunger. Just as she succeeded, a blow to her head sent her sprawling to the floor. Listening to the ear-splitting noise, Marissa tried to struggle to her feet. Then she heard Tad's voice shouting at the intruder. She turned groggily, to see him struggling with a tall, heavyset man.

Covering her ears against the incessant screech of the alarm, she rushed to the front door and threw it open, screaming for help from the Judsons. She ran across the lawn and through the shrubs that divided the properties. As she neared the Judsons' house, she saw Mr. Judson opening his front door. She yelled for him to call the police but didn't wait to explain. She turned on her heel and ran back to her

129

house. The sound of the alarm echoed off the trees that lined the street. Bounding up the front steps two at a time, she returned to her living room, only to find it empty. Panicked, she rushed down the hall to the kitchen. The back door was ajar. Reaching over to the panel, she turned the alarm off.

"Tad," she shouted, going back to the living room and looking into the first-floor guest room. There was no sign of him.

Mr. Judson came running through the open front door, brandishing a poker. Together they went through the kitchen and out the back door.

"My wife is calling the police," said Mr. Judson.

"There was a friend with me," gasped Marissa, her anxiety increasing. "I don't know where he is."

"Here comes someone," said Mr. Judson, pointing.

Marissa saw a figure approaching through the evergreen trees. It was Tad. Relieved, she ran to him and threw her arms around his neck, asking him what had happened.

"Unfortunately, I got knocked down," he told her, touching the side of his head. "When I got up, the guy was outside. He had a car waiting."

Marissa took Tad into the kitchen and cleaned the side of his head with a wet towel. It was only a superficial abrasion.

"His arm felt like a club," said Tad.

"You're lucky you're not hurt worse. You never should have gone after him. What if he'd had a gun?"

"I wasn't planning on being a hero," said Tad. "And all he had with him was a briefcase."

"A briefcase? What kind of burglar carries a briefcase?"

"He was well dressed," said Tad. "I'd have to say that about him."

"Did you get a good enough look at him to identify him?" asked Mr. Judson.

Tad shrugged. "I doubt it. It all happened so quickly."

In the distance, they heard the sound of a police siren approaching. Mr. Judson looked at his watch. "Pretty good response time."

"Taffy!" cried Marissa, suddenly remembering the dog. She ran back into the living room, with Tad and Mr. Judson close behind.

The dog had not moved, and Marissa bent down and gingerly lifted the animal. Taffy's head dangled limply. Her neck had been broken.

Up until that moment Marissa had maintained cool control of her emotions. But now she began to weep hysterically. Mr. Judson finally coaxed her into releasing the dog. Tad put his arms around her, trying to comfort her as best he could.

The police car pulled up with lights flashing. Two uniformed policemen came inside. To their credit, Marissa found them sensitive and efficient. They found the point of entry, the broken living room window, and explained to Marissa the reason why the alarm hadn't sounded initially: The intruder had knocked out the glass and had climbed through without lifting the sash.

Then, in a methodical fashion, the police took all the relevant information about the incident. Unfortunately, neither Marissa nor Tad could give much of a description of the man, save for his stiff arm. When asked if anything was missing, Marissa had to say that she had not yet checked. When she told them about Taffy, she began to cry again.

The police asked her if she'd like to go to the hospital, but she declined. Then, after saying they'd be in touch, the police left. Mr. Judson also departed, telling Marissa to call if she needed anything and not to concern herself about Taffy's remains. He also said he'd see about getting her window repaired tomorrow.

Suddenly Marissa and Tad found themselves alone, sitting at the kitchen table with the groceries still in their bags.

"I'm sorry about all this," said Marissa, rubbing her sore head.

"Don't be silly," protested Tad. "Why don't we just go out for dinner?"

"I really am not up to a restaurant. But I don't want to stay here either. Would you mind if I fixed the meal at your place?"

"Absolutely not. Let's go!"

"Just give me a moment to change," said Marissa.

10

MAY 20

It was Monday morning, and Marissa was filled with a sense of dread. It had not been a good weekend. Friday had been the worst day of her life, starting with the episode with Dubchek, then being attacked and losing Taffy. Right after the assault, she'd minimized the emotional impact, only to pay for it later. She'd made dinner for Tad and had stayed at his house, but it had been a turbulent evening filled with tears and rage at the intruder who'd killed her dog.

Saturday had found her equally upset, despite first Tad's and then the Judsons' attempts to cheer her up. Saturday night she'd seen Ralph as planned, and he'd suggested she ask for some time off. He even offered to take her to the Caribbean for a few days. He felt that a short vacation might let things at the CDC cool down. When Marissa insisted that she go back to work, he suggested she concentrate on something other than Ebola, but Marissa shook her head to that, too. "Well at least don't make more waves," Ralph counseled. In his opinion, Dubchek was basically a good man who was still recovering from the loss of the wife he'd adored. Marissa should give him another chance. On this point at least, Marissa agreed.

Dreading another confrontation with Dubchek, but resolved to try her best to make amends, Marissa went to her office only to find another memorandum already waiting for her on her desk. She assumed

132

it was from Dubchek, but when she picked up the envelope, she noticed it was from Dr. Carbonara, the administrator of the EIS program and hence Marissa's real boss. With her heart pounding, she opened the envelope and read the note which said that she should come to see him immediately. That didn't sound good.

Dr. Carbonara's office was on the second floor, and Marissa used the stairs to get there, wondering if she were about to be fired. The office was large and comfortable, with one wall dominated by a huge map of the world with little red pins indicating where EIS officers were currently assigned. Dr. Carbonara was a fatherly, soft-spoken man with a shock of unruly gray hair. He motioned for Marissa to sit while he finished a phone call. When he hung up, he smiled warmly. The smile made Marissa relax a little. He didn't act as though he were about to terminate her employment. Then he surprised her by commiserating with her about the assault and the death of her dog. Except for Tad, Ralph and the Judsons, she didn't think anyone knew.

"I'm prepared to offer you some vacation time," continued Dr. Carbonara. "After such a harrowing experience a change of scene might do you some good."

"I appreciate your consideration," said Marissa. "But to tell you the truth, I'd rather keep working. It will keep my mind occupied, and I'm convinced the outbreaks are not over."

Dr. Carbonara took up a pipe and went through the ritual of lighting it. When it was burning to his satisfaction he said, "Unfortunately, there are some difficulties relating to the Ebola situation. As of today we are transferring you from the Department of Virology to the Department of Bacteriology. You can keep your same office. Actually it's closer to your new assignment than it was to your old one. I'm certain you will find this new position equally as challenging as your last." He puffed vigorously on his pipe, sending up clouds of swirling gray smoke.

Marissa was devastated. In her mind the transfer was tantamount to being fired.

"I suppose I could tell you all sorts of fibs," said Dr. Carbonara, "but the truth of the matter is that the head of the CDC, Dr. Morrison, personally asked that you be moved out of virology and away from the Ebola problem."

"I don't buy that," snapped Marissa. "It was Dr. Dubchek!"

"No, it wasn't Dr. Dubchek," said Dr. Carbonara with emphasis. Then he added: ". . . although he was not against the decision."

Marissa laughed sarcastically.

"Marissa, I am aware that there has been an unfortunate clash of personalities between you and Dr. Dubchek, but—"

"Sexual harassment is more accurate," interjected Marissa. "The man has made it difficult for me ever since I stepped on his ego by resisting his advances."

"I'm sorry to hear you say that," said Dr. Carbonara calmly. "Perhaps it would be in everyone's best interests if I told you the whole story. You see, Dr. Morrison received a call from Congressman Calvin Markham, who is a senior member of the House Appropriations Subcommittee for the Department of Health and Human Services. As you know, that subcommittee handles the CDC's annual appropriations. It was the congressman who insisted that you be put off the Ebola team, not Dr. Dubchek."

Marissa was again speechless. The idea of a United States Congressman calling the head of the CDC to have her removed from the Ebola investigation seemed unbelievable. "Congressman Markham used my name specifically?" asked Marissa, when she found her voice.

"Yes," said Dr. Carbonara. "Believe me, I questioned it, too."

"But why?" asked Marissa.

"There was no explanation," said Dr. Carbonara. "And it was more of an order than a request. For political reasons, we have no choice. I think you can understand."

Marissa shook her head. "That's just it, I don't understand. But it does make me change my mind about that vacation offer. I think I need the time after all."

"Splendid," said Dr. Carbonara. "I'll arrange it—effective immediately. After a rest you can make a fresh start. I want to reassure you that we have no quarrel with your work. In fact we have been impressed by your performance. Those Ebola outbreaks had us all terrified. You'll be a significant addition to the staff working on enteric bacteria, and I'm sure you will enjoy the woman who heads the division, Dr. Harriet Samford."

Marissa headed home, her mind in turmoil. She'd counted on work to distract her from Taffy's brutal death; and while she'd thought there'd been a chance she'd be fired, she'd never considered she'd be given a vacation. Vaguely she wondered if she should ask Ralph if he was serious about that Caribbean trip. Yet such an idea was not without disadvantages. While she liked him as a friend, she wasn't sure if she were ready for anything more.

Her empty house was quiet without Taffy's exuberant greeting. Marissa had an overwhelming urge to go back to bed and pull the covers over her head, but she knew that would mean yielding to the depression she was determined to fight off. She hadn't really accepted Dr. Carbonara's story as an excuse for shuffling her off the Ebola case. A casual recommendation from a congressman usually didn't produce such fast results. She was sure if she checked she would discover Markham was a friend of Dubchek's. Eyeing her bed with its tempting ruffled pillows, she resolved not to give in to her usual pattern of withdrawal. The last reactive depression, after Roger left, was too fresh in her mind. Instead of just giving in and accepting the situation, which was what she'd done then, she told herself that she had to do something. The question was what.

Sorting her dirty clothes, intending to do a therapeutic load of wash, she spotted her packed suitcase. It was like an omen.

Impulsively, she picked up the phone and called Delta to make a reservation for the next flight to Washington, D.C.

"There's an information booth just inside the door," said the knowledgeable cab driver as he pointed up the stairs of the Cannon Congressional Office Building.

Once inside, Marissa went through a metal detector while a uniformed guard checked the contents of her purse. When she asked for Congressman Markham's office she was told that it was on the fifth floor. Following the rather complicated directions—it seemed that the main elevators only went to the fourth floor—Marissa was struck by the general dinginess of the interior of the building. The walls of the elevator were actually covered with graffiti.

Despite the circuitous route, she had no trouble finding the office. The outer door was ajar, so she walked in unannounced, hoping an element of surprise might work in her favor. Unfortunately, the congressman was not in.

"He's not due back from Houston for three days. Would you like to make an appointment?"

"I'm not sure," said Marissa, feeling a little silly after having flown all the way from Atlanta without checking to see if the man would be in town, let alone available.

"Would you care to talk with Mr. Abrams, the congressman's administrative assistant?"

"I suppose," said Marissa. In truth she hadn't been certain how to confront Markham. If she merely asked if he had tried to do Dubchek a favor by figuring out a way to remove her from the Ebola case, obviously he would deny it. While she was still deliberating, an earnest young man came up to her and introduced himself as Michael Abrams. "What can I do for you?" he asked, extending a hand. He looked about twenty-five, with dark, almost black, hair and a wide grin that Marissa suspected could not be as sincere as it first seemed.

"Is there somewhere we can talk privately?" she asked him. They were standing directly in front of the secretary's desk.

"By all means," said Michael. He guided her into the congressman's office, a large, high-ceilinged room with a huge mahogany desk flanked by an American flag on one side and a Texas state flag on the other. The walls were covered with framed photos of the congressman shaking hands with a variety of celebrities including all the recent presidents.

"My name is Dr. Blumenthal," began Marissa as soon as she was seated. "Does that name mean anything to you?"

Michael shook his head. "Should it?" he asked in a friendly fashion.

"Perhaps," said Marissa, unsure of how to proceed.

"Are you from Houston?" asked Michael.

"I'm from Atlanta," said Marissa. "From the CDC." She watched to see if there was any unusual response. There wasn't.

"The CDC," repeated Michael. "Are you here in an official capacity?"

"No," admitted Marissa. "I'm interested in the congressman's association with the Center. Is it one of his particular concerns?"

"I'm not sure 'particular' is the right word," said Michael warily. "He's concerned about all areas of health care. In fact Congressman Markham has introduced more health-care legislation than any other congressman. He's recently sponsored bills limiting the immigration of foreign medical school graduates, a bill for compulsory arbitration of malpractice cases, a bill establishing a federal ceiling on malpractice awards and a bill limiting federal subsidy of HMO—Health Maintenance Organization—development . . ." Michael paused to catch his breath.

"Impressive," said Marissa. "Obviously he takes a real interest in American medicine."

"Indeed," agreed Michael. "His daddy was a general practitioner, and a fine one at that."

"But as far as you know," continued Marissa, "he does not concern himself with any specific projects at the CDC."

"Not that I know of," said Michael.

"And I assume that not much happens around here without your knowing about it."

Michael grinned.

"Well, thank you for your time," said Marissa, getting to her feet. Intuitively, she knew she wasn't going to learn anything more from Michael Abrams.

Returning to the street, Marissa felt newly despondent. Her sense of doing something positive about her situation had faded. She had no idea if she should hang around Washington for three days waiting for Markham's return, or if she should just go back to Atlanta.

She wandered aimlessly toward the Capitol. She'd already checked into a hotel in Georgetown, so why not stay? She could visit some museums and art galleries. But as she gazed at the Capitol's impressive white dome, she couldn't help wondering why a man in Markham's position should bother with her, even if he were a friend of Dubchek's. Suddenly, she got the glimmer of an idea. Flagging a cab, she hopped in quickly and said, "Federal Elections Commission; do you know where that is?"

The driver was a handsome black who turned to her and said, "Lady, if there's some place in this city that I don't know, I'll take you there for nothin'."

Satisfied, Marissa settled back and let the man do the driving. Fifteen minutes later they pulled up in front of a drab semimodern office building in a seedy part of downtown Washington. A uniformed guard paid little heed to Marissa other than to indicate she had to sign the register before she went in. Uncertain which department she wanted, Marissa ended up going into a first-floor office. Four women were typing busily behind gray metal desks.

As Marissa approached, one looked up and asked if she could be of assistance.

"Maybe," said Marissa with a smile. "I'm interested in a congressman's campaign finances. I understand that's part of the public record."

"Certainly is," agreed the woman, getting to her feet. "Are you interested in contributions or disbursements?"

"Contributions, I guess," said Marissa with a shrug.

The woman gave her a quizzical look. "What's the congressman's name?"

"Markham," said Marissa. "Calvin Markham."

The woman padded over to a round table covered with black loose-leaf books. She found the appropriate one and opened it to the *M*'s, explaining that the numbers following the congressman's name referred to the appropriate microfilm cassettes. She then led Marissa to an enormous cassette rack, picked out the relevant one and loaded it into the microfilm reader. "Which election are you interested in?" she asked, ready to punch in the document numbers.

"The last one, I suppose," said Marissa. She still wasn't sure what she was after—just some way to link Markham either to Dubchek or the CDC.

The machine whirred to life, documents flashing past on the screen so quickly that they appeared as a continuous blur. Then the woman pressed a button and showed Marissa how to regulate the speed. "It's five cents a copy, if you want any. You put the money in here." She pointed to a coin slot. "If you run into trouble, just yell."

Marissa was intrigued by the apparatus as well as the information available. As she reviewed the names and addresses of all the contributors to Markham's considerable reelection coffers, Marissa noted that he appeared to get fiscal support on a national scale, not just from his district in Texas. She did not think that was typical, except perhaps for the Speaker of the House or the Chairman of the House Ways and Means Committee. She also noted that a large percentage of the donors were physicians, which made sense in light of Markham's record on health legislation.

The names were alphabetized, and though she carefully scanned the *D*'s, she failed to find Dubchek's name. It had been a crazy idea anyway, she told herself. Where would Cyrill get the money to influence a powerful congressman? He might have some hold on Markham, but not a financial one. Marissa laughed. To think she considered Tad naive!

Still, she made a copy of all the contributors, deciding to go over the list at her leisure. She noticed that one doctor with six children had donated the maximum amount allowable for himself and for each member of his family. That was real support. At the end of the individual contributors was a list of corporate supporters. One called the

"Physicians' Action Congress Political Action Committee" had donated more money than any number of Texas oil companies. Going back to the previous election, Marissa found the same group. Clearly it was an established organization, and it had to be high on Markham.

After thanking the woman for her help, Marissa went outside and hailed a cab. As it inched through rush-hour traffic, Marissa looked again at the list of individual names. Suddenly, she almost dropped the sheets. Dr. Ralph Hempston's name leapt out from the middle of a page. It was a coincidence, to be sure, and made her feel what a small world it was, but thinking it over she was not surprised. One of the things that had always troubled her about Ralph was his conservatism. It would be just like him to support a congressman like Markham.

It was five-thirty when Marissa crossed the pleasant lobby of her hotel. As she passed the tiny newsstand, she saw the *Washington Post*'s headline: EBOLA STRIKES AGAIN!

Like iron responding to a magnet, Marissa was pulled across the room. She snatched up a paper and read the subhead: NEWEST SCOURGE TERRIFIES THE CITY OF BROTHERLY LOVE.

Digging up change from the bottom of her purse to buy the paper, she continued reading as she walked toward the elevators. There were three presumed cases of Ebola at the Berson Clinic Hospital in Abington, Pennsylvania, just outside of Philadelphia. The article described widespread panic in the suburban town.

As she pressed the button for her floor, Marissa saw that Dubchek was quoted as saying that he believed the outbreak would be contained quickly and that there was no need for concern: The CDC had learned a lot about controlling the virus from the three previous outbreaks.

Peter Carbo, one of Philadelphia's Gay Rights leaders, was quoted as saying that he hoped Jerry Falwell had noticed that not a single known homosexual had contracted this new and far more dangerous disease that had come from the same area of Africa as AIDS had.

Back in her room, Marissa turned to an inside photo section. The picture of the police barricade at the entrance to the Berson Hospital reminded her of Phoenix. She finished the article and put the paper down on the bureau, looking at herself in the mirror. Although she was on vacation and was officially off the Ebola team, she knew she had to get the details firsthand. Her commitment to the Ebola problem left her with little choice. She rationalized her decision to go by telling herself that Philadelphia was practically next door to Washington; she could even go by train. Turning into the room, Marissa began collecting her belongings.

Leaving the station in Philadelphia, Marissa took a cab to Abington, which turned out to be a far more expensive ride than she'd anticipated. Luckily she had some traveler's checks tucked in her wallet, and the driver was willing to accept them. Outside the Berson Hospital, she was confronted by the police barricade pictured in the newspaper. Before she attempted to cross, she asked a reporter if the place was quarantined. "No," said the man, who had been trying to interview a doctor who had just sauntered past. The police were there in case a quarantine was ordered. Marissa flashed her CDC identity card at one of the guards. He admitted her without question.

The hospital was a handsome, new facility much like the sites of the Ebola outbreaks in L.A. and Phoenix. As Marissa headed toward the information booth, she wondered why the virus seemed to strike these elegant new structures rather than the grubby inner-city hospitals in New York or Boston.

There were a lot of people milling about the lobby, but nothing like the chaos that she'd seen in Phoenix. People seemed anxious but not terrified. The man at the information booth told Marissa that the cases were in the hospital's isolation unit on the sixth floor. Marissa had started toward the elevators when the man called out, "I'm sorry, but there are no visitors allowed." Marissa flashed her CDC card again. "I'm sorry, Doctor. Take the last elevator. It's the only one that goes to six."

When Marissa got off the elevator, a nurse asked her to don protective clothing immediately. She didn't question Marissa as to why she was there. Marissa was particularly glad to put on the mask; it gave her anonymity as well as protection.

"Excuse me, are any of the CDC doctors available?" she asked, startling the two women gossiping behind the nurses' station.

"I'm sorry. We didn't hear you coming," said the older of the two.

"The CDC people left about an hour ago," said the other. "I think they said they were going down to the administrator's office. You could try there."

"No matter," said Marissa. "How are the three patients?"

"There are seven now," said the first woman. Then she asked Marissa to identify herself.

"I'm from the CDC," she said, purposely not giving her name. "And you?"

"Unfortunately, we're the RN's who normally run this unit. We're used to isolating patients with lowered resistance to disease, not cases of fatal contagious disease. We're glad you people are here."

"It *is* a little frightening at first," commiserated Marissa, as she boldly entered the nurses' station. "But if it's any comfort, I've been involved with all three previous outbreaks and haven't had any problems." Marissa did not admit to her own fear. "Are the charts here or in the rooms?"

"Here," said the older nurse, pointing to a corner shelf.

"How are the patients doing?"

"Terribly. I know that doesn't sound very professional, but I've never seen sicker people. We've used round-the-clock special-duty nursing, but no matter what we try, they keep getting worse."

Marissa well understood the nurse's frustration. Terminal patients generally depressed the staff.

"Do either of you know which patient was admitted first?"

The older nurse came over to where Marissa was sitting and pushed the charts around noisily before pulling out one and handing it to Marissa. "Dr. Alexi was the first. I'm surprised he's lasted the day."

Marissa opened the chart. There were all the familiar symptoms but no mention of foreign travel, animal experiments or contact with any of the three previous outbreaks. But she did learn that Alexi was the head of ophthalmology! Marissa was amazed; was Dubchek right after all?

Unsure of how long she dared stay in the unit, Marissa opted to see the patient right away. Donning an extra layer of protective clothing, including disposable goggles, she entered the room.

"Is Dr. Alexi conscious?" she asked the special-duty nurse, whose name was Marie. The man was lying silently on his back, mouth open, staring at the ceiling. His skin was already the pasty yellow shade that Marissa had learned to associate with near-death.

"He goes in and out," said the nurse. "One minute he's talking, the next he's unresponsive. His blood pressure has been falling again. I've been told that he's a 'no code.' "

Marissa swallowed nervously. She'd always been uncomfortable with the order not to resuscitate.

"Dr. Alexi," called Marissa, gingerly touching the man's arm. Slowly he turned his head to face her. She noticed a large bruise beneath his right eye.

"Can you hear me, Dr. Alexi?"

The man nodded.

"Have you been to Africa recently?"

Dr. Alexi shook his head "no."

"Did you attend an eyelid surgery conference in San Diego a few months back?"

The man mouthed the word "yes."

Perhaps Dubchek really was right. It was too much of a coincidence: each outbreak's primary victim was an ophthalmologist who'd attended that San Diego meeting.

"Dr. Alexi," began Marissa, choosing her words carefully. "Do you have friends in L.A., St. Louis or Phoenix? Have you seen them recently?"

But before Marissa had finished, he'd slipped back into unconsciousness.

"That's what he's been doing," said the nurse, moving to the opposite side of the bed to take another blood-pressure reading.

Marissa hesitated. Perhaps she'd wait a few minutes and try to question him again. Her attention returned to the bruise beneath the man's eye, and she asked the nurse if she knew how he'd gotten it.

"His wife told me he'd been robbed," said the nurse. Then she added, "His blood pressure is even lower." She shook her head in dismay as she put down the stethoscope.

"He was robbed just before he got sick?" asked Marissa. She wanted to be sure she'd heard correctly.

"Yes. I think the mugger hit him in the face even though he didn't resist."

An intercom sputtered to life. "Marie, is there a doctor from the CDC in your room?"

The nurse looked from the speaker to Marissa, then back to the speaker again. "Yes, there is."

Over the continued crackle of static, indicating that the line was still open, Marissa could hear a woman saying, "She's in Dr. Alexi's room." Another voice said, "Don't say anything! I'll go down and talk with her."

Marissa's pulse raced. It was Dubchek! Frantically, she looked around the room as if to hide. She thought of asking the nurse if there were another way out, but she knew it would sound ridiculous, and it was too late. She could already hear footsteps in the hall.

Cyrill walked in, adjusting his protective goggles.

"Marie?" he asked.

"Yes," said the nurse.

Marissa started for the door. Dubchek grabbed her by the arm. Marissa froze. It was ridiculous to have a confrontation of this sort in the presence of a dying man. She was scared of Dubchek's reaction, knowing how many rules she had probably broken. At the same time, she was angry at having been forced to break them.

"What the hell do you think you're doing?" he growled. He would not let go of her arm.

"Have some respect for the patient, if not for anyone else," said Marissa, finally freeing herself and leaving the room. Dubchek was right behind her. She pulled off the goggles, the outer hood and gown, then the gloves, and deposited them all in the proper receptacle. Dubchek did the same.

"Are you making a career out of flouting authority?" he demanded, barely controlling his fury. "Is this all some kind of game to you?"

"I'd rather not talk about it," said Marissa. She could tell that Dubchek, for the moment, was beyond any reasonable discussion. She started toward the elevators.

"What do you mean, you'd 'rather not talk about it'?" yelled Dubchek. "Who do you think you are?"

He grabbed Marissa's arm again and yanked her around to face him.

"I think we should wait until you are a little less upset," Marissa managed to say as calmly as she could.

"Upset?" exploded Dubchek. "Listen, young lady, I'm calling Dr. Morrison first thing in the morning to demand that he make you take a forced leave of absence rather than a vacation. If he refuses, I'll demand a formal hearing."

"That's fine by me," said Marissa maintaining a fragile control. "There is something extraordinary about these Ebola outbreaks, and I think you don't want to face it. Maybe a formal hearing is what we need."

"Get out of here before I have you thrown out," snapped Dubchek.

"Gladly," said Marissa.

As she left the hospital, Marissa realized she was shaking. She hated confrontations, and once again she was torn between righteous anger and guilty humiliation. She was certain she was close to the real cause of the outbreaks, but she still could not clearly formulate her suspicions—not even to her own satisfaction, much less someone else's.

Marissa tried to think it through on her way to the airport, but all she could think of was her ugly scene with Dubchek. She couldn't get it out of her head. She knew she had taken a risk by going into the Berson Hospital when she was specifically unauthorized to do so. Cyrill had every right to be enraged. She only wished she had been able to talk to him about the strange fact that each of the index cases had been mugged just before becoming ill.

Waiting for her plane back to Atlanta, Marissa went to a pay phone to call Ralph. He answered promptly, saying he'd been so worried about her that he'd gone to her house when she had failed to answer the phone. He asked her where she'd been, pretending to be indignant that she'd left town without telling him.

"Washington and now Philadelphia," explained Marissa, "but I'm on my way home."

"Did you go to Philly because of the new Ebola outbreak?"

"Yes," said Marissa. "A lot has happened since we talked last. It's a long story, but the bottom line is that I wasn't supposed to go, and when Dubchek caught me, he went crazy. I may be out of a job. Do you know anybody who could use a pediatrician who's hardly been used?"

"No problem," said Ralph with a chuckle. "I could get you a job right here at the University Hospital. What's your flight number? I'll drive out to the airport and pick you up. I'd like to hear about what was so important that you had to fly off without telling me you were going."

"Thanks, but it's not necessary," said Marissa. "My Honda is waiting for me."

"Then stop over on your way home."

"It might be late," said Marissa, thinking that it might be more pleasant at Ralph's than in her own empty house. "I'm planning on stopping by the CDC. There is something I'd like to do while Dubchek is out of town."

"That doesn't sound like a good idea," said Ralph. "What are you up to?"

"Believe me, not much," said Marissa. "I just want one more quick visit to the maximum containment lab."

"I thought you didn't have authorization."

"I can manage it, I think," she told him.

"My advice is to stay away from the CDC," said Ralph. "Going into that lab is what caused most of your problems in the first place."

"I know," admitted Marissa, "but I'm going to do it anyway. This Ebola affair is driving me crazy."

"Suit yourself, but stop over afterwards. I'll be up late."

"Ralph?" Marissa said, screwing up her courage to ask the question. "Do you know Congressman Markham?"

There was a pause. "I know of him."

"Have you ever contributed to his campaign fund?"

"What an odd question, particularly for a long-distance call."

"Have you?" persisted Marissa.

"Yes," said Ralph. "Several times. I like the man's position on a lot of medical issues."

After promising again to see him that night, Marissa hung up feeling relieved. She was pleased she'd broached the subject of Markham and was even happier that Ralph had been so forthright about his contributions.

Once the plane took off, though, her sense of unease returned. The theory still undeveloped in the back of her mind was so terrifying, she was afraid to try to flesh it out.

More horrifying yet, she was beginning to wonder if her house being broken into and her dog killed was something more than the random attack she'd taken it for.

11

MAY 20—EVENING

Marissa left the airport and headed directly for Tad's house. She'd not called, thinking it would be better just to drop in, even though it was almost nine.

She pulled up in front of his house, pleased to see lights blazing in the living room on the second floor.

"Marissa!" said Tad, opening the front door of the building, a medical journal in his hand. "What are you doing here?"

"I'd like to see the man of the house," said Marissa. "I'm doing a home survey on peanut butter preference."

"You're joking."

"Of course I'm joking," said Marissa with exasperation. "Are you going to invite me in or are we going to spend the night standing here?" Marissa's new assertiveness surprised even herself.

"Sorry," said Tad, stepping aside. "Come on in."

He'd left his apartment door open, so after climbing the stairs Marissa entered ahead of him. Glancing at the shelf in the foyer, she saw that his lab access card was there.

"I've been calling you all day," said Tad. "Where have you been?"

"Out," said Marissa vaguely. "It's been another interesting day."

"I was told you'd been transferred from Special Pathogens," said Tad. "Then I heard a rumor that you were on vacation. What's happening?"

146

"I wish I knew," said Marissa, dropping onto Tad's low-slung sofa. His cat materialized out of nowhere and leaped into her lap. "What about Philadelphia? Is it Ebola?"

"I'm afraid so," said Tad, sitting down next to her. "The call came in on Sunday. I got samples this morning and they're loaded with the virus."

"Is it the same strain?"

"I won't know that for some time," said Tad.

"You still think it's all coming from that San Diego eye meeting?" she asked him.

"I don't know," said Tad with a slight edge to his voice. "I'm a virologist, not an epidemiologist."

"Don't be cross," said Marissa. "But you don't have to be an epidemiologist to recognize that something strange is happening. Do you have any idea why I've been transferred?"

"I'd guess that Dubchek requested it."

"Nope," said Marissa. "It was a U.S. Congressman from Texas named Markham. He called Dr. Morrison directly. He sits on the appropriations committee that decides on the CDC budget, so Morrison had to comply. But that's pretty weird, isn't it? I mean I'm only an EIS officer."

"I suppose it is," agreed Tad. He was becoming more and more nervous.

Marissa reached out and put her hand on his shoulder. "What's the matter?"

"All this worries me," said Tad. "I like you; you know that. But trouble seems to follow you around, and I don't want to be drawn into it. I happen to like my job."

"I don't want to involve you, but I need your help just one last time. That's why I came here so late."

Tad shook off her hand. "Please don't ask me to break any more rules."

"I have to get back into the maximum containment lab," said Marissa. "Only for a few minutes."

"No!" said Tad decisively. "I simply can't take the risk. I'm sorry."

"Dubchek is out of town," said Marissa. "No one will be there at this hour."

"No," said Tad. "I won't do it."

147

Marissa could tell he was adamant. "Okay," she said. "I understand."

"You do?" said Tad, surprised that she'd given in so easily.

"I really do, but if you can't take me into the lab, at least you could get me something to drink."

"Of course," said Tad, eager to please. "Beer, white wine. What's your pleasure?"

"A beer would be nice," said Marissa.

Tad disappeared into the kitchen. When she heard the sound of the refrigerator opening, Marissa stood and quickly tiptoed to the front door. Glancing at the shelf, she was pleased to see Tad had two access cards. Maybe he wouldn't even notice that she'd borrowed one, she thought to herself, as she slipped one of the two into her jacket pocket. She was back on the couch before Tad returned with the beers.

Tad handed Marissa a bottle of Rolling Rock, keeping one for himself. He also produced a package of potato chips that he popped open and set on the coffee table. To humor him, Marissa asked about his latest research, but it was obvious she wasn't paying close attention to his answers.

"You don't like Rolling Rock?" asked Tad, noticing that she'd hardly touched hers.

"It's fine," said Marissa, yawning. "I guess I'm more tired than thirsty. I suppose I ought to be going."

"You're welcome to spend the night," said Tad.

Marissa pushed herself to her feet. "Thanks, but I really should go home."

"I'm sorry about the lab," said Tad, bending to kiss her.

"I understand," said Marissa. She headed out the door before he could get his arms around her.

Tad waited until he heard the outer door close before going back inside his apartment. On the one hand, he was glad that he'd had the sense to resist her manipulations. On the other, he felt badly that he'd disappointed her.

From where Tad was standing he was looking directly at the shelf where he'd left his access card and keys. Still thinking about Marissa, he realized that one of his cards was gone. He carefully looked through all the junk he'd removed from his pockets and then searched the shelves above and below. His spare card was gone.

"Damn!" said Tad. He should have expected a trick when she'd given up so easily. Opening the door, he ran down the stairs and out into the street, hoping to catch her, but the street was empty. There wasn't even a breath of air in the humid night. The leaves on the trees hung limp and still.

Tad went back to his apartment, trying to decide what to do. He checked the time, then went to the phone. He liked Marissa, but she'd gone too far. He picked up the phone and began dialing.

Driving to the Center, Marissa hoped Dubchek hadn't warned the guards she was no longer working in virology. But when she flashed her identity card the guard on duty just smiled and said, "Working late again?"

So far so good; but as a precaution, Marissa first went to her own office in case the man decided to follow her. She turned her light on and sat behind her desk, waiting, but there were no footsteps in the hall.

There were a few letters on her blotter: two advertisements from pharmaceutical houses and a third from Lab Engineering in South Bend. Marissa ripped this third one open. A salesman thanked her for her inquiry concerning their type 3 HEPA Containment Hoods and went on to say that such equipment was only built to custom specifications. If she was interested, she should retain an architectural firm specializing in health-care construction. He ended by answering the question that had prompted her letter: Lab Engineering had built only one system in the last year and that had been for Professional Labs in Grayson, Georgia.

Marissa looked at a map of the United States that her office's previous occupant had left hanging and which she'd never bothered to take down. Poring over Georgia, she tried to find Grayson. It wasn't there. She searched through her drawers, thinking she had a Georgia road map somewhere. Finally she found it in the file cabinet. Grayson was a small town a few hours east of Atlanta. What on earth were they doing with a type 3 HEPA Containment Hood?

After putting the road map back in the file cabinet and the letter in her blazer pocket, Marissa checked the hallway. It was quiet, and the elevator was still at her floor; it had not been used. She decided that the time was right to make her move.

Taking the stairs to descend one floor, Marissa left the main building and crossed to the virology building by the catwalk. She was pleased that there were no lights on in any of the offices. When she passed Dubchek's door, she stuck out her tongue. It was childish but satisfying. Turning the corner, she confronted the airtight security door. Involuntarily, she held her breath as she inserted Tad's card and tapped out his access number: 43-23-39. There was a resounding mechanical click and the heavy door swung open, Marissa caught a whiff of the familiar phenolic disinfectant.

Marissa felt her pulse begin to race. As she crossed the threshold, she had the uncomfortable feeling she was entering a house of horrors. The dimly lit cavernous two-story space, filled with its confusion of pipes and their shadows, gave the impression of a gigantic spiderweb.

As she'd seen Tad do on her two previous visits, Marissa opened the small cabinet by the entrance and threw the circuit breakers, turning on the lights, and activating the compressors and ventilation equipment. The sound of the machinery was much louder than she'd recalled, sending vibrations through the floor.

Alone, the futuristic lab was even more intimidating than Marissa remembered. It took all her courage to proceed, knowing in addition that she was breaking rules when she was already on probation. Every second, she feared that someone would discover her.

With sweaty palms, she grasped the releasing wheel on the airtight door to the dressing rooms and tried to turn it. The wheel would not budge. Finally, using all her strength, she got it to turn. The seal broke with a hiss and the door swung outward. She climbed through, hearing the door close behind her with an ominous thud.

She felt her ears pop as she scrambled into a set of scrub clothes. The second door opened more easily, but the fewer problems she encountered, the more she worried about the real risks she was taking.

Locating a small plastic isolation suit among the twenty or so hanging in the chamber, Marissa found it much harder to get into without Tad's help. She was sweaty by the time she zipped it closed.

At the switch panel, she only turned on the lights for the main lab; the rest were unnecessary. She had no intention of visiting the animal area. Then, carrying her air hose, she crossed the disinfecting chamber and climbed through the final airtight door into the main part of the lab.

Her first order of business was to hook up to an appropriately positioned manifold and let the fresh air balloon out her suit and clear her mask. She welcomed the hissing sound. Without it the silence had been oppressive. Orienting herself in relation to all the high-tech hardware, she spotted the freezer. She was already sorry that she'd not turned on all the lights. The shadows at the far end of the lab created a sinister backdrop for the deadly viruses, heightening Marissa's fear.

Swinging her legs wide to accommodate the inflated and bulky isolation suit, Marissa started for the freezer, again marveling that with all the other "high-tech," up-to-the-minute equipment, they had settled for an ordinary household appliance. Its existence in the maximum containment lab was as unlikely as an old adding machine at a computer convention.

Just short of the freezer, Marissa paused, eyeing the insulated bolted door to the left. After learning the viruses were not stored behind it, she had wondered just what it did protect. Nervously, she reached out and drew the bolt. A cloud of vapor rushed out as she opened the door and stepped inside. For a moment she felt as if she had stepped into a freezing cloud. Then the heavy door swung back against her air hose, plunging her into darkness.

When her eyes adjusted, she spotted what she hoped was a light switch and turned it on. Overhead lights flicked on, barely revealing a thermometer next to the switch. Bending over she was able to make out that it registered minus fifty-one degrees centigrade.

"My God!" exclaimed Marissa, understanding the source of the vapor: as soon as the air at room temperature met such cold, the humidity it contained sublimated to ice.

Turning around and facing the dense fog, Marissa moved deeper into the room, fanning the air with her arms. Almost immediately a ghastly image caught her eye. She screamed, the sound echoing horribly within her suit. At first she thought she was seeing ghosts. Then she realized that, still more horrible, she was facing a row of frozen, nude corpses, only partially visible through the swirling mist. At first she thought they were standing on their own in a row, but it turned out they were hung like cadavers for an anatomy course—caliperlike devices thrust into the ear canals. As she came closer, Marissa recognized the first body. For a moment she thought she was going to pass out: it was the Indian doctor whom Marissa had seen in Phoenix, his face frozen into an agonized death mask.

There were at least a half-dozen bodies. Marissa didn't count. To the right, she saw the carcasses of monkeys and rats, frozen in equally grotesque positions. Although Marissa could understand that such freezing was probably necessary for the viral study of gross specimens, she had been totally unprepared for the sight. No wonder Tad had discouraged her from entering.

Marissa backed out of the room, turning off the light, and closing and bolting the door. She shivered both from distaste and actual chill.

Chastised for her curiosity, Marissa turned her attention to the freezer. In spite of the clumsiness afforded by the plastic suit and her own tremulousness, she worked the combination on the bicycle lock and got it off with relative ease. The link chain was another story. It was knotted, and she had to struggle to get it through the handle. It took longer than she would have liked, but at last it was free and she lifted the lid.

Rubbing the frost off the inner side of the lid, Marissa tried to decipher the index code. The viruses were in alphabetical order. "Ebola, Zaire '76" was followed by "97, E11–E48, F1–F12." Marissa guessed that the first number referred to the appropriate tray and that the letters and numbers that followed located the virus within the tray. Each tray held at least one thousand samples, which meant that there were fifty individual vials of the Zaire '76 strain.

As carefully as possible, Marissa lifted tray 97 free and set it on a nearby counter top while she scanned the slots. Each was filled with a small black-topped vial. Marissa was both relieved and disappointed. She located the Zaire '76 strain and lifted out sample E11. The tiny frozen ball inside looked innocuous, but Marissa knew that it contained millions of tiny viruses, any one or two of which, when thawed, were capable of killing a human being.

Slipping the vial back in its slot, Marissa lifted the next, checking to see if the ice ball appeared intact. She continued this process without seeing anything suspicious until finally she reached vial E39. The vial was empty!

Quickly, Marissa went through the rest of the samples: All were as they should be. She held vial E39 up to the light, squinting through her face mask to make sure she wasn't making a mistake. But there was no doubt: there was definitely nothing in the vial. Although one of the scientists might have misplaced a sample, she could think of no reason a vial might be empty. All her inarticulated fears that the outbreaks had stemmed from accidental or even deliberate misuse of a CDC vial filled with an African virus seemed to be confirmed.

A sudden movement caught Marissa's attention. The wheel to the door leading into the disinfecting chamber was turning! Someone was coming in!

Marissa was gripped with a paralyzing panic. For a moment she just stared helplessly. When she'd recovered enough to move, she put the empty vial back in the tray, returned it to the freezer and closed the lid. She thought about running, but there was no place to go. Maybe she could hide. She looked toward the darkened area by the animal cages. But there was no time. She heard the seal break on the door and two people entered the lab, dressed anonymously in plastic isolation suits. The smaller of the two seemed familiar with the lab, showing his larger companion where he should plug in his air hose.

Terrified, Marissa stayed where she was. There was always the faint chance that they were CDC scientists checking on some ongoing experiment. That hope faded quickly when she realized they were coming directly toward her. It was at that point she noticed that the smaller individual was holding a syringe. Her eyes flicked to his companion, who lumbered forward, his elbow fixed at an odd angle, stirring an unpleasant memory.

Marissa tried to see their faces, but the glare off the face plates made it impossible.

"Blumenthal?" asked the smaller of the two in a harsh, masculine voice. He reached out and rudely angled Marissa's mask against the light. Apparently he recognized her, because he nodded to his companion, who reached for the zipper on her suit.

"No!" screamed Marissa, realizing these men were not security. They were about to attack her just as she'd been attacked in her house. Desperately, she snatched the bicycle lock from the freezer and threw it. The confusion gave Marissa just enough time to detach her air hose and run toward the animal area.

The larger man was after her in less than a second, but as he was about to grab her, he was pulled up short by his air hose, like a dog on a leash.

Marissa moved as quickly as she could into the dark corridors between the stacked animal cages, hearing the frightened chatter of monkeys, rats, chickens and God knew what else. Trapped within the confines of the lab, she was desperate. Hoping to create a diversion, she began opening the monkey cages. The animals who weren't too sick to move immediately fled. Soon, her breathing became labored.

Finding an air manifold, which was not easy in the darkness, Marissa plugged in, welcoming the rush of cool, dry air. It was obvious the larger man was unaccustomed to being in the lab, but she didn't really see that it would give her much of an advantage. She moved down the line of cages to where she could see into the main area of the room. Silhouetted against the light, he was moving toward her. She had no idea if he could see her or not, but she stayed still, mentally urging the man down a different aisle. But he was unswerving. He was walking right at her. The hairs on the back of her neck stood on end.

Reaching up, she detached her air hose and tried to move around the far end of the row of cages. Before she could, the man caught her left arm.

Marissa looked up at her assailant. All she could see was the slight gleam of his face plate. The strength of his grip made resistance seem useless, but over his shoulder she glimpsed a red handle marked Emergency Use Only.

In desperation, Marissa reached up with her free hand and pulled the lever down. Instantly an alarm sounded, and a sudden shower of phenolic disinfectant drenched the whole lab, sending up clouds of mist and reducing the visibility to zero. Shocked, the man released Marissa's arm. She dropped to the floor. Discovering that she could slither beneath the row of cages, she crawled away from the man, hoping she was headed back toward the main lab. She got to her feet, moving forward by feel. The disinfectant shower was apparently going to continue until someone replaced the lever. Her breathing was becoming painfully labored. She needed fresh air.

Something jumped in front of her, and she nearly screamed. But it was only one of the monkeys, tortured by the lethal atmosphere. The animal held on to her for a minute, then slid off her plastic-covered shoulder and disappeared.

Gasping, Marissa reached up and ran her hand along the pipes. Touching an air manifold, she connected her line.

Over the sound of the alarm, Marissa heard a commotion in the next aisle, then muffled shouts. She guessed that her pursuer could not find a manifold.

Gambling that the second man would go to the aid of his accomplice, Marissa detached her own air hose and moved toward the light, her arms stretched out in front of her like a blind man. Soon the illumination was uniform and she guessed she had reached the main part of the lab. Moving toward the wall, she banged into the freezer and remembered seeing a manifold just above it. She hooked up for several quick breaths. Then she felt her way to the door. The second she found it, she released the seal and pulled it open. A minute later she was standing in the disinfecting room.

Having already been drenched with phenolic disinfectant, she didn't wait through the usual shower. In the next room, she struggled out of her plastic suit, then ran into the room beyond, where she tipped the lockers holding the scrub clothes over against the pressure door. She didn't think it would stop the door from being opened, but it might slow her pursuers down.

Racing into her street clothes, she flicked all the circuit breakers, throwing even the dressing rooms into darkness and turning off the ventilation system.

Once outside the maximum containment lab, Marissa ran the length of the virology building, across the catwalk, and to the stairs to the main floor, which she bounded down two at a time. Taking a deep breath, she tried to look relaxed as she went through the front lobby. The security guard was sitting at his desk to the left. He was on the phone, explaining to someone that a biological alarm had gone off, not a security door alarm.

Even though she doubted her pursuers would have enlisted security's help after having tried to kill her, she'd trembled violently while signing out. She heard the guard hang up after he explained to the person he was talking to that the operators were busy searching for the head of the virology department.

"Hey!" yelled the guard, as Marissa started for the door. Her heart leapt into her mouth. For a moment, she thought about fleeing; she was only six feet from the front door. Then she heard the guard say, "You forgot to put the time."

Marissa marched back and dutifully filled in the blank. A second later she was outside, running to her car.

She was halfway to Ralph's before she was able to stop shaking and think about her terrible discovery. The missing ball of frozen Ebola couldn't have been a coincidence. It was the same strain as each of the recent outbreaks across the country. Someone was using the virus, and whether intentionally or by accident, the deadly disease was infecting doctors and hospitals in disparate areas at disparate times.

That the missing sample from vial E39 was the mysterious reservoir for the Ebola outbreaks in the United States was the only explanation that answered the questions posed by the apparently long incubation periods and the fact that, though the virus tended to mutate, all of the outbreaks involved the same strain. Worse yet, someone did not want that information released. That was why she'd been taken off the Ebola team and why she had just been nearly killed. The realization that frightened her most was that only someone with maximum containment lab access—presumably someone on the CDC staff—could have found her there. She cursed herself for not having had the presence of mind to look in the log book as she signed out to see who'd signed in.

She had already turned down Ralph's street, anxious to tell him her fears, when she realized that it wasn't fair to involve him. She'd already taken advantage of Tad's friendship, and by the next day, when he saw her name on the log, she would be a total pariah. Her one hope was that her two assailants would not report her presence in the lab, since they would then be implicated in the attempt on her life. Even so, she couldn't count on their not devising a plausible lie about what had gone on. It would be their word against hers, and by tomorrow, her word wouldn't mean much at the CDC. Of that she was sure. For all she knew the Atlanta police might be looking for her by morning.

Remembering her suitcase was still in the trunk of her car, Marissa headed for the nearest motel. As soon as she reached the room assigned her, she put in a call to Ralph. He answered sleepily on the fifth ring.

"I stayed up as long as I could," he explained. "Why didn't you come by?"

"It's a long story," said Marissa. "I can't explain now, but I'm in serious trouble. I may even need a good criminal lawyer. Do you know of one?"

"Good God," said Ralph, suddenly not sleepy. "I think you'd better tell me what's going on."

"I don't want to drag you into it," said Marissa. "All I can say is that the whole situation has become decidedly serious and, for the moment, I'm not ready to go to the authorities. I guess I'm a fugitive!" Marissa laughed hollowly.

"Why don't you come over here?" said Ralph. "You'd be safe here."

"Ralph, I'm serious about not wanting to involve you. But I do need a lawyer. Could you find me one?"

"Of course," said Ralph. "I'll help you any way I can. Where are you?"

"I'll be in touch," said Marissa evasively. "And thanks for being my friend."

Marissa disconnected by pushing the button on top of the phone, trying to build up her courage to call Tad and apologize before he found out from someone else that she'd taken his access card. Taking a deep breath, she dialed. When there was no answer after several rings, she lost her nerve and decided not to wake him up.

Marissa took the letter from Lab Engineering from her pocket and smoothed it out. Grayson was going to be her next stop.

12

MAY 21

Although she was exhausted, Marissa slept poorly, tortured by nightmares of being chased through alien landscapes. When the early light coming through the window awakened her, it was a relief. She looked out and saw a man filling the coin-operated newspaper dispenser. As soon as he left, she ran out and bought the *Atlanta Journal and Constitution*.

There was nothing in it about the CDC, but halfway through the morning television news, the commentator said that there had been a problem at the Center. There was no mention of the maximum containment lab, but it was repeated that a technician had been treated at Emory University Hospital after inhaling phenolic disinfectant and then released. The segment continued with a phone interview with Dr. Cyrill Dubchek. Marissa leaned forward and turned up the volume.

"The injured technician was the only casualty," Cyrill said, his voice sounding metallic. Marissa wondered if he was in Philadelphia or Atlanta. "An emergency safety system was triggered by accident. Everything is under control, and we are searching for a Dr. Marissa Blumenthal in relation to the incident."

The anchorperson capped the segment with the comment that if anyone knew the whereabouts of Dr. Blumenthal, they should notify the Atlanta police. For about ten seconds they showed the photograph that had accompanied her CDC application.

Marissa turned off the TV. She'd not considered the possibility of seriously hurting her pursuers and she was upset, despite the fact that the man had been trying to harm her. Tad was right when he'd said that trouble seemed to follow her.

Although Marissa had joked about being a fugitive, she'd meant it figuratively. Now, having heard the TV announcer request information about her whereabouts, she realized the joke had become serious. She was a wanted person; at least by the Atlanta police.

Quickly getting her things together, Marissa went to check out of the motel. The whole time she was in the office, she felt nervous since her name was there in black and white for the clerk to see. But all he said was: "Have a nice day."

She grabbed a quick coffee and donut at a Howard Johnson's, and drove to her bank, which luckily had early hours that day. Although she tried to conceal her face at the drive-in window in case the teller had seen the morning news, the man seemed as uninterested as usual. Marissa extracted most of her savings, amounting to $4,650.

With the cash in her purse, she relaxed a little. Driving up the ramp to Interstate 78, she turned on the radio. She was on her way to Grayson, Georgia.

The drive was easy, although longer than she'd expected, and not terribly interesting. The only sight of note was that geological curiosity called Stone Mountain. It was a bubble of bare granite sticking out of the wooded Georgia hills, like a mole on a baby's bottom. Beyond the town of Snellville, Marissa turned northeast on 84, and the landscape became more and more rural. Finally she passed a sign: WELCOME TO GRAYSON. Unfortunately it was spotted with holes, as if someone had been using it for target practice, reducing the sincerity of the message.

The town itself was exactly as Marissa had imagined. The main street was lined with a handful of brick and wood-frame buildings. There was a bankrupt movie theater, and the largest commercial establishment was the hardware and feed store. On one corner, a granite-faced bank sported a large clock with Roman numerals. Obviously it was just the kind of town that needed a type 3 HEPA Containment Hood!

The streets were almost empty as Marissa slowly cruised along. She saw no new commercial structures and realized that Professional Labs was probably a little ways from town. She would have to inquire, but whom could she approach? She was not about to go to the local police.

159

At the end of the street, she made a U-turn and drove back. There was a general store that also boasted a sign that read U.S. Post Office.

"Professional Labs? Yeah, they're out on Bridge Road," said the proprietor. He was in the dry-goods section, showing bolts of cotton to a customer. "Turn yourself around and take a right at the firehouse. Then after Parsons Creek, take a left. You'll find it. It's the only thing out there 'cept for cows."

"What do they do?" asked Marissa.

"Darned if I know," said the storekeeper. "Darned if I care. They're good customers and they pay their bills."

Following the man's directions, Marissa drove out of the town. He was right about there being nothing around but cows. After Parsons Creek the road wasn't even paved, and Marissa began to wonder if she were on a wild-goose chase. But then the road entered a pine forest, and up ahead she could see a building.

With a thump, Marissa's Honda hit asphalt as the road widened into a parking area. There were two other vehicles: a white van with Professional Labs, Inc., lettered on the side, and a cream-colored Mercedes.

Marissa pulled up next to the van. The building had peaked roofs and lots of mirror glass, which reflected the attractive tree-lined setting. The fragrant smell of pine surrounded her as she walked to the entrance. She gave the door a pull, but it didn't budge. She tried to push, but it was as if it were bolted shut. Stepping back, she searched for a bell, but there was none. She knocked a couple of times, but realized she wasn't making enough noise for anyone inside to hear. Giving up on the front door, Marissa started to walk around the building. When she got to the first window, she cupped her hands and tried to look through the mirror glass. It was impossible.

"Do you know you are trespassing?" said an unfriendly voice.

Marissa's hands dropped guiltily to her sides.

"This is private property," said a stocky, middle-aged man dressed in blue coveralls.

"Ummm . . . ," voiced Marissa, desperately trying to think of an excuse for her presence. With his graying crew cut and florid complexion, the man looked exactly like a red-neck stereotype from the fifties.

"You did see the signs?" asked the man, gesturing to the notice by the parking lot.

"Well, yes," admitted Marissa. "But you see, I'm a doctor . . ."

She hesitated. Being a physician didn't give her the right to violate someone's privacy. Quickly she went on: "Since you have a viral lab here, I was interested to know if you do viral diagnostic work."

"What makes you think this is a viral lab?" questioned the man.

"I'd just heard it was," said Marissa.

"Well, you heard wrong. We do molecular biology here. With the worry of industrial espionage, we have to be very careful. So I think that you'd better leave unless you'd like me to call the police."

"That won't be necessary," said Marissa. Involving the police was the last thing she wanted. "I certainly apologize. I don't mean to be a bother. I would like to see your lab, though. Isn't there some way that could be arranged?"

"Out of the question," the man said flatly. He led Marissa back to her car, their footsteps crunching on the crushed-stone path.

"Is there someone that I might contact to get a tour?" asked Marissa as she slid behind the wheel.

"I'm the boss," said the man simply. "I think you'd better go." He stepped back from the car, waiting for Marissa to leave.

Having run out of bright ideas, Marissa started the engine. She tried smiling good-bye, but the man's face remained grim as she drove off, heading back to Grayson.

He stood waiting until the little Honda was lost in the trees. With an irritated shake of his head, he turned and walked back to the building. The front door opened automatically.

The interior was as contemporary as the exterior. He went down a short tiled corridor and entered a small lab. At one end was a desk, at the other was an airtight steel door like the one leading into the CDC's maximum containment lab, behind which was a lab bench equipped with a type 3 HEPA filtration system.

Another man was sitting at the desk, torturing a paper clip into grotesque shapes. He looked up: "Why the hell didn't you let me handle her?" Speaking made him cough violently, bringing tears to his eyes. He raised a handkerchief to his mouth.

"Because we don't know who knows she was here," said the man in the blue coveralls. "Use a little sense, Paul. Sometimes you scare me." He picked up the phone and punched the number he wanted with unnecessary force.

"Dr. Jackson's office," answered a bright, cheerful voice.

"I want to talk to the doctor."

"I'm sorry, but he's with a patient."

"Honey, I don't care if he's with God. Just put him on the phone."

"Who may I say is calling?" asked the secretary coolly.

"Tell him the Chairman of the Medical Ethics Committee. I don't care; just put him on!"

"One moment, please."

Turning to the desk, he said: "Paul, would you get my coffee from the counter."

Paul tossed the paper clip into the wastebasket, then heaved himself out of his chair. It took a bit of effort because he was a big man and his left arm was frozen at the elbow joint. He'd been shot by a policeman when he was a boy.

"Who is this?" demanded Dr. Joshua Jackson at the other end of the phone.

"Heberling," said the man in the blue coveralls. "Dr. Arnold Heberling. Remember me?"

Paul gave Arnold his coffee, then returned to the desk, taking another paper clip out of the middle drawer. He pounded his chest, clearing his throat.

"Heberling!" said Dr. Jackson. "I told you never to call me at my office!"

"The Blumenthal girl was here," said Heberling, ignoring Jackson's comment. "She drove up pretty as you please in a red car. I caught her looking through the windows."

"How the hell did she find out about the lab?"

"I don't know and I don't care," said Heberling. "The fact of the matter is that she was here, and I'm coming into town to see you. This can't go on. Something has to be done about her."

"No! Don't come here," said Jackson frantically. "I'll come there."

"All right," said Heberling. "But it has to be today."

"I'll be there around five," said Jackson, slamming down the receiver.

Marissa decided to stop in Grayson for lunch. She was hungry, and maybe someone would tell her something about the lab. She stopped in front of the drugstore, went in and sat down at the old-fashioned soda fountain. She ordered a hamburger, which came on a freshly toasted roll with a generous slice of Bermuda onion. Her Coke was made from syrup.

162

While Marissa ate, she considered her options. They were pretty meager. She couldn't go back to the CDC or the Berson Clinic Hospital. Figuring out what Professional Labs was doing with a sophisticated 3 HEPA filtration system was a last resort, but the chances of getting in seemed slim: the place was built like a fortress. Perhaps it was time to call Ralph and ask if he'd found a lawyer, except . . .

Marissa took a bite of her dill pickle. In her mind's eye she pictured the two vehicles in the lab's parking lot. The white van had had Professional Labs, Inc., printed on its side. It was the Inc. that interested her.

Finishing her meal, Marissa walked down the street to an office building she remembered passing. The door was frosted glass: RONALD DAVIS, ATTORNEY AND REALTOR was stenciled on it in gold leaf. A bell jangled as she entered. There was a cluttered desk, but no secretary.

A man dressed in a white shirt, bow tie and red suspenders came out from an inside room. Although he appeared to be no more than thirty, he was wearing wire-rimmed glasses that seemed almost grandfatherly. "Can I help you?" he asked, with a heavy Southern accent.

"Are you Mr. Davis?" asked Marissa.

"Yup." The man hooked his thumbs through his suspenders.

"I have a couple of simple questions," said Marissa. "About corporate law. Do you think you could answer them?"

"Maybe," said Mr. Davis. He motioned for Marissa to come in.

The scene looked like a set for a 1930s movie, complete with the desk-top fan that slowly rotated back and forth, rustling the papers. Mr. Davis sat down and leaned back, putting his hands behind his head. Then he said: "What is it you want to know?"

"I want to find out about a certain corporation," began Marissa. "If a business is incorporated, can someone like myself find out the names of the owners?"

Mr. Davis tipped forward, resting his elbows on the desk. "Maybe and maybe not," he said, smiling.

Marissa groaned. It seemed that a conversation with Mr. Davis was going to be like pulling teeth. But before she could rephrase her question, he continued: "If the company in question is a public corporation, it would be hard to find out all the stockholders, especially if a lot of the stock is held in trust with power of attorney delegated to a third party. But if the company is a partnership, then it would be easy. In any case, it is always possible to find out the name of the service agent if you have in mind to institute some sort of litigation. Is that what you have in mind?''

"No," said Marissa. "Just information. How would I go about finding out if a company is a partnership or a public corporation?''

"Easy," said Mr. Davis, leaning back once more.

"All you have to do is go to the State House in Atlanta, visit the Secretary of State's office and ask for the corporate division. Just tell the clerk the name of the company, and he can look it up. It's a matter of public record, and if the company is incorporated in Georgia, it will be listed there.''

"Thank you," said Marissa, seeing a glimmer of light at the end of the dark tunnel. "How much do I owe you?''

Mr. Davis raised his eyebrows, studying Marissa's face. "Twenty dollars might do it, unless . . .''

"My pleasure," said Marissa, pulling out a twenty-dollar bill and handing it over.

Marissa returned to her car and drove back toward Atlanta. She was pleased to have a goal, even if the chances of finding significant information were not terribly good.

She stayed just under the speed limit. The last thing she wanted was to be stopped by the police. She made good time and was back in the city by 4:00. Parking in a garage, she walked to the State House.

Distinctly uncomfortable in the presence of the capitol police, Marissa sweated nervously as she started up the front steps, certain she would be recognized.

"Dr. Blumenthal," called a voice.

For a split second, Marissa considered running. Instead, she turned to see one of the CDC secretaries, a bright young woman in her early twenties, walking toward her.

"Alice MacCabe, Dr. Carbonara's office. Remember me?''

Marissa did, and for the next few nerve-wracking minutes was forced to engage in small talk. Luckily, Miss MacCabe was oblivious to the fact that Marissa was a "wanted" person.

As soon as she could, Marissa said good-bye and entered the building. More than ever, she just wanted to get whatever information she could and leave. Unfortunately, there was a long line at the corporate division. With dwindling patience, Marissa waited her turn, keeping a hand to her face with the mistaken notion that it might keep her from being recognized.

"What can I do for you?" asked the white-haired clerk when it was finally Marissa's turn.

"I'd like some information about a corporation called Professional Labs."

"Where is it located?" asked the clerk. He slipped on his bifocals and entered the name at a computer terminal.

"Grayson, Georgia," said Marissa.

"Okay," said the clerk. "Here it is. Incorporated just last year. What would you like to know?"

"Is it a partnership or a public corporation?" asked Marissa, trying to remember what Mr. Davis had said.

"Limited partnership, subchapter S."

"What does that mean?" asked Marissa.

"It has to do with taxes. The partners can deduct the corporate losses, if there are any, on their individual returns."

"Are the partners listed?" asked Marissa, excitement overcoming her anxiety for the moment.

"Yup," said the clerk. "There's Joshua Jackson, Rodd Becker . . ."

"Just a second," said Marissa. "Let me write this down." She got out a pen and began writing.

"Let's see," said the clerk, staring at the computer screen. "Jackson, Becker; you got those?"

"Yes."

"There's Sinclair Tieman, Jack Krause, Gustave Swenson, Duane Moody, Trent Goodridge and the Physicians' Action Congress."

"What was that last one?" asked Marissa, scribbling furiously.

The clerk repeated it.

"Can an organization be a limited partner?" She had seen the name Physicians' Action Congress on Markham's contributions list.

"I'm no lawyer, lady, but I think so. Well, it must be so or it wouldn't be in here. Here's something else: a law firm by the name of Cooper, Hodges, McQuinllin and Hanks."

"They're partners too?" asked Marissa, starting to write down the additional names.

"No," said the clerk. "They're the service agent."

"I don't need that," said Marissa. "I'm not interested in suing the company." She erased the names of Cooper and Hodges.

Thanking the clerk, Marissa beat a hasty retreat and hurried back to the parking garage. Once inside her car, she opened her briefcase and took out the photocopies of Markham's contributors list. Just as she'd remembered, the Physicians' Action Congress (PAC) was listed. On the one hand it was a limited partner in an economic venture, on the other, a contributor to a conservative politician's reelection campaign.

Curious, Marissa looked to see if any of the other partners of Professional Labs were on Markham's list. To her surprise, they all were. More astonishing, the partners, like Markham's contributors, came from all over the country. From Markham's list, she had all their addresses.

Marissa put her key in the ignition, then hesitated. Looking back at Markham's list she noted that the Physicians' Action Congress was listed under corporate sponsors. Much as she hated to tempt fate by passing the capitol police again, she forced herself to get out of the car and walk back. She waited in line for the second time, for the same clerk, and asked him what he could tell her about the Physicians' Action Congress.

The clerk punched in the name on his terminal, waited for a moment, then turned to Marissa. "I can't tell you anything. It's not in here."

"Does that mean it's not incorporated?"

"Not necessarily. It means it's not incorporated in Georgia."

Marissa thanked the man again, and again ran out of the building. Her car felt like a sanctuary. She sat for a few minutes, trying to decide what to do next. She really didn't have all that much information, and she was getting rather far afield from the Ebola outbreaks. But her intuition told her that in some weird way everything she had learned was related. And if that were the case, then the Physicians' Action Congress was the key. But how could she investigate an organization she'd never heard of?

Her first thought was to visit the Emory Medical School library. Perhaps one of the librarians might know where to look. But then, remembering running into Alice MacCabe, she decided the chance of being recognized was too great. She would do much better to go out of town for a few days. But where?

Starting the car, Marissa had an inspiration: the AMA! If she couldn't get information about a physicians' organization at the AMA, then it wasn't available. And Chicago sounded safe. She headed south toward the airport, hoping the meager supply of clothing in her suitcase would hold up.

Joshua Jackson's heavy sedan thundered over the wood-planked bridge spanning Parsons Creek, then veered sharply to the left, the tires squealing. The pavement stopped, and the car showered the shoulder of the road with pebbles as it sped down the tree-lined lane. Inside, Jackson's fury mounted with each mile he traveled. He didn't want to visit the lab, but he had no intention of being seen in town with Heberling. The man was proving increasingly unreliable, and even worse, unpredictable. Asked to create minor confusion, he resorted to atomic warfare. Hiring him had been a terrible decision, but there wasn't much any of them could do about the fact now.

Pulling up to the lab, Jackson parked across from Heberling's Mercedes. He knew that Heberling had bought it with some of the funds he'd been given for technical equipment. What a waste!

Jackson walked up to the front of the building. It was an impressive affair, and Jackson, perhaps better than anyone, knew how much money it had all cost. The Physicians' Action Congress had built Dr. Arnold Heberling a personal monument, and for what: a hell of a lot of trouble, because Heberling was a nut.

There was a click, the door opened and Jackson stepped inside.

"I'm in the conference room," shouted Heberling.

Jackson knew the room Heberling meant, and it was hardly a conference room. Jackson paused at the door, taking in the high ceiling, glass wall and stark furnishings. Two Chippendale couches faced one another on a large Chinese rug. There was no other furniture. Heberling was on one of the couches.

"I hope this is important," said Jackson, taking the initiative. The two men sat facing each other. Physically, they couldn't have been more different. Heberling was stocky with a bloated face and coarse features. Jackson was tall and thin with an almost ascetic face. Their clothes helped heighten the contrast: Heberling in coveralls; Jackson in a banker's pinstripes.

"The Blumenthal girl was right here in the yard," said Heberling, pointing over his shoulder for effect. "Obviously she didn't see anything, but just the fact that she was here suggests that she knows something. She's got to be removed."

"You had your chance," snapped Jackson. "Twice! And each time, you and your thugs made a mess of things. First at her house and then last night at the CDC."

"So we try again. But you've called it off."

"You're darn right. I found out you were going to give her Ebola."

"Why not?" said Heberling. "She's been exposed. There'd be no questions."

"I don't want an Ebola outbreak in Atlanta," shouted Jackson. "The stuff terrifies me. I've got a family of my own. Leave the woman to us. We'll take care of her."

"Oh, sure," scoffed Heberling. "That's what you said when you got her transferred off Special Pathogens. Well, she's still a threat to the whole project, and I intend to see that she's eliminated."

"You are not in charge here," said Jackson menacingly. "And when it comes to fixing blame, none of us would be in this mess if you'd stuck to the original plan of using influenza virus. We've all been in a state of panic since we learned you took it upon yourself to use Ebola!"

"Oh, we're back to that complaint," said Heberling disgustedly. "You were pretty pleased when you heard the Richter Clinic was closing. If PAC wanted to undermine the public's growing confidence in prepaid health clinics, they couldn't have done better. The only difference from the original plan was that I got to carry out some field research that will save me years of lab research time."

Jackson studied Heberling's face. He'd come to the conclusion the man was a psychopath, and loathed him. Unfortunately the realization was a bit late. Once the project had started, there was no easy way to stop it. And to think that the plan had sounded so simple back when the PAC executive committee had first suggested it.

Jackson took a deep breath, knowing he had to control himself despite his anger. "I've told you a dozen times the Physicians' Action Congress is not pleased and, on the contrary, is appalled at the loss of life. That had never been our intent and you know it, Dr. Heberling!"

"Bullshit!" shouted Heberling. "There would have been loss of life with influenza, given the strains we would have had to use. How many would you have tolerated? A hundred? And what about the loss of life you rich practitioners cause when you turn your backs on unnecessary surgery, or allow incompetent doctors to keep their hospital privileges?"

"We do not sanction unnecessary surgery or incompetence," snapped Jackson. He'd had about as much of this psychopath as he could tolerate.

"You do nothing to stop them," said Heberling, with disgust. "I haven't believed any of this crap you and PAC feed me about your concern for the negative drift of American medicine away from its traditional values. Give me a break! It's all an attempt to justify your own economic interests. All of a sudden there are too many doctors and not enough patients. The only reason I've cooperated with you is because you built me this lab.'' Heberling made a sweeping gesture with his hand. "You wanted the image of prepaid health plans tarnished, and I delivered. The only difference is that I did it my way for my own reasons.''

"But we ordered you to stop," yelled Jackson. "Right after the Richter Clinic outbreak.''

"Half-heartedly, I might add," said Heberling. "You were pleased with the results. Not only did the Richter Clinic fold, but new subscribers to California health plans have leveled off for the first time in five years. The Physicians' Action Congress feels an occasional twinge of conscience, but basically you're all happy. And I've vindicated my beliefs that Ebola is a premier biological weapon despite the lack of vaccine or treatment. I've shown that it is easily introduced, relatively easy to contain and devastatingly contagious to small populations. Dr. Jackson, we are both getting what we want. We just have to deal with this woman before she causes real trouble.''

"I'm telling you once and for all," said Jackson. "We want no further use of Ebola. That's an order!''

Heberling laughed. "Dr. Jackson," he said, leaning forward, "I have the distinct impression that you are ignoring the facts. PAC is no longer in a position to give me orders. Do you realize what would happen to your careers if the truth gets out? And I'm telling you that it will unless you let me handle Blumenthal in my own way.''

For a moment, Jackson struggled with his conscience. He wanted to grab Heberling by the neck and choke him. But he knew the man was right: PAC's hands were tied. "All right," he said reluctantly. "Do whatever you think is best about Dr. Blumenthal. Just don't tell me about it and don't use Ebola in Atlanta.''

"Fine." Heberling smiled. "If that will make you feel better, I'll give you my word on both accounts. After all, I'm a very reasonable man.''

Jackson stood up. "One other thing. I don't want you phoning my office. Call me at home on my private line if you have to reach me.''

"My pleasure," said Heberling.

Since the Atlanta-Chicago run was heavily traveled, Marissa only had to wait half an hour for the next available flight. She bought a

Dick Francis novel, but she couldn't concentrate. Finally, she decided to call Tad and at least attempt an apology. She wasn't sure how much to tell him about her growing suspicions, but decided to play it by ear. She dialed the lab, and as she suspected, he was working late.

"This is Marissa," she said when he answered. "Are you mad at me?"

"I'm furious."

"Tad, I'm sorry . . ."

"You took one of my access cards."

"Tad, I'm truly sorry. When I see you, I'll explain everything."

"You actually went into the maximum containment lab, didn't you?" Tad said, his voice uncharacteristically hard.

"Well, yes."

"Marissa, do you know that the lab is a shambles, all the animals are dead, and someone had to be treated at Emory Emergency?"

"Two men came into the lab and attacked me."

"Attacked you?"

"Yes," said Marissa. "You have to believe me."

"I don't know what to believe. Why does everything happen to you?"

"Because of the Ebola outbreaks. Tad, do you know who got hurt?"

"I assume one of the techs from another department."

"Why don't you find out. And maybe you could also find out who else went into the lab last night."

"I don't think that's possible. No one will tell me anything right now because they know we're friends. Where are you?"

"I'm at the airport," said Marissa.

"If what you say about being attacked is true, then you should come back here and explain. You shouldn't be running away."

"I'm not running away," insisted Marissa. "I'm going to the AMA in Chicago to research an organization called the Physicians' Action Congress. Ever hear of them? I believe they are involved somehow."

"Marissa, I think you should come directly back to the Center. You're in real trouble, in case you don't know."

"I do, but for the time being what I'm doing is more important. Can't you please ask the Office of Biosafety who else went into the maximum containment lab last night?"

"Marissa, I'm in no mood to be manipulated."

"Tad, I . . ." Marissa stopped speaking. Tad had hung up. Slowly she replaced the receiver. She couldn't really blame him.

She glanced at the clock. Five minutes until boarding. Making up her mind, she dialed Ralph's home number.

He picked up on the third ring. In contrast to Tad, he was concerned, not angry. "My God, Marissa, what is going on? Your name is in the evening paper. You're in serious trouble, the Atlanta police are looking for you!"

"I can imagine," said Marissa, thinking that she'd been wise to use a false name and pay cash when she'd bought her airline ticket. "Ralph, have you gotten the name of a good lawyer yet?"

"I'm sorry. When you asked, I didn't realize it was an emergency."

"It's becoming an emergency," said Marissa. "But I'll be out of town for a day or two. So if you could do it tomorrow I'd really appreciate it."

"What's going on?" asked Ralph. "The paper gave no details."

"Like I said last night, I don't want to involve you."

"I don't mind," Ralph insisted. "Why don't you come over here. We can talk and I can get you a lawyer in the morning."

"Have you ever heard of an organization called the Physicians' Action Congress?" asked Marissa, ignoring Ralph's offer.

"No," said Ralph. "Marissa, please come over. I think it would be better to face this problem, whatever it is. Running away makes you look bad."

Marissa heard her flight called.

"I'm going to the AMA to find out about the organization I just mentioned," said Marissa quickly. "I'll call tomorrow. I've got to run." She hung up, picked up her briefcase and book and boarded the plane.

13

MAY 22

Arriving in Chicago, Marissa decided to treat herself to a nice hotel and was happy to find the Palmer House had a room. She risked using her credit card and went straight upstairs to bed.

The next morning, she ordered fresh fruit and coffee from room service. While waiting, she turned on the *Today Show* and went into the bathroom to shower. She was drying her hair when she heard the anchorman mention Ebola. She rushed into the bedroom, expecting to see the news commentator giving an update on the situation in Philadelphia. Instead, he was describing a new outbreak. It was at the Rosenberg Clinic on upper Fifth Avenue in New York City. A doctor by the name of Girish Mehta had been diagnosed as having the disease. Word had leaked to the press, and a widespread panic had gripped the city.

Marissa shivered. The Philadelphia outbreak was still in progress and another one had already started. She put on her makeup, finished fixing her hair and ate her breakfast. Marissa got the AMA's address and set out for Rush Street.

A year ago if someone had told her she'd be visiting the association, she never would have believed it. But there she was, going through the front door.

The woman at the information booth directed her to the Public

Relations office. The director, a James Frank, happened by as Marissa was trying to explain her needs to one of the secretaries. He invited her to his office.

Mr. Frank reminded Marissa of her high-school guidance counselor. He was of indeterminate age, slightly overweight and going bald, but his face had a lived-in look that exuded friendliness and sincerity. His eyes were bright, and he laughed a lot. Marissa liked him instantly.

"Physicians' Action Congress," he repeated when Marissa asked about the organization. "I've never heard of it. Where did you come across it?"

"On a congressman's contributions list," said Marissa.

"That's funny," said Mr. Frank. "I'd have sworn that I knew all the active political action committees. Let me see what my computer says."

Mr. Frank punched in the name. There was a slight delay, then the screen blinked to life. "What do you know! You're absolutely right. It's right here." He pointed to the screen. "Physicians' Action Congress Political Action Committee. It's a registered separate segregated fund."

"What does that mean?" asked Marissa.

"Less than it sounds. It just means that your Physicians' Action Congress is an incorporated membership organization because it has legally set up a committee to dispense funds as campaign contributions. Let's see who they have been supporting."

"I can tell you one candidate," said Marissa. "Calvin Markham."

Mr. Frank nodded. "Yup, here's Markham's name along with a number of other conservative candidates. At least we know the political bent."

"Right wing," said Marissa.

"Probably very right wing," said Mr. Frank. "I'd guess they are trying to knock off DRGs—Diagnosis-Related Groups—limit immigration of foreign medical school graduates, stop HMO start-up subsidies and the like. Let me call someone I know at the Federal Elections Commission."

After some chitchat, he asked his friend about the Physicians' Action Congress. He nodded a few times while he listened, then hung up and turned to Marissa. "He doesn't know much about PAC either, except he looked up their Statement of Organization and told me they are incorporated in Delaware."

"Why Delaware?" questioned Marissa.

"Incorporation is cheapest there."

"What are the chances of finding out more about the organization?" asked Marissa.

"Like what? Who the officers are? Where the home office is? That kind of stuff?"

"Yes," said Marissa.

Picking up the phone again, Frank said: "Let's see what we can learn from Delaware."

He was quite successful. Although initially a clerk in the Delaware State House said that he'd have to come in person for the information, Mr. Frank managed to get a supervisor to bend the rules.

Mr. Frank was on the line for almost fifteen minutes, writing as he listened. When he was done, he handed Marissa a list of the board of directors. She looked down: President, Joshua Jackson, MD; vice-president, Rodd Becker, MD; treasurer, Sinclair Tieman, MD; secretary, Jack Krause, MD; directors, Gustave Swenson, MD; Duane Moody, MD; and Trent Goodridge, MD. Opening her briefcase, she took out the list of partners for Professional Labs. They were the same names!

Marissa left the AMA with her head spinning. The question that loomed in her mind was almost too bizarre to consider: what was an ultraconservative physicians' organization doing with a lab that owned sophisticated equipment used only for handling deadly viruses? Purposely, Marissa did not answer her own question.

Her mind churning, Marissa began walking in the direction of her hotel. Other pedestrians jostled her, but she paid no heed.

Trying to pick holes in her own theory, Marissa ticked off the significant facts: each of the outbreaks of Ebola had occurred in a private group prepaid health-care facility; most of the index patients had foreign-sounding names; and in each case where there was an index patient, the man had been mugged just prior to getting sick. The one exception was the Phoenix outbreak, which she still believed was foodborne.

Out of the corner of her eye, she saw a display of Charles Jourdan shoes—her one weakness. Stopping abruptly to glance in the store window, she was startled when a man behind her almost knocked her over. He gave her an angry look, but she ignored him. A plan was forming in her mind. If her suspicions had any merit, and the previous outbreaks had not been the result of chance, then the index patient in New York was probably working for a prepaid health-care clinic and had been mugged a few days previous to becoming ill. Marissa decided she had to go to New York.

Looking around, she tried to figure out where she was in relation to her hotel. She could see the el in front of her and remembered that the train traveled the Loop near the Palmer House.

She began walking briskly when she was suddenly overwhelmed with fear. No wonder she'd been attacked in her home. No wonder the man who'd caught her in the maximum containment lab had tried to kill her. No wonder Markham had had her transferred. If her fears were true, then a conspiracy of immense proportions existed and she was in extreme jeopardy.

Up until that moment she'd felt safe in Chicago. Now, everywhere she looked she saw suspicious characters. There was a man pretending to window-shop she was sure was watching her in the reflection. She crossed the street, expecting the man to follow. But he didn't.

Marissa ducked into a coffee shop and ordered a cup of tea to calm down. She sat at a window table and stared out at the street. The man who had scared her came out of the store with a shopping bag and hailed a cab. So much for him. It was at that moment that she saw the businessman. It was the way he was carrying his briefcase that caught her attention, his arm at an awkward angle, as though he couldn't flex his elbow.

In a flash, Marissa was back in her own home, desperately fighting the unseen figure whose arm seemed frozen at the joint. And then there was the nightmare in the lab . . .

As Marissa watched, the man took out a cigarette and lit it, all with one hand, the other never leaving his briefcase. Marissa remembered that Tad had said the intruder had carried a briefcase.

Covering her face with her hands, Marissa prayed she was imagining things. She sat rubbing her eyes for a minute, and when she looked again, the man was gone.

Marissa finished her tea, then asked directions to the Palmer House. She walked quickly, nervously switching her own briefcase from hand to hand. At the first corner, she looked over her shoulder: the same businessman was coming toward her.

Immediately changing directions, Marissa crossed the street. Out of the corner of her eye, she watched the man continue to the middle of the block and then cross after her. With a rising sense of panic, she looked for a taxi, but the street was clear. Instead, she turned around and ran back to the elevated train. Hurriedly she climbed the stairs, catching up to a large group. She wanted to be in a crowd.

Once on the platform, she felt better. There were lots of people standing about, and Marissa walked a good distance away from the entrance. Her heart was still pounding, but at least she could think. Was it really the same man? Had he been following her?

As if in answer to her question, the man popped into her line of vision. He had large features and coarse skin and a heavy five-o'clock shadow. His teeth were square and widely spaced. He coughed into a closed fist.

Before she could move, the train thundered into the station, and the crowd surged forward, taking Marissa along with the rest. She lost sight of the man as she was carried into the car.

Fighting to stay near the door, Marissa hoped she could detrain at the last moment as she'd seen people do in spy movies, but the crush of people hampered her, and the doors closed before she could get to them. Turning, she scanned the faces around her, but she did not see the man with the stiff elbow.

The train lurched forward, forcing her to reach for a pole. Just as she grabbed it, she saw him again. He was right next to her, holding onto the same pole with the hand of his good arm. He was so close, Marissa could smell his cologne. He turned and their eyes met. A slight smile formed at the corners of his mouth as he let go of the pole. He coughed and reached into his jacket pocket.

Losing control, Marissa screamed. Frantically, she tried to push away from the man, but she was again hindered by the crush of people. Her scream died, and no one moved or spoke. They just stared at her. The wheels of the train shrieked as they hit a sharp bend, and Marissa and the man had to grab the pole to keep from falling. Their hands touched.

Marissa let go of the pole as if it were red hot. Then, to her utter relief, a transit policeman managed to shove his way over to her.

"Are you all right?" yelled the policeman over the sounds of the train.

"This man has been following me," said Marissa, pointing.

The policeman looked at the businessman. "Is this true?"

The man shook his head. "I've never seen her before. I don't know what she's talking about."

The policeman turned back to Marissa as the train began to slow. "Would you care to file a complaint?"

"No," yelled Marissa, "as long as he leaves me alone."

The screech of the wheels and the hiss of the air brakes made it impossible to hear until the train stopped. The doors opened instantly.

"I'll be happy to get off if it would make the lady feel better," said the businessman.

A few people got off. Everyone else just stared. The policeman kept the door from closing with his body and looked questioningly at Marissa.

"I would feel better," said Marissa, suddenly unsure of her reactions.

The businessman shrugged his shoulders and got off. Almost immediately, the doors closed and the train lurched forward once again.

"You all right now?" asked the policeman.

"Much better," said Marissa. She was relieved the businessman was gone, but afraid the cop might ask for her identification. She thanked him then looked away. He took the hint and moved on.

Realizing that every eye within sight was still on her, Marissa was acutely embarrassed. As soon as the train pulled in to the next station, she got off. Descending to the street, and irrationally afraid the man had found a way to follow her, she caught the first cab she could to take her to the Palmer House.

Within the security of the taxi, Marissa was able to regain a degree of control. She knew she was in over her head, but she had no idea to whom in authority she could go. She was presupposing a conspiracy but had no idea of its extent. And worst of all, she had no proof; nothing—just a few highly suggestive facts.

She decided she might as well continue on to New York. If her suspicions about that outbreak proved to be correct, she'd decide there whom to contact. Meanwhile, she hoped that Ralph had found her a good lawyer. Maybe he could handle the whole thing.

As soon as she got back to the hotel, Marissa went directly to her room. With her present paranoia, she wanted out as soon as possible, criticizing herself for having used a credit card and, hence, her own name. She'd used an assumed name and paid cash for the flight from Atlanta to Chicago, and she should have done the same at the hotel.

Going up in the elevator, Marissa had decided she would pack her few things and go right to the airport. She opened her door and headed straight for the bathroom, tossing her purse and briefcase onto the desk. Out of the corner of her eye, she saw movement and ducked automatically. Even so, she was struck so hard she was knocked forward over the nearest twin bed, ending up on the floor between them. Looking up, she saw the man from the train coming toward her.

Frantically, she tried to scramble beneath one of the beds, but the man got ahold of her skirt with his good arm and yanked her back.

Marissa rolled over, kicking furiously. Something fell out of the man's hand and hit the floor with a metallic thud. A gun, thought Marissa, compounding her terror.

The man bent to retrieve the gun, and Marissa slithered beneath the bed closest to the door. The man returned, checking first under one bed, then under the one where Marissa was cowering. His large hand reached for her. When he couldn't grab her, he got down on his knees and lunged under the bed, catching Marissa by an ankle and pulling her toward him.

For the second time that day, Marissa screamed. She kicked again and loosened the man's grip. In a flash she was back under the bed.

Tiring of the tug of war, he dropped his gun onto the bed and came after her. But Marissa rolled out the other side. She scrambled to her feet and ran for the door. She had just wrenched it open when the man leaped across the bed and caught her hair. Whipping her around, he threw her against the bureau with such force that the mirror fell with a crash.

The man checked the hall quickly, then closed and secured the door. Marissa ran to the bathroom, grabbing what she thought was the gun off the far bed. She had almost managed to get the bathroom door closed before the man reached it.

Marissa wedged her back against the sink and tried to keep her attacker from opening the door farther. But, little by little, his greater strength prevailed. The door cracked open, enabling him to get the arm with the frozen elbow hooked around the jamb.

Marissa eyed the wall phone but couldn't reach it without taking her feet off the door. She looked at the weapon in her hand, wondering if it would scare the man if she were to fire a bullet at the wall. That was when she realized she was holding an air-powered vaccination gun of the kind used for mass inoculations in her old pediatrics clinic.

The door had opened enough for the man to move his arm more freely. He blindly groped until he got a grip on one of Marissa's ankles. Feeling she had little choice, Marissa pressed the vaccination gun against the man's forearm and discharged it. The man screamed. The arm was withdrawn, and the door slammed shut.

She heard him run across the room, open the door to the hall and rush out. Going back into the bedroom, Marissa breathed a sigh of relief, only to be startled by a strong odor of phenolic disinfectant. Turning the vaccinator toward herself with a shaky hand, she examined the circular business end. Intuitively, she sensed the gun contained Ebola virus, and she guessed that the disinfectant she smelled was part of a mechanism to prevent exposure to the operator. Now she was truly terrified. Not only had she possibly killed a man, she might also have triggered a new outbreak. Forcing herself to remain calm, she carefully placed the gun in a plastic bag that she took from the wastebasket and then got another plastic bag from the basket under the desk and placed it over the first, knotting it closed. For a moment she hesitated, wondering if she should call the police. Then she decided there was nothing they could do. The man was far away by now, and if the vaccination gun did contain Ebola, there was no way they could find him quietly if he didn't want to be found.

Marissa looked out into the hall. It was clear. She put a Do Not Disturb sign on the door, then carried her belongings, including the plastic bag with the vaccination gun, down to housekeeping. There were no cleaning people in sight. She found a bottle of Lysol and disinfected the outside of the plastic bag. Then she washed and disinfected her hands. She couldn't think of anything else to do prophylactically.

In the lobby, where there were enough people to make Marissa feel reasonably safe, she called the Illinois State Epidemiologist. Without identifying herself, she explained that room 2410 at the Palmer House might have been contaminated with Ebola virus. Before the man could gasp out a single question, she hung up.

Next, she called Tad. All this activity was enabling her to avoid thinking about what had just happened. Tad's initial coolness thawed when he realized that she was on the verge of hysteria.

"What on earth is going on now?" he asked. "Marissa, are you all right?"

"I have to ask two favors. After the trouble I've caused you, I'd

179

vowed that I wouldn't bother you again. But I have no choice. First, I need a vial of the convalescent serum from the L.A. outbreak. Could you send it by overnight carrier to Carol Bradford at the Plaza Hotel in New York?''

"Who the hell is Carol Bradford?''

"Please don't ask any questions,'' said Marissa, struggling to keep from bursting into tears. "The less you know at this point, the better.'' Carol Bradford had been one of Marissa's college roommates; it was the name she'd used on the flight from Atlanta to Chicago.

"The next favor involves a parcel I'm sending you by overnight carrier. Please, do not open it. Take it inside the maximum containment lab and hide it.'' Marissa paused.

"Is that it?'' asked Tad.

"That's it,'' said Marissa. "Will you help me, Tad?''

"I guess,'' said Tad. "Sounds reasonably innocuous.''

"Thank you,'' said Marissa. "I'll be able to explain everything in a few days.''

She hung up and called the Westin Hotel toll-free number and reserved a room at the Plaza for that night under the name of Carol Bradford. That accomplished, she scanned the Palmer House lobby. No one seemed to be paying her any heed. Trusting that the hotel would bill her on her credit card, she did not bother to check out.

The first stop was a Federal Express office. The people were extremely nice when she told them it was a special vaccine needed in Atlanta by the next day. They helped her pack her plastic bags in an unbreakable metal box and even addressed it, when they saw how badly her hand was trembling.

Back on the street, she flagged a cab to O'Hare. As soon as she was seated, she began checking her lymph nodes and testing her throat for soreness. She'd been close to Ebola before, but never this close. She shuddered to think that the man had intended to infect her with the virus. It was a cruel irony that the only way she'd escaped was to have infected him. She hoped that he realized the convalescent serum had a protective effect if it was given prior to the appearance of symptoms. Maybe that was why the man had left so precipitately.

During the long ride to the airport, she began to calm down enough to think logically. The fact that she'd been attacked again gave more credence to her suspicions. And if the vaccination gun proved to contain Ebola, she'd have her first real piece of evidence.

The taxi driver dropped Marissa at the American Airlines terminal, explaining that they had hourly flights to New York. Once she got her ticket, passed through security and hiked the long distance to the gate, she found she had nearly half an hour to wait. She decided to call Ralph. She badly needed to hear a friendly voice, and she wanted to ask about the lawyer.

Marissa spent several minutes struggling with Ralph's secretary, who guarded him as if he were the Pope, pleading with the woman to at least let him know she was on the line. Finally, Ralph picked up the phone.

"I hope you're back in Atlanta," he said before she could say hello.

"Soon," promised Marissa. She explained that she was at the American terminal in Chicago, on her way to New York, but that she'd probably be back in Atlanta the following day, particularly if he'd found her a good lawyer.

"I made some discreet inquiries," said Ralph, "and I think I have just the man. His name is McQuinllin. He's with a large firm here in Atlanta."

"I hope he's smart," said Marissa. "He's going to have his hands full."

"Supposedly he's one of the best."

"Do you think that he will require a lot of money up front?"

"Chances are he'll want a retainer of some sort," said Ralph. "Will that be a problem?"

"Could be," said Marissa. "Depends on how much."

"Well, don't worry," said Ralph. "I'll be happy to lend a hand."

"I couldn't ask you to do that," said Marissa.

"You're not asking, I'm offering," said Ralph. "But in return, I'd like you to stop this crazy trip. What's so important in New York? I hope it's not the new Ebola outbreak. You don't want a repeat of Philadelphia. Why don't you just fly back to Atlanta. I'm worried about you.

"Soon," said Marissa. "I promise."

After hanging up, Marissa kept her hand on the receiver. It always made her feel good to talk with Ralph. He cared.

Like most of the businesspeople who constituted ninety percent of the passengers, Marissa ordered herself a drink. She was still a bundle of nerves. The vodka tonic calmed her considerably, and she actually got into one of those "where you from?" and "what do you do?" conversations with a handsome young bond dealer from Chicago, named Danny. It turned out he had a sister who was a doctor in Hawaii. He chatted so enthusiastically, Marissa finally had to close her eyes and feign sleep in order to find time to put her thoughts in order.

The question that loomed in her mind was: how had the man with the frozen arm known she was in Chicago? And, assuming it was the same man, how had he known when she'd been in the maximum containment lab? To answer both questions, Marissa's mind reluctantly turned to Tad. When Tad had discovered the missing card, he must have known she would use it that night. Maybe he told Dubchek to avoid getting into trouble himself. Tad had also known she was flying to Chicago, but she simply couldn't believe he had intentionally set a murderer on her trail. And much as she resented Dubchek, she respected him as a dedicated scientist. It was hard to connect him with the financially oriented, right-wing Physicians' Action Congress.

Thoroughly confused as to what was intelligent deduction and what paranoid delusion, Marissa wished she hadn't let the vaccination gun out of her hands. If Tad was somehow involved, then she'd lost her only hard evidence, provided it tested positive for Ebola.

As her plane touched down at La Guardia airport, Marissa decided that if the New York outbreak confirmed her theories about the origin of the Ebola outbreaks, she would go directly to Ralph's lawyer and let him and the police sort things out. She just wasn't up to playing Nancy Drew any longer. Not against a group of men who thought nothing of risking entire populations.

When the plane stopped and the seat-belt sign went off, indicating that they had arrived at the gate, Marissa stood and wrestled her suitcase out of the overhead bin. Danny insisted on helping her down the jetway, but when they said good-bye, Marissa vowed she would be more careful in the future. No more conversations with strangers, and she would not tell anyone her real name. In fact, she decided not to check into the Plaza as Carol Bradford. Instead, she'd stay overnight at the nearby Essex House, using the name of her old high-school chum, Lisa Kendrick.

George Valhala stood by the Avis Rent-a-Car counter and casually scanned the crowds in the baggage area. His employers had nicknamed him The Toad, not because of any physical characteristic, but rather because of his unusual patience, enabling him to sit still for hours on a stakeout, like a toad waiting for an insect.

But this job was not going to utilize his special talent. He'd only been at the airport for a short time, and his information was that the girl would arrive on the five o'clock or the six o'clock flight from Chicago. The five o'clock had just landed, and a few passengers were beginning to appear around the appropriate carousel.

The only minor problem that George foresaw was that the description he'd been given was vague: a cute, short, thirty-year-old female with brown hair. Usually he worked with a photo, but in this case there hadn't been time to get one.

Then he saw her. It had to be her. She was almost a foot shorter than everyone else in the army of attaché-case-toting travelers swarming the baggage area. And he noticed that she was bypassing the carousel, having apparently carried her suitcase off the plane.

Pushing off the Avis counter, George wandered toward Marissa to get a good fix on her appearance. He followed her outside, where she joined the taxi queue. She definitely was cute, and she definitely was little. George wondered how on earth she'd managed to overpower Paul in Chicago. The idea that she was some kind of martial-arts expert flitted through his mind. One way or another, George felt some respect for this little trick. He knew Al did too, otherwise Al wouldn't be going through all this trouble.

Having gotten a look at her up close, George crossed the street in front of the terminal and climbed into a taxi waiting opposite the taxi stand.

The driver twisted around, looking at George. "You see her?" He was a skinny fellow with birdlike features, quite a contrast to George's pear-shaped obesity.

"Jake, do I look like an idiot? Start the car. She's in the taxi line."

Jake did as he was told. He and George had been working for Al for four years, and they got along fine, except when George started giving orders. But that wasn't too often.

"There she is," said George, pointing. Marissa was climbing into a cab. "Pull up a little and let her cab pass us."

"Hey, I'm driving," said Jake. "You watch, I drive." Nonetheless, he put the car in gear and started slowly forward.

George watched out the rear window, noticing Marissa's cab had a dented roof, he said, "That will be easy to follow." The taxi passed

183

them on the right, and Jake pulled out behind. He allowed one car to get between them before they entered the Long Island Expressway.

There was no problem keeping Marissa's cab in sight even though the driver took the Queensborough Bridge, which was crowded with rush-hour traffic. After forty minutes they watched her get out in front of the Essex House. Jake pulled over to the curb fifty feet beyond the hotel.

"Well, now we know where she's staying," said Jake.

"Just to be certain, I'm going in to see that she registers," said George. "I'll be right back."

14

MAY 23

Marissa did not sleep well. After the incident in the room at the Palmer House, she might never feel comfortable in a hotel again. Every noise in the hall made her fearful, thinking someone would try to break in. And there were plenty of noises, what with people returning late and ordering from room service.

She also kept imagining symptoms. She could not forget the feel of the vaccination gun in her hand, and each time she woke up, she was certain she had a fever or was otherwise ill.

By the next morning, she was totally exhausted. She ordered fresh fruit and coffee, which arrived with a complimentary *New York Times*. The front page carried an article about the Ebola outbreaks. In New York, the number of cases had risen to eleven with one death, while in Philadelphia the count stood at thirty-six with seventeen deaths. The single death in New York was the initial case, Dr. Girish Mehta.

Starting at ten, Marissa repeatedly called the Plaza Hotel to inquire after a parcel for Carol Bradford. She intended to keep calling until noon: the overnight carriers generally guaranteed delivery by that time. If the parcel arrived, she would be less wary of Tad's betraying her and would then go up to the Rosenberg Clinic. Just after eleven, she was told that the package was there and that it was being held for the guest's arrival.

As Marissa prepared to leave the hotel, she didn't know whether to be surprised that Tad had sent the serum or not. Of course the package could be empty, or its arrival only a ruse to get her to reveal her whereabouts. Unfortunately, there was no way for Marissa to be sure, and she wanted the serum enough to make her doubts academic. She would have to take a chance.

Taking only her purse, Marissa tried to think of a way of obtaining the package that would involve the least risk. Unfortunately, she didn't have any bright ideas other than to have a cab waiting and to be sure there were plenty of people around.

George Valhala had been in the lobby of the Essex House since early that morning. This was the kind of situation that he loved. He'd had coffee, read the papers and ogled some handsome broads. All in all, he'd had a great time, and none of the house detectives had bothered him, dressed as he was in an Armani suit and genuine alligator shoes.

He was considering ducking into the men's room when he saw Marissa get off the elevator. He dropped his *New York Post* and beat her out the revolving door. Dodging Fifty-ninth Street traffic, he jogged across to the taxi where Jake was waiting and climbed into the front seat.

Jake had spotted Marissa and had already started the car. "She looks even cuter in daylight," he said, preparing to make a U-turn.

"You sure that's Blumenthal?" asked the man who had been waiting in the backseat. His name was Alphonse Hicktman, but few people teased him about his first name, just calling him Al, as he requested. He'd grown up in East Germany and had fled to the West over the Berlin Wall. His face was deceptively youthful. His hair was blond, and he wore it short in a Julius Caesar-style shag. His pale blue eyes were as cold as a winter sky.

"She registered under the name of Lisa Kendrick, but she fits the description," said George. "It's her all right."

"She's either awfully good or awfully lucky," said Al. "We've got to isolate her without any slipups. Heberling says she could blow the whole deal."

They watched as Marissa climbed into a taxi and headed east.

Despite the traffic, Jake made his U-turn, then worked his way up to a position only two cars behind Marissa's taxi.

"Look, lady, you got to tell me where you want to go," said Marissa's driver, eyeing her in his rearview mirror.

Marissa was twisted around, still watching the entrance to the Essex House. No one had come out who appeared to be following her. Facing forward, she told the driver to go around the block. She was still trying to think of a safe way to get the serum.

The driver muttered something under his breath as he proceeded to turn right at the corner. Marissa looked at the Fifth Avenue entrance to the Plaza. There were loads of cars, and the little park in front of the hotel was crowded with people. Horse-drawn hansom cabs lined the curb, waiting for customers. There were even several mounted policemen with shiny blue and black helmets. Marissa felt encouraged. There was no way anybody could surprise her in such a setting.

As they came back down Fifty-ninth Street, Marissa told the driver that she wanted him to stop at the Plaza and wait while she ran inside.

"Lady, I think . . . ."

"I'll only be a moment," said Marissa.

"There are plenty of cabs," pointed out the driver. "Why don't you get another?"

"I'll add five dollars to the metered fare," said Marissa, "and I promise I won't be long." Marissa treated the man to the largest smile she could muster under the circumstances.

The driver shrugged. His reservations seemed adequately covered by the five-dollar tip and the smile. He pulled up to the Plaza. The hotel doorman opened the door and Marissa got out.

She was extremely nervous, expecting the worst at any second. She watched as her cab pulled up about thirty feet from the entrance. Satisfied, she went inside.

As she'd hoped, the ornate lobby was busy. Without hesitating, Marissa crossed to a jewelry display window and pretended to be absorbed. Scanning the reflection in the glass, she checked the area for signs anyone was watching her. No one seemed to notice her at all.

Crossing the lobby again, she approached the concierge's desk and waited, her heart pounding.

"May I see some identification?" asked the man, when Marissa requested the parcel.

Momentarily confused, Marissa said she didn't have any with her.

"Then your room key will be adequate," said the man, trying to be helpful.

"But I haven't checked in yet," said Marissa.

The man smiled. "Why don't you check in and then get your parcel. I hope you understand. We do have a responsibility."

"Of course," said Marissa, her confidence shaken. She obviously had not thought this out as carefully as she should have. Recognizing she had little choice, she walked to the registration desk.

Even that process was complicated when she said she didn't want to use a credit card. The clerk made her go to the cashier to leave a sizable cash deposit before he would give her a room key. Finally, armed with the key, she got her Federal Express package.

Tearing open the parcel as she walked, Marissa lifted out the vial and glanced at it. It seemed authentic. She threw the wrapping in a trash can and pocketed the serum. So far so good.

Emerging from the revolving door, Marissa hesitated while her eyes adjusted to the midday glare. Her cab was still where she'd last seen it. The doorman asked if she wanted transportation, and Marissa smiled and shook her head.

She looked up and down Fifty-ninth Street. If anything, the traffic had increased. On the sidewalk hundreds of people rushed along as if they were all late for some important meeting. It was a scene of bright sun and purposeful bustle. Satisfied, Marissa descended the few steps to the street and ran the short distance to her cab.

Reaching the car and grasping the rear door handle, she cast one last look over her shoulder at the Plaza entrance. No one was following her. Her fears about Tad had been unfounded.

She was about to slide inside when she found herself staring into the muzzle of a gun held by a blond man who'd apparently been lying on the backseat. The man started to speak, but Marissa didn't give him time. She swung herself clear of the cab and slammed the door. The weapon discharged with a hiss. It was some kind of sophisticated air gun. The cab window shattered, but Marissa was no longer looking. She took off, running as she'd never run before. Out of the corner of her eye, she noticed that the cab driver had bolted out of his car and was running diagonally away from her. The next time she looked over her shoulder, she saw the blond man headed in her direction, pushing his way through the crowds.

The sidewalk was an obstacle course of people, luggage, pushcarts, baby carriages and dogs. The blond man had pocketed his weapon, but she no longer was convinced the crowds provided the protection she had hoped for. Who would even notice the air gun's soft hiss? She'd just fall to the ground, and her attacker would escape before anyone realized she'd been shot.

People shouted as she crashed by them, but she kept going. The confusion she caused hampered the blond man, but not dramatically. He was gaining on her.

Running across the drive east of the Plaza, Marissa dodged taxis and limos, reaching the edge of the small park with its central fountain. She was in a full panic with no destination. But she knew she had to do something. It was at that moment that she saw the mounted policeman's horse. It was loosely tethered to the link chain fence that bordered the tiny patch of grass in the park. As Marissa ran toward the horse, she searched desperately for the policeman. She knew he had to be near, but there was so little time. She could hear the blond man's heels strike the sidewalk, then hesitate. He'd arrived at the drive separating the park from the hotel.

Reaching the horse, Marissa grabbed the reins and ducked underneath as the animal nervously tossed its head. Looking back, Marissa saw the man was in the street, rounding a limo.

Frantically, Marissa's eyes swept the small park. There were plenty of people, many of them looking in her direction, but no policeman. Giving up, she turned and started running across the park. There was no chance to hide. Her pursuer was too close.

A good crowd was seated by the fountain, watching her with studied indifference. New Yorkers, they were accustomed to any form of excess, including panic-filled flight.

As Marissa rounded the side of the fountain, the blond man was so close she could hear him breathe. Turning again, Marissa collided with the people streaming into the park. Pushing and shoving, Marissa forced her way through the pedestrians, hearing people muttering, "Hey, you!" "The nerve," and worse.

Breaking into a clear space, she thought she was free, until she realized she was in the center of a circle of several hundred people. Three muscular blacks were break dancing to a rap song. Marissa's desperate eyes met those of the youths. She saw only anger: She'd crashed their act.

Before anyone could move, the blond man stumbled into the circle, coming to an off-balance halt. He started to raise his air gun, but he didn't get far. With a practiced kick, one of the infuriated dancers sent the weapon on a low arc into the crowd. People began to move away as Marissa's pursuer countered with a kick of his own. The dancer caught the blow on his forearm and fell to the ground.

Three of his friends who'd been watching from the sidelines leaped to their feet and rushed the blond man from behind.

Marissa didn't wait. She melted into the crowd that had backed away from the sudden brawl. Most of the people were crossing Fifth Avenue, and she did the same. Once north of Fifty-ninth Street, she hailed another taxi and told the driver she wanted the Rosenberg Clinic. As the cab turned on Fifty-ninth, Marissa could see a sizable crowd near the fountain. The mounted policeman was finally back on his horse, and she hoped he would keep the blond man occupied for several weeks.

Once again, Marissa looked over at the Plaza entrance. There was no unusual activity going on as far as she could see. Marissa sat back and closed her eyes. Instead of fear she was suddenly consumed with anger. She was furious with everyone, particularly with Tad. There could be little doubt now that he was telling her pursuers her whereabouts. Even the serum that she'd gone to so much trouble to obtain was useless. With her current suspicions, there was no way she'd inject herself with it. Instead, she'd have to take her chances that the vaccination gun had been designed to adequately protect the user.

For a short time, she considered skipping her visit to the Rosenberg Clinic, but the importance of proving, at least to herself, that the Ebola was being deliberately spread won out. She had to be sure. Besides, after the last elaborate attack, no one would be expecting her.

Marissa had the cab drop her off a little way from the clinic and went the remaining block on foot. The place certainly was not hard to find. It was a fancy, renovated structure that occupied most of a city block. A mobile TV truck and several police cruisers were parked out front. A number of officers lounged on the granite steps. Marissa had to flash her CDC identity card before they let her through.

The lobby was in the same state of confusion as the other hospitals that had suffered an Ebola outbreak. As she threaded her way through the crowd, she began to lose her resolve. The anger she'd felt in the taxi waned, replaced with the old fear of exposing herself to Ebola. Also, her exhilaration at escaping her pursuer faded. In its stead was the reality of being caught in a dangerous web of conspiracy and intrigue. She stopped, eyeing the exit. For a moment she debated leaving, but decided her only hope was to be absolutely sure. She had to remove any of her own doubts before she could possibly convince anyone else.

She thought she would check the easiest piece of information first. She walked down to the business office, where she found a desk with a sign, New Subscribers. Although it was unoccupied, it was loaded with printed literature. It only took a moment for her to learn that the Rosenberg Clinic was an HMO, just as she'd suspected.

The next questions she wanted answered would be more difficult, since the initial patient had already died. Retracing her steps back to the main lobby, Marissa stood watching the stream of people coming and going until she figured out where the doctor's coatroom was. Timing her approach, Marissa arrived at the door along with a staff doctor who paused to signal the man at the information booth. The coatroom door buzzed open and Marissa entered behind the doctor.

Inside, she was able to obtain a long white coat. She put it on and rolled up the sleeves. There was a name tag on the lapel that said Dr. Ann Elliott. Marissa took it off and placed it in the coat's side pocket.

Going back to the lobby, Marissa was startled to see Dr. Layne. Turning away, she expected any moment to hear a cry of recognition. Luckily, when she glanced back, Dr. Layne was leaving the hospital.

Seeing him had made Marissa more nervous than ever. She was terrified of running into Dubchek as she had in Philadelphia, but she knew she had to find out more about the dead index case.

Going over to the directory, she saw that the Department of Pathology was on the fourth floor. Marissa took the next elevator. The Rosenberg Clinic was an impressive place. Marissa had to walk through the chemistry lab to get to the pathologists' offices. En route, she noticed that they had the latest and most expensive automated equipment.

Going through a pair of double doors, Marissa found herself surrounded by secretaries busily typing from Dictaphones. This was the center of the pathology department, where all the reports were prepared.

One of the women removed her earpiece as Marissa approached. "May I help you?"

"I'm one of the doctors from the CDC," Marissa said warmly. "Do you know if any of my colleagues are here?"

"I don't think so," said the secretary, starting to rise. "I can ask Dr. Stewart. He's in his office."

"I'm right here," said a big, burly man with a full beard. "And to answer your question, the CDC people are down on the third floor in our isolation wing."

"Well, perhaps you can help me," said Marissa, purposely avoiding introducing herself. "I've been looking into the Ebola outbreaks from the beginning, but unfortunately I was delayed getting to New York. I understand that the first case, a Dr. Mehta, has already died. Did you do a post?"

"Just this morning."

"Would you mind if I asked a few questions?"

"I didn't do the autopsy," said Dr. Stewart. Then, turning to the secretary, he asked, "Helen, see if you can round up Curt."

He led Marissa to a small office furnished with a modern desk and white Formica lab bench, holding a spanking new double-headed Zeiss binocular microscope.

"Did you know Dr. Mehta?" asked Marissa.

"Quite well," said Stewart, shaking his head. "He was our medical director, and his death will be a great loss." Stewart went on to describe Dr. Mehta's contributions in establishing the Rosenberg Clinic and his enormous popularity among staff and patients alike.

"Do you know where he did his training?" asked Marissa.

"I'm not certain where he went to medical school," said Stewart. "I think it was in Bombay. But I know he did his residency in London. Why do you ask?"

"I was just curious if he was a foreign medical school graduate," said Marissa.

"Does that make a difference?" asked Stewart, frowning.

"It might," said Marissa vaguely. "Are there a large percentage of foreign medical school graduates on staff here?"

"Of course," said Stewart. "All HMOs started by hiring a large proportion of foreign medical graduates. American graduates wanted private practice. But that's changed. These days we can recruit directly from the top residencies."

The door opened and a young man came in.

"This is Curt Vandermay," said Stewart.

Reluctantly, Marissa gave her own name.

"Dr. Blumenthal has some questions about the autopsy," explained Dr. Stewart. He pulled a chair away from his microscope bench for Dr. Vandermay, who sat down and gracefully crossed his legs.

"We haven't processed the sections yet," explained Dr. Vandermay. "So I hope the gross results will do."

"Actually, I'm interested in your external exam," said Marissa. "Were there any abnormalities?"

"For sure," said Dr. Vandermay. "The man had extensive hemorrhagic lesions in his skin."

"What about trauma?" asked Marissa.

"How did you guess?" said Dr. Vandermay, surprised. "He had a broken nose. I'd forgotten about that."

"How old?" asked Marissa.

"A week, ten days. Somewhere in that range."

"Did the chart mention a cause?"

"To tell the truth, I didn't look," said Dr. Vandermay. "Knowing the man died of Ebola Hemorrhagic Fever took precedence. I didn't give the broken nose a lot of thought."

"I understand," said Marissa. "What about the chart? I assume it's here in pathology. Can I see it?"

"By all means," said Vandermay. He stood up. "Why don't you come down to the autopsy area. I have some Polaroids of the broken nose, if you'd like to see them."

"Please," said Marissa.

Stewart excused himself, saying he had a meeting to attend, and Marissa followed Vandermay as he explained that the body had been disinfected and then double-bagged in special receptacles to avoid contamination. The family had requested that the body be shipped home to India, but that permission had been refused. Marissa could understand why.

The chart wasn't as complete as Marissa would have liked, but there was reference to the broken nose. It had been set by one of Dr. Mehta's colleagues, an ENT surgeon. Marissa also learned that Dr. Mehta was an ENT surgeon himself, a terrifying fact given the way the epidemic had spread in the previous outbreaks. As far as the cause of the broken nose was concerned, there was nothing.

Vandermay suggested that they phone the man who set it. While he put through the call, Marissa went through the rest of the chart. Dr. Mehta had no history of recent travel, exposure to animals or connection to any of the other Ebola outbreaks.

"The poor man was robbed," said Dr. Vandermay, hanging up the phone. "Punched out and robbed in his own driveway. Can you believe it? What a world we live in!"

If you only knew, thought Marissa, now absolutely certain that the Ebola outbreaks were deliberately caused. A wave of fear swept over her, but she forced herself to continue questioning the pathologist. "Did you happen to notice a nummular lesion on Dr. Mehta's thigh?"

"I don't recall," said Dr. Vandermay. "But here are all the Polaroids." He spread a group of photos out as if he were laying out a poker hand.

Marissa looked at the first one. They brutally portrayed the naked corpse laid out on the stainless-steel autopsy table. Despite the profusion of hemorrhagic lesions, Marissa was able to pick out the same circular lesion she had seen on Dr. Richter's thigh. It corresponded in size to the head of a vaccination gun.

"Would it be possible for me to take one of these photos?" asked Marissa.

Dr. Vandermay glanced at them. "Go ahead. We've got plenty."

Marissa slipped the photo into her pocket. It wasn't as good as the vaccination gun, but it was something. She thanked Dr. Vandermay and got up to leave.

"Aren't you going to tell me your suspicions?" Vandermay asked. There was a slight smile on his face, as if he knew that something was up.

An intercom system crackled to life, informing Dr. Vandermay that he had a phone call on line six. He picked up, and Marissa overheard him say, "That's a coincidence, Dr. Dubchek, I'm talking with Dr. Blumenthal right this moment . . ."

That was all Marissa needed to hear. She got up and ran for the elevators. Vandermay called after her, but she didn't stop. She passed the secretaries at a half-jog and raced through the double doors, clutching the pens in the pocket of the white coat to keep them from falling out.

Facing the elevators and fire stairs, she decided to risk the elevator. If Dubchek had been on the third floor, he probably would think it faster to use the stairs. She pushed the Down button. A lab tech was waiting with his tray of vacu-containers. He watched Marissa frantically push the already illuminated elevator button several more times. "Emergency?" he asked as their eyes met.

An elevator stopped and Marissa squeezed on. The doors seemed to take forever to close, and she expected at any moment to see Dubchek running to stop them. But finally they started down, and Marissa began to relax only to find herself stopping on three. She moved deeper into the car, for once appreciating her small stature. It would have been difficult to see her from outside the elevator.

As the elevator began to move again, she asked a gray-haired technician where the cafeteria was. He told her to turn right when she got off the elevator and follow the main corridor.

Marissa got off and did as she had been told. A short distance down the hall, she smelled the aroma of food. For the rest of the way she followed her nose.

She had decided it was too dangerous to risk the front entrance to the clinic. Dubchek could have told the police to stop her. Instead, she ran into the cafeteria, which was crowded with people having lunch. She headed directly for the kitchen. The staff threw her a few questioning looks, but no one challenged her. As she'd imagined, there was a loading dock, and she exited directly onto it, skirting a dairy truck that was making a delivery.

Dropping down to the level of the driveway, Marissa walked briskly out onto Madison Avenue. After going north for half a block, she turned east on a quiet tree-lined street. There were few pedestrians, which gave Marissa confidence that she was not being trailed. When she got to Park Avenue, she hailed a cab.

To be sure that no one was following her, Marissa got off at Bloomingdale's, walked through the store to Third Avenue and hailed a second cab. By the time she pulled up at the Essex House, she was confident that she was safe, at least for the time being.

Outside her room, with its Do Not Disturb sign still in place, Marissa hesitated. Even though no one knew she was registered under an assumed name, the memory of Chicago haunted her. She opened the door carefully, scanning the premises before going in. Then she propped the door open with a chair and warily searched the room. She checked under the beds, in the closet and in the bathroom. Everything was as she'd left it. Satisfied, Marissa closed and locked her door, using all the bolts and chains available.

15

MAY 23—continued

Marissa ate some of the generous portion of fruit she'd ordered from room service for her breakfast that morning, peeling an apple with the sharp paring knife that had come with it. Now that her suspicions appeared to be true, she wasn't sure what to do next. The only thing she could think of was to go to Ralph's lawyer and tell him what she believed: that a small group of right-wing physicians were introducing Ebola into privately owned clinics to erode public trust in HMOs. She could hand over the meager evidence she had and let him worry about the rest of the proof. Maybe he could even suggest a safe place for her to hide while things were being sorted out.

Putting down the apple, she reached for the phone. She felt much better having come to a decision. She dialed Ralph's office number and was pleasantly surprised to be immediately put through to him.

"I gave my secretary specific instructions," explained Ralph. "In case you don't know it, I'm concerned about you."

"You're sweet," said Marissa, suddenly touched by Ralph's sympathy. It undermined the tight control she'd been holding over her emotions. For a second she felt like the child who didn't cry after a fall until she saw her mother.

"Are you coming home today?"

"That depends," said Marissa, biting her lip and taking a deep breath. "Do you think I can talk to that lawyer today?" Her voice wavered.

"No," said Ralph. "I called his office this morning. They said he had to go out of town but that he's expected back tomorrow."

"Too bad," said Marissa, her voice beginning to shake.

"Marissa, are you all right?" asked Ralph.

"I've been better," admitted Marissa. "I've had some awful experiences."

"What happened?"

"I can't talk now," said Marissa, knowing if she tried to explain, she'd burst into tears.

"Listen to me," said Ralph. "I want you to come here immediately. I didn't want you going to New York in the first place. Did you run into Dubchek again?"

"Worse than that," said Marissa.

"Well, that settles it," said Ralph. "Get the next flight home. I'll come and pick you up."

The idea had a lot of appeal, and she was about to say as much when there was a knock on her door. Marissa froze.

The knock was repeated.

"Marissa, are you there?"

"Just a minute," said Marissa into the phone. "There's someone at the door. Stay on the line."

She put the phone down on the night table and warily approached the door. "Who is it?"

"A delivery for Miss Kendrick." Marissa opened the door a crack but kept the safety catch on. One of the uniformed bellmen was standing there, holding a large package covered with white paper.

Flustered, she told the bellman to wait while she went back to the phone. She told Ralph that someone was at her door and that she'd call back as soon as she knew what flight she was taking home to Atlanta that evening.

"You promise?" asked Ralph.

"Yes!" said Marissa.

Returning to the door, Marissa looked out into the hall again. The bellman was leaning against the wall opposite, still holding the package. Who could have sent "Miss Kendrick" flowers when as far as Marissa knew her friend was living happily on the West Coast?

Returning to the phone, she called the desk and asked if she'd gotten any flowers. The concierge said, yes, they were on their way up.

Marissa felt a little better, but not enough to take off the chain. Instead, she called through the crack, "I'm terribly sorry, but would you mind leaving the flowers? I'll get them in a few minutes."

"My pleasure, madam," said the bellman, setting down the package. Then he touched his hat and disappeared down the hall.

Removing the chain, Marissa quickly picked up the basket and relocked the door. She ripped off the paper and found a spectacular arrangement of spring blossoms. On a green stake pushed into the Styrofoam base was an envelope addressed to Lisa Kendrick.

Removing it, Marissa pulled out a folded card addressed to Marissa Blumenthal! Her heart skipped a beat as she began to read:

> Dear Dr. Blumenthal,
> Congratulations on your performance this morning. We were all impressed. Of course, we will have to make a return visit unless you are willing to be reasonable. Obviously, we know where you are at all times, but we will leave you alone if you return the piece of medical equipment you borrowed.

Terror washed over Marissa. For a moment she stood transfixed in front of the flowers, looking at them in disbelief. Then in a sudden burst of activity, she began to pack her belongings, opening the drawers of the bureau, pulling out the few things that she'd placed there. But then she stopped. Nothing was exactly where she'd left it. They had been in her room, searching through her belongings! Oh, God! She had to get away from there.

Rushing into the bathroom, she snatched up her cosmetics, dumping them haphazardly into her bag. Then she stopped again. The implications of the note finally dawned on her. If they did not have the vaccination gun, that meant Tad was not involved. And neither he nor anyone else knew she was staying at the Essex House under a second assumed name. The only way they could have found her was by following her from the airport in Chicago.

The sooner she was out of the Essex House the better. After flinging the rest of her things into her suitcase, she found she had packed so badly it wouldn't close. As she sat on it, struggling with the latch, her eyes drifted back to the flowers. All at once she understood. Their purpose was to frighten her into leading her assailants to the vaccination gun, which was probably just what she would have done.

She sat on the bed and forced herself to think calmly. Since her adversaries knew she didn't have the vaccination gun with her, and were hoping she would lead them to it, she felt she had a little room to maneuver. Marissa decided not to bother taking the suitcase with her. She stuffed a few essentials in her purse and pulled the various papers she needed from her briefcase so she could leave that, too.

The only thing that Marissa felt absolutely certain of was that she would be followed. Undoubtedly her pursuers expected her to leave in a panic, making it that much easier for them. Well, thought Marissa, they were in for a surprise.

Looking again at the magnificent flowers, she decided she might well use the same strategy her enemies had. Thinking along those lines, she began to develop a plan that might give the answers that would provide the solution to the whole affair.

Unfolding the list of officers of the Physicians' Action Congress, Marissa reassured herself that the secretary was based in New York. His name was Jack Krause, and he lived at 426 East Eighty-fourth Street. Marissa decided that she'd pay the man an unannounced visit. Maybe all the doctors didn't know what was going on. It was hard to think of a group of physicians being willing to spread plague. In any case, her appearance on his doorstep should spread a lot more panic than any bouquet.

Meanwhile, she decided to take some steps to protect her departure. Going to the phone, she called the hotel manager, and in an irritated voice, complained that the desk had given her room number to her estranged boyfriend and that the man had been bothering her.

"That's impossible," said the manager. "We do not give out room numbers."

"I have no intention of arguing with you," snapped Marissa. "The fact of the matter is that it happened. Since the reason I stopped seeing him was because of his violent nature, I'm terrified."

"What would you like us to do?" asked the manager, sensing that Marissa had something specific in mind.

"I think you could at least move me to another room," said Marissa.

"I'll see to it myself," said the manager.

"One other thing," said Marissa. "My boyfriend is blond, athletic-looking, sharp features. Perhaps you could alert your people."

"Certainly," said the manager.

* * *

Alphonse Hicktman took one last draw on his cigarette and tossed it over the granite wall that separated Central Park from the sidewalk. Looking back at the taxi with its off-duty light on, Al could just make out George's features. He was hunkered down, relaxed as usual. Waiting never seemed to bother the man. Looking across the street at the Essex House entrance, Al hoped to God that Jake was properly situated in the lobby so that Marissa could not leave unseen by a back entrance.

Al had been so sure that the flowers would send the woman flying out of the hotel. Now he was mystified. Either she was super smart or super stupid.

Walking over to the taxi, he whacked its roof with an open palm, making a noise like a kettledrum. George was instantly half out of the car on the other side.

Al smiled at him. "Little tense, George?" His patience made Al's frustration that much harder to bear.

"Jesus Christ!" exclaimed George.

The two men got into the cab.

"What time is it?" asked Al, taking out another cigarette. He'd already gone through most of a pack that afternoon.

"Seven-thirty."

Al flicked the used match out the open window. The job was not going well. Since the vaccination gun had not been in the woman's hotel room, his orders were to follow her until she retrieved it, but it was all too apparent that Dr. Blumenthal was not about to accommodate them, at least not immediately.

At that moment a group of revelers came stumbling out of the Essex House, arm in arm, swaying, laughing and generally making fools of themselves. They were obviously conventioneers, dressed in dark suits with name tags, and wearing plastic sun visors that said SANYO.

The doorman signaled a group of limousines waiting just up the street. One by one, they drove to the door to pick up their quota.

Al slapped George on the shoulder, frantically pointing toward the largest group to emerge through the revolving door. Among them two men were supporting a woman wearing a Sanyo visor who seemed too drunk to walk. "Is that the mark hanging onto those guys?" he asked.

George squinted, and before he could answer, the woman in question disappeared into one of the limousines. He turned back to Al. "I don't think so. Her hair was different. But I couldn't be sure."

"Damn!" said Al. "Neither could I." After a moment's hesitation, Al jumped out of the taxi. "If she comes out, follow her." Al then dodged the traffic and raced across to get in another cab.

From the back of the limousine, Marissa watched the entrance to the hotel. Out of the corner of her eye she saw someone alight from a parked taxi and run across the street. Just as her limousine pulled in front of a bus, blocking her view, she saw the man climbing into another taxi, a vintage Checker.

Marissa turned to face forward. She was certain she was being followed. She had several options, but with almost a full block's head start, she decided it would be best to get out.

As soon as the limousine turned on Fifth, Marissa shocked her companions by shouting at the driver to pull over.

The driver complied, figuring she was about to be sick, but before any of the men knew what was happening, she had the door open and jumped out, telling the driver to go on without her.

Spying a Doubleday bookstore, which, happily, was keeping late hours, she ducked inside. From the store window she saw the Checker cab speed by and caught a glimpse of a blond head in the backseat. The man was sitting forward, staring straight ahead.

The house looked more like a medieval fortress than a New York luxury townhouse. Its leaded windows were narrow and covered with twisted wrought-iron grilles. The front door was protected by a stout iron gate that was fashioned after a portcullis. The fifth floor was set back and the resulting terrace was crenellated like a castle tower.

Marissa eyed the building from across the street. It was hardly a hospitable sight, and for a moment she had second thoughts about visiting Dr. Krause. But safely ensconced in her new room at the Essex House that afternoon, she'd made some calls and learned that he was a prominent Park Avenue internist. She could not imagine that he would be capable of harming her directly. Perhaps through an organization like PAC, but not with his own two hands.

She crossed the street and climbed the front steps. Casting one last glance up and down the quiet street, she rang the bell. Behind the gate was the heavy wooden door, its center decorated with a family crest carved in relief.

She waited a minute and rang again. All at once a bright light went on, blinding her so that she could not see who was opening the door.

ROBIN COOK

"Yes?" said a woman's voice.

"I would like to see Dr. Krause," said Marissa, trying to sound authoritative.

"Do you have an appointment?"

"No," admitted Marissa. "But tell the doctor that I'm here on emergency Physicians' Action Congress business. I think he'll see me."

Marissa heard the door close. The hard light illuminated most of the street. After a couple of minutes, the door was reopened.

"The doctor will see you." Then there was the painful sound of the iron gate opening on hinges that needed oil.

Marissa went inside, relieved to get away from the glare. She watched the woman, who was dressed in a maid's black uniform, close the gate, then come toward her.

"If you'll follow me, please."

Marissa was led through a marbled and chandeliered entrance, down a short corridor to a paneled library.

"If you'll wait here," said the woman, "the doctor will be with you shortly."

Marissa glanced around the room, which was beautifully furnished with antiques. Bookcases lined three of the walls.

"Sorry to keep you waiting," said a mellow voice.

Marissa turned to look at Dr. Krause. He had a fleshy face with deep lines, and as he gestured for her to sit, she noticed his hands were unusually large and square, like those of an immigrant laborer. When they were sitting, she could see him better. The eyes were those of an intelligent, sympathetic man, reminding her of some of her internal medicine professors. Marissa was amazed that he could have gotten mixed up in something like the Physicians' Action Congress.

"I'm sorry to bother you at such an hour," she began.

"No problem," said Dr. Krause. "I was just reading. What can I do for you?"

Marissa leaned forward to watch the man's face. "My name is Dr. Marissa Blumenthal."

There was a pause as Dr. Krause waited for Marissa to continue. His expression did not change. Either he was a good actor or her name was not familiar.

"I'm an Epidemiology Intelligence Service officer at the CDC," added Marissa. His eyes narrowed just a tad.

"My maid said that you were here on PAC business," said Dr. Krause, a measure of the hospitality disappearing from his voice.

"I am," said Marissa. "Perhaps I should ask if you are aware of anything that PAC might be doing that could concern the CDC."

This time, Krause's jaw visibly tightened. He took a deep breath, started to speak, then changed his mind. Marissa waited as if she had all the time in the world.

Finally, Dr. Krause cleared his throat. "PAC is trying to rescue American medicine from the economic forces that are trying to destroy it. That's been its goal from the start."

"A noble goal," admitted Marissa. "But how is PAC attempting to accomplish this mission?"

"By backing responsible and sensible legislation," said Dr. Krause. He stood up, presumably to escape Marissa's stare. "PAC is providing an opportunity for more conservative elements to exert some influence. And it's about time; the profession of medicine is like a runaway train." He moved over to the fireplace, his face lost in shadow.

"Unfortunately, it seems PAC is doing more than sponsoring legislation," said Marissa. "That's what concerns the CDC."

"I think we have nothing more to discuss," said Dr. Krause. "If you'll excuse me—"

"I believe PAC is responsible for the Ebola outbreaks," blurted Marissa, standing up herself. "You people have some misguided idea that spreading disease in HMOs will further your cause."

"That's absurd!" said Dr. Krause.

"I couldn't agree more," said Marissa. "But I have papers linking you and the other officers of PAC to Professional Labs in Grayson, Georgia, which has recently purchased equipment to handle the virus. I even have the vaccination gun used to infect the index cases."

"Get out of here," ordered Dr. Krause.

"Gladly," said Marissa. "But first let me say that I intend to visit all the officers of PAC. I can't imagine they all agreed to this idiotic scheme. In fact, it's hard for me to imagine that a physician like yourself—any physician—could have allowed it."

Maintaining a calm she did not feel, Marissa walked to the door. Dr. Krause did not move from the fireplace. "Thank you for seeing me," said Marissa. "I'm sorry if I've upset you. But I'm confident that one of the PAC officers I see will want to help stop this horror. Perhaps by turning state's evidence. It could be you. I hope so. Good night, Dr. Krause."

Marissa forced herself to walk slowly down the short corridor to the foyer. What if she misjudged the man and he came after her? Luckily, the maid materialized and let her out. As soon as Marissa was beyond the cone of light, she broke into a run.

For a few moments Dr. Krause didn't move. It was as if his worst nightmare were coming true. He had a gun upstairs. Maybe he should just kill himself. Or he could call his lawyer and ask for immunity in return for turning state's evidence. But he had no idea what that really meant.

Panic followed paralysis. He rushed to his desk, opened his address book and, after looking up a number, placed a call to Atlanta.

The phone rang almost ten times before it was picked up. Joshua Jackson's smooth accent oiled its way along the wires as he said hello and asked who was calling.

"Jack Krause," said the distraught doctor. "What the hell is going on? You swore that aside from Los Angeles, PAC had nothing to do with the outbreaks of Ebola. That the further outbreaks sprang from accidental contact with the initial patients. Joshua, you gave me your word."

"Calm down," said Jackson. "Get ahold of yourself!"

"Who is Marissa Blumenthal?" asked Krause in a quieter voice.

"That's better," said Jackson. "Why do you ask?"

"Because the woman just showed up on my doorstep accusing me and PAC of starting all the Ebola epidemics."

"Is she still there?"

"No. She's gone," said Krause. "But who the hell is she?"

"An epidemiologist from the CDC who got lucky. But don't worry, Heberling is taking care of her."

"This affair is turning into a nightmare," said Krause. "I should remind you that I was against the project even when it only involved influenza."

"What did the Blumenthal girl want with you?" asked Jackson.

"She wanted to frighten me," said Krause. "And she did a damn good job. She said she has the names and addresses of all the PAC officers, and she implied that she was about to visit each one."

"Did she say who was next?"

"Of course she didn't. She's not stupid," said Krause. "In fact she's extremely clever. She played me like a finely tuned instrument. If she sees us all, somebody's going to fold. Remember Tieman in San Fran? He was even more adamantly against the project than I was."

"Try to relax," urged Jackson. "I understand why you're upset. But let me remind you that there is no real evidence to implicate anyone. And as a precautionary measure, Heberling has cleaned out his whole lab except for his bacterial studies. I'll tell him that the girl plans to visit the other officers. I'm sure that will help. In the meantime, we'll take extra precautions to keep her away from Tieman."

Krause hung up. He felt a little less anxious, but as he stood up and turned off the desk lamp, he decided he'd phone his attorney in the morning. It couldn't hurt to inquire about the procedure for turning state's evidence.

As her cab whizzed over the Triborough Bridge, Marissa was mesmerized by Manhattan's nighttime skyline. From that distance it was beautiful. But it soon dropped behind, then out of sight altogether as the car descended into the sunken portion of the Long Island Expressway. Marissa forced her eyes back to the list of names and addresses of the PAC officers, which she had taken from her purse. They were hard to make out as the taxi shot from one highway light to the next.

There was no logical way to choose who to visit after Krause. The closest would be easiest, but also probably the most obvious to her pursuers, and therefore the most dangerous. For safety's sake, she decided to visit the man farthest away, Dr. Sinclair Tieman in San Francisco.

Leaning forward, Marissa told the driver she wanted Kennedy rather than LaGuardia airport. When he asked what terminal, she chose at random: United. If they didn't have space on a night flight, she could always go to another terminal.

At that time in the evening there were few people at the terminal, and Marissa got rapid service. She was pleased to find a convenient flight to San Francisco with just one stop, in Chicago. She bought her ticket with cash, using yet another false name, bought some reading material from a newsstand and went to the gate. She decided to use the few moments before takeoff to call Ralph. As she anticipated, he was upset she hadn't called him back sooner, but was pleased at first to learn she was at the airport.

"I'll forgive you this one last time," he said, "but only because you are on your way home."

Marissa chose her words carefully: "I wish I could see you tonight, but . . ."

"Don't tell me you are not coming," said Ralph, feigning anger to conceal his disappointment. "I made arrangements for you to meet with Mr. McQuinllin tomorrow at noon. You said you wanted to see him as soon as possible."

"It will have to be postponed," said Marissa. "Something has come up. I must go to San Francisco for a day or two. I just can't explain right now."

"Marissa, what on earth are you up to?" said Ralph in a tone of desperation. "Just from the little you've told me, I'm absolutely certain you should come home, see the lawyer; then, if Mr. McQuinllin agrees, you can still go to California."

"Ralph, I know you're worried. The fact you care makes me feel so much better, but everything is under control. What I'm doing will just make my dealings with Mr. McQuinllin that much easier. Trust me."

"I can't," pleaded Ralph. "You're not being rational."

"They're boarding my plane," said Marissa. "I'll call as soon as I can."

Marissa replaced the receiver with a sigh. He might not be the world's most romantic man, but he certainly was sensitive and caring.

Al told Jake to shut up. He couldn't stand the man's incessant gab. If it wasn't about baseball, it was about the horses. It never stopped. It was worse than George's eternal silence.

Al was sitting with Jake in the taxi while George still waited in the Essex House lobby. Something told Al that things were screwed up. He'd followed the limo all the way to a restaurant in Soho, but then the girl he'd seen get in didn't get out. Coming back to the hotel, he'd had Jake check to see if Miss Kendrick was still registered. She was, but when Al went up and walked past the room, he'd seen it being cleaned. Worse, he'd been spotted by the house detectives, who claimed he was the broad's boyfriend and that he'd better leave her alone. You didn't have to be a brain surgeon to know something was wrong. His professional intuition told him that the girl had fled and that they were wasting their time staking out the Essex House.

"You sure you don't want to put a small bet on the fourth at Belmont today?" said Jake.

Al was about to bounce a couple of knuckles off the top of Jake's head when his beeper went off. Reaching under his jacket, he turned the thing off, cursing. He knew who it was.

"Wait here," he said gruffly. He got out of the car and ran across the street to the Plaza where he used one of the downstairs pay phones to call Heberling.

Heberling did not even try to hide his contempt. "For Chrissake, the woman's only a hundred pounds or so. It's not like I'm asking you to take out Rambo. Why the hell is PAC paying you fellows a thousand dollars a day?"

"The woman's been lucky," said Al. He'd be patient, but only to a point.

"I don't buy that," said Heberling. "Now tell me, do you have any idea where she is at this moment?"

"I'm not positive," admitted Al.

"Meaning you've lost her," snapped Heberling. "Well, I can tell you where she's been. She's seen Dr. Krause and scared him shitless. Now we're afraid she's planning to visit the other PAC officers. Dr. Tieman's the most vulnerable. I'll worry about the other physicians. I want you and your orangutans to get your asses to San Francisco. See if she's there, and whatever you do, don't let her get to Tieman."

16

MAY 24

It was just beginning to get light as Al followed Jake and George down the jetway to San Francisco's central terminal. They'd taken an American flight that first stopped for an hour and a half at Dallas, then was delayed in Las Vegas on what should have been a brief touchdown.

Jake was carrying the suitcase with the vaccination gun they'd used on Mehta. Al wondered if he looked as bad as his colleagues. They needed to shave and shower, and their previously sharply pressed suits were badly wrinkled.

The more Al thought about the current situation, the more frustrated he became. The girl could be in any one of at least four cities. And it wasn't even a simple hit. If they did find her, they first had to get her to tell them where she'd hidden the vaccination gun.

Leaving Jake and George to get the luggage, he rented a car, using one of the several fake IDs he always carried. He decided the only thing they could do was stake out Tieman's house. That way, even if they didn't find the girl, she wouldn't get to the doctor. After making sure he could get a car with a cellular phone, he spread out the map the girl at Budget had given him. Tieman lived in some out-of-the-way place called Sausalito. At least there wouldn't be much traffic; it wasn't even 7:00 A.M. yet.

208

* * *

The operator at the Fairmont placed Marissa's wakeup call at 7:30 as she'd requested. Marissa had been lucky the night before. A small convention group had canceled out at the last minute, and she'd had no trouble getting a room.

Lying in bed waiting for her breakfast she wondered what Dr. Tieman would be like. Probably not much different from Krause: a selfish, greedy man whose attempt to protect his own wallet had gotten out of control.

Getting up, she opened the drapes to a breathtaking scene that included the Bay Bridge, the hills of Marin County, with Alcatraz Island looking like a medieval fortress in the foreground. Marissa only wished that she was visiting under more pleasant circumstances.

By the time she'd showered and wrapped herself in the thick white terrycloth robe supplied by the hotel, her breakfast had arrived, an enormous selection of fresh fruit and coffee.

Peeling a peach, she noticed they had given her an old-fashioned paring knife—wood-handled and very sharp. As she ate, she looked at Tieman's address and wondered if it wouldn't be better to visit him at his office rather than at home. She was sure someone had contacted him after her visit to Dr. Krause, so she couldn't count on really surprising the man. Under such conditions, it seemed safer to go to his office.

The Yellow Pages was in one of the desk drawers. Marissa opened it to Physicians and Surgeons, found Tieman's name and noted that his practice was limited to OB-GYN.

Just to be certain the man was in town, Marissa dialed his office. The service operator said that the office didn't open until eight-thirty. That was about ten minutes away.

Marissa finished dressing and dialed again. This time she got the receptionist, who told her the doctor wasn't expected until three. This was his day for surgery at San Francisco General.

Hanging up, Marissa stared out at the Bay Bridge while she considered this new information. In some ways confronting Tieman in the hospital might even be better than at his office. It would certainly be safer if the doctor had any idea of trying to stop her himself.

She looked at herself in the mirror. Except for her underwear, she had been wearing the same clothes for two days, and she realized she'd have to stop somewhere and get some fresh things.

She put up the Do Not Disturb sign as she left the room, less nervous here than in New York, since she was certain she was several jumps ahead of her pursuers.

The site of San Francisco General was gorgeous, but once inside, the hospital was like any other large city hospital, with the same random mixture of old and modern. There was also that overwhelming sense of bustle and disorganization characteristic of such institutions. It was easy for Marissa to walk unnoticed into the doctor's locker room.

As she was selecting a scrub suit, an attendant came over and asked, "Can I help you?"

"I'm Dr. Blumenthal," said Marissa. "I'm here to observe Dr. Tieman operate."

"Let me give you a locker," said the attendant without hesitation, and gave her a key.

After Marissa changed, her locker key pinned to the front of her scrub dress, she walked to the surgical lounge. There were about twenty people there, drinking coffee, chatting and reading newspapers.

Passing through the lounge, Marissa went directly into the operating area. In the vestibule, she put on a hood and booties, then stopped in front of the big scheduling board. Tieman's name was listed for room eleven. The man was already on his second hysterectomy.

"Yes?" inquired the nurse behind the OR desk. Her voice had that no-nonsense tone of a woman in charge.

"I'm here to watch Dr. Tieman," said Marissa.

"Go on in. Room eleven," said the nurse, already devoting her attention to another matter.

"Thank you," said Marissa, starting down the wide central corridor. The operating rooms were on either side, sharing scrub and anesthesia space. Through the oval windows in the doors, Marissa caught glimpses of gowned figures bent over their patients.

Entering the scrub area between rooms eleven and twelve, Marissa put on a mask and pushed into Tieman's operating room.

There were five people besides the patient. The anesthesiologist was sitting at the patient's head, two surgeons were standing on either side of the table, a scrub nurse perched on a footstool and there was one circulating nurse. As Marissa entered, the circulating nurse was sitting in the corner, waiting for orders. She got up and asked Marissa what she needed.

"How much longer for the case?"

"Three-quarters of an hour," shrugged the nurse. "Dr. Tieman is fast."

"Which one is Dr. Tieman?" asked Marissa. The nurse gave her a strange look.

"The one on the right," she said. "Who are you?"

"A doctor friend from Atlanta," said Marissa. She didn't elaborate. Moving around to the head of the table and looking at Dr. Tieman, she understood why the nurse had been surprised by her question: the man was black.

How odd, thought Marissa. She would have suspected that all the PAC officers were old-guard, white and probably racially prejudiced.

For a while she stood above the ether screen and watched the course of the operation. The uterus was already out, and they were starting repair. Tieman was good. His hands moved with that special economy of motion that could not be taught. It was a talent, a gift from God, not something to be learned even with practice.

"Start the damn car," said Al, hanging up the cellular phone. They were parked across from a sprawling redwood house that clung to the hillside above the town of Sausalito. Between the eucalyptus trees they could see blue patches of the Bay.

Jake turned the key in the ignition. "Where to?" He knew Al was pissed, and when he was in that kind of mood, it was better to say as little as possible.

"Back to the city."

"What did Tieman's office say?" asked George from the backseat.

Jake wanted to tell George to shut up, but he was afraid to speak.

"That the doctor was in surgery at San Francisco General," said Al, almost white with anger. "His first operation was scheduled for seven-thirty, and he's not expected at the office until three."

"No wonder we missed him," said George disgustedly. "The guy must have left his house an hour before we got here. What a waste of time. We should have gone to a hotel like I said."

With blinding speed Al twisted around in the front seat and grabbed George's pink Dior tie. George's eyes bulged and his face turned red. "If I want your advice, I'll ask for it. Understand?"

Al released the tie and shoved George back down in his seat. Jake hunkered down like a turtle into his sports jacket. He hazarded a glance in Al's direction.

"And what are you gawking at?" demanded Al.

Jake didn't say a word, and after what had just happened, he hoped George had learned the wisdom of silence.

They were almost at the bridge before anyone spoke.

"I think we should get another car," Al said, his voice as calm as if the outburst had never happened. "Just in case we run into a problem and have to split up. Then we'll go to San Francisco General. The sooner we spot Tieman the better."

With plenty of time to spare and feeling confident that she'd have no problem recognizing Dr. Tieman now that she'd seen him, Marissa left the operating room as the assistant was closing. She changed back to her street clothes. She wanted to be able to leave right after she spoke to the man. Going into the surgical lounge, she found a seat by the window. A few people smiled at her but no one spoke.

A half hour went by before Dr. Tieman appeared, coming into the room with the same effortless grace that had characterized his surgical technique.

Marissa walked over to where he was pouring a cup of coffee. In his short-sleeved scrub top, Marissa could see his beautifully muscled arms. His color was a rich brown, like polished walnut.

"I'm Dr. Marissa Blumenthal," she said, watching the man for a reaction.

He had a broad, masculine face with a well-trimmed mustache and sad eyes, as if he'd seen more of life than he cared to know. He looked down at Marissa with a smile. It was obvious from his expression that he had no idea who she was.

"May I speak to you in private?" asked Marissa.

Tieman glanced at his assistant, who was just approaching. "I'll see you in the OR," Tieman said, leading Marissa away.

He took her to one of the dictation cubicles separated from the lounge by two swinging doors. There was one chair, and Dr. Tieman turned it around, gesturing for Marissa to sit. He leaned against a counter, holding his coffee in his right hand.

Acutely conscious of her short stature and its psychological handicap, Marissa pushed the chair back to him, insisting that he sit since he'd been standing in surgery since early that morning.

"Okay, okay," he said with a short laugh. "I'm sitting. Now what can I do for you?"

"I'm surprised you don't recognize my name," said Marissa, watching the man's eyes. They were still questioning, still friendly.

"I'm sorry," said Dr. Tieman. He laughed again, but with a tinge of embarrassment. He was studying Marissa's face. "I do meet a lot of people . . ."

"Hasn't Dr. Jack Krause called you about me?" asked Marissa.

"I'm not even sure I know a Dr. Krause," said Dr. Tieman, directing his attention to his coffee.

The first lie, thought Marissa. Taking a deep breath, she told the doctor exactly what she'd told Krause. From the moment she mentioned the L.A. Ebola outbreak, he never lifted his eyes. She could tell that he was nervous. The surface of the coffee shook slightly in the cup in his hand, and Marissa was suddenly glad she was not the man's next patient.

"I haven't the slightest idea why you are telling me this," said Dr. Tieman, starting to rise. "And unfortunately I have another case."

With uncharacteristic forwardness, Marissa gently touched his chest, forcing him back in his seat. "I'm not finished," she said, "and whether you realize it or not, you are intimately involved. I have evidence that Ebola is being deliberately spread by the Physicians' Action Congress. You are their treasurer, and I'm shocked that a man of your reputation could be connected to such a sordid affair."

"You're shocked," countered Dr. Tieman, finally rising to his feet and towering over her. "I'm amazed that you have the nerve to make such irresponsible allegations."

"Save your breath," said Marissa. "It's public knowledge that you are an officer of PAC as well as a limited partner in one of the only labs in the country equipped to handle viruses like Ebola."

"I hope you have plenty of insurance," warned Dr. Tieman, his voice rising. "You'll be hearing from my lawyer."

"Good," said Marissa, ignoring the threat. "Maybe he will persuade you that your best course is to cooperate with the authorities." She stepped back and looked directly up at his face. "Having met you, I cannot believe you approved the idea of spreading a deadly disease. It will be a double tragedy for you to lose everything you've worked for because of someone else's poor judgment. Think about it, Dr. Tieman. You don't have a lot of time."

Pushing through the swinging doors, Marissa left a stunned doctor desperately heading for the phone. She realized she had forgotten to tell Tieman that she was planning to visit the other PAC officers, but she decided it didn't matter. The man was terrified enough.

* * *

"There's the girl!" yelled Al, slapping Jake on the shoulder. They were parked across the street from the main entrance to the hospital. George waited behind them in the second car. When Al turned to look at him, George gave a thumbs-up sign, meaning that he'd also seen Marissa.

"She won't get away today," said Al.

Jake started the car and, as Marissa got into a cab, he pulled out into the street, heading back into town. Al watched as Marissa's cab pulled out behind them, followed neatly by George. Now things were working as they should.

"She must have seen Tieman if she's leaving," said Jake.

"Who cares?" said Al. "We got her now." Then he added, "It would make things easier if she'd go back to her hotel."

Marissa's cab went by them with George in pursuit. Jake began to speed up. Ahead he saw George overtake Marissa. They would continue leapfrogging until Marissa reached her destination.

About fifteen minutes later, Marissa's taxi stopped behind a line of cars waiting to pull up to the Fairmont. "Looks like your prayers have been answered," said Jake, stopping across the street from the hotel.

"I'll handle the car," said Al. "You get your ass in there and find out what room she's in."

Jake got out as Al slid behind the wheel. Dodging the midmorning traffic, Jake reached the front of the hotel before Marissa had even gotten out of her cab. In the lobby, he picked up a newspaper and, folding it commuter-style, positioned himself so that he could see everyone coming into the hotel.

Marissa walked directly to the front desk. He quickly moved behind her, expecting her to ask for her room key. But she didn't. Instead she asked to use her safe-deposit box.

While the receptionist opened a gate allowing Marissa into the office behind the front desk, Jake wandered toward the board announcing the various convention meetings. Presently Marissa reappeared, busily closing her shoulder purse. Then, to Jake's consternation, she came directly toward him.

In a frantic moment of confusion, Jake thought she'd recognized him, but she passed right by, heading down a hall lined with gift shops.

Jake took off after her, passing her in a corridor lined with old photos

214

of the San Francisco earthquake. Guessing she was headed to the elevators, he made sure he beat her there, mingling with the crowd already waiting.

An elevator arrived, which Jake boarded before Marissa, making certain there was plenty of room. He stepped in front of the self-service buttons. Holding his newspaper as if he were reading, he watched as Marissa pressed eleven. As more passengers got on, Marissa was pushed farther back into the car.

As the elevator rose, stopping occasionally, Jake continued to keep his nose in the newspaper. When the car stopped at the eleventh floor, he strolled off, still absorbed in his paper, allowing Marissa and another guest to pass him. When she stopped in front of room 1127, Jake kept walking. He didn't turn and go back to the elevators until he'd heard her door close.

Back on the street, Jake crossed over to Al's car.

"Well?" said Al, momentarily worried something had gone wrong.

"Room 1127," said Jake with a self-satisfied smile.

"You'd better be right," said Al, getting out of the car. "Wait here. This shouldn't take long at all." He smiled so broadly that Jake noticed for the first time Al's gums had receded almost to the roots of his front teeth.

Al walked over to George's car and leaned on the window. "I want you to drive around and cover the back entrance. Just in case."

Feeling better than he had in several days, Al crossed the street to the posh, red-and-black lobby.

He went over to the front desk and eyed the mailbox for 1127. There was an extra set of keys, but there wasn't enough of a crowd for him to chance the receptionist's turning them over without asking questions. Instead, he headed for the elevators.

On the eleventh floor, he searched for the housekeeping cart. He found it outside of a suite, with its usual complement of clean sheets, towels and cleaning materials. Taking one of the hand towels, he carefully folded it on the diagonal, creating a stout rope. Gripping an end in each hand, he entered the open suite where the maid presumably was working.

The living room was empty. There was a vacuum cleaner in the middle of the bedroom and a pile of linens on the floor, but he still didn't see anyone. Advancing to the dressing room, he heard running water.

The maid was on her knees in front of the bathtub, scrubbing its interior. A can of Comet was on the floor by her knees.

Without a moment's hesitation, Al stepped behind the woman and, using the folded towel as a garrote, strangled her. She made some muffled noises but they were covered by the sound of the bathwater. Her face turned red, then purple. When Al let up the tension on the ends of the towel, she slumped to the floor like a limp rag doll.

Al found the passkeys in her pocket on a brass ring the size of a bracelet. Back in the hall, he hung a Do Not Disturb sign on the knob and closed the door to the suite. Then he pushed the housekeeping cart out of sight into the stairwell. Flexing his fingers like a pianist preparing for a recital, he started for room 1127.

17

MAY 24

Marissa peeled the last of the breakfast fruit with the wooden-handled paring knife, leaving the knife and rinds on her night table. She was on the phone to Northwest Airlines trying to make a reservation to Minneapolis. She had decided PAC and company would figure she'd probably go to L.A. next, so Minneapolis seemed as good a bet as any.

The agent finally confirmed her on an afternoon flight. Flopping back on the bed, she began to debate how she should spend the next hour or so, but while she was thinking, exhaustion overtook her and she fell asleep.

She was awakened by a metallic click. It sounded like the door, but she knew she'd left up the Do Not Disturb sign. Then she saw the knob silently begin to turn.

She remembered being caught in the hotel room in Chicago by the man with the vaccination gun. Panic danced through her like an electrical current. Pulling herself together, she reached for the phone.

Before Marissa could lift the receiver, the door burst open, splintering part of the jamb as the screws holding the chain lock plate were yanked out of the molding. A man slammed the door shut then hurled himself onto Marissa. He grabbed her by the neck with both hands and shook her like a mad dog in a frenzy. Then he pulled her ashen face close to his. "Remember me?" he snarled furiously.

Marissa remembered him. It was the blond man with the Julius Caesar haircut.

"You have ten seconds to produce the vaccination gun," hissed Al, loosening the death grip he had on Marissa's throat. "If you don't, I'll snap your neck." To emphasize his point, he gave her head a violent jolt, sending a flash of pain down her spine.

Barely able to breathe, Marissa fruitlessly clawed at the man's powerful wrists. He shook her again, hitting her head against the wall. By reflex Marissa's hands extended behind her to cushion her body.

The lamp fell off the bedside table and crashed to the floor. The room swam as her brain cried for oxygen.

"This is your last chance," shouted Al. "What did you do with that vaccinator?"

Marissa's hand touched the paring knife. Her fingers wrapped around the tiny haft. Holding it in her fist, she hammered it up into the man's abdomen as hard as she could. She had no idea if she'd penetrated anything, but Al stopped speaking in midsentence, let go of Marissa and rocked back on his haunches. His face registered surprise and disbelief. She switched the tiny knife to her right hand, keeping it pointed at Al, who seemed confused when he saw the blood staining his shirt.

She hoped to back up to the door and run, but before she reached it he leaped at her like an enraged animal, sending her racing to the bathroom. It seemed as if only hours before she'd been in the same predicament in Chicago.

Al got his hand around the door before it shut. Marissa hacked blindly, feeling the tip of her knife strike bone. Al screamed and yanked his hand away, leaving a smear of blood on the panel. The door slammed shut, and Marissa hastily locked it.

She was about to dial the bathroom phone when there was a loud crash and the entire bathroom door crashed inward. Al forced Marissa to drop the phone, but she hung on to the knife, still stabbing at him wildly. She hit his abdomen several times, but if it had any effect, it wasn't apparent.

Ignoring the knife, Al grabbed Marissa by her hair and flung her against the sink. She tried to stab him again, but he grabbed her wrist and bashed it against the wall until her grip loosened and the weapon clattered to the floor.

He bent down to pick it up, and as he straightened, Marissa grabbed the phone that was swinging on its cord and hit him as hard as she could with the receiver. For a brief instant, she wasn't sure who was hurt more. The blow had sent a bolt of pain right up to her shoulder.

For a moment Al stood as if he were frozen. Then his blue eyes rolled upward, and he seemed to fall in slow motion into the bathtub, striking his head on the faucets.

As Marissa watched, half expecting Al to get up and come at her again, a beeping noise snapped her into action. She reached over and hung up the receiver. Glancing back into the tub, she was torn between fear and her medical training. The man had a sizable gash over the bridge of his nose, and the front of his shirt was covered with bloodstains. But terror won out, and Marissa grabbed her purse and ran from the room. Remembering the man had not been alone in New York, she knew she had to get away from the hotel as soon as possible.

Descending to the ground floor, Marissa avoided the front entrance. Instead, she went down a flight of stairs and followed arrows to a rear exit. Standing just inside the door, she waited until a cable car came into view. Timing her exit to give herself the least exposure, she ran out of the hotel and jumped onto the trolley.

Marissa forced her way through the crowd to the rear. She looked back at the hotel as the car began to move. No one came out.

George blinked in disbelief. It was the girl. Quickly he dialed Jake's car.

"She just came out of the hotel," said George, "and jumped on a cable car."

"Is Al with her?" asked Jake.

"No," said George. "She's by herself. It looked like she was limping a little."

"Something is weird."

"You follow her," said George. "The cable car is just starting. I'll go into the hotel and check on Al."

"Right on," said Jake. He was more than happy to let George deal with Al. When Al found out the girl had flown, he was going to be madder than shit.

Marissa looked back at the hotel for any sign of being followed. No one came out of the door, but as the cable car began to move, she saw a man get out of an auto and run for the hotel's rear entrance. The timing was suggestive, but as the man didn't even look in her direction, she dismissed it as a coincidence. She continued to watch until the cable car turned a corner and she could no longer see the Fairmont. She'd made it.

She relaxed until a loud clang almost made her jump out of her skin. She started for the door before she realized it was just the overhead bell that the conductor rang as he collected fares.

A man got off, and Marissa quickly took his seat. She was shaking and suddenly scared she might have bloodstains on her clothes. The last thing she wanted was to call attention to herself.

As her fear abated, she became more aware of the pain where her hip had hit the sink, and her neck was exquisitely tender and probably turning black and blue.

"Fare please," said the conductor.

Without lifting her eyes, Marissa fished around in her purse for some change. That was when she saw the blood caked on the back of her right hand. Quickly, she changed the way she was holding her purse and used her left hand to give the money to the man.

When he moved off, Marissa tried to figure out how they had found her. She'd been so careful . . . Suddenly it dawned on her. They must have been guarding Tieman. It was the only possible explanation.

Her confidence shattered, Marissa began to have second thoughts about having fled the hotel. Perhaps she would have been safer if she had stayed and faced the police. Yet fleeing had become an instinct of late. She felt like a fugitive, and it made her act like one. And to think she'd thought she would be able to outwit her pursuers. Ralph had been right. She never should have gone to New York, let alone San Francisco. He had said she was in serious trouble before she'd visited both cities. Well, it was a lot worse now—for all she knew she'd killed two men. It was all too much. She wasn't going to Minneapolis. She would go home and turn everything that she knew, such as it was, and everything that she suspected, over to the attorney.

The cable car slowed again. Marissa looked around. She was some-place in Chinatown. The car stopped, and just as it was starting again, Marissa stood up and swung off. As she ran to the sidewalk, she saw the conductor shaking his head in disgust. But no one got off after her.

Marissa took a deep breath and rubbed her neck. Glancing around, she was pleased to see that both sides of the street were crowded. There were pushcart vendors, trucks making deliveries and a variety of stores with much of their merchandise displayed on the sidewalk. All the signs were written in Chinese. She felt as if the short cable-car ride had mysteriously transported her to the Orient. Even the smells were different: a mixture of fish and spices.

She passed a Chinese restaurant and, after hesitating a second, went inside. A woman dressed in a Mandarin-collared, red silk dress slit to the knee came out and said the restaurant was not yet open for lunch. "Half hour," she added.

"Would you mind if I used your restroom and your phone?" asked Marissa.

The woman studied Marissa for a moment, decided she meant no harm and led her to the rear of the restaurant. She opened a door and stepped aside.

Marissa was in a small room with a sink on one side and a pay phone on the other. There were two doors in the back with Ladies stenciled on one, and Gents on the other. The walls were covered with years of accumulated graffiti.

Marissa used the phone first. She called the Fairmont and reported to the operator that there was a man in room 1127 who needed an ambulance. The operator told her to hold on, but Marissa hung up. Then she paused, debating whether she should call the police and explain everything to them. No, she thought, it was too complicated. Besides, she'd already fled the scene. It would be better to go back to Atlanta and see the attorney.

Washing her hands, Marissa glanced at herself in the mirror. She was a mess. Taking out her comb, she untangled her hair and braided a few strands to keep it off her face. She'd lost her barrette when the blond man had yanked her by the hair. When she was finished, she straightened her blazer and the collar of her blouse. That was about all she could do.

Jake dialed George's car for the hundredth time. Mostly the phone went unanswered, but occasionally he'd get a recording telling him that the party he was calling was not presently available.

He could not figure out what was going on. Al and George should have been back in the car long ago. Jake had followed the girl, practically running her over when she'd leaped unexpectedly from the cable car, and had watched her go into a restaurant called Peking Cuisine. At least he hadn't lost her.

He scrunched down in the driver's seat. The girl had just come out of the restaurant and was flagging a cab.

An hour later, Jake watched helplessly as Marissa handed over her ticket and boarded a Delta nonstop to Atlanta. He had thought about buying a ticket himself, but scrapped the idea without Al's okay. She'd spent the last half hour closeted in the ladies' room, giving Jake ample time to try the mobile phone at least ten more times, hoping for some instructions. But still no one answered.

As soon as the plane taxied down the runway, Jake hurried back to his car. There was a parking ticket under the windshield wiper, but Jake didn't give a shit. He was just glad the car hadn't been towed away. Climbing in, he thought he'd drive back to the Fairmont and see if he could find the others. Maybe the whole thing had been called off, and he'd find both of them in the bar, laughing their asses off while he ran all over the city.

Back on the freeway, he decided to try calling the other mobile phone one last time. To his astonishment, George answered.

"Where the hell have you been?" Jake demanded. "I've been calling you all goddamn morning."

"There's been a problem," said George, subdued.

"Well, I hope to hell there's been something," said Jake. "The girl is on a plane to Atlanta. I was going crazy. I didn't know what the hell to do."

"Al was knifed, I guess by the girl. He's at San Francisco General, having surgery. I can't get near him."

"Christ!" said Jake incredulously, unable to imagine that the pint-sized broad could have knifed Al and gotten away.

"He's not supposed to be hurt that bad," continued George. "What's worse is that apparently Al wasted a maid. He had the woman's passkeys in his pocket. He's being charged with murder."

"Shit," said Jake. Things were going from bad to worse.

"Where are you now?" asked George.

"Just on the freeway, leaving the airport," said Jake.

"Go back," said George. "Book us on the next flight to Atlanta. I think we owe Al a bit of revenge."

18

MAY 24

"Reading material?" asked the smiling cabin attendant.

Marissa nodded. She needed something to keep her from thinking about the horrible scene in the hotel.

"Magazine or newspaper?" asked the attendant.

"Newspaper, I guess," said Marissa.

"*San Francisco Examiner* or *New York Times*?"

Marissa was in no mood to make decisions. "*New York Times*," she said finally.

The big jet leveled off, and the seat-belt sign went out. Marissa glanced through the window at rugged mountains stretching off into dry desert. It was a relief to have gotten onto the plane finally. At the airport, she had been so scared of either being attacked by one of the blond man's friends or being arrested, she had simply hidden in a toilet in the ladies' room.

Unfolding the newspaper, Marissa glanced at the table of contents. Continuing coverage of the Ebola outbreaks in Philadelphia and New York was listed on page 4. Marissa turned to it.

The article reported that the Philadelphia death toll was up to fifty-eight and New York was at forty-nine, but that many more cases had been reported there. Marissa was not surprised since the index case was an ear, nose and throat specialist. She also noted that the Rosenberg Clinic had already filed for bankruptcy.

On the same page as the Ebola article was a photograph of Dr. Ahmed Fakkry, head of epidemiology for the World Health Organization. The article next to the picture said that he was visiting the CDC to investigate the Ebola outbreaks because World Health was fearful that the virus would soon cross the Atlantic.

Maybe Dr. Fakkry could help her, thought Marissa. Perhaps the lawyer Ralph was lining up for her would be able to arrange for her to speak with him.

Ralph was catching up on his journals when the doorbell rang at 9:30 P.M. Glancing at his watch, he wondered who could possibly be visiting at that hour. He looked out of the glass panel on the side of the door and was shocked to find himself staring directly into Marissa's face.

"Marissa!" he said in disbelief, pulling open the door. Behind her, he could see a yellow cab descending his long, curved driveway.

Marissa saw him hold out his arms and ran into them, bursting into tears.

"I thought you were in California," said Ralph. "Why didn't you call and let me know you were coming? I would have met you at the airport."

Marissa just held onto him, crying. It was so wonderful to feel safe.

"What happened to you?" he asked, but was only greeted by louder sobs.

"At least let's sit down," he said, helping her to the couch. For a few minutes, he just let her cry, patting her gently on the back. "It's okay," he said for lack of anything else. He eyed the phone, willing it to ring. He had to make a call, and at this rate she was never going to let him get up. "Perhaps you'd like something to drink?" he asked. "How about some of that special cognac? Maybe it will make you feel better."

Marissa shook her head.

"Wine? I have a nice bottle of Chardonnay open in the refrigerator." Ralph was running out of ideas.

Marissa just held him tighter, but her sobs were lessening, her breathing becoming more regular.

Five minutes went by. Ralph sighed. "Where is your luggage?"

Marissa didn't answer, but did fish a tissue out of her pocket and wipe her face.

"I've got some cold chicken in the kitchen."

At last Marissa sat up. "Maybe in a little bit. Just stay with me a little longer. I've been so scared."

"Then why didn't you call me from the airport? And what happened to your car? Didn't you leave it there?"

"It's a long story," said Marissa. "But I was afraid that someone might be watching it. I didn't want anybody to know I was back in Atlanta."

Ralph raised his eyebrows. "Does that mean you'd like to spend the night?"

"If you don't mind," said Marissa. "Nothing like inviting myself, but you've been such a good friend."

"Would you like me to drive you over to your house to get some things?" asked Ralph.

"Thanks, but I don't want to show up there for the same reason I was afraid to go to my car. If I were to drive anyplace tonight, I'd run over to the CDC and get a package that I hope Tad put away for me. But to tell you the truth, I think it all can wait until morning. Even that criminal lawyer, who I hope will be able to keep me out of jail."

"Good grief," said Ralph. "I hope you're not serious. Don't you think it's time you told me what's going on?"

Marissa picked up Ralph's hand. "I will. I promise. Let me just calm down a little more. Maybe I should eat something."

"I'll fix you some chicken," he said.

"That's all right. I know where the kitchen is. Maybe I'll just scramble some eggs."

"I'll join you in a minute. I have to make a call."

Marissa dragged herself through the house. In the kitchen, she glanced around at all the appliances and space and thought it was a waste just to be making eggs. But that was what sounded best. She got them out of the refrigerator, along with some bread for toast. Then she realized she hadn't asked Ralph if he wanted some too. She was about to call out but decided he wouldn't hear her.

Putting the eggs down, she went over to the intercom and began pushing the buttons on the console to see if she could figure out how it worked. "Hello, hello," she said as she held down different combinations. Stumbling onto the correct sequence, she suddenly heard Ralph's voice.

"She's not in San Francisco," he was saying. "She's here at my house."

Pause.

"Jackson, I don't know what happened. She's hysterical. All she said was that she has a package waiting for her at the CDC. Listen, I can't talk now. I've got to get back to her."

Pause.

"I'll keep her here, don't worry. But get over here as soon as you can."

Pause.

"No, no one knows she's here. I'm sure of that. 'Bye."

Marissa clutched the counter top, afraid she was going to faint. All this time Ralph—the one person she'd trusted—had been one of "them." And Jackson! It had to be the same Jackson she'd met at Ralph's dinner party. The head of PAC, and he was on his way over. Oh, God!

Knowing Ralph was on his way to the kitchen, Marissa forced herself to go on with her cooking. But when she tried to break an egg on the side of the skillet, she smashed it shell and all into the pan. She had the other egg in her hand when Ralph appeared with some drinks. She broke the second egg a bit more deftly, mixing it all together, including the first egg's shell.

"Smells good," he said brightly. He put down her glass and touched her lightly on the back. Marissa jumped.

"Wow, you really are uptight. How are we going to get you to relax?"

Marissa didn't say anything. Although she was no longer the slightest bit hungry, she went through the motions of cooking the eggs, buttering the toast and putting out jam. Looking at Ralph's expensive silk shirt, the heavy gold cuff links, the tasseled Gucci loafers, everything about him suddenly seemed a ridiculous affectation, as did the whole elaborately furnished house. It all represented the conspicuous consumption of a wealthy doctor, now fearful of the new medical competition, of changing times, of medicine no longer being a seller's market.

Obviously, Ralph was a member of PAC. Of course he was a supporter of Markham. And it was Ralph, not Tad, who had always known where she was. Serving the eggs, Marissa thought that even if she could escape there was no one to go to. She certainly couldn't use a lawyer Ralph recommended. In fact, now that she knew Ralph was implicated, she remembered why the name of the law firm he'd suggested had sounded familiar: Cooper, Hodges, McQuinllin and Hanks had been listed as the service agent of PAC.

OUTBREAK

Marissa felt trapped. The men pursuing her had powerful connections. She had no idea how deeply they had penetrated the CDC. Certainly the conspiracy involved the congressman who exerted control over the CDC budget.

Marissa's mind reeled. She was terrified no one would believe her, and she was acutely aware that the only piece of hard evidence she had—the vaccination gun—was resting somewhere in the maximum containment lab, to which she knew from painful experience her pursuers had access. The only thing that was crystal clear was that she had to get away from Ralph before Jackson and maybe more thugs arrived.

Picking up her fork, she had a sudden vision of the blond man hurling himself through the bathroom door in San Francisco. She dropped the fork, again afraid she was about to faint.

Ralph grabbed her elbow and helped her to the kitchen table. He put the food on a plate and placed it in front of her and urged her to eat.

"You were doing so well a minute ago," he said. "You'll feel better if you get something in your stomach." He picked up the fork she'd dropped and tossed it into the sink, then got another from the silver drawer.

Marissa dropped her head into her hands. She had to get herself under control. Valuable time was ticking away.

"Not hungry after all?" asked Ralph.

"Not very," admitted Marissa. The very smell of the eggs was enough to make her sick. She shuddered.

"Maybe you should take a tranquilizer. I've got some upstairs. What do you think?"

"Okay," said Marissa.

"Be right back," said Ralph, squeezing her shoulder.

This was the chance she had prayed for. As soon as he was out of the room, Marissa was on her feet, snatching the phone off its hook. But there was no dial tone. Ralph must have disconnected it somehow! So much for the police. Replacing the phone, she rushed around the kitchen searching for Ralph's car keys. Nothing. Next she tried the adjoining family room. There was a tiny marble urn on the room divider with a few keys, but none for a car. Going back through the kitchen, Marissa went to the small foyer by the back door. There was a cork bulletin board, an antique school desk and an old bureau. There was also a door that led to the bathroom.

Trying the desk first, she lifted its cover and rummaged through its contents. There were some odd-shaped house keys, but that was all.

227

Turning to the small bureau, she began opening drawers, finding a jumble of gloves, scarves and rain gear.

"What do you need?" asked Ralph, suddenly appearing behind her. Guiltily she straightened up, searching for an alibi. Ralph waited, looking at her expectantly. His right hand was closed. His left hand held a glass of water.

"I thought maybe I could find a sweater," said Marissa.

Ralph eyed her curiously. If anything, the house was too warm. After all, it was almost June.

"I'll turn the heat on in the kitchen," he said, guiding her back to her chair. He extended his right hand. "Here, take this." He dropped a capsule into Marissa's palm. It was red and ivory in color.

"Dalmane?" questioned Marissa. "I thought you were getting me a tranquilizer."

"It will relax you *and* give you a good night's sleep," explained Ralph.

Shaking her head and handing the capsule back to Ralph, Marissa said, "I'd prefer a tranquilizer."

"What about Valium?"

"Fine," said Marissa.

As soon as she heard him climbing the back stairs, Marissa ran to the front foyer. There were no keys on the elaborate marble half-table or in the one central drawer. Opening the closet, Marissa rapidly patted jacket pockets. Nothing.

She was back in the kitchen just in time to hear Ralph start down the back stairs.

"There you go," he said, dropping a blue tablet into Marissa's hand.

"What dose is this?"

"Ten milligrams."

"Don't you think that's a little much?"

"You're so upset. It won't affect you as it would normally," said Ralph, handing her a glass of water. She took it from him, then pretended to take the Valium, but dropped it into the pocket of her jacket instead.

"Now let's try the food again," said Ralph.

Marissa forced herself to eat a little as she tried to figure out a way to escape before Jackson arrived. The food tasted awful, and she put down her fork after a few bites.

"Still not hungry?" said Ralph.

Marissa shook her head.

"Well, let's go into the living room."

She was glad to leave the cooking smells, but the moment they were seated, Ralph urged her to have a fresh drink.

"I don't think I should after the Valium."

"A little won't hurt."

"Are you sure you're not trying to get me drunk?" said Marissa. She forced a laugh. "Maybe you'd better let me fix the drinks."

"Fine by me," said Ralph, lifting his feet to the coffee table. "Make mine scotch."

Marissa went directly to the bar and poured Ralph a good four fingers of scotch. Then, checking to see that he was absorbed, she took out the Valium tablet, broke it in half and dropped the pieces into the alcohol. Unfortunately, they did not dissolve. Fishing the pieces out, she pulverized them with the scotch bottle and swept the powder into the drink.

"You need any help?" called Ralph.

"No," she said, pouring a little brandy into her own glass. "Here you go."

Ralph took his drink and settled back on the couch.

Sitting down beside him, Marissa racked her brains to figure out where he might have put his car keys. She wondered what he would say if she suddenly demanded them, but decided it was too great a risk. If he realized she knew about him, he might forcibly restrain her. This way, she still had a chance, if she could just find the keys.

A horrible thought occurred to her: he probably had just put them in his pants pocket. As distasteful as it was, Marissa forced herself to snuggle against him. Provocatively, she placed her hand on his hip. Sure enough, she could feel the keys through the light gabardine. Now, how on earth was she going to get them?

Gritting her teeth, she tilted her face to his, encouraging him to kiss her. As his arms circled her waist, she let her fingers slide into his pocket. Scarcely breathing she felt the edge of the ring and pulled. The keys jangled a little and she began frantically kissing him. Sensing his response she decided she had to take the chance. Please God, please God, she prayed and pulled out the keys and hid them in her own pocket.

Ralph had obviously forgotten Jackson was coming, or he'd decided sex was the best way to keep Marissa quiet. In any case, it was time to stop him.

"Darling," she said. "I hate to do this to you, but that pill is getting to me. I think I'm going to have to go to sleep."

"Just rest here. I'll hold you."

"I'd love to, but then you'd have to carry me upstairs." She pulled herself out of his embrace, and he solicitously helped her up the stairs to the guest bedroom.

"Don't you want me to stay with you?" he asked.

"I'm sorry, Ralph. I'm about to pass out. Just let me sleep." She forced a smile. "We can always continue when the Valium wears off." As if to end any further conversation, she lay on the bed fully clothed.

"Don't you want to borrow pajamas?" he asked hopefully.

"No, no. I can't keep my eyes open."

"Well, call if you need anything. I'll just be downstairs."

The moment he closed the door, she tiptoed over and listened to him go down the front stairs. Then she went to the window and opened it. The balcony outside was just as she remembered. As quietly as possible, she slipped out into the warm spring night. Above was an inverted bowl of stars. The trees were just dark silhouettes. There was no wind. In the distance, a dog barked. Then Marissa heard a car.

Quickly she surveyed her position. She was about fifteen feet above the asphalt drive. There was no possibility of jumping. The balcony was surrounded by a low balustrade, separating it from the sloped roof of the porch. To the left the porch roof abutted the tower and to the right it swept around the corner of the building.

Climbing over the balustrade, Marissa inched her way to the corner. The porch roof ended about twenty feet away. The fire escape descended from the third floor, but it was out of reach. Turning, she started back for the balcony. She was halfway there when the car she'd heard earlier turned into Ralph's drive.

Marissa lay still on the sloped roof. She knew that she was in full view of anybody coming up the driveway if they happened to look up. The car's lights played against the trees, then swept across the front of the house, bathing her in light before it pulled up to the front steps. She heard the doors open and several voices. They were not excited; apparently no one had seen her sprawled on the roof. Ralph answered the door. There was more conversation, and then the voices disappeared inside.

Marissa scampered along the roof and climbed back over the balustrade to the balcony. She ducked into the guest room and eased open the door to the hallway. Stepping into the hall, she could hear Ralph's voice though she could not make out what he was saying. As quietly as possible, she started toward the back stairs.

The light from the vestibule did not penetrate beyond the second turn in the hallway, and Marissa had to make her way by running her hands along the walls. She passed a number of dark bedrooms before she rounded a final corner and saw the kitchen light shining below.

At the head of the stairs, she hesitated. The sounds in the old house were confusing her. She still heard voices, but she also heard footsteps. The problem was, she couldn't tell where they were coming from. At that moment she caught sight of a hand on the newel post below.

Changing direction, Marissa went up the stairs and was halfway to the third floor in seconds. One of the treads squeaked under her foot, and she hesitated, heart pounding, listening to the relentless approach of the figure below. When he reached the second floor and turned down the hall toward the front of the house, she let out her breath.

Marissa continued up the stairs, wincing at every sound. The door to the servants' apartment at the top was closed but not locked.

As quietly as possible, she made her way across the dark living room and into the bedroom that she guessed looked out on the fire escape.

After struggling to raise the window, she climbed out onto the flimsy metal grate. Never fond of heights, it took all her courage to stand upright. Hesitantly, she started down, one step at a time, leading with her right foot. By the time she reached the second story, she heard excited voices inside the house and the sound of doors opening and slamming shut. Lights began going on in the darkened rooms. They had already realized that she had fled.

Forcing herself to hurry, Marissa rounded the second-story platform and was stopped by what seemed to be a large jumble of metal. Feeling with her hands, she realized that the last flight of stairs had been drawn up to protect the house from burglars. Desperately, she tried to figure out how to lower them. There didn't seem to be any release mechanism. Then she noticed a large counterweight behind her.

Gingerly, she put her foot on the first step. There was a loud squeak of metal. Knowing she had no choice, Marissa shifted her full weight to the step. With a nerve-shattering crash, the stairs shot to the ground and she ran down them.

As soon as her feet touched the grass, she ran for the garage, arms swinging wildly. There was no way the men inside the house could not have heard the fire escape's descent. In seconds they would be looking for her.

She ran to a side door to the garage, praying to heaven that it was not locked. It wasn't. As she raced inside, she heard the back door of the house open. Desperately, she stepped into the dark interior, pulling the door shut behind her. Turning, she moved forward, colliding almost immediately with Ralph's 300SDL sedan. Feeling for the car door, she opened it and slipped behind the wheel. She fumbled with the key until it slid into the ignition, and turned it. Several indicator lights flashed on, but the car didn't start. Then she remembered Ralph explaining how you had to wait for the orange light to go out because the engine was a diesel. She switched the ignition back off, then turned the key part way. The orange light went on, and Marissa waited. She heard someone raise the garage door; frantically, she hit the button locking all four doors of the car.

"Come on!" she urged through clenched teeth. The orange light went out. She turned the key, and the car roared to life as she stomped on the gas. There was a series of loud thumps as someone pounded her window. She shifted to reverse and floored the accelerator. There was a second's delay before the big car leaped backward with such force that she was flung against the wheel. She braced herself as the car shot out the door, sending two men diving sideways for safety.

The car careened wildly down the drive. Marissa jammed on the brakes as the car screeched around the front of the house, but it was too late. She rammed Jackson's car with the back of hers. Shifting to forward, Marissa thought she was free, until one of the men, taking advantage of her momentary halt, flung himself across the hood. Marissa accelerated. The tires spun, but the car did not move. She was caught on the car behind. Putting the Mercedes into reverse, then into drive, she rocked the car as if she were stuck in snow. There was a scraping sound of metal; then she shot forward, dislodging her attacker as she careened down the drive.

"Forget it," said Jake, crawling out from under Jackson's car, wiping grease from his hands. "She busted your radiator," he told the doctor. "There's no coolant, so even if it started, you couldn't drive it."

"Damn," said Jackson, getting out. "That woman lives a charmed life." He looked furiously at Heberling. "This probably wouldn't have happened if I'd come here directly instead of waiting for your goons to get in from the airport."

"Yeah?" said Heberling. "And what would you have done? Reasoned with her? You needed Jake and George."

"You can use my 450 SL," offered Ralph. "But it's only a two-seater."

"She got too big a head start," said George. "We'd never catch her."

"I don't know how she escaped," said Ralph apologetically. "I'd just left her to sleep. She's had ten milligrams of Valium, for Chrissake." He noticed he felt a little dizzy himself.

"Any idea where she might go?" asked Jackson.

"I don't think she'll go to the police," said Ralph. "She's terrified of everyone, especially now. She might try the CDC. She said something about a package being there."

Jackson looked at Heberling. They had the same thought: the vaccination gun.

"We may as well send Jake and George," said Heberling. "We're pretty sure she won't go home, and after what she did to Al, the boys are most eager for revenge."

Fifteen minutes from the house, Marissa began to calm down enough to worry about where she was. She had made so many random turns in case she was being pursued, she had lost all sense of direction. For all she knew, she could have driven in a full circle.

Ahead, she saw street lights and a gas station. Marissa pulled over, lowering her window. A young man came out wearing an Atlanta Braves baseball hat.

"Could you tell me where I am?" asked Marissa.

"This here's a Shell station," said the young man, eyeing the damage to Ralph's car. "Did you know that both your taillights is busted?"

"I'm not surprised," said Marissa. "How about Emory University. Could you tell me how to get there?"

"Lady, you look like you've been in a demolition derby," he said, shaking his head in dismay.

Marissa repeated her question, and finally the man gave her some vague directions.

Ten minutes later Marissa cruised past the CDC. The building seemed quiet and deserted, but she still wasn't sure what she should do or who she could trust. She would have preferred going to a good lawyer, but she had no idea how to choose one. Certainly McQuinllin was out of the question.

The only person she could envision approaching was Dr. Fakkry, from the World Health Organization. He certainly was above the conspiracy, and, conveniently, he was staying at the Peachtree Plaza. The problem was, would he believe her or would he just call Dubchek or someone else at the CDC, putting her back into the hands of her pursuers?

Fear forced her to do what she felt was her only logical choice. She had to get the vaccination gun. It was her only piece of hard evidence. Without it she doubted anyone would take her seriously. She still had Tad's access card, and if he was not involved with PAC, the card might still be usable. Of course there was always the chance that security wouldn't allow her into the building.

Boldly, Marissa turned into the driveway and pulled up just past the entrance to the CDC. She wanted the car handy in case anyone tried to stop her.

Looking in the front door, she saw the guard sitting at the desk, bent over a paperback novel. When he heard her come in, he looked up, his face expressionless.

Rolling her lower lip into her mouth and biting on it, Marissa walked deliberately, trying to hide her fear. She picked up the pen and scrawled her name in the sign-in book. Then she looked up, expecting some comment, but the man just stared impassively.

"What are you reading?" asked Marissa, nerves making her chatter.

"Camus."

Well, she wasn't about to ask if it was *The Plague*. She started for the main elevators, conscious of the man's eyes on her back. She pushed the button to her floor, turned and looked at him. He was still watching her.

The moment the doors shut, he snatched up the phone and dialed. As soon as someone answered, he said, "Dr. Blumenthal just signed in. She went up in the elevator."

"Wonderful, Jerome," said Dubchek. His voice was hoarse, as if he were tired or sick. "We'll be right there. Don't let anyone else in."

"Whatever you say, Dr. Dubchek."

Marissa got off the elevator and stood for a few minutes, watching the floor indicators. Both elevators stayed where they were. The building was silent. Convinced that she wasn't being followed, she went to the stairs and ran down a flight, then out into the catwalk. Inside the virology building, she hurried down the long cluttered hall, rounded the corner and confronted the steel security door. Holding her breath, she inserted Tad's access card and tapped out his number.

There was a pause. For a moment she was afraid an alarm might sound. But all she heard was the sound of the latch releasing. The heavy door opened, and she was inside.

After flipping the circuit breakers, she twisted the wheel on the airtight door, climbed into the first room and, instead of donning a scrub suit, went directly into the next chamber. As she struggled into a plastic suit, she wondered where Tad might have hidden the contaminated vaccination gun.

Dubchek drove recklessly, braking for curves only when absolutely necessary, and running red lights. Two men had joined him; John, in the front seat, braced himself against the door; Mark, in the back, had more trouble avoiding being thrown from side to side. The expressions on all three faces were grim. They were afraid they would be too late.

"There it is," said George, pointing at the sign that said Centers for Disease Control.

"And there's Ralph's car!" he added, pointing at the Mercedes in the semicircular driveway. "Looks like luck is finally on our side." Making up his mind, he pulled into the Sheraton Motor Inn lot across the street.

George drew his S & W .357 Magnum, checking to see that all the chambers were filled. He opened the door and stepped out, holding the gun down along his hip. Light gleamed off the stainless-steel barrel.

"You sure you want to use that cannon?" asked Jake. "It makes so goddamn much noise."

"I wish I had had this thing when she was driving around with you on the hood," George snapped. "Come on!"

Jake shrugged and got out of the car. Patting the small of his back, he felt the butt of his own Beretta automatic. It was a much neater weapon.

Air line in hand, Marissa hastily climbed through the final door to the maximum containment lab. She plugged into the central manifold and looked around. The mess she'd helped create on that other fateful night had all been cleared away, but the memory of that episode flooded

235

back with horrifying clarity. Marissa was shaking. All she wanted was to find her parcel and get the hell out. But that was easier said than done. As in any lab, there was a profusion of places where a package that size could be hidden.

Marissa started on the right, working her way back, opening cabinet doors and pulling out drawers. She got about halfway down the room, when she straightened up. There had to be a better way. At the central island, she went to the containment hood that Tad considered his own. In the cupboards below, she found bottles of reagents, paper towels, plastic garbage bags, boxes of new glassware and an abundance of other supplies. But there was no package resembling hers. She was about to move on when she looked through the glass of the containment hood itself. Behind Tad's equipment, she could just barely make out the dark green of a plastic garbage bag.

Turning on the fan over the hood, Marissa pulled up the glass front. Then, careful not to touch Tad's setup, she lifted out the bag. Inside was the Federal Express package. To be sure, she checked the label. It was addressed to Tad in her handwriting.

Marissa put the package in a new garbage bag, sealing it carefully. Then she put the used bag back inside the containment hood and pulled the glass front into place. At the central manifold, she hurriedly detached her air hose, then headed for the door. It was time to find Dr. Fakkry or someone else in authority she could trust.

Standing under the shower of phenolic disinfectant, Marissa tried to be patient. There was an automated timing device, so she had to wait for the process to finish before she could open the door. Once in the next room, she struggled out of her plastic suit, pulling frantically each time the zipper stuck. When she finally got it off, her street clothes were drenched with sweat.

Dubchek came to a screeching halt directly in front of the CDC entrance. The three men piled out of the car. Jerome was already holding open one of the glass doors.

Dubchek didn't wait to ask questions, certain that the guard would tell them if Marissa had left. He ran into the waiting elevator with the other two men on his heels, and pressed the button for the third floor.

Marissa had just started across the catwalk when the door to the main building opened and three men burst out. Spinning around, she ran back into virology.

236

"Stop, Marissa," someone yelled. It sounded like Dubchek. Oh, God, was he chasing her too?

She latched the door behind her and looked about for a place to hide. To her right was an elevator, to her left, a stairwell. There was no time to debate.

By the time Dubchek forced open the door, all he could see was the elevator light pointing down. Marissa was already on the lobby level as the three men began pounding down the stairs.

Knowing Dubchek was close behind, Marissa knew she had no time to slow down to avoid alerting the security guard when she'd reached the main building. His head popped up from his book, just in time to catch her streaking past. He stood up but that was all, and she was already gone when he decided that Dr. Dubchek might have wanted her stopped by force.

Outside, she fumbled for the keys to Ralph's car, switching her parcel to her left hand. She heard shouts and then the doors to the CDC crash open. Wrestling the car door open, she started to slide behind the wheel. She was so programmed for flight that it took a minute for her to realize that the passenger seat was occupied. There was also someone in the back. But worse was the sight of an enormous revolver pointing at her.

Marissa tried to reverse her direction, but it was as if she were caught in a heavy, viscous fluid. Her body wouldn't respond. She saw the gun coming up at her, but she could do nothing. She saw a face in the half-light, and she heard someone start to say "good-bye." But the gun went off with a fearful concussion, and time stopped.

When Marissa regained consciousness, she was lying on something soft. Someone was calling her name. Slowly opening her eyes, she realized that she'd been carried back inside to the couch in the CDC lobby.

Flashing red and blue lights washed the room like a tawdry, punk discotheque. There seemed to be many people coming in and out of the room. It was too confusing. She closed her eyes again and wondered what had happened to the men with the guns.

"Marissa, are you all right?"

Her lids fluttered open, and she saw Dubchek bending over her, his dark eyes almost black with fear.

"Marissa," he said again. "Are you all right? I've been so worried. When you finally made us realize what was going on, we were afraid they'd try to kill you. But you never stayed still long enough for us to find you.''

Marissa was still too shocked to speak.

"Please say something," Dubchek pleaded. "Did they hurt you?''

"I thought you were part of it. Part of the conspiracy," was all she could manage to utter.

"I was afraid of that," groaned Dubchek. "Not that I didn't deserve it. I was so busy protecting the CDC, I just dismissed your theories. But believe me, I had nothing to do with any of it.''

Marissa reached for his hand. "I guess I never gave you much chance to explain, either. I was so busy breaking all the rules.''

An ambulance attendant came up to them. "Does the lady want to go to the hospital?''

"Do you, Marissa?" asked Dubchek.

"I guess so, but I think I'm okay.''

As another attendant came up to help lift her onto a stretcher, she said, "When I heard the first bang, I thought I'd been shot.''

"No, one of the FBI men I'd alerted shot your would-be killer instead.''

Marissa shuddered. Dubchek walked beside the stretcher as they took her to the ambulance. She reached out and took his hand.

EPILOGUE

Marissa was unpacking from a two-week vacation, taken at Dr. Carbonara's insistence, when the doorbell rang. She had just returned from Virginia, where her family had done everything they could to spoil her, even giving her a new puppy that she'd immediately named Taffy Two.

As she walked downstairs, she couldn't imagine who might be at the door. She hadn't told anyone the exact date of her return. When she opened the door, she was surprised to see Cyrill Dubchek and a stranger.

"I hope you don't mind our turning up like this, but Dr. Carbonara said you might be home, and Dr. Fakkry from World Health wanted to meet you. This is his last day in America. Tonight he is flying back to Geneva."

The stranger stepped forward and dipped his head. Then he looked directly at Marissa. His eyes reminded her of Dubchek's: dark and liquid.

"I am deeply honored," said Dr. Fakkry, with a crisp, English accent. "I wanted to thank you personally for your brilliant detective work."

"And with no help from us," admitted Dubchek.

"I'm flattered," said Marissa, at a loss for words.

Dubchek cleared his throat. Marissa found his new lack of confidence appealing. When he wasn't making her furious, she could admit that he was actually very handsome.

"We thought you'd like to know what's been happening," he said. "The press has been given as little detail as possible, but even the police agree you are entitled to the truth."

"I'd love to hear everything," said Marissa. "But please come in and sit down. Can I get you something to drink?"

When they were settled, Dr. Fakkry said, "Thanks to you, almost everyone connected to the Ebola conspiracy has been arrested. The man you stabbed in San Francisco implicated Dr. Heberling the minute he recovered from surgery."

"The police think he wanted to be sent to jail so you couldn't find him again," said Dubchek, with a hint of his old sardonic grin.

Marissa shivered, remembering the terrible episode of stabbing the man in the bathroom at the Fairmont. For a moment the image of his ice-blue eyes froze her. Then, pulling herself together, she asked what had happened to Heberling.

"He'll be going before a grand jury on multiple counts of murder with intent," said Dubchek. "The judge refused to set bail, no matter how high, saying that he was as dangerous to society as the Nazi war criminals."

"And the man I hit with the vaccination gun?" Marissa had been afraid to ask this question. She didn't want to be responsible for killing anyone or for spreading Ebola.

"He'll live to stand trial. He did use the serum in time, and it proved effective, but he came down with a severe case of serum sickness. As soon as he's better, he'll also be off to jail."

"What about the other officers of the Physicians' Action Congress?" asked Marissa.

"A number of them have offered to turn state's evidence," said Dubchek. "It's making the investigation inordinately easy. We are beginning to believe that the regular members of the organization thought they were supporting just an ordinary lobbying campaign."

"What about Tieman? He certainly didn't seem the type to be mixed up in such an affair. Or at least his conscience really seemed to bother him."

"His lawyer has been making arrangements for a lighter sentence in return for his cooperation. As for PAC itself, the group's bankrupt. The families of the victims have almost all filed suit. They're also suing the doctors individually. Most of the officers are being prosecuted as criminals. So they should be behind bars a good while, particularly Jackson."

"He and Dr. Heberling would be—I think your word is lynched—if the public got ahold of them," added Dr. Fakkry.

"I guess Ralph will also be sentenced," Marissa said slowly. She was still trying to come to terms with the fact that the man she considered a protector had tried to kill her.

"He was one of the first to cooperate with the prosecution. He'll get some breaks, but I doubt he'll be released for a long time. Aside from his connection with PAC, he is directly linked to the attacks on you."

"I know," Marissa sighed. "So it's really over."

"Thanks to your persistence," said Dubchek. "And the outbreak in New York is definitely under control."

"Thank God," she said.

"So when will you be coming back to the CDC?" asked Dubchek. "We've already gotten you clearance for the maximum containment lab." This time there was no doubt about his grin. "No one relished the thought of your stumbling around in there at night anymore."

Marissa blushed in spite of herself. "I haven't decided yet. I'm actually considering going back into pediatrics."

"Back to Boston?" Dubchek's face fell.

"It will be a loss to the field," said Dr. Fakkry. "You've become an international epidemiological hero."

"I'll give it more thought," promised Marissa. "But even if I do go back to pediatrics, I'm planning to stay in Atlanta." She nuzzled her new puppy. There was a pause, then she added, "But I've one request."

"If we can be of any help . . ." said Dr. Fakkry.

Marissa shook her head. "Only Cyrill can help on this one. Whether I go back to pediatrics or not, I was hoping he'd ask me to dinner again."

Dubchek was taken off guard. Then, laughing at Fakkry's bemused expression, he leaned over and hugged Marissa to his side.

MORTAL
FEAR

ACKNOWLEDGMENTS

This book could not have been written without
the support and encouragement of all my friends
who have helped me in a difficult time.
You all know who you are,
and you all have my heartfelt thanks.

*For my older brother, Lee, and
my younger sister, Laurie.
I've never been between two nicer people.*

PROLOGUE

OCTOBER 11, WEDNESDAY P.M.

The sudden appearance of the foreign proteins was the molecular equivalent of the Black Plague. It was a death sentence with no chance of reprieve, and Cedric Harring had no idea of the drama about to happen inside him.

In sharp contrast, the individual cells of Cedric Harring's body knew exactly what disastrous consequences awaited them. The mysterious new proteins that swept into their midst and through their membranes were overwhelming, and the small amounts of enzymes capable of dealing with the newcomers were totally inadequate. Within Cedric's pituitary gland, the deadly new proteins were able to bind themselves to the repressors that covered the genes for the death hormone. From that moment, with the fatal genes exposed, the outcome was inevitable. The death hormone began to be synthesized in unprecedented amounts. Entering the bloodstream, the hormone coursed out into Cedric's body. No cell was immune. The end was only a matter of time. Cedric Harring was about to disintegrate into his stellar elements.

1

The pain was like a white-hot knife starting somewhere in his chest and quickly radiating upward in blinding paroxysms to paralyze his jaw and left arm. Instantly Cedric felt the terror of the mortal fear of death. Cedric Harring had never felt anything like it.

By reflex he gripped the steering wheel of his car more tightly and somehow managed to stay in control of the weaving vehicle as he gasped for breath. He'd just entered Storrow Drive from Berkeley Street in downtown Boston, and had accelerated westward, merging with the maddening Boston traffic. The images of the road swam before him and then receded, as if they existed at the end of a long tunnel.

By sheer strength of will, Cedric resisted the darkness that threatened to engulf him. Gradually, the scene brightened. He was still alive. Instead of pulling over, instinct told him his only chance was to get to a hospital as fast as possible. By lucky coincidence the Good Health Plan Clinic was not too far off. Hold on, he told himself.

Along with the pain came a drenching sweat that started on Cedric's forehead but soon spread to the rest of his body. Sweat stung his eyes, but he dared not loosen his grip on the steering wheel to wipe it away. He exited the highway onto the Fenway, a parklike complex in Boston, as the pain returned, squeezing his chest like a cinch of steel wire. Ahead cars were slowing for a traffic light. He couldn't stop. There was no time. Leaning forward, he depressed the horn and shot through the intersection. Cars went by, missing him by inches. He could see

251

the faces of the startled and enraged drivers. He was now on Park Drive with the Back Bay Fens and the scruffy victory gardens on his left. The pain was constant now, strong and overpowering. He could hardly breathe.

The hospital was ahead on the right, on the previous site of a Sears building. Only a little further. Please. . . . A large white sign with a red arrow and red letters that said EMERGENCY loomed above.

Cedric managed to drive directly up to the emergency room platform, braking belatedly and crashing into the concrete abutment. He slumped forward, hitting the horn and gasping for breath.

The first person to reach his car was the security guard. He yanked open the door and after a glance at Cedric's frightening pallor yelled for help. Cedric barely choked out the words, "Chest pain." The head nurse, Hilary Barton, appeared and called for a gurney. By the time the nurses and the security man had Cedric out of the car, one of the emergency room residents had appeared and helped maneuver him onto the stretcher. His name was Emil Frank and he'd been a resident for only four months. A few years previously he would have been called an intern. He too noticed Cedric's cream-colored skin and profuse perspiration.

"Diaphoresis," he said with authority. "Probably a heart attack."

Hilary rolled her eyes. Of course it was a heart attack. She rushed the patient inside, ignoring Dr. Frank, who'd plugged his stethoscope into his ears and was trying to listen to Cedric's heart.

As soon as they reached the treatment room, Hilary ordered oxygen, IV fluids and electrocardiographic monitoring, attaching the three main EKG leads herself. As soon as Emil had the IV going, she suggested to him that he order 4 mg. of morphine to be given IV immediately.

As the pain receded a little, Cedric's mind cleared. Even though no one had told him, he knew he'd had a heart attack. He also knew he'd come very close to dying. Even now, staring at the oxygen mask, the IV, and the EKG machine as it spewed paper out onto the floor, Cedric had never felt so vulnerable in his life.

"We're going to move you to the coronary care unit," Hilary said. "Everything is going to be okay." She patted Cedric's hand. He tried to smile. "We've called your wife. She's on her way."

The coronary intensive care unit was similar to the emergency room as far as Cedric was concerned—and just as frightening. It was filled with esoteric, ultramodern electronic technology. He could hear his heartbeat being echoed by a mechanical beep, and when he turned his head he could see a phosphorescent blip trace across a round TV screen.

Although the machines were frightening, it was a source of some reassurance to know all that technology was there. Even more reassuring was the fact that his own doctor, who had been paged shortly after Cedric's arrival, had just come into the ICU.

Cedric had been a patient of Dr. Jason Howard's for five years. He had begun going when his employers, the Boston National Bank, insisted that senior executives have yearly physicals. When Dr. Howard suddenly sold his private practice several years previously and joined the staff of the Good Health Plan (GHP), Cedric had dutifully followed. The move required changing his health plan from Blue Cross to the prepaid variety, but it was Dr. Howard that had attracted him, not GHP, and Cedric had let Dr. Howard know it in no uncertain terms.

"How are you doing?" Jason asked, grasping Cedric's arm but paying more attention to the EKG screen.

"Not . . . great," Cedric rasped. It took several breaths to get out the two words.

"I want you to try to relax."

Cedric closed his eyes. *Relax! What a joke.*

"Do you have a lot of pain?"

Cedric nodded. Tears were running down his cheeks.

"Another dose of morphine," Jason ordered.

Within minutes of the second dose, the pain became more tolerable. Dr. Howard was talking with the resident, making sure all the appropriate blood samples had been drawn and asking for some kind of catheter. Cedric watched him, reassured just seeing Howard's handsome, hawklike profile and sensing the man's confidence and authority. Best of all, he could feel Dr. Howard's compassion. Dr. Howard cared.

"We have to do a little procedure," Jason was saying. "We want to insert a Swan-Ganz catheter so we can see what's going on inside. We'll use a local anesthesia so it won't hurt, okay?"

Cedric nodded. As far as he was concerned, Dr. Howard had carte blanche to do whatever he felt was necessary. Cedric appreciated Dr. Howard's approach. He never talked down to his patients—even when Cedric had had his physical three weeks ago and Howard had lectured him about his high-cholesterol diet, his two-pack-a-day cigarette habit, and his lack of exercise. *If only I'd listened*, Cedric thought. But despite Dr. Howard's doomsday approach to Cedric's lifestyle, the doctor had admitted that the tests were okay. His cholesterol was not too high, and his electrocardiogram had been fine. Reassured, Cedric put off attempts to stop smoking and start exercising.

Then, less than a week after his physical, Cedric felt as if he were coming down with the flu. But that had been only the beginning. His digestive system began acting up, and he suffered terrible arthritis. Even his eyesight seemed to deteriorate. He remembered telling his wife it was as though he had aged thirty years. He had all the symptoms his father had endured during his final months in the nursing home. Sometimes when he caught an unexpected glimpse of his reflection, it was as if he were staring at the old man's ghost.

Despite the morphine, Cedric felt a sudden stab of white-hot, crushing pain. He felt himself receding into a tunnel as he had in the car. He could still see Dr. Howard, but the doctor was far away, and his voice was fading. Then the tunnel started to fill with water. Cedric choked and tried to swim to the surface. His arms frantically grappled the air.

Later, Cedric regained consciousness for a few moments of agony. As he struggled back to awareness, he felt intermittent pressure on his chest, and something in his throat. Someone was kneeling beside him, crushing his chest with his hands. Cedric started to cry out when there was an explosion in his chest and darkness descended like a lead blanket.

Death had always been Dr. Jason Howard's enemy. As a resident at Massachusetts General, he'd carried that belief to the extreme, never giving up on a cardiac arrest until a superior ordered him to stop.

Now he refused to believe that the fifty-six-year-old man whom he'd examined only three weeks earlier and had declared generally healthy was about to die. It was a personal affront.

Glancing up at the monitor, which still showed normal EKG activity, Jason touched Cedric's neck. He could feel no pulse. "Let me have a cardiac needle," he demanded. "And someone get a blood pressure." A large cardiac needle was thrust into his hand as he palpated Cedric's chest to locate the ridge on the sternum.

"No blood pressure," reported Philip Barnes, an anesthesiologist who had responded to the code call that automatically went out when Cedric arrested. He'd placed an endotracheal tube into Cedric's trachea and was ventilating him with oxygen by compressing the Ambu bag.

To Jason, the diagnosis was obvious: cardiac rupture. With the EKG still being recorded, yet no pumping action of the heart, a situation of electromechanical dissociation prevailed. It could mean only one thing. The portion of Cedric's heart that had been deprived of its blood supply had split open like a squashed grape. To prove this horrendous diagnosis, Jason plunged the cardiac needle into Cedric's chest, piercing the heart's pericardial covering. When he drew back on the plunger, the syringe filled with blood. There was no doubt. Cedric's heart had burst open inside his chest.

"Let's get him to surgery," Jason shouted, grabbing the end of the bed. Philip rolled his eyes at Judith Reinhart, the coronary care head nurse. They both knew it was futile. At best they might get Cedric on the heart-lung machine, but what then?

Philip stopped ventilating the patient. But instead of helping to push the bed, he walked over to Jason and gently put an arm on his shoulder, restraining him. "It's got to be cardiac rupture. You know it. I know it. We've lost this one, Jason."

Jason made a motion to protest, but Philip tightened his hold. Jason glanced at Cedric's ivory-colored face. He knew Philip was right. As much as he hated to admit it, the patient was lost.

"You're right," he said, and reluctantly let Philip and Judith lead him from the unit, leaving the other nurses to prepare the body.

As they walked over to the central desk, Jason admitted that Cedric was the third patient to die just weeks after having a clean physical. The first had been another heart attack, the other a massive stroke. "Maybe I should think about changing professions," Jason said half seriously. "Even my inpatients have been doing poorly."

"Just bad luck," Philip said, giving Jason a playful poke in the shoulder. "We all have our bad times. It'll get better."

"Yeah, sure," Jason said.

Philip left to return to surgery.

Jason found an empty chair and sat down heavily. He knew he'd have to get ready to face Cedric's wife, who would be arriving at the hospital at any moment. He felt drained. "You'd think by now I'd have gotten a little more accustomed to death," he said aloud.

"The fact that you don't is what makes you a good doctor," said Judith, attending to the paperwork associated with a death.

Jason accepted the compliment, but he knew his attitude toward death went far beyond the profession. Just two years ago death had destroyed all that Jason held dear. He could still remember the sound of the phone at quarter past midnight on a dark November night. He'd fallen asleep in the den trying to catch up on his journals. He thought it would be his wife, Danielle, calling from Children's Hospital, saying she'd be delayed. She was a pediatrician and had been called back to the hospital that evening to attend to a preemie in respiratory distress. But it had been the turnpike police. They called to say that a semi coming from Albany with a load of aluminum siding had jumped the central divider and rammed into his wife's car head-on. She had never had a chance.

Jason could still remember the trooper's voice, as if it had been yesterday. First there'd been shock and disbelief, followed by anger. Then his own terrible guilt. If only he'd gone with Danielle as he sometimes had, and read at Countway Medical Library. Or if only he'd insisted she sleep at the hospital.

A few months later he'd sold the house that was haunted by Danielle's presence and his private practice and the office he'd shared with her. That was when he had joined the Good Health Plan. He'd done everything Patrick Quillan, a psychiatrist friend, had suggested he do. But the pain was still there, and the anger, too.

"Excuse me, Dr. Howard?"

Jason looked up into the broad face of Kay Ramn, the unit secretary.

"Mrs. Harring is in the waiting room," Kay said. "I told her you'd be out to talk with her."

"Oh, God," Jason said, rubbing his eyes. Speaking to the relatives after a patient died was difficult for any doctor, but since Danielle's death, Jason felt the families' pain as if it were his own.

Across from the coronary care unit was a small sitting room with outdated magazines, vinyl chairs and plastic plants. Mrs. Harring was staring out the window that faced north toward Fenway Park and the Charles River. She was a slight woman with hair that had been allowed to go naturally gray. When Jason entered, she turned and looked at him with red-rimmed, terrified eyes.

"I'm Dr. Howard," Jason said, motioning for her to sit. She did, but on the very edge of the chair.

"So it is bad . . ." she began. Her voice trailed off.

"I'm afraid it is very bad," Jason said. "Mr. Harring has passed away. We did all we could. At least he didn't suffer." Jason hated himself for voicing those expected lies. He knew Cedric had suffered.

He'd seen the mortal fear in his face. Death was always a struggle, rarely the peaceful ebbing of life portrayed in film.

The color drained from Mrs. Harring's face, and for a moment Jason thought she would faint. Finally, she said, "I can't believe it."

Jason nodded. "I know." And know he did.

"It's not right," she said. She looked at Jason defiantly, her face reddening. "I mean, you just gave him a clean bill of health. You gave him all those tests and they were normal! Why didn't you find something? *You might have prevented this.*"

Jason recognized the anger, the familiar precursor to grief. He felt great compassion for her. "I didn't exactly give him a clean bill of health," he said gently. "His lab studies were satisfactory, but I warned him as I always did about his smoking and diet. And I reminded him that his father had died of a heart attack. All these factors put him in a high-risk category despite his lab values."

"But his father was seventy-four when he died. Cedric is only fifty-six! What's the point of a physical if my husband dies just three weeks later?"

"I'm sorry," Jason said softly. "Our predictive abilities are limited. We know that. We can only do the best we can."

Mrs. Harring sighed, letting her breath out. Her narrow shoulders sagged forward. Jason could see the anger fading. In its place came the crushing sadness. When she spoke, her voice was shaking. "I know you do the best you can. I'm sorry."

Jason leaned forward and put his hand on her shoulder. She felt delicate under her thin silk dress. "I know how hard this is for you."

"Can I see him?" she asked through her tears.

"Of course." Jason got to his feet and offered her a hand.

"Did you know Cedric had made an appointment to see you?" Mrs. Harring said as they walked into the corridor. She wiped her eyes with a tissue she'd taken from her purse.

"No, I didn't," Jason admitted.

"Next week. It was the first available appointment. He wasn't feeling well."

Jason felt the uncomfortable stirring of defensive concern. Although he was certain no malpractice had been committed, that was no guarantee against a suit.

"Did he complain of chest pain when he called?" Jason asked. He stopped Mrs. Harring in front of the CCU door.

257

"No, no. Just a lot of unrelated symptoms. Mostly exhaustion."
Jason breathed a sigh of relief.

"His joints ached," Mrs. Harring continued. "And his eyes were bothering him. He was having trouble driving at night."

Trouble driving at night? Although such a symptom did not relate to a heart attack, it rang some kind of a bell in Jason's mind.

"And his skin got very dry. And he had lost a great deal of hair—"

"Hair naturally replaces itself," Jason said mechanically. It was obvious that this litany of nonspecific complaints had nothing to do with the man's massive heart attack. He pushed open the heavy door to the unit and motioned Mrs. Harring to follow him. He guided her into the appropriate cubicle.

Cedric had been covered with a clean white sheet. Mrs. Harring put her thin, bony hand on her husband's head.

"Would you like to see his face?" Jason asked.

Mrs. Harring nodded, tears reappearing and streaming down her face. Jason folded back the sheet and stepped back.

"Oh, God!" she cried. "He looks like his father did before he died!" She turned away and murmured, "I didn't realize how death aged a person."

It doesn't usually, Jason thought. Now that he wasn't concentrating on Cedric's heart, he noticed the changes in his face. His hair had thinned. And his eyes appeared to have receded deep into their orbits, giving the dead man's face a hollow, gaunt look, a far cry from the appearance Jason remembered when he'd done Cedric's physical three weeks earlier. Jason replaced the sheet and led Mrs. Harring back to the small sitting room. He sat her back down and took a seat across from her.

"I know it's not a good time to bring this up," he said, "but we would like permission to examine your husband's body. Maybe we can learn something that will help someone in the future."

"I suppose if it could help others . . ." Mrs. Harring bit her lip. It was hard for her to think, much less make a decision.

"It will. And we really appreciate your generosity. If you'd just wait here, I'll have someone bring out the forms."

"All right," Mrs. Harring said, with resignation.

"I'm sorry," Jason told her again. "Please call me if there is anything I can do."

Jason found Judith and told her that Mrs. Harring had agreed to an autopsy.

"We called the medical examiner's office and spoke to a Dr. Danforth. She said they want the case," Judith told him.

"Well, make sure they send us all the results." Jason hesitated. "Did you notice anything odd about Mr. Harring? I mean, did he appear unusually old for a man of fifty-six?"

"I didn't notice," Judith said, hurrying away. In a unit with eleven patients, she was already involved in another crisis.

Jason knew that Cedric's emergency was putting him behind schedule, but Cedric's unexpected death continued to disturb him. Making up his mind, he called Dr. Danforth, who had a deep resonant voice, and convinced her to let the postmortem be done in house, saying death was due to a long family history of heart disease and that he wanted to compare the heart pathology with the stress EKGs that had been done. The medical examiner graciously released the case.

Before leaving the unit, Jason used the opportunity to check another of his patients who was not doing well.

Sixty-one-year-old Brian Lennox was another heart attack victim. He had been admitted three days previously, and although he'd done well initially, his course had taken a sudden turn for the worse. That morning when Jason had made rounds he had planned to move Lennox from CCU, but the man was in the early throes of congestive heart failure. It was an acute disappointment for Jason, since Brian Lennox had to be added to the list of Jason's inpatients who had recently gone sour. Instead of transferring the patient, Jason had instituted aggressive treatment for the heart failure.

Any hope of a rapid return by Mr. Lennox to his previous state was dashed when Jason saw him. He was sitting up, breathing rapidly and shallowly in an oxygen mask. His face had an evil grayness that Jason had learned to fear. A nurse attending him straightened up from adjusting the IV.

"How are things going?" Jason asked, forcing a smile. But he didn't have to ask. Lennox lifted a limp hand. He couldn't talk. All his attention was directed toward his breathing efforts.

The nurse pulled Jason from the cubicle into the center of the room. Her name tag said Miss Levay, RN. "Nothing seems to be working," she said, concernedly. "The pulmonary wedge pressure has gone up despite everything. He's had the diuretic, the hydralazine and the nitroprusside. I don't know what to do."

Jason glanced over Miss Levay's shoulder into the room. Mr. Lennox was breathing like a miniature locomotive. Jason didn't have any ideas save for a transplant, and of course, that was out of the question. The man was a heavy smoker and undoubtedly had emphysema as well as heart trouble. But Mr. Lennox should have responded to the medication. The only thing Jason could imagine was the area of the heart involved with the heart attack was extending.

"Let's get a cardiology consult stat," Jason said. "Maybe they'll be able to see if the coronary vessels are more involved. It's the only thing I can think of. Maybe he's a candidate for bypass."

"Well at least it's something," said Miss Levay. Without hesitation, she went to the central desk to call.

Jason returned to the cubicle to dispense some compassion to Brian Lennox. He wished he had more to give but the diuretic was supposed to reduce fluid while the hydralazine and nitroprusside were supposed to reduce pre-load and after-load on the heart. All of this was geared to lower the effort the heart had to expend to pump the blood. This would allow the heart to heal after the insult of the heart attack. But it wasn't working. Lennox was slipping downhill despite all the efforts and all the technology. His eyes now had a sunken, glazed appearance.

Jason put his hand on Brian's forehead and pushed the hair back from his perspiring brow. To Jason's surprise, some of the hair came out in his hand. Momentarily confused, Jason stared at it, then he carefully pulled on a few other strands. They came out as well with almost no resistance. Checking the pillow behind Brian's head, Jason noticed more hair. Not an enormous amount but more than he would suspect. It made him wonder if any of the medications he'd ordered had hair loss as a potential side effect. He made a mental note to look that up in the evening. Obviously hair loss was not a major concern at the time. But it reminded him of Mrs. Harring's comment. Curious!

After leaving word that he should be called after the cardiology consult on Brian Lennox and after one more masochistic glance at the sheet-wrapped corpse of Cedric Harring, Jason left the coronary care unit and took the elevator down to the second floor, which connected the hospital with the outpatient building. The GHP Medical Center was the impressive central facility of the large prepaid health plan. It incorporated a four-hundred-bed hospital with an ambulatory surgery center, separate outpatient department, a small research wing, and a floor of administrative offices. The main building, originally designed as a Sears office building, had an art deco flair. It had been gutted and totally renovated to incorporate the hospital and the administrative offices. The outpatient and research building was new, but it had been built to match the old structure, with the same careful details. It was built on pillars over a parking lot. Jason's office was on the third floor, along with the rest of the department of internal medicine.

There were sixteen internists at the GHP Center. Most were specialists, though a few like Jason maintained a generalized practice. Jason had always felt that the whole panoply of human illness interested him, not just specific organs or systems.

The doctors' offices were spread around the perimeter, with a central desk surrounded by a waiting area with comfortable seating. Examining rooms were clustered between the offices. At one end were small treatment rooms. There was a pool of support personnel who were supposed to rotate positions, but in actual fact the nurses and secretaries tended to work for one or another of the doctors. Such a situation promoted efficiency since there could be some adaptation to each doctor's eccentricities. A nurse by the name of Sally Baunan and a secretary by the name of Claudia Mockelberg had aligned themselves with Jason. He got along well with both women, but particularly Claudia, who took an almost motherly interest in Jason's well-being. She had lost her only son in Vietnam and contended that Jason looked just like him despite the age difference.

Both women saw Jason coming and followed him to his office. Sally had an armload of charts of waiting patients. She was the compulsive one, and Jason's absence had disturbed her carefully planned routine. She was eager to "get the show on the road," but Claudia restrained her and sent her out of the room.

"Was it as bad as you look?" Claudia asked.

"Is it that obvious?" Jason said as he washed his hands at the sink in the corner of the room.

She nodded. "You look like you've been run over by an emotional train."

"Cedric Harring died," he said. "Do you remember him?"

"Vaguely," Claudia admitted. "After you got called to the emergency room, I pulled his chart. It's on your desk."

Jason glanced down and saw it. Claudia's efficiency was sometimes unnerving.

"Why don't you sit down for a few moments," Claudia suggested. More than anyone else at GHP, Claudia knew Jason's reaction to death.

She was one of only two people at the Center in whom Jason had confided about his wife's fatal accident.

"We must be really behind schedule," Jason said. "Sally will get her nose bent out of shape."

"Oh, screw Sally." Claudia came around Jason's desk and pushed him gently into the seat. "Sally can hold her water for a few minutes."

Jason smiled in spite of himself. Leaning forward, he fingered Cedric Harring's chart. "Do you remember last month the two others who died just after their physicals?"

"Briggs and Connoly," Claudia said without hesitation.

"How about pulling their charts? I don't like this trend."

"Only if you promise me you're not going to let yourself"—Claudia paused, struggling for a word—"get into a dither over this. People die. Unfortunately it happens. It's the nature of the business. You understand? Why don't you just have a cup of coffee."

"The charts," Jason repeated.

"Okay, okay," Claudia said, going out.

Jason opened Cedric Harring's chart, glancing through the history and physical. Except for his unhealthy living habits, there was nothing remarkable. Turning to the EKG and the stress EKG, Jason scanned the tracing, looking for some sign of the impending disaster. Even armed as he was with hindsight, he could find nothing.

Claudia came back and opened the door without knocking. Jason could hear Sally whine, "Claudia . . ." but Claudia shut the door on her and came over to Jason's desk. She plopped down Briggs's and Connoly's charts in front of him.

"The natives are getting restless," she said, then left.

Jason opened the two charts. Briggs had died of a massive heart attack probably similar to Harring's. Autopsy had shown extensive occlusion of all of the coronary vessels despite the EKG done during his physical four weeks prior to his death being as normal-looking as Harring's. Also like Harring's, his stress EKG had been normal. Jason shook his head in dismay. Even more than the normal EKG, the stress EKG was supposed to pick up such potentially fatal conditions. It certainly suggested that the executive physical was an exercise in futility. Not only was the examination failing to pick up these serious problems, but it was giving the patients a false sense of security. With the results being normal, there wasn't motivation for the patients to change their unhealthy lifestyles. Briggs, like Harring, had been in his late fifties, was a heavy smoker, and never exercised.

The second patient, Rupert Connoly, had died of a massive stroke. Again, it had been a short time after an executive-style physical, which in his case had also revealed no alarming abnormalities. In addition to a generally unhealthy lifestyle, Connoly had been a heavy drinker, though not an alcoholic. Jason was about to close the chart when he noticed something he had missed before. In the autopsy report the pathologist had recorded significant cataract development. Thinking that he'd not remembered the man's age correctly, Jason flipped to the information page. Connoly was only fifty-eight. Now cataracts were not entirely unknown at fifty-eight, but it was nonetheless rare. Turning to the physical, Jason checked to see if he'd noted cataracts. Embarrassingly he'd failed to include them, noting he described the "eyes, ears, nose, and throat" as being within normal limits. Jason wondered if he were getting sloppy in his "old" age. But then he noticed he described the retinas as appearing normal as well. In order to have visualized the retinas, Jason would have had to have sighted through a cataract. Not being an ophthalmologist, he knew his limitations in this regard. He wondered if certain kinds of cataracts impede the passage of light more than others. He added that question to his mental list of things to investigate.

Jason stacked the charts. Three apparently healthy men had all died a month after their physicals. *Jesus*, he thought. People were often scared of going to hospitals. If this got out, they might stop getting checkups.

Grabbing all three charts in his arms, Jason emerged from his office. He saw Sally stand up in the central desk area and look at him expectantly. Jason silently mouthed "two minutes" as he walked the length of the waiting area. He passed several patients whom he treated with nods and smiles. He slipped into the hall leading to Roger Wanamaker's office. Roger was an internist who specialized in cardiology and whose opinion Jason held in high esteem. He found the man leaving one of the examination rooms. He was an obese man with a face like an old hound dog with wattles and lots of extra skin.

"How about a sidewalk consult?" Jason asked.

"It'll cost ya," Roger teased. "Whatcha got?"

Jason followed the man into his disheveled office.

"Unfortunately, some pretty embarrassing evidence." Jason opened the charts of his three late patients to the EKG sections and placed them in front of Roger. "I'm ashamed to even discuss this, but I've had three middle-aged men die right after their fancy executive physicals showed them in pretty good health. One was today. Cardiac rupture after a massive MI. I did the physical exam three weeks ago. This is the one. Even knowing what I do now, I can't find even a bit of trouble or any of the tracings. What do you think?''

There was a moment of silence while Roger studied the EKGs. ''Welcome to the club,'' he finally said.

''Club?''

''These EKGs are fine,'' Roger said. ''All of us have had the same experience. I've had four such cases over the last few months. Just about everybody who's willing to bring it up has had at least one or two.''

''How come it's not come up?''

''You tell me,'' Roger said, with a wry smile. ''You haven't exactly been advertising your experience, have you? It's dirty laundry. We'd all rather not call attention to it. But you're acting chief of service. Why don't you call a meeting?''

Jason nodded glumly. Under the aegis of the GHP administration, which made all of the major organizational decisions, chief of service was not a desirable position. It was rotated on a yearly basis among all the internists, and had fallen onto Jason's shoulders two months previously.

''I guess I should,'' Jason said, collecting his charts from Roger's desk. ''If nothing else, the other doctors should know they're not alone if they've had the same experience.''

''Sounds good,'' Roger agreed. He heaved his considerable bulk to his feet. ''But don't expect everybody to be quite as open as you are.''

Jason headed back to the central desk, motioning to Sally to ready the next patient. Sally took off like a sprinter. He then turned to Claudia.

''Claudia, I need a favor. I want you to make a list of all the annual physicals I've done over the last year, pull their charts, and check on their state of health. I want to be sure none of the others have had serious medical problems. Apparently some of the other doctors have been having similar episodes. I think it's something we should look into.''

''It's going to be a big list,'' Claudia warned.

Jason was aware of that. In its desire to promote what it called preventive medicine, GHP had been strongly advocating such physicals and had streamlined the process to take care of the maximum number of people. Jason knew that he did, on the average, between five and ten a week.

For the next several hours, Jason devoted himself to his patients, who treated him to an endless stream of problems and complaints. Sally was relentless, filling examining rooms the moment the previous patient vacated. By skipping lunch, Jason was actually able to catch up.

In the middle of the afternoon, as Jason was returning from one of the treatment rooms where he had done a sigmoidoscopy on a patient with recurrent ulcerative colitis, Claudia caught his attention and motioned for him to come over to the central desk. She was sporting a cocky smile as Jason approached. He knew something was brewing.

"You have an honored visitor," Claudia said with pursed lips, imitating a Lily Tomlin character.

"Who?" Jason asked, reflexively scanning the adjacent waiting room area.

"He's in your office," Claudia said.

Jason shifted his eyes toward his office. The door was closed. It wasn't like Claudia to put someone in there. He looked back at his secretary. "Claudia?" he questioned, extending her name out as if it were more than three syllables. "How come you allowed someone in my office?"

"He insisted," said Claudia, "and who am I to refuse?"

Obviously whoever it was had offended her. Jason knew her that well. And whoever it was certainly had some kind of stature at GHP. But Jason was tiring of the game. "Are you going to tell me who it is or am I supposed to be surprised?"

"Dr. Alvin Hayes," Claudia said. She batted her eyes and made a sneer. Agnes, the secretary who worked for Roger, snickered.

Jason waved at them in disgust and headed for his office. A visit by Dr. Alvin Hayes was a unique occurrence. He was the GHP token and star researcher, hired by the Plan to promote its image. It had been a move reminiscent of the Humana Corporation's hiring Dr. William DeVries, the surgeon of artificial-heart fame. GHP, as a health-maintenance organization (HMO), did not support research per se, yet it had hired Hayes at a prodigious salary in order to expand and augment its image, especially in the Boston academic community. After all, Dr. Alvin Hayes was a world-class molecular biologist who had been on the cover of *Time* magazine after having developed a method of making

ROBIN COOK

human growth hormone from recombinant DNA technology. The growth hormone he had made was exactly like the human variety. Earlier attempts had resulted in a hormone that was similar but not exactly the same. It had been considered an important breakthrough.

Jason reached his office and opened the door. He could not fathom why Hayes would be paying him a visit. Hayes had all but ignored Jason from the day he had been hired over a year previously, despite the fact they'd been in the same Harvard Medical School class. After graduation they had gone their separate ways, but when Alvin Hayes had been hired by GHP, Jason had sought the man out and personally welcomed him. Hayes had been distant, obviously impressed by his own celebrity status and openly contemptuous of Jason's decision to stay in clinical medicine. Except for a few chance meetings, they ignored each other. In fact, Hayes ignored everyone at the GHP, becoming more and more what people referred to as the mad scientist. He'd even gone to the extreme of letting his personal appearance suffer by wearing baggy, unpressed clothes and allowing his unkempt hair to grow long like a throwback to the turbulent sixties. Although people gossiped, and he had few friends, everyone respected him. Hayes worked long hours and produced an unbelievable number of papers and scientific articles.

Alvin Hayes was sprawled in one of the chairs facing Jason's antique desk. About Jason's height, with pudgy, boyish features, Hayes's unkempt hair hung about his face, which appeared more sallow than ever. He'd always had that peculiar academic pallor that characterizes scientists who spend all their time in their laboratories. But Jason's clinical eye noted an increased yellowishness as well as a laxness that made Hayes look ill and overly exhausted. Jason wondered if this was a professional visit.

"Sorry to bother you," Hayes said, struggling to his feet. "I know you must be busy."

"Not at all," Jason lied, skirting his desk and sitting down. He removed the stethoscope draped around his neck. "What can we do for you?" Hayes appeared nervous and fatigued, as if he hadn't slept for several days.

"I have to talk to you," he said, lowering his voice and leaning forward in a conspiratorial fashion.

Jason flinched back. Hayes's breath was fetid and his eyes had a glassy, unfocused look that gave him a slightly crazed appearance. His

266

white laboratory coat was wrinkled and stained. Both sleeves were pushed up above his elbows. His watch fitted so loosely that Jason wondered how he kept from losing it.

"What's on your mind?"

Hayes leaned farther forward, knuckles resting on Jason's blotter. He whispered, "Not here. I want to talk with you tonight. Outside of GHP."

There was a moment of strained silence. Hayes's behavior was obviously abnormal, and Jason wondered if he should try to get the man to talk to his friend Patrick Quillan, thinking a psychiatrist might have more to offer him. If Hayes wanted to talk away from the hospital, it couldn't be about his health.

"It's important," Hayes added, striking Jason's desk impatiently.

"All right," Jason said quickly, afraid Hayes might throw a tantrum if he hesitated any longer. "How about dinner?" He wanted to meet the man in a public place.

"All right. Where?"

"Doesn't matter." Jason shrugged. "How about the North End for some Italian food?"

"Fine. When and where?"

Jason ran down the list of restaurants he knew in the North End section of Boston, a warren of crooked streets that made you feel you'd been mystically transplanted to southern Italy. "How about Carbonara?" he suggested. "It's on Rachel Revere Square, across from Paul Revere House."

"I know it," Hayes said. "What time?"

"Eight?"

"That's fine." Hayes turned and walked somewhat unsteadily toward the door. "And don't invite anyone else. I want to talk with you alone." Without waiting for a reply, he left, pulling the door shut behind him.

Jason shook his head in amazement and went back to his patients.

Within a few minutes, he was again absorbed in his work, and the bizarre episode with Hayes slipped into his unconscious. The afternoon drifted on without unwelcome surprises. At least Jason's outpatients seemed to be doing well and responding to the various regimens he'd ordered. That gave a needed boost to his confidence that the Harring affair had undermined. With only two more patients to be seen, Jason crossed the waiting room after having done a minor surgical procedure in one of the treatment rooms. Just before he disappeared into his office to dictate the procedure, he caught sight of Shirley Montgomery leaning on the central desk and chatting with the secretaries. Within the clinical environment, Shirley stood out like Cinderella at the ball. In contrast to the other women, who were dressed in white skirts and blouses or white pants suits, Shirley wore a conservative silk dress that tried but failed to hide her attractive figure. Although few people could guess when seeing her, Shirley was the chief executive officer of the entire Good Health Plan organization. She was as attractive as any model, and she had a PhD in hospital administration from Columbia and a master's degree from the Harvard Business School.

With her physical and mental attributes, Shirley could have been intimidating, but she wasn't. She was outgoing and sensitive and as a result she got along with everyone: maintenance people, secretaries, nurses, and even the surgeons. Shirley Montgomery could take personal credit for providing a good portion of the glue that held GHP together and made it work so smoothly.

When she spotted Jason, she excused herself from the secretaries. She moved toward him with the ease and grace of a dancer. Her thick brown hair was swept back from her forehead and layered along the side into a heavy mane. Her makeup was applied so expertly that she didn't seem to be wearing any. Her large blue eyes shone with intelligence.

"Excuse me, Dr. Howard," she said formally. At the very corners of her mouth there was the faint hint of a smile. Unknown to the staff, Shirley and Jason had been seeing each other on a social basis for several months. It had started during one of the semiannual staff meetings when they had met each other over cocktails. When Jason learned that her husband had recently died of cancer, he felt an immediate bond.

During the dinner that followed, she told Jason that one morning three years ago her husband had awakened with a severe headache. Within months he was dead from a brain tumor that had been unresponsive to any treatment. At the time they had both been working at the Humana Hospital Corporation. Afterward, like Jason, she had felt compelled to move and had come to Boston. When she told Jason the story, it had affected him so deeply that he'd broken his own wall of silence. That same evening he shared his own anguish concerning his wife's accident and death.

Fueled by this extraordinary commonality of emotional experience, Jason and Shirley began a relationship that hovered somewhere between friendship and romance. Each knew the other was too emotionally raw to move too quickly.

Jason was perplexed. She had never sought him out in such a fashion. As usual, he had only the vaguest notion of what was going on inside her expansive mind. In so many ways she was the most complicated woman he'd ever met. "Can I be of assistance?" he asked, watching for some hint of her intent.

"I know you must be busy," she was saying now, "but I was wondering if you were free tonight." She lowered her voice, turning her back on Claudia's unwavering stare. "I'm having an impromptu dinner party tonight with several Harvard Business School acquaintances. I'd like you to join us. How about it?"

Jason immediately regretted having made plans to eat with Alvin Hayes. If only he'd agreed to see the man for drinks.

"I know it's short notice," Shirley added, sensing Jason's hesitation.

"That's not the problem. The trouble is that I promised to have dinner with Alvin Hayes."

"Our Dr. Hayes?" Shirley said with obvious surprise.

"None other. I know it sounds peculiar, but he seemed almost distraught. And though he's hardly been friendly, I felt sorry for the man. Dinner was my suggestion."

"Damn!" Shirley said. "You'd have enjoyed this group. Well, next time . . ."

"I'll take a rain check," Jason said. She was about to leave when he remembered his conversation with Roger Wanamaker. "I probably should tell you I'm going to call a staff meeting. A number of patients have died of coronary disease which our physicals have missed. As acting chief of service I thought I should look into it. Dropping dead within a month of receiving a clean bill of health from us doesn't make for good PR."

"Dear God," Shirley said. "Don't go spreading rumors like that!"

"Well, it's a bit unnerving when someone you've examined with all your resources and declared essentially healthy comes back to the hospital with a catastrophic condition and dies. Avoiding such an event is the whole purpose of the executive physical. I think we should try to increase the sensitivity of our stress testing."

"An admirable goal," Shirley agreed. "All I ask is that you keep it low key. Our executive physicals play a major role in our campaign to lure some of the larger corporate clients in the area. Let's keep this an in-house issue."

"Absolutely," said Jason. "Sorry about tonight."

"Me too," Shirley said, lowering her voice. "I didn't think Dr. Hayes socialized much. What's up with him?"

"It's a mystery to me," Jason admitted, "but I'll let you know."

"Please," Shirley said. "I'm one of the main reasons GHP hired the man. I feel responsible. Talk to you soon." She moved off, smiling to nearby patients.

Jason watched her for a moment, then caught Claudia's stare. She guiltily looked down at her work. Jason wondered if the secret was out. With a shrug he went back to his last two patients.

2

Late fall in Boston was an exhilarating season for Jason despite the bleak winter it heralded. Dressed in his Indiana Jones–style fedora and his "lived-in" Burberry trench coat, he was adequately protected from the chilly October night.

Gusts of wind blew the yellowed remains of the elm leaves around Jason's feet as he trudged up Mt. Vernon Street and passed through the columned passageway under the State House. Crossing the Government Center promenade, he skirted the Faneuil Hall Marketplace with its street performers and entered the North End, Boston's Little Italy. People were everywhere: men standing on street corners and talking with animated gestures; women leaning out the windows gossiping with their friends on the opposite side of the street. The air was filled with the smell of ground coffee and almond-flavored baked goods. Like Italy itself, the neighborhood was a delight to the senses.

Two blocks down Hanover Street, Jason turned right and quickly found himself in sight of Paul Revere's modest wood clapboard house. The cobblestoned square was defined by a heavy black nautical chain looped between metal stanchions. Directly across from Paul Revere's house was Carbonara, one of Jason's favorite restaurants. There were two other restaurants in the square but neither was as good as the Carbonara. He mounted the front steps and was greeted by the maître d', who led him to his table by the front window, affording him a view of the quaint square. Like many Boston locations the scene had an unreal quality, as though it were the set for some theme park.

271

ROBIN COOK

Jason ordered a bottle of Gavi white wine and munched on a dish of antipasto while waiting for Hayes to appear. Within ten minutes, a cab pulled up and Hayes got out. For a few moments after the cab had left, he just stood on the sidewalk and peered back up North Street from the direction he had come. Jason watched, wondering what the man was waiting for. Eventually, he turned and entered the restaurant.

As the maître d' escorted him to the table, Jason noted how out of place Hayes seemed in the elegant decor and among the fashionably dressed diners. In place of his stained lab coat, Hayes was wearing a baggy tweed jacket with a torn elbow patch. He seemed to be having trouble walking, and Jason wondered if the man had been drinking.

Without acknowledging Jason's presence, Hayes threw himself into the empty seat and stared out the window, again looking up North Street. A couple had appeared, strolling arm in arm. Hayes watched them until they disappeared from view down Prince Street. His eyes still appeared glassy, and Jason noted that a web of new, red capillaries had spread out over his nose like a sea fan. His skin was pale as ivory, not too dissimilar to Harring's when Jason had seen him in the CCU. It seemed certain that Hayes was not well.

Fumbling in one of the bulging pockets of his tweed jacket, Hayes brought out a crumpled pack of unfiltered Camels. He lit one with trembling hands and said, his eyes glittering with some strong emotion, "Someone is following me."

Jason wasn't sure how to react. "Are you sure?"

"No doubt," Hayes said, taking a long drag on his cigarette. A smoldering ash fell onto the white tablecloth. "A dark guy, smooth—a sharp dresser, a foreigner," he added with venom.

"Does that make you concerned?" Jason asked, trying to play psychiatrist. Apparently, on top of everything else, Hayes was acutely paranoid.

"Christ, yes!" Hayes shouted. A few heads turned and Hayes lowered his voice. "Wouldn't you be upset if someone wanted to kill you?"

"Kill you?" Jason echoed, now sure Hayes had gone mad.

"Absolutely positive. And my son, too."

"I didn't know you had a son," Jason said. In fact, he hadn't even been aware Hayes was married. It was rumored in the hospital that Hayes frequented the disco scene on the rare occasions he wanted distraction.

Hayes mashed out his cigarette in the ashtray, cursed under his breath, and lit another, blowing the smoke away in short, nervous puffs. Jason realized that Hayes was at the breaking point and he'd have to tread carefully. The man was about to decompensate.

"I'm sorry if I sound dumb," Jason said, "but I would like to help. I presume that's why you wanted to talk to me. And frankly, Alvin, you don't look too well."

Hayes leaned the back of his right wrist on his forehead, his elbow on the table. His lit cigarette was dangerously close to his disheveled hair. Jason was tempted to move either the hair or the cigarette; he didn't want the man lighting himself like a pyre. But fearful of Hayes's distraught state, he did neither.

"Would you gentlemen like to order?" asked a waiter, silently materializing at the table.

"For Christ's sake!" Hayes snarled, his head popping up. "Can't you see we're talking?"

"Excuse me, sir," the waiter said, bowing and moving off.

After taking a deep breath, Hayes returned his attention to Jason. "So I don't look well?"

"No. Your color isn't good, and you seem exhausted as well as upset."

"Ah, the clairvoyant clinician," Hayes said sarcastically. Then he added, "I'm sorry—I don't mean to be nasty. You're right. I'm not feeling well. In fact, I'm feeling terrible."

"What's the problem?"

"Just about everything. Arthritis, GI upset, blurred vision. Even dry skin. My ankles itch so much they're driving me insane. My body is literally falling apart."

"Perhaps it would have been better to meet in my office," Jason said. "Maybe we should check you out."

"Maybe later—but that's not why I wanted to see you. It may be too late for me, anyway, but if I could save my son . . ." He broke off, pointing out the window. *"There he is!"*

Twisting in his seat, Jason barely caught sight of a figure disappearing up North Street. Turning back to Hayes, Jason asked, "How could you tell it was him?"

"He's been following me from the moment I left GHP. I think he plans on killing me."

With no way to tell fact from delusion, Jason studied his colleague.

273

The man was acting weird, to put it mildly, but the old cliché "even paranoids have enemies" echoed in his brain. Maybe someone was in fact following Hayes. Fishing the chilled bottle of Gavi from the ice bucket, Jason poured Hayes a glass and filled his own. "Maybe you'd better tell me what this is all about."

Tossing back the wine as if it were a shot of aquavit, Hayes wiped his mouth with the back of his hand. "It's such a bizarre story. . . . How about a little more of the wine?"

Jason refilled the glass as Hayes continued. "I don't suppose you know too much of what my research interests are. . . ."

"I have some idea."

"Growth and development," Hayes said. "How genes turn on and off. Like puberty; what turns on the appropriate genes. Solving the problem would be a major achievement. Not only could we potentially influence growth and development, but we'd probably be able to 'turn off' cancers, or, after heart attacks, 'turn on' cellular division to create new cardiac muscle. Anyway, in simplified terms, the turning on and off of growth and development genes has been my major interest. But like so often in research, serendipity played a role. About four months ago, in the process of my research I stumbled onto an unexpected discovery, ironic but astounding. I'm talking about a major scientific breakthrough. Believe me: it is Nobel material."

Jason was willing to suspend disbelief, although he wondered if Hayes was exhibiting symptoms of a delusion of grandeur to go along with his paranoia.

"What was your discovery?"

"Just a moment," Hayes said. He put his cigarette in the ashtray and pressed his right hand against his chest.

"Are you all right?" Jason asked. Hayes appeared to have become a shade grayer, and a line of perspiration had formed at his hairline.

"I'm okay," Hayes assured him. He let his hand drop to the table. "I didn't report this discovery because I realized it was the first step toward an even bigger breakthrough. I'm talking about something akin to antibiotics or the helical structure of DNA. I've been so excited I've been working around the clock. But then I found out my original discovery was no longer a secret. That it was being used. When I suspected this, I . . ." Hayes stopped in midsentence. He stared at Jason with an expression that started out as confusion but rapidly changed to fear.

"Alvin, what's the matter?" Jason asked. Hayes didn't reply. His right hand again pressed against his chest. A moan escaped from his lips, then both hands shot out and gripped the tablecloth, clawing it toward him. The wineglasses fell over. He started to get to his feet but he never made it. With a violent choking cough, he spewed a stream of blood across the table, drenching the cloth and spraying Jason, who jumped backward, knocking over his chair. The blood didn't stop. It came in successive waves, splattering everything as nearby diners began to scream.

As a physician, Jason knew what was happening. The blood was bright red and was literally being pumped out of Hayes's mouth. That meant it was coming directly from his heart. In the seconds that followed, Hayes remained upright in his chair, confusion and pain replacing the fear in his eyes. Jason skirted the table and grabbed him by the shoulders. Unfortunately there was no way to staunch the flow of blood. Hayes was either going to exsanguinate or drown. There was nothing Jason could do but hold the man as his life flowed out of him.

When Hayes's body went flaccid, Jason let it slump to the floor. Although the human body contains about six quarts of blood, the amount on the table and floor appeared to be considerably more. Jason turned to a neighboring table that had been vacated and took a napkin to wipe his hands.

For the first time since the initial catastrophe, Jason became aware of his surroundings. The other patrons of the restaurant had all leaped from their tables and were crowded at the other end of the room. Unfortunately, several people had gotten sick.

The maître d' himself, with a green complexion, was swaying on his feet. "I've called for an ambulance," he managed to say through a hand clamped over his mouth.

Jason looked down at Hayes. Without an operating room right there, with a heart and lung machine primed and ready to go, there was no chance of saving him. An ambulance at this point was futile. But at least it could take the body away. Glancing again at the still body, Jason decided the man must have had a lung cancer. A tumor could have eroded through his aorta, causing the bleeding. Ironically, Hayes's cigarette was still lit in the ashtray that was now full of frothy blood. A bit of smoke languidly rose to the ceiling.

In the distance Jason heard the undulating sound of an approaching ambulance. But before it arrived, a police cruiser with a flashing blue

light pulled up outside, and two uniformed policemen came bounding
into the dining room. They both pulled up short when confronted by
the bloody scene. The younger one, Peter Carbo, a blond-haired boy
who looked about nineteen, immediately turned green. His partner,
Jeff Mario, quickly sent him to interview the patrons. Jeff Mario was
Jason's age, give or take a couple of years. "What the hell happened?"
he asked, astounded at the amount of blood.

"I'm a physician," Jason offered. "The man is dead. He bled out.
There was nothing that could have been done."

After squatting over Hayes, Jeff Mario gingerly felt for a pulse.
Satisfied, he stood up and directed his attention to Jason. "You a
friend?"

"More a colleague," said Jason. "We both work for Good Health
Plan."

"He a physician also?" Jeff Mario asked, motioning toward Hayes
with his thumb.

Jason nodded.

"Was he sick?"

"I'm not certain," Jason said. "If I had to guess, I'd say cancer.
But I don't know."

Jeff Mario took out a pad and a pencil. He opened the pad. "What's
the man's name?"

"Alvin Hayes."

"Does Mr. Hayes have a family?"

"I guess," Jason said. "To tell you the truth, I don't know too
much about his private life. He mentioned a son, so I presume he has
a family."

"Do you know his home address?"

"I'm afraid not."

Officer Mario regarded Jason for a moment, then reached down and
carefully searched Hayes's pockets, coming up with a billfold. He
went through Hayes's cards.

"The guy doesn't have a driver's license," Jeff Mario said. He
looked at Jason for confirmation.

"I wouldn't know." Jason could feel himself begin to tremble. The
horror of the episode was starting to affect him.

The sound of the ambulance, which had gotten progressively louder,
trailed off outside the window. There was now a red flashing light in
addition to the blue. Within a minute two uniformed emergency techs

came into the room, one carrying a metal case that looked like a tackle box. They went directly over to Hayes.

"This man's a doctor," Jeff Mario said, pointing at Jason with his pencil. "He says it's all over. He says the guy bled out from cancer."

"I'm not sure it was cancer," Jason said. His voice was higher than he intended. He was visibly trembling now, so he clasped his hands together.

The EMTs examined Hayes briefly, then stood up. The one who'd been carrying the case told the other to go down and get the stretcher.

"Okay, here's his address," said Jeff Mario, who had gone back to searching Hayes's wallet. He held up a card. "He lives over near Boston City Hospital." He copied the address down on his note pad. The younger policeman was taking down names and addresses, including Jason's.

When they were ready to leave, Jason asked if he could go along with the body. He felt bad sending Hayes to the morgue all alone. The cops said it was fine with them. As they emerged onto the square, Jason could see that a considerable crowd had formed. News like this traveled around the North End like wildfire, but the crowd was silent, awed by the presence of death.

Jason's eye caught one nattily dressed man who seemed to melt backward into the crowd. He looked like a businessman—more Latin American or Spanish than Italian—particularly his clothing—and for a moment Jason wondered at himself for even noticing.

Then one of the emergency techs said, "Want to ride with your friend?" Jason nodded and climbed into the back of the ambulance. He sat on a low seat across from Hayes, down near his feet. One of the EMTs sat on a similar seat closer to Hayes's head. With a lurch, the ambulance moved. Through the back window Jason saw the restaurant and the crowd recede. As they turned onto Hanover Street, he had to hold on. The siren had not been turned on, but the flashing light was still functioning. Jason could see it reflected in the glass of the store windows.

The trip was short; about five minutes. The EMT tried to make small talk, but Jason made it apparent he was preoccupied. Staring at the covered body of Hayes, Jason attempted to come to terms with the experience. He couldn't help but think that death was stalking him. It made him feel curiously responsible for Hayes, as if the man would still be alive if he'd not had the misfortune of meeting with Jason.

Jason knew such thoughts were ridiculous on a rational level. But feelings didn't always rely on rationality.

After a sharp turn to the left, the ambulance backed up, then stopped. When the rear door was opened, Jason recognized where they were. They'd arrived at the courtyard of the Massachusetts General Hospital. It was a familiar place for Jason. He'd done his internal medicine residency there years ago. Jason climbed out. The two EMTs unloaded Hayes efficiently and the wheels dropped down under the stretcher. Silently, they pushed the body into the emergency room, where a triage nurse directed them to an empty trauma room.

Despite his being a physician, Jason did not know the protocol for handling a situation like Hayes's death. He was a bit surprised they'd even come to an emergency room, since Hayes was beyond care. But thinking about it, he realized Hayes had to be formally pronounced dead. He'd remembered doing it when he'd been a house officer.

The trauma room was set up in the usual fashion, with all sorts of equipment ready for instant use. In a corner was a scrub sink. Jason washed Hayes's blood off his hands. A small mirror over the sink revealed a significant amount of dried blood that had splattered his face as well. After rinsing his face, he dried himself with paper towels. There was blood on his jacket and shirtfront as well as his pants, but there was little he could do about that. As he was finishing washing, a house officer breezed into the room with a clipboard. He unceremoniously yanked back the sheet covering Hayes, then pulled his stethoscope from around his neck. Hayes's face looked eerily pale in the raw fluorescent light.

"You related?" asked the resident casually as he listened to Hayes's chest.

When the resident took the stethoscope from his ears, Jason spoke. "No, I'm a colleague. We worked together at Good Health."

"You an MD?" the resident asked, sounding a degree more deferential.

Jason nodded.

"What happened to your friend?" He shined a penlight into Hayes's eyes.

"He exsanguinated at the dinner table," Jason said, being deliberately blunt, mildly offended at the callous attitude of the resident.

"No kidding. Far out! Well, he sure is dead." He pulled the sheet back over Hayes's head.

It took all of Jason's self-control not to tell the resident what he thought of his insensitivity, but he knew it would be a waste of time. Instead, he wandered out into the hallway and watched the bustle of the emergency room, remembering his own days as a resident. It seemed a long time ago, but nothing had really changed.

Thirty minutes later, Hayes's body was wheeled back out to the ambulance. Jason followed and watched as it was reloaded.

"Do you mind if I still tag along?" he asked, uncertain as to his motives, realizing he was probably acting out of shock.

"We're just going to the morgue," the driver said, "but be my guest."

As they pulled out of the courtyard, Jason was suddenly surprised to see what looked like the same sharply dressed businessman he'd spotted outside the restaurant. Then he shrugged. That would be too much of a coincidence. Odd, though, the man's face had the same Hispanic cast.

Jason had never been to the city morgue. As they wheeled Hayes's body through scarred and battered swinging doors and entered the storage room, he wished he had not come on this occasion. The atmosphere was as unpleasant as his imagination had suggested it would be. The storage room was large and lined on both sides with square, refrigerator-like doors that had once been white. The walls and floor were surfaced with old, stained, and cracked tiles. There were a number of gurneys, some occupied by corpses covered with sheets, a few of which were bloody. The room reeked with an antiseptic, fishy smell that made Jason reluctant to breathe. A heavyset, florid man wearing a rubber apron and gloves came over to Hayes and helped transfer the corpse to one of the morgue's ancient and stained gurneys. Then they all disappeared to attend to the necessary paperwork.

For a few moments Jason stood in the body room and thought about the sudden end to Hayes's distinguished life. Then, pursued by a vivid image of his trip to the hospital after Danielle's death, he walked after the emergency technicians.

At the time the Boston City Morgue had been built a half century ago, it had been considered a state-of-the-art facility. As Jason mounted the wide steps leading up to the offices, he noticed some architectural detail work with ancient Egyptian motifs. But the building had suffered over the years. Now it was dark, dirty, and inadequate. What horrors it had seen was beyond Jason's imagination.

In a shabby office he found the two EMTs and the florid morgue worker. They had finished the paperwork and were laughing about something, completely oblivious to the oppressive atmosphere of death.

Jason interrupted their conversation to ask if any of the medical examiners were there at the moment.

"Yup," said the attendant. "Dr. Danforth's finishing up an emergency case in the autopsy room."

"Is there someplace I can wait for her?" Jason asked. He was in no condition to visit the autopsy room.

"There's a library upstairs," the attendant said. "Right next to Dr. Danforth's office."

The library was a dark, musty place with large bound volumes of autopsy reports that dated back to the eighteenth century. In the center of the room was a large oak table with six captain's chairs. More important, there was a telephone. After some thought, Jason decided to call Shirley. He knew she was in the middle of entertaining, but he thought she would want to know.

"Jason!" she exclaimed. "Are you coming over?"

"Unfortunately, no. There's been some trouble."

"Trouble?"

"This is going to be a shock," Jason warned. "I hope you're sitting down."

"Stop teasing me," Shirley said. The concern in her voice rose a notch.

"Alvin Hayes is dead."

There was a pause. Inappropriate-sounding laughter could be heard in the background.

"What happened?"

"I'm not entirely sure," Jason said, wanting to shield her from the horrible details. "Some kind of internal medical catastrophe."

"Like a heart attack?"

"Something like that," Jason said evasively.

"My God! The poor man."

"Do you know anything about his family? They've asked me, but I don't know anything."

"I don't know much either. He's divorced. He has children, but I believe the wife has custody. She lives somewhere near Manhattan and that's about all I know. The man was very private about his personal life."

280

"I'm sorry to bother you about this now."

"Don't be silly. Where are you?"

"At the morgue."

"How did you get there?"

"I rode in the ambulance with Hayes's body."

"I'll come and pick you up."

"No need," Jason said. "I'll get a cab after I talk to the medical examiner."

"How are you feeling?" Shirley asked. "It must have been an awful experience."

"Well," Jason admitted, "I've been better."

"That settles it. I'm coming to pick you up."

"What about your guests?" Jason protested half-heartedly. He felt guilty ruining her party, but not guilty enough to refuse her offer. He knew he wasn't ready to be alone with tonight's memory.

"They can take care of themselves," Shirley said. "Where are you exactly?"

Jason gave her directions, then hung up. He let his head sink into his hands and closed his eyes.

"Excuse me," said a deep voice softened by a slight brogue. "Are you Dr. Jason Howard?"

"That's correct," Jason said, sitting up with a start.

A heavyset figure advanced into the room. The man had a broad face with lidded eyes, wide nose, and square teeth. His hair was dark with glints of red. "I'm Detective Michael Curran, Homicide." He stuck out a broad, callused hand.

Jason shook it, flustered by the sudden appearance of the plainclothes detective. He realized he was being evaluated as the detective's eyes went from his face to his feet and back again.

"Officer Mario reported that you were with the victim," Detective Curran said, taking a chair.

"Are you investigating Hayes's death?"

"Just routine," Curran said. "Rather a dramatic scene, according to Officer Mario's description. I don't want my detective sergeant on my back if there's any questions later on."

"Oh, I see," Jason said. In truth, Detective Curran's appearance made him remember Hayes's insistence that someone was trying to kill him. Though the man's death seemed a natural disaster rather than murder, Jason realized Hayes's fear in part had motivated Jason to come to the morgue to check the cause of death.

"Anyway," Detective Curran said, "I got to ask the usual questions. In your opinion, was Dr. Hayes's death expected? I mean, was he ill?"

"Not that I know of," Jason said, "though when I saw him this afternoon and then again this evening, I did have the feeling he wasn't well."

Detective Curran's heavy eyelids lifted slightly. "What do you mean?"

"He looked terrible. And when I mentioned the fact to him, he admitted he wasn't feeling well."

"What were the symptoms?" asked the detective. He'd taken out a small pad.

"Fatigue, stomach upset, joint discomfort. I thought he might have had a fever, but I couldn't be sure."

"What did you think about these symptoms?"

"They worried me," Jason admitted. "I told him that it might be better if we met in my office so I could have run a few tests. But he insisted we meet away from the hospital."

"And why was that?"

"I'm not sure." Then Jason went on to describe what was probably Hayes's paranoia and his statements about having made a breakthrough.

After writing all this down, Curran looked up. He seemed more alert. "What do you mean, 'paranoia'?"

"He said that someone was following him and wanted him and his son dead."

"Did he say who?"

"No," Jason said. "To be honest, I thought that he was delusional. He was acting strangely. I thought he was about to decompensate."

"Decompensate?" Curran asked.

"Nervous breakdown," Jason said.

"I see," Curran said, returning to his note pad. Jason watched as he wrote. He had the curious habit of licking the end of his pencil at odd intervals.

At that moment another figure appeared in the doorway. She walked around the table to Jason's right. Both Jason and the detective got to their feet. The newcomer was a diminutive woman barely five feet tall. She introduced herself as Dr. Margaret Danforth. In contrast to her size, her voice resounded in the small room.

"Sit down," she commanded, smiling at Curran, whom she obviously knew.

Jason guessed the woman to be in her upper thirties. She had small, delicate features with highly arched eyebrows that gave her an innocent appeal. Her hair was short and very curly. She wore a dark, demure dress with a lace collar. Jason had trouble associating her appearance with her position as one of the medical examiners of the city of Boston.

"What's the problem?" she asked, getting right to business. There were dark circles under her eyes, and Jason guessed she'd been working since early that morning.

Detective Curran tipped his chair back and teetered. "Sudden death of a physician in a North End restaurant. Apparently he vomited a large amount of blood . . ."

"Coughed up would be a better term," interrupted Jason.

"How so?" Detective Curran asked, coming forward with a thump. He licked the end of his pencil to make a correction.

"Vomiting would mean it came from his digestive system," Jason said. "This blood obviously came from his lungs. It was bright red and frothy."

"Frothy! I like that word," Curran said. He bent over his pad, making a correction.

"I presume it was arterial blood," Dr. Danforth said.

"I believe so," Jason said.

"Which means . . . ?" Curran questioned.

"Probably a rupture of the aorta," Danforth answered. She had her hands folded in her lap as if she were at a tea party. "The aorta is the main vessel that leaves the heart," she added for Curran's benefit. "It carries oxygenated blood out to the body."

"Thank you," Curran said.

"Sounds like either lung cancer or aneurysm," Danforth added. "An aneurysm is an abnormal outpocketing of the blood vessel."

"Thank you again," Curran said. "It's so handy when people know I'm ignorant."

Jason had a momentary flash of Peter Falk playing Detective Columbo. He was quite sure that Curran was anything but ignorant.

"Would you agree, doctor?" Danforth asked, looking directly at Jason.

"I'd vote for lung cancer," Jason said. "Hayes was a prodigious smoker."

"That does raise the probability."

"Any possibility of foul play?" Curran asked, looking at the medical examiner from under his heavy lids.

283

Dr. Danforth gave a short laugh. "If the diagnosis is what I think it is, the only foul play involved would have been perpetrated by his Maker—or the tobacco industry."

"That's what I thought," Curran said, flipping his notebook closed and pocketing his pencil.

"Are you going to do an autopsy now?" Jason asked.

"Heavens no," Dr. Danforth said. "If there were some pressing reason, we could. But there isn't. We'll get to it first thing in the morning. We should have some answers by ten-thirty or so, if you'd like to call about then."

Curran put his hands on the table as if he were about to stand. Instead, he said, "Dr. Howard has alleged that the victim thought someone was trying to kill him. Am I right, doctor?"

Jason nodded.

"So . . ." Curran said. "Could you keep that in mind when you do the autopsy?"

"Absolutely," Dr. Danforth said. "We keep an open mind in all cases we do. That's our job. Now, if you'll excuse me, I'd like to get home. I haven't even had a chance to eat dinner."

Jason felt a mild wave of nausea. He wondered how Margaret Danforth could feel hungry after spending her day cutting up corpses. Curran actually said as much to Jason as they descended to the first floor. He offered Jason a lift, but Jason told him he was expecting a friend. No sooner had he said it than the street door opened and Shirley walked in. "Some friend," Curran whispered with a wink as he left.

Once again Shirley stood out like a mirage. For entertaining she'd dressed in a red, fitted, silk shirt-dress, cinched with a wide black leather belt. Her appearance bespoke so strongly of life and vitality that her presence in the dirty morgue was a collision of opposites. Jason had the unnatural urge to get her out of there as soon as possible, lest some evil force touch her. But she was resistant to his urging. She'd thrown her arms around him and pressed his head against hers in a genuine show of sympathy. Jason melted. His response surprised him. He found himself fighting back tears like an adolescent. It was embarrassing.

She pulled back and looked him in the eyes. He managed a crooked smile. "What a day," he said.

"What a day!" she agreed. "Any reason you have to stay here?"

Jason shook his head.

"Come on, I'm taking you home," she said, hurrying him outside to where her BMW was parked in a no-parking zone. They got in and the car roared to life.

"Are you okay?" Shirley asked as they headed toward Massachusetts Avenue.

"I'm much better now." Jason looked at Shirley's profile as the city lights illuminated it in flashes. "I'm just overwhelmed by all the deaths. As if I should be doing something better."

"You're too hard on yourself. You can't take responsibility for everyone. Besides, Hayes wasn't your patient."

"I know."

They drove for a while in silence. Then Shirley said, "It is a tragedy about Hayes. He was pretty close to a genius, and he couldn't have been more than forty-five."

"He was my age," Jason said. "He was in my class in medical school."

"I didn't know that," Shirley said. "He looked a lot older."

"Especially lately," Jason said. They passed Symphony Hall. Some affair was just getting out, and men in black tie were emerging on the front steps.

"What did the medical examiner have to say?" Shirley asked.

"Probably cancer. But they aren't going to do the autopsy until morning."

"Autopsy? Who gave the authorization?"

"No need if the medical examiner thinks there is some question about the death."

"But what kind of question? You said the man had a heart attack."

"I didn't say it was a heart attack. I said it was something like that. At any rate, it's apparently protocol for them to do a postmortem on any unexpected death. A detective actually questioned me."

"Seems like a waste of taxpayers' money," Shirley said as they turned left on Beacon Street.

"Where are we going?" Jason asked suddenly.

"I'm taking you home with me. My guests will still be there. It will be good for you."

"No way," Jason said. "I'm in no shape to be social."

"Are you sure? I don't want you brooding. These people will understand."

"Please," Jason said. "I'm not strong enough to argue. I just need to sleep. Besides, look at me, I'm a wreck."

"Okay, if you put it that way," Shirley said. She turned left on the

285

next block, then left again on Commonwealth Avenue, heading back to Beacon Hill. After a period of silence, she said, "I'm afraid Hayes's death is going to be a big blow to GHP. We were counting on him to produce some exciting results. The fallout is going to be especially tough for me, since I was responsible for his being hired."

"Then take some of your own advice," Jason said. "You can't hold yourself responsible for his medical condition."

"I know. But try telling that to the board."

"In that case I guess I should tell you. There's more bad news," Jason said. "Apparently Hayes believed he'd made a real scientific breakthrough. Something extraordinary. Do you know anything about it?"

"Not a thing," Shirley said with alarm. "Did he tell you what it was?"

"Unfortunately no," Jason said. "And I wasn't sure whether to believe him or not. He was acting rather bizarre, to say the least, claiming someone wanted him dead."

"Do you think he was having a nervous breakdown?"

"It crossed my mind."

"The poor man. If he did make some sort of discovery, then GHP is going to have a double loss."

"But if he had made some dramatic discovery, wouldn't you be able to find out what it was?"

"Obviously you didn't know Dr. Hayes," Shirley said. "He was an extraordinarily private man, personally and professionally. Half of what he knew he carried around in his head."

They skirted the Boston Garden, then navigated the roundabout route to get into Beacon Hill, a residential enclave of brick-fronted townhouses in the center of Boston, whose one-way streets made driving a nightmare.

After crossing Charles Street, Shirley drove up Mt. Vernon Street and turned into the cobblestoned Louisburg Square. When he'd decided to give up suburban living and try the city, Jason had been lucky enough to find a one-bedroom apartment overlooking the square. It was in a large townhouse whose owner had a unit in the building, but was rarely there. It was a perfect location for Jason, since the apartment came with a true urban prize: a parking place.

Jason got out of the car and leaned in the open window. "Thanks for picking me up. It meant a lot." He reached in and gave Shirley's shoulder a squeeze.

Shirley suddenly reached out and grabbed Jason by the tie, pulling his head down to her. She gave him a hard kiss, gunned the motor, and was off.

Jason stood at the curb in a pool of light from the gas lamp and watched her disappear down Pinckney Street. Turning to his door, he fumbled for his keys. He was pleased she had come into his life, and for the first time considered the possibility of a real relationship.

3

It had not been a good night. Every time Jason had closed his eyes, he'd seen Hayes's quizzical expression just before the catastrophe and re-experienced the awful feeling of helplessness as he watched Hayes's lifeblood pump out of his mouth.

The scene haunted him as he drove to work, and he remembered something he'd forgotten to tell either Curran or Shirley. Hayes had said his discovery was no longer a secret and it was being used. Whatever that meant. Jason planned to call the detective when he reached GHP, but the moment he entered he was paged to come directly to the coronary care unit.

Brian Lennox was much worse. After a brief examination, Jason realized there was little he could do. Even the cardiac consult he'd requested the day before was not optimistic, though Harry Sarnoff had scheduled an emergency coronary study for that morning. The only hope was if immediate surgery might have something to offer.

Outside Brian's cubicle the nurse asked, "If he arrests, do you want to code him? Even his kidneys seem to be failing."

Jason hated such decisions, but said firmly that he wanted the man resuscitated at least until they had the results from the coronary study.

The remainder of Jason's rounds were equally as depressing. His diabetes cases, all of whom had multisystem involvement, were doing very poorly. Two of them were in kidney failure and the third was threatening. The depressing part was that they had not entered the hospital for that reason. The kidney failure had developed while Jason was treating them for other problems.

Jason's two leukemia patients were also not responding to treatment as he'd expected. Both had developed significant heart conditions even though they had been admitted for respiratory symptoms. And his two AIDS sufferers had made very distinct turns for the worse. The only patients doing well were two young girls with hepatitis. The last patient was a thirty-five-year-old man in for an evaluation of his heart valves. He'd had rheumatic fever as a child. Thankfully he was unchanged.

Arriving at his office, Jason had to be firm with Claudia. News of Hayes's death had already permeated the entire GHP complex, and Claudia was beside herself with curiosity. Jason told her that he wasn't going to talk about it. She insisted. He ordered her out of his office. Later he apologized and gave her an abridged version of the event. By ten-thirty he got a call from Henry Sarnoff with depressing news. Brian Lennox's coronary arteries were much worse but without focal blockage. In other words, they were uniformly filling up with athero-sclerosis at a rapid rate, and there was no chance for surgery. Sarnoff said he'd never seen such rapid progression and asked Jason's permission to write it up. Jason said it was fine with him.

After Sarnoff's call, Jason kept himself locked in his office for a few minutes. When he felt emotionally prepared, he called the coronary care unit and asked for the nurse taking care of Brian Lennox. When she came on the line, he discussed with her the results of the coronary artery study. Then he told her that Brian Lennox should be a no-code. Without hope, the man's suffering had to be curtailed. She agreed. After he'd hung up, he stared at the phone. It was moments like that that made him wonder why he'd gone into medicine in the first place.

When the lunch break came, Jason decided to check out Hayes's autopsy results in person. In the daylight, the morgue was not such an eerie place—just another aging, run-down, not-too-clean building. Even the Egyptian architectural details were more comical than impos-ing. Yet Jason avoided the body storage room and went directly to find Margaret Danforth's narrow office next to the library. She was hunched over her desk eating what looked like a Big Mac. She waved him in, smiling. "Welcome."

"Sorry to bother you," Jason said, sitting down. Once again he marveled how small and feminine Margaret seemed in light of her job.

"No bother," she said. "I did the post on Dr. Hayes this morning."

She leaned back in her chair, which squeaked softly. "I was a little surprised. It wasn't cancer."

"What was it?"

"Aneurysm. Aortic aneurysm that broke into the tracheobronchial tree. The man never had syphilis, did he?"

Jason shook his head. "Not that I know of. I'd kinda doubt it."

"Well, it looked strange," Margaret said. "Do you mind that I continue eating? I have another autopsy in a few minutes."

"Not at all," Jason said, wondering how she could. His own stomach did a little flip-flop. The whole building had a slightly fishy odor. "What looked strange?"

Margaret chewed, then swallowed. "The aorta looked kind of cheesy, friable. So did the trachea, for that matter. I'd never seen anything quite like it, except in this one guy I'd posted who was one hundred and fourteen. Can you believe it? It was written up in *The Globe*. He was forty-four when the First World War started. Amazing."

"When will you have a microscopic report?"

Margaret made a gesture of embarrassment. "Two weeks," she said. "We're not funded for adequate support personnel. Slides take quite a while."

"If you could give me some samples, I could have our path department process them."

"We have to process them ourselves. I'm sure you understand."

"I don't mean for you not to do it," Jason said. "I just meant we could too. It would save some time."

"I don't see why not." Standing up, Margaret took another large bite out of her hamburger and motioned for Jason to follow her. They used the stairwell and went up a floor to the autopsy room.

It was a long rectangular room with four stainless-steel tables oriented perpendicular to the long axis. The smell of formaldehyde and other unspeakable fluids was overpowering. Two tables were occupied, and the two others were in the process of being cleaned. Margaret, perfectly at home in the environment, was still chewing her last bite of lunch as she led Jason over to the sink. After scanning through a profusion of plastic-capped specimen bottles, she separated a number from the rest. Then, taking each in turn, she fished out the contents, placed them on a cutting board, and sliced off a piece of each with a blade that looked very much like a standard kitchen carving knife. Then she got new specimen bottles, labeled them, poured in formaldehyde, and dropped in the respective samples. When she was done, she packed them in a brown paper bag and handed it to Jason. It had all been done with remarkable efficiency.

Back at GHP, Jason headed to pathology, where he found Dr. Jackson Madsen at his microscope. Dr. Madsen was a tall, gaunt man who at sixty was still proudly running marathons. As soon as he saw Jason, he commiserated with him about Jason's experience with Hayes.

"Not many secrets around here," Jason said a little sourly.

"Of course not," Jackson said. "Socially, the medical center is like a small town. It thrives on gossip." Eyeing the brown paper bag, he added, "You have something for me?"

"In a manner of speaking." Jason went on to explain what the specimens were, and added that since it was going to take two weeks for the slides to be processed at the city lab, he wondered if Jackson would mind running them at the GHP lab.

"I'd be happy to," Jackson said, taking the bag. "By the way, are you interested in hearing the results of the Harring case now?"

Jason swallowed. "Of course."

"Cardiac rupture. First case I've seen in years. Split open the left ventricle. It appeared as if most of the heart had been involved in the infarct, and when I sectioned the heart, I had the impression that all of the coronary vessels were involved. That man had the worst coronary heart disease I've seen in years."

So much for our wonderful predictive tests, Jason thought. He felt defensive enough to explain to Jackson that he'd gone back and reviewed Harring's record and still couldn't find any evidence of the impending problem on an EKG taken less than a month before Harring's death.

"Maybe you'd better check your machines," Jackson said. "I'm telling you, this man's heart was in bad shape. The microscopic sections should be ready tomorrow if you're interested."

Leaving the pathology department, Jason considered Jackson's comment. The idea of a defective EKG machine hadn't occurred to him. But by the time he got to his office, he discarded the notion. There would be too many ways to tell if the EKG machine wasn't functioning properly. Besides, two different machines were used for the resting EKG and the stress EKG. But in thinking about it, he remembered something. Like Jason himself, on joining the GHP staff, Hayes would have been given a complete physical. Everyone was.

After Claudia had given Jason his phone messages, he asked her to see if Dr. Alvin Hayes had a patient chart, and if he did, to get it.

Meanwhile, he avoided Sally and headed up to radiology. With the help of one of the department secretaries, he located Alvin Hayes's folder. As he'd expected, it contained a routine chest X ray taken six months previously. He looked at it briefly. Then, armed with the film, he sought out one of the four staff radiologists. Milton Perlman, MD, was emerging from the fluoroscopy room when Jason buttonholed him, described Hayes's death and the results of the autopsy, and handed Milton the chest film. Milton took the film back to his office, placed it on the viewing box, and flipped on the light. He scanned the film for a full minute before turning to Jason.

"There ain't no aneurysm here," he said. He was from West Virginia and liked to talk as if he'd left the farm the day before. "Aorta looks normal, no calcification."

"Is that possible?" Jason asked.

"Must be." Milton checked the name and unit number on the film. "I guess there's always a chance we could have mixed up the names, but I doubt it. If the man died of an aneurysm, then he developed it in the last month."

"I never heard of that happening."

"What can I say?" Milton extended his hands, palms up.

Jason returned to his office, mulling over the problem. An aneurysm could balloon quickly, especially if the victim had a combination of vessel disease and high blood pressure, but when he checked Hayes's physical exam, his blood pressure and heart sounds were, as he suspected, normal. With no signs of vascular disease, Jason realized that there was little he could do at that point besides wait for the microscopic sections. Maybe Hayes had contracted some strange infectious disease that had attacked his blood vessels, including his aorta. For the first time, Jason wondered if they were seeing the beginnings of a new and terrible disease.

Changing his suit jacket for a white coat, Jason left his office, practically bumping into Sally.

"You're behind schedule!" she scolded.

"So what else is new?" Jason said, heading for exam room A.

By a combination of hard work and luck, Jason caught up to his schedule. The luck involved not having any new patients that needed extensive workups or old patients with new problems. By three there was even a break. Someone had canceled.

The whole afternoon, Jason could not get the Hayes affair out of his mind. And with a little extra time on his hands, he headed up to the sixth floor. That was where Dr. Alvin Hayes's lab was located. Jason thought perhaps Hayes's assistant would have some idea if the big breakthrough Hayes had mentioned had any basis in fact.

As soon as he stepped from the elevator, Jason felt as if he were in another world. As part of Hayes's incentive to come to GHP, the GHP board had built him a brand new lab which occupied a good portion of the sixth floor.

The area near the elevator was furnished with comfortable leather seating, deep-pile carpets, and even a large glass-fronted bookcase filled with current references in molecular biology. Beyond this reception room was a clean room where visitors were expected to don long white coats and protective coverings over their shoes. Jason tried the door. It was open, so he entered.

Jason put on the coat and booties and tried the inner door. As he expected, it was locked. Next to the door was a buzzer. He pushed it and waited. Above the lintel a small red light blinked on over a closed-circuit TV camera. Then the door buzzed open and Jason entered.

The lab was divided into two main sections. The first section was constructed of white Formica and white tile and included a large central room with several offices on one side. With overhead fluorescent lighting, the effect was dazzling. The room was filled with sophisticated equipment, most of which Jason did not recognize. A locked steel door separated the first section from the second. A sign next to the door read: ANIMAL ROOM AND BACTERIAL INCUBATORS: NO ENTRY!

Sitting at one of the extensive lab benches in the first section was a very blond woman Jason had seen on several occasions in the GHP cafeteria. She had sharp features, a slightly aquiline nose, and her hair was tightly pulled back into a French knot. Jason saw that her eyes were red, as if she had been crying.

"Excuse me, I'm Dr. Jason Howard," he said, extending his hand. She took it. Her skin was cool.

"Helene Brennquivist," she said with a slight Scandinavian accent.

"Do you have a moment?"

Helene didn't answer. Instead, she closed her notebook and pushed away a stack of petri dishes.

"I'd like to ask a few questions," Jason continued. He saw that she had an uncanny ability to maintain an absolutely neutral facial expression.

"This is, or was, Dr. Hayes's lab?" Jason asked, with a short wave of his hand to the surroundings.

She nodded.

"And I presume you worked with Dr. Hayes?"

Another nod, less perceptible than the first. Jason had the feeling he'd already evoked a defensiveness in the woman.

"I'm assuming that you've heard the bad news about Dr. Hayes," Jason said. This time she blinked, and Jason thought he saw the glint of tears.

"I was with Dr. Hayes when he died," Jason explained, watching Helene carefully. Except for the watery eyes, she seemed strangely devoid of emotion, and Jason wondered if it was a form of grief. "Just before Hayes died, he told me that he'd made a major scientific breakthrough . . ."

Jason let his comment hang in the air, hoping for some appropriate response. There was none. Helene merely stared back at him.

"Well, was there?" Jason said, leaning forward.

"I didn't know you were finished speaking," Helene said. "It wasn't a question, you know."

"True," Jason admitted. "I was merely hoping you'd respond. I do hope you know what Dr. Hayes meant."

"I'm afraid I don't. Other people in the administration have already been up here asking me the same question. Unfortunately, I have no idea what Dr. Hayes could have been referring to."

Jason imagined that Shirley had been to see Helene first thing that morning.

"Are you the only person besides Dr. Hayes who works in this lab?"

"That's right," Helene said. "We had a secretary, but Dr. Hayes dismissed her three months ago. He thought she talked too much."

"What was he afraid she'd talk about?"

"Anything and everything. Dr. Hayes was an intensely private person. Especially about his work."

"So I'm learning," Jason said. His initial impression that Hayes had become paranoid seemed to be substantiated. Yet Jason persisted: "What exactly do you do, Miss Brennquivist?"

"I'm a molecular biologist. Like Dr. Hayes, but nowhere near his ability. I use recombinant DNA techniques to alter E. coli bacteria to produce various proteins that Dr. Hayes was interested in."

Jason nodded as if he understood. He'd heard the term "recombinant DNA," but had only the vaguest notion what it really meant. Since he'd been in medical school there had been a virtual explosion of knowledge in the field. But there was one thing he did remember, and that was a fear that recombinant DNA studies might produce bacteria capable of causing new and unknown diseases. With Hayes's sudden death in mind, he asked, "Had you come up with any new and potentially dangerous strains?"

"No," Helene said without hesitation.

"How can you be so sure?"

"For two reasons. First of all, I did all the recombinant bacterial work, not Dr. Hayes. Secondly, we use a strain of E. coli bacteria that cannot grow outside of the laboratory."

"Oh," Jason said, nodding encouragingly.

"Dr. Hayes was interested in growth and development. He spent most of his time isolating the growth factors from the hypothalamic-pituitary axis responsible for puberty and sexual development. Growth factors are proteins. I'm sure you know that."

"Of course," Jason said. *What a curious woman*, he thought. At first, conversation had been like pulling teeth. Now that she was on scientific ground, she was extremely vocal.

"Dr. Hayes would give me a protein and I'd set out to produce it by recombinant DNA techniques. That's what I'm doing here." She turned to the stacks of petri dishes, and, lifting one, removed the cover. She extended it toward Jason. On the surface were whitish clumps of bacterial colonies.

Helene replaced the dish on its appropriate stack. "Dr. Hayes was fascinated by the on/off switching of genes, the balance between repression and expression, and the role of repressor proteins and where they bind to the DNA. He's used the growth hormone gene as the prototype. Would you like to see his latest map of chromosome 17?"

"Sure," Jason said, forcing a smile.

A buzzer resounded in the lab, momentarily drowning out the low hum of the electronic equipment. A screen in front of Helene flashed to life, showing four people and a dog in the foyer. Jason recognized two of them immediately—Shirley Montgomery and Detective Michael Curran. The other two were strangers.

"Oh, dear," Helene said, as she reached for the buzzer.

Jason stood as the new arrivals filed into the room. Shirley registered a momentary flash of surprise when she saw Jason, but calmly introduced Detective Curran to Helene. As he began to question her, Shirley took Jason by the arm and steered him into the nearest office, which Jason realized must have been Hayes's. Covering the walls were progressive close-up photos of human genitalia going through the anatomical evolution of puberty. They were all nicely framed in stainless steel squares.

"Interesting decor," Jason commented wryly.

Shirley acted as if she didn't even see the photos. Her usually calm face wore an expression of concern and irritation. "This affair is getting out of hand."

"What do you mean?" Jason asked.

"Apparently last night the police got an anonymous tip that Dr. Alvin Hayes dealt drugs. They searched his apartment and found a significant amount of heroin, cocaine, and cash. Now they have a warrant to search his lab."

"My God!" Jason suddenly understood the dog's presence.

"And as if that's not enough, they found out he's been living with a woman by the name of Carol Donner."

"That name sounds familiar," Jason said.

"Well, it shouldn't be," Shirley said sternly. "Carol Donner is an exotic dancer at the Club Cabaret in the Combat Zone."

"Well, I'll be damned." Jason chuckled.

"Jason!" Shirley snapped. "This is not a laughing matter."

"I'm not laughing," he protested. "I'm just astounded."

"If you think *you're* astounded, what's the board of directors going to say? And to think I insisted on hiring Hayes. The man's death alone was bad enough. This is fast becoming a public relations nightmare."

"What are you going to do?" Jason asked.

"I haven't the slightest idea," Shirley admitted. "At the moment my intuition tells me the less we do, the better."

"What are your thoughts about Hayes's supposed breakthrough?"

"I think the man was fantasizing," Shirley said. "I mean, he was involved with drugs and an exotic dancer, for God's sake!"

Exasperated, she returned to the main part of the lab, where Detective Curran was still talking intently with Helene. The other two men and the dog were methodically searching the lab. Jason watched for a few moments, then excused himself to finish office hours. He still had a handful of outpatients to see as well as hospital rounds to do.

On the way home, even though he was more convinced than ever that Hayes had been on the verge of a nervous breakdown, rather than a breakthrough, Jason stopped at the library and took out a slim volume titled *Recombinant DNA: An Introduction for the Nonscientist*.

Rush hour traffic was the usual dog-eat-dog Boston rally, and when Jason stepped on the emergency brake in his parking place in front of his townhouse, he felt the usual relief that he'd survived unscathed. He carried his briefcase up to his apartment, and put it on the desk in the small study that looked out onto the square. The now leafless elms were like skeletons against the night sky. Daylight Saving was already over, and it was dark outside even though it was only six forty-five. Changing into his jogging clothes, Jason ran down Mt. Vernon Street, crossed over Storrow Drive on the Arthur Fiedler Bridge, and ran along the Charles. He ran to the Boston University Bridge before turning. In contrast to the summer, there were few joggers. On the way back he stopped at De Luca's Market and picked up some fresh, local bluefish, makings for a salad, and a cold bottle of California Chardonnay.

Jason liked to cook, and after taking his shower, he prepared the fish by broiling it with a small amount of garlic and virgin olive oil. He tossed the salad, then rescued the wine from the freezer where he'd put it to give it an icy kick. He poured himself a glass. When all was ready he carried it into the study on a tray. Thus prepared, he opened the small book on recombinant DNA and settled in for the night.

The first part of the book served as a review. Jason was well aware that deoxyribonucleic acid, better known as DNA, was a molecule, shaped like a twisted, double-stranded string. It was made up of repeating subunits called bases that had the property of pairing with each other in very specific ways. Particular areas of the DNA were called genes, and each gene was associated with the production of a specific protein.

Jason felt encouraged as he took a sip of his wine. The book was well written and made the subject matter seem clear. He liked the little tidbits like the fact that each human cell had four billion base pairs. The next part of the book dealt with bacteria, and the fact that bacteria reproduce easily and rapidly. Within days, trillions of identical cells could be made from a single initial cell. This was important, because in genetic engineering bacteria served as the recipient of small fragments of DNA. This "foreign" DNA was incorporated into the bacterium's own DNA, and then, as the cell divided, it manufactured the original fragments. The bacterium with the newly incorporated DNA was called a recombinant strain and the new DNA molecule was called recombinant DNA. So far so good.

Jason ate some of his fish and salad and washed it down with wine. The next chapter got a little more complicated. It talked about how the genes in the DNA molecule went about producing their respective proteins. The first part entailed making a copy of the segment of DNA with a molecule called messenger RNA. The messenger RNA then directed the production of the protein in a process called transcription. Jason drank a little more wine. The last part of the chapter got particularly interesting, since it explained the elaborate mechanisms that turned genes on and off.

Getting up from his desk, Jason walked across his living room into the kitchen. Opening the freezer, he poured himself another glass of wine. Back in his study he stared out the window, seeing the lights across the square in St. Margaret's Convent. It always amused him that there was a convent on the most desirable residential square in Boston: Give up the material world, become a nun, and move to Louisburg! Jason smiled, then looked back down at the recombinant DNA book. Sitting down again, he reread the section on the timing of gene expression. It was complicated and fascinating. Apparently, a host of proteins had been discovered that served as repressors of gene function. These proteins attached to the DNA or caused the DNA to coil, to cover up the involved genes.

Jason closed the book. He'd had enough for one night. Besides, the section on the control of gene function was what he'd been unconsciously looking for. Reading that section brought back Hayes's comment that his main interest was "how genes turned on and how they turned off." Helene had said the same thing but in different words.

Taking his wine, Jason wandered into his living room. Absently fondling the cut-glass sconces over the fireplace, he allowed his mind to consider the possibilities. What could Hayes have meant when he said he'd made a major scientific breakthrough? For the moment Jason dismissed the idea of Hayes having delusions of grandeur. After all, he was a world-class researcher, and he was working prodigious hours. So there was a chance he'd been telling the truth. If he'd made a discovery, it would be in the area of turning genes on and off, and probably have to do with growth and development. The image of the photos of the genitals clouded Jason's mind for a moment.

Jason was brought out of his reverie by the phone. It was the head nurse in the coronary care unit. "Brian Lennox just died. He had a terminal episode of V-tack that progressed to asystole."

"I'll be right over," Jason said. He hung up and thought of the nurse's scientific jargon, recognizing that it was an emotional defense. Once again the shadow of death hung over him like a noxious cloud.

4

The radio alarm blasted Jason out of bed. He'd turned up the volume for fear of oversleeping. He'd spent a good portion of the night consoling Brian Lennox's wife. Retrieving his newspaper from the front steps, he shaved and showered while his Mr. Coffee performed its usual morning miracle. By the time he was dressed, the apartment was filled with the aromatic smell of the freshly brewed coffee. With mug in hand, he retreated to the den, slipping the *Boston Globe* out of its protective clear plastic sheath.

Planning to turn directly to the sports section, he stopped at a front-page headline—DOCTOR, DRUGS AND DANCER. It was not a flattering article about Dr. Alvin Hayes. It played up Hayes's shocking death and unfairly associated it with the drugs found in his apartment, even likening his affair with the dancer to the case involving the Tufts Medical School professor who had been convicted of murdering a prostitute. Along with the article there were two photos: the *Time* cover shoot of Hayes and another of a woman entering the Club Cabaret, captioned, "Carol Donner entering her place of business." Jason tried to see what Carol Donner looked like, but it was impossible. She had one hand up, shielding her face. In the background was a sign that said, TOPLESS COLLEGE GIRLS. *Sure*, thought Jason with a smile.

He read the rest of the article, feeling sorry for Shirley. The police reported that a significant amount of heroin and cocaine was found at the South End apartment that Hayes had shared with Carol Donner.

Jason went to the hospital to find his inpatients generally in poor shape. Matthew Cowen, who had had a cardiac catheterization the day before, displayed odd symptoms alarmingly like the late Cedric Harring: arthritis, constipation, and dry skin. None of these would normally cause Jason much concern. But in view of recent events, they made him feel uneasy. They again brought up the specter of some new unknown infectious disease that he could not control. He had the feeling Matthew's course was about to change for the worse.

After ordering a dermatology consult for Cowen, Jason gloomily went down to his office, where Claudia greeted him with the information that she had pulled the executive physicals through the letter P. She had called the patients and discovered that only two complained of health problems.

Jason reached for the charts and opened them. The first one was Holly Jennings, the other Paul Klingler. Both had had their physicals within a month. "Call them back," Jason said, "and ask both to come in as soon as they can without alarming them."

"It's going to be hard not to upset them. What should I say?"

"Tell them we want to repeat some test. Use your imagination."

Later in the day he decided to see if he could charm some more information on Hayes out of his lab technician, but the moment he saw Helene she made it clear she was not about to be charmed.

"Did the police find anything?" he asked, already knowing the answer was no. Shirley had called him and told him after the police had departed, saying, "Thank God for small favors."

Helene shook her head.

"I know you're busy," Jason said, "but do you think you could spare a minute? I'd like to ask a few more questions."

She finally stopped working and turned toward him.

"Thank you," he said, and smiled. Her expression didn't change. It wasn't unpleasant, just neutral.

"I hate to belabor the subject," Jason said, "but I keep thinking of what Dr. Hayes said about a significant breakthrough. Are you sure you have no idea what it could be? It would be tragic if a real medical discovery were lost."

"I told you what I know," Helene said. "I could show you the latest map he did of chromosome 17. Would that help?"

"Let's give it a try."

Helene led the way into Hayes's office. She ignored the photos that covered the walls, but Jason couldn't. He wondered what kind of man could work in such an environment. Helene produced a large sheet of paper covered with minute printing, giving the sequence of base pairs of the DNA molecule constituting a portion of chromosome 17. There was a staggering number of base pairs: hundreds and hundreds of thousands.

"Dr. Hayes's area is here." She pointed to a large section where the pairs were done in red. "These are the genes associated with growth hormone. It's very complex."

"You're right there," Jason said. He knew he'd have to do a lot more reading to make any sense of it all.

"Is there any chance this mapping could have led to a major scientific breakthrough?"

Helene thought for a moment, then shook her head. "The technique has been known for some time."

"What about cancer?" Jason asked, giving the idea a shot. "Could Dr. Hayes have discovered something about cancer?"

"We didn't work with cancer at all," Helene said.

"But if he was interested in cell division and maturation, it's possible he could have discovered something about cancer. Especially with his interest in the switching on and off of genes."

"I suppose it's possible," Helene said without enthusiasm.

Jason was sure that Helene was not being as helpful as she could be. As Hayes's assistant, she should have had a better idea of what Hayes was doing. But there was no way he could force the issue.

"What about his lab books?"

Helene returned to her spot at the lab bench. Opening the second drawer at the table, she pulled out a ledger. "This is all I have," she said, and handed it to Jason.

The book was three-quarters filled. Jason could see it was only a data book without experimental protocols, and without those, the data was meaningless.

"Aren't there other lab books?"

"There were some," Helene admitted, "but Dr. Hayes kept them with him, especially over the last three months. Mostly he kept everything in his head. He had a fabulous memory, especially for figures. . . ." For a brief moment Jason saw a light in Helene's eyes and thought she might open up, but it didn't last.

She trailed off into silence. She took the data book from Jason and replaced it in its drawer.

"Let me ask one other question," Jason said, struggling over the wording. "As far as you could tell, did Dr. Hayes act normally over the last few weeks? He seemed anxious and overtired when I saw him." Jason deliberately understated Hayes's condition.

"He seemed normal to me," said Helene flatly.

Oh, brother, Jason thought. Now he was sure Helene wasn't being open with him. Unfortunately, there was nothing he could do about it. Thanking her and excusing himself, he retreated from Hayes's lab. He descended in the elevator, avoided being seen by Sally, crossed to the main building, and rode up to Pathology.

He found Jackson Madsen in the chemistry lab, where there was a problem with one of the automated machines. Two company reps were there, and Jackson was happy to return to his office with Jason to show him the slides of Harring's heart.

"Wait until you see this," he said as he positioned a slide under his microscope. He peered through the eyepiece, moving the slide deftly with his thumb and index finger. Then he stepped back and let Jason take a look.

"See that vessel?" he asked. Jason nodded. "Notice the lumen is all but obliterated. It's some of the worst atherosclerosis I've seen. That pink stuff looks like amyloid. It's amazing, especially if you say his EKG was okay. And let me show you something else." Jackson substituted another slide. "Take a look now."

Jason peered into the microscope. "What am I supposed to see?"

"Notice how swollen the nuclei are," Jackson said. "And the pink stuff. That's amyloid for certain."

"What does that mean?"

"It's as if the guy's heart was under siege. Notice the inflammatory cells."

Unaccustomed to looking at microscopic sections, Jason hadn't noticed them at first, but now they jumped out at him. "What do you make of it?" he asked.

"I'm not sure. How old did you say this guy was?"

"Fifty-six." Jason straightened up. "Is there any chance, in your estimation, that we are seeing some new infectious disease?"

Jackson thought for a moment, then shook his head. "I don't think there's enough inflammation for that. It looks more metabolic, but that's all I can say. Oh, one more thing," he added, putting in another slide. While he focused he said: "This is part of the red nucleus in the brain. Tell me what you see." He leaned back for Jason. Jason peered into the scope. He saw a neuron. Within the neuron was a prominent nucleus as well as a darkly stained granular area. He described it to Jackson.

"That's lipofuscin," said Jackson. He removed the slide.

Jason straightened up. "What does it all mean?"

"Wish I knew," said Jackson. "All nonspecific, but certainly a suggestion that your Mr. Harring was a sick cookie. These slides could have belonged to my grandfather."

"That's the second time I've heard something like that," said Jason slowly. "Can't you give me anything more specific?"

"I'm sorry," said Jackson. "I wish I could be more cooperative. I'll be running some tests to be sure these deposits in the heart and elsewhere are amyloid. I'll let you know."

"Thanks," said Jason. "What about the slides on Hayes?"

"Not ready yet," said Jackson.

Jason returned to the second floor and walked over to the outpatient area. As a doctor he'd always had questions about the efficacy of certain tests, procedures, and drugs. But he had never had reason to question his general competence. In fact, in most situations he'd always thought of himself as well above average. Now, he wasn't so sure. Such misgivings were disturbing, especially because he'd been using work as his major sense of self since Danielle's death.

"Where have you been?" demanded Sally, catching up to Jason as he tried to slip into his office. Within minutes Sally had Jason buried beneath a host of minor problems that thankfully absorbed his attention. By the time he could catch his breath, it was just after twelve. He saw his last patient, who wanted advice and shots for a trip to India, and then he was free.

Claudia tried to get him to join her and some other secretaries for lunch, but Jason declined. He retreated to his office and brooded. The worst part for Jason was the frustration. He felt something was terribly wrong, but he didn't know what it was or what to do about it. A loneliness descended over him.

"Damn," said Jason, slapping the top of his desk with his open palm, hard enough to send unattached papers flying. He had to avoid slipping into a depression. He had to do something. Changing from his white coat to his jacket, he grabbed his beeper and descended to his car. He drove around the Fenway, passing the Gardner Museum and then the Museum of Fine Arts on his right. Then, heading south on Storrow Drive, he got off at Arlington. His destination was Boston Police Headquarters.

At police headquarters a policeman directed Jason to the fifth floor. As soon as he got off the elevator, he saw the detective coming down the hall, balancing a full mug of coffee. Curran was jacketless, with the top button of his shirt open and his tie loosened. Under his left arm dangled a worn leather holster. When he saw Jason he seemed perplexed until Jason reminded him that they'd met at the morgue and at GHP.

"Ah, yes," Curran said, with his slight brogue. "Alvin Hayes business."

He invited Jason into his office, which was starkly utilitarian with a metal desk and metal file cabinet. On the wall was a calendar with the Celtics' basketball schedule.

"How about some coffee?" Curran suggested, putting his mug down.

"No, thank you," Jason said.

"You're smart," Curran said. "I know everybody complains about institutional coffee, but this stuff is lethal." He pulled a metal chair away from the wall and motioned to it for Jason to sit.

"So what can I do for you, doctor?"

"I'm not sure. This Hayes business disturbs me. Remember I told you that Dr. Hayes said he'd made a major discovery? Well, now I think there's a good chance he did. After all, the man was a world-famous researcher, and he was working in a field with a lot of potential."

"Wait a minute. Didn't you also tell me you thought Hayes was having a nervous breakdown?"

"At the time I thought he was displaying inappropriate behavior," Jason said. "I thought he was paranoid and delusional. Now I'm not sure. What if he did make a major discovery which he hadn't revealed because he was still perfecting it? Suppose someone found out and for some reason wanted it suppressed?"

"And had him killed?" Curran interrupted patronizingly. "Doctor, you're forgetting one major fact: Hayes died of natural causes. There was no foul play, no gunshot wounds to the head, no knife in the back. And on top of that, he was dealing. We found heroin, coke, and cash in his Southie pad. No wonder he acted paranoid. The drug scene is a serious world."

"Wasn't that anonymous tip a bit strange?" Jason asked, suddenly curious.

"It happens all the time. Somebody's pissed about something so they call us to get even."

Jason stared at the detective. He thought the drug connection was out of character, but didn't know why. Then he remembered that Hayes had been living with an exotic dancer. Maybe it wasn't so out of character after all.

As if reading Jason's thoughts, Curran said, "Listen, doctor, I appreciate you taking the time to come down, but facts are facts. I don't know if this guy made a discovery or not, but let me tell you something. If he was dealing drugs, he was taking them too. That's the pattern. I had the Vice department run his name through their computers. They came up with zip, but that just means he hadn't been caught yet. He's lucky he got to die of natural causes. In any case, I can't justify spending Homicide time on the death."

"I still think there's more to it."

Curran shook his head.

"Dr. Hayes was trying to tell me something," Jason persisted. "I think he wanted help."

"Sure," Curran said. "He probably wanted to pull you into his drug ring. Listen, doctor, take my advice. Forget this affair." He stood up, indicating the interview was over.

Descending to the street, Jason removed the parking ticket from his windshield wiper. Sliding in behind the wheel, he thought about his conversation with Detective Curran. The man had been cordial, but he obviously gave little credence to Jason's thoughts and intuition. As Jason started his car, he remembered something else Hayes had said about his discovery. He'd said it was "ironic." Now that was a weird way to characterize a major scientific breakthrough, especially if someone were contriving the story.

Back at the GHP, Jason returned to his patients, going from room to room listening, touching, sympathizing, and advising. That was what he loved about medicine. People opened themselves to him, literally and figuratively. He felt privileged and needed. Some of his confidence ebbed back.

It was close to four when he approached exam room C and took the chart. He remembered the name. It was Paul Klingler, the man whose physical exam he had done. Before entering the room, Jason quickly reviewed his workup. The man appeared to be healthy, with low normal cholesterol and triglycerides and normal EKG. Jason entered the room.

Klingler was slender, with sandy blond hair and the quiet confidence of an old moneyed Yankee. "What was wrong with my tests?" he asked, concerned.

"Nothing, really."

"But your secretary told me you wanted to repeat some. That I had to come today."

"Sorry about that. There was no need for alarm. When she heard you weren't feeling well, she thought we should take a look."

"I'm just getting over the flu," Paul said. "Kids brought it home from school. I'm much better. The only problem is that it has kept me from exercise for over a week."

The flu didn't scare Jason. Healthy people didn't die of it. But he still examined Paul Klingler carefully and repeated the various cardiac tests. Finally he told Klingler that he'd call if the blood work revealed any abnormalities.

Two patients later, Jason confronted Holly Jennings, a fifty-four-year-old executive from one of the largest Boston advertising firms. She was not happy and certainly not shy about expressing her feelings. And although there was a sign specifically forbidding it, she'd been smoking in the exam room while she had been waiting.

"What the hell is going on?" she demanded as Jason entered the room. Her physical a month ago had given her a clean bill of health, though Jason had warned her to stop smoking and take off the twenty to thirty extra pounds she had put on in the last five years.

"I'd heard you weren't feeling well," Jason said mildly. He noticed she looked tired, and saw the dark circles under her eyes.

"Is that what this is all about?" she snapped. "The secretary told me you wanted to repeat some tests. What was wrong with them?"

"Nothing. We just wanted to do some follow-up. Tell me about your health."

"Jesus Christ! You drag me down here, scaring the hell out of me, making me miss two important presentations, just to have a conversation. Couldn't this have been done on the phone?"

"Well, since you're here, why don't you tell me how you've been feeling."

"Tired."

"Anything else?"

"Just generally lousy. I haven't been able to sleep. My appetite's been poor. Nothing specific . . . well, that's not true. My eyes have been bothering me. I've had to wear sunglasses a lot, even in the office."

"Anything else?" Jason asked, feeling an uncomfortable prickle of fear.

Holly shrugged. "For some goddamn reason my hair's been thinning."

As carefully as possible, Jason examined the woman. Her pulse and blood pressure were up, although that could have been due to stress. Her skin was dry, particularly on her extremities. When he repeated her EKG, he thought there might have been some very mild ST changes suggesting reduced oxygen to her heart. When he suggested they do another stress test, she declined.

"Can I come back for that?"

"I'd rather do it now," Jason said. "In fact, would you consider staying in the hospital for a couple of days?"

"Are you kidding? I don't have time. Besides, I don't feel that bad. Why do you even suggest it?"

"Just to get everything done. I'd like you to see a cardiologist and an ophthalmologist as well."

"Next week. Monday or Tuesday. But I've got some big deadlines."

Reluctantly, Jason let Holly go after drawing some blood. There was no way he could force her to stay, and he had nothing specific enough to convince her she was in trouble. It was just a feeling: a bad feeling.

Following his usual routine after returning home, Jason jogged, stopped into Dè Luca's Market where he got a Perdue chicken, put his meal in the oven, showered and retreated to his den with an ice-cold beer. Making himself comfortable, he continued his reading on DNA. He began to understand how Hayes could isolate specific genes. That was what Helene Brennquivist had probably been doing that morning. Once an appropriate bacterial colony was found, it was cultivated to produce trillions of bacteria. Then, using enzymes, the bacteria DNA was separated, fragmented, and the desired gene was isolated and purified. Later, it could be spliced back into different bacteria into regions of the DNA that could be "switched on" by the researcher. In that form, the recombinant strain of bacteria acted like miniature factor-

307

ies to produce the protein the gene was coded for. It had been this method that Hayes had used to produce his human growth hormone. He had started with a piece of human DNA, the gene that made growth hormone, cloned it by the help of bacteria, then spliced it into bacteria DNA in an area controlled by a gene responsible for digesting lactose. By adding lactose to the culture, Hayes's recombinant strain of bacteria had been "turned on" to produce human growth hormone.

Jason drained his beer and went into the kitchen and popped another. He was overwhelmed by what he'd learned. No wonder scientists like Hayes were strange. They knew they had the power to manipulate life. This comprehension thrilled Jason and disturbed him at the same time. The DNA technology had awesome potential to do good and harm. The direction, he thought, was a toss-up.

Armed with this information, Jason was even more inclined to believe that Hayes, though under general stress, had been telling the truth—at least about the scientific breakthrough. Jason was not so sure about Hayes's statement that someone wanted him dead. He wished he'd spent more time with the man over the last months. He wished he knew more about him.

Opening the oven, Jason checked his chicken. It was browning nicely and looked delicious. He put water on to boil for rice, then went back to the den. Lifting his legs onto the desktop and tilting back his chair, he started the next chapter on the laboratory techniques of genetic engineering. The first part dealt with the methods by which DNA molecules were fragmented with enzymes called restriction endonucleases. Jason had to read the section several times. It was difficult material.

The shrill whine of the smoke detector startled Jason. Leaping up from the desk where he'd fallen fast asleep, he dashed into the kitchen. The water for the rice had boiled away, and the Teflon lining was smoking, filling the kitchen with acrid vapors. Jason shoved it under running water, where it spattered and hissed. Turning on the exhaust fan and opening one of the living room windows slowly emptied the kitchen of smoke, and finally the smoke detector fell silent. Jason was glad the landlord was out of town as usual.

When his dinner was finally prepared, without rice, Jason carried it to his desk in the den, pushing papers and books aside. As he started eating he found himself looking at the front of the *Boston Globe* with the article "Doctor, Drugs and Dancer" staring him in the face. Picking the paper up in his left hand, he looked at Carol Donner again. The idea that Hayes would have been living with the woman confounded him. Jason wondered if Hayes had fallen prey to the age-old male fantasy of rescuing the prostitute who, despite her work, had a heart of gold. Thinking of Hayes as a colleague with similar background including the same medical school, Jason found the idea of his falling for such a cliché farfetched. But as Curran had said, facts were facts. Obviously Hayes had been living with the girl. Jason tossed the paper aside.

After reading what he could find about dry skin, which wasn't much, Jason carried his soiled dishes to the kitchen and rinsed them. The image of Carol Donner with her hand in front of her face kept popping up in his mind. He looked at his watch. It was ten-thirty. "Why not," he said aloud. After all, if Hayes had been living with the woman, maybe she knew something that could give Jason a clue about Hayes's breakthrough. At any rate, he had nothing to lose. Donning a sweater and a tweed jacket, Jason left the apartment.

From Beacon Hill it was only a fifteen-minute walk to the Combat Zone. But fifteen minutes took Jason an enormous social distance. Beacon Hill was the epitome of comfortable wealth and propriety, with its cobblestone streets and gas lamps. The Combat Zone was the sordid opposite. To get there, Jason skirted the edge of the Boston Common, reaching Washington Street with its row of bottomless bars by way of Boylston Street. There were roaming packs of street people mixing uneasily with groups of boisterous students and leather-jacketed blue-collar workers from Dorchester. The Club Cabaret was in the middle of the block, nestled between an X-rated cinema and an adult bookstore with a variety of supposed sexual aids on display in its window. The TOPLESS COLLEGE GIRLS sign glowed with fluorescent paint.

Jason walked up to the door and went inside. He found himself in the bar, a long, dark room illuminated in the center to spotlight a wooden runway. The bar itself was U-shaped and surrounded the runway. Behind there were small booths, and rock music thudded into the room from large speakers flanking the stairs that led to the runway from the floor above.

The air was foul with cigarette smoke and that peculiar chemical odor which smells like cheap room-deodorant. The place was almost filled with men hunched over drinks at the bar. It was difficult to see into the booths, but as Jason passed, he glimpsed numerous women in low-cut spaghetti-strap dresses. He found a stool at the bar. A waitress wearing a white shirt and tight black shorts took his order almost instantly.

As she brought his beer and a glass, a seminude dancer came down the stairs and pranced along the runway. Jason gazed up at her, catching her eye for a brief instant. She looked bored. Her face was heavily made up, and her bleached hair had the consistency of straw. Jason guessed her age to be over thirty, certainly no coed.

Glancing around the room, he noticed equivalent expressions of boredom on the faces of the men as their eyes reflexively followed the progress of the dancer up and down the runway. Jason sipped his beer from the bottle. There was no way he'd allow his lips to touch a glass in that place.

When the rock-and-roll piece ended, the dancer acted as if she'd been momentarily stranded. Self-consciously, she shifted her weight from one four-inch heel to the other, waiting for the next number. Jason noticed a tattooed heart on her right thigh.

Heralded by the heavy beat of drums, the next number began, and the blonde immediately recommenced her gyrations. As she did so, she slipped off her brief top. Now all she had on was a G-string and her shoes. Still, the men at the bar appeared carved in stone. The only movements were those necessary to bring their drinks or cigarettes to their lips. At least until the dancer began moving along the runway. Then a few customers would hold out dollar bills.

Jason watched for a while, then scanned the room again. About twenty feet away was a booth occupied by a man in a dark suit with a cigar, studying a ledger through dark glasses. Jason had no idea how the man could see anything at all, but decided he was management. Several body-builder types with eighteen-inch necks, wearing white T-shirts, stood on either side of the booth, their beefy arms crossed and their heads constantly turning to survey the room.

As the music ended, the blond stripper picked up her things and ran up the stairs. There was scattered applause. When the music began again, a new dancer descended the stairs and whirled about the runway. Dressed in a flashy, voluminous gypsy costume, she could have been the first dancer's sister—her older sister.

Very quickly, Jason got the hang of the program. A girl would appear in some wild costume and dance, taking off more of her clothes as the number progressed. Forty-five minutes passed and Jason wondered if Carol Donner was scheduled to appear that night. He asked one of the waitresses.

"She should be next. Want another round, mister?"

Jason shook his head. He was content to nurse his first beer for the entire visit. Looking around, he noticed that several of the strippers had come back down to the floor. They would stop and talk to the man in the dark glasses and then wander around the room, chatting up the customers. Jason tried to imagine Hayes, the famous molecular biologist, there at the bar. Try as he might, he couldn't.

There was a pause in the music and the runway lights dimmed. A PA system crackled to life for the first time and announced the next performer: the famous Carol Donner. The bored patrons propped up on the bar suddenly seemed to wake up. There were a few catcalls.

The music changed to a softer rock and a figure appeared on the runway. As the lights came up, Jason was stunned. To his amazement, Carol Donner was a beautiful young woman. Her skin had a healthy glow and her eyes sparkled. She was dressed in a body suit, headband, and leg warmers as though she were in an aerobics class. Her feet were bare. She moved down the runway with effortless grace, and Jason noticed that her smile held genuine enjoyment.

As her number progressed, she removed her leg warmers, a silk sash around her waist, and then the body suit. The sodden audience actually cheered as she danced topless back up the stairs. As soon as she disappeared, the customers sank back into their torpor. Jason kept waiting for Carol to appear on the floor like the other girls, but after twenty minutes he decided she might not. He pushed off his stool and walked back to the man in the sunglasses. One of the body-builders noticed his approach and unfolded his arms. "Excuse me," Jason said to the man with the ledger. "Would it be possible to talk with Carol Donner?"

The man removed his cigar. "Who the hell are you?" Jason was reluctant to give his real name, and while he hesitated, the man in the dark glasses motioned to one of the body-builders. Jason felt large hands take hold of his arm and urge him toward the door. "I only want . . ." But he didn't get to say any more. He was grabbed by his jacket and hastily escorted the length of the bar and through the dark curtain, his feet barely touching the floor. With a good deal of humiliation, he found himself propelled out into the street.

5

After the radio alarm had awakened him, Jason had to stand under the shower for several minutes to feel capable of facing the day. The night before, after he'd returned from the unpleasant visit to the Club Cabaret, he'd been called back to the hospital. One of his AIDS patients, a man named Harvey Rachman, had arrested. When Jason had arrived, the staff had been giving CPR for fifteen minutes. They'd kept it up for two hours before conceding defeat. The head nurse's comment that at least the man didn't have to suffer anymore was not much consolation to a stricken Jason. For Jason it seemed that death was winning the competition.

The only positive side of inpatient rounds later that morning was the discharge of one of his hepatitis cases. Jason was sorry to see the girl go. Now he had only a single patient who was doing well.

In the CCU, Matthew Cowen was no better. In addition to his other complaints, he was now having trouble seeing. The symptom bothered Jason. Harring and Lennox had also complained of impaired vision in the weeks before their deaths, and again the possibility of some new multisystem illness crossed Jason's mind. He ordered an ophthalmology consult. After finishing rounds, Jason headed to pathology to see if the slides from Hayes's autopsy were done. Maybe they would help explain why so many seemingly healthy people were suffering cardiovascular catastrophe.

312

He had to wait while Jackson called a report on a frozen section down to the OR. It was a breast biopsy and it was positive.

"That always makes me feel terrible," Jackson said, hanging up the phone. Then, in a more cheerful voice, he added, "I bet you want to see the Hayes slides." He searched around on his desk until he found the right folder. Opening it up, he took out a slide and focused it for Jason. "Wait until you see this.

"That's Alvin Hayes's aorta," Jackson explained as Jason looked in. The cellular death and disorganization were evident even to his unpracticed eye. "It's no wonder it blew," Jackson continued. "I've never seen such deterioration in anyone under seventy except with established aortic disease. And let me show you something else." He replaced the slide with another. "That's Hayes's heart. Look at the coronary vessel. It's like Cedric Harring's. All the coronary vessels are almost closed. If Hayes's aorta hadn't blown, he'd have died of a heart attack. The man was a walking time bomb. And not only that, he had inflammation in the thyroid, again like Harring. In fact, there were so many parallels that I went back and looked at Harring's aorta. And guess what? Harring's aorta was on the verge of blowing too."

"What exactly are you saying?" Jason asked.

Jackson spread his hands. "I don't know. There are strong similarities between these two cases. The widespread inflammation—but I don't think it's infectious. It has more the look of autoimmunity, as if their immune system had started attacking their own organs."

"You mean like lupus?"

"Yeah, something like that. Anyway, Alvin Hayes was in terrible shape. Just about every organ was in a state of deterioration. He was falling apart at the seams."

"He said he wasn't feeling too well," Jason said.

"Ha!" Jackson exclaimed. "That's the understatement of the year."

Jason left pathology, trying to make sense of Jackson's statement. Again he considered the possibility of an unknown infectious disease despite Jackson's opinion. After all, what kind of an autoimmune disease could work so quickly? Jason answered his own question: none.

Before starting the office patients, Jason decided to stop by Hayes's lab. Not that he expected Helene to be helpful, but he thought she might be interested in the fact that Hayes had been so ill the last few weeks of his life. To his surprise, he saw Helene had been crying.

"What's the matter?"

313

Helene shook her head. "Nothing."

"Aren't you working?"

"I finished," Helene said.

All at once Jason realized that without Hayes there to give her instructions, she was lost. Apparently she'd not been apprised of the big picture, a fact that made Jason pessimistic that she would have knowledge of Hayes's breakthrough, if there'd been one. The man's penchant for secrecy was to be society's loss.

"Do you mind if I talk with you for a few minutes?" Jason asked.

"No," Helene said in her usual laconic manner. She motioned him into Hayes's office. Jason followed, assaulted once again by the graphic genital photos.

"I've just come from pathology," Jason began, once they were seated. "Dr. Hayes apparently was a very sick man. Are you sure he didn't complain of feeling ill?"

"He did," Helene admitted, reversing her previous stand. "He kept saying he felt weak."

Jason stared across at her. She seemed softer, more open, and he realized that in contrast to the previous times he'd seen her, her hair was loose, falling to her shoulders instead of severely pulled back.

"Last time you said his behavior was unchanged," he said.

"It was. But he said he felt terrible."

Frustrated by this semantic distinction, Jason again was convinced that she was covering up something. He wondered why, but he felt he'd get nowhere by confronting her.

"Miss Brennquivist," Jason said, speaking patiently, "I want to ask once again. Are you absolutely certain you have no idea what Dr. Hayes could have been referring to when he told me he'd made a major scientific breakthrough?"

She shook her head. "I really don't know. The truth was that things had not been going well in the lab. About three months ago, the rats receiving growth-hormone–releasing factors had mysteriously begun to die."

"Where did the releasing factors come from?"

"Dr. Hayes extracted them himself from rat brains. Mostly the hypothalamus. Then I produced them by recombinant DNA techniques."

"So the experiments were a failure?"

"Completely," Helene said. "But, like any great researcher, Dr.

Hayes was not daunted. Instead he worked harder. He tried different proteins, but unfortunately with the same fatal results.''

"Do you think Dr. Hayes was lying when he told me he'd made a breakthrough?''

"Dr. Hayes never lied,'' Helene said indignantly.

"Well, how do you explain it?'' Jason asked. "At first I thought Hayes was having a nervous breakdown. Now I'm not so sure. What do you think?''

"Dr. Hayes was not having a nervous breakdown,'' Helene said, rising to make it clear the conversation was over. Jason had hit a raw nerve. She was not about to listen to her late boss be calumniated.

Frustrated, Jason went down to his office, where Sally already had two patients waiting for physicals. Between them Jason escaped Sally long enough to check the laboratory values on Holly Jennings. The only significant change from her earlier tests was an elevated gamma globulin, again making Jason consider a non-AIDS-related epidemic involving the autoimmune system. Instead of turning the immune system off, as with AIDS, this problem seemed to turn it on in a destructive fashion.

Midmorning Jason got a call from Margaret Danforth, who stated without preamble, "Thought you should know that Dr. Hayes's urine showed moderate levels of cocaine.''

So Curran was right, Jason realized, hanging up. Hayes was using drugs. But whether that was related to his claim of discovery, his fear of being attacked, or even his actual death, Jason couldn't tell.

He was forced to put aside his speculation as the heavy patient load pushed him further and further behind. The pressure was heightened by a call from Shirley, who had apparently learned of his visit to Helene.

"Jason,'' she said with an edge to her voice, "please don't stir the pot. Just let the Hayes affair calm down.''

"I think Helene knows more than she's telling us,'' Jason said.

"Whose side are you on?'' Shirley asked.

"Okay, okay,'' he said, rudely cutting her off as he was confronted by Madaline Krammer, an old patient who had been squeezed in as an emergency. Up until now her heart condition had been stable. Suddenly she was presenting swollen ankles and chest rales. Despite strong medication, her congestive heart disease had increased in severity to the point that Jason insisted on hospitalization.

"Not this weekend,'' Madaline protested. "My son is coming from California with his new baby. I've never seen my granddaughter.

Please!'' Madaline was a cheerful woman in her mid-sixties with silver-gray hair. Jason had always been fond of her, since she rarely complained and was extraordinarily grateful for his ministrations.

"Madaline, I'm sorry. I wouldn't do this unless I thought it was necessary. But the only way we can adjust your medications is with constant monitoring."

Grumbling but resigned, Madaline agreed. Jason told her he'd see her later, and left her in the capable hands of Claudia. By four P.M., Jason had just about caught up to his appointment schedule. Emerging from his office, Jason ran into Roger Wanamaker, whose impressive bulk completely blocked the narrow hallway.

"My turn," Roger said. "Got a minute for a chat?"

"Sure," said Jason, who never said no to a colleague. He led the way back to his office. Roger ceremoniously dropped a chart on his desk.

"Just so you don't feel lonely," he said. "That's the chart of a fifty-three-year-old executive from Data General who was just brought into the emergency room deader than a doorknob. I'd given him one of our full-scale executive physicals less than three weeks ago."

Jason opened the chart and glanced through the physical, including the EKG and laboratory values. The cholesterol was high but not terrible. "Another heart attack?" he asked, flipping to the report of the chest X ray. It was normal.

"Nope," Roger said. "Massive stroke. The guy had a seizure right in the middle of a board meeting. His wife is madder'n hell. Made me feel terrible. She said he'd been feeling crummy ever since he'd seen us."

"What were his symptoms?"

"Nothing specific," Roger said. "Mostly insomnia and tension, the kind of stuff executives complain about all the time."

"What the hell is going on?" Jason asked rhetorically.

"Beats me," Roger said. "But I'm getting a bad feeling—like we're on the edge of some kind of epidemic or something."

"I've talked with Madsen in pathology. I asked him about an unknown infectious disease. He said no. He said it was metabolic, maybe autoimmune."

"I think we'd better do something. What about the meeting you suggested?"

"I haven't called it yet," Jason admitted. "I'm having Claudia pull all my physicals over the last year and checking to see how the patients are doing. Maybe you should do the same."

"Good idea."

"What about the autopsy on this case?" Jason asked, handing the chart back to Roger.

"The medical examiner has it."

"Let me know what they find."

When Roger left, Jason made a note to call a meeting of the other internists early the following week. Even if he didn't want to know how widespread the problem was, he knew he couldn't sit back and watch while patients with seemingly healthy checkups ended up in the morgue.

En route to his final patient, Jason found himself again thinking of Carol Donner. Suddenly getting an idea, he made a detour to the central desk and found Claudia. He asked her to go down to personnel and see if she could get Alvin Hayes's home address. Jason was confident that if anybody could do it, Claudia could.

Once again heading for his last outpatient, Jason wondered why he'd not thought of getting Hayes's address sooner. If Carol Donner had been living with the man, it would be vastly easier to talk with her at her apartment than at the Club Cabaret, where they obviously felt rather protective. Maybe she'd have some ideas about Hayes's breakthrough, or if nothing else, his health. By the time Jason had finished with his last patient, Claudia had the address. It was in the South End.

After all the outpatients had been seen, and Jason had dictated the necessary correspondence, he headed up the main elevator to begin his inpatient rounds. He saw Madaline Krammer first.

She was already looking better. An increased diuretic had reduced her swollen feet and hands considerably, but when he went over her again he was disturbed to find that her pupils seemed widely dilated and unreactive to light. He made a note on her chart before continuing his rounds.

Before he went in to see Matthew Cowen, Jason pulled his chart to see what the ophthalmology consult had said about his eyes. Shocked, Jason read, "Mild cataract formation in both eyes. Check again in six months." Jason couldn't believe what he was seeing. Cataracts at thirty-five? He remembered the autopsy had noted cataracts in Connoly's eyes. He also remembered just seeing Madaline Krammer's dilated pupils. What the hell were they dealing with? He was further confused when he went down the hall to see Matthew.

"Are you giving me any weird drugs?" he demanded as soon as he glimpsed Jason.

"No. Why do you ask?"

"Because my hair is coming out." To make his point, he tugged on a few strands, which indeed came right out. He scattered them on the pillow.

Jason picked one up, rolling it slowly between his thumb and index finger. It looked normal save for a grayness at the root. Then he examined Matthew's scalp. It too was normal, with no inflammation or soreness.

"How long has this been going on?" he asked, remembering Brian Lennox with startling vividness, as well as Mrs. Harring's comment that her husband's hair had started to fall out.

"It's gotten much worse today," Matthew said. "I don't mean to sound paranoid, but everything seems to be happening to me."

"It's just coincidence," Jason said, trying to buoy his own confidence as much as Matthew's. "I'll have the dermatologist take another look. Maybe it's associated with your dry skin. Has that improved?"

"It's worse, if anything. I shouldn't have come into the hospital."

Jason tended to agree, especially since so many of his patients were doing poorly. By the time he finished rounds, he was exhausted. He almost forgot that some well-meaning friends had insisted he attend a dinner party that night so they could fix him up with a cute thirty-four-year-old lawyer named Penny Lambert. With an hour to kill, Jason decided it wasn't worth going home. Instead, he pulled out the Boston map he kept in his car and located Springfield Street, where Hayes's apartment was located. It was off Washington Street. Thinking it would be a good time to catch Carol Donner, he decided to drive directly there. But that was easier said than done. Heading south, he found himself caught in bumper-to-bumper traffic on Massachusetts Avenue. With persistence, he reached Washington Street and turned left, then left again at Springfield. He located Hayes's building, then found a parking spot.

The neighborhood was a mixture of renovated and unrenovated buildings. Hayes's was in the latter category. Graffiti was spray-painted on the front steps. Jason entered the foyer and noted that several of the mailboxes were broken and that the inner door was unlocked. In fact, the lock had been broken sometime in the distant past and never replaced. Hayes's apartment was on the third floor. Jason started up the poorly lit steps. The smell was musty and damp.

The building was large, with single apartments on each floor. On three Jason tripped over several *Boston Globes* still in their plastic covers. There was no bell so Jason knocked. Hearing no response, he knocked again, harder. The door squeaked open about an inch. Looking down, Jason saw that the lock had recently been forced and that part of the doorjamb was missing. Using his index finger, Jason gingerly pushed the door open. It squeaked again as if in pain. "Hello," he called. There was no answer. He stepped into the apartment. "Hello." There was no noise except a running toilet. He closed the door behind him and started across a dark hall toward a partially opened door.

Jason took one look and almost fled. The place had been trashed. The living room, once decorated with attractive antiques and reproductions, was a wreck. All the drawers in the desk and sideboard had been pulled out and dumped. The sofa cushions had been slashed, and the contents of a large bookcase were strewn about the floor.

Picking his way carefully through the mess, Jason peered into a small bedroom, which was in the same condition as the living room, then went down the hall to what he assumed was the master bedroom. It too was a wreck. Every drawer had been dumped, and the clothes in the walk-in closet had been ripped from hangers and thrown on the floor. Picking some up, he noted they were all men's clothes.

Suddenly the front door squeaked, sending a shiver down Jason's spine. He let the clothes fall to the floor. He started to call out again, hoping that it was Carol Donner, but for a moment he was too scared to speak. He froze, his ears straining for sound. Maybe a draft had pushed the door. . . . Then he heard a thud, like the sound of a shoe knocking against a book or an overturned drawer. Someone was definitely in the apartment, and Jason had the feeling whoever it was knew he was there. Perspiration appeared on his forehead and ran down the side of his nose. Detective Curran's warning that the drug world was dangerous flashed through his mind. He wondered if there was a way to sneak out. Then he realized he was at the end of a long hallway.

All at once a large figure filled the doorway. Even in the darkness Jason could tell that it was carrying a gun.

Panic filled Jason as his heart raced. But still he did not move. A second, smaller figure joined the first and together they stepped into the room. Then they advanced toward Jason, inexorably, step by step. It seemed like an eternity. Jason wanted to cry out or run.

6

The next instant Jason thought he'd died. There was a flash. But then he realized it was not the gun, but a light bulb over his head. He was still alive. Two uniformed policemen stood before him. Jason could have hugged them in his relief.

"Am I glad to see you guys," Jason said.

"Turn around," the larger cop ordered, ignoring Jason's comment.

"I can explain . . ." Jason began, but he was told to shut up and put his hands on the wall, his feet spread apart.

The second cop searched him, removing his wallet. When they were satisfied Jason was unarmed, they pulled his arms off the wall and handcuffed him. Then they marched him back through the apartment, down the stairs, and into the street. Some passersby stopped to watch as Jason was forced into the back seat of an unmarked car.

The cops remained silent during the ride to the stationhouse, and Jason decided there was no point trying to explain until they got there. Now that he had calmed down, he began to think of what he should do. He guessed he'd be able to make a phone call, and he wondered if he should call Shirley or the lawyer he'd used when he'd sold his house and practice.

But when they arrived, the cops just marched Jason to a small, bare room and left him there. The door clicked when they went out and Jason realized he was locked in. He'd never been in jail before and it did not feel good.

As the minutes slipped by, Jason realized the gravity of the situation. He remembered Shirley's request that he not stir the pot. God knows the effect his arrest would have on the clinic if it became public.

Finally the door to the room opened and Detective Michael Curran came in, followed by the smaller policeman. Jason was glad to see Curran, but he was immediately aware the detective did not reciprocate the emotion. The lines on his face seemed deeper than ever.

"Uncuff him," Curran said without smiling. Jason stood up while the uniformed policeman released his hands. He watched Curran's face, trying to fathom his thoughts, but he remained impenetrable.

"I want to talk with him alone," he said to the policeman, who nodded and left.

"Here's your goddamn wallet," Curran said, slapping it into Jason's palm. "You don't take advice too well, do you? What do I have to do to convince you this drug business is serious stuff?"

"I was only trying to talk with Carol Donner . . ."

"Wonderful. So you butt in and screw things up for us."

"Like what?" Jason asked, beginning to feel his temper rise.

"Vice has been staking out Hayes's apartment since we learned it had been searched. We hoped to pull in someone a bit more interesting than you."

"I'm sorry."

Curran shook his head in frustration. "Well, it could have been worse. You could have gotten yourself hurt. Please, doctor—would you get back to your doctoring?"

"Am I free to go?" Jason asked with disbelief.

"Yeah," Curran said, turning to the door. "I'm not going to book you. No sense wasting our time."

Jason left the police station and took a cab back to Springfield Street, where he retrieved his car. He glanced up at Hayes's building and shivered. It had been an unnerving experience.

With enough adrenaline in his system now to run a four-minute mile, Jason was glad he had plans for the evening. His friends the Alics had invited a lively group of people, and the food and wine were really good. The girl they wanted him to meet, Penny Lambert, struck him as a bit of a yuppie, conservatively dressed in a blue suit with a voluminous silk bow tie. Luckily, she was cheerful and talkative and willingly filled the gap left by Jason's inability to stop thinking about Hayes's apartment and his need to speak to Carol Donner.

When coffee and brandy were cleared away, Jason had an idea. Maybe if he offered to take Penny home, he could persuade her to stop at Carol's club. Obviously, Carol was no longer living at Hayes's apartment, and Jason figured he might have a better chance talking to her if he were accompanied by another woman. Penny happily accepted his offer of a lift, and when they were in the car, he asked her if she were feeling adventurous.

"What do you mean?" she asked cautiously.

"I thought you might like to see another side of Boston."

"Like a disco?"

"Something like that," Jason said. In a mildly perverse way, Jason thought the experience might be good for Penny. She was nice enough, but a bit too predictable.

She relaxed, smiling and chatting until they pulled up in front of the Club Cabaret. "Are you sure this is a good idea?" she asked.

"Come on," Jason urged. He'd given her a little background en route, explaining that he wanted to see the girl Dr. Hayes had been involved with. Penny had remembered the story from the newspapers and it had not buoyed her confidence, but with a bit more cajoling he persuaded her to let him park and go in.

Friday was obviously a big night. Gripping Penny's hand, Jason worked his way down the room, hoping to avoid the man with the dark glasses and his two he-man bodyguards. With the help of a five-dollar bill he got one of the waitresses to give them a booth against the side wall, several steps up from the floor. They could see the runway while remaining partially concealed from the dancers by the dark silhouettes of men standing two deep at the bar.

They'd entered between numbers. They had just ordered drinks when the speakers roared to life. Jason's eyes had adjusted to the darkness, and he could just make out Penny's face. What he could see best were the whites of her eyes. She wasn't doing much blinking.

A stripper appeared in a swirl of diaphanous crepe. There were a few catcalls. Penny remained silent. As he paid the waitress for their drinks, Jason asked if Carol Donner was dancing that night. The waitress said her first set was at eleven. Jason was relieved—at least she hadn't been trashed along with Hayes's apartment.

When the waitress left he saw the dancer was down to her G-string and that Penny's lips were tightly pursed.

"This is disgusting," she spat.

322

"It's not the Boston Symphony," Jason agreed.

"She even has cellulite."

Jason looked more carefully when the dancer went back up the stairs. Sure enough, the backs of her thighs were heavily dimpled. Jason smiled. It was curious what a woman noticed.

"Are these men really enjoying themselves?" Penny asked with distaste.

"Good question. I don't know. Most of them look bored."

But not one was bored when Carol came out. Like the night before, the crowd came alive when she began her routine.

"What do you think?" Jason asked.

"She's a good dancer, but I can't believe your friend was involved with her."

"That's exactly what I thought," Jason said. But now he wasn't so sure. Carol Donner projected a very different personality than he had expected.

After Carol finished, and again did not appear among the patrons, Jason had had enough. Penny was eager to leave, and Jason noticed she had little to say on the way home. He guessed the Club Cabaret hadn't made a great impression. When he left her at her door, he didn't even bother to say he'd call. He knew the Alics would be disappointed, but he figured they should have known better than to fix him up with a bow tie.

Back in his own apartment, Jason undressed and picked up the DNA book from the den. He got into bed and started reading. Remembering his exhaustion that afternoon, he thought he'd drop off to sleep quickly. But that wasn't the case. He read about bacteriophages, the viral particles that infected bacteria, and how they were used in genetic engineering. Then he read a chapter on plasmids, which he'd never even heard of before he'd started reading about DNA. He marveled that plasmids were small circular DNA molecules that existed in bacteria and reproduced faithfully when the bacteria reproduced. They, too, served an enormously important function as vehicles for introducing segments of DNA into bacteria.

Still wide awake, Jason looked at the time. It was after two A.M., and sleep was out of the question. Getting up, he went into his living room and stared out at Louisburg Square. A car pulled up. It was the tenant who occupied the garden apartment in Jason's building. He, too, was a doctor and although they were friendly, Jason knew little about the man other than he dated a lot of beautiful women. Jason wondered where he found them all. True to form, the man emerged from his car with an attractive blonde and amid soft laughter disappeared out of sight below. Jason heard the front door to the building close. Silence returned. He could not get Carol Donner out of his mind, wishing he could speak with her. Looking at the clock on the mantel, Jason had an idea. Quickly, he returned to the bedroom, redressed, and went out to his car.

With some misgivings about the possible consequences, Jason drove back to the Combat Zone. In contrast to the rest of the city, it was still very much awake. He drove past the Club Cabaret once, then circled and backed into a side street and parked. He switched off the motor. There were some unsavory types lingering in doorways and on the side street who made Jason feel uncomfortable. He made sure all his doors were locked.

Within a quarter hour of his arrival, a large group of people emerged from the club and went their separate ways. About ten minutes later, a group of dancers appeared. They chatted together in front of the club, then split up. Carol was not among them. Just when Jason had begun to worry that he'd missed her, Carol came out with one of the body-builders. He wore a leather jacket over his T-shirt, but it was not zipped up. They turned right, heading up Washington Street toward Filene's.

Jason started his car, unsure of what to do. Luckily there was plenty of traffic, both cars and pedestrian. To keep Carol in sight, he nudged out into the street, staying to the side. A policeman saw him and waved him on. Carol and her friend turned left on Boylston Street, walked into an open parking lot, and got into a large black Cadillac.

Well, at least he'll be easy to keep in sight, Jason thought. But, never having followed anyone, he discovered it wasn't as easy as he'd imagined, especially if he didn't want to be observed. The Cadillac skirted the edge of the Common, went north on Charles Street, then made a left on Beacon, passing the Hampshire House. Several blocks later, the car pulled over to the left side of the street and double-parked. This was an area of town called Back Bay, composed of large, turn-of-the-century brownstones, most of which had been converted into rental units or condos. Jason passed the Cadillac as Carol alighted. Slowing, he watched in the rearview mirror as she ran up the steps of a building with a large bay window. Jason turned left on Exeter, then left on Marlborough. After waiting about five minutes, he rounded the block. Arriving back on Beacon Street, he looked for the black Cadillac. It was gone.

Jason parked in front of a fire hydrant half a block from Carol's building. At three A.M. Back Bay was peaceful—no pedestrians and only an occasional passing car. Turning in to the walk leading to Carol's building, Jason surveyed the six-story façade and saw no lights in any of the windows. Entering the building's outer foyer, he scanned the names opposite the buzzers. There were fourteen. To his disappointment there was no Donner listed.

Stepping back outside, Jason debated what he should do. Remembering there was an alley running between Beacon and Marlborough, he walked around the block, counting the buildings until he located Carol's. There was a light in the window on the fourth floor. He guessed that had to be Carol's since it was unlikely anyone else would be up.

Intending to go back to the entrance and press the appropriate buzzer, Jason turned and headed back up the alley. He saw the lone figure immediately, but he kept walking, hoping the man would merely pass by. As the distance between them closed, Jason's steps slowed, then stopped. To his dismay he realized it was the body-builder. His leather motorcycle jacket was unzipped, showing a white T-shirt stretched tight across powerful muscles. It was the same individual who had thrown him out of the Club Cabaret the night before.

The man kept coming at Jason, his fingers flexing in apparent anticipation. Jason guessed him to be in his mid-twenties, with a full face that suggested he took steroids. It obviously spelled trouble. And Jason's hope that the man might not recognize him was banished as the goon growled, "What the fuck you doing, creep?"

That was all Jason needed. He spun on his heels and started for the other end of the alley. Unfortunately, his leather-soled loafers were no competition for the body-builder's Nikes. "You goddamn pervert!" he shouted, pulling Jason to a stop.

Jason ducked a roundhouse left hook and grabbed the goon's thigh, hoping to trip him. Unfortunately, it was like grabbing a piano leg. Instead, Jason was jerked upright. The unevenness of the match was already apparent to Jason, who decided he'd prefer some kind of dialogue. "Why don't you find someone your own size!" he yelled in exasperation.

"Because I don't like perverts," the body-builder said, practically lifting Jason off his feet.

Twisting to one side, then the other, Jason wriggled out of his jacket and shot off down the alley, knocking over a garbage can as he fled.

"I'll teach you not to come sniffing around Carol!" the goon shouted, kicking aside the garbage can as he started off after Jason. But Jason's years of jogging paid off. Although the body-builder was quick despite his size, Jason could hear the man's breathing becoming increasingly labored. Jason was almost at the end of the alley when he skidded on loose pebbles, momentarily losing his balance. He scrambled back to his feet just as a heavy hand grabbed his shoulder and spun him around.

7

"Hold it! Police!" A voice shattered the stillness of the Boston night. Jason froze and so did the body-builder. The doors of an unmarked police car parked next to the mouth of the alley suddenly opened and three plainclothesmen leaped out. Once again Jason was ordered, "Up against the wall. Feet apart!" He obeyed, but the body-builder thought about it for a moment. Finally he growled to Jason, "You're a lucky son of a bitch." He then complied.

"Shut up!" a policeman yelled. Jason and his pursuer were quickly searched, then turned around and told to put their hands behind their heads. One cop took out a flashlight and checked their identification.

"Bruno DeMarco?" questioned the man holding the light on the body-builder. Bruno nodded. The light switched to Jason.

"Dr. Jason Howard?"

"That's correct."

"What's going on here?" the policeman asked.

"This little creep was trying to bother my girlfriend," Bruno informed him in an outraged voice. "He followed her."

The policeman looked back and forth between Jason and Bruno, then walked over to the car, opened the door, and took something from the back seat. When he returned, he handed Bruno his wallet and told him to go home and get some sleep. At first Bruno acted as though he hadn't understood, but then he took his wallet.

"I'll remember you, asshole!" he shouted at Jason as he disappeared toward Beacon Street.

"You," the policeman said, pointing to Jason. "In the car!"

Jason was stunned. He couldn't believe they let the bouncer go and not him. He was about to complain when the policeman grasped his arm and forced him into the back seat.

"You are becoming one big pain in the ass," Detective Curran said. He was sitting stolidly, smoking. "I should have let that hunk work you over."

Jason was at a loss for words.

"I hope you have some idea," Curran continued, "of just how much you are screwing up this case. First we have Hayes's apartment covered. You blew that. Then we're watching Carol Donner and you blow that. We might as well bag the whole operation. We're certainly not going to learn anything from her at this point. Where the hell is your car? I presume you came in a car?"

"Just around the corner," Jason said meekly.

"I suggest you get in it and go home," Curran said slowly. "Then I suggest you get back to doctoring and leave this investigation to us. You're making our job impossible."

"I'm sorry," Jason began. "I didn't think . . ."

"Just leave!" Curran said with a wave of dismissal.

Jason climbed out of the police car, feeling pretty dumb. Of course they'd be watching Carol. If she had been living with Hayes, she was probably involved with drugs too. In fact, with her line of work, it was almost a given. Getting into his own car, Jason thought about his jacket, said the hell with it, and drove home.

It was three-thirty when he trudged up the stairs to his apartment and dutifully called his service. He hadn't taken his beeper with him when he left to follow Carol Donner, and he hoped there had been no calls. He was too tired to handle an emergency. There was nothing from the hospital, but Shirley had left a message asking him to call the moment he got in, no matter what time. The page operator told him it was urgent.

Perplexed, Jason dialed. Shirley answered on the first ring. *"Where on earth have you been?"*

"That's a story in itself."

"I want you to do me a favor. Come over right now."

"It's three-thirty," Jason pleaded.

"I wouldn't ask if it weren't important."

Jason put on another jacket, returned to his car, and drove out to Brookline, wondering what emergency couldn't have waited a little longer. The only certainty was that it involved Hayes.

Shirley lived on Lee Street, a road that curved around Brookline Reservoir and wound its way up into a residential area of fine old homes. Her house was a fieldstone building of comfortable proportions with a gambrel roof and twin gables. As Jason entered the cobblestone driveway, he saw that the house was ablaze with light. He pulled up across from the entrance, and by the time he was out of the car, Shirley had the door open.

"Thank you for coming," she said, giving him a hug. She was dressed in a white cashmere sweater and faded jeans and seemed, for the first time since Jason had met her, totally distraught.

She led him into a large living room and introduced him to two GHP executives who also seemed visibly upset. Jason shook hands first with Bob Walthrow, a small, balding man, and then Fred Ingelnook, a Robert Redford lookalike.

"How about a cocktail?" Shirley asked. "You look like you need it."

"Just soda," Jason said. "I'm dead on my feet. What's going on?"

"More trouble. I got a call from security. Hayes's lab was broken into tonight and practically demolished."

"Vandalism?"

"We're not sure."

"Hardly," Bob Walthrow said. "It was searched."

"Was anything taken?" Jason asked.

"We don't know yet," Shirley said. "But that's not the problem. We want to keep this out of the papers. Good Health can't take much more bad publicity. We have two large corporate clients on the fence about joining the Plan. They might be scared off if they hear that the police think Hayes's lab was searched for drugs."

"It's possible," Jason said. "The medical examiner told me Hayes had cocaine in his urine."

"Shit," Bob Walthrow said. "Let's hope the newspapers don't get ahold of this."

"We've got to limit the damage!" Shirley said.

"How do you propose to do that?" Jason asked, wondering why he'd been called.

"The governing board wants us to keep this latest incident quiet."

"That might be difficult," Jason said, taking a sip of his soda. "The papers will probably get it from the police blotter."

"That's exactly the point," Shirley said. "We've decided not to tell the police. But we wanted your opinion."

"Mine?" Jason asked, surprised.

"Well," Shirley said, "we want the opinion of the medical staff. You're a current chief. We thought you could quietly find out how the others felt."

"I suppose," said Jason, wondering how he'd go about polling the other internists and still keep the episode undercover. "But if you want my personal opinion, I don't think it's a good idea at all. Besides, you won't be able to collect insurance unless you inform the police."

"That's a point," Fred Ingelnook said.

"True," Shirley said, "but it's still minor in relation to the public relations problem. For now we will not report it. But we'll check with insurance and hear from the department chiefs."

"Sounds good to me," Fred Ingelnook said. "Fine," Bob Walthrow said.

The conversation wound down and Shirley sent the two executives home. She held Jason back when he tried to follow, suggesting he meet her at eight o'clock that morning. "I've asked Helene to come in early. Maybe we can make some sense out of what's going on."

Jason nodded, still wondering why Shirley couldn't have told him all this on the phone. But he was too tired to care, and after giving her a brief kiss on the cheek, he staggered back out to his car, hoping for two or three hours' sleep.

8

It was just after eight that Saturday morning when Jason, bleary-eyed, entered Shirley's office. It was paneled in dark mahogany, with dark green carpet and brass fixtures, and looked more like it belonged to a banker than to the chief executive of a health care plan. Shirley was on the phone talking to an insurance adjuster, so Jason sat and waited. After she hung up she said, "You were right about the insurance. They have no intention of paying a claim unless the break-in is reported."

"Then report it."

"First let's see how bad the damage is and what's missing."

They crossed into the outpatient building and took the elevator up to the sixth floor. A security guard was waiting for them and unlocked the inner door. They dispensed with the booties and white coat.

Like Hayes's apartment, the lab was a mess. All the drawers and cabinets had been emptied onto the floor, but the high-tech equipment appeared untouched, so it was obvious to both of them that it had been a search and not a destructive visit. Jason glanced into Hayes's office. It was equally littered, with the contents of the desk and several file cabinets strewn about the floor.

Helene Brennquivist appeared in the doorway to the animal room, her face white and drawn. Her hair was again severely pulled back from her face, but without her usual shapeless lab coat, Jason could see she had an attractive figure.

"Can you tell if anything is missing?" Shirley asked.

"Well, I don't see my data books," Helene said. "And some of the E. coli bacterial cultures are gone. But the worst is what's happened to the animals."

"What about them?" Jason asked, noting that her usually emotionless face was trembling with fear.

"Maybe you should look. They've all been killed!"

Jason stepped around Helene and through the steel door into the animal area. He was immediately confronted with a pungent, zoolike stench. He turned on the light. It was a larger room, some fifty feet long and thirty feet wide. The animal cages were organized in rows and stacked one on top of the other, sometimes as many as six high.

Jason started down the nearest row, glancing into individual cages. Behind him the door closed with a decisive click. Helene had not been exaggerating: all the animals that Jason saw were dead, hideously curled in contorted positions, often with bloodied tongues as if they'd chewed them in their final agony.

Suddenly Jason stopped short. Staring into a group of large cages, he saw something that made his stomach turn: rats the likes of which he had never seen. They were huge, almost the size of pigs, and their bald, whiplike tails were as thick as Jason's wrists. Their exposed teeth were four inches long. Moving along, Jason came to rabbits the same size, and then white mice the size of small dogs.

This side of genetic engineering horrified Jason. Although he was afraid of what he might see, morbid curiosity drove him on. Slowly, he looked into other cages, seeing distortions of familiar creatures that made him sick. It was science gone mad: rabbits with several heads and mice with supernumerary extremities and extra sets of eyes. For Jason, genetic manipulation of primitive bacteria was one thing; distortion of mammals was quite another.

He retreated back to the central part of the lab, where Shirley and Helene had been checking the scintillation cultures.

"Have you seen the animals?" Jason asked Shirley with disgust.

"Unfortunately. When Curran was here. Don't remind me."

"Did the GHP authorize those experiments?" Jason demanded.

"No," Shirley said. "We never questioned Hayes. We never thought we had to."

"The power of celebrity," Jason said cynically.

"The animals were part of Dr. Hayes's growth hormone work," Helene said defensively.

"Whatever," Jason said. He was not interested in any ethical argument with Helene at the moment. "At any rate, they're all dead."

"All of them?" Shirley questioned. "How bizarre. What do you think happened?"

"Poison," Jason said grimly. "Though why anyone searching for drugs would bother to kill lab animals beats me."

"Do you have any explanation for all of this?" Shirley said angrily, turning to Helene.

The younger woman shook her head, her eyes darting nervously about the room.

Shirley continued to stare at Helene, who was now shifting uncomfortably from foot to foot. Jason watched, intrigued by Shirley's suddenly aggressive behavior.

"You'd better cooperate," she was saying, "or you're going to be in a lot of trouble. Dr. Howard is convinced you're keeping something from us. If that's true and we find out, I hope you realize what that can do to your career."

Helene's anxiety was finally apparent. "I just followed Dr. Hayes's orders," she said, her voice breaking.

"What orders?" Shirley asked, lowering her voice threateningly.

"We did some free-lance work here . . ."

"What kind?"

"Dr. Hayes moonlighted for a company called Gene, Inc. We developed a recombinant strain of E. coli to produce a hormone for them."

"Were you aware that moonlighting was specifically forbidden under Dr. Hayes's contract?"

"That's what he told me," Helene admitted.

Shirley glared at Helene for another minute. Finally she said, "I don't want you to speak of this to anyone. I want you to make a detailed list of every animal and item missing or damaged in this lab and bring it directly to me. Do you understand?"

Helene nodded.

Jason followed Shirley out of the lab. She had obviously succeeded where he had failed, in breaking through Helene's façade. But she hadn't asked the right questions.

"Why didn't you press her about Hayes's breakthrough?" he said as they arrived at the elevator. Shirley hit the down button repeatedly, obviously furious.

"I didn't think of it. Every time I think the Hayes problem is under control, something new comes up. I had specifically demanded the no-moonlighting clause in his contract.''

"It doesn't much matter now," Jason said, boarding the elevator after Shirley. "The man is dead."

She sighed. "You're right. Maybe I'm overreacting. I just wish this whole affair was over.''

"I still think Helene knows more than she's telling."

"I'll talk to her again."

"And after seeing those animals, you don't think you should call the police?''

"With the police come the newspapers," Shirley reminded him. "With the newspapers comes trouble. Aside from the animals, it doesn't appear that anything terribly valuable is damaged.''

Jason held his tongue. Obviously, reporting the break-in was an administrative decision. He was more concerned about discovering Hayes's breakthrough, and he knew the police and newspapers wouldn't help in finding that. He wondered if the breakthrough could have involved the monstrous animals. The thought gave him a shiver.

Jason started rounds with Matthew Cowen. Unfortunately, there'd been a new development. Besides his other problems, Matthew was now acting bizarrely. Only a few minutes earlier the nurses had found him wandering in the halls, mumbling nonsense to himself. When Jason entered the room he was restrained in the bed, regarding Jason as a stranger. The man was acutely disoriented as to time, place, and person. As far as Jason was concerned, that could have meant only one thing. The man had thrown emboli, probably blood clots, from his injured heart valves into his brain. In other words he'd had a stroke or perhaps even multiple strokes.

Without delay, Jason placed a call for a neurology consult. He also called the cardiac surgeon who'd seen the case. Although he debated immediate anticoagulation, he decided to wait for the neurologist's opinion. In the interim, he started the patient on aspirin and Persantine to reduce platelet adhesiveness. Strokes were a disturbing development and a very bad sign.

Jason did the rest of his rounds quickly and was about to leave for home and for some much-needed sleep when he was paged by the emergency room for one of his patients. Cursing under his breath, he ran downstairs, hoping whatever the problem was, it could be easily solved. Unfortunately, that was not to be the case.

Arriving breathless in the main treatment room, he found a group of residents giving CPR to a comatose patient. A quick look at the monitor screen told him there was no cardiac activity at all.

Jason stepped over to Judith Reinhart, who told him the patient had been found unconscious by her husband when he tried to waken her in the morning.

"Did the EMTs see any cardiac or respiratory activity?"

"None," Judith said. "In fact, she feels cold to me."

Jason touched the woman's leg and agreed. Her face was turned away from him.

"What's the patient's name?" Jason asked, intuitively bracing himself for the blow.

"Holly Jennings."

Jason felt like he'd been hit in the stomach. "My God!" he murmured.

"Are you all right?" Judith asked.

Jason nodded, but he insisted that the ER team maintain the CPR long past any reasonable time. He'd suspected trouble when he'd seen Holly on Thursday, but not this. He just couldn't accept the fact that, like Cedric Harring, Holly would die less than a month after her fancy GHP physical told her she was okay, and two days after he'd seen her again.

Shaken, Jason picked up the phone and called Margaret Danforth.

"So once again there's no cardiac history?" Margaret asked him.

"That's correct."

"What are you people doing down there?" Margaret demanded.

Jason didn't answer. He wanted Margaret to release the case so they could do the autopsy at GHP, but Margaret hesitated.

"We'll do the case today," Jason said. "You'll have a report early next week."

"I'm sorry," Margaret said, making a decision. "There are questions in my mind, and I think I'm obligated by law to do the autopsy."

"I understand. But I suppose you wouldn't mind supplying us with specimens so we can process them here as well."

"I suppose," Margaret said without enthusiasm. "To tell the truth, I don't even know the legality. But I'll find out. I'd rather not wait two weeks for the microscopic."

Jason went home and fell into bed. He slept for four hours, interrupted by a call from the neurologist concerning Matthew. He wanted to anticoagulate and CAT-scan the patient. Jason implored him to do whatever he thought was best.

Jason tried to go back to sleep, but he couldn't. He felt shell-shocked and anxious. He got up. It was a gloomy, late fall day with a slight drizzle that made Boston look dreadful. Fighting a depression, he paced his apartment, searching for something to occupy his mind. Realizing he couldn't stay there, he put on casual clothes and went down to his car. Knowing he was probably asking for trouble, he drove over to Beacon Street and parked in front of Carol's apartment.

Ten minutes later, as if God had finally decided to give him a break, Carol emerged. Dressed in jeans and a turtleneck, with her thick brown hair gathered in a ponytail, she seemed the young college student the Club Cabaret advertised. Feeling the light drizzle, she opened a flower print umbrella and started up the street, passing within a few feet of Jason, who scrunched down in his car seat, unreasonably afraid she'd recognize him.

Giving her a good lead, Jason got out of his car to follow on foot. He lost sight of her on Dartmouth Street, but picked her up at Commonwealth Avenue. As he continued to follow her, he kept a sharp eye out for the likes of Bruno or Curran. At the corner of Dartmouth and Boylston, Jason stopped at a magazine stand and thumbed through a periodical. Carol passed him, waited for the light, then hurried across Boylston. Jason studied the people and the cars, looking for anything suspicious. But there was no indication that Carol was not alone.

She was now passing the Boston Public Library, and Jason guessed she was heading for the Copley Plaza Shopping Mall. After buying the magazine, which turned out to be *The New Yorker*, Jason continued after her. When she folded her umbrella and went into the Copley Plaza, Jason quickened his step. It was a large shopping and hotel complex, and he knew he could easily lose her.

For the next three-quarters of an hour, Jason busied himself by pretending to study window displays, reading his *New Yorker*, and eyeing the crowds. Carol happily hopped from Louis Vuitton to Ralph Lauren to Victoria's Secret. At one point Jason thought she was being tailed, but it turned out the man in question was simply trying to pick her up. She apparently rebuffed his advance when he finally approached her, because he quickly disappeared.

At a little after three-thirty, Carol took her bags and umbrella and retreated into Au Bon Pain. Jason followed, standing next to her as they waited to order and taking the opportunity to note her lovely oval face, smooth olive complexion, and dark liquid eyes. She was a handsome young woman. Jason guessed she was about twenty-four.

"Good day for coffee," he said, hoping to start a conversation.

"I prefer tea."

Jason smiled sheepishly. He wasn't good at pick-ups or small talk. "Tea's good, too," he said, afraid he was making a fool of himself.

Carol ordered soup, tea, and a plain croissant, then carried her tray to one of the large communal tables.

Jason ordered a cappuccino and then, hesitating as though he could find no place to sit, approached her table.

"Do you mind?" he asked, pulling back a chair.

Several of the people at the table looked up, including Carol. A man moved several of his packages. Jason sat down, giving everyone a limp smile.

"What a coincidence," Jason said to Carol. "We meet again."

Carol eyed him over her teacup. She didn't say anything, but she didn't have to. Her expression reflected her irritation.

At once Jason recognized that his whole act appeared to be a come-on and that he was about to be sent packing. "Excuse me," he said. "I don't mean to be a bother. My name is Dr. Jason Howard. I was a colleague of Dr. Alvin Hayes. You're Carol Donner, and I'd like very much to talk with you."

"You're with GHP?" Carol asked suspiciously.

"I'm the current chief of the medical staff." It was the first time Jason had ever used the title. At a regular academic hospital it had great significance, but at GHP the job was a bothersome sinecure.

"How can I be sure?" Carol asked.

"I can show you my license."

"Okay."

Jason reached behind for his wallet, but Carol grasped his arm.

"Never mind," she said. "I believe you. Alvin used to speak of you. Said you were the best clinician there."

"I'm flattered," Jason said. He was also surprised, considering the little contact he'd had with Hayes.

"Sorry to be so suspicious," Carol said, "but I get hassled a lot, especially the last few days. What would you like to talk about?"

"Dr. Hayes," Jason said. "First, I'd like to say that his death was a real loss to us. You have my sympathy."

Carol shrugged.

Jason wasn't sure what to make of her response. "I still have trouble believing Dr. Hayes was involved with drugs. Did you know about that?" he asked.

"I did. But the newspapers had it wrong. Alvin was a minimal user, usually marijuana but occasionally cocaine. Certainly not heroin."

"Not a dealer?"

"Absolutely not. Believe me, I would have known."

"But a lot of drugs and cash were found in his apartment."

"The only explanation I can think of is that the police put both the drugs and the money in the apartment. Alvin was always short of both. If he ever had extra cash, he sent it to his family."

"You mean his ex-wife?"

"Yes. She had custody of his children."

"Why would the police do such a thing?" Jason asked, thinking her comment echoed Hayes's paranoia.

"I don't know, really. But I can't think of any other way the drugs could have gotten there. I can assure you, he didn't have them when I left at nine o'clock that evening."

Jason leaned forward, lowering his voice. "The night Dr. Hayes died he told me he'd made a major discovery. Did he tell you anything about it?"

"He mentioned something. But that was three months ago."

For a moment Jason allowed himself to feel optimistic. Then Carol explained that she didn't know what the discovery was.

"He didn't confide in you?"

"Not lately. We'd kinda drifted apart."

"But you were living together—or did the newspapers get that wrong too?"

"We were living together," Carol admitted, "but in the end just as roommates. Our relationship had deteriorated. He really changed. It wasn't just that he felt physically ill; his whole personality was different. He seemed withdrawn, almost paranoid. He kept talking about seeing you, and I tried to get him to do it."

"You really have no idea what the discovery was?" Jason persisted.

"Sorry," Carol said, spreading her hands in apology. "The only thing I remember was that he said the breakthrough was ironic. I remembered because it seemed an odd way to describe success."

"He said the same to me."

"At least he was consistent. His only other comment was that if all went well, I would appreciate it because I was beautiful. Those were his exact words.''

"He didn't elaborate?''

"That was all he said.''

Taking a sip of his cappuccino, Jason stared at Carol's face. How could an ironic discovery help her beauty? His mind tried to reconcile that statement with his guess that Hayes's discovery had something to do with a cancer cure. It didn't fit.

Finishing her tea, Carol stood up. "I'm glad to have met you,'' she said, thrusting out her hand.

Jason stood up, awkwardly catching his chair to keep it from falling over. He was nonplussed by her sudden departure.

"I don't mean to be rude,'' she said, "but I have an appointment. I hope you solve the mystery. Alvin worked very hard. It would be a tragedy if he'd discovered something important and it was lost.''

"My feelings exactly,'' said Jason, frantic not to see her disappear. "Can we meet again? There's so much more I'd like to discuss.''

"I suppose. But I'm quite busy. When did you have in mind?''

"How about tomorrow?'' Jason suggested eagerly. "Sunday brunch.''

"It would have to be late. I work at night and Saturday is the busiest.''

Jason could well imagine. "Please,'' he said. "It could be important.''

"All right. Let's say two P.M. Where?''

"How about the Hampshire House?''

"Okay,'' Carol said, gathering up her bags and umbrella. With a final smile she left the café.

Glancing at her watch, Carol quickened her step. The impromptu meeting with Jason hadn't figured in her tight schedule, and she didn't want to be late for the meeting with her PhD adviser. She'd spent the late evening and early afternoon polishing the third chapter of her dissertation and she was eager to hear her professor's response. Carol took the escalator down to the street level, thinking about her conversation with Dr. Howard.

It had been a surprise to meet the man after hearing about him for so long. Alvin had told her that Jason had lost his wife and had reacted to the tragedy by completely changing his environment and submerging himself in his work. Carol had found the story fascinating because her thesis involved the psychology of grief. Dr. Jason Howard sounded like a perfect case study.

The Weston Hotel doorman blew his whistle with a shriek that hurt Carol's ears, making her wince. As the taxi lumbered toward her, she admitted that her response to Dr. Jason Howard went a bit further than pure professional interest. She'd found the man unusually attractive, and realized that her knowledge of his vulnerabilities contributed to his appeal. Even his social awkwardness had an endearing quality.

"Harvard Square," Carol said as she got into the cab. She found herself looking forward to brunch the following morning.

Still seated in front of his cooling coffee, Jason admitted to being totally bowled over by Carol's unexpected intelligence and charm. He'd expected an unsophisticated small-town girl who'd somehow been lured away from high school by money or drugs. Instead she was a lovely, mature woman quite capable of holding her own in any conversation. What a tragedy that a person with her obvious assets had become mixed up in the sordid world she inhabited. . . .

The insistent and jarring sound of his beeper snapped Jason back to reality. He switched it off and looked at the LCD display. The word "urgent" blinked twice, followed by a telephone number Jason did not recognize. After seeing his medical identification, the Au Bon Pain manager allowed Jason to use the phone behind the cash register.

"Thank you for calling, Dr. Howard. This is Mrs. Farr. My husband, Gerald Farr, has developed terrible chest pains and he's having trouble breathing."

"Call an ambulance," Jason said. "Bring him to the GHP emergency. Is Mr. Farr a patient of mine?" Jason thought the name sounded familiar but he couldn't place it.

"Yes," Mrs. Farr said. "You did a physical on him two weeks ago. He's the senior vice president of the Boston Banking Company."

Oh, no, Jason thought as he hung up the receiver. *It's happening again*. Deciding to leave his car on Beacon Street until he'd handled the emergency, he ran from the café, dashed over the pedestrian connection to the hotel side of the Copley Plaza complex, and leaped into a cab.

Jason arrived at the GHP emergency room before the Farrs. He told Judith what he expected and even called anesthesia, pleased to learn Philip Barnes was on call.

When he saw Gerald Farr, Jason knew immediately that his worst fears were realized. The man was in agonizing pain and was pale as skim milk, with crystalline beads of perspiration on his forehead.

The initial EKG showed that a large area of the man's heart had been damaged. It was not going to be an easy case. Morphine and oxygen helped to calm the patient, and lidocaine was given for prophylaxis against irregular heartbeats. But, despite everything, Farr wasn't responding. Studying another EKG, Jason had the feeling that the infarcted area of the heart was expanding.

In desperation, he tried everything. But it was all for naught. At five minutes to four, Gerald Farr's eyes rolled up inside his head and his heart stopped.

Unwilling as usual to give up, Jason commanded the resuscitative efforts. They got the heart to start several more times, but each time it would slip back into a deadly pattern and fail again.

Farr never regained consciousness. At six-fifteen, Jason finally declared the patient dead.

"Shit!" said Jason with disgust at himself and life in general. He was unaccustomed to swearing, and the effect of his doing so was not lost on Judith Reinhart. She leaned her forehead against Jason's shoulder and put her arm around his neck.

"Jason, you did the best you could," she said softly. "You did the best anybody could. But our powers are limited."

"The man's only fifty-eight," said Jason, choking back tears of frustration.

Judith cleared the room of the other nurses and residents. Coming back to Jason, she put her hand on his shoulder. "Look at me, Jason!" she said.

Reluctantly, Jason turned his face toward the nurse. A single tear had run down from the corner of his eye, along the crease of his nose. Softly but firmly she told Jason that he could not take these episodes so personally. "I know that two in one day is an awful burden," she added. "But it's not your fault."

Jason knew intellectually that she was right, but emotionally it was another story. Besides, Judith had no idea how badly his inpatients were doing, especially Matthew Cowen, and Jason was embarrassed to tell her. For the first time, he seriously contemplated giving up medicine. Unfortunately, he had no idea of what else he could do. He wasn't trained for anything else.

After promising Judith that he was okay, Jason went out to face

Mrs. Farr, steeling himself against the expected anger. But Mrs. Farr, in the depths of her grief, had decided to take the burden of guilt on herself. She said her husband had been complaining of feeling ill for a week, but that she'd ignored his complaints because, frankly, he'd always been a bit of a hypochondriac. Jason tried to comfort the woman as Judith had tried to comfort him. He was about equally successful.

Confident that the medical examiner would take the case, Jason didn't burden Mrs. Farr with an autopsy request. By law, the ME didn't need authorization to do a postmortem in cases of questionable death. But to be sure, he called Margaret Danforth. The response was as expected: she indeed wanted the case, and while she had Jason on the phone, she spoke to him about Holly Jennings.

"I take back that snide comment I made this morning," Margaret said. "You people are just having bad luck. The Jennings woman was as bad off as Cedric Harring. All her vessels looked terrible, not just the heart."

"That's not a lot of consolation," Jason said. "I had just given her a physical showing everything was fine. I did a follow-up EKG on Thursday, but that showed only minimal changes."

"No kidding? Wait till you see the sections. Grossly the coronary vessels looked ninety percent occluded, and it was disseminated, not focal. Surgery wouldn't have done a damn thing. Oh, by the way, I checked and it's okay for us to give you small specimens from Jennings's case. But I should have a formal request in writing."

"No problem," Jason said. "Same with Farr?"

"Sure thing."

Jason took a cab back to his car and drove home. Despite the fog and rain, when he got home, he went for a jog. Getting mud-spattered and soaked had a mild cathartic effect, and after a shower he felt some relief from his burdensome emotions and depressive feelings. Just when he was starting to think about food, Shirley called and asked him over for dinner. Jason's first response was to say no. But then he recognized he felt too depressed to be alone, so he accepted. After changing into more reasonable clothes, he went down to his car and headed west toward Brookline.

Eastern's flight #409, nonstop from Miami to Boston, banked sharply before lining up for the final approach. It touched down at seven thirty-seven as Juan Díaz closed his magazine and looked out at the fog-shrouded Boston skyline. It was his second trip to Boston and he wasn't all that pleased. He wondered why anyone would choose to live in such predictably bad weather. It had rained on his previous trip just a few days ago. Looking down on the tarmac, he saw the wind and rain in the puddles and thought nostalgically of Miami, where late fall had finally put an end to the searing summer heat.

Getting his bag from under the seat in front of him, Juan wondered how long he'd be in Boston. He remembered that on the previous trip he'd been there only two days, and he hadn't had to do a thing. He wondered if he'd have the same good fortune. After all, he got his five thousand no matter what.

The plane taxied toward the terminal. Juan looked around the compartment with a sense of pride. He wished his family back in Cuba could see him now. Would they be surprised! There he was, flying first class. After being sentenced to life in prison by the Castro government, he'd been released after only eight months and sent first to Mariel and then, to his astonishment, to the USA. That was to be his punishment for having been convicted of multiple murder and rape— being sent to the USA! It was so much easier to do his type of work in the United States. Juan felt that the one person in the world whose hand he'd most like to shake was a peanut farmer someplace in Georgia.

The plane gave a final lurch, then was still. Juan rose to his feet and stretched. Taking his carry-on bag, he headed for baggage. After retrieving his suitcase, he caught a cab to the Royal Sonesta Hotel, where he registered as Carlos Hernández from Los Angeles. He even had a credit card in that name, with a legitimate number. He knew the number was good, since he'd taken it off a receipt he'd found at the Bal Harbour shopping plaza in Miami.

Once he was comfortably relaxed in his room, with his second silk suit hanging in the closet, Juan sat at the desk and called a number he'd been given in Miami. When the phone was answered, he told the person he needed a gun, preferably a .22 caliber. With that business taken care of, he got out the name and address of the hit and looked up the location on the map supplied by the hotel. It wasn't far away.

The evening with Shirley was a great success. They dined on roast chicken, artichokes, and wild rice. Afterward they had Grand Marnier in front of the fire in the living room and talked. Jason learned that

Shirley's father had been a doctor and that back in college she'd entertained the idea of following in his footsteps.

"But my father talked me out of it," Shirley said. "He said that medicine was changing."

"He was right about that."

"He told me that it would be taken over by big business and that someone who cared about the profession should go into management. So I switched to business courses, and I believe I made the right choice."

"I'm sure you did, too," Jason agreed, thinking about the explosion of paperwork and the malpractice dilemma. Medicine had indeed changed. The fact that he now worked for a salary for a corporation stood as testament to that change. When he'd been in medical school he'd always imagined he'd work for himself. That had been part of the appeal.

At the end of the evening, there was a bit of awkwardness. Jason said he'd best be going, but Shirley encouraged him to stay.

"You think that would be a good idea?" Jason asked.

She nodded.

Jason wasn't so sure, saying he'd have to get up early for rounds and wouldn't want to disturb her. Shirley insisted she was up at seven-thirty as a matter of course, Sundays included.

They stared at each other for a time, the firelight making Shirley's face glow.

"There's no obligation," Shirley said softly. "I know we both have to be slow about this. Let's just be together. We've both been under stress."

"Okay," Jason said, recognizing he did not have the strength to resist. Besides, he was flattered that Shirley was so insistent. He was becoming more open to the idea that not only could he care about another person but another person could care about him.

But Jason did not get to sleep the whole night through. At three-thirty he felt a hand on his shoulder, and he sat up, momentarily confused as to his whereabouts. In the half-light, he could just make out Shirley's face.

"I'm sorry to have to bother you," she said gently, "but I'm afraid the phone is for you." She handed him the receiver from the nightstand.

Jason took the phone and thanked her. He hadn't even heard the phone ring. Propping himself on one elbow, he put the receiver to his ear. He was certain it would be bad news, and he was right. Matthew Cowen had been found dead in his bed, apparently having suffered a final, massive stroke.

"Has the family been notified?" Jason asked.

"Yes," said the nurse. "They live in Minneapolis. They said they'd come in the morning."

"Thanks," Jason said, absently giving the phone back to Shirley.

"Trouble?" Shirley asked. She set the receiver back in the cradle.

Jason nodded. Trouble had become his middle name. "A young patient died. Thirty-five or so. He had rheumatic heart disease. He was in for evaluation for surgery."

"How bad was his heart disease?" asked Shirley.

"It was bad," Jason said, seeing Matthew's face, remembering him as he'd been when he entered the hospital. "Three of his four valves were affected. They would have had to replace all of them."

"So there were no guarantees," Shirley said.

"No guarantees," Jason agreed. "Three valve replacements can be tricky. He's had congestive heart failure for a long time, undoubtedly affecting his heart, lungs, kidneys and liver. There would have been problems, but he had age on his side."

"Maybe it was for the best," Shirley suggested. "Maybe he's been spared from a lot of suffering. Sounds like he would have been in and out of the hospital for the rest of his life."

"Maybe so," Jason said without conviction. He knew what Shirley was doing: she was trying to make him feel better. Jason appreciated her effort. He patted the thigh through the thin cover of her robe. "Thanks for your support."

The night seemed awfully cold when Jason ran out to his car. It was still raining, in fact, harder than before. Turning up the heat, he rubbed his thighs to get his circulation going. At least there was no traffic. At four A.M., Sunday morning, the city was deserted. Shirley had tried to get him to stay, arguing that there was nothing for Jason to do if the man had died and the family was not available. As true as this was, Jason felt an obligation to his patient that he could not dismiss. Besides, he knew he'd not be able to get back to sleep. Not with yet another death on his conscience.

The GHP parking lot was mostly empty. Jason was able to park close to the hospital entrance rather than under the outpatient building where he usually parked. As he stepped out of his car, preoccupied with thoughts of Matthew Cowen, he didn't notice a darkened figure hunched over at the side of the hospital door. Rounding the front of his car, the figure lunged at Jason. Caught completely unaware, Jason screamed. But the figure turned out to be one of the drunken street people who frequented the GHP emergency room, asking for spare change. With a shaking hand, Jason gave him a dollar, hoping he'd at least buy himself a little food.

Shirley had been right. There was nothing for Jason to do but write a final note in Matthew Cowen's chart. He went in and viewed his body. At least Matthew's face looked calm, and as Shirley suggested, he was now spared further suffering. Silently, Jason apologized to the dead man.

Paging the resident on call, Jason instructed him to ask the family for an autopsy. Jason explained he might not be immediately available. Then, feeling as ineffectual as ever, after these deaths, he left the hospital and returned to his apartment. He lay for some time, staring at the ceiling, unable to sleep. He wondered what kind of job he could get in the pharmaceutical industry.

9

Cedric Harring, Brian Lennox, Holly Jennings, Gerald Farr, and now Matthew Cowen. Jason had never lost so many patients in such a short period of time. All night the parade of their faces had interrupted his dreams, and when he awakened about eleven he was as exhausted as though he'd never slept at all. He forced himself to do his regular Sunday six miles, then showered and dressed carefully in a pale yellow shirt with white collar and cuffs, dark brown pants, and a muted brown plaid jacket of linen and silk. He was glad he had the meeting with Carol to distract him.

The Hampshire House was on Beacon Street, overlooking the Boston Public Gardens. In contrast to Saturday's rain, the sky was filled with bright sunshine and scudding clouds. The American flag flying over the Hampshire entrance snapped in the late autumn breeze. Jason arrived early and asked for a table in the front room on the first floor. A fire crackled comfortably and a piano player kept up a stream of old favorites.

Jason regarded the people around him. They were all respectably dressed and were engaged in lively conversation, obviously unaware of whatever new medical horror was sweeping their city. . . . Then Jason warned himself not to let his imagination run wild. Half a dozen deaths didn't mean an epidemic. Besides, he wasn't even sure it was infectious. Still, he couldn't get the fatalities out of his mind.

Carol arrived at five minutes after two. Jason stood up, waving to get her attention. She was appealingly dressed in a white silk blouse with black wool pants. Her fresh, young innocent appearance away from the club always amazed Jason. Noticing him, she smiled broadly and made her way over to the table. She acted mildly out of breath.

"Sorry I'm late," she said, arranging her things, which included a suede jacket, a canvas bag full of papers, and a shoulder handbag. As she did so, she glanced frequently at the entrance.

"Are you expecting someone?" Jason asked.

"I certainly hope not. But I have this crazy boss who insists on being overprotective. Especially since Alvin died. He's keeping someone with me most of the time, supposedly for my protection. At night I don't mind, but during the day I don't like it. Mr. Muscle showed up this morning, but I sent him on his way. He may have followed me anyway."

Jason wondered if he should mention he'd met Bruno, but decided against it. It was only after they had been served without glimpsing Bruno's hulk that they both began to relax a bit.

"I probably should be more grateful to my boss," Carol said. "He's been so good to me. Right now I'm living in one of his apartments on Beacon Street. I don't even pay rent."

Jason didn't want to consider all the reasons for which Carol's boss might want her to have a nice apartment. Embarrassed, he turned his attention to his omelette.

"So . . ." Carol said, brandishing her fork. "What else did you want to ask me?" She took a sizable bite of her French toast.

"Have you remembered anything else about Alvin Hayes's discovery?"

"Nope," Carol said, swallowing. "Besides, even when he used to discuss his work with me, I found it incomprehensible. He always forgot that not everyone is a nuclear physicist." Carol laughed, her eyes sparkling attractively.

"I've been told that Alvin free-lanced for another bioengineering company," Jason said. "Did you know anything about that?"

"I guess you're referring to Gene, Inc." Carol paused, her smile fading. "That was supposed to be a big secret." She cocked her head to the side. "But now that he's gone, I guess it doesn't matter. He'd worked for them for about a year."

"Do you know what he did for them?"

"Not really. Something with growth hormone. But lately they'd gotten into a row. Something to do with finances. I don't know the details. . . ."

Jason realized that he'd been right after all. Helene had been holding back. If Hayes had been feuding with Gene, Inc., she must have known.

"What do you know about Helene Brennquivist?"

"She's a nice lady." Carol put down her fork. "Well . . . that's not quite sincere. She's probably okay. But to tell you the truth, Helene is the reason Alvin and I stopped being lovers. Because they worked together so much, she started coming over to the apartment. Then I found out they were having an affair. That I couldn't handle. It irked me she'd been so secret about it, especially right under my nose in my own house."

Jason was amazed. He'd guessed that Helene was withholding information, but it had never dawned on him that she was sleeping with Hayes. Jason studied Carol's face. He could see that mentioning the affair had brought back unpleasant feelings. Jason wondered if Carol had been as angry with Hayes as she was with Helene.

"What about Hayes's family?" he asked, deliberately changing the subject.

"I don't know much about them. I spoke to his ex-wife on the phone once or twice, but never in person. They'd been divorced for five years or so."

"Did Hayes have a son?"

"Two. Two boys and a girl."

"Do you know where they lived?"

"A small town in New Jersey. Leonia or something like that. I remember the street though—Park Avenue. I remembered that because it sounded so pretentious."

"Did he ever say anything about one of his sons being sick?"

Carol shook her head. Motioning to a waitress, Carol indicated she wanted more coffee. They ate in silence for a while, enjoying the food and the atmosphere.

When Jason's beeper went off, it startled them both. Luckily, it was just his service saying Cowen's family had finally arrived from Minneapolis and hoped to meet him at the hospital around four.

Returning from the phone, Jason suggested they take advantage of the nice weather and walk in the garden. After they'd crossed Beacon Street, she surprised him by taking his arm. He surprised himself by enjoying it. Despite her somewhat dubious profession, Jason had to admit he enjoyed her company immensely. Aside from her wholesome good looks, her vitality was infectious.

They skirted the swan boat pond, passed under the mounted bronze statue of Washington, then crossed the bridge spanning the central neck of the waterway. The swan boats had been retired for the season. Finding an empty bench under a now naked willow tree, Jason turned the conversation back to Hayes.

"Did he do anything out of the ordinary over the last three months? Anything unexpected . . . out of character?"

Carol picked up a pebble and tossed it into the water. "That's a hard question," she said. "One of the things I liked about Alvin was his impulsiveness. We would do a lot of things on the spur of the moment, like taking trips."

"Had he done much traveling recently?"

"Oh, yes," Carol said, searching for another stone. "Last May he went to Australia."

"Did you go?"

"No. He didn't take me. He said it was strictly business—and that he needed Helene to help him with various tests. At the time I believed him, chump that I was."

"Did you ever find out what his business was?"

"Something involving Australian mice. I remember him saying they had peculiar habits. But that's all I knew. He had lots of mice and rats in his lab."

"I know," Jason said, vividly picturing the revolting dead animals. Jason had asked if Hayes had been behaving oddly. A sudden trip to Australia might be considered bizarre, but without knowing his current studies it was hard to be sure. He'd have to take the issue up with Helene.

"Any other trips?"

"I got to go to Seattle."

"When was that?"

"In the middle of July. Apparently old Helene wasn't feeling up to par, and Alvin needed a driver."

"A driver?"

"That was another weird thing about Alvin," Carol said. "He couldn't drive. He said he'd never learned and never would."

Jason recalled the police commenting the night he died that Hayes had no driver's license.

"What happened in Seattle?"

"Not a lot. We were only in the city a couple of days. We did visit the University of Washington. Then we headed up into the Cascades. Now, that's beautiful country, but if you think it rains a lot in Boston, wait until you visit the Pacific Northwest. Have you?"

"No," Jason said absently. He tried to imagine a discovery that would involve trips to Seattle and Australia.

"How long were you away?"

"Which time?"

"You went more than once?"

"Twice," Carol said. "The first trip was for five days. We visited the University of Washington and saw the sights. On the second trip, which was several weeks later, we only stayed two nights."

"Did you do the same things both times?"

Carol shook her head. "The second trip we bypassed Seattle and went directly into the Cascades."

"What on earth did you do?"

"I just hung out, relaxed. We went to a lodge. It was gorgeous."

"What about Alvin? What did he do?"

"About the same. But he was interested in the ecology and all that stuff. You know, always the scientist."

"So it was like a vacation?" Jason asked, thoroughly perplexed.

"I suppose." She tossed another stone.

"What did Alvin do at the University of Washington?" Jason asked.

"He saw an old friend. Can't think of his name. Someone he trained with at Columbia."

"A molecular geneticist like Alvin?"

"I believe so. But we weren't there very long. I visited the Psychology Department while they were talking."

"That must have been interesting." Jason smiled, thinking the Psychology Department would have enjoyed getting their academic hands on the likes of Carol Donner.

"Damn," she said, suddenly checking her watch. "I've got to run. I have another appointment."

Jason stood up, taking her hand. He was impressed by the delicacy with which Carol described her work. "An appointment" sounded so professional. They walked to the edge of the park.

Refusing a ride, Carol said good-bye and started up Beacon Street. Jason watched as her figure receded in the distance. She seemed so carefree and happy. *What a tragedy*, he thought. *Time, which seems boundless to her youthful mind, will soon catch up with her*. What kind of life was topless dancing and dates with men? He didn't like to think about it. Turning in the opposite direction, Jason walked to De Luca's Market and bought the makings for a simple supper: barbecued chicken and salad greens. All the while he went over his conversation with Carol. He had a lot more information, but it provided more questions than conclusions. Still, he was now sure of two things. One, Hayes had definitely made a discovery, and two, the key was Helene Brennquivist.

In less than twenty-four hours, Juan had the whole scenario planned out. Since this was not supposed to look like a traditional hit, it required more thought. The usual ploy was to nail the victim in a crowd, putting a low-caliber pistol to the head, and pow, it was all over. That kind of operation needed little planning, only the right circumstances. The whole performance relied on the peculiar mentality of crowds. After any shocking event, everyone was so intent on the victim that the perpetrator could melt away unnoticed, even pretending to be one of the curious onlookers. All he had to do was drop the gun.

But the instructions on this job were different. The hit was to be staged as a rape, Juan's specialty. He smiled to himself, amazed that he could get paid for something he used to do as a sport. The United States was a strange and wonderful place, where the law often gave the felon more consideration than the victim.

This time Juan realized he'd have to get his victim alone. That was what made it a challenge. It was also what made it fun, because without witnesses he could do what he liked with the woman, as long as when he left she was dead.

Juan decided to follow the victim and accost her in the foyer of her building. The threat of immediate bodily injury made in a soft, reasonable voice should be enough to persuade her to take him up to her apartment. Once inside, it would be all fun and games.

He followed the mark on a short shopping excursion in Harvard Square. She bought a magazine at a corner kiosk, then headed for a grocery store called Sages. Juan lingered across the street, examining the window of a bookstore, surprised the place was open on Sunday. The mark came out of the grocery store with a plastic shopping bag, cut diagonally across the street, and disappeared into a bakery café. Juan followed—coffee sounded good, even if it was the American kind. He preferred Cuban coffee: thick, sweet, and rich.

While he sipped the watery brew, he stared at his victim. He was astounded at his good luck. The woman was beautiful. He guessed mid-twenties. *What a deal*, he thought. He could already feel himself getting hard. He wouldn't have to fake this one.

Half an hour later, the mark finished, paid, and walked out of the café. Juan tossed a ten-dollar bill on the table. He felt generous. After all, he'd be five thousand richer when he got back to Miami.

To his delight, the woman continued up Brattle Street. Juan slowed his pace, content to just keep her in view. When she turned onto Concord, he speeded up, knowing she was almost home. When she reached Craigie Arms Apartment Complex, Juan was right behind her. A quick glance up and down Concord Avenue suggested the timing was perfect. Now it depended on what was happening inside the building.

Juan paused long enough to be sure the inner door had been opened. With split-second timing he was in the foyer and had one foot over the threshold of the inner door. It was then that he spoke.

"Miss Brennquivist?"

Momentarily startled, Helene looked into Juan's darkly handsome Hispanic face.

"Ja," she said with her Scandinavian accent, thinking he must be a fellow tenant.

"I've been dying to meet you. My name is Carlos."

Helene paused fatally, her keys still in her hand. "Do you live here?" she asked.

"Sure do," Juan said with practiced ease. "Second floor. How about you?"

"Third," Helene said. She stepped through the door, Juan directly behind her.

"Nice to meet you," she added. She debated using the stairs or the elevator. Juan's presence made her feel uncomfortable.

"I was hoping we could talk," Juan said, coming alongside her. "How about inviting me up for a drink?"

"I don't think that . . ." Helene saw the gun and gasped.

"Please don't make me angry, miss," Juan said in a soothing voice. "I do things I regret when I'm angry." He hit the elevator button. The doors opened. He motioned for Helene to enter and stepped in behind her. Everything was working perfectly.

As the elevator clanked and thumped upward, Juan smiled warmly. It was best to keep everything calm.

Helene was paralyzed by panic. Not knowing what to do, she did nothing. The man terrified her, yet he seemed reasonable, and he was very well dressed. He looked like a successful businessman. Maybe he was associated with Gene, Inc., and they wanted to search her apartment. She thought briefly about screaming or trying to run, but then she remembered the gun.

The elevator grated open on the third floor. Juan graciously motioned for her to proceed. With her keys in her shaking hand, she walked toward her door and opened it. Juan immediately put his foot over the threshold, just as he'd done downstairs. After they'd both entered, he closed the door and locked it, using all three latches. Helene stood dumbly in the small entrance hall, unable to move.

"Please," Juan said, politely motioning for her to enter the living room. To his surprise, a plump blonde was sitting on the sofa. Juan had been told Helene lived alone. *Never mind*, he thought. "What is that saying you people have?" he murmured. "When it rains, it pours. This party is going to be twice as good as I expected."

He brandished his weapon, motioning for Helene to sit opposite her roommate. The women exchanged anxious looks. Then Juan yanked the telephone line from the wall, leaving the three color-coded wires to dangle nakedly in the air. He went over to Helene's stereo and turned on the tuner. A classical station came on. Figuring out the digital controls, he switched to a hard-rock station and turned up the volume.

"What kind of party is it without some music?" he shouted as he took some thin rope out of his pocket.

10

Jason got to the hospital early Monday morning and suffered through rounds. No one was doing well. After he got to his office, he began calling Helene at every spare moment. She never answered. At mid-morning he even ran up to the sixth floor lab only to find it dark and deserted. Returning to his office, Jason was irritated. He felt that Helene had been obstructive from the start, and now by not making herself available, she was compounding the problem.

Jason picked up the telephone, called personnel, and got Helene's home address and phone number. He called immediately. After the phone rang about ten times, he slammed the receiver down in frustration. He then called Personnel and asked to speak to the director, Jean Clarkson. When she came on the line, Jason inquired about Helene Brennquivist: "Has she called in sick? I've been trying to reach her all morning."

"I'm surprised," Ms. Clarkson said. "We haven't heard from her, and she's always been dependable. I don't think she's missed a day in a year and a half."

"But if she were ill," Jason asked, "you would expect her to call?"

"Absolutely."

Jason hung up the phone. His irritation changed to concern. He had a bad feeling about Helene's absence.

His office door opened and Claudia stuck her head in. "Dr. Danforth's on line two. Do you want to talk with her?"

Jason nodded.

"Do you need someone's chart?"

"No, thanks," Jason said as he lifted the phone.

Dr. Danforth's resonant voice came over the line: "I'd say Good Health had better start screening their patients. I've never seen corpses in such bad shape. Gerald Farr is as bad as the rest. He didn't have an organ that appeared less than one hundred years old!"

Jason didn't answer.

"Hello?" Margaret said.

"I'm here," Jason said. Once again he was embarrassed to tell Margaret that a month ago he'd done a complete physical on Farr and found nothing wrong despite the man's unhealthy lifestyle.

"I'm surprised he didn't have a stroke several years ago," Margaret said. "All his vessels were atheromatous. The carotids were barely open."

"What about Roger Wanamaker's patient?" Jason asked.

"What was the name?"

"I don't know," he admitted. "The man died on Friday of a stroke. Roger said you were getting the case."

"Oh, yes. He also presented almost total degeneration. I thought health plans were supposed to provide largely preventive medicine. You people aren't going to make much money if you sign up such sick patients." Margaret laughed. "Kidding aside, it was another case of multisystem disease."

"Do you people do routine toxicology?" Jason asked suddenly.

"Sure. Especially nowadays. We test for cocaine, that sort of stuff."

"What about doing more toxicology on Gerald Farr? Would that be possible?"

"I think we still have blood and urine," Margaret said. "What do you want us to look for?"

"Just about everything. I'm fishing, but I have no idea what's going on here."

"I'll be happy to run a battery of tests," Margaret said, "but Gerald Farr wasn't poisoned, I can tell you that. He just ran out of time. It was as if he were thirty years older than his actual age. I know that doesn't sound very scientific, but it's the truth."

"I'd appreciate the toxicology tests just the same."

"Will do," Margaret said. "And we'll be sending some specimens for your people to process. I'm sorry it takes us so long to do our microscopics."

Jason hung up and went back to work, vacillating between self-doubt and the discomfiting sense that something was going on that was beyond his comprehension. Every time he got a moment, he dialed Hayes's lab. There was still no answer. He called Jean Clarkson again, who said that she'd call if she heard from Miss Brennquivist and to please stop bothering her. Then she slammed down the phone. Nostalgically Jason remembered those days when he got more respect from the hospital staff.

After seeing the last morning patient, Jason sat at his desk nervously drumming his fingers. All at once a wave of certainty spread through him, telling him that Helene's absence was not only significant, it was serious. In fact, he was convinced that it was so serious that he should inform the police immediately.

Jason traded his white coat for his suit jacket, and went to his car. He decided he'd better see Detective Curran in person. After their last encounter, he didn't think Curran would take him seriously over the phone.

Jason remembered the way to Curran's office without difficulty. Glancing into the sparsely furnished room, he saw the detective working over a form at his metal desk, his large fist gripping his pencil as if it were a prisoner trying to escape.

"Curran," Jason said, hoping the man would be in a better mood than he'd been the other night.

Curran glared up. "Oh, no!" he exclaimed, tossing his pencil onto the uncompleted form. "My favorite doctor!" He made an exaggerated expression of exasperation, then waved Jason into his office.

Jason pulled a metal-backed chair over to Curran's desk. The detective eyed him with obvious misgiving.

"There's been a new development," Jason said. "I thought you should know."

"I thought you were going back to doctoring."

Ignoring the cut, Jason went on. "Helene Brennquivist hasn't been at work all day."

"Maybe she's sick. Maybe she's tired. Maybe she's been sick and tired of you and all your questions."

Jason tried to hold on to his temper. "Personnel says she's extremely reliable. She'd never take a day off without calling. And when I tried her apartment, there was no answer."

Detective Curran gave Jason a disdainful look. "Have you considered the possibility that the attractive young lady might have taken a long weekend with a boyfriend?"

"I don't think so. Since I saw you I've learned she was having an affair with Hayes."

Curran sat up and for the first time gave Jason his full attention.

"I always felt she was covering for Hayes," Jason continued. "Now I know why. And I also believe she knows a lot more about his work than she's saying, and why his places were searched. I think Hayes made a major breakthrough and someone is after his notes—"

"If there was a breakthrough."

"I'm sure there was," Jason said. "And it adds to my suspicions about Hayes's death. It was too convenient."

"You're jumping to conclusions."

"Hayes said someone was trying to kill him," Jason said. "I think he made a major scientific discovery and was murdered because of it."

"Hold on!" Curran shouted, banging his fist on his desk. "The medical examiner determined that Dr. Alvin Hayes died of natural causes."

"An aneurysm, to be exact. But he was still being followed."

"He *thought* he was," Curran corrected, his voice rising in anger.

"I think he was too," Jason said with equal vehemence. "That would explain why someone ransacked his apartment and his—"

"We *know* why his apartment was tossed," Curran interrupted. "Only we found the drugs and the money first!"

"Hayes may have used cocaine." Jason was shouting now. "But he wasn't a dealer! And I think those drugs were planted, and—" He started to mention his conversation with Carol, then stopped. He wasn't ready to tell Curran that he had persisted in seeing the dancer. "In any case," he said more quietly, "I think the reason the lab was torn apart was that someone was searching for his lab books."

"What was that about a lab?" Curran's heavy-lidded eyes opened wide and his face turned a mottled red.

Jason swallowed.

"Dammit!" Curran yelled. "You mean to tell me Hayes's lab was tossed and it wasn't reported? What do you people think you're doing?"

"The clinic was concerned about negative press," Jason said, forced to defend the decision he did not condone.

"When did this happen?"

"Friday night."

"What was taken?"

"Several data books and some bacterial cultures. But none of the valuable equipment. And it wasn't a robbery." Jason watched Curran's hound-dog face for some sign his concern for Helene was vindicated.

"Any damage, vandalism?" was all he said.

"Well, they turned the place upside down and dumped everything on the floor. So the lab was a mess. But the only deliberate destruction involved those, uh, animals."

"Good," Curran said. "Those monsters should have been destroyed. They made me sick. How were they killed?"

"Probably poisoned. Our pathology department is checking that out."

Detective Curran ran his thick fingers through his once-red hair. "You know something?" he asked rhetorically. "With the amount of cooperation I've gotten from you eggheads, I'm goddamned glad I turned this case over to Vice. They can have it. Maybe you'd like to go down the hall and rant and rage at them. Maybe they'll get a charge out of the fact that your mad scientist was humping his lab assistant as well as the exotic dancer—"

"Hayes and the dancer were no longer lovers."

"Oh, really?" Curran asked with a short, hollow laugh that ended in a belch. "Why don't you go over to the Vice department and leave me alone, doctor. I have a lot of genuine homicides to ponder."

Curran picked up his pencil and went back to his forms. Enraged, Jason returned to the ground floor and surrendered his visitor's pass. Then he went out to his car. Driving along Storrow Drive, with the Charles River lazily spread out on the right, Jason finally began to calm down. He was still convinced something had happened to Helene, but he decided that if the police weren't concerned, there was little he could do.

He pulled into the GHP parking lot and went back to his office. Claudia and Sally hadn't returned from their lunch break yet. A few patients were already waiting. Jason changed back to his white coat and called to check on Madaline Krammer's cardiac consult. Harry Sarnoff had agreed with Jason's appraisal, and Madaline was having an angiogram.

As soon as Sally returned, Jason went to work seeing his scheduled patients. He was on his third afternoon patient when Claudia ducked into the exam room.

"You have a visitor," she announced.

"Who?" Jason asked, tearing off a prescription.

"Our fearless leader. And she's foaming at the mouth. I thought I should warn you."

Jason handed the prescription to the patient, tossed his stethoscope around his neck, and walked down the corridor to his office. Shirley was standing by the window. The moment she heard Jason she turned to face him. She was without question furious.

"I certainly hope you have a good explanation, Dr. Howard," she said. "I just got a call from the police. They're on their way here to get a formal statement on why I didn't report the break-in of Hayes's lab. They said they heard about it from you—and they're threatening obstruction of justice."

"I'm sorry," said Jason. "It was an accident. I was at the police station. I didn't mean to mention it . . ."

"And just what the hell were you doing down at the station?"

"I wanted to see Curran," Jason said guiltily.

"Why?"

"There was some information I thought he should have."

"About the break-in?"

"No," Jason said, letting his hands fall to his sides. "Helene Brennquivist hasn't shown up today. I found out that she and Hayes were having an affair, and I guess I jumped to conclusions. The break-in just slipped out."

"I think it would be best if you stayed with doctoring," Shirley said, her voice softening a degree.

"That's what Curran said," sighed Jason.

"Well," Shirley said, reaching out and touching Jason's arm, "at least you didn't do it on purpose. For a while there I was wondering whose side you were on. I tell you, this Hayes affair has a life of its own. Every time I think the problem is contained, something else breaks."

"I'm sorry," Jason said sincerely. "I didn't mean to make things worse."

"It's okay. But remember—Hayes's death is already hurting this institution. Let's not compound our difficulties." She gave Jason's hand a squeeze, then walked to the door.

Jason went back to his patients, determined to leave the investigation to the police. It was nearly four when Claudia interrupted again.

"You have a call," she whispered.

"Who is it?" Jason asked nervously. The usual modus operandi was for Claudia to take messages and for Jason to return the calls at the end of the day. Unless, of course, it was an emergency. But Claudia didn't whisper when it was an emergency.

"Carol Donner," she said.

Jason hesitated, then said he'd take it in his office. Claudia followed, still whispering.

"Is that *the* Carol Donner?"

"Who is *the* Carol Donner?"

"The dancer in the Combat Zone," Claudia said.

"I wouldn't know," Jason said, entering his office. He closed the door on Claudia and picked up the phone. "Dr. Howard," he said.

"Jason, this is Carol Donner. I'm sorry to bother you."

"No bother." Her voice brought back the pleasant image of her sitting across from him at the Hampshire House. He heard a click. "Just a moment, Carol." He put the phone down, opened the door, and looked across the room at Claudia. With an irritated expression, he motioned for her to hang up.

"Sorry," Jason said, returning to the phone.

"I wouldn't call you unless I thought it might be important," Carol said. "But I came across a package in my locker at work. I'm a dancer at the Club Cabaret, by the way. . . ."

"Oh," Jason said vaguely.

"Anyway," Carol said, "I had to go in to the club today and I found it. Alvin had asked me to put it in my locker several weeks ago and I'd forgotten all about it."

"What's in it?"

"Bound ledgers, papers and correspondence. That type of stuff. There were no drugs, if that's what you were wondering."

"No," Jason said, "that's not what I was wondering. But I'm glad you called. The books might be important. I'd like to see them."

"Okay," Carol said. "I'll be at the club tonight. I'll have to think of some way to get them to you. My boss is giving me a lot of trouble about protection. Something weird is going on, which they won't tell me about, but I'm stuck with this goon following me around. I'd just as soon not involve you in that."

"Maybe I could come and pick it up?"

"No, I don't think that would be a good idea. I'll tell you what. If you give me your number, I'll call when I get home tonight."

Jason gave her the number.

"One other thing," Carol said. "Last night I realized there was something else I didn't tell you. About a month ago, Alvin said he was going to break up with Helene. He said he wanted her to concentrate on their work."

"Do you think he told her?"

"Haven't the slightest idea."

"Helene hasn't shown up for work today."

"No kidding!" Carol said. "That's strange. From what I'd heard, she was compulsive about work. Maybe she's the reason my boss is acting so crazy."

"How would your boss know about Helene Brennquivist?"

"He has a great informational network. He knows what's going on in the whole city."

Hanging up, Jason pondered the confusing inconsistencies between Carol's job and her intellectual sophistication. "Informational network" was a computer-age term—unexpected from an exotic dancer.

Going back to his patients, Jason studiously avoided Claudia's questioning gaze. He knew she was overwhelmingly curious, but he wasn't about to give her any satisfaction.

Toward the very end of the afternoon, Dr. Jerome Washington, a burly black physician who specialized in gastrointestinal disorders, interrupted Jason, asking for a quick consult.

"Sure," Jason said, taking him back to his office.

"Roger Wanamaker suggested I speak to you about this case." He took a bulky chart from under his arm and put it on the desk. "A few more like this and I'm going into the aluminum siding business."

Jason opened the chart. The patient was male, sixty years old.

"I did a physical on Mr. Lamborn twenty-three days ago," Jerome said. "The guy was a little overweight, but aren't we all? Otherwise I thought he was okay and told him so. Then, a week ago, he comes in looking like death warmed over. He'd dropped twenty pounds. I put him in the hospital, thinking he had a malignancy I'd missed. I gave him every test in the book. Nothing. Then three days ago he died. I put a lot of pressure on the family for an autopsy. And what did it show?"

"No malignancy."

"Right," Jerome said. "No malignancy—but every organ he had was totally degenerated. I told Roger and he said to see you, that you'd commiserate."

"Well, I've had some similar problems," Jason said. "So has Roger. To be truthful, I'm worried we're on the brink of some unknown medical disaster."

"What are we going to do?" Jerome asked. "I can't take too much of this kind of emotional abuse."

"I agree. With all the deaths I've had lately, I've been thinking of changing professions too. And I don't understand why we're not picking up symptoms on our physicals. I told Roger I'd call a meeting next week, but now I think we can't afford to wait." An image of Hayes's blood pumping over the dinner table flashed through Jason's mind. "Let's get together tomorrow afternoon. I'll have Claudia set it up, and I'll tell the secretaries to put together a list of all the physicals we've done over the last year and see what's happened to the patients."

"Sounds good to me," Jerome said. "Cases like this don't do much for a man's confidence."

After Jerome left, Jason went out to the central desk to make plans for the staff conference. He knew that a few people would have to put in some overtime, and he thanked providence for providing computers. There were a few groans when he explained what was needed, including rebooking all the afternoon patients, but Claudia took it on herself to be the ringleader. Jason was confident things would get done as well as the short time would permit.

At five-thirty, after seeing his last patient, Jason tried Helene's home number. Still no answer. Impulsively, he decided to stop by her apartment on his way home. He looked at the address he'd gotten from personnel and noted she lived in Cambridge on Concord Avenue. Then he recognized the address. It was the Craigie Arms apartment building.

What a coincidence, he thought. Before meeting Danielle he'd dated a girl at the Craigie Arms.

Descending to his car, Jason headed over to Cambridge. The traffic was terrible, but thanks to his familiarity with the area he had no trouble locating the address. He parked his car and went into the familiar lobby. Scanning the names, he found Brennquivist and pressed the buzzer. There was always the outside chance Helene wasn't picking up her phone, but would respond to the door. There was no answer. Jason looked at the tenant list, but Lucy Hagen's name was gone. After all, it had been fifteen years.

Instead, he reached for the super's buzzer and pressed it. A small speaker above the door buzzers crackled to life, and the gruff voice of Mr. Gratz grated out into the tiled foyer.

"There's no soliciting."

Jason quickly identified himself, admitting that Mr. Gratz might not remember him since it had been a few years. He said he was concerned about a colleague who was a tenant. Mr. Gratz didn't say anything, but the door buzzed open. Jason had to run a few steps to get it. Inside, Jason confronted the unmistakable odor, which he'd remembered for fifteen years. It was the smell of grilled onions. A metal door opened down the tiled hall and Mr. Gratz appeared dressed, as always, in a tank-top undershirt and soiled jeans. He sported a two-day growth of beard. He studied Jason's face, demanded his name again, then asked, "Didn't you used to date the Hagen girl in 2-J?"

Jason was impressed. The man certainly wouldn't win any beauty contests, but he apparently had a memory like a steel trap. Jason had gotten to know him because Lucy had chronic problems with her drains and Larry Gratz was in and out of her apartment.

"What can I do for you?" Larry asked.

Jason explained that Helene Brennquivist hadn't shown up for work and wasn't answering her phone. Jason said he was worried.

"I can't let you in her apartment."

"Oh, I understand," Jason said. "I just want to make sure everything is okay."

Gratz regarded him for a moment, grunted, then started toward the elevator. He pulled a ring of keys out of his pocket that looked adequate enough to open half the doors in Cambridge. They rode the elevator without speaking.

Helene's apartment was at the end of a long hall. Even before they got to the door, they could hear loud rock and roll.

"Sounds like she's having a party," Gratz said. He rang the bell for a full minute, but there was no response. Gratz put his ear to the door and rang again. "Can't even hear the door chimes," he said. "Wonder no one's complained about the music."

Lifting a hairy fist, he pounded on the door. Finally he selected a key and turned the lock. As the door opened, the volume of the music increased dramatically. "Shit," Gratz said. Then he yelled, *"Hello!"* There was no answer.

The apartment had a small foyer with an arched opening to the left, but even from where he stood Jason recognized the unmistakable smell of death. He started to speak, but Gratz stopped him.

"You better wait here," Gratz said over the pounding music as he advanced toward the living room.

"Oh, *Christ!*" he shouted a second later. His eyes opened wide as his face contorted with horror. Jason looked between the arch and Larry's body. The room was a nightmare.

The super ran for the kitchen, his hand clasped over his mouth. Even with his medical training, Jason felt his own stomach turn over. Helene and another woman were side by side on the couch, naked, with their hands tied behind their back. Their bodies had been unspeakably mutilated. A large, stained kitchen knife was jammed into the coffee table.

Jason turned and looked into the kitchen. Larry was bent over the kitchen sink, heaving. Jason's first response was to help him, but he thought better of it. Instead, he went to the door to the hall and opened it, thankful for the fresh air. In a few minutes Larry stumbled past him.

"Why don't you go call the police," Jason said, allowing the door to close behind him. The relative quiet was refreshing. His nausea abated.

Thankful for something to do, Larry ran down the stairs. Jason leaned against the wall and tried not to think. He was trembling.

Two policemen arrived in short order. They were young and turned several shades of green when they looked into the living room. But they set about sealing off the scene and carefully questioning Jason and Gratz. With care not to disturb anything else, they finally pulled the plug on the stereo. More police arrived, including plainclothes detectives. Jason suggested Detective Curran might be interested in the case and someone called him. A police photographer arrived and began snapping shot after shot of the devastated apartment. Then the Cambridge medical examiner arrived.

Jason was waiting in the hall when Curran came lumbering toward Helene's apartment.

Seeing Jason, he paused only to shout, "What the hell are you doing here?"

Jason held his tongue, and Curran turned to the policeman standing by the door. "Where's the detective in charge?" he snapped, flashing his badge. The policeman jerked his thumb in the direction of the living room. Curran went in, leaving Jason in the hall.

The press appeared with their usual tangle of cameras and spiral notebooks. They tried to enter Helene's apartment, but the uniformed policeman at the door restrained them. That reduced them to interviewing anybody in the area, including Jason. Jason told them he knew nothing, and they eventually left him alone.

After a while Curran reappeared. Even he looked a little green. He came over to Jason. He took a cigarette out of a crumpled pack and made a production out of finding a match. Finally, he looked at Jason.

"Don't tell me 'I told you so,' " he said.

"It wasn't just a rape murder, was it?" Jason asked quietly.

"That's not for me to say. Sure, it was a rape. What makes you think it was more?"

"The mutilation was done after death."

"Oh? Why do you say that, doctor?"

"Lack of blood. If the women had been alive, there would have been a lot of bleeding."

"I'm impressed," Curran said. "And while I hate to admit it, we don't think it was your ordinary loony. There's evidence I can't discuss but it looks like a professional job. A small-caliber weapon was involved."

"Then you agree Helene's death is tied to Hayes."

"Possibly," Curran said. "They told me you discovered the bodies."

"With the help of the superintendent."

"What brought you over here, doctor?"

Jason didn't answer immediately. "I'm not sure," he said finally. "As I told you, I had an uncomfortable feeling when Helene didn't show up for work."

Curran scratched his head, letting his attention wander around the hallway. He took a long drag on his cigarette, letting the smoke out through his nose. There was a crowd of police, reporters, and curious tenants. Two gurneys were lined up against the wall, waiting to take the bodies away.

"Maybe I won't turn the case over to Vice," Curran said at last. Then he wandered off.

Jason approached the policeman standing guard at the door to Helene's apartment. "I was wondering if I could go now."

"Hey, Rosati!" yelled the cop. The detective in charge, a thin, hollow-faced man with a shock of dark, unruly hair, appeared almost immediately.

"He wants to leave," said the cop, nodding at Jason.

"We got your name and address?" Rosati asked.

"Name, address, phone, social security, driver's license—everything."

"I suppose it's okay," Rosati said. "We'll be in touch."

Jason nodded, then walked down the hallway on shaky legs. When he emerged outside on Concord Avenue, he was surprised it had already gotten dark. The cold evening air was heavy with exhaust fumes. As one final slap in the face, Jason found a parking ticket under his windshield wiper. Irritated, he pulled it out, realizing he'd parked in a zone that required a Cambridge resident sticker.

It took much longer for him to return to GHP than it had taken to drive to Helene's apartment. The traffic on Storrow Drive was backed up exiting at Fenway, so it was about seven-thirty P.M. when he finally parked and entered the building. Going up to his office, he found a large computer printout on his desk listing all the GHP patients who had received executive physicals in the last year, along with a notation of the patient's current physical status. *The secretaries did a great job*, Jason thought, putting the printout in his briefcase.

He went up to the floor for inpatient rounds. One of the nurses gave him the results of Madaline Krammer's arteriogram. All the coronary vessels showed significant, diffuse, nonfocal encroachment. When the results were compared with a similar study done six months previously, it showed significant deterioration. Harry Sarnoff, the consulting cardiologist, did not feel she was a candidate for surgery, and with her current low levels of both cholesterol and fatty acids, had little to suggest with regard to her management. To be one hundred percent certain, Jason ordered a cardiac surgery consult, then went in to see her.

As usual, Madaline was in the best of moods, minimizing her symptoms. Jason told her that he'd asked a surgeon to take a look at her, and promised to stop by the next day. He had the awful sense that the woman was not going to be around much longer. When he checked her ankles for edema, Jason noted some excoriations.

"Have you been scratching yourself?" he asked.

"A little," Madaline admitted, grasping the sheet and pulling it up as if she were embarrassed.

"Are your ankles itchy?"

"I think it's the heat in here. It's very dry, you know."

Jason didn't know. In fact, the air-conditioning system of the hospital kept the humidity at a constant, normal level.

With a horrible sense of déjà vu, Jason went back to the nurses' station and ordered a dermatology consult as well as a chemistry screen

367

that included some forty automated tests. There had to be something he was missing.

The rest of rounds was equally depressing. It seemed all his patients were in decline. When he left the hospital he decided to take a run out to Shirley's. He felt like talking and she'd certainly made it clear she enjoyed seeing him. He also felt he should break the news of Helene's murder before she heard it from the press. He knew it was going to devastate her.

It took about twenty minutes before he pulled into her cobblestone driveway. He was pleased to see lights on.

"Jason! What a pleasant surprise," Shirley said, answering the bell. She was dressed in a red leotard with black tights and a white headband. "I was just on my way to aerobics."

"I should have called."

"Nonsense," Shirley said, grabbing his hand and pulling him inside. "I'm always looking for an excuse not to exercise." She led him into the kitchen, where a mountain of reports and memoranda covered the table. Jason was reminded of what an enormous amount of work went into running an organization like GHP. As always, he was impressed by Shirley's skills.

After she brought him a drink, Jason asked if she'd heard the news.

"I don't know," Shirley said, pulling off her headband and shaking out her thick hair. "News about what?"

"Helene Brennquivist," Jason said. He let his voice trail off.

"Is this news I'm going to like?" Shirley asked, picking up her drink.

"I hardly think so," Jason said. "She and her roommate were murdered."

Shirley dropped her drink on the couch and then mechanically occupied herself cleaning up the mess. "What happened?" she asked after a long silence.

"It was a rape murder. At least ostensibly." He felt ill as he recalled the scene.

"How awful," Shirley said, clutching her hand to her chest.

"It was gruesome," agreed Jason.

"It's every woman's worst nightmare. When did it happen?"

"They seem to think it happened last night."

Shirley stared off into the middle distance. "I'd better phone Bob Walthrow. This is only going to add to our PR woes."

Shirley heaved herself to her feet and walked shakily to the phone. Jason could hear the emotion in her voice as she explained what had happened.

"I don't envy you your job," he said when she hung up. He could see her eyes were bright with unshed tears.

"I feel the same about yours," she said. "Every time I see you after a patient dies, I'm glad I didn't go into medicine myself."

Although neither Shirley nor Jason was particularly hungry, they made a quick spaghetti dinner. Shirley tried to talk Jason into staying the night, but though he had found comfort being with her, helping him to endure the horror of Helene's death, he knew he couldn't stay. He had to be home for Carol's call. Pleading a load of unfinished work, he drove back to his apartment.

After a late jog and a shower, Jason sat down with the printouts of all patients who'd had GHP physicals in the last year. Feet on his desk, he went over the list carefully, noting that the number of physicals had been divided evenly among all the internists. Since the list had been printed in alphabetical order rather than chronologically, it took some time for Jason to realize that the poor predictive results were much more common in the last six months than in the beginning of the year. In fact, without graphing the material, it appeared that there had been a marked increase in unexpected deaths over the last few months.

Taking a pencil, Jason began writing down the unit numbers of the recent deaths. He was shocked by the number. Then he called the main operator at GHP and asked to be connected to Records. When he had one of the night secretaries on the line, he gave the list of unit numbers and asked if the outpatient charts could be pulled and put on his desk. The secretary told him there would be no problem at all.

Putting the computer printout back into his briefcase, Jason took down his Williams' *Textbook of Endocrinology* and turned to the chapters on growth hormone. Like so many other subjects, the more he read, the less he knew. Growth hormone and its relation to growth and sexual maturation were enormously complicated. So complicated, in fact, that he fell asleep, the heavy textbook pressing against his abdomen.

The phone shocked him awake—so abruptly that he knocked the book to the floor. He snatched up the receiver, expecting his service. It took another moment before he realized the caller was Carol Donner. Jason looked at the time—eleven minutes to three.

"I hope you weren't asleep," Carol said.

"No, no!" Jason lied. His legs were stiff from being propped up on the desk. "I've been waiting for your call. Where are you?"

"I'm at home," Carol said.

"Can I come get that package?"

"It's not here," Carol said. "To avoid problems, I gave it to a friend who works with me. Her name is Melody Andrews. She lives at 69 Revere Street on Beacon Hill." Carol gave him Melody's phone number. "She's expecting a call and should just be getting home. Let me know what you think of the material, and if there's any trouble, here's my number"—which she recited.

"Thanks," said Jason, writing everything down. He was surprised how disappointed he felt not to be seeing her.

"Take care," Carol said, hanging up.

Jason remained at his desk, still trying to fully wake up. As he did so, he realized he hadn't mentioned Helene's death to Carol. *Well, that might be a good excuse to call Carol back*, he reflected as he dialed her friend's number.

Melody Andrews answered her phone with a strong South Boston accent. She told Jason that she had the package, and he was welcome to come over and get it. She said she'd be up for another half hour or so.

Jason put on a sweater and down vest, left the house, walked down Pinckney Street, along West Cedar, and up Revere. Melody's building was on the left. He rang her bell, and she appeared at the door in pin curls. Jason didn't think anyone still used those things. Her face was tired and drawn.

Jason introduced himself. Melody merely nodded and handed over a parcel wrapped in brown paper and tied with string. It weighed about ten pounds. When Jason thanked her she just shrugged and said, "Sure."

Returning home, Jason pulled off his vest and sweater. Eagerly eyeing the package, he got scissors from the kitchen and cut the string. Then he carried the package into the den and placed it on his desk. Inside he found two ledgers filled with handwritten instructions, diagrams, and experimental data. One of the books had *Property of Gene, Inc.* printed on the cover; the other merely the word *Notebook*. In addition there was a large manila envelope filled with correspondence. The first letters Jason read were from Gene, Inc., demanding that

370

Hayes live up to his contractual agreements and return the Soma-tomedin protocol and the recombinant E. coli strain of bacteria that he'd illegally removed from their laboratory. As Jason continued reading, it was apparent that Hayes had a significant difference of opinion concerning the ownership of the procedure and the strain, and that he was in the process of patenting the same. Jason also found a number of letters from an attorney by the name of Samuel Schwartz. Half of them involved the application for the patent on the Somatomedin-producing E. coli and the rest dealt with the formation of a corporation. It seemed that Alvin Hayes owned fifty-one percent of the stock, while his children shared the other forty-nine percent along with Samuel Schwartz.

So much for the correspondence, Jason thought. He returned the letters to the manila envelope. Next he took up the ledger books. The one that had "Gene, Inc." on the cover seemed to be the protocol referred to in the correspondence. As Jason flipped through it, he realized that it detailed the creation of the recombinant strain of bacteria to produce Somatomedin. From his reading, he knew that Somatomedins were growth factors produced by the liver cells in response to the presence of growth hormone.

Putting the first book aside, Jason picked up the second. The experiments outlined were incomplete, but they concerned the production of a monoclonal antibody to a specific protein. The protein was not named, but Jason found a diagram of its amino-acid sequence. Most of the material was beyond his comprehension, but it was clear from the crossing out of large sections and the scribbling in the margins that the work was not progressing well and that at the time of the last entry, Hayes had obviously not created the antibody he'd desired.

Stretching, Jason got up from his desk. He was disappointed. He had hoped the package from Carol would offer a clearer picture of Hayes's breakthrough, but except for the documentation of the controversy between Hayes and Gene, Inc., Jason knew little more than he had before opening the package. He did have the protocol for producing the Somatomedin E. coli strain, but that hardly seemed a major discovery, and all the other lab book outlined was failure.

Exhausted, Jason turned out the lights and went to bed. It had been a long, terrible day.

11

Nightmares involving gross permutations of the terrible scene in Helene's apartment drove Jason out of bed before the sun paled the eastern sky. He put on coffee and as he waited for it to filter through his machine, he picked up his paper and read about the double murder. There was nothing new. As he'd expected, the emphasis was on the rape. Putting the Gene, Inc., ledger in his briefcase, Jason started out for the hospital.

At least there was no traffic at that early hour as he drove to the GHP, and he had his choice of parking places. Even the surgeons who usually arrived at such an uncivilized hour were not there yet.

When he arrived at GHP, he went directly to his office. As he'd requested, his desk was piled with charts. He took off his jacket and began to go through them. Keeping in mind these were patients who had died within a month of getting a fairly clean bill of health from doctors who'd completed the most extensive physicals GHP had to offer, Jason searched for commonalities. Nothing caught his eye. He compared EKGs and the levels of cholesterol, fatty acids, immunoglobulins, and blood counts. No common group of compounds, elements, or enzymes varied from the normal in any predictable pattern. The only shared trait was that most of the patients' deaths occurred within a month of having the physical. More upsetting, Jason noticed, was that in the last three months the number of deaths increased dramatically.

Reading the twenty-sixth chart, one correlation suddenly occurred

372

to Jason. Although the patients did not share physical symptoms, their charts showed a predominance of high-risk social habits. They were overweight, smoked heavily, used drugs, drank too much, and failed to exercise, or combined any and all of these unhealthy practices; they were men and women who were eventually destined to have severe medical problems. The shocking fact was that they deteriorated so quickly. And why the sudden upswing in deaths? People weren't indulging in vices more than they were a year ago. Maybe it was a kind of statistical equalizing: they'd been lucky and now the numbers were catching up to them. But that didn't make a whole lot of sense, for there seemed to be too many deaths. Jason was not an experienced statistician, so he decided to ask a better mathematician than he was to look at the numbers.

When he knew he wouldn't be waking the patients, Jason left his office and made rounds. Nothing had changed. Back in his office and before he saw the first scheduled patient, he called Pathology and inquired about the dead animals from Hayes's lab, and waited several minutes while the technician looked for the report.

"Here it is," the woman said. "They all died of strychnine poisoning."

Jason hung up and called Margaret Danforth at the city morgue. A technician answered, since Margaret was busy doing an autopsy. Jason asked if the toxicology on Gerald Farr revealed anything interesting.

"Toxicology was negative," the tech said.

"One more question. Would strychnine have shown up?"

"Just a moment," the technician said.

In the background Jason could hear the woman shouting to the medical examiner. She returned to the phone. "Dr. Danforth said yes, strychnine would have shown up if it had been present."

"Thank you," Jason said.

He hung up the phone, then stood up. At the window, he examined the developing day. He could see the traffic snarled on the Riverway from his window. The sky was light but overcast. It was early November. Not a pretty month for Boston. Jason felt restless and anxious and disconsolate. He thought about the parcel from Carol and wondered if he should turn it over to Curran. Yet for what purpose? They weren't even investigating Hayes except as a drug pusher.

Walking back to the desk Jason took out his phone directory and looked up the phone number of Gene, Inc. He noted the company was located on Pioneer Street in East Cambridge next to the MIT campus. Impulsively, he sat down and dialed the number. The line was answered by a woman receptionist with an English accent. Jason asked for the head of the company.

"You mean Dr. Leonard Dawen, the president?"

"Dr. Dawen will be fine," Jason said. He heard the extension ring. It was picked up by a secretary.

"Dr. Dawen's office."

"I'd like to speak to Dr. Dawen."

"Who may I say is calling?"

"Dr. Jason Howard."

"May I tell him what this is in reference to?"

"It's about a lab book I have. Tell Dr. Dawen I'm from the Good Health Plan and was a friend of the late Alvin Hayes."

"Just a moment, please," the secretary said in a voice that sounded like a recording.

Jason opened the center drawer to his desk and toyed with his collection of pencils. There was a click on the phone, then a powerful voice came over the line, "This is Leonard Dawen!"

Jason explained who he was and then described the lab book.

"May I ask how it came into your possession, sir?"

"I don't think that's important. The fact is I have it." He was not about to implicate Carol.

"That book is our property," Dr. Dawen said. His voice was calm but with a commanding and threatening undercurrent.

"I'll be happy to turn the book over in exchange for some information about Dr. Hayes. Do you think we might meet?"

"When?"

"As soon as possible," Jason said. "I could get over just before lunch."

"Will you have the book with you?"

"I will indeed."

For the rest of the morning Jason had trouble concentrating on the steady stream of patients. He was pleased Sally hadn't scheduled him through lunch. The minute he finished his last exam, he hurried out to his car.

Reaching Cambridge, Jason threaded his way past MIT and among the new East Cambridge corporate skyscrapers, some with dramatically modern architecture that contrasted sharply with the older and more traditional New England brick structures. Making a final turn on Pioneer Street, Jason found Gene, Inc., housed in a startlingly modern building of polished black granite. Unlike its neighbors, the structure was only six floors high. Its windows were narrow slits alternating with circles of bronze mirrored glass. It had a solid, powerful look, like a castle in a science fiction movie.

Jason got out of his car with his briefcase and gazed up at the striking façade. After reading so much about recombinant DNA and seeing Hayes's grossly deformed zoo, Jason was afraid he was about to enter a house of horrors. The front entrance was circular, defined by radiating spikes of granite, giving the illusion of a giant eye, the black doors being the pupil. The lobby was also black granite: walls, floor, even ceiling. In the center of the reception area was a dramatically illuminated modern sculpture of the double-helix DNA molecule opening like a zipper.

Jason approached an attractive Korean woman sitting behind a glass wall and in front of a control panel that looked like something out of the *Starship Enterprise*. She wore a tiny earpiece along with a small microphone that snaked around from behind her neck. She greeted Jason by name and told him he was expected in the fourth-floor conference room. Her voice had a metallic sound as she spoke into the microphone.

The minute the receptionist stopped speaking, one of the granite panels opened, revealing an elevator. As he thanked her, Jason suddenly fancied that she was a lifelike robot. Smiling, he boarded the elevator and looked for the floor buttons. The door closed behind him. There was no floor-selector panel, but the elevator started upward.

When the doors reopened, Jason found himself in a doorless black foyer. He assumed the entire building was controlled from a central location, perhaps by the receptionist downstairs. To his left a granite panel slid open. Within the doorway stood a man with coarse features, impeccably dressed in a dark pinstripe suit, white shirt, and red paisley tie.

"Dr. Howard, I'm Leonard Dawen," the man said, motioning Jason into the room. He didn't offer to shake hands. His voice had the same commanding quality Jason remembered from the phone conversation. Compared to the tomblike austerity of the rest of the building, the conference room looked more like a wood-paneled library and seemed positively cozy until you looked at the fourth wall, which was glass.

It looked out on what appeared to be a large ultramodern lab. There was another man in the room, an Oriental, wearing a white zippered jumpsuit. Dawen introduced the man as Mr. Hong, a Gene, Inc., engineer. After they were all seated around a small conference table, Dawen said, "I assume you have the lab book. . . ."

Jason opened his briefcase and handed the ledger to Dawen, who handed it to Hong. The engineer began studying it page by page. A heavy silence ensued.

Jason looked back and forth between the two men. He'd expected things to be a bit more cordial. After all, he was doing them a favor.

He turned and peered through the glass wall. The floor of the room beyond was a story below. Much of the area was filled with stainless-steel vats, reminding Jason of a visit he'd once made to a brewery. He guessed they were the incubators for the culture of the recombinant bacteria. There was a lot of other equipment and complicated piping. People in white jumpsuits with white hoods were moving about checking gauges, making adjustments.

Hong closed the lab book with a snap. "It seems complete," he said.

"That's a nice surprise," Dr. Dawen said. Turning to Jason he said, "I hope you realize everything in this book is confidential."

"Don't worry," Jason said, forcing a smile. "I didn't understand much of it. What I'm interested in is Dr. Hayes. Just before he died he said he'd made a major discovery. I'm curious to know if what is described in those pages would be considered as such."

Dawen and Hong exchanged glances. "It's more of a commercial breakthrough," Hong said. "There's no new technology here."

"That's what I suspected. Hayes was so distraught I couldn't tell if he was entirely rational. But, if he made a major breakthrough, I'd hate to have it lost to humanity."

Dawen's blunt features softened for the first time since Jason had arrived.

Jason continued, directing his attention to the engineer. "Any idea what Hayes could have been talking about?"

"Unfortunately, no. Hayes was always rather secretive." Dawen folded his hands on the table and looked directly at Jason. "We were afraid you were going to extort us with this material—make us pay to get it back," he said, touching the cover of the lab book. "You have to understand that Dr. Hayes had been giving us a rather difficult time."

"What was Dr. Hayes's role here?" Jason asked.

"We hired him to produce a recombinant strain of bacteria," Dawen explained. "We wanted to produce a certain growth factor in commercial quantities."

Jason guessed that was the Somatomedin.

"We agreed to pay him a flat fee for the project, as well as letting him use the Gene, Inc., facilities for his own research. We have some very unique equipment."

"Any idea what his own research involved?" Jason asked.

Hong spoke up. "He spent most of his time isolating growth-factor proteins. Some of them exist in such minute quantities that the most sophisticated equipment is required to isolate them."

"Would the isolation of one of these growth factors be considered a major scientific discovery?" Jason asked.

"I can't see how," Hong replied. "Even if they've never been isolated, we know their effects."

Another dead end, Jason thought wearily.

"There's just one thing I remember that might be significant," Hong said, pinching the bridge of his nose. "About three months ago Hayes got very excited about some side effect. He said it was ironic."

Jason straightened. There was that word again. "Any idea what caused his excitement?" he asked.

Hong shook his head. "No," he said, "but after that we didn't see him for a time. When we did see him, he said he'd been to the Coast. Then he set up an elaborate extraction process on some material he'd brought back with him. I don't know if it worked, but then he abruptly switched to monoclonal antibody technology. At that point his excitement seemed to die."

The words "monoclonal antibody" reminded Jason of the second lab book, and he wondered if he shouldn't have brought it after all. Maybe Mr. Hong could have made more out of it than he had.

"Did Dr. Hayes leave any other research material here?" Jason asked.

"Nothing significant," Leonard Dawen answered. "And we checked carefully, because he'd walked off with our lab book and the cultures. In fact, we were suing Dr. Hayes. We never anticipated he would try and contend he owned the strains that we'd hired him to produce."

"Did you get your cultures back?" Jason asked.

"We did."

"Where did you find them?"

"Let's say we looked in the right place," Dawen said evasively. "But even though we have the strain, we still appreciate getting the protocol book back. On behalf of the company, I'd like to thank you. I hope we have helped you in some small way."

"Perhaps," Jason said vaguely. He had an idea he'd inadvertently found out who had searched Hayes's lab and apartment. But why would the scientists from Gene, Inc., want to kill the animals? He wondered if the huge animals had been treated with Gene, Inc.'s, Somatomedin. "I appreciate your time," he said to Dawen. "You have an impressive setup here."

"Thank you. Things are going well. We plan to have recombinant strains of farm animals soon."

"You mean like pigs and cows?"

"That's right. Genetically we can produce leaner pigs, cows that produce more milk, and chickens that have more protein, just to give you a few examples."

"Fascinating," Jason said without enthusiasm. How far away could they be from genetically engineering people? He shivered again, seeing Hayes's outsized rats and mice, especially those with supernumerary eyes.

Back in the car, Jason glanced at his watch. He still had an hour before the staff meeting being held to go over recent patient deaths, so he decided to visit Samuel Schwartz, Hayes's attorney.

Starting the car, Jason backed out of the Gene, Inc., parking lot and worked his way over to Memorial Drive. He crossed the Charles River, stopping at Philip's Drug Store on Charles Circle. Double-parking with his emergency light blinking, he ran into the store and looked up Schwartz's address. Ten minutes later he was in the lawyer's waiting room, flipping the pages of an outdated *Newsweek*.

Samuel Schwartz was an enormously obese man with a glistening bald head. He motioned Jason into his office as if he were directing traffic. Settling himself into his chair and adjusting his wire-rimmed glasses, he studied Jason, who had seated himself in front of the massive mahogany partner's desk.

"So you are a friend of the late Alvin Hayes. . . ."

"We were more colleagues than friends."

"Whatever," Schwartz said with another wave of his chubby hand. "So what can I do for you?"

Jason retold Hayes's story of a purported breakthrough. He explained that he was trying to figure out what Hayes had been working on and had come across correspondence from Samuel Schwartz.

"He was a client. So what?"

"No need to be defensive."

"I'm not defensive. I'm just bitter. I did a lot of work for that bum and I'm going to have to write it all off."

"He never paid?"

"Never. He conned me into working for stock in his new company."

"Stock?"

Samuel Schwartz laughed without humor. "Unfortunately, now that Hayes is dead, the stock is worthless. It might have been worthless even if he had lived. I should have my head examined."

"Was Hayes's corporation going to sell a service or a product?" Jason asked.

"A product. Hayes told me he was on the verge of developing the most valuable health product ever known. And I believed him. I figured a guy who'd been on the cover of *Time* had to have something on the ball."

"Any idea what this product was?" Jason asked, trying to keep the excitement out of his voice.

"Not the foggiest. Hayes wouldn't tell me."

"Do you know if it involved monoclonal antibodies?" Jason asked, unwilling to give up.

Schwartz laughed again. "I wouldn't know a monoclonal antibody if I walked into it."

"Malignancies?" Jason was only fishing, but he hoped he could jog the lawyer's memory. "Could the product have involved a cancer treatment?"

The obese man shrugged. "I don't know. Possibly."

"Hayes told someone that his discovery would enhance their beauty. Does that mean anything to you?"

"Listen, Dr. Howard. Hayes told me nothing about the product. I was just setting up the corporation."

"You were also applying for a patent."

"The patent had nothing to do with the corporation. That was to be in Hayes's name."

Jason's beeper startled both men. He watched the tiny screen. The word "urgent" blinked twice, followed by a number at the GHP hospital. "Would it be possible to use your phone?" Jason asked.

Schwartz pushed it across the desk. "Be my guest, doctor."

The call was from Madaline Krammer's floor. She'd arrested and they were giving her CPR. Jason said he'd be right there. Thanking Samuel Schwartz, Jason ran from the lawyer's office and impatiently waited for the elevator.

When he got to Madaline's room, he saw an all too familiar scene. The patient was unresponsive. Her heart refused to respond to anything, including external pacing. Jason insisted they continue life support while his mind went over various drugs and treatments, but after an hour of frantic activity, even he was forced to give up and he reluctantly called a halt to the proceedings.

Jason remained at Madaline's bedside after everyone else had left. She'd been an old friend, one of the first patients he'd treated in his private practice. One of the nurses had covered her face with a sheet. Madaline's nose poked it up like a miniature snow-covered mountain. Gently, Jason turned it back. Even though she had been only in her early sixties, he couldn't get over how old she looked. Since she'd entered the hospital, her face had lost all its cheerful plumpness and taken on the skeletal cast of those nearing death.

Needing some time by himself, Jason retreated to his office, avoiding both Claudia and Sally, who each had a hundred urgent questions about the upcoming conference and the problems of rescheduling so many patients. Jason locked his door and settled himself at his desk. As such an old patient, Madaline's passing seemed like the severing of one more connection to Jason's former life. Jason felt poignantly alone, fearful, yet relieved, that Danielle's memory was receding.

Jason's phone rang, but he ignored it. He looked over his desk, which was a mass of stacked hospital charts of deceased patients, including Hayes's. Involuntarily, Jason's mind went back to the Hayes affair. It was frustrating that the package from Carol, which had held such hope, had added so little information. It did give a bit more credence to the idea Hayes had made a discovery that at least he thought was stupendous. Jason cursed Hayes's secrecy.

Leaning back, Jason put his hands behind his head and stared up at the ceiling. He was running out of ideas about Hayes. But then he remembered the Oriental engineer's comment that Hayes had brought something back from the Coast, presumably Seattle. It must have been a sample of something because Hayes had subjected it to a complicated extraction process. From Hong's comments, it seemed to Jason that Hayes had probably been isolating some kind of growth factor which would stimulate growth, or differentiation, or maturation, or all three.

Jason came forward with a thump. Remembering that Carol had said Hayes had visited a colleague at the University of Washington, Jason suddenly entertained the idea that Hayes had obtained some kind of sample from the man.

All at once, Jason decided he'd go to Seattle, provided, of course, Carol would go along. She might. After all, she'd be the key to finding this friend. Besides, a few days away sounded extremely therapeutic to Jason. With a little time left before the staff meeting, Jason decided to stop by and see Shirley.

Shirley's secretary at first insisted that her boss was too busy to see Jason, but he convinced her to at least announce his presence. A moment later he was ushered inside. Shirley was on the phone. Jason took a seat, gradually catching the drift of the conversation. She was dealing with a union leader, handling the person with impressive ease. Absently she ran her fingers through her thick hair. It was a wonderfully feminine gesture, reminding Jason that underneath the professional surface was a very attractive woman, complicated but lovely.

Shirley hung up and smiled. "This is a treat," she said. "You *are* filled with surprises these days, aren't you, Jason? I suppose you're here to apologize for not having spent more time with me last night."

Jason laughed. Her directness was disarming. "Maybe so. But there's something else. I'm thinking of taking a few days off. I lost another patient this morning and I think I need some time away."

Shirley clicked her tongue in sympathy. "Was it expected?"

"I guess so. At least over the last few days. But when I'd admitted her I had no idea she was terminal."

Shirley sighed. "I don't know how you deal with this sort of thing."

"It's never easy," Jason agreed. "But what's made it particularly hard lately is the frequency."

Shirley's phone rang, but she buzzed her secretary to take a message.

"Anyway," Jason said, "I've decided to take a few days off."

"I think it's a good idea," Shirley said. "I wouldn't mind doing the same if these damned union negotiations conclude. Where are you planning to go?"

"I'm not sure," Jason lied. The trip to Seattle was such a long shot that he was ashamed to mention it.

"I have some friends who own a resort in the British Virgin Islands. I could give them a call," Shirley offered.

"No, thanks. I'm not a sun person. What's happened about the Brennquivist tragedy? Much fallout?"

"Don't remind me," Shirley said. "To tell you the truth, I couldn't face it. Bob Walthrow is handling that."

"I had nightmares all night," admitted Jason.

"Not surprising," Shirley said.

"Well, I've got a meeting," Jason said, getting to his feet.

"Would you have time for dinner tonight?" Shirley asked. "Maybe we can cheer each other up."

"Sure. What time?"

"Let's say around eight."

"Eight it is," Jason said, heading for the door. As he left, Shirley called after him.

"I'm really sorry about your patient."

The staff meeting was better attended than Jason had expected, given such short notice. Fourteen of the sixteen internists were there, and several had brought along their nurses. It seemed obvious they all recognized they were facing a serious problem.

Jason started with the statistics that he'd extracted from the computer printout listing all patients who'd died within a month of a complete physical. He pointed out that the number of deaths had increased in the last three months, and said he was trying to check up on all GHP clients who'd had executive physicals in the last sixty days.

"Were the physicals evenly distributed among us?" Roger Wanamaker asked.

Jason nodded.

A number of the doctors spoke out, making it clear they feared the start of a nationwide epidemic. No one could understand the connection with the physicals, and why the deaths were not being anticipated. The acting chief of cardiology, Dr. Judith Rolander, tried to take much of the blame on herself, admitting that in most of the cases she'd reviewed, the EKG done during the physical did not predict the imminent problems, even when she was armed with hindsight.

The conversation then switched to stress testing as the main key to predicting catastrophic cardiac events. There were many opinions on this issue; all were duly discussed. Upon recommendation from the floor, an ad hoc committee was formed to look into specific ways to alter their stress testing in hopes of increasing its prognostic value.

Jerome Washington then took the floor. Getting heavily on his feet, he said, "I think we're overlooking the significance of unhealthy life-styles. That's one factor that all these patients seem to share."

There were a few joking references to Jerome's weight and his affection for cigars. "All right, you guys," he said. "You know patients should do what we say and not what we do." Everyone laughed. "Seriously," he continued. "We all know the dangers of poor diet, heavy smoking, excess alcohol and lack of exercise. Such social factors have far more predictive value than a mild EKG abnormality."

"Jerome is right," Jason said. "The poor risk-factor profile was the only negative commonality I could find."

By a vote, it was decided to form a second committee to investigate risk-factor contribution to the current problem and come up with specific recommendations.

Harry Sarnoff, the current month's consulting cardiologist, raised his hand, and Jason recognized him. When he got to his feet, he began to talk about noticing an increase in morbidity and mortality for his inpatients. Jason interrupted him.

"Excuse me, Harry," Jason said. "I can appreciate your concern, and frankly I've had experience apparently similar to yours. However, this current meeting involves the problem with the outpatient executive physicals. We can schedule a second meeting if the staff desires to discuss any potential inpatient problem. They very well may be related."

Harry threw up his hands, and reluctantly sat back down.

Jason then encouraged the staff to be sure to autopsy any patients who met unexpected deaths if the medical examiner didn't take them. Jason then told the audience that the results from the medical examiner's office on his patients suggested that the people were suffering multisystem disease including extensive cardiovascular problems. Of course, that fact only undermined the concern that their conditions had not been picked up on either resting or exercise EKGs. Jason added that Pathology thought there was an autoimmune component.

After the meeting broke up, the doctors gravitated to smaller groups to discuss the problem. Jason collected his printout and searched for Roger Wanamaker. He was in an animated conversation with Jerome.

"May I interrupt?" Jason asked. The two men separated to allow Jason to join them. "I'm about to leave town for a few days."

Roger and Jerome exchanged glances. Roger spoke: "Seems like a poor time to be leaving."

"I need it," Jason said without elaborating. "But I have five patients in house. Would either of you gentlemen be willing to cover? I'll admit right up front that they're all pretty sick."

"Wouldn't much matter," Roger said. "I've been in here night and day trying to keep my own half dozen alive. I'll be happy to cover."

With that problem solved, Jason went into his office and called Carol Donner, thinking late afternoon would be a good time to catch her. The phone rang a long time and he was about to give up when she answered, out of breath. She told him she'd been in the bath.

"I want to see you tonight," Jason said.

"Oh," Carol said noncommittally. She hesitated. "That might be difficult." Then she added angrily, "Why didn't you tell me about Helene Brennquivist last night? I read in the paper that you were the one who found the bodies."

"I'm sorry," Jason said defensively. "To be perfectly honest, you woke me last night and all I could think about was the package."

"Did you get it?" Carol asked, her voice softening.

"I did," Jason said. "Thank you."

"And . . . ?"

"The material wasn't as enlightening as I'd hoped."

"I'm surprised," said Carol. "The ledgers must have been important or Alvin wouldn't have asked me to keep them. But that's beside the point. What an awful thing about Helene. My boss is so distressed he won't let me go anywhere without one of the club bouncers. He's outside the building at this very moment."

"It's important that I see you alone," Jason said.

"I don't know if I can. This behemoth takes orders from my boss, not me. And I don't want any trouble."

"Well, call me the minute you get home," Jason said. "Promise! We'll think of something."

"It'll be late again," Carol warned.

"That doesn't matter. It's important."

"All right," Carol agreed before hanging up.

Jason made one more call, to United Airlines, and checked on service from Boston to Seattle. He learned there was a daily flight at four P.M.

Gathering his stethoscope, Jason left his office and headed for the hospital to make rounds. He knew he needed to thoroughly update his charts if Roger was going to cover. None of his patients was doing very well, and Jason was disturbed to find that another patient had developed advanced cataracts. Troubled, he arranged an ophthalmol- ogy consult. This time he was certain he hadn't noticed the problem on admission. How could the cataracts have progressed so far so fast?

At home, he changed into jogging clothes and ran a good hour, trying to sort out his thoughts. By the time he showered, changed, and drove over to Shirley's, he was in a better mood.

Shirley outdid herself with the dinner, and Jason began to think she'd fit into the Superwoman category. She'd worked all day running a multimillion-dollar company and conducting crucial union negotia- tions, yet somehow she'd gotten home, put together a fabulous feast of roast duck with fresh pasta and artichoke. And on top of that she'd dressed herself in a black silk chemise that would have been appropriate for the opera. Jason felt embarrassed that he'd put on jeans and a rugby shirt over a turtleneck after his shower.

"You wore what you wanted and so did I," Shirley said with a laugh. She gave him a Kir Royale and told him to wash the radicchio and the arugula for their salad. She checked the duck and said it was about done. To Jason, it smelled heavenly.

They ate in the dining room, sitting at opposite ends of a long table with six empty chairs on either side. Every time Jason poured more wine, he had to get up and walk several steps. Shirley thought it was amusing.

As they ate, Jason described the staff meeting and added that all the doctors were going to intensify the quality of their stress testing. Shirley was pleased, reminding Jason that the executive physical was an im- portant part of GHP's sales pitch to corporate clients. She told Jason that there would be a new emphasis on preventive medicine for execu- tive customers.

Later, over coffee, she said, "Michael Curran came by this after- noon."

"Really," said Jason. "I'm sure that was unpleasant. What did he want?"

"Background material on the Brennquivist woman. We gave him everything we had. He even interviewed the woman in personnel who'd hired her."

"Did he mention if they had any suspects?"

"He didn't say," Shirley said. "I just hope it's all over."

"I wish I'd gotten to talk with Helene again. I still think she was covering for Hayes."

"Do you still think he discovered something?"

"Absolutely." Jason went on to describe the lab ledgers and his visit to Gene, Inc., and to Samuel Schwartz. He told Shirley that Schwartz had set up a corporation for Hayes that was to market the new discovery, whatever it was.

"Didn't the lawyer know what the product was?"

"Nope. Apparently Hayes trusted no one."

"But he would have needed seed capital. He would have had to trust *someone* if he was planning to manufacture and distribute."

"Maybe so," Jason admitted. "But I can't find anyone he told—at least not yet. Unfortunately, Helene was the best bet."

"Are you still looking?"

"I guess so," he admitted. "Does that sound stupid?"

"Not stupid," Shirley said, "just disturbing. It would be a tragedy if an important discovery were lost, but I definitely think it's time to put the Hayes affair to rest. I hope you're taking time off to relax, not to continue this wild-goose chase."

"Now why would you suggest that?" Jason asked, surprised at his own transparency.

"Because you don't give up easily." She moved over and put her hand on his shoulder. "Why don't you go to the Caribbean? Maybe I could get away over the weekend and join you. . . ."

Jason experienced an excitement he'd not felt since Danielle's death. The idea of the hot sun and cool, clear water sounded wonderful, especially if Shirley were there too. But then he hesitated. He didn't know if he was ready for the emotional commitment that would entail. And, more important, he'd promised himself he'd visit Seattle.

"I want to go out to the West Coast," he said finally. "There's an old friend out there I'd like to see."

"That sounds innocent enough. But the Caribbean sounds better to me."

"Maybe soon." He gave Shirley's arm a squeeze. "How about a cognac?"

As Shirley got up to get the Courvoisier, Jason studied her figure with increasing interest.

When Carol called at two-thirty in the morning, Jason was wide awake. He'd been so worried that she might forget, he hadn't been able to sleep.

"I'm exhausted, Jason," Carol announced, instead of saying hello.

"I'm sorry, but I must see you," he said. "I can be over in ten minutes."

"I don't think that would be a good idea. As I told you this afternoon, I'm not alone. There's someone outside watching my building. Why do you have to see me tonight? Maybe we can work something out tomorrow."

Jason thought about asking her on the phone to go to Seattle, but decided he'd have a better chance convincing her in person. It was a bit out of the ordinary asking a young woman to accompany him to Seattle after only two meetings.

"Is this bodyguard alone?"

"Yes. But what difference does that make? The guy's built like an ox."

"There's an alley in back of your building. I could come up the fire escape."

"The fire escape! This is crazy! What on earth is so important that you have to see me tonight?"

"If I told you, I wouldn't have to see you."

"Well, I'm not crazy about men coming to my apartment at night."

Oh, sure, Jason thought. "Look," he said aloud, "I'll tell you this much. I've been trying to figure out what Hayes could have discovered and I'm down to my last idea. I need your help."

"That's quite a line, Dr. Jason Howard."

"It's true. You're the only one who can help me."

Carol laughed. "When you put it that way, who could refuse? All right, come along. But you're coming at your own risk. I have to warn you, I don't have much control over Atlas outside."

"My disability insurance is all paid up."

"I live at . . ." Carol began.

"I know where you live," Jason interrupted. "In fact, I've already had a run-in with Bruno, if that's the charming fellow guarding your door."

"You've met Bruno?" Carol asked incredulously.

"Lovely man. Such a wonderful conversationalist."

"Let me warn you, then," Carol said. "It was Bruno who walked me home."

"Luckily he's pretty easy to spot. Watch out your back window. I don't want to be stranded on your fire escape."

"This is really insane," Carol said.

Jason changed into dark slacks and sweater. He'd be visible enough on the fire escape without wearing light colors. He donned running shoes and went down to his car. Driving along Beacon Street, he kept an eye out for Bruno. He went left on Gloucester Street and left again on Commonwealth. When he crossed Marlborough, he slowed. He knew there was no chance to find a parking place, so he pulled in at the nearest hydrant. He left the doors unlocked; if need be the firemen could run the hoses right through the car.

Getting out of his car, Jason peered down the alleyway between Beacon and Marlborough streets. Intermittent lights formed pools of illumination. There were lots of dark areas, and trees threw spider-weblike shadows. Jason could vividly remember his last attempted flight from Bruno down the same alley.

Marshaling his courage, Jason started into the alley as tense as a sprinter waiting for the starting gun. A sudden movement to his left made him gasp. It was a rat the size of a small cat, and Jason felt the hairs on the back of his neck spring up. He kept walking, happy to see no sign of Bruno. It was so quiet he could hear his breathing.

Arriving at Carol's building, he noted the familiar light in the fourth-floor window before taking a good look at the fire escape. Unfortunately, it had one of those ladder mechanisms that have to be lowered from the first floor. Jason glanced around for something to stand on. The only thing available was a trash can, and that meant turning it over and dumping it. Despite the fact it would make a lot of noise, he realized he had no choice. But he shuddered as the metal clanged against the pavement and a number of beer cans clattered down the street.

Holding his breath, he looked up. No lights had come on. Satisfied, he climbed up on the garbage can and got hold of the lowest rung of the raised ladder.

"Hey!" someone yelled. Jason's head turned and he saw a familiar bulky figure coming down the alley on the run, his thick arms pumping, his breaths coming in puffs like a steam engine. At that moment Bruno looked like a fullback for the Washington Redskins.

"Shit," Jason said. With all his strength he pulled himself up on the ladder, half expecting it to drop under his weight. Luckily it didn't. Hand over hand, he lifted himself until he could put his foot on the first rung and scamper up to the first floor.

"Hey, you goddamned little pervert!" Bruno was yelling. "You get the hell down here!"

Jason hesitated. He could hold the man off by stepping on his fingers if he tried to come up, but that wouldn't get him in to see Carol. And somebody would call the police if there were enough ruckus. Jason decided to take the chance. He ran up the next two flights of the fire escape, arriving at Carol's window. She was looking out and raised the sash the second she spotted him. Before she could speak, Jason gasped, "Your neo-Nazi is on his way up. Do you think he has a gun?" Jason found himself standing in a large kitchen.

"I don't know."

"He's going to be here in a moment," Jason said, slamming down the window and locking it. That was going to delay Bruno just about ten seconds.

"Maybe I should talk to him," Carol suggested.

"Will he listen?"

"I'm not sure. He's kinda bullheaded. . . ."

"That's my impression," Jason said. "And I know he's not fond of me. I think I need something like a baseball bat."

"You can't hit him, Jason."

"I don't want to, but I don't think Bruno wants to sit down and talk this over. I need something to threaten him with to keep him away from me."

"I have a fire poker."

"Get it." Jason turned the light out in the kitchen. Putting his nose to the glass, he could see Bruno struggling to pull himself onto the first ladder. He was strong but he was also bulky. Carol returned with the fire poker. Jason hefted it. With a little luck he might be able to convince the guy to listen.

"I knew this was a bad idea," Carol said.

Jason glanced around the room and noticed that the floor was old-fashioned linoleum. He looked at the door leading from the kitchen to the rest of the apartment. It was thick and solid, with a lock and key. At one point the room had been something other than a kitchen.

"Carol, would you mind if I made a mess? I mean, I'll be happy to pay to have it cleaned up."

"What are you talking about?"

"Do you have a big can of vegetable oil?"

"I suppose."

"Can I have it?"

Perplexed, Carol opened the pantry door and lifted out a gallon can of imported Italian olive oil.

"Perfect," Jason said. After another quick check out the window, he hurriedly pulled the two chairs and table out of the kitchen. Carol watched him with growing confusion.

"Okay, out," Jason ordered. Carol stepped into the hall.

Jason uncorked the olive oil and began pouring the contents over the floor in wide, sweeping movements. As he closed and locked the door, he heard banging on the kitchen window, followed by the crash of glass.

He wedged the kitchen table between the door and the opposite hall.

"Come on," he said, taking Carol's hand. In his other he still held the poker. He led her to the front door of the apartment, which was adequately secured with double latches and a metal-pole police lock. In the kitchen they heard a tremendous crash. Bruno had fallen down for the first time.

"That was ingenious," laughed Carol.

"When you're one hundred and sixty pounds, you have to compensate." Jason's heart was still racing. "Anyway, I have no idea how long Bruno will be entertained in there, so this has to be fast. I need you. The last chance I have of reconstructing Alvin Hayes's discovery is to go to Seattle and try to find out what he did there. Apparently, he . . ."

There was another crash followed by a volley of swear words, some of which were appropriately in Italian.

"He's going to be in a foul mood," Jason said as he undid the locks on the front door.

"So you want me to go to Seattle with you. That's what this is all about?"

"I knew you'd understand. Hayes brought back a biological sample from there, which he processed at Gene, Inc. I have to find out what it was. The best bet is the man he saw out at the University of Washington."

"The man whose name I can't remember."

"But you saw him and could recognize him?"

"Probably."

"I know it's presumptuous to ask you to come," Jason said. "But I really do believe Hayes made some sort of breakthrough. And considering his previous track record, it has to be significant."

"And you really think going to Seattle might solve it?"

"It's a long shot. But the only one left."

The door to the kitchen rattled and they heard Bruno begin a steady pounding.

"I think I've overstayed my welcome," Jason said. "Bruno won't hurt you, will he?"

"Heavens, no. My boss would skin him alive. That's why he's so rabid now. He thinks I'm in danger."

"Carol, would you come with me to Seattle?" Jason asked while removing the pole to the police lock.

"When would you want to go?" Carol asked, vacillating.

"Late today. We wouldn't stay long. Would it be possible for you to get off on short notice?"

"I have in the past. I just say I want to go home. Besides, after Helene's murder my boss might be relieved to have me out of town."

"Then say you'll go?" Jason pleaded.

"All right." Carol gave him one of her heartwarming smiles. "Why not?"

"There's a flight to Seattle at four this afternoon. We'll meet at the gate. I'll get the tickets. How does that sound?"

"Insane," Carol said, "but fun."

"See you there." Jason ran down the stairs to his car, fearful that Bruno might have reversed direction and gone back out the window.

12

Jason woke early and called Roger to brief him on his patients. He wasn't going to the hospital today. He had another trip he wanted to take before meeting Carol for the four o'clock flight to Seattle. He packed quickly, being careful to take clothes for rainy, chilly weather, and called a cab to the airport, getting there just in time to store his bag in a locker and take the ten o'clock Eastern shuttle to La Guardia. At La Guardia he rented a car and drove to Leonia, New Jersey. It was probably even less of a possibility than Seattle, but Jason was going to see Hayes's former wife. He was not about to leave even the smallest stone unturned.

Leonia turned out to be a surprisingly sleepy little town that belied its proximity to New York. Within ten minutes of the George Washington Bridge, he found himself on a wide street lined with one-story commercial establishments fronted by angled parking. It could have been Main Street, USA. Instead, it was called Broad Avenue. There was a drugstore, a hardware store, a bakery, and even a luncheonette. It looked like a movie set from the fifties. Jason went into the luncheonette, ordered a vanilla malted, and used the phone directory. There was a Louise Hayes on Park Avenue. While he drank his malted, Jason debated the wisdom of calling or just dropping by. He opted for the latter.

Park Avenue bisected Broad and rose up the hillside that bordered Leonia on the east. After Pauline Boulevard, it arched to the north. That was where Jason found Louise Hayes's house. It was a modest, dark-brown, shingled structure, much in need of repair. The grass in the front yard had gone to seed.

Jason rang the bell. The door was opened by a smiling, middle-aged woman in a faded red house-dress. She had stringy brown hair, and a little girl of five or six, a thumb buried to the second knuckle in her mouth, clung to her thigh.

"Mrs. Hayes?" Jason asked. The woman was a far cry from Hayes's two other girlfriends.

"Yes."

"I'm Dr. Jason Howard, a colleague of your late husband." He'd not rehearsed what he was going to say.

"Yes?" Mrs. Hayes repeated, reflexively pushing the young girl behind her.

"I'd like to talk to you if you have a moment." Jason took out his wallet and handed over his driver's license with its photo and his GHP staff identity card. "I went to medical school with your husband," he added for good measure.

Louise looked at the cards and handed them back. "Would you like to come in?"

"Thank you."

The interior of the house also looked in need of work. The furniture was worn and the carpet was threadbare. Children's toys littered the floor. Louise hastily cleared a spot on the couch and motioned for Jason to sit down.

"Can I offer you something? Coffee, tea?"

"Coffee would be nice," he said. The woman seemed anxious, and he thought the activity would calm her. She went into the kitchen, where Jason could hear the sound of running water. The little girl had hung behind, regarding Jason with large brown eyes. When Jason smiled at her, she fled into the kitchen.

Jason gazed around the room. It was dark and cheerless, with a few mail-order prints on the walls. Louise returned with her daughter in tow. She gave Jason a mug of coffee and placed sugar and cream on the small coffee table. Jason helped himself to both.

Louise sat down across from Jason. "I'm sorry if I didn't seem hospitable at first," she said. "I don't have many visitors asking about Alvin."

"I understand," Jason said. He looked at her more carefully. Underneath the frowsy exterior, Jason could see the shadow of an attractive woman. Hayes had good taste, that was for sure. "I'm sorry to barge in like this, but Alvin had spoken of you. Since I was in the area I thought I'd drop by." He thought a few untruths might help.

"Did he?" Louise said indifferently.

Jason decided to be careful. He wasn't there to dredge up painful emotions.

"The reason I wanted to talk to you," he said, "is that your husband told me he'd made an important scientific discovery." Jason went on to explain the circumstances of Alvin Hayes's death, and how he, Jason, had made it a personal crusade to try to find out if her husband had indeed made a scientific breakthrough. He explained that it would be a tragedy if Alvin had come across something that could help mankind, only to have it lost. Louise nodded, but when Jason asked if she had any idea of what the discovery could have been, she said she didn't.

"You and Alvin didn't speak much?"

"No. Only about the children and financial matters."

"How are your children?" Jason asked, remembering Hayes's concern about his son.

"They are both fine, thank you."

"Two?"

"Yes," Louise said. "Lucy here"—she patted her daughter's head—"and John is in school."

"I thought you had three children."

Jason saw the woman's eyes film over. After an uncomfortable silence she said, "Well . . . there is another. Alvin Junior. He's severely retarded. He lives at a school in Boston."

"I'm sorry."

"It's all right. You'd think I'd have adjusted by now, but I guess I never will. I guess it was the reason Alvin and I got divorced—I couldn't deal with it."

"Where exactly is Alvin Junior?" Jason asked, knowing he was probing a painful area.

"At the Hartford School."

"How is he doing?" Jason knew of the Hartford School. It was an institution acquired by GHP when the corporation purchased an associated acute-care proprietary hospital. Jason also knew the school was for sale. It was a money-loser for GHP.

"Fine, I guess," Louise said. "I'm afraid I don't visit too often. It breaks my heart."

"I understand," Jason said, wondering if this was the son Hayes had been referring to the night he died. "Would it be possible for us to call and inquire how the boy is doing?"

"I suppose," Louise said, not reacting to the extraordinary nature of the question. She got stiffly to her feet and, with her daughter still clinging to her, went to the telephone and called the school. She asked for the pre-teen dormitory and, when they answered, talked for a while about her son's condition. When she hung up, she said, "They feel he's doing as well as can be expected. The only new problem is some arthritis, which has interfered with his physical therapy."

"Has he been there long?"

"Just since Alvin went to work for GHP. Being able to place Alvin Junior at Hartford was one of the reasons he accepted the job."

"And your other son? You say he's fine."

"Couldn't be better," Louise said with obvious pride. "He's in the third grade and considered one of the brightest in the class."

"That's wonderful," Jason said, trying to think back to the night Hayes died. Alvin had said that someone wanted him and his son dead. That it was too late for him but maybe not for his son. What on earth had he meant? Jason had assumed one of his sons had been physically sick, but apparently that was not the case.

"More coffee?" Louise asked.

"No, thank you," Jason said. "There's just one more thing I wanted to ask. At the time of his death, Alvin was involved in setting up a corporation. Your children were to be stockholders. Did you know anything at all about that?"

"Not a thing."

"Oh, well," Jason said. "Thanks for the coffee. If there's anything I can do for you in Boston, like look in on Alvin Junior, don't hesitate to call." He got up and the little girl buried her head in Louise's skirt.

"I hope Alvin didn't suffer," she said.

"No, he didn't," Jason lied. He could still remember the look of agony on Alvin's face.

They were at the door when Louise suddenly said, "Oh, there's one thing I didn't tell you. A few days after Alvin died, someone broke in here. Luckily we were out."

"Was anything taken?" Jason wondered if it could have been Gene, Inc.

"No," Louise said. "They probably saw the usual mess and just

395

moved on.'' She smiled. ''But they seemed to have searched through everything. Even the children's bookcases.''

As Jason drove out of Leonia, New Jersey, and made his way back to the George Washington Bridge, he thought about his meeting with Louise Hayes. He should have been more discouraged than he was. After all, he'd learned nothing of importance to have justified the trip. But he realized there had been more to his wanting to go. He'd been genuinely curious about Hayes's wife. Having had his own wife rudely taken away from him, Jason couldn't understand why someone like Hayes would split up voluntarily. But Jason had never experienced the trauma of a retarded child.

Jason was able to catch the two o'clock afternoon shuttle back to Boston. He tried to read on the plane, but couldn't concentrate. He began to worry that Carol wouldn't meet him at the Boston airport, or, worse yet, that she'd show up with Bruno.

Unfortunately, the two o'clock shuttle that was supposed to land in Boston at two-forty didn't even leave La Guardia until two-thirty. By the time Jason got off the plane it was three-fifteen. He got his luggage from the locker and ran from the Eastern terminal over to United.

There was a long line at the ticket window, and Jason couldn't imagine what the airline agents were doing to make each transaction so lengthy. It was now twenty to four and no sign of Carol Donner.

At last it was Jason's turn. He tossed over his American Express card, asking for two round-trip tickets to Seattle for the flight leaving at four, with open returns.

At least with Jason the agent was efficient. Within three minutes Jason had the tickets and boarding cards and was running for Gate 19. It was now five minutes to four. The flight was in the final stages of boarding. Arriving at Gate 19, Jason breathlessly asked if anyone had asked for him. When the girl at the desk said no, he quickly described Carol and asked if the agent had seen her.

''She's very attractive,'' he added.

''I'm sure she is,'' smiled the agent. ''Unfortunately, I haven't noticed her. But if you are planning to go to Seattle you'd better board.''

Jason watched the second hand sweep around the face of the wall clock behind the check-in counter. The agent was busy counting the tickets. Another agent made the final announcement for the departure to Seattle. It was two minutes before four.

With his carry-on bag draped over his shoulder, Jason looked up the concourse toward the terminal proper. At the point he was about to give up all hope, he saw her. She was running in his direction. Jason should have been elated. The only problem was that a few steps behind her was the impressive hulk of Bruno. Farther down the hall was a policeman, lounging at the point where bags were picked up from the X-ray machine. Jason made a mental note: that would be his direction of flight if the need arose.

With her own carry-on shoulder bag, Carol was having some difficulty running. Bruno made no attempt to assist her. Carol came directly up to Jason. Jason saw the expression on Bruno's broad face go from vexation to confusion to anger.

"Did I make it?" she panted.

The agent was now at the door to the jetway, kicking out the doorstop.

"What the hell are *you* doing here, creep?" Bruno shouted, looking up at the destination sign. He turned accusingly on Carol. "You said you were going home, Carol."

"Come on," Carol urged, grasping Jason's arm and pulling him toward the jetway.

Jason stumbled backward, his eyes on Bruno's pudgy face, which had turned an unattractive shade of red. The veins in his temple swelled to the size of cigars.

"Just a moment!" Carol called to the agent. The agent nodded and shouted something down the jetway. Jason watched Bruno until the very last second. He saw him lumber over to a bank of telephones.

"You people like to cut it close," the agent said, ripping off a part of each boarding card. Jason finally turned to face ahead, at last convinced that Bruno had decided not to cause a scene. Carol was still pulling Jason's arm as they descended the jetway. They had to wait while the jetway operator pounded on the side of the plane to get the cabin attendant inside to reopen the already sealed aircraft. "This is about as close as you can make it," he said, frowning.

Once they were seated, Carol apologized for being late. "I'm furious," she said, jamming her carry-on under the seat ahead of her. "I appreciate Arthur's concern for my well-being, but this is ridiculous."

"Who's Arthur?"

"He's my boss," Carol said disgustedly. "He told me if I left now he might actually fire me. I think I'll quit when we get back."

"Would you be able to do that?" Jason asked, wondering just what

Carol's work involved besides dancing. It was his understanding that women like Carol lost control of their lives.

"I was planning on stopping soon anyway," said Carol.

The plane lurched as it was towed backward out of the gate.

"You do know what kind of work I do?" Carol asked.

"Well, sort of," Jason said vaguely.

"You've never mentioned it," Carol said. "Most people bring it up."

"I figured it was your business," Jason said. Who was he to judge?

"You're a little strange," Carol said, "likable but strange."

"I thought I was pretty normal," Jason said.

"Ha!" Carol said playfully.

There was a good bit of air traffic and they waited for over twenty minutes before they lifted off the ground and headed west.

"I didn't think we were going to make it," Jason said, finally beginning to relax.

"I'm sorry," Carol said again. "I tried to lose Bruno, but he stuck like glue. I didn't want him to know I wasn't heading back to Indiana. But what could I do?"

"It doesn't matter," Jason said, although in the back of his mind it disturbed him that anyone but Shirley knew where he was going. He'd meant it to be a secret. At the same time he couldn't figure out how it would make any difference.

Taking notes on a yellow pad, Jason began quizzing Carol as to Hayes's schedule on each of his two trips to Seattle. The first visit was the more interesting. They'd stayed at the Mayfair Hotel and among other things had visited a club called the Totem, similar to the Cabaret in Boston. He asked her what it was like.

"It was okay," Carol said, "nothing special. But it didn't have the excitement of the Club Cabaret. Seattle seems a bit conservative."

Jason nodded, wondering why Hayes would waste his time at a place like that when he was traveling with Carol. "Did Alvin talk to anyone there?" he asked.

"Yes. Arthur arranged for him to speak to the owner."

"Your boss did? Did Alvin know your boss?"

"They were friends. That was how I met Alvin."

Jason recalled the rumors about Alvin's taste for discos and the like. Apparently they'd been true. But the idea of a world-famous molecular biologist being chummy with a man who managed a topless bar seemed ludicrous.

"Do you know what Alvin spoke to this man about?"

"No, I don't," Carol said. "They didn't talk very long. I was busy watching the dancers. They were quite good."

"And you visited the University of Washington, correct?"

"That's right. We did that the first day."

"And you think you can find the man Alvin saw there?" Jason asked, just to be sure.

"I think so. He was a tall, good-looking fellow."

"And then what?"

"We went up into the mountains."

"And that was vacation time?"

"I suppose."

"Did Alvin meet anyone up there?"

"No one in particular. But he talked to a lot of people."

Jason settled back after the cocktail service. He thought about what Carol had told him, believing the most critical event was the visit to the University of Washington. But the visit to the club was also curious and deserved to be checked out.

"One other thing," Carol said. "On the second trip we had to spend some time looking for dry ice."

"Dry ice? What on earth for?"

"I didn't know and Alvin didn't tell me. Alvin had a cooler and he wanted it full of dry ice."

Perhaps to transport the specimen, Jason thought. *This sounds promising*.

When they touched down in Seattle, they dutifully changed their watches to Pacific Coast time. Jason looked out the airplane window. True to expectations, it was raining. He could see the drops in the darkened pools of water on the runway. Soon, even the window was streaked with moisture.

They rented a car and once they were clear of the airport traffic, Jason said, "In case it helps your memory, I thought we'd stay at the same hotel you did last time. Separate rooms, of course."

Carol turned to eye him in the half-light of the car. Jason wanted it very clear this trip was all business.

Two cars behind Jason and Carol was a dark blue Ford Taurus. Behind the wheel was a middle-aged man dressed in a turtleneck sweater, suede jacket, and checked slacks. He'd gotten a call only about five hours earlier to meet the United flight from Boston. He was supposed to spot a forty-five-year-old doctor who'd be arriving with a beautiful young woman. The names were Howard and Donner, and he was to keep them under surveillance. The operation had been easier than he'd expected. He'd confirmed their identity simply by coming up behind them at the Avis counter.

Now all he had to do was keep them in sight. Supposedly he'd be contacted by somebody who'd be coming from Miami. For this he was being paid his usual fifty dollars an hour plus expenses. He wondered if it were some kind of domestic problem.

The hotel was elegant. Judging from Hayes's usual disheveled appearance, Jason wouldn't have expected the man to have such expensive tastes. They got separate rooms, but Carol insisted they open the connecting door. "Let's not be prudish," she said. Jason didn't know how to take that.

Since they'd barely touched the airplane food, Jason suggested they have dinner before heading out to the Totem Club. Carol changed, and as they entered the dining room, Jason was pleased at how young and lovely she looked. The maître d' even checked her ID when Jason ordered a bottle of California chardonnay. The episode thrilled Carol, who complained of looking as if she were already over the hill at age twenty-five.

By ten P.M., one o'clock East Coast time, they were ready to leave for the Totem Club. Jason was already beginning to feel sleepy, but Carol felt fine. To avoid difficulty, they left the rental car in the hotel parking lot and took a taxi. Carol admitted she had trouble finding the place with Hayes.

The Totem Club was outside of the downtown area of Seattle, on the border of a pleasant residential neighborhood. There was none of the sordid color of the Boston Combat Zone. The club was surrounded by a large asphalt parking area that wasn't even littered, and there were no street people panhandling. It looked like any restaurant or bar, except for several ersatz totem poles flanking the entrance. When Jason got out of the car, he could feel the beat of the rock music. They ran through the rain to the entrance.

Inside, the club seemed much more conservative than the Cabaret. The first thing Jason noticed was that the crowd consisted mostly of couples rather than the heavy-drinking men who lined the runway in

Boston. There was even a small dance floor. The only real similarity was the configuration of the bar, which was also U-shaped with a runway for the dancers in the center.

"They don't dance topless here," Carol whispered.

They were shown to a booth on the first level, away from the bar. There was another level behind them. A waitress placed a cardboard coaster in front of each and asked for their drink order.

After they'd been served, Jason asked if Carol saw the owner. At first she didn't, but after a quarter hour she grasped Jason's arm and leaned across the table.

"There he is." She pointed to a young man, probably in his early thirties, dressed in a tuxedo with a red tie and cummerbund. He had olive skin and thick blue-black hair.

"Do you remember his name?"

She shook her head.

Jason eased out from the booth and walked toward the owner, who had a friendly, boyish face. As Jason came up to him, he laughed and patted the back of a man sitting at the bar.

"Excuse me," Jason said. "I'm Dr. Jason Howard. From Boston."
The owner turned to him. He wore a plastic smile.

"I'm Sebastian Frahn," the owner said. "Welcome to the Totem."

"Could I speak to you for a moment?"

The man's smile waned. "What's on your mind?"

"It will take a minute or two to explain."

"I'm awfully busy. Maybe later."

Unprepared for such a quick brush-off, Jason stood for a moment watching Frahn move among his customers. His smile had immediately returned.

"Any luck?" Carol asked when Jason returned to their booth and sat down again.

"None. Three thousand miles and the guy won't talk to me."

"People have to be careful in this business. Let me try."

Without waiting for Jason's reply, she slid from the booth. Jason watched her gracefully make her way over to the owner. She touched his arm and spoke briefly. Jason saw him nod, then gaze in his direction. The man nodded again and moved off. Carol returned.

"He'll be over in a minute."

"What did you say?"

"He remembered me," Carol said simply.

Jason wondered what that meant. "Did he remember Hayes?"

"Oh, yes," Carol said. "No problem."

Sure enough, within ten minutes Sebastian Frahn made a swing around the room and stopped at their table.

"Sorry to have been so curt. I didn't know you people were friends."

"That's all right," Jason said. He didn't know exactly what the man meant, but it sounded cordial.

"What can I do for you?"

"Carol says you remember Dr. Hayes."

Sebastian turned to Carol. "Was that the man you were here with last time?" he asked.

Carol nodded.

"Sure I remember him. He was a friend of Arthur Koehler."

"Do you think you could tell me what you talked about? It might be important."

"Jason worked with Alvin," Carol interjected.

"I don't have any problem at all telling you what we discussed. The man wanted to go salmon fishing."

"Fishing!" Jason exclaimed.

"Yup. He said he wanted to catch some big chums but he didn't want to drive too far. I told him to go to Cedar Falls."

"Was that all?" Jason asked, his heart sinking.

"We talked about the Seattle Supersonics for a few minutes."

"Thank you," Jason said. "I appreciate your time."

"Not at all," Sebastian said with a smile. "Well, got to circulate." He stood up, shook hands, and told them to come back again. Then he moved off.

"I can't believe it," Jason said. "Every time I think I have a lead, it turns out to be a joke. Fishing!"

At Carol's request they stayed for another half hour to watch the show, and by the time they got back to the hotel, Jason was totally exhausted. By East Coast time it was four o'clock Thursday morning. Jason got ready for bed and climbed between the sheets with relief. He'd been disappointed by the results of his visit to the Totem Club, but there was still the University of Washington. He was about to drop off to sleep when there was a soft knock on the connecting door. It was Carol. She said she was starving and couldn't sleep. Could they order room service? Feeling obliged to be a good sport, Jason agreed. They ordered a split of champagne and a plate of smoked salmon.

Carol sat on the edge of Jason's bed in a terrycloth robe, eating salmon and crackers. She described her childhood growing up outside of Bloomington, Indiana. Jason had never heard her talk so much. She'd lived on a farm and had to milk cows before going to school in the morning. Jason could see her doing that. She had that freshness about her that suggested such a life. What he had trouble with was relating that former life to her current one. He wanted to know how things got on the wrong track, but he was afraid to ask. Besides, exhaustion took over and try as he might, he could not keep his eyes open. He fell asleep and Carol, after covering him with a blanket, returned to her own room.

13

Awakening with a start, Jason checked his watch, which said five A.M. That meant eight in Boston, the time he usually left for the hospital. He opened the drapes and looked out on a crystal-clear day. In the distance a ferry was making its way across Puget Sound toward Seattle, leaving a sparkling wake.

After showering, Jason knocked on the adjoining door. There was no answer. He knocked again. Finally he opened it a crack, allowing a swath of bright sunlight to fall into the cool, darkened room. Carol was still fast asleep, clutching her pillow. Jason watched her for a moment. She looked angelically lovely. Silently, he closed the door so as to not waken her.

He went back to his bed, dialed room service, and ordered fresh orange juice, coffee, and croissants for two. Then he called GHP and paged Roger Wanamaker.

"Everything okay?"

"Not quite," Roger admitted. "Marge Todd threw a big embolus last night. She went into a coma and died. Respiratory arrest."

"My God," Jason said.

"Sorry to be the bearer of sad tidings," Roger said. "Try to enjoy yourself."

"I'll give you a call in a day or so," Jason said.

Another death. Except for one young woman with hepatitis, he was beginning to think the only way his patients could leave the hospital was feetfirst. He wondered if he should fly directly back to Boston. Yet Roger was right. There was nothing he could do, and he might as well see the Hayes business through, even though he wasn't very optimistic.

Two hours later Carol knocked at the door and came in, her hair still wet from the shower. "Top of the morning," she said in her cheerful voice. Jason ordered fresh coffee.

"Guess we're lucky," he said, pointing out at the bright sunlight.

"Don't be so sure. The weather around here can change mighty quickly."

While Carol breakfasted, Jason had another cup of coffee.

"Hope I didn't talk your ear off last night," Carol said.

"Don't be silly. I'm sorry I fell asleep."

"What about you, doctor?" Carol asked, putting jam on a croissant. "You haven't told me much about yourself." She didn't mention that Hayes had told her a good deal about him.

"Not much to tell."

Carol raised her eyebrows. When she saw his smile, she laughed. "For a second I thought you were serious."

Jason told Carol about his boyhood in Los Angeles, his education at Berkeley and Harvard Medical School, and his residency at Massachusetts General. Without meaning to, he found himself describing Danielle and the awful November night when she'd been killed. No one had ever drawn him out the way Carol did, not even Patrick, the psychiatrist he'd seen after Danielle's death. Jason even heard himself describing his current depression over his increased patient mortality and then Roger's news that morning about Marge Todd's death.

"I'm flattered that you've told me this," Carol said sincerely. She hadn't expected such openness and trust. "You've had a lot of emotional pain."

"Life can be like that," Jason said with a sigh. "I don't know why I've bored you with all this."

"It hasn't been boring," Carol said. "I think you've made an extraordinary adjustment. I think it was difficult yet very positive that you changed your work and living environment."

"Do you?" Jason asked. He hadn't remembered saying that. He hadn't expected to be so personal with Carol, but now that he'd done so, he felt better.

Enjoying their time together, it wasn't until ten-thirty that they emerged from their respective rooms dressed for the day. Jason asked the bellman to bring their car to the front entrance, and they took the elevator down to the lobby. True to Carol's prediction, when they emerged from the hotel the sky had darkened and a steady rain was falling.

With the help of an Avis map and Carol's memory, they drove out to the University of Washington's Medical School. Carol pointed out the research building Hayes had visited. They went in the front entrance and were immediately challenged by a uniformed security man. They had no University of Washington identity badges.

"I'm a doctor from Boston," Jason said, removing his wallet to show his ID.

"Hey, man, I don't care where you're from. No badge, no entry. Simple as that. If you want to come in here, you have to go to Central Administration."

Seeing it was fruitless to argue, they went to Central Administration. En route, Jason asked how Hayes had handled security.

"He called his friend beforehand," Carol said. "The man met us in the parking lot."

The woman at Central Administration was friendly and accommodating, and even showed Carol a faculty book to see if she could pick out Hayes's friend. But faces weren't enough, and Carol couldn't identify him. Instead, armed with security badges, they returned to the research building.

Carol led Jason up to the fifth floor. The corridor was crowded with spare equipment, and the walls were in need of fresh paint. There was a pungent chemical smell, akin to formaldehyde.

"Here's the lab," Carol said, stopping by an open doorway. The names to the left of the door were Duncan Sechler, MD, PhD; and Rhett Shannon, MD, PhD. The department was, as Jason might have guessed, molecular genetics.

"Which name?" Jason asked.

"I don't know," Carol said, going up to a young technician and asking if either of the doctors was in.

"Both. They're in the animal room." He pointed over his shoulder, then turned as Carol walked by so he could catch the view from the rear. Jason was surprised by his blatancy.

The door to the animal room had a large glass panel. Inside were two men in white coats drawing blood from a monkey.

"It was the tall one with the gray hair," Carol said, pointing. Jason moved closer to the window. The man Carol indicated was handsome and athletic-appearing, of approximately Jason's age. His hair was a uniform silver color that gave him a particularly distinguished look. The other man, in contrast, was almost bald. What hair he had was combed over the top of his head in a vain attempt to cover the thinning spot.

"Will he remember you?"

"Possibly. We only met for a moment before I went off to the Psychology Department."

They waited until the doctors finished their task and emerged from the animal room. The tall gray-haired man was carrying the vial of blood.

"Excuse me," Jason said. "Could I possibly have a moment of your time?"

The man glanced at Jason's badge. "Are you a drug rep?"

"Heavens, no." Jason smiled. "I'm Dr. Jason Howard and this is Miss Carol Donner."

"What can I do for you?"

"I'll see you in a minute, Duncan," interrupted the balding man.

"Okay," Duncan said. "I'll run the blood immediately." Then, turning to Jason, he said, "Sorry."

"Quite all right. I wanted to talk to you about an old acquaintance."

"Oh?"

"Alvin Hayes. Do you remember him visiting you here?"

"Sure," Duncan said, turning to Carol. "And weren't you with him?"

Carol nodded. "You have a good memory."

"I was shocked to hear he'd died. What a loss."

"Carol said Hayes came to ask you something important," Jason said. "Could you tell me what it was about?"

Duncan looked upset, glancing nervously around at the technicians. "I'm not sure I want to talk about it."

"I'm sorry to hear that. Was it business or a personal matter?"

"Maybe you'd better come into my office."

Jason had trouble containing his excitement. It finally sounded as if he'd stumbled onto something significant.

After entering the office, Duncan closed the door. There were two metal-backed chairs. Removing stacks of journals, he motioned for Jason and Carol to sit.

"To answer your question," he said, "Hayes came to see me for personal reasons, not business."

"We've come three thousand miles just to talk with you," Jason said. He wasn't going to give up so easily, but it wasn't sounding encouraging.

"If you'd called, I could have saved you the trip." Some of Duncan's friendliness had disappeared from his voice.

"Maybe I should tell you why we are so interested," Jason said. He explained the mystery of Hayes's possible discovery and his own futile attempts to figure out what it might have been.

"You think Hayes came to me for help in his research?" Duncan asked.

"That's what I'd hoped."

Duncan gave a short, unpleasant laugh. He looked at Jason out of the corner of his eye. "You wouldn't be a narc, would you?"

Jason was confused.

"All right, I'll tell you what Hayes wanted. A place to buy marijuana. He said he was terrified to fly with the stuff and couldn't bring any with him. As a favor, I set him up with a kid on campus."

Jason was stunned. His excitement dwindled like air seeping out of a balloon, leaving him deflated.

"I'm sorry to have taken your time. . . ."

"Not at all."

Carol and Jason walked out of the research building, surrendering their visitor's badges to the security guard. Carol was smiling slyly.

"It isn't so funny, you know," Jason said as they got into the car.

"But it is," Carol said. "You just can't see it right at this moment."

"We might as well go home," he said gloomily.

"Oh, no! You dragged me all the way out here, and we're not leaving until you see the mountains. It's only a short drive."

"Let me think about it," Jason told her moodily.

Carol prevailed. They went back to the hotel, got their belongings, and before Jason knew it, they were on a freeway heading out of town. She insisted on driving. Soon the suburbs gave way to misty green forest, and the rolling hills became mountains. The rain stopped and Jason could see snow-capped peaks in the distance. The scenery was so beautiful he forgot his disappointment.

"It gets even prettier," Carol said as they left the freeway, heading toward Cedar Falls. She remembered the route now and happily pointed out the sights. Taking an even smaller road, Carol drove along the Cedar River.

It was a nature fairyland, with deep forests, craggy rocks, distant mountains, and rushing rivers. As dusk fell, Carol turned off the road and bumped across a crushed-stone driveway, coming to a halt in front of a picturesque mountain lodge constructed like an enormous five-story log cabin. Smoke curled up lazily from a huge fieldstone chimney. A sign over the steps leading to the porch said SALMON INN.

"Is this where you and Alvin stayed?" Jason asked, peering through the windshield. There was a huge porch with raw pine furniture.

"This is it." Carol reached around to get her bag from the back seat.

They got out of the car. There was a chill to the air and the pungent smell of woodsmoke. Jason heard a distant sound of rushing water.

"The river's on the other side of the lodge," Carol said, mounting the steps. "Just a little way up there's a cute waterfall. You'll see it tomorrow."

Jason followed her, suddenly wondering what the hell he was doing. The trip had been a mistake; he belonged back in Boston with his critically ill patients. Yet here he was in the Cascade Mountains with a girl he had no business admiring.

The interior of the inn was every bit as charming as the exterior. The central room was a large, two-story affair dominated by a gargantuan fireplace. It was furnished with chintz, animal heads, and scattered bearskin rugs. There were several people reading in front of the fire and a family playing Scrabble. A few heads turned as Jason and Carol approached the registration desk.

"Do you people have a reservation?" asked the man behind the desk.

Jason wondered if the man was joking. The place was immense, it was in the middle of nowhere, it was early November, and it wasn't a weekend. He couldn't imagine the demand would be very high.

"No reservations," Carol said. "Is that a problem?"

"Let me see," said the man, bending over his book.

"How many rooms are there in the hotel?" Jason asked, still bemused.

"Forty-two and six suites," the receptionist said without looking up.

"Is there a shoe convention in town?"

The man laughed. "It's always full this time of year. The salmon are running."

Jason had heard of the Pacific salmon and how they'd mysteriously return to the particular freshwater breeding grounds that had spawned them. But he'd thought the phenomenon occurred in the spring.

"You're in luck," the receptionist said. "We have a room, but you might have to move tomorrow night. How many nights are you planning to stay?"

Carol looked at Jason. Jason felt a rush of anxiety—only one room! He didn't know what to say. He started to stammer.

"Three nights," Carol said.

"Fine. And how will you settle your bill?"

There was a pause.

"Credit card," Jason said, fumbling for his wallet. He couldn't believe what was happening.

As they followed the bellboy down the second-floor hallway, Jason wondered how he'd gotten himself into this. He hoped there would at least be twin beds. Much as he admired Carol's looks, he wasn't prepared for an affair with an exotic dancer who did God knows what else on the side.

"You people have a wonderful view," the bellboy said.

Jason went in, but his eyes shifted immediately to the sleeping arrangements, not the windows. He was relieved to see separate beds.

When the boy left, Jason finally went over to admire the dramatic vista. The Cedar River, which at that point widened to what appeared to be a small lake, was bordered by tall evergreens that glowed a dark purple in the fading light. Immediately below was a lawn that sloped down to the water's edge. Extending out into the river was a maze of docks used to moor twenty to thirty rowboats. On racks, out of the water, were canoes. Four large rubber boats with outboard motors were tied to the end of a dock. Jason could tell there was a significant current in the river despite its placid appearance, since all four of the rubber boats had their sterns pointed downriver, their bowlines taut.

"Well, what do you think?" Carol said, clapping her hands. "Isn't it cozy?"

The room was papered with a flower print. The floor was broad-planked pine with scattered rag rugs. The beds were covered with comforters printed to appear like quilts.

"It's wonderful," Jason said. He glanced into the bathroom, hoping for robes. "You seem to be the tour director. What now?"

"I vote for dinner immediately. I'm starved. And I think the dining room only serves until seven. People turn in early here."

The restaurant had a curved, windowed wall facing the river. In the center of the wall were double doors leading to a wide porch. Jason guessed that in the summer the porch was used for dining. There were steps from the porch down to the lawn, and at the docks the lights had come on, illuminating the water.

About half of the two dozen tables in the room were filled. Most of the people were already on their coffee. It seemed to Jason that everyone stopped talking the moment he and Carol appeared.

"Why do I feel we're on display?" Jason whispered.

"Because you're anxious about sleeping in the same room with a young woman whom you barely know," Carol whispered. "I think you feel defensive and a little guilty and unsure of what's expected of you."

Jason's lower jaw slowly sank. He tried to look into Carol's warmly liquid eyes to comprehend what was in there. He knew he was blushing. How on earth could a girl who danced half nude be so perceptive? Jason had always prided himself on his ability to evaluate people: after all, it was his job. As a physician, he had to have a sense of his patients' inner dynamics. Yet why did he feel there was something about Carol that didn't fit?

Glancing at Jason's red face, Carol laughed. "Why don't you just relax and enjoy yourself. Let down your hair, doctor—I'm certainly not going to bite."

"Okay," Jason said. "I'll do just that."

They dined on salmon, which was offered in bewilderingly tempting varieties. After great deliberation, they both had it baked in a pastry shell. For authenticity, they sampled a Washington State Chardonnay which Jason found surprisingly good. At one point he heard himself laughing aloud. It had been a long time since he'd felt so free. It was at that point they both realized they were alone in the dining room.

Later that night when Jason was in bed, looking up at the dark ceiling, he again felt confused. It had been a comedy of sorts getting to bed, juggling towels as coverups, flipping a coin to see who used the bathroom first, and having to get out of bed to turn out the light. Jason had never remembered feeling quite so body conscious. Jason rolled over. In the darkness, he could just make out the outline of Carol's form. She was on her side. He could hear the faint sound of her rhythmical breathing against the background sound of the distant waterfall. She was obviously asleep. Jason envied her honest acceptance of herself and her untroubled slumber. But what confused him was not the inconsistencies of Carol's personality, but rather the fact that he was enjoying himself. And it was Carol who was making it happen.

14

Weatherwise, their luck held. When they opened the drapes in the morning, the river sparkled with the brilliance of a million gemstones. The minute they finished breakfast, Carol announced they were going on a hike.

With box lunches from the hotel, they walked up the Cedar River on a well-marked trail alive with birds and small animals. About a quarter of a mile from the lodge they came upon the waterfall Carol had mentioned. It was a series of rocky ledges, each about five feet high. They joined several other tourists on a wooden viewing platform and watched in awed silence as the wild water cascaded downward. Just below them, a magnificent rainbow-colored fish, three to four feet long, broke the turbulent surface of the water, and in defiance of gravity leaped up the face of the first ledge. Within seconds it had leaped again, clearing the second ledge by a wide margin.

"My God," Jason exclaimed. He'd remembered reading that salmon were capable of running through rapids against the current, but he had no idea that they could navigate such high falls. Jason and Carol stayed mesmerized as several other salmon leaped. He could only marvel at the physical stamina the fish were displaying. The genetically determined urge to procreate was a powerful force.

"It's unbelievable," he said as a particularly large fish began to swim the watery gauntlet.

"Alvin was fascinated too," Carol said.

Jason could well imagine, especially with Hayes's interest in developmental and growth hormones.

"Come on," Carol said, taking Jason's hand. "There's more."

They continued up the trail, which left the river's edge for a quarter of a mile, taking them deep into a forest. When the trail returned to the river, the Cedar had widened into another small lake like the one in front of the Salmon Inn. It was about a quarter of a mile across and a mile long, and its surface was dotted with fishermen.

A cabin much like a miniature Salmon Inn lay nestled in a stand of large pines. In front of it at the water's edge was a short dock with half a dozen rowboats. Carol took Jason up the flagstone walk and through the front door.

The cabin was a fishing concession run by the Salmon Inn. There was a long, glass-fronted counter to the right, presided over by a bearded man in a red-checkered wool shirt, red suspenders, faded trousers, and caulked boots. Jason guessed he was in his late sixties, and that he would have made a perfect department store Santa Claus. Arranged along the wall behind him was an enormous selection of fishing poles. Carol introduced Jason to the older man, whose name was Stooky Griffiths, saying that Alvin had enjoyed visiting with Stooky while she fished.

"Hey," Carol said suddenly. "How about trying your hand at some salmon fishing?"

"Not for me," Jason said. Hunting and fishing had never interested him.

"I think I'll try. Come on—be a sport."

"You go ahead," Jason urged. "I can entertain myself."

"Okay." She turned to Stooky and made arrangements for a pole and some bait, then tried once more to talk Jason into joining her, but he shook his head.

"Is this where you and Alvin fished?" he asked, looking out the window at the river.

"Nope," Carol said, collecting her gear. "Alvin was like you. He wouldn't join me. But I caught a big one. Right off the dock."

"Alvin didn't fish at all?" Jason asked, surprised.

"No," said Carol. "He just watched the fish."

"I thought Alvin told Sebastian Frahn he wanted to go fishing."

"What can I say? Once we got here, Alvin was content to wander around and observe. You know, the scientist."

Jason shook his head in confusion.

"I'll be on the dock," Carol said brightly. "If you change your mind, come on down. It's fun!"

Jason watched her run down the flagstone walk, wondering why Alvin would have made such elaborate inquiries about fishing and then never cast a line. It was weird.

Two men came into the cabin and made arrangements with Stooky for gear, bait, and a boat. Jason stepped outside onto the porch. There were several rocking chairs. Stooky had hung a bird feeder from the eaves and dozens of birds circled it. Jason watched for a while, then wandered down to join Carol. The water was crystal clear and he could see rocks and leaves on the bottom. Suddenly, a huge salmon flashed out of the dark emerald green of the deeper water and shot under the dock, heading for a shallow, shady area fifty feet away.

Looking after it, Jason noticed a disturbance on the surface of the water. Curious, he walked over along the shore. When he got close, he saw another large salmon lying on its side in a few feet of water, its tail flapping weakly. Jason tried pushing it with a stick into deeper water, but it didn't help. The fish was obviously ill. A few feet away he spotted another salmon lying immobile in just a few inches of water, and, still closer to shore, a dead fish being eaten by a large bird.

Jason walked back up the flagstone path. Stooky had come out of the cabin and was sitting in one of the rockers with a pipe stuck between his teeth. Leaning on the rail, Jason asked him about the sick fish, wondering if there was some problem with pollution upriver.

"Nope," Stooky said. He took several puffs on his well-chewed pipe. "No pollution here. Them fish just spawned and now it's time for 'em to die."

"Oh, yeah," Jason said, suddenly remembering what he'd read about the salmon's life cycle. The fish pushed themselves to their limits to return to their spawning grounds, but once they laid their eggs and fertilized them, they died. No one knew exactly why. There had been theories about the physiological problems of going from saltwater to freshwater, but no one knew for certain. It was one of nature's mysteries.

Jason looked down at Carol. She was busy trying to cast her line out from the dock. Turning back to Stooky, he asked, "Do you by any chance remember talking with a doctor by the name of Alvin Hayes?"

"Nope."

"He was about my height," Jason continued. "Had long hair. Pale skin."

"I see a lot of people."

"I bet you do," Jason said. "But the man I'm talking about was with that girl." He pointed toward Carol. Jason guessed Stooky didn't see too many girls who looked like Carol Donner.

"The one on the dock?"

"That's right. She's a looker."

Smoke came out of Stooky's mouth in short puffs. His eyes narrowed. "Could the fella you're talking about come from Boston?"

Jason nodded.

"I remember him," Stooky said. "But he didn't look like no doctor."

"He did research."

"Maybe that explains it. He was real strange. Paid me a hundred bucks to get him twenty-five salmon heads."

"Just the heads?"

"Yup. Gave me his telephone number back in Boston. Told me to call collect when I had 'em."

"Then he came back here to get them?" Jason asked, remembering Hayes and Carol had made two trips.

"Yup. Told me to clean 'em good and pack 'em in ice."

"Why did it take so long?" Jason asked. With all the fish available, it seemed twenty-five heads could have been collected in a single afternoon.

"He only wanted certain salmon," Stooky said. "They had to have just spawned—and spawning salmon don't take bait. You have to net 'em. Them people fishing out there are catching trout."

"A particular species of salmon?"

"Nope. They'd just had to have spawned."

"Did he say why he wanted those heads?"

"He didn't and I didn't ask," Stooky said. "He was payin' and I figured it was his business."

"And just fishheads—nothing else."

"Just fishheads."

Jason left the porch frustrated and mystified. The idea that Hayes had come three thousand miles for fishheads and marijuana seemed preposterous.

Carol spotted him at the edge of the dock and waved at him to join her.

"You have to try this, Jason," she said. "I almost caught a salmon."

"The salmon don't bite here," Jason said. "It must have been a trout."

Carol looked disappointed.

Jason studied her lovely, high-cheekboned face. If his original premise was correct, the salmon heads had to have been associated with Hayes's attempts to create a monoclonal antibody. But how could that help Carol's beauty as Hayes had told her? It didn't make any sense.

"I guess it doesn't matter whether it's trout or salmon," Carol said, turning her attention back to her fishing. "I'm having fun."

A circling hawk plunged down into the shallow water and tried to grasp one of the dying salmon with its talons, but the fish was too big and the bird let go and soared back into the sky. As Jason watched, the salmon stopped struggling in the water and died.

"I got one!" Carol cried as her pole arched over.

The excitement of the catch cleared Jason's mind. He helped Carol land a good-sized trout—a beautiful fish with steely black eyes. Jason felt sorry for it. After he'd gotten the hook out of its lower lip, he talked Carol into throwing it back into the water. It was gone in a flash.

For lunch they walked along the banks of the widened river to a rocky promontory. As they ate, they could not only see the entire expanse of the river, but the snow-capped peaks of the Cascade Mountains. It was breathtaking.

It was late afternoon when they started back to the Salmon Inn. As they passed the cabin they saw another large fish in its death throes. It was on its side, its glistening white belly visible.

"How sad," Carol said, gripping Jason's arm. "Why do they have to die?"

Jason didn't have any answers. The old cliché, "It's nature's way," occurred to him, but he didn't say it. For a few moments they watched the once magnificent salmon as several smaller fish darted over to feed on its living flesh.

"Ugh!" Carol said, giving Jason's arm a tug. They continued walking. To change the subject, Carol started talking about another diversion the hotel had to offer. It was white-water rafting. But Jason didn't hear. The horrid image of the tiny predators feeding from the dying larger fish had started the germ of an idea in Jason's mind. Suddenly, like a revelation, he had a sense of what Hayes had discovered. It wasn't ironic—it was terrifying.

The color drained from Jason's face and he stopped walking.

"What's the matter?" Carol asked.

Jason swallowed. His eyes stared, unblinking.

"Jason, what is it?"

"We have to get back to Boston," he said with urgency in his voice. He set off again at a fast pace, almost dragging Carol with him.

"What are you talking about?" she protested.

He didn't respond.

"Jason! What's going on?" She jerked him to a stop.

"I'm sorry," he said, as if waking from a trance. "I suddenly have an idea of what Alvin may have stumbled onto. We have to get back."

"What do you mean—tonight?"

"Right away."

"Now wait just a minute. There won't be any flights to Boston tonight. It's three hours later there. We can stay over and leave early in the morning if you insist."

Jason didn't reply.

"At least we can have dinner," Carol added irritably.

Jason allowed her to calm him down. *After all, who knows? I could be wrong*, he thought. Carol wanted to discuss it, but Jason told her she wouldn't understand.

"That's pretty patronizing."

"I'm sorry. I'll tell you all about it when I know for sure."

By the time he had showered and dressed, Jason realized Carol was right. If they'd driven to Seattle, they'd have gotten to the airport around midnight Boston time. There wouldn't have been any flights until morning.

Descending to the dining room, they were escorted to a table directly in front of the doors leading to the veranda. Jason sat Carol facing the doors, saying she deserved the view. After they'd been given their menu, he apologized for acting so upset and gave her full credit for being right about not leaving immediately.

"I'm impressed you're willing to admit it," Carol said.

For variety, they ordered trout instead of salmon, and in place of the Washington State wine, they had a Napa Valley Chardonnay. Outside, the evening slowly darkened into night and the lights went on at the docks.

Jason had trouble concentrating on the meal. He was beginning to realize that if his theory was correct, Hayes had been murdered and Helene had not been the victim of random violence. And if Hayes was right and someone was using his accidental and terrifying discovery, the result could be far worse than any epidemic.

While Jason's mind was churning, Carol was carrying on a conversation, but when she realized he was off someplace, she reached across and gripped his arm. "You are not eating," she said.

Jason looked absently at her hand on his arm, his plate, and then Carol. "I'm preoccupied, I'm sorry."

"It doesn't matter. If you're not hungry, maybe we should go and find out about flights to Boston in the morning."

"We can wait until you're through eating," Jason said.

Carol tossed her napkin on the table. "I've had more than enough, thank you."

Jason looked for their waiter. His eyes roamed the room and then stopped. They became riveted on a man who had just entered the dining room and paused by the maître d's lectern. The man was slowly scanning the room, his eyes moving from table to table. He was dressed in a dark blue suit with a white shirt open at the collar. Even from the distance, Jason could tell the man wore a heavy gold necklace. He could see the sparkle from the overhead lights.

Jason studied the man. He looked familiar, but Jason couldn't place him. He was Hispanic, with dark hair and deeply tanned skin. He looked like a successful businessman. Suddenly, Jason remembered. He'd seen the face on that awful night when Hayes had died. The man had been outside the restaurant and then outside the Massachusetts General Hospital emergency room.

Just then the man spotted Jason, and Jason felt a sudden chill descend his spine. It was apparent the man recognized Jason because he immediately started forward, his right hand casually thrust into his jacket pocket. He walked deliberately, closing the distance quickly. Having just thought of Helene Brennquivist's murder, Jason panicked. His intuition told him what was coming, but he couldn't move. All he could do was look at Carol. He wanted to scream and tell her to run, but he couldn't. He was paralyzed. Out of the corner of his eye, he saw the man round the nearby table.

"Jason?" questioned Carol, tilting her head to one side.

The man was only steps away. Jason saw his hand come out of his pocket and the glint of metal as his hand covered the gun. The sight of the weapon finally galvanized Jason into action. In a sudden explosion of activity, he snatched the tablecloth from the table, sending the dishes, glasses, and silverware flying to the floor. Carol leaped to her feet with a scream.

Jason rushed the man, flinging the tablecloth over his head, pushing him backward into a neighboring table and knocking it over in a shower of china and glass. The people at the table screamed and tried to get away, but several were caught in the tangle of overturned chairs.

In the commotion, Jason grabbed Carol's hand and yanked her through the doors to the porch. Having managed to break his panic-filled paralysis, Jason was now a torrent of directed action. He knew who the Hispanic-looking businessman had been: the killer Hayes claimed was on his trail. Jason had no doubt his next targets were Carol and himself.

He pulled Carol down the front steps, intending to run around the hotel to the parking lot. But then he realized they'd never make it. They had a better chance running for one of the boats at the dock.

"Jason!" Carol yelled as he changed direction and dragged him down the lawn. "What's wrong with you?"

Behind them, Jason could hear the doors to the dining room crash open, and assumed they were being chased.

When they reached the dock, Carol tried to stop. "Come on, dammit," Jason shouted through gritted teeth. Looking back at the inn, he could see a figure run to the porch railing, then start down the stairs.

Carol tried to jerk her hand free, but Jason tightened his clasp and yanked her forward. "He wants to kill us!" he shouted. Stumbling ahead, they raced to the end of the dock, ignoring the rowboats. Jason shouted to Carol to help untie three of the rubber boats and push them off. They were already drifting downstream by the time their pursuer hit the dock. Jason helped Carol into the fourth boat and scrambled after her, pushing them away from the dock with his foot. They too drifted downstream, slowly at first, then gathering speed. Jason forced Carol to lie down, then covered her body with his own.

An innocent-sounding pop was immediately followed by a dull thud somewhere in the boat. Almost simultaneously there was the sound of escaping air. Jason groaned. The man was shooting at them with a silenced pistol. Another pop was followed by a ringing sound as a bullet ricocheted off the outboard motor, and another made a slapping sound in the water.

To Jason's relief, he realized the rubber boat was compartmentalized. Although a bullet had deflated one section, the boat wouldn't sink. A few more shots fell short, then Jason heard a thump of wood against the dock. Jason lifted his head cautiously and looked back. The man had pulled one of the canoes from the rack and was pushing it into the water.

Jason was again gripped with fear—the man could paddle much faster than they were drifting. Their only chance was to start the motor—an old-fashioned outboard with a pull cord. Jason shifted the gear lever to "start" and tugged the cord. The engine didn't even turn over. The killer had already boarded the canoe and was starting toward them. Jason pulled the cord again: nothing. Carol lifted her head and said nervously, "He's getting closer."

For the next fifteen seconds, Jason frantically jerked the starter cord over and over. He could see the silhouette of the oncoming canoe moving silently through the water. He checked to make sure the lever was at "start," then tried again without success. His eyes drifted to the gas tank, which he prayed was full. Its black cap appeared to be loose, so he tightened it. Just to its side was a button he guessed was to increase pressure in the tank. He pushed it a half dozen times, noticing that it became increasingly harder to depress. Looking up again, he saw the canoe was almost to them.

Grasping the starter cord again, Jason pulled with all his strength. The motor roared to life. Then he reached for the lever and pushed it to "reverse," as they were floating downstream backward. He jammed the throttle forward and threw himself back onto the bottom of the boat, pinning Carol beneath him. As expected, there were several more shots, two of which hit the rubber boat. When Jason dared to look out again, the gap had widened. In the darkness, he could barely see the canoe.

"Stay down," he commanded to Carol, while he checked the extent of the damage. A section of the right side of the bow was soft, as was a portion of the left gunwale. Otherwise the boat was intact. Moving back to the outboard, Jason cut the throttle, put the motor into "forward," then angled the tiller to head downstream, steering out to the center of the river. The last thing he wanted to do was hit rocks.

"Okay," he called to Carol. "It's safe to sit up."

Carol rose gingerly from the bottom of the boat and ran her fingers through her hair. "I really don't believe this," she shouted over the noise of the outboard. "Just what the hell are we going to do?"

"We'll head downriver until we see some lights. There's got to be plenty of places along here."

As they motored along, Jason wondered if it would be safe to stop at another dock. After all, their pursuer might get into his car and drive along the river. *Maybe there's a light on the opposite side*, he thought.

From the silhouettes of the trees lining the lakelike expanse of the river, Jason could gauge their speed. It seemed to be about a fast walk. He also had the feeling the river was again gradually narrowing, especially when it appeared that their speed was increasing. After a half hour, there were still no lights. Just a dark forest bordering a star-strewn, moonless sky.

"I don't see a thing," yelled Carol.

"It's okay," reassured Jason.

After traveling another quarter hour, the bordering trees closed in rather suddenly, suggesting the lakelike expanse was coming to an end. When the trees were closer, Jason realized he had misjudged their speed; they were moving much faster than he'd thought. Reaching back he cut the throttle. The small outboard whined down. As soon as the sound of the outboard fell, Jason heard another more ominous noise. It was the deep growling roar of white water.

"Oh, God," he said to himself, remembering the falls upriver from the Salmon Inn. He pushed the small outboard to the side and turned the boat around. Then he gave it full throttle. To his surprise and consternation, it slowed, but did not stop their rush downriver. Next he tried to angle the boat toward shore. Slowly, it moved laterally. But then all hell broke loose. The river narrowed to a rocky gorge, and Jason and Carol were unwittingly sucked into it.

Around the top edge of the rubber boat was a short rope secured at intervals by eyelets. Jason grabbed a hold on either side, spanning the craft with his outstretched arms. He yelled for Carol to do the same. She couldn't hear over the roar of the water, but when she saw what he was doing, she attempted to do the same. Unfortunately, she couldn't quite reach. She held on to one side and hooked a leg under one of the wooden seats. At that moment, they hit the first real turbu-lence, and the boat was tossed into the air like a cork. Water came into the boat in a blinding, drenching sheet. Jason sputtered. The darkness and water in his eyes made it all but impossible to see. He felt Carol's body hit up against his and he tried to anchor her with his leg. Then they thudded into a rock and the boat spun counter-clockwise. Through all this violent activity, Jason kept seeing the image of the falls, know-ing that at any second they could plummet to their death.

Jason and Carol clutched at the ropes in utter terror. They bounced from side to side and end to end, in rapid gyrations, completely at the mercy of the water. At every moment he thought they were going over. Water filled the cockpit. It was stingingly cold.

After what seemed like an eternity of hell, the water smoothed out. They were still spinning and careening downriver, but without the sudden violent upheavals. Jason glanced out. He could make out the sheer falls of rock on either side. He knew it wasn't over.

With a tremendous upward surge, the violent dubbing recommenced. Jason could feel his fingers begin to pain him; a combination of constant muscular contraction and the cold was having its effect. He gripped the rope holds with all his strength, trying to tighten his hold on Carol with his legs. The pain in his hands was so intense that for an instant he thought he'd have to let go.

Then, as suddenly as the nightmare began, it was over. Still spinning, the boat shot out onto relatively placid water. The thundering noise of the rapids lessened. The sides of the river fell away, opening up a clear view to the starry sky. Inside the boat there was a half foot of icy water, but Jason realized the outboard was chugging as smoothly as if nothing had happened.

With shaking hands, Jason straightened the boat and stopped its nauseating rotation. His fingers touched a button just inside the transom. He took a chance and pressed it; the water in the boat slowly receded.

Jason kept his eye on the silhouettes of the bordering trees. Ahead, the river bent sharply to the left, and as they rounded the point, they finally saw lights. Jason steered to shore.

As they approached, he could see several well-lit buildings, docks, and a number of rubber boats like their own. He was still afraid the killer might have driven down to intercept them, but he knew they had to land. Jason pulled alongside the second dock and cut the engine.

"You sure know how to entertain a girl," Carol said through chattering teeth.

"I'm glad you still have your sense of humor," Jason said.

"Don't count on it lasting much longer. I want to know what in heaven's name is going on."

Jason stood up stiffly, holding on to the dock. He helped Carol out of the boat, got out himself, and tied the line to a cleat. The sound of country music drifted from one of the buildings.

"It must be a bar," said Jason. He took her hand. "We have to get warm before we get pneumonia.'' Jason led the way up the gravel path, but instead of going inside, he walked into the parking lot and began looking in the parked vehicles.

"Hold on," said Carol with irritation. "What are you doing now?"

"I'm looking for keys," Jason said. "We need a car."

"I don't believe this," said Carol, throwing up her hands. "I thought we were going to get warm. I don't know about you, but I'm going in that restaurant." Without waiting for a response, she started for the entrance.

Jason caught up to her and grabbed her arm. "I'm afraid he'll be back—the man who was shooting at us."

"Then we'll call the police," Carol said. She pulled out of Jason's grasp and entered the restaurant.

The Hispanic was not in the restaurant, so, following Carol's suggestion, they called the police, who happened to be a local sheriff. The proprietor of the restaurant refused to believe that Jason and Carol had navigated Devil's Chute in the dark—"Nobody ain't done that before," he said. He found chef's smocks and oversized black and white checkered kitchen pants for them to change into, and a plastic garbage bag for their wet clothes. He also insisted they have steaming hot rum toddies, which finally stopped their shivering.

"Jason, you've got to tell me what's going on," Carol insisted as they waited for the sheriff. They sat at a table across from a Wurlitzer jukebox playing fifties music.

"I don't know for sure," Jason said. "But the man shooting at us was outside the restaurant where Alvin died. My guess is that Alvin was a victim of his own discovery, but if he hadn't died that night, the same man would have eventually killed him anyway. So Alvin was telling the truth when he said someone wanted him dead."

"This doesn't sound real," Carol said, trying to smooth her hair, which was drying in tangled ringlets.

"I know. Most conspiracies don't."

"What about Hayes's discovery?"

"I don't know for sure, but if my theory is right, it's almost too scary to contemplate. That's why I want to get back to Boston."

Just then the door opened and the sheriff, Marvin Arnold, walked in. He was a mountain of a man dressed in a wrinkled brown uniform that sported more buckles and straps than Jason had ever seen. More important to Jason was the .357 Magnum strapped to Marvin's oversized left thigh. That was the kind of cannon Jason wished he'd had back at the Salmon Inn.

Marvin had already heard about the commotion at the Salmon Inn, and had been there to check things out. What he hadn't heard about was any man with a gun, and no one had heard any gunshots. When Jason described what had happened, he could tell that Marvin regarded him with a good deal of skepticism. Marvin was surprised and impressed, however, when he heard that Jason and Carol had come down Devil's Chute by themselves in the dark. "Ain't a lot of people going to believe that," he said, shaking his massive head in admiration.

Marvin drove Jason and Carol back to the Salmon Inn, where Jason was surprised to find out there was a question of charges being filed against him, holding him responsible for the damages in the dining room. No one had seen any gun. And even more shocking, no one remembered an olive-complexioned man in a dark blue suit. But in the end, the management decided to drop the issue, saying they'd let their insurance take care of the damages. With that decided, Marvin tipped his hat, preparing to leave.

"What about protection?" asked Jason.

"From what?" asked Marvin. "Don't you think it is a little embarrassing that no one can corroborate your story? Listen, I think you people have caused enough trouble tonight. I think you should go up to your room and sleep this whole thing off."

"We need protection," said Jason. He tried to sound authoritative. "What do we do if the killer returns?"

"Look, friend, I can't sit here all night and hold your hand. I'm the only one on this shift and I got the whole damned county to keep my eye on. Lock yourself in your room and get some shut-eye."

With a final nod toward the manager, Marvin lumbered out the front door.

The manager in turn smiled condescendingly at Jason and went into his office.

"This is unreal," Jason said with a mixture of fear and irritation. "I can't believe nobody noticed the Hispanic guy." He went to the public phone booth and looked up private detective agencies. He found several in Seattle, but when he dialed he just got their answering machines. He left his name and the hotel number, but he didn't have much hope of reaching someone that night.

Emerging from the phone booth, he told Carol that they were leaving immediately. She followed him up the stairs.

"It's nine-thirty at night," she protested, entering the room behind him.

"I don't care. We're leaving as fast as we can. Get your things together."

"Don't I have any say in the matter?"

"Nope. It was your decision to stay tonight and your decision to call the helpful local police. Now it's my turn. We're leaving."

For a minute, Carol stood in the center of the room watching Jason pack, then she decided he probably had a point. Ten minutes later, changed into their own clothes, they carried their luggage downstairs and checked out.

"I have to charge you for tonight," the man at the desk informed them.

Jason didn't bother to argue. Instead, he asked the man if he'd bring their car around to the front entrance. He tipped him five dollars and the clerk was happy to oblige.

Once in the car, Jason had hoped he'd feel less anxious and less vulnerable. Neither was the case. As he pulled out of the hotel parking lot and started down the dark mountain road, he quickly recognized how isolated they were. Fifteen minutes later, in the rearview mirror, he saw headlights appear. At first Jason tried to ignore them, but then it became apparent that they were relentlessly gaining on them despite Jason's gradual acceleration. The terror Jason had felt earlier crept back. His palms began to perspire.

"There's someone behind us," Jason said.

Carol twisted in the front seat and looked out the back. They rounded a curve and the headlights disappeared. But on the next straightaway they reappeared. They were closer. Carol faced forward. "I told you we should have stayed."

"That's helpful!" said Jason sarcastically.

He inched the accelerator closer to the floor. They were already going well over sixty on the curvy road. He tightened his grip on the steering wheel, then looked up at the rearview mirror. The car was close, its lights like eyes of a monster. He tried to think of what he could do, but he could think of nothing other than trying to outrun the car behind them. They came to another curve. Jason turned the wheel. He saw Carol's mouth open in a silent scream. He could feel the car start to fishtail. He braked, and they skidded first to one side and then to the other. Carol grabbed the dash to steady herself. Jason felt his seat belt tighten.

Fighting the car, Jason managed to keep it on the road. Behind him the pursuing car gained considerably. Now it was directly behind, its headlights filling Jason's car with unearthly light. In a panic, Jason floored the accelerator, pulling his car out of its careening course. They shot forward down a small hill. But the car behind stayed right with them, hounding them like a hunting dog at the heels of a deer.

Then to both Jason and Carol's bewilderment, their car filled with flashing red light. It took them a moment to realize that the light was coming from the top of the car behind them. When Jason recognized what it was, he slowed, watching in the rearview mirror. The car behind slowed proportionately. Ahead, at a turnout, Jason pulled off the road and stopped. Sweat stood out in little droplets along his hairline. His arms were trembling from his death grip on the steering wheel. Behind them, the other car stopped as well, its flashing light illuminating the surrounding trees. In the rearview mirror, Jason saw the door open, and Marvin Arnold stepped out. He had the safety strap off his .357 Magnum.

"Well, I'll be a pig's ass," he said, shining his flashlight into Jason's embarrassed face. "It's lover boy."

Furious, Jason shouted, "Why the hell didn't you turn on your blinker at the start?"

"Wanted to catch me a speeder." Marvin chuckled. "Didn't know I was chasing my favorite lunatic."

After an unsolicited lecture and a ticket for reckless driving, he let Jason and Carol continue. Jason was too angry to talk, and they drove in silence to the freeway, where Jason announced, "I think we should drive to Portland. God knows who may be waiting for us at the Seattle airport."

"Fine by me," Carol said, much too tired to argue.

They stopped for a couple hours' sleep at a motel near Portland, and at the first light of dawn, went on to the airport, where they boarded a flight to Chicago. From Chicago, they flew to Boston, touching down a little after five-thirty Saturday evening.

In the cab in front of Carol's apartment, Jason suddenly laughed. "I wouldn't even know how to apologize for what I've put you through."

Carol picked up her shoulder bag. "Well, at least it wasn't boring.

Look, Jason, I don't mean to be sarcastic, or a nag, but please tell me what's going on."

"As soon as I'm sure," Jason said. "I promise. Really. Just do me one favor. Stay put tonight. Hopefully, no one knows we're back, but all hell might break loose if and when they find out."

"I don't plan on going anywhere, doctor." Carol sighed. "I've had it."

15

Jason never even stopped at his apartment. As soon as Carol disappeared into her building, he told the cabdriver to drop him at his car and drove directly to GHP. He crossed immediately into the outpatient building. It was seven P.M. and the large waiting room was deserted. Jason went directly to his office, pulled off his jacket, and sat down at his computer terminal. GHP had spent a fortune on their computer system and was proud of it. Each station accessed the large mainframe where all patient data was entered. Although the individual charts were still the best source of patient information, most of the material could be obtained from the computer. Best of all, the sophisticated machinery could scan the entire patient base of GHP and graphically display the data on the screen, analyzed in almost any way one could wish.

Jason first called up the current survival curves. The graph that the computer drew was shaped like the steep slope of a mountain, starting high, then rounding and falling off. The graph compared the survival rate of GHP users by age. As one might expect, subscribers at the oldest end of the graph had the lowest survival rate. Over the past five years, although the median age of the GHP population had gradually increased, the survival curves stayed about the same.

Next, Jason asked the computer to print month-by-month graphs for the last half year. As he had feared, he saw the death rate rise for patients in their late fifties and early sixties, particularly during the last three months.

ROBIN COOK

A sudden crash made him jump from his seat, but when he looked out in the hall he saw it was just the cleaning service.

Relieved, Jason returned to the computer. He wished he could separate the data on patients who had been given executive physicals, but he couldn't figure out how to do it. Instead, he had to be content with crude death rates. These graphs compared the percentages of deaths associated with age. This time the curve went the other way. It started low, then as the age increased the percentage of deaths went up. But then Jason asked the computer to print out a series of such graphs over the previous several months, month by month. The results were striking, particularly over the last two months. The death curves rose sharply starting at age fifty.

Jason sat at the computer terminal for another half hour, trying to coax the machine into separating out the executive physicals. What he expected he would see if he'd been able, was a rapid increase in death rates for people fifty and over who had high-risk factors such as smoking, alcohol abuse, poor diets, and lack of exercise. But the data was not available. It had not been programmed to be extracted en masse. Jason would have to take each individual name and laboriously obtain the data himself, but he didn't have time to do that. Besides, the crude death-rate curves were enough to corroborate his suspicions. He now knew he was right. But there was one more way to prove it. With enormous unease, he left his office and returned to his car.

Driving out the Riverway, Jason headed for Roslindale. The closer he got, the more nervous he became. He had no idea what he was about to confront, but he suspected it was not going to be pleasant. His destination was the Hartford School, the institution run by GHP for retarded children. If Alvin Hayes had been right about his own condition, he must have been right about his retarded son's.

The Hartford School backed onto the Arnold Arboretum, an idyllic setting of graceful wooded hills, fields, and ponds. Jason turned into the parking lot, which was all but deserted, and stopped within fifty feet of the front entrance. The handsome, Colonial-style building had a deceptively serene look that belied the personal family tragedies it housed. Severe retardation was a hard subject even for professionals to deal with. Jason vividly remembered examining some of the children on previous visits to the school. Physically many were perfectly formed, which only made their low IQs that much more disturbing.

The front door was closed and locked, so Jason rang the buzzer and

430

waited. The door was opened by an overweight security guard in a soiled blue uniform.

"Can I help you?" he said, making it clear he had no wish to.

"I'm a doctor," Jason said. He tried to push by the security man, who stepped back to bar his way.

"Sorry—no visitors after six, doctor."

"I'm hardly a visitor," Jason said. He pulled out his wallet and produced his GHP identity card.

The guard didn't even look at the ID. "No visitors after six," he repeated, adding, "and no exceptions."

"But I . . ." Jason began. He stopped in midsentence. From the man's expression, he knew discussion was futile.

"Call in the morning, sir," the guard said, slamming the door.

Jason walked back down the front steps and gazed up at the five-story building. It was brick, with granite window casings. He wasn't about to give up. Assuming the guard was watching, Jason went back to his car and drove out the driveway. About a hundred yards down the road, he pulled over to the side. He got out, and with some difficulty made his way through the Arboretum back to the school.

He circled the building, staying in the shadows. There were fire escapes on all sides but the front. They went right up to the roof. Unfortunately, as at Carol's building, none was at ground level, and Jason couldn't find anything to stand on to reach the first rung.

On the right side of the building, he spotted a flight of stairs that went down to a locked door. Feeling with his hands in the dark, he discovered the door had a central glass pane. He went back up the stairs and felt around the ground until he found a rock the size of a softball.

Holding his breath, Jason went back to the door and smashed the glass. In the quiet evening, the clatter seemed loud enough to wake the dead. Jason fled to the nearby trees and hid, watching the building. When no one appeared after fifteen minutes, he ventured out and returned to the door. Gingerly, he reached in and undid the latch. No alarm sounded.

For the next half hour Jason stumbled around a large basement he guessed was a storage area. He found a stepladder and debated taking it outside to use to reach a fire escape, but gave up that idea and continued feeling about blindly for a light. His hands finally touched a switch and he flicked it on.

He was in a maintenance room filled with lawnmowers, shovels, and other equipment. Next to the light switch was a door. Slowly, Jason eased it open. Beyond was a much larger furnace room that was dimly illuminated.

Moving quickly, Jason crossed the second room and mounted a steep steel stairway. He opened the door at the top and immediately realized he had reached the front hall. From his previous visits he knew the stairs to the wards were to his right. On his left was an office where a middle-aged woman in a bulging white uniform was reading at a desk. Looking down toward the front entrance, Jason could see the guard's feet perched on a chair. The man's face was out of sight.

As quietly as possible, Jason slipped through the basement door and let it ease back into place. For a moment he was in full view of the woman in the office, but she didn't look up from her book. Forcing himself to move slowly, he silently crossed the hall and entered the stairwell. He breathed a sigh of relief when he was completely out of sight of both the woman and the guard. Taking the stairs on tiptoe two at a time, he headed for the third floor, where the ward for boys aged four to twelve was located.

The stairs were marble, and even though he tried to be quiet, his footsteps echoed in the otherwise silent, cavernous space. Above him was a skylight, which at that time looked like a black onyx set into the ceiling.

On the third floor, Jason carefully opened the stairwell door. He remembered there was a glassed-in nurses' office to the right at the end of a long hallway and noticed that although the corridor was dark, the office still blazed with light. A male attendant was, like the woman downstairs, busy reading.

Looking diagonally across the hall, Jason eyed the door to the ward. He noted it had a large central window with embedded wire. After one last check on the attendant, Jason tiptoed across the hall and let himself into the darkened room. Immediately, he was confronted by a musty smell. After waiting a moment to be sure the attendant hadn't been disturbed, he began searching for the light. To confirm his suspicions, he would have to turn it on even if it meant being caught.

The drab room was suddenly flooded with raw, white fluorescent light. The ward was some fifty feet long, with low iron beds lined up on either side, leaving a narrow aisle. There were windows, but they were high, near the ceiling. At the end of the room were tiled toilet facilities with a coiled hose for cleaning and a bolted door to the fire escape. Jason walked down the aisle looking at the nameplates attached to the ends of beds: Harrison, Lyons, Gessner. . . . The children, disturbed by the light, began to sit up, staring with wide, vacant, and unknowing eyes at the intruder.

Jason stopped, and a terrible sense of revulsion that expanded to terror gripped him. It was worse than he'd imagined. Slowly, his eyes went from one pitiful face to another of the unwanted creatures. Instead of looking like the children they were, they all looked like miniature senile centenarians with beady eyes, wrinkled dry skin, and thinned white hair, showing scaly patches of scalp. Jason spotted the name Hayes. Like the others, the child appeared prematurely aged. He'd lost most of his eyelashes and his lower lids hung down. In place of his pupils were the glass-white reflection of dense cataracts. Except for light perception, the child was blind.

Some of the children began getting out of their beds, balancing precariously on wasted limbs. Then, to Jason's horror they began to move toward him. One of them began to say feebly the word "*please*" over and over in a high-pitched, grating voice. Soon the others joined in a terrifying, unearthly chorus.

Jason backed up, afraid to be touched. Hayes's son got out of his bed and began to feel his way forward, his bony, uncoordinated little arms making helpless swirling motions in the air.

The mob of children backed Jason up against the ward door and began to tug at his clothes. Frightened and nauseated, Jason pushed open the ward door and retreated into the hall. After he closed the door, the children pressed their mummylike faces against the glass, still silently voicing the word "please."

"Hey, you!" Jason heard a rasping voice behind him.

Turning his head, he saw the attendant standing outside his office, waving his open book in astonishment. "What's goin' on?" the man yelled.

Jason ran across the hall to the stairwell, but he'd descended only a few steps before a second voice echoed up from below. "Kevin? What gives?"

Looking over the railing, Jason saw the guard down on the first-floor landing.

"Well, I'll be damned," the guard said, and charged up the stairs, club in hand.

Reversing direction, Jason returned to the third floor. The attendant was still standing in the doorway of his office, apparently too dumbfounded to move as Jason sprinted across the hall and back into the ward. Some of the children were wandering aimlessly about the room; others had collapsed back on their beds. Jason frantically beckoned them over, opened the door, and as the attendant and guard appeared, they were immediately surrounded by a swarm of boys.

They tried to shove their way through the crowd, but the children clung to them, shouting their eerie, monotonous chorus of *please*.

Reaching the emergency door at the opposite end of the room, Jason depressed its lever which, for safety's sake, was positioned six feet off the floor. At first the door wouldn't open. Obviously, it had not been used for years. Jason could see that paint had sealed it shut. Putting his shoulder against it, he finally got it to swing free. Stepping out into the dark night, he pushed several of the boys back into the ward before closing the heavy door.

Wasting no time, he clambered down the fire escape. There was no need to be quiet now. He was at the second level when the door above him opened. Once again he heard the shrieking of the children. Then he felt the vibration of heavy boots on the fire escape.

Pulling out a pin caused the final ladder to descend with a deep thud, as it hit the asphalt of the parking lot below. Even before it had touched down, Jason was on it. The slight delay enabled the guard behind Jason to close the distance between them.

Once on the lawn, though, Jason's running ability soon left the beefy guard far behind, and by the time Jason reached his car, he had plenty of time to start the engine, put it in gear, and pull away. In his rearview mirror he could barely see the man just reaching the edge of the road, shaking his fist in the light of a street lamp.

Jason could barely control his disgust and fury at what he'd seen. He drove directly to Boston police headquarters and brazenly left his car in a no-parking zone in front of the building.

"I want to see Detective Curran," Jason told the officer at the desk, then identified himself.

The policeman calmly checked his watch, then called up to Homicide. He spoke for a minute, then covered the receiver with his hand. "Would anyone else do?"

"No. I want Curran. And now, please."

The policeman spoke into the phone a few minutes more, then hung up. "Detective Curran isn't available, sir."

"I think he'll talk with me. Even if he's off duty."

"That's not the problem," the policeman said. "Detective Curran is on a double homicide in Revere. He should be calling in within an hour or so. If you want, you can wait or leave your number. It's up to you, sir."

Jason thought for a moment. He'd been up most of the night, his nerves were shot, and the idea of a shower, a change of clothes, and food had a lot of appeal. Besides, once he got together with Curran, he would be busy for some time. He left his home number, asking that Curran call as soon as possible.

The United flight from Seattle had been delayed considerably, and by the time it landed at Logan, Juan Díaz was in a sour mood. He'd not screwed up an assignment so badly since he hit the wrong man in New York. That fiasco was excusable, but his current one was not. He'd been within a few seconds of popping both the doctor and the nightclub *puta* when Jason, an amateur, had outsmarted him. Juan had no excuse and had told the contact as much. He knew he had to redeem himself or else, and he looked forward to it eagerly. As soon as he got off the plane, he went to the phone. It was answered on the second ring.

Jason drove the short distance from the police station to Louisburg Square, trying to erase the horrible image of the prematurely aged children at the school. He didn't even want to think about Hayes and his discovery until he was safely in Curran's presence.

When he got to his building, he drove around the block a couple of times to make sure no one was watching it. Finally, convincing himself that the guard at the school had not looked at his ID, and hence had no idea who he was, Jason parked his car, carried his luggage up to his apartment, and turned on the lights. To his relief, the place was exactly as he'd left it. When he glanced out at the square, it seemed as peaceful as ever.

Jason was about to get into the shower when he remembered the one other person he should speak to besides the detective. He dialed Shirley. She finally answered on the eighth ring. Jason could hear animated voices in the background.

435

"Jason!" she exclaimed. "When did you get back from vacation?"

"I got in tonight."

"What's the matter?" she asked, picking up on the exhaustion and worry in his voice.

"Big trouble. I think I've figured out not only Hayes's discovery, but how it was being misused. It involves the GHP in a far worse way than you could ever imagine."

"Tell me."

"Not over the phone."

"Then come right over. I have guests here, but I'll get rid of them."

"I'm waiting to speak to Curran in Homicide."

"I see . . . you've already contacted him?"

"He's out on a case, but he should be calling shortly."

"Then why don't I come to your apartment? You've got me really terrified now."

"Welcome to the club," Jason said with a short, bitter laugh. "You might as well come over. You probably should be present when I talk to Curran."

"I'm on my way."

"Oh, one other thing. Do you remember who's currently medical director at the Hartford School?"

"Dr. Peterson, I believe," Shirley said. "I can find out for certain tomorrow."

"Wasn't Peterson closely involved in Hayes's clinical studies?" Jason asked, suddenly remembering that Peterson was the doctor who had done the physical on Hayes.

"I think so. Is it important?"

"I'm not sure," Jason said. "But if you're coming, hurry. Curran should be calling any minute."

Jason hung up and was again about to take his shower when he realized Carol too might be in danger. Picking up the phone again, he dialed her number.

"I want you to be sure to stay at home," he said the moment she answered. "I'm not fooling. Don't answer your door—don't go out."

"Now what is it?"

"The Hayes conspiracy is worse than anything I could imagine."

"You sound anxious, Jason."

In spite of himself, Jason smiled. Sometimes Carol could sound like a psychiatrist.

"I'm not anxious, I'm scared to death. But I'll be talking with the police shortly."

"Will you let me know what's going on?" Carol demanded.

"I promise." Jason hung up and finally went into the bathroom and turned on the shower.

16

The buzzer sounded and Jason ran downstairs to see Shirley smiling at him through the glass side panel of his front door. He stepped back to let her in, admiring her usual impeccable dress. Tonight she was wearing a black leather miniskirt and a long, red suede jacket.

"Has Curran called?" she asked as they walked upstairs.

"Not yet," Jason said, carefully double-locking his apartment door.

"Now fill me in," Shirley said, slipping out of her jacket. Underneath she was wearing a soft cashmere sweater. She sat on the edge of Jason's sofa, her hands clasped in her lap, and waited.

"You're not going to like this," Jason said, sitting next to her.

"I've tried to prepare myself. Shoot."

"First let me give you a little background. If you don't understand the current research on aging, what I'm about to say may not make much sense.

"In the last few years, scientists like Hayes have spent a lot of time trying to slow the aging process. Most of their work has focused on cells in cell cultures, although some work has been done with rats and mice. Most of the researchers have concluded that aging is a natural process with a genetic basis regulated by neuroendocrine, immune, and humoral factors."

"You've lost me already," Shirley admitted, lifting her hands in mock surrender.

"How about a drink, then?" Jason suggested, getting to his feet.

"What are you having?"

"A beer. But I have wine, hard stuff, you name it."

"A beer might be nice."

Jason went to the kitchen, opened the refrigerator, and took out two cold Coors.

"You doctors are all the same," Shirley complained, taking a sip. "You make everything sound complicated."

"It is complicated," Jason said, sitting back down. "Molecular genetics concerns the fundamental basis of life. Research in this area is scary, not just because scientists might accidentally create a new and deadly bacterium or virus. It is just as scary if it goes right, because we are playing with life itself. Hayes's tragedy was not that he failed; the problem was that he succeeded."

"What did he discover?"

"In a moment," Jason said, taking a long drink of beer and wiping his mouth with the back of his hand. "Let me put the story another way. We all reach puberty at about the same time, and if disease or accident doesn't intervene, we all age and die in about the same life-span."

Shirley nodded.

"Okay," Jason said, leaning toward her. "This happens because our bodies are genetically programmed to follow an internal timetable. As we develop, different genes are turned on while others are turned off. This is what fascinated Hayes. He had been studying the ways humoral signals from the brain control growth and sexual maturation. By isolating one after another of these humoral proteins, he discovered what they did to peripheral tissues. He was hoping to find out what caused cells to either start dividing or stop dividing."

"That much I do understand," Shirley said. "It's one of the reasons we hired him. We hoped he'd make a breakthrough in cancer treatment."

"Now let me digress a moment," Jason said. "There was another researcher by the name of Denckla, who was experimenting on ways to retard the aging process. He took out the pituitary glands of rats, and after replacing the necessary hormones, found that the rats had an increased life-span."

Jason stopped and looked expectantly at Shirley.

"Am I supposed to say something?" she asked.

"Doesn't Denckla's experiment suggest something to you?"

"Why don't you just tell me."

"Denckla deduced that not only does the pituitary secrete the hormones for growth and puberty, but it also secretes the hormone for aging. Denckla called it the death hormone."

Shirley laughed nervously. "That sounds cheerful."

"Well, I believe that while Hayes was researching growth factors, he stumbled onto Denckla's postulated death hormone," Jason said. "That was what he meant by an ironic discovery. While looking for growth stimulators, he finds a hormone that causes rapid aging and death."

"What would happen if this hormone were given to someone?" Shirley asked.

"If it were given in isolation, probably not much. The subject might experience some symptoms of aging, but the hormone would probably be metabolized and its effect limited. But Hayes wasn't studying the hormone in isolation. He realized that in the same way the secretion of the sex and growth hormone is triggered, there had to be a releasing factor for the death hormone. He was immediately drawn to the life cycle of salmon, which die within hours of spawning. I believe he collected salmon heads and isolated the death hormone's releasing factor from the brains. This was the free-lance work I think he did at Gene, Inc. Once he had isolated the releasing factor, he had Helene reproduce it in quantity by recombinant DNA techniques at his GHP lab."

"Why would Hayes want to produce it?"

"I believe he hoped to develop a monoclonal antibody that would prevent the secretion of the death hormone and halt the aging process." All at once Jason realized what Hayes meant about his discovery becoming a beauty aid. It would preserve youthful good looks, like Carol's.

"What would happen if the releasing factor were given to someone?"

"It would turn on the death gene, releasing the aging hormone just the way it is in salmon—with pretty much the same results. The subject would age and die in three or four weeks. And nobody would know why. And this brings me to the worst thing of all. I believe someone obtained the artificially created hormone Helene was producing at our lab and started giving it to our patients. Whoever it is must be insane—but that's what I think has been happening. Hayes caught on—probably when he visited his son—and was given the aging factor himself. If he hadn't died that night, I think he'd have been killed some other way." Jason shuddered.

"How did you find out?" Shirley whispered.

"I followed Hayes's experimental trail. When Helene was murdered I guessed that Hayes had been telling the truth both about his discovery and the fact that someone wanted him dead."

"But Helene was raped by an unknown intruder."

"Sure. But only to mislead the police as to the motive for her murder. I always felt she knew more than she was telling about Hayes's work. When I learned that she'd been having an affair with him, I was sure."

"But who would want to kill our patients?" Shirley asked desperately.

"A sociopath. The same kind of nut who puts cyanide in Tylenol. Tonight at the clinic I had the computer print out survival curves and death curves. The results were incredible. There's been a significant increase in the death rate at GHP for patients over fifty who are chronically ill or who have high-risk lifestyles." Suddenly Jason stopped. "Damn!"

"What's the matter?" Shirley asked, looking about nervously, as if the danger were just around the corner.

"I forgot something. I printed the curves month by month—I didn't look at them doctor by doctor."

"You think a physician's behind this?" Shirley asked incredulously.

"Must be. A doctor—or maybe a nurse. The releasing factor would be a polypeptide protein. It would have to be injected. If it was administered orally, the gastric juices would degrade it."

"Oh, my God." Shirley dropped her head into her hands. "And I thought we had troubles before." She took a breath and looked up. "Isn't there a chance you could be wrong, Jason? Maybe the computer made a mistake. God knows, data processing breaks down often enough. . . ."

Jason put his hand on her shoulder. He knew that her hard-won empire was about to come crashing down. "I'm not wrong," he said gently. "I also did something else tonight. I saw Hayes's son at Hartford."

"And . . . ?"

"It's a horror. All the kids on his ward must have been given the releasing factor. Apparently it acts more slowly on prepubescent subjects, so the boys are still alive. There must be some kind of hormonal competition with growth hormone. But they all look one hundred years old.''

Shirley shuddered.

''That's why I wanted to know the name of the current medical director.''

''You think Peterson's responsible?''

''He'd have to be a prime suspect.''

''Maybe we should go to the clinic and double-check the computer. We could even rerun your survival curves by doctor.''

Before Jason could answer, the door buzzer shattered the silence and made them both jump. Jason got to his feet, his heart pounding.

Shirley dropped her drink on the table. ''Who could that be?''

''I don't know.'' Jason had told Carol not to leave her apartment, and Curran would have called before coming over.

''What should we do?'' Shirley asked urgently.

''I'm going downstairs and have a look.''

''Is that such a good idea?''

''Got a better one?''

Shirley shook her head. ''Just don't open the door.''

''What do you think I am—crazy? Oh—and one thing I didn't tell you. Someone tried to kill me.''

''No! Where?''

''In a remote country inn east of Seattle.''

He unlocked his apartment door.

''Maybe you'd better not go down,'' Shirley said hurriedly.

''I've got to find out who it is.'' Jason went out to the railed landing and looked down at the front door. He could see a figure through one of the glass panels.

''Be careful,'' Shirley said.

Jason silently started down the stairs. The closer he got, the bigger the shadow of the individual in the foyer became. He was facing the nameplates and angrily hitting the buzzer. Suddenly he whirled around and pressed his face to the glass. For a moment, Jason's and the stranger's faces were only inches apart. There was no mistaking the massive face and tiny, closely set eyes. Their visitor was Bruno, the body-builder. Jason turned and fled back upstairs as the door rattled furiously behind him.

"Who is it?"

"A muscle-bound thug I know," Jason told her, double-locking his door, "and the only person who knew I went to Seattle." That point had just occurred to him with terrifying force. He ran into the den and snatched up the phone. "Damn!" he said after a minute. He dropped the receiver and tried the one in the bedroom. Again, there was no dial tone. "The phones are dead," he said with disbelief to Shirley, who had followed him, sensing his panic.

"What are we going to do?"

"We're leaving. I'm not getting trapped here." Rummaging in the hall closet, he found the key to the gate separating his building from the narrow alley that ran out to West Cedar Street. He opened the bedroom window, climbed onto the fire escape, and helped Shirley out after him. Single file, they descended to the small garden where the leafless white birches stood out like ghosts in the dark. Once in the alley, they ran to the gate, where Jason frantically fumbled to insert the key. When they emerged onto the narrow street, it was quiet and empty, the gloom pierced at intervals by the soft Beacon Hill gas lamps. Not a soul was stirring.

"Let's go!" Jason said, and started down West Cedar to Charles.

"My car is back on Louisburg Square," Shirley panted, struggling to match Jason's pace.

"So is mine. But obviously we can't go back. I have a friend whose car I can take."

On Charles Street there were a few pedestrians outside the 7-Eleven. Jason thought about calling the police from the store, but now that he was out of his apartment he felt less trapped. Besides, he wanted to check the GHP computer again before he spoke with Curran.

They walked down Chestnut Street, lined with its old Federal buildings. There were several people walking dogs, which made Jason feel safer. Just before Brimmer Street, Jason turned in to a parking garage where he gave the attendant ten dollars and asked for the car that belonged to a friend. Luckily, the man recognized Jason and brought out a blue BMW.

"I think it would be a good idea to go to my place," Shirley said, sliding into the front seat. "We can call Curran from there and let him know where you are."

"First I want to go back to the clinic."

With almost no traffic, they reached the hospital in less than ten minutes. "I'll only be a minute," Jason said, pulling up to the entrance. "Do you want to come in or wait here?"

"Don't be silly," Shirley said, opening her side of the car. "I want to see these graphs myself."

They waved ID cards at the security guard and took the elevator, even though they were going up only one floor.

The cleaning service had left the clinic in pristine condition—magazines in racks, wastepaper baskets empty, and the floor glistening with fresh wax. Jason went directly into his office, sat down at his desk, and booted up his computer terminal.

"I'll call Curran," Shirley said, going out to the secretaries' station.

Jason gave a wave to indicate he'd heard her. He was already engrossed in data on the computer. First he called up the various clinic physicians' identification numbers. He was particularly interested in Peterson's. When he had all the numbers, he instructed the computer to separate the GHP patient population by doctor and then start drawing death curves on each group for the past two months, months that had shown the greatest changes when all the patients had been listed. He expected Peterson's patients to show either a higher or lower death rate, believing that a psychopath would experiment either significantly more or less with his own patients.

Shirley came back into the office and stood watching him enter the data.

"Your friend Curran's not back yet," she said. "He called in to the station and said he might be tied up a couple more hours."

Jason nodded. He was more interested in the emerging curves. It took about fifteen minutes to produce all the graphs. Jason separated the continuous sheets and lined them up.

"They all look the same," Shirley said, leaning on his shoulder.

"Just about," Jason admitted. "Even Peterson's. It doesn't rule out his involvement, but it doesn't help us either." Jason eyed the computer, trying to think of any other data that might be useful. He drew a blank.

"Well, that's all the bright ideas for the moment. The police will have to take over from here."

"Let's go, then," Shirley said. "You look exhausted."

"I am," Jason admitted. Pushing himself out of the chair was an effort.

"Are these the graphs you produced earlier?" Shirley asked, pointing to the stack of printouts by the terminal.

Jason nodded.

"How about bringing them along? I'd like you to explain them to me."

Jason stuffed the papers into a large manila envelope.

"I gave Curran's office my phone number," Shirley said. "I think that's the best place to wait. Have you had a chance to eat anything?"

"Some dreadful airplane food, but that seems like days ago."

"I have a little leftover cold chicken."

"Sounds great."

When they got to the car, Jason asked Shirley if she'd mind driving so he could relax and think a little.

"Not at all," she said, taking his keys.

Jason climbed into the passenger side, tossing the envelope into the back seat. He fastened his seat belt, leaned back, and closed his eyes. He let his mind play over the various ways the clinic patients might have been given the releasing factor. Since it couldn't be administered orally, he wondered how the criminal could have injected the patients undergoing executive physicals. Blood was drawn for lab workups, but vacuum tubes provided no way to inject a substance. For inpatients it was a different story—they were always getting injections and intravenous fluids.

He had reached no plausible conclusion when Shirley drew up before her house. Jason staggered and almost fell as he got out of the car. The short rest had exaggerated his fatigue. He reached into the back seat for the envelope.

"Make yourself at home," Shirley said, leading him into the living room.

"First let's make sure Curran hasn't called."

"I'll check my service in a moment. Why don't you make yourself a drink while I rustle up that chicken."

Too tired to argue, Jason went over to the bar and poured some Dewar's over ice, then retreated to the couch. While he waited for Shirley, he again pondered the ways the releasing factor might have been administered. There weren't many possibilities. If it wasn't injected, it had to be through rectal suppositories or some other direct contact with a mucous membrane. Most of the patients having a complete executive physical got a barium enema, and Jason wondered if that was the answer.

He began sipping his Scotch as Shirley came in with a cold chicken and salad.

"Can I make you a drink?" Jason asked. Shirley put the tray down on the coffee table. "Why not?" Then she added, "Don't move. I'll get it."

Jason watched her add a drop of vermouth to her vodka, and that was when he thought of eyedrops. All patients having executive physicals had complete eye exams, including eyedrops to dilate their pupils. If someone wished to introduce the death gene's releasing factor, the mucous membrane in the eye would absorb it perfectly. Even better, since the releasing factor could be secretly introduced to the regular eye medication, the fatal drops could be administered unwittingly by any innocent doctor or technician.

Jason felt his head begin to pound. Finding a plausible explanation of what might have been the key to it all made the possibility of a psychopathic mass murderer suddenly real. Shirley returned from the bar, swirling her drink. For the moment, Jason decided to spare her this newest revelation.

"Any message from Curran?" he asked instead.

"Not yet," Shirley said, looking at him oddly. For a moment he wondered if she could read his mind.

"I have a question," she said hesitantly. "Isn't this supposed releasing factor for the death hormone part of a natural process?"

"Yes," Jason said. "That's why pathology hasn't been much help. All the victims, including Hayes, died of what are called natural causes. The releasing factor merely takes the gene activated at puberty and turns it on full force."

"You mean we start aging at puberty?" Shirley asked with dismay.

"That's the current theory," said Jason. "But obviously it is gradual, picking up speed only in later life, as the levels of growth hormone and sex hormones fall. The releasing factor apparently switches on the death hormone gene all at once, and in an adult without high titers of growth hormone to counter it, it causes rapid aging just like the salmon. My guess is about three weeks. The limiting factor seems to be the cardiovascular system. That's what apparently gives out first and causes death. But it could be other organ systems, as well."

"But aging is a natural process," she repeated.

"Aging is a part of life," agreed Jason. "Evolutionarily it is as important as growth. Yes, it is a natural process." Jason laughed hollowly. "Hayes certainly was right when he described his discovery as ironic. With all the work being done to slow aging down, his work on growth resulted in a way to speed it up."

"If aging and death have an evolutionary value," Shirley persisted, "perhaps they have a social one as well."

Jason looked at her with a growing sense of alarm. He wished he weren't so tired. His brain was sending danger signals he felt too exhausted to decode. Taking his silence as assent, Shirley continued. "Let me put it another way. Medicine in general is faced with the challenge of providing quality care at low cost. But because of increasing life-spans, hospitals are swamped with an elderly population that they keep alive at an enormous price, draining not just their economic resources, but the energy of the medical personnel as well. GHP, for example, did very well when it first started, because the bulk of the subscribers were young and healthy. Now, twenty years later, they are all older and require a great deal more health care. If aging were speeded up in certain circumstances, it might be best for both the patients and the hospitals.

"The important point," emphasized Shirley, "is that the old and infirm should age and die rapidly to avoid suffering as well as to avoid the overutilization of expensive medical care."

As Jason's numb brain began to understand Shirley's reasoning, he felt himself becoming paralyzed with horror. Although he wanted to shout that what she was implying was legalized murder, he found himself sitting dumbly on the edge of the couch like a bird confronted by a poisonous snake and frozen with fear.

"Jason, do you have any idea how much it costs to keep people alive during their last months of life in a hospital?" Shirley said, again mistaking his silence for acquiescence. "Do you? If medicine didn't spend so much on the dying, it could do so much more to help the living. If GHP wasn't swamped with middle-aged patients destined to be ill because of their unhealthy lifestyles, think what we could do for the young. And aren't patients who fail to take care of themselves, like heavy smokers and drinkers, or people who use drugs, voluntarily speeding up their own demise? Is it so wrong to hasten their deaths so they don't burden the rest of society?"

Jason's mouth finally opened in protest, but he couldn't find the words to refute her. All he could do was shake his head in disbelief.

"I can't believe you won't accept the fact that medicine can no longer survive under the crushing burden of the chronic health problems presented by physically unfit people—those very patients who have spent thirty or forty years abusing the bodies God gave them."

"That's not for me or you to decide," Jason shouted at last.

"Even if the aging process is simply speeded up by a natural substance?"

"That's murder!" Jason stumbled to his feet. Shirley rose too, moving swiftly to the double doors leading to the dining room. "Come in, Mr. Díaz," she said, flinging them open. "I've done what I could."

Jason's mouth went dry as he turned to face the man he'd last seen at the Salmon Inn. Juan's darkly handsome face was alive with anticipation. He was carrying a small, German-made automatic muzzled with a cigar-sized silencer.

Jason backed up clumsily until his back struck the far wall. His eyes went from the gun to the killer's strikingly handsome face, to Shirley, who eyed him as calmly as if she were in a board meeting.

"No tablecloth this time," Díaz said, grinning to show movie-star-perfect white teeth. He advanced on Jason, putting the muzzle of the gun six inches from Jason's head. "Good-bye," he said with a friendly flick of his head.

17

"Mr. Díaz," Shirley said.

"Yes," Juan answered without taking his eyes off Jason.

"Don't shoot him unless he forces you to. It will be better to deal with him the way we did with Mr. Hayes. I'll bring you the material from the clinic tomorrow."

Jason breathed out. He hadn't realized he was holding his breath.

The smile vanished from Juan's face. His nostrils flared; he was disappointed and angry. "I think it would be much safer if I killed him right now, Miss Montgomery."

"I don't care what you think—and I'm paying you. Now let's get him into the cellar. And no rough stuff—I know what I'm doing."

Juan moved the pistol so the cold metal touched Jason's temple. Jason knew the man was hoping for the slightest excuse to shoot; he remained perfectly still, petrified by fear.

"Come on!" called Shirley from the front hall.

"Go!" said Juan, pulling the gun back from Jason's head.

Jason walked stiffly, his arms pressed against his sides. Juan fell in behind, occasionally touching Jason's back with the gun.

Shirley opened a door under the staircase across from the front entrance. Jason could see a flight of steps leading to the basement.

As Jason approached, he tried to catch Shirley's eye, but she turned away. He stepped through the door and started down, Juan directly behind him.

449

"Doctors amaze me," said Shirley, turning on the cellar light and closing the door behind her. "They think medicine is just a question of helping the sick. The truth is unless something is done about the chronically unhealthy, there won't be money or manpower to help those who can actually recover."

Looking at her calm, pretty face, the perfect clothes, Jason couldn't believe it was the same woman he'd always admired.

She interrupted herself to direct Juan down a long narrow hallway to a heavy oak door. Squeezing by Juan and Jason, she unlocked it and flicked on the light, illuminating a large square room. Jason was pushed inside, where he saw an open doorway to the left, a workbench, and another heavy closed door to the right. Then the light went out, the door slammed, and total darkness surrounded him.

For a few minutes, Jason stood still, immobilized by shock and lack of vision. He could hear small sounds; water coursing through pipes, the heating system kicking on, and footsteps above his head. The darkness remained absolute: he could not even tell if his eyes were open or closed.

When Jason was finally able to move, he stepped back to the door through which he'd entered. He grabbed the doorknob and tried to turn it. He pulled on the door. There was no doubt it was secure. Running his hands around the jamb, he felt for hinges. He gave that up when he remembered the door opened into the hall.

Leaving the door, Jason worked his way laterally, taking baby steps and gingerly sliding his hands along the wall. He came to the corner and turned ninety degrees. He continued moving step by miniature step until he felt the doorway of the open door. Carefully reaching inside, he felt for a wall switch. On the left side, about chest height, he found one. He threw the switch. Nothing happened.

Advancing into the side room, he began to feel the walls, trying to ascertain the dimensions. His fingers hit on a metal object on the wall whose front was glass. Feeling down at waist height he touched a sink. Over to the right was a toilet. The room was only about five by seven.

Returning to the main room, Jason continued his slow circuit. He encountered a second small room with a closed door just beyond the bathroom. When he opened the door, his nose told him it was a cedar closet. Inside he felt several garment bags filled with clothes.

Back in the main room, Jason came to another corner, and he turned again. Within a dozen small steps, he gently hit against the workbench, which stuck out about three feet into the room. Skirting the end of the bench, he felt beneath it, finding cabinets. The workbench, he estimated, was about ten to fifteen feet long. Beyond the workbench, he returned to the wall, encountering shelving with what felt like paint cans. Beyond the shelving was another corner.

In the middle of the fourth wall, Jason came to another heavy door that was tightly closed and secured. He could feel a lock, but it needed a key. There were no hinges. Continuing his circuit, Jason came to the fourth corner. After a few minutes, he was back at the entrance.

Getting down on his hands and knees, Jason felt the floor. It was poured concrete. Standing up again, he tried to think of what else he could do. He had no good ideas. Suddenly, he felt an overwhelming sense of mortal fear like he was being smothered. He'd never suffered from claustrophobia, but it descended on him with crushing severity. ''HELP!'' he shouted, only to have his voice echo back to his ears. Losing control, he groped madly for the entrance door and pounded on it with closed fists. ''PLEASE!'' he shouted. He pounded until he became aware of pain in his hands. He stopped abruptly with a wince and clutched his bruised hands to his chest. Leaning forward, Jason touched the door with his forehead. Then the tears came.

Jason could not remember crying since he'd been a child. Even after Danielle's death. And all those years of denying that emotion came out as he crouched in the blackness of Shirley's basement. He lost complete control and slowly sank to the floor, where he curled up in front of the door like an imprisoned dog, choking on his own tears.

The ferocity of Jason's emotional reaction surprised him. And after ten minutes of sobbing, he began to regain his composure. He was embarrassed at himself, having always believed he had more self-control. Finally, he sat up with his back against the door. In the darkness, he wiped his tears from his damp cheeks.

Instead of surrendering to utter despair, he thought about the room he was in. He tried to guess the dimensions and picture the location of things he'd encountered on his exploratory circuit. He began to wonder if there were any other light switches. Getting to his feet, he slowly returned to the second locked door that was to his right. When he got there, he felt along the walls on both sides, but there was no light switch.

Striking out across the room, he returned to the bathroom. He tried the switch in there several more times. Then he felt for the fixture, thinking he could exchange the bulb provided he could locate the lights in the ceiling of the main room. But there was no fixture, either as part of the medicine cabinet or as part of the ceiling. Discouraged, Jason returned to the large room.

"Ahhh!" cried Jason, as he walked directly into a lolly column, hitting his nose against the six-inch diameter metal surface. Momentarily off balance, he felt his nose already beginning to swell. There was a bony ridge along the right side: he'd broken it. Once more, tears involuntarily filled his eyes, but this time it was from reflex, not emotion. When he recovered enough to proceed, Jason had become disoriented. Reverting to baby steps, he moved until he encountered a wall. Only then was he able to find the workbench.

Bending down, Jason began opening the cabinets, then carefully exploring each with his hands. Each cabinet was about four feet wide and contained a single removable shelf. He found more cans of what he thought was paint, but no tools whatsoever. Standing up, Jason leaned over the workbench and felt the wall above it. There was some narrow shelving to the right with small jars and boxes. Moving to the central part, Jason felt the wall again, hoping to encounter a pegboard or the like with screwdrivers, hammers and chisels. Instead, his hand encountered a glass bowl facing away from him. Curious as to what it was, Jason felt around it, ascertaining that the glass bowl was secured to a metal box. Pipes entered the metal box. Jason realized it was the electric meter.

Moving down to the left end of the workbench, Jason again felt the wall. There was more shelving containing plastic and ceramic flower pots, but there were no tools.

Discouraged, Jason wondered what else he could do. He thought about finding something to stand on so that he could explore the walls close to the ceiling in case there was a blacked-out window. Then his mind went back to the electric meter. Climbing up on the workbench, he located the meter and traced the wires to a second rectangular metal box. Feeling the surface, Jason immediately encountered a hinged metal ring. Giving it a slight tug, Jason opened the box.

Inside was the service panel for the house. Slowly he reached inside, hoping he was not about to touch a live wire. Instead, his fingers touched the low row of circuit breaker switches.

For the next five minutes Jason thought about how to make use of his discovery. Getting off the bench, he opened the door to the cabinet underneath and removed its contents, storing the cans in the two side cabinets. Then he removed the single shelf, which luckily was not nailed down, and climbed in. He had plenty of room.

He got out, climbed back on the workbench and, one by one, threw all the circuit breakers. Then he closed the service panel, scrambled into the empty cabinet, pulled the door shut behind him, and prayed. If they'd already gone to bed, the lack of power wouldn't bother them.

After what Jason guessed was another five minutes, he heard a door opening. Then he heard voices, and through a crack in the cabinet door saw a line of flickering light. Then there was the sound of a key in the entrance door and it swung open. His eye to the crack, he could plainly see two figures. One was holding a flashlight which slowly swung around the room.

"He's hiding," said Juan.

"I don't need you to tell me that," said Shirley with irritation.

"Where is your fuse box?" asked Juan.

The flashlight swung around above the workbench.

"You stay here," said Juan. He started into the room, coming between Jason and the light which Shirley must have been holding. Jason suspected Juan's hands were busy with his gun.

Jason leaned against the back wall of the cabinet and lifted his feet. As soon as he heard the circuit breakers being turned back on, Jason kicked the cabinet doors with all the force and power his runner's legs could muster. The doors caught Juan Díaz entirely by surprise, hitting him in the groin. He gasped with pain and staggered back against the cedar closet.

Jason lost no time. He crawled out and raced across the room, catching the door before Shirley had a chance to close it. He hit it with full force, running directly into Shirley and knocking the two of them onto the floor. Shirley cried as her head hit the concrete. The flashlight rolled out of her hand.

Scrambling to his feet, Jason raced down the hallway toward the stairs, thankful that this area of the house again had lights. He grabbed the banister and used it to catapult himself up the first steps. That was when he heard the dull pop. Simultaneously he felt a pain in his thigh and his right leg crumbled beneath him. Pulling himself upright, he hopped up the rest of the stairs. He was almost at the foyer; he could not give up.

His right leg dragging, Jason struggled over to the front door. Below, he heard someone start up the stairs.

The dead bolt opened and Jason stumbled out into the raw November night. He knew he'd been shot. He could feel the blood from his bullet wound running down his leg into his shoe.

Jason only got as far as the center of the driveway when Juan caught up to him and knocked him to the cobblestones with the butt of his pistol. Jason fell to his hands and knees. Before he could rise, Juan kicked him over onto his back. Once again, the pistol was pointed directly at Jason's head.

Suddenly, both men were bathed in brilliant light. Keeping the gun on Jason, Juan tried to shield his eyes from the glare of two high-beam headlights. A second later, there was the sound of car doors opening, followed by the ominous sound of shotguns being cocked. Juan backed up several steps like a cornered animal.

"Hold it, Díaz," called a voice unfamiliar to Jason. It was thick with a South Boston accent. "Don't do anything stupid. We don't want trouble with you or Miami. All we want you to do is walk to your car nice and easy and leave. Can you do that?"

Juan nodded. His left hand was still vainly trying to shield his eyes from the light.

"Then do it!" commanded the voice.

After taking two or three uncertain steps backward, Juan turned and fled to his car. He started the engine, gunned it, then roared out of the driveway.

Jason rolled onto his stomach. As soon as Juan left, Carol Donner ran out of the circle of light and dropped to her knees in front of him.

"My God, you're hurt!" A large bloodstain had formed on Jason's thigh.

"I suppose," said Jason vaguely. Too much had happened too quickly. "But it doesn't hurt too much," he added.

Another figure emerged from the glare; Bruno came up hefting a pump-action Winchester shotgun.

"Oh, no!" said Jason, trying to sit up.

"Don't worry," said Carol. "He knows you're a friend now."

At that moment, Shirley appeared on her front porch. Her clothing was disheveled and her hair spiked up like a punk rocker. For a second, she took in the scene. Then she stepped back and slammed the door. Locks were heard being engaged.

"We have to get him to a hospital," said Carol, pointing to Jason.

A second body-builder appeared. Gingerly they picked Jason up.

"I don't believe this," said Jason.

Jason found himself carried behind the glare of the lights. The vehicle turned out to be a white stretch Lincoln with a ''V''-shaped TV antenna on the rear deck. The two muscle men eased Jason into the back seat where a man with dark glasses, slicked-back hair, and an unlit cigar was waiting. It was Arthur Koehler, Carol's boss. Carol jumped in after Jason and introduced him to Arthur. The muscle men got in the front seat and started the limo.

''Am I glad to see you two,'' said Jason. ''But what in God's name brought you here?'' Jason winced as the car bumped out of the driveway.

''Your voice,'' explained Carol. ''That last time you called, I knew you were in trouble again.''

''But how did you know I was here in Brookline?''

''Bruno followed you,'' said Carol. ''After you called, I called my lovable boss here.'' Carol slapped Arthur's leg.

Arthur said, ''Cut it out!'' It had been his voice that had terrified Juan Díaz.

''I asked Arthur if he would protect you and he said he would under one condition. I have to dance for at least another two months or until he finds a replacement.''

''Yeah, but she got me down to one month,'' complained Arthur.

''I'm very grateful,'' said Jason. ''Are you really going to stop dancing, Carol?''

''She's a goddamn brat,'' said Arthur.

''I'm amazed,'' said Jason. ''I didn't think girls like you could stop whenever you wanted.''

''What are you talking about?'' asked Carol indignantly.

''I'll tell you what he means,'' laughed Arthur, reaching forward and returning Carol's slap on the thigh. ''He thinks you're a goddamn hooker.'' Arthur collapsed into paroxysms of laughter that changed to coughing. Carol had to pound him on the back several times before he got control of himself. ''I used to have more fits like that when I lit these things,'' said Arthur, holding up his cigar. Then he looked at Jason in the half-light of the car. ''You think I would have let her go to Seattle if she were a prostitute? Be reasonable, man.''

''I'm sorry,'' Jason said. ''I just thought . . .''

''You thought because I was dancing at the club I was a hooker,'' said Carol with somewhat less indignation. ''Well, I suppose that's not entirely unfair. A couple of them are. But most aren't. For me, it was a great opportunity. My family name isn't Donner. It's Kikonen. We're Finnish and we've always had a healthier attitude to nudity than you Americans.''

"And she's my wife's sister's kid," said Arthur. "So I gave her a job.''

"You two are related?" asked Jason, amazed.

"We don't like to admit it," said Arthur, starting to laugh again.

"Come on," Carol said.

But Arthur continued, saying, "We hate the idea of any of our people going to Harvard. It hurts our image.''

"You're going to Harvard?" asked Jason, turning to Carol.

"For my doctorate. The dancing covers my tuition.''

"I guess I should have known Alvin would never have lived with your average exotic dancer," said Jason. "In any case, I'm grateful to you both. God knows what would have happened if you hadn't come along. I know the police will take care of Shirley Montgomery, but I wish you hadn't let Juan go.''

"Don't worry," said Arthur with a wave of his cigar. "Carol told me what happened in Seattle. He won't be around for long. But I don't want trouble with my people in Miami. We'll deal with Juan through channels or I can give you enough information for the Miami police to pick him up. They'll have enough stuff on him down there to put him away. Believe me.''

Jason looked at Carol. "I don't know how I can make it up to you.''

"I have a few ideas," she said brightly.

Arthur had another laughing fit. When he was finally under control, Bruno lowered the glass to the front compartment.

"Hey, pervert," he called with a chuckle. "Where do you want us to take you? GHP emergency?''

"Hell, no," said Jason. "For the moment, I'm a little down on prepaid health care. Take me to Mass General.''

EPILOGUE

Jason had never enjoyed ill health, as the saying goes, but currently he was loving it. He'd been hospitalized for three days following surgery on the wound in his leg. The pain had lessened significantly and the nursing staff at General was superbly competent and attentive. Several of them even remembered Jason as a resident.

But the best part of his hospitalization was that Carol spent most of each day with him, reading out loud, regaling him with funny stories, or just sitting in companionable silence.

"When you're all better," she said on the second day as she rearranged flowers that had come from Claudia and Sally, "I think we should go back to the Salmon Inn."

"What on earth for?" Jason said. After their experience, he couldn't imagine wanting to revisit the place.

"I'd like to try Devil's Chute again," Carol said cheerfully. "But this time in daylight."

"You're kidding!"

"Really. I bet it's a gas when the sun's shining."

A soft cough made them turn to the doorway. Detective Curran's disheveled bulk looked distinctly out of place in the hospital. His large hands were clutching a khaki rain hat that looked as if it had been run over by a truck.

"I hope I'm not bothering you, Dr. Howard," he said with uncharacteristic politeness.

Jason guessed that Curran was as intimidated by the hospital as Jason had been by the police station.

"Not at all," Jason said, pushing himself up to a sitting position. "Come in. Sit down."

Carol pulled a chair away from the wall and positioned it next to the bed. Curran lowered himself into it, still clutching the hat.

"How's the leg coming?" he asked.

"Fine," Jason said. "Mostly muscle injury. Not going to be a problem at all."

"I'm glad."

"Candy?" Carol asked, extending a box of chocolates that the GHP secretaries had sent.

Curran examined them carefully, chose a chocolate-covered cherry, and plopped it whole into his mouth. Swallowing, he said, "I thought you'd like to know how the case is developing."

"Absolutely," Jason said. Carol went around to the other side of the bed and sat on the edge.

"First of all, they picked Juan up in Miami. He has a sheet a mile long. You name it. He's one of Castro's gifts to America. We're going to try to get him extradited to Massachusetts for Brennquivist's and Lund's murders, but it'll be tough. Seems four or five other states want the creep for similar capers, including Florida."

"Can't say I feel very sorry for him," Jason said.

"The guy's a psychopath," Curran agreed.

"What about GHP?" Jason asked. "Have you been able to prove that the releasing factor for the death gene was introduced into the eyedrops used by the ophthalmological office?"

"We're working closely with the DA's office on it," Curran said. "It's turning out to be quite a story."

"How much do you feel will be made public?"

"At this point we aren't certain. Some will have to come out. The Hartford School's closed and the parents of those kids aren't blind. Furthermore, as the DA points out, there's a slew of local families with million-dollar lawsuits to file against the GHP. Shirley and her crew are finished."

"Shirley . . ." Jason said wistfully. "You know, there was a time, if I hadn't met Carol, I might have gotten involved with the lady."

Carol shook a playful fist at him.

"I guess I owe you an apology, doctor," Curran said. "At first I thought you were just a pain in the ass. But it turns out you're responsible for busting the deadliest conspiracy I've ever heard of.''

"It was mostly luck," Jason said. "If I hadn't been with Hayes the night he died, we doctors would have thought we were battling some new epidemic."

"This guy Hayes must have been a smart cookie," Curran said.

"A genius," Carol said.

"You know what bugs me the most?" Curran said. "Until the end Hayes thought he was working on a discovery to help mankind. Probably thought he'd be a hero, like Salk. Nobel prizes and all that. Save the world. I'm not a scientist, but it seems to me Hayes's whole field of research is pretty damned scary. You know what I mean?''

"I know exactly what you mean," Jason said. "Medical science has always assumed its research would save lives and reduce suffering. But now science has awesome potential. Things can go either way."

"As I understand it," Curran said, "Hayes found a drug that makes people age and die in a couple of weeks—and he wasn't even looking for it. Makes me think you eggheads are out of control. Am I wrong?''

"I agree," Jason said. "Maybe we're getting too smart for our own good. It's like eating the forbidden fruit all over again."

"Yeah, and we're going to get kicked right out of paradise," Curran added. "Incidentally, doesn't Uncle Sam have watchdogs overseeing guys like Hayes?''

"They don't have a very good record on this sort of thing," Jason explained. "Too many conflicts of interest. Besides, both doctors and laymen tend to believe all medical research is inherently good."

"Wonderful," snorted Curran. "It's like a car barreling down the freeway at a hundred miles an hour with no driver."

"That's probably the best analogy I've ever heard," Jason said.

"Oh, well." The detective shrugged his huge shoulders. "At least we can deal with GHP. Formal indictments are coming down soon. Of course, the whole pack is out on bail. But the case has broken wide open, with all the principals stabbing each other in the back and trying to plea-bargain. Seems that friend Hayes originally approached some guy by the name of Ingelbrook."

"Ingelnook. He's one of the GHP vice presidents," Jason said. "I think he's in finance."

"Must be," Curran said. "Apparently Hayes approached him for seed capital to front a company."

"I know," Jason said.

The detective looked hard at him. "Did you, now? And just how did you know about that, Dr. Howard?"

"It's unimportant. Go on."

"Anyway," Curran said, "Hayes must have told Ingelnook that he was about to develop some kind of elixir of youth."

"That would have been an antibody to the death-hormone releasing factor," Jason said.

"Hold it a minute," Curran said. "Maybe you should be telling me this stuff rather than vice versa."

"I'm sorry," Jason said. "It's all finally making sense to me. Please—go on."

"Ingelnook must have liked the death hormone better than the elixir of youth," Curran continued. "For some time he'd been racking his brains about lowering costs at GHP to keep them competitive. So far the conspiracy only involves six people, but there may be more. They've been responsible for eliminating a lot of patients they thought were going to use more than their fair share of medical services. Nice, huh?"

"So they killed them," Carol said with horror.

"Well, they kept telling themselves that the process was natural," Curran said.

"Some excuse for murder—we're all going to die anyway," Jason commented bitterly. The faces of some of his recently deceased patients rose to haunt him.

"In any case, it's the end of GHP," Curran said. "The criminal charges notwithstanding, malpractice claims are through the roof. GHP is already filing for Chapter Eleven. So I think you'll be looking for a job."

"Looks like it." Then, looking up at Carol, Jason added, "Carol's finishing her studies in clinical psychology. We thought we'd open an office together. I think I want to get back to private practice. No more corporations for a while."

"That sounds cozy," Curran said. "Then I can get my head and my ticker fixed at the same place."

"You can be our first patient."

MUTATION

*Thanks to Jean, who provided lots of
literal and figurative nourishment.*

TO GRANDPARENTS

For Mae and Ed,
whom I wish I had known better
For Esther and John,
who welcomed me into their family
For Louise and Bill,
who adopted me out of pure generosity.

"HOW DARE YOU SPORT THUS WITH LIFE."

Mary Wollstonecraft Shelley
Frankenstein (1818)

Energy had been building within the millions of neurons since they'd first formed six months previously. The nerve cells were sizzling with electrical energy steadily galvanizing toward a voltaic threshold. The arborization of the nerve cells' dendrites and the supporting microglia cells had been increasing at an exponential rate, with hundreds of thousands of new synaptic connections arising every hour. It was like a nuclear reactor on the brink of hypercriticality.

At last it happened! The threshold was reached and surpassed. Microbolts of electric charges spread like wildfire through the complicated plexus of synaptic connections, energizing the whole mass. Intracellular vesicles poured forth their neurotransmitters and neuromodulators, increasing the level of excitation to another critical point.

Out of this complex microscopic cellular activity emerged one of the mysteries of the universe: consciousness! Mind had once more been born of matter.

Consciousness was the faculty that provided foundation for memory and meaning; and also terror and dread. With consciousness came the burden of knowledge of eventual death. But at that moment, the consciousness created was consciousness without awareness. Awareness was next and soon to come.

PROLOGUE

OCTOBER 11, 1978

"Oh, God!" Mary Millman said, gripping the sheets with both hands. The agony was starting again in her lower abdomen, spreading rapidly into her groin and into her lower back like a shaft of molten steel.

"Give me something for the pain! Please! I can't stand it!" Then she screamed.

"Mary, you're doing fine," Dr. Stedman said calmly. "Just take deep breaths." He was putting on a pair of rubber gloves, snapping the fingers into place.

"I can't take it," Mary cried hoarsely. She twisted herself into a different position, but it didn't provide any relief. Each second the pain intensified. She held her breath and, by reflex, contracted every muscle in her body.

"Mary!" Dr. Stedman said firmly, grabbing Mary's arm. "Don't push! It won't help until your cervix is dilated. And it might hurt the baby!"

Mary opened her eyes and tried to relax her body. Her breath came out in an agonized groan. "I can't help it," she whimpered through tears. "Please—I can't take it. *Help me!*" Her words were lost in another shriek.

Mary Millman was a twenty-two-year-old secretary who worked for a department store in downtown Detroit. When she'd seen the advertisement to be a surrogate mother, the idea of the money had seemed like a godsend—a perfect way for her to finally settle the seemingly endless debts left from her mother's long illness. But never having been pregnant or seen a birth, except in movies, she'd had no idea what it would be like. At the moment she couldn't think about the thirty thousand dollars she was to receive when it was all over, a figure much higher than the "going" fee for surrogacy in Michigan, the one state where an infant could be adopted before birth. She thought she was going to die.

The pain peaked, then leveled off. Mary was able to snatch a few shallow breaths. "I need a pain shot," she said with some difficulty." Her mouth was dry.

"You've already had two," Dr. Stedman answered. He was preoccupied with removing the pair of gloves he'd contaminated by grabbing her arm, replacing them with a new and sterile pair.

"I don't feel them," Mary moaned.

"Maybe not at the height of a contraction," Dr. Stedman said, "but just a few moments ago you were asleep."

"I was?" Mary looked up for confirmation into the face of Marsha Frank, one of the adoptive parents, who was gently wiping her forehead with a cool, damp washcloth. Marsha nodded. She had a warm, empathetic smile. Mary liked her and was thankful Marsha had insisted on being present at the birth. Both Franks had made that a condition of the agreement, though Mary was less enthusiastic about the prospective father, who was constantly barking orders at her.

"Remember, the baby gets whatever medications you get," he was now saying sharply. "We can't jeopardize his life just to ease your pain."

Dr. Stedman gave Victor Frank a quick look. The man was getting on his nerves. As far as Dr. Stedman was concerned, Frank was the worst prospective father he'd ever allowed in the labor room. What made it particularly astounding was that Frank was a physician himself and had had obstetric training before going into research. If he had had such experience, it certainly didn't show in his bedside manner. A long sigh from Mary brought Dr. Stedman's attention back to his patient.

The grimace that had distorted Mary's face slowly faded. The contraction was obviously over. "Okay," Dr. Stedman said, motioning for the nurse to lift the sheet covering Mary's legs. "Let's see what's going on." He bent over and positioned Mary's legs.

"Maybe we should do an ultrasound?" Victor suggested. "I don't think we're making much progress."

Dr. Stedman straightened up. "Dr. Frank! If you don't mind . . ." He let his sentence trail off, hoping that his tone conveyed his irritation.

Victor Frank looked up at Dr. Stedman, and Stedman suddenly realized the man was terrified. Frank's face was porcelain white, with beads of perspiration along his hairline. Perhaps using a surrogate was a unique strain even for a doctor.

"Oh!" exclaimed Mary. There was a sudden gush of fluid onto the bed, drawing Dr. Stedman's attention back to his patient. For the moment he forgot about Frank.

"That's the rupture of the membranes," Dr. Stedman said. "It's entirely normal, as I explained before. Let's see where we are with this baby."

Mary closed her eyes. She felt fingers going back inside of her. Lying in sheets drenched with her own fluid, she felt humiliated and vulnerable. She'd told herself she was doing this not just for the money but to bring happiness to a couple who couldn't have another baby. Marsha had been so sweet and persuasive. Now she wondered if she'd done the right thing. Then another contraction forced all thought from her head.

"Well, well!" Dr. Stedman exclaimed. "Very good, Mary. Very good indeed." He snapped off the rubber gloves and tossed them aside. "The baby's head is now engaged and your cervix is almost entirely dilated. Good girl!" He turned to the nurse. "Let's move the show into the delivery room."

"Can I have some pain medicine now?" Mary asked.

"Just as soon as we get in the delivery room," Dr. Stedman said cheerfully. He was relieved. Then he felt a hand on his arm.

"Are you sure the head isn't too big?" asked Victor abruptly, pulling Dr. Stedman aside.

Dr. Stedman could feel a tremor in the hand that gripped his arm. He reached up and peeled away the fingers. "I said the head was engaged. That means the head has passed through the pelvic inlet. I'm certain you remember that!"

"Are you sure the head is engaged?" asked Victor.

A wave of resentment wafted through Dr. Stedman. He was about to lose his temper, but he saw that Frank was trembling with anxiety. Holding his anger in check, Stedman just said, "The head is engaged.

I'm certain.'' Then he added: ''If this is upsetting you, perhaps it would be best if you went to the waiting room.''

''I couldn't!'' Victor said with emphasis. ''I've got to see this thing through.''

Dr. Stedman gazed at Dr. Frank. From the first meeting, he'd had a strange feeling about this man. For a while, he'd attributed Frank's uneasiness to the surrogacy situation, but it was more than that. And Dr. Frank was more than the worried father. ''I've got to see this thing through'' was a strange comment for a father-to-be, even a surrogate one. He made it sound as if this was some kind of mission, not a joyous—if traumatic—experience involving human beings.

Marsha was vaguely aware of her husband's curious behavior as she followed Mary's bed down the hall to the delivery room. But she was so absorbed in the birth itself she didn't focus on it. With all her heart she wished it were she in the hospital bed. She would have welcomed the pain, even though the birth of their son, David, five years earlier had ended in such a violent hemorrhage her doctor had had to perform an emergency hysterectomy to save her life. She and Victor had so desperately wanted a second child. Since she could not bear one, they had weighed the options. After some deliberation, they settled on surrogacy as the preferable one. Marsha had been happy about the arrangement, and glad that even before birth, the child was legally theirs, but she still would have given anything to have carried this much-longed-for baby herself. For a moment she wondered how Mary could bear to part with him. For that reason she was particularly pleased about Michigan law.

Watching the nurses move Mary to the delivery table, Marsha said softly, ''You're doing just fine. It's almost over.''

''Let's get her on her side,'' said Dr. Whitehead, the anesthesiologist, to the nurses. Then, gripping Mary's arm, she said: ''I'm going to give you that epidural block we discussed.''

''I don't think I want epidural,'' said Victor, moving to the opposite side of the delivery table. ''Especially not if you're planning on using a caudal approach.''

''Dr. Frank!'' Dr. Stedman said sternly. ''You have a choice: either stop interfering or leave the delivery room. Take your pick.'' Dr. Stedman had had enough. He'd already put up with a number of Frank's orders, such as performing every known prenatal test, including amniocentesis and chorionic villus biopsy. He'd even permitted Mary to take an antibiotic called cephaloclor for three weeks in the early part of the pregnancy. Professionally, he'd felt none of these things were indicated, but he'd gone along with them because Dr. Frank had insisted and because the surrogacy status made the situation unique. Since Mary did not object, saying it was all part of the deal she'd struck with the Franks, he didn't mind complying. But that was during the pregnancy. The delivery was a different story, and Dr. Stedman was not about to compromise his methodology for a neurotic colleague. Just what kind of medical training had Frank gone through? he wondered. Surely he could abide by standard operating procedures. But here he was questioning each of Stedman's orders, second-guessing every step.

For a few tense seconds, Victor and Dr. Stedman stood glaring at each other. Victor's fists were clenched, and for a brief moment Dr. Stedman thought that the man was about to strike him. But the moment passed, and Victor slouched away to stand nervously in the corner.

Victor's heart was racing and he felt an unpleasant sensation in his abdomen. "Please make the baby normal," he prayed to himself. He looked over at his wife as his eyes clouded with tears. She had wanted another baby so much. He felt himself begin to tremble again. He chided himself inwardly. "I shouldn't have done it. But please, God— let this baby be all right." He looked up at the clock. The second hand seemed to drag slowly around the face. He wondered how much longer he could stand the tension.

Dr. Whitehead's skilled hands had the caudal analgesic in place in seconds. Marsha held Mary's hand, smiling encouragement as the pain began to ease. The next thing Mary knew was that someone was waking her, telling her it was time to push. The second stage of labor went quickly and smoothly, and at 6:04 P.M. a vigorous Victor Frank Jr. was born.

Victor was standing directly behind Dr. Stedman at the moment of birth, holding his breath, trying to see as best he could. As the child came into view, he rapidly scanned the infant as Dr. Stedman clamped and cut the cord. Stedman handed the infant to the waiting resident pediatrician, whom Victor followed to the thermostatically controlled infant care unit. The resident put the silent infant down and began to examine him. Victor felt a rush of relief. The child appeared normal.

"Apgar of ten," the resident called out, indicating that Victor Jr. had the highest possible rating.

"Wonderful," said Dr. Stedman, who was busy with Mary and the imminent delivery of the afterbirth.

"But he's not crying," questioned Victor. Doubt clouded his euphoria.

The resident lightly slapped the soles of Victor Jr.'s feet, then rubbed his back. Still the infant stayed quiet. "But he's breathing fine."

The resident picked up the bulb syringe and tried to suction Victor Jr.'s nose once again. To the doctor's astonishment, the newborn's hand came up and yanked the bulb away from the fingers of the resident and dropped it over the side of the infant care unit.

"Well that settles that," said the resident with a chuckle. "He just doesn't want to cry."

"Can I?" asked Victor, motioning toward the baby.

"As long as he doesn't get cold."

Gingerly, Victor reached into the unit and scooped up Victor Jr. He held the infant in front of him with both hands around his torso. He was a beautiful baby with strikingly blond hair. His chubby, rosy cheeks gave his face a picturesquely cherubic quality, but by far the most distinctive aspect of his appearance was his bright blue eyes. As Victor gazed into their depths he realized with a shock that the baby was looking back at him.

"Beautiful, isn't he?" said Marsha over Victor's shoulder.

"Gorgeous," Victor agreed. "But where did the blond hair come from? Ours is brown."

"I was blond until I was five," Marsha said, reaching up to touch the baby's pink skin.

Victor glanced at his wife as she lovingly gazed at the child. She had dark brown hair peppered with just a few strands of gray. Her eyes were a sultry gray-blue; her features quite sculptured: they contrasted with the rounded, full features of the infant.

"Look at his eyes," Marsha said.

Victor turned his attention back to the baby. "They are incredible, aren't they? A minute ago I'd have sworn they were looking right back at me."

"They are like jewels," Marsha said.

Victor turned the baby to face Marsha. As he did so he noticed the baby's eyes remained locked on his! Their turquoise depths were as cold and bright as ice. Unbidden, Victor felt a thrill of fear.

The Franks felt triumphant as Victor pulled his Oldsmobile Cutlass into the crushed-stone driveway leading to their clapboard farmhouse.

476

All the planning and anguish of the in-vitro fertilization process had paid off. The search for an appropriate surrogate mother, the dreary trips to Detroit had worked. They had a child, and Marsha cradled the infant in her arms, thanking God for His gift.

Marsha watched as the car rounded the final bend. Lifting the child up and pulling aside the edge of the blanket, she showed the boy his home. As if comprehending, Victor Jr. stared out of the car windshield at the pleasant but modest house. He blinked, then turned to smile at Victor.

"You like it, huh, Tiger?" said Victor playfully. "He's only three days old but I'd swear he'd talk to me if he could."

"What would you have him say?" Marsha asked as she lowered VJ into her lap. They had nicknamed him that to help distinguish him from his father, Victor Sr.

"I don't know," said Victor, bringing the car to a stop at the front door. "Maybe say he wanted to grow up and become a doctor like his old man."

"Oh, for goodness' sake," said Marsha, opening the passenger-side door.

Victor jumped out to help her. It was a beautiful, crystal-clear October day, filled with bright sunshine. Behind the house the trees had turned a brilliant profusion of fall colors; scarlet maples, orange oaks and yellow birches all competed with their beauty. As they came up the walk the front door opened and Janice Fay, their live-in nanny, ran down the front steps.

"Let me see him," she begged, stopping short in front of Marsha. Her hand went to her mouth in admiration.

"What do you think?" Victor asked.

"He's angelic!" Janice said. "He's gorgeous, and I don't think I've ever seen such blue eyes." She held out her arms. "Let me hold him." Gently she took the child from Marsha and rocked him back and forth. "I certainly didn't expect blond hair."

"We didn't either," Marsha said. "We thought we'd surprise you like he surprised us. But it comes from my side of the family."

"Oh sure," kidded Victor. "There were a lot of blonds with Genghis Khan."

"Where's David?" asked Marsha.

"Back in the house," said Janice without taking her eyes from VJ's face.

"David!" Marsha called.

The little boy appeared at the doorway, holding one of his previously discarded teddy bears. He was a slight child of five with dark, curly hair.

"Come out here and see your new brother."

Dutifully David walked out to the cooing group.

Janice bent down and showed the newborn to his brother. David looked at the infant and wrinkled his nose. "He smells bad."

Victor chuckled, but Marsha kissed him, saying that when VJ was a little older he'd smell nice like David.

Marsha took VJ back from the nanny and started into the house. Janice sighed. It was such a happy day. She loved newborn babies. She felt David take her hand. She looked down at the boy. He had his head tilted up toward hers.

"I wish the baby hadn't come," he said.

"Shush now," said Janice gently, hugging David to her side. "That's not a nice way to act. He's just a tiny baby and you are a big boy."

Hand in hand, they entered the house just as Marsha and Victor were disappearing into the newly decorated baby's room at the top of the stairs. Janice took David into the kitchen where she had started dinner preparation. He climbed up onto one of the kitchen chairs, placing the teddy bear on the one just opposite. Janice went back to the sink.

"Do you love me more or the baby?"

Janice quickly put down the vegetables she was rinsing and picked David up in her arms. She leaned her forehead on his and said: "I love you more than anybody in the whole world." Then she hugged him forcefully. David hugged her back.

Neither realized that they only had a few more years to live.

1

MARCH 19, 1989
SUNDAY, LATE AFTERNOON

Long, lacy shadows from the leafless maple trees lining the driveway inched across the broad cobblestone courtyard that separated the sprawling white colonial mansion from the barn. A wind had sprung up as the dusk approached, moving the shadows in undulating patterns and making them look like giant spiderwebs. Despite the fact it was almost officially spring, winter still gripped the land in North Andover, Massachusetts.

Marsha stood at the sink in the large country kitchen, staring out at the garden and the fading light. A movement by the driveway caught her eye, and she turned to see VJ pedaling home on his bicycle.

For a second, she felt her breath catch in her throat. Since David's death nearly five years ago, she never took her family for granted. She would never forget the terrible day the doctor told her that the boy's jaundice was due to cancer. His face, yellow and wizened from the disease, was etched on her heart. She could still feel his small body clinging to her just before he died. She had been certain he had been trying to tell her something, but all she'd heard was his uneasy gasps as he tried to hold on to life.

Nothing had really been the same since then. And things got even

479

worse just a year later. Marsha's extreme concern for VJ stemmed partly from the loss of David, and partly from the terrible circumstances surrounding Janice's death only a year after his. Both had contracted an extremely rare form of liver cancer, and despite assurances that the two cancers were in no way contagious, Marsha couldn't shake the fear that lightning, having struck twice, might flash a third time.

Janice's death was all the more memorable because it had been so gruesome.

It had been in the fall, just after VJ's birthday. Leaves were falling from the trees, an autumn chill was in the air. Even before she got sick, Janice had been behaving strangely for some time, only willing to eat food that she prepared herself and which came from unopened containers. She'd become fiercely religious, embracing a particularly fanatic strain of born-again Christianity. Marsha and Victor might not have put up with her had she not become practically one of the family in the many years she'd worked for them.

During David's final, critical months, she'd been a godsend. But soon after David's passing, Janice started carrying her Bible everywhere, pressing it to her chest as if it might shield her from unspeakable ills. She'd only put it aside to do her chores, and then reluctantly. On top of that, she'd become sullen and withdrawn, and would lock herself in her room at night.

What was worse was the attitude that she'd developed toward VJ. Suddenly she'd refused to have anything to do with the boy, who was five at the time. Even though VJ was an exceptionally independent child, there were still times when Janice's cooperation was needed, but she refused to help. Marsha had had several talks with her, but to no avail. Janice persisted in shunning him. When pressed, she'd rave about the devil in their midst and other religious nonsense.

Marsha was at her wits' end when Janice got sick. Victor had been the first to notice how yellow her eyes had become. He brought it to Marsha's attention. With horror, Marsha realized Janice's eyes had the same jaundiced cast that David's had had. Victor rushed Janice to Boston so that her condition could be evaluated. Even with her yellow eyes, the diagnosis had come as a tremendous shock: she had liver cancer of the same particularly virulent type that David had died of.

Having two cases of such a rare form of liver cancer in the same household within a year prompted extensive epidemiological investigations. But the results had all been negative. There was no environmental hazard present. The computers determined that the two cases were simply rare chance occurrences.

At least the diagnosis of liver cancer helped explain Janice's bizarre behavior. The doctors felt she might have already suffered brain metastasis. Once she was diagnosed, her downhill course proved swift and merciless. She'd rapidly lost weight despite therapy, became skin and bones within two weeks. But it had been the last day before she'd gone to the hospital to die that had been most traumatic.

Victor had just arrived home and was in the bathroom off the family room. Marsha was in the kitchen preparing dinner, when the house had reverberated with a blood-chilling scream.

Victor shot out of the bathroom. "What in God's name was that?" he yelled.

"It came from Janice's room," said Marsha, who'd turned very pale.

Marsha and Victor exchanged a knowing, fateful glance. Then they dashed out to the garage and up the narrow stairs to Janice's separate studio apartment.

Before they reached her room, a second scream shattered the silence. Its primeval force seemed to rattle the windows.

Victor reached the room first with Marsha on his heels.

Janice was standing in the middle of her bed, clutching her Bible. She was a sorry sight. Her hair, which had become brittle, stood straight out from her head, giving her a demonic appearance. Her face was hollow, her jaundiced skin stretched tautly across her all-too-visible bones. Her eyes were like yellow neon lights and they were transfixed.

For an instant, Marsha was mesmerized by this vision of Janice as a harpy. Then she followed the woman's line of sight. Standing in the doorway to Janice's rear entry was VJ. He didn't even blink but calmly returned Janice's stare with one of his own.

Marsha immediately surmised what had happened: VJ had innocently come up Janice's back stairs, apparently frightening her. In her illness-induced psychosis, Janice had screamed her terrible scream.

"He is the devil!" Janice snarled through clenched teeth. "He is a murderer! Get him away from me!"

"You try to calm Janice," Marsha shouted, running for VJ. She scooped the six-year-old up into her arms, and retreated down the stairs, rushing him into the family room and kicking the door shut

481

behind her. She pressed VJ's head against her chest, thinking how stupid she'd been to keep the crazed woman at home.

Finally Marsha released VJ from her bear hug. VJ pushed away from her and looked up at her with his crystal eyes.

"Janice doesn't mean what she said," Marsha told him. She hoped this awful moment would have no lasting effect.

"I know," VJ said with amazingly adult maturity. "She's very sick. She doesn't know what she's saying."

Since that day, Marsha could never relax and enjoy her life as she had before. If she did she was afraid God might strike again and if anything happened to VJ, she didn't think she could bear the loss.

As a child psychiatrist, she knew she could not expect her child to develop in a certain way, but she often found herself wishing VJ were a more openly affectionate child. Since he had been an infant he had been unnaturally independent. He would occasionally let her hug him, but sometimes she longed for him to climb onto her lap and cuddle the way David had.

Now, watching him get off his bike, she wondered if VJ was as self-absorbed as he sometimes appeared. She waved to get his attention but he didn't look up as he snapped off the saddlebags, letting them fall to the cobblestones. Then he pushed open the barn door and disappeared from sight as he parked his bike for the night. When he reappeared he picked up the saddlebags and started toward the house. Marsha waved again, but although he was walking directly toward her he did not respond. He had his chin pressed down against the cold wind that constantly funneled through the courtyard.

She started to knock on the window, then dropped her hand. Lately she had this terrible premonition there was something wrong with the boy. God knows she couldn't have loved him more if she'd delivered him herself, but sometimes she feared he was unnaturally cold and unfeeling. Genetically he was her own son, but he had none of the warmth and carefree ways she remembered in herself as a child. Before going to sleep she was often obsessed with the thought that being conceived in a petri dish had somehow frozen his emotions. She knew it was a ridiculous idea, but it kept returning.

Shaking off her thoughts, she called, "VJ's home," to Victor, who was reading in front of a crackling fire in the family room next to the kitchen. Victor grunted but didn't look up.

The sound of the back door slamming heralded VJ's entrance into the house. Marsha could hear him taking off his coat and boots in the mud room. Within minutes he appeared at the doorway to the kitchen. He was a handsome boy, about five feet tall, somewhat large for a ten-year-old. His golden blond hair had not darkened like Marsha's had, and his face had retained its angelic character. And just like the day he was born, his most distinctive feature remained his ice-blue eyes. For as cherubic as he seemed, those intense eyes hinted at an intelligence wiser than his years.

"All right, young man," Marsha scolded in mock irritation. "You know you are not supposed to be out on your bike after dark."

"But it's not dark yet," VJ said defensively in his clear, soprano voice. Then he realized his mother was joking. "I've been at Richie's," he added. He put his saddlebags down and came over to the sink.

"That's nice," Marsha said, obviously pleased. "Why didn't you call? Then you could have stayed as long as you liked. I'd have been happy to come and get you."

"I wanted to come home anyway," VJ said as he picked up one of the carrots Marsha had just cleaned. He took a noisy bite.

Marsha put her arms around VJ and gave him a squeeze, aware of the strength in his wiry young body. "Since you have no school this week I'd have thought you would have wanted to stay with Richie and have some fun."

"Nah," VJ said as he wormed his way out of his mother's grasp.

"Are you worrying your mother again?" Victor asked in a teasing tone. He appeared at the doorway to the family room, holding an open scientific journal, his reading glasses perched precariously on the end of his nose.

Ignoring Victor, Marsha asked, "What about this week? Did you make some plans with Richie?"

"Nope. I'm planning on spending the week with Dad at the lab. If that's okay, Dad?" VJ moved his eyes to his father.

"Fine by me as usual," Victor said with a shrug.

"Why in heaven's name do you want to go to the lab?" Marsha asked. But it was a rhetorical question. She didn't expect an answer. VJ had been going to the lab with his father since he'd been an infant. First to take advantage of the superb day-care services offered at Chimera, Inc., and later to play in the lab itself. It had become a routine, even more so after Janice Fay had died.

"Why don't you call up some of your friends from school, and you and Richie and a whole group do something exciting?"

"Let him be," Victor said, coming to VJ's assistance. "If VJ wants to come with me, that's fine."

"Okay, okay," Marsha said, knowing when she was outnumbered. "Dinner will be around eight," she said to VJ, giving his bottom a playful slap.

VJ picked up the saddlebags he'd parked on the chair next to the phone and headed up the back stairs. The old wooden risers creaked under his seventy-four-pound frame. VJ went directly to the second-floor den. It was a cozy room paneled in mahogany. Sitting down at his father's computer, he booted up the machine. He listened intently for a moment to make sure his parents were still talking in the kitchen and then went through an involved procedure to call up a file he'd named STATUS. The screen blinked, then filled with data. Zipping open each saddlebag in turn, VJ stared at the contents and made some rapid calculations, then entered a series of numbers into the computer. It took him only a few moments.

After completing the entry, VJ exited from STATUS, zipped up the saddlebags, and called up Pac-Man. A smile spread across his face as the yellow ball moved through the maze, gobbling up its prey.

Marsha shook the water from her hands, then dried them on the towel hanging from the refrigerator handle. She couldn't get her growing concern for VJ out of her mind. He wasn't a difficult child; there certainly weren't any complaints from teachers at school, yet tough as it was to put her finger on it, Marsha was increasingly certain something was wrong. It was time she brought it up. Picking up Kissa, their Russian Blue cat who'd been doing figure eights around her legs, Marsha walked into the family room where Victor was sprawled on the gingham couch, perusing the latest journals as was his habit after work.

"Can I talk to you for a moment?" Marsha asked.

Victor lowered his magazine cautiously, peering at Marsha over the tops of his reading glasses. At forty-three, he was a slightly built, wiry man with dark, wavy, academically unkempt hair and sharp features. He'd been a reasonably good squash player in college and still played three times a week. Chimera, Inc., had its own squash courts, thanks to Victor.

"I'm worried about VJ," Marsha said as she sat down on the wing chair next to the couch, still petting Kissa, who was momentarily content to remain on her lap.

"Oh?" said Victor, somewhat surprised. "Something wrong?"

"Not exactly," Marsha admitted. "It's a number of little things. Like it bothers me that he has so few friends. A few moments ago when he said he'd been with this Richie boy, I was so pleased, like it was an accomplishment. But now he says he doesn't want to spend any time with him over his spring break. A child VJ's age needs to be with other kids. It's an important part of normal latency development."

Victor gave Marsha one of his looks. She knew he hated this kind of psychological discussion, even if psychiatry was her field. He didn't have the patience for it. Besides, talk of any problems related to VJ's development had always seemed to fuel anxieties Victor preferred not to fire. He sighed, but didn't speak.

"Doesn't it worry you?" Marsha persisted when it was apparent Victor wasn't about to say anything. She stroked the cat, who took the attention as if it were a burden.

Victor shook his head. "Nope. I think VJ is one of the best-adapted kids I've ever met. What's for dinner?"

"Victor!" Marsha said sharply. "This is important."

"All right, all right!" Victor said, closing his magazine.

"I mean, he gets along fine with adults," Marsha continued, "but he never seems to spend time with kids his own age."

"He's with kids his own age at school," Victor said.

"I know," Marsha admitted. "But that's so highly structured."

"To tell the truth," Victor said, knowing he was being deliberately cruel, but given his own anxiety about VJ—anxiety very different from his wife's—he couldn't bear to stay on the subject, "I think you're just being neurotic. VJ's a great kid. There's nothing wrong with him. I think you're still reacting to David's death." He winced inwardly as he said this, but there was no getting around it: the best defense was an offense.

The comment hit Marsha like an open-hand slap. Emotion bubbled up instantly. Blinking back tears, she forced herself to continue. "There are other things besides his apparent lack of friends. He never seems to need anyone or anything. When we bought Kissa we told VJ it was to be his cat, but he's never given her a second glance. And since you've brought up David's death, do you think it normal that VJ

485

has never mentioned his name? When we told him about David he acted as if we'd been talking about a stranger.''

''Marsha, he was only five years old. I think you're the one who's disturbed. Five years is a long time to grieve. Maybe you should see a psychiatrist.''

Marsha bit her lip. Victor was usually such a kind man, but any time she wanted to discuss VJ, he just cut her off.

''Well, I just wanted to tell you what was on my mind,'' she said, getting up. It was time to go back into the kitchen and finish dinner. Hearing the familiar sounds of Pac-Man from the upstairs den, she felt slightly reassured.

Victor got up, stretched, and followed her into the kitchen.

2

MARCH 19, 1989
SUNDAY, EARLY EVENING

Dr. William Hobbs was looking across the chessboard at his son, marveling over him as he did almost every day, when the boy's intensely blue eyes rolled back into his head, and the child fell backward off his seat. William didn't see his son hit the floor, but he heard the sickening thud.

"Sheila!" he screamed, jumping up and rushing around the table. To his horror, he saw that Maurice's arms and legs were flailing wildly. He was in the throes of a grand mal seizure.

As a Ph.D., not an M.D., William was not certain what to do. He vaguely remembered something about protecting the victim's tongue by putting something between his teeth, but he had nothing appropriate.

Kneeling over the boy, who was just days short of his third birthday, William yelled again for his wife. Maurice's body contorted with surprising force; it was hard for William to keep the child from injuring himself.

Sheila froze at the sight of her husband juggling the wildly thrashing child. By this time Maurice had bitten his tongue badly, and as his head snapped up and down, a spray of frothy blood arched onto the rug.

"Call an ambulance!" shouted William.

487

Sheila broke free of the paralyzing spell and rushed back to the kitchen phone. Maurice hadn't felt well from the moment she'd picked him up from Chimera Day Care. He'd complained of a headache—one of a pounding variety, like a migraine. Of course most three-year-olds wouldn't describe a headache that way, but Maurice wasn't most three-year-olds. He was a true child prodigy, a genius. He'd learned to talk at eight months, read at thirteen months, and now could beat his father at their nightly chess game.

"We need an ambulance!" shouted Sheila into the phone when a voice finally answered. She gave their address, pleading with the operator to hurry. Then she rushed back into the living room.

Maurice had stopped convulsing. He was lying quite still on the couch where William had placed him. He'd vomited his dinner along with a fair amount of bright red blood. The awful mess had become matted in his blond hair and drooled from the corners of his mouth. He'd also lost control of his bladder and bowels.

"What should I do?" William pleaded in frustration. At least the child was breathing and his color, which had turned a dusky blue, was returning to normal.

"What happened?" Sheila asked.

"Nothing," William answered. "He was winning as usual. Then his eyes rolled up and back and he fell over. I'm afraid he hit his head pretty hard on the floor."

"Oh, God!" Sheila said, wiping Maurice's mouth with the corner of her apron. "Maybe you shouldn't have insisted he play chess tonight with his headache and everything."

"He wanted to," William said defensively. But that wasn't quite true. Maurice had been lukewarm to the idea. But William couldn't resist an opportunity to watch the child use his phenomenal brain. Maurice was William's pride and joy.

He and Sheila had been married for eight years before they finally were willing to admit they were unable to conceive. Since Chimera had its own fertility center, Fertility, Inc., and since William was an employee of Chimera, he and Sheila had gone there free of charge. It hadn't been easy. They had to face the fact that both of them were infertile, but eventually, via a surrogate and gamete-donation plans, they got their long-awaited child: Maurice, their miracle baby with an IQ right off the charts.

"I'll get a towel and clean him up," Sheila said, starting for the kitchen. But William grabbed her arm.

"Maybe we shouldn't move him around."

The couple sat watching the child helplessly, until they heard the ambulance scream down their street. Sheila rushed to let the medics in.

A few moments later, William found himself balancing on a seat in the back of the lurching vehicle with Sheila following behind in the family car.

When they reached Lowell General Hospital, the couple waited anxiously while Maurice was examined and evaluated, then declared stable enough for transfer. William wanted the child to go to Children's Hospital in Boston, about a half hour's drive. Something told him that his child was deathly ill. Maybe they had been too proud of his phenomenal brilliance. Maybe God was making them pay.

"Hey, VJ!" Victor shouted up the back stairs. "How about a swim!" He could hear his voice carom off the walls of their spacious house. It had been built in the eighteenth century by the local land-owner. Victor had bought and renovated it shortly after David's death. Business at Chimera had begun to boom after the company had gone public, and Victor felt Marsha would be better off if she didn't have to face the same rooms where David had grown up. She'd taken David's passing even harder than he had.

"Want to go in the pool?" Victor shouted again. It was at times like this that he wished they'd put in an intercom system.

"No, thanks," came VJ's answer echoing down the stairwell.

Victor remained where he was for a moment, one hand on the handrail, one foot on the first step. His earlier conversation with Marsha had reawakened all his initial fears about his son. The early unusual development, the incredible intelligence which had made him a chess master at three years of age, the precipitous drop in intelligence before he was four; VJ's was by no means a standard maturation. Victor had been so guilt-ridden since the moment of the child's birth that he had been almost relieved at the disappearance of the little boy's extraordinary powers. But now he wondered if a normal kid wouldn't jump at the chance to swim in the family's new pool. Victor had decided to add a pool for exercise. They'd built it off the back of the house in a type of greenhouse affair. Construction had just been completed the previous month.

Making up his mind not to take no for an answer, Victor bounded up the stairs two at a time in his stocking feet. Silently, he whisked down the long hall to VJ's bedroom, which was located in the front of the house overlooking the driveway. As always, the room was neat and orderly, with a set of the Encyclopaedia Britannica lining one wall and a chemical chart of the elements on the wall opposite. VJ was lying on his stomach on his bed, totally absorbed in a thick book.

Advancing toward the bed, Victor tried to see what VJ was reading. Peering over the top of the book, all he could make out was a mass of equations, hardly what he expected.

"Gotcha!" he said, playfully grabbing the boy's leg.

At his touch, VJ leaped up, his hands ready to defend himself.

"Whoa! Were you concentrating or what?" Victor said with a laugh.

VJ's turquoise eyes bore into his father. "Don't ever do that again!" he said.

For a second, Victor felt a familiar surge of fear at what he had created. Then VJ let out a sigh and dropped back onto the bed.

"What on earth are you reading?" Victor asked.

VJ closed the book as if it had been pornography. "Just something I picked up on black holes."

"Heavy!" Victor said, trying to sound hip.

"Actually, it's not very good," VJ said. "Lots of errors."

Again, Victor felt a cold chill. Lately he had wondered if his son's precocious intelligence wasn't returning. Attempting to shrug off his worries, Victor said firmly, "Listen, VJ, we're going for a swim."

He went over to VJ's bureau and extracted a pair of bathing trunks and tossed them at his son. "Come on, I'll race you."

Victor walked down to his own bedroom, where he pulled on a bathing suit, then called for VJ. VJ appeared and came down the hall toward his father. Victor noted with pride that his son was well built for a ten-year-old. For the first time Victor thought that VJ could be an athlete if he were so inclined.

The pool had that typical humid chlorine smell. The glass that constituted the ceiling and walls of its enclosure reflected back the image of the pool; the wintry scene outside was not in view. Victor tossed his towel over the back of an aluminum deck chair as Marsha appeared at the door to the family room.

"How about swimming with us?" Victor asked.

Marsha shook her head. "You boys enjoy yourself. It's too cold for me."

"We're going to race," Victor said. "How about officiating?"

"Dad," VJ said plaintively. "I don't want to race."

"Sure you do," Victor said. "Two laps. The loser has to take out the garbage."

Marsha came out onto the deck and took VJ's towel, rolling her eyes at the boy in commiseration.

"You want the inside lane or the outside one?" Victor asked him, hoping to draw him in.

"It doesn't matter," VJ said as he lined up next to his father, facing down the length of the pool. The surface swirled gently from the circulator.

"You start us," Victor said to Marsha.

"On your mark, get set," Marsha said, pausing, watching her husband and her son teeter on the side of the pool. "Go!"

After backing up to avoid the initial splash, Marsha sat down in one of the deck chairs and watched. Victor was not a good swimmer, but even so she was surprised to see that VJ was leading through the first lap and the turn. Then, on the second lap, VJ seemed to hold back and Victor won by half a length.

"Good try," Victor said, sputtering and triumphant. "Welcome to the garbage detail!"

Perplexed at what she thought she had witnessed, Marsha eyed VJ curiously as he hoisted himself from the water. As their eyes met, VJ winked, confusing her even more.

VJ took his towel and dried himself briskly. He really would have liked to be the sort of son his mother longed for, the kind David had been. But it just wasn't in him. Even times he tried to fake it, he knew he didn't get it quite right. Still, if moments like this one at the pool gave his parents a sense of family happiness, who was he to deny them?

"Mother, it hurts even more," Mark Murray said to Colette. He was in his bedroom on the third floor of the Murray townhouse on Beacon Hill. "Whenever I move I feel pressure behind my eyes and in my sinuses." The precise terms were a startling contrast to the tiny toddler's palms with which the child clutched his head.

"It's worse than before dinner?" Colette asked, smoothing back his tightly curled blond hair. She was no longer startled by her toddler's exceptional vocabulary. The boy was lying in a standard-size bed, even though he was only two and a half years old. At thirteen months he'd demanded that the crib be put in the basement.

"It's much worse," Mark said.

"Let's take your temperature once more," Colette said, slipping a thermometer into his mouth. Colette was becoming progressively alarmed even though she tried to reassure herself it was just the beginning of a cold or flu. It had started about an hour after her husband, Horace, had brought Mark home from the day-care center at Chimera. Mark told her he wasn't hungry, and for Mark that was distinctly abnormal.

The next symptom was sweating. It started just as they were about to sit down to eat. Although he told his parents that he didn't feel hot, the sweat poured out of him. A few minutes later he vomited. That was when Colette put him to bed.

As an accountant who'd been too queasy even to take biology in college, Horace was happy to leave the sickroom chores to Colette, not that she had any real experience. She was a lawyer and her busy practice had forced her to start Mark at day care when he was only a year old. She adored their brilliant only child, but getting him had been an ordeal the likes of which she had never anticipated.

After three years of marriage, she and Horace had decided to start a family. But after nearly a year of trying with no luck, they'd both gone in for fertility consultation. It was then they learned the hard truth: Colette was infertile. Mark resulted from their last resort: in-vitro fertilization and the use of a surrogate mother. It had been a nightmare, especially with all the controversy generated by the Baby M case.

Colette slipped the thermometer from Mark's lips, then rotated the cylinder, looking for the column of mercury. Normal. Colette sighed. She was at a loss. "Are you hungry or thirsty?" she asked.

Mark shook his head. "I'm starting not to see very well," he said.

"What do you mean, not see very well?" she asked, alarmed. She covered Mark's eyes alternately. "Can you see out of both eyes?"

"Yes," Mark responded. "But things are getting blurry. Out of focus."

"Okay, you stay here and rest," Colette said. "I'm going to talk with your father."

Leaving the child, Colette went downstairs and found Horace hiding in the study, watching a basketball game on the miniature TV.

When Horace saw his wife in the doorway, he guiltily switched it off. "The Celtics," he said as an explanation.

Colette dismissed a fleeting sense of irritation. "He's much worse," she said hoarsely. "I'm worried. He says he can't see well. I think we should call the doctor."

"Are you sure?" Horace asked. "It is Sunday night."

"I can't help that!" Colette said sharply.

Just then an earsplitting shriek made them rush for the stairs.

To their horror, Mark was writhing around in the bed, clutching his head as if in terrible agony, and screaming at the top of his lungs. Horace grabbed the child by the shoulders and tried to restrain him as Colette went for the phone.

Horace was surprised at the boy's strength. It was all he could do to keep the child from hurling himself off the bed.

Then, as suddenly as it had begun, the screaming stopped. For a moment, Mark lay still, his small hands still pressed against his temples, his eyes squeezed shut.

"Mark?" Horace whispered.

Mark's arms relaxed. He opened his blue eyes and looked up at his father. But recognition failed to register in them and when he opened his mouth he spouted pure gibberish.

Sitting at her vanity, brushing her long hair, Marsha studied Victor in the mirror. He was at the sink, brushing his teeth with rapid, forceful strokes. VJ had long since gone to bed. Marsha had checked him when she'd come upstairs fifteen minutes earlier. Looking at his angelic face, she again considered his apparent ploy in the pool.

"Victor!" she called suddenly.

Victor spun around, toothpaste foaming out of his mouth like a mad dog. She'd startled him.

"Do you realize VJ let you win that race?"

Victor spat noisily into the sink. "Now just a second. It might have been close, but I won that contest fair and square."

"VJ had the lead through most of the race," said Marsha. "He deliberately slowed down to let you win."

"That's absurd," Victor said indignantly.

"No it's not. He does things that just don't make sense for a ten-year-old. It's like when he was two and a half and started playing chess. You loved it, but it bothered me. In fact, it scared me. I was relieved when his intelligence dropped, at least after it stabilized at its high normal. I just want a happy, normal kid." Tears suddenly welled up in her eyes. "Like David," she added, turning away.

Victor dried his face quickly, tossed the towel aside, and came over to Marsha. He put his arms around her. "You're worrying about nothing. VJ's a fine boy."

"Maybe he acts strange because I left him with Janice so much when he was a baby," Marsha said, fighting her tears. "I was never home enough. I should have taken a leave from the office."

"You certainly are intent on blaming yourself," Victor said, "even if there's nothing wrong."

"Well," Marsha said, "there is something odd about his behavior. If it were one episode, it would be okay. But it's not. The boy just isn't a normal ten-year-old. He's too secretive, too adult." She began to weep. "Sometimes he just frightens me."

Leaning over to comfort his wife, Victor remembered the terror he'd felt when VJ had been born. He'd wanted his son to be exceptional, not abnormal in any kind of deviant way.

3

MARCH 20, 1989
MONDAY MORNING

Breakfast was always casual at the Franks'. Fruit, cereal, coffee, and juice on the run. The major difference on this particular morning was that it wasn't a school day for VJ so he wasn't in his usual rush to catch the bus. Marsha was the first to leave, around eight, in order to give her time to see her hospital patients before starting office hours. As she went out the door she passed Ramona Juarez, the cleaning lady who came on Mondays and Thursdays.

Victor watched his wife get into her Volvo station wagon. Each exhale produced a transient cloud of vapor in the crisp morning air. Even though spring was supposed to arrive the next day, the thermometer registered a chilly 28 degrees.

Upending his coffee mug in the sink, Victor turned his attention to VJ, who was alternately watching TV and leafing through one of Victor's scientific journals. Victor frowned. Maybe Marsha was right. Maybe the boy's initial brilliance was returning. The articles in that journal were fairly sophisticated. Victor wondered just how much his son might be gleaning.

He debated saying something, then decided to leave it alone. The kid was fine, normal. "You sure you want to come to the lab today?"

he asked. "Maybe you could find something more exciting to do with your friends."

"It's exciting to come to the lab," said VJ.

"Your mother thinks you ought to spend more time with kids your own age," Victor said. "That's the way you learn to cooperate and share and all that kind of stuff."

"Oh, please!" VJ said. "I'm with kids my own age every day at school."

"At least we think alike," Victor said. "I told your mother the same thing. Well, now that we have that cleared up, how do you want to get to the lab—ride with me or bike?"

"Bike," VJ answered.

Despite the chill in the air, Victor had the sunroof open on his car and the wind tousled his hair. With the radio tuned to the only classical station he could get, he thundered over an ancient bridge spanning the swollen Merrimack River. The river was a torrent of eddies and white water, and it was rising daily thanks to winter snow melting in the White Mountains of New Hampshire, a hundred miles to the north.

On the street before Chimera, Inc., Victor turned left and drove the length of a long brick building that crowded the side of the road. At the end of the building, he took another left, then slowed as he drove past a manned security checkpoint. Recognizing the car, the uniformed man waved as Victor passed under the raised black and white gate onto the grounds of a vast private biotechnology firm.

Entering the nineteenth-century red-brick mill complex, Victor always felt a rush of pride that came with ownership. It was an impressive place, especially since many of the buildings had had their exteriors restored rather than renovated.

The tallest buildings of the compound were five stories high, but most were three, and they stretched off in both directions like studies in perspective. Rectangular in shape, they enclosed a huge inner court which was spotted with newer buildings in a variety of shapes and sizes.

At the western corner of the property and dominating the site was an eight-story clock tower designed as a replica of Big Ben in London. It soared above the other buildings from the top of a three-story structure built partially over a concrete dam across the Merrimack. With the river as swollen as it was, the millpond behind the dam was filled to overflowing. A thunderous waterfall at the spillway in the center of the dam filled the air with a fine mist.

Back in the old days when the mill turned out textiles from southern cotton, the clock tower building had been the power station. The entire complex had been run by waterpower until electrification had shut the main sluice and quieted the huge paddle wheels and gears in the basement of the building. The Big Ben replica had chimed its last years before, but Victor was thinking of having it restored.

When Chimera had purchased the abandoned complex in 1976, it had renovated less than half of the available square feet, leaving the rest for future expansion. In anticipation of growth, however, all the buildings had been equipped with water, sanitation, and power. There was no doubt in Victor's mind that it would be easy to get old Big Ben going again. He made a mental note to bring it up at the next development meeting.

As Victor pulled into his assigned parking spot in front of the administration building and pulled the sunroof shut, he paused to review his day. Despite the pride the expansive site evoked, he recognized he had some mixed feelings about the success of Chimera. In his heart Victor was a scientist, yet as one of the three founding partners of Chimera, he was required to assume his share of the administrative responsibilities. Unfortunately, these obligations were increasingly taking more time.

Victor entered the building through the elaborate Georgian entranceway, replete with columns and pediments. The architects had paid painstaking attention to detail in the restoration. Even the furnishings were from the early nineteenth century. The lobby was a far cry from the utilitarian halls of MIT where Victor was teaching back in 1973 when he first started talking with a fellow academician, Ronald Beekman, about the opportunities afforded by the explosion of biotechnology. Technically, it was a good marriage, since Victor was in biology and Ronald was in biochemistry. They had combined forces with a businessman by the name of Clark Fitzsimmons Foster, and in 1975 founded Chimera. The result was better than their wildest expectations. In 1983, under the guidance of Clark, the company went public and they'd all become enormously wealthy.

But with success came responsibilities that kept Victor away from his first love: the lab. As a founding partner, he was a member of the Board of Directors of the parent company, Chimera. He was also senior vice president of the same company in charge of research. At the same time he was acting director of the Department of Developmental Biology. In addition to those duties he was the president and managing director of the enormously lucrative subsidiary, Fertility, Inc., which owned an expanding chain of infertility clinics.

Victor paused at the top of the main stairs and gazed out of the multipaned arched window at the sprawling factory complex that had been brought back to life. There was no doubt about the satisfaction he felt. In the nineteenth century the factory had been a huge success, but it had been based on exploitation of an immigrant working class. Now its success rested on firmer ground. Chimera's foundation stood on the laws of science and the ingenuity of the human mind in its endeavor to unlock the mysteries of life. Victor knew that science in the form of biotechnology was the wave of the future, and he gloated that he was at the epicenter. In his hands was a lever that could move the world, maybe the universe.

VJ whistled as he freewheeled down Stanhope Street. He had his down parka zipped up to keep out the cold wind, and his hands were crammed into mittens filled with the same insulation the astronauts used.

Switching his bike into the highest gear possible, he caught up to the pedals. With the swish of the wind and the whine from the tires, he felt like he was going a hundred miles an hour. He was free. No more school for a week. No more need to pretend in front of the teachers and those kids. He could spend his time doing what he'd been born to accomplish. He smiled a strange, unchildlike grin. His blue eyes blazed and he was happy his mother was nowhere near to see him. He had a mission, just like his father. And he could not let anything interfere.

VJ had to slow when he reached the small town of North Andover. He pedaled up the center of the main shopping street and stopped in front of the local bank, where he parked his bike in a metal rack and locked it with his Kryptonite lock. Slinging his saddlebags over his shoulder, he climbed the three brownstone steps and went inside.

"Good morning, Mr. Frank," the manager said, twisting around in his swivel desk chair. His name was Harold Scott and VJ generally tried to avoid him, but since his desk was just to the right of the entrance, it was difficult. "May I talk with you, young man?"

VJ paused, considered his options, then reluctantly detoured to the man's desk.

"I know you are a good customer of the bank," Harold said, "so I thought it would be appropriate if I discussed with you some of the benefits of banking here. Do you understand the concept of interest, young man?"

"I believe so," VJ answered.

"If so, then I wanted to ask why you don't have a savings account for your paper route money?"

"Paper route?" VJ questioned.

"Yes," Harold answered. "You told me some time ago that you had a paper route. I assume you still have it since you are still coming into the bank on a fairly regular basis."

"Of course I still have it," VJ answered. Now he remembered having been previously cornered by the same man. It must have been a year ago.

"Once your money is in a savings account, it begins to work for you. In fact your money grows. Let me give you an example."

"Mr. Scott," VJ said as the manager got some paper from a drawer at his desk. "I don't have a lot of time. My father expects me at his lab."

"This won't take long," Harold said. He then proceeded to show Victor what happened to twenty dollars left in The North Andover National Bank for twenty years. When he was finished, he asked: "What do you say? Does this convince you?"

"Absolutely," VJ said.

"Well then," Harold said. He took some forms from another drawer and quickly filled them in. Then he pushed them in front of VJ and pointed to a dotted line near the bottom. "Sign here."

Dutifully VJ took the pen and signed his name.

"Now then," Harold repeated. "How much would you like to deposit?"

VJ chewed his cheek, then extracted his wallet. He had three dollars in it. He took them out and gave them to Harold.

"Is this all?" Harold questioned. "How much do you make a week with your paper route? You have to start a habit of savings early in your life."

"I'll add to it," VJ said.

Taking the forms and the bills, Harold went behind the teller's window. He had to be buzzed in through the plexiglass door. When he returned, he handed VJ a deposit slip. "This is an important day in your life," Harold said.

VJ nodded, pocketed the slip, then went to the rear of the bank. He watched Mr. Scott. Thankfully a customer came in and sat down at his desk.

VJ buzzed for the attendant for the safe deposit vault. A few minutes later he was safely in one of the privacy cubicles with his large safe deposit box. Putting his saddlebags carefully on the floor, he unzipped them. They were filled with tightly bound stacks of hundred-dollar bills. When he was finished adding them to those already there, he had to use both hands to heave the box back up and into its slot in the vault.

Back on his bike, VJ left North Andover, heading west. He pedaled steadily and was soon in Lawrence. Crossing the Merrimack, he eventually entered the grounds of Chimera. The security man at the gate waved with the same kind of respect he reserved for Dr. Frank.

As soon as Victor reached his office, his very pretty and very efficient secretary, Colleen, cornered him with a stack of phone messages.

Victor silently groaned. Mondays were all too frequently like this, keeping him from the lab, sometimes for the entire day. Victor's current and primary research interest involved the mysteries of how a fertilized egg got implanted in a uterus. No one knew how it worked and what were the factors necessary to facilitate it. Victor had picked the project many years ago because its solution would have major academic and major commercial importance. But with his current rate of progress he would be working on it for many years to come.

"This is probably the most important message," Colleen said, handing over a pink slip.

Victor took the paper, which said for him to call Ronald Beekman ASAP. "Oh, wonderful," Victor thought. Although he and Ronald had been the best of friends during the initial phases of the founding of Chimera, Inc., their relationship was now strained over their differing views about the future of the company. Currently they were arguing about a proposed stock offering that was being championed by Clark Foster as a means of raising additional capital for expansion.

Ronald was adamantly opposed to any dilution of the stock, fearing a hostile takeover in the future. It was his belief that expansion should be tied directly to current revenues and current profits. Once again, Victor's vote was to be the swing vote, just as it had been back in 1983 over the question of going public. Victor had voted against

Ronald then, siding with Clark. Despite the incontrovertible success of going public, Ronald still felt Victor had sold out his academic integrity.

Victor put Ronald's message in the center of his blotter. "What else?" he asked.

Before Colleen could respond, the door opened and VJ stuck his head in, asking if anybody had seen Philip.

"I saw him earlier at the cafeteria," Colleen said.

"If anybody sees him," VJ said, "tell him that I'm here."

"Certainly," Colleen said.

"I'll be around," VJ said.

Victor waved absently, still wondering what he would say to Ronald. Victor was certain they needed capital now, not next year.

VJ closed the door behind him.

"No school?" Colleen questioned.

"Spring vacation," Victor said.

"Such an exceptional child," Colleen said. "So undemanding. If my son were here, he'd be underfoot the entire time."

"My wife thinks differently," Victor said. "She thinks VJ has some kind of problem."

"That's hard to believe," Colleen said. "VJ is so polite, so grown up."

"Maybe you should talk to Marsha," Victor said. Then he stuck his hand out, anxious to move on. "What's the next message?"

"Sorry," Colleen said. "This is the phone number for Jonathan Marronetti, Gephardt's attorney."

"Lovely!" Victor said. George Gephardt was the director of personnel for Fertility, Inc., and had been supervisor of purchasing for Chimera until three years ago. Currently, he was on a leave of absence, pending an investigation regarding the disappearance of over one hundred thousand dollars from Fertility, Inc. Embarrassingly enough, it had been the IRS that had first discovered that Gephardt was banking the paychecks of a deceased employee. As soon as he had heard, Victor ordered an audit of the man's purchasing bills for Chimera from 1980 to 1986. Sighing, Victor put the attorney's number behind Ronald's.

"What's next?" Victor asked.

Colleen shuffled through the remaining messages. "That's about all the important ones. The rest of these I can handle."

"That's it?" Victor questioned with obvious disbelief.

501

Colleen stood up and stretched. "That's all the messages, but Sharon Carver is waiting to see you."

"Can't you handle her?" Victor asked.

"She's demanded to see you," Colleen said. "Here's her file."

Victor didn't need the file, but he took it and placed it on his desk. He knew all about Sharon Carver. She'd been an animal handler in Developmental Biology before she'd been "terminated because of dereliction of duty." "Let her wait," Victor said, standing up. "I'll see her after I see Ronald."

Using the rear entrance to his office, Victor started off for his partner's office. Maybe Ronald would be reasonable face to face.

Rounding a corner, Victor spotted a familiar figure backing out of a doorway and pulling a cart. It was Philip Cartwright, one of the retarded persons whom Chimera had hired to work to the extent of their abilities; they were all valuable employees. Philip did custodial and messenger work, and had been popular from his first day on. In addition, he'd taken a particular liking to VJ over the years and had spent lots of time with him, particularly before VJ started school. They made an improbable pair. Philip was a big, powerfully built man with scant hair, closely set eyes, and a broad neck that sloped from just behind his ears to the tip of his shoulders. His long arms ended in spadelike hands, with all the fingers the same length.

As soon as Philip saw Dr. Frank, there was a wide smile of recognition, displaying a mouthful of square teeth. The man could have been frightening, but he had such a pleasant personality, his demeanor overcame his appearance.

"Good morning, Mr. Frank," Philip said. He had a surprisingly childlike voice despite his size.

"Good morning, Philip," Victor said. "VJ is here someplace and was looking for you. He'll be here all week."

"That makes me happy," Philip said with sincerity. "I'll find him right away. Thank you."

Victor watched him hurry off with his cart, wishing all the Chimera employees were as dependable as Philip.

Reaching Ronald's office, which was a mirror image of his, Victor said hello to Ronald's private secretary and asked if her boss was available. She kept Victor waiting for a few minutes before ushering him in.

"Does Brutus come to praise Caesar?" Ronald asked, looking up at Victor from under bushy brows. He was a heavyset man with a thick mat of unkempt hair.

"I thought we could discuss the stock offering," Victor suggested. From Ronald's manner and tone, it was clear he was in no mood for conversation.

"What's there to talk about?" Ronald said with thinly disguised resentment. "I've heard you're for a dilution of stock."

"I'm for raising more capital," Victor said.

"It's the same thing," Ronald said.

"Are you interested in my reasons?" Victor asked.

"I think your reasons are very clear," Ronald said. "You and Clark have been plotting against me since we went public!"

"Oh, really?" Victor questioned, unable to keep the sarcasm from his voice. Such ridiculous paranoia began to give him the idea the man was cracking under the strain of his administrative duties. He certainly had as much if not more than Victor and neither one of them was trained for such work.

"Don't 'oh, really' me!" Ronald said, heaving his bulk to his feet. He leaned forward on his desk. "I'm warning you, Frank. I'll get even with you."

"What on earth are you talking about?" Victor said with disbelief. "What are you going to do to me, let the air out of my tires? Ronald, it's me, Victor. Remember?" Victor waved his hand in front of Ronald's face.

"I can make your life just as miserable as you're making mine," Ronald snapped. "If you continue to press me to sell more stock, I promise I'll get even with you."

"Please!" Victor said, backing up. "Ronald, when you wake up, call me. I'm not going to stand here and be threatened."

Victor turned and left the office. He could hear Ronald start to say something else, but Victor didn't stop to hear it. He was disgusted. For a moment he considered throwing in the towel, cashing in his stock, and going back to academia. But by the time he got back to his desk, he felt differently. He wasn't about to let Ronald's personality problems deny him access to the excitement of the biotechnology industry. After all, there were limitations in academia as well; they were just of a different sort.

Staring up at Victor from his desk blotter was the telephone number for Jonathan Marronetti, Gephardt's attorney. Resigned, Victor dialed

503

the number and got the lawyer on the phone. The man had a distinctive New York accent that grated on Victor's nerves.

"Got good news for you people," Jonathan said.

"We can use some," Victor said.

"My client, Mr. Gephardt, is willing to return all the funds that mysteriously ended up in his checking account, plus interest. This is not to imply guilt; he just wants the matter to be closed."

"I will discuss the offer with our attorneys," Victor said.

"Wait, there's more," Jonathan said. "In return for transferring these funds, my client wants to be reinstated, and he wants all further harassment ceased, including any current investigation of his affairs."

"That's out of the question," Victor said. "Mr. Gephardt can hardly expect reinstatement without our completing the investigation."

"Well," Jonathan said, pausing, "I suppose I can reason with my client and talk him out of the reinstatement proviso."

"I'm afraid that wouldn't make much difference," Victor said.

"Listen, we're trying to be reasonable."

"The investigation will proceed as scheduled," Victor said.

"I'm sure there is some way—" Jonathan began.

"I'm sorry," Victor interrupted. "When we have all the facts, we can talk again."

"If you're not willing to be reasonable," Jonathan said, "I'll be forced to take action you may regret. You are hardly in a position to play holier than thou."

"Good-bye, Mr. Marronetti," Victor said, slamming down the phone.

Slumping back in his chair, Victor buzzed Colleen and told her to send in the Carver woman. Even though he was familiar with the case, he opened up her folder. She'd been a problem practically from the first day on the job. She had been undependable, with frequent absences. The folder contained five letters from various people complaining about her poor performance.

Victor looked up. Sharon Carver came into the room wearing a skin-tight mini with a silk top. She oozed into the chair opposite Victor, showing a lot of leg.

"Thank you for seeing me," she whispered.

Victor glanced at the Polaroid shot in her file. She'd been dressed in baggy jeans and a flannel shirt.

"What can I do for you?" Victor asked, looking her directly in the eye.

"I'm sure you could do a lot of things," Sharon said coyly. "But what I'm most interested in right now is having my job back. I want to be rehired."

"That's not possible," Victor said.

"I believe it is," Sharon persisted.

"Miss Carver," Victor began, "I must remind you that you were fired for failing to perform your job."

"How come the man I was with when we were caught in the stock-room wasn't fired?" Sharon asked, uncrossing her legs and leaning forward defiantly. "Answer me that!"

"Your amorous activities on your last day were not the sole basis for your termination," Victor explained. "If that had been the only problem, you would not have been fired. And the man you mentioned had never neglected his responsibilities. Even on the day in question he was on his official break. You were not. At any rate, what is done is done. I'm confident you will find employment elsewhere, so if you will excuse me . . ." Victor rose from his seat and motioned toward the door.

Sharon Carver did not move. She looked up at Victor with cold eyes. "If you refuse to give me my job back I'll serve you with a sex-discrimination suit that will make your head spin. I'll make you suffer."

"You're already doing a pretty good job," Victor said. "Now if you'll excuse me."

Like a cat about to attack, Sharon rose slowly from the chair, glaring at Victor out of the corner of her eye. "You've not seen the last of me!" she spat.

Victor waited until the door closed before buzzing Colleen to tell her that he was heading over to his lab and that she shouldn't call him for anybody less than the Pope.

"Too late," said Colleen. "Dr. Hurst is in the waiting room. He wants to see you and he's quite upset."

William Hurst was the acting chief of the Department of Medical Oncology. He, too, was the subject of a newly ordered investigation. But contrary to Gephardt's, Hurst's involved possible research fraud, a growing menace in the scientific world. "Send him in," Victor said reluctantly. There was no place to hide.

Hurst came through the door as if he planned to assault Victor, and rushed up to the desk. "I just heard that you ordered an independent lab to verify the results on the last paper I published in the journal."

"I don't think that's surprising in light of the article in Friday's *Boston Globe*," Victor said. He wondered what he'd do if this maniac came around behind the desk.

"Damn the *Boston Globe!*" Hurst shouted. "They based that cockamamie story on the remarks of one disgruntled lab tech. You don't believe it, do you?"

"My beliefs are immaterial at this point," Victor said. "The *Globe* reported that data in your paper were deliberately falsified. That kind of allegation can be detrimental to you and Chimera. We have to nip such a rumor before it gets out of hand. I don't understand your anger."

"Well then, I'll explain," Hurst snapped. "I expected support from you, not suspicion. The mere ordering of a verification of my work is tantamount to ascribing guilt. Besides, some insignificant graphite statistics can sneak into any collaborative paper. Even Isaac Newton himself was later known to have improved some planetary observations. I want that verification request canceled."

"Look, I'm sorry you're upset," Victor said. "But Isaac Newton notwithstanding, there is no relativity when it comes to research ethics. The public's confidence in research—"

"I didn't come in here to get a lecture!" Hurst yelled. "I tell you I want that investigation stopped."

"You make yourself very clear," Victor said. "But the fact remains that if there is no fraud, you have nothing to fear and everything to gain."

"Are you telling me that you will not cancel the verification?"

"That's what I'm telling you," Victor said. He'd had enough of trying to appease this man's ego.

"I'm shocked by your lack of academic loyalty," Hurst said finally. "Now I know why Ronald feels as he does."

"Dr. Beekman advocates the same ethics of research as I do," said Victor, finally letting his anger show. "Good-bye, Dr. Hurst. This conversation is over."

"Let me tell you something, Frank," said Hurst, leaning over the desk. "If you persist in dragging my name through the mud, I'll do the same to you. Do you hear me? I know you're not the 'white knight' scientific savior you pretend to be."

"I'm afraid I've never published falsified data," Victor said sarcastically.

"The point is," Hurst said, "you're not the white knight you want us to believe."

"Get out of my office."

"Gladly," Hurst said. He walked to the door, opened it and said: "Just remember what I've told you. You're not immune!" Then he slammed the door behind him with such force that Victor's medical school diploma tilted on its hanger.

Victor sat at his desk for a few moments, trying to regain a sense of emotional equilibrium. He'd certainly had enough threats for one day. He wondered what Hurst was referring to when he said that Victor was not a "white knight." What a circus!

Pushing back his chair, Victor got up and pulled on his white lab coat. He opened the door, expecting to lean out and tell Colleen he was heading over to the lab. Instead he practically bumped into her as she was on her way in to see him.

"Dr. William Hobbs is here and he's an emotional wreck," Colleen said quickly.

Victor tried to see around Colleen. He spotted a man sitting in the chair next to her desk, hunched over, holding his head.

"What's the problem?" Victor whispered.

"Something about his son," Colleen said. "I think something has happened to the boy and he wants to take some time off."

Victor felt perspiration appear in the palms of his hands and a constriction in his throat. "Send him in," he managed.

He couldn't help but feel a twinge of empathy, having gone through the same extraordinary measures to get a child himself. The thought that something might now be wrong with the Hobbs boy revived all of his apprehensions concerning VJ.

"Maurice . . ." Hobbs began, but he had to stop while he choked back tears. "My boy was about to turn three. You never met him. He was such a joy. The center of our life. He was a genius."

"What happened?" Victor asked, almost afraid to hear.

"He died!" Hobbs said with sudden anger breaking through his sadness.

Victor swallowed hard. His throat was as dry as sandpaper. "An accident?" he asked.

Hobbs shook his head. "They don't know exactly what happened. It started with a seizure. When we got him to the Children's Hospital, they decided he had edema of the brain: brain swelling. There was

507

nothing they could do. He never regained consciousness. Then his heart stopped.''

A heavy silence hung over the office. Finally, Hobbs said, "I'd like to take some time off."

"Of course," said Victor.

Hobbs slowly got up and went out.

Victor sat staring after him for a good ten minutes. For once the last place in the world he wanted to go was the lab.

4

LATER MONDAY MORNING

The small alarm on Marsha's desk went off, signaling the end of the fifty-minute session with Jasper Lewis, an angry fifteen-year-old boy with a smudge of whiskers along his chin line. He was slouched in the chair opposite Marsha's, acting bored. The fact of the matter was that the kid was heading for real trouble.

"What we haven't discussed yet is your hospitalization," Marsha said. She had the boy's file open on her lap.

Jasper hooked a thumb over his shoulder toward Marsha's desk. "I thought that bell means the session is over."

"It means it is almost over," Marsha said. "How do you feel about your three months in the hospital now that you are back home?" Marsha's impression was that the boy had benefited from the hospital's structured environment, but she wanted to learn his opinion.

"It was okay," Jasper said.

"Just okay?" asked Marsha encouragingly. It was so tough to draw this boy out.

"It was like fine," Jasper said, shrugging. "You know, no big deal."

Obviously it was going to take a bit more effort to extract the boy's opinion, and Marsha made a note of reminder to herself in the margin of the boy's file. She'd start the next session with that issue. Marsha closed the file and made eye contact with Jasper. "It's been good to see you," Marsha said. "See you next week."

"Sure," Jasper said, avoiding Marsha's eyes as he got up and awkwardly left the room.

Marsha went back to her desk to dictate her notes. Flipping open the chart, she looked at her preadmission summary. Jasper had had a conduct disorder since early childhood. Once he hit age eighteen, the diagnosis would change to an antisocial personality disorder. On top of that, he also had what appeared to Marsha as a schizoid personality disorder.

Reviewing the salient features of the boy's history, Marsha noted the frequent lying, the fights at school, the record of truancy, the vindictive behavior and fantasies. Her eye stopped at the statement: *cannot experience affection or show emotion*. She suddenly pictured VJ pulling away from her embrace, looking at her coldly, his blue eyes frigid as mountain lakes. She forced her eyes back down on the chart. *Chooses solitary activities, does not desire close relationships, has no close friends*.

Marsha's pulse quickened. Was she reading a summary of her own son? With trepidation, she reread the review of Jasper's personality. There were a number of uncomfortable correlations. She was happy when her train of thought was interrupted by her nurse and secretary, Jean Colbert, a prim and proper New Englander with auburn hair. As she looked up, her eye caught a sentence that she had underlined in red: *Jasper was essentially reared by an aunt, since his mother worked two jobs to support the family*.

"You ready for your next patient?" Jean asked.

Marsha took a deep breath. "Remember those articles I saved on day care and its psychological effects?" she asked.

"Sure do," Jean said. "I filed them in the storage room."

"How about pulling them for me," Marsha said, trying to mask her concern.

"Sure," Jean said. She paused, then asked: "Are you okay?"

"I'm fine," Marsha said, picking up the next chart. As she scanned her recent notes, twelve-year-old Nancy Traverse slunk into the room and tried to disappear into one of the chairs. She pulled her head low into her shoulders like a turtle.

Marsha moved over to the therapy area, taking the seat opposite Nancy. She tried to remember where the girl had left off at the previous visit, describing her forays into sex.

510

The session began and dragged on. Marsha tried to concentrate, but fears for VJ floated at the back of her mind along with guilt for having worked when he had been little. Not that he'd ever minded when she'd left. But as Marsha well knew, that in itself could be a symptom of psychopathology.

After Hobbs left, Victor tried to busy himself with correspondence, partly to avoid the lab, partly to take his mind off the terrible news that Hobbs had told him. But his thoughts soon drifted back to the circumstances of the boy's death. Edema of the brain, meaning acute brain swelling, had been the immediate cause. But what could have been the cause of the edema? He wished Hobbs had been able to give him more details. It was the lack of a specific diagnosis that fed Victor's fears.

"Damn!" Victor yelled as he slammed his open palm on the top of his desk. He stood up abruptly and stared out the window. He had a good view of the clock tower from his office. The hands had been frozen in the distant past at quarter past two.

"I should have known better!" Victor said to himself, pounding his right fist into his left palm with enough strength to make them both tingle. The Hobbs child's death brought back all the concern Victor had had for VJ—concern he had finally put to rest. While Marsha fretted over the boy's psychological state, Victor's worries had more to do with the boy's physical being. When VJ's IQ dropped, then stabilized at what was still an exceptional level, Victor had felt terror. It had taken years for him to overcome his fear and relax. But the Hobbs boy's sudden death raised his fears again. Victor was particularly concerned since the parallels between VJ and the Hobbs boy did not stop with their conception. Victor understood that, like VJ, the Hobbs boy was something of a child prodigy. Victor had been keeping surreptitious tabs on the child's progress. He was curious to see if the boy would suffer as precipitous a drop in IQ as VJ had. But now, Victor only wanted to learn the circumstances of the child's tragic death.

Victor went to his computer terminal and cleared the screen. He called up his personal file on Baby Hobbs. He wasn't looking for anything in particular, he just thought that if he scanned the data, some explanation for the child's death might occur to him. The screen stayed dark past the usual access time. Confused, Victor hit the Execute button again. Answering him, the word SEARCHING blinked in the screen's lower-right-hand corner. Then, to Victor's surprise, the computer told him there was no such file.

"What the devil?" Victor said. Thinking he might have made an entry error, Victor tried again, typing BABY-HOBBS very deliberately. He pressed execute and after a pause during which the computer searched all its storage banks, he got the exact same response: NO FILE FOUND.

Victor turned off the computer, wondering what could have happened to the information. It was true that he hadn't accessed it for some time, but that shouldn't have made a difference. Drumming his fingers on the desk in front of the keyboard, Victor thought for a moment, then accessed the computer again. This time he typed in the words BABY-MURRAY.

There was the same pause as with the Hobbs file and ultimately the same response appeared: NO FILE FOUND.

The door to the office opened and Victor twisted around. Colleen was standing in the doorway. "This is not a day for fathers," she said, gripping the edge of the door. "You have a phone call from a Mr. Murray from accounting. Apparently his baby isn't doing well either and he's crying too."

"I don't believe it," Victor blurted. The timing was so coincidental.

"Trust me," Colleen said. "Line two."

Dazed, Victor turned to his phone. The light was blinking insistently, each flash causing a ringing sensation in Victor's head. This couldn't be happening, not after everything had gone so well for so long. He had to force himself to pick up the receiver.

"I'm sorry to bother you," Murray managed, "but you've been so understanding when we were trying to get a baby. I thought you'd want to know. We brought Mark to the Children's Hospital and he is dying. The doctors tell me there is nothing they can do."

"What happened?" Victor asked, barely able to speak.

"Nobody seems to know," Horace said. "It started with a headache."

"He didn't hit his head or anything?" Victor questioned.

"Not that we know of," Horace said.

"Would you mind if I came over?" Victor asked.

A half hour later, Victor was parking his car in the garage opposite the hospital. He went inside and stopped at the information desk. The receptionist told him Mark Murray was in the surgical intensive-care unit, and gave him directions to the waiting room. Victor found Horace and Colette distraught with worry and lack of sleep. Horace got to his feet when he saw Victor.

"Any change?" Victor asked hopefully.

Horace shook his head. "He's on a respirator now."

Victor conveyed his condolences as best he could. The Murrays seemed touched that Victor had taken the time to come to the hospital, especially since they never socialized.

"He was such a special child," Horace said. "So exceptional, so intelligent . . ." He shook his head. Colette hid her face in her hands. Her shoulders began to quiver. Horace sat back down and put an arm around his wife.

"What's the name of the doctor taking care of Mark?" Victor asked.

"Nakano," Horace answered. "Dr. Nakano."

Victor excused himself, left his coat with the Murrays, and departed the waiting room with its anxious parents. He walked toward Pediatric Surgical Intensive Care, which was at the end of the corridor, behind a pair of electronic doors. As Victor stepped on the rubberized area in front of the doors, they automatically opened.

The room inside was familiar to Victor from his days as a resident. There was the usual profusion of electronic gear and scurrying nurses. The constant hiss of the respirators and bleeps of the cardiac monitors gave the room an aura of tension. Life here was in the balance.

Since Victor acted at ease in the environment, no one questioned his presence, despite the fact that he was not wearing an ID. Victor went to the desk and asked if Dr. Nakano was available.

"He was just here," a pert young woman replied. She half stood and leaned over the counter to see if she could spot him. Then she sat down and picked up the phone. A moment later the page system added Dr. Nakano's name to the incessant list that issued from speakers in the ceiling.

Walking about the room, Victor tried to locate Mark, but too many of the kids were on respirators that distorted their faces. He returned to the desk just as the ward clerk was hanging up the phone. Seeing Victor, she told him that Dr. Nakano was on his way back to the unit.

Five minutes later, Victor was introduced to the handsome, deeply tanned Japanese-American. Victor explained that he was a physician and friend of the Murray family, and that he hoped to get some idea of what was happening to Mark.

"It's not good," Dr. Nakano said candidly. "The child is dying. It's not often we can say that, but in this case the problem is unresponsive to any treatment.''

"Do you have any idea of what's going on?" Victor asked.

"We know what's happening," Dr. Nakano said. "What we don't know is what's causing it. Come on, I'll show you."

With the hurried step of a busy doctor, Dr. Nakano took off toward the rear of the ICU. He stopped outside a cubicle separated from the main portion of the ICU.

"The child's on precautions," Dr. Nakano explained. "There's been no evidence of infection, but we thought just in case . . ." He handed Victor a gown, hat, and mask. Both men donned the protective gear and entered the small room.

Mark Murray was in the center of a large crib with high side rails. His head was swathed in a gauze bandage. Dr. Nakano explained that they'd tried a decompression and a shunt, hoping that might help, but it hadn't.

"Take a look," Dr. Nakano said, handing Victor an ophthalmo-scope. Leaning over the stricken two-year-old, Victor lifted Mark's eyelid and peered through the dilated, fixed pupil. Despite his inexperi-ence with the instrument, he saw the pathology immediately. The optic nerve was bulging forward as if being pushed from behind.

Victor straightened up.

"Pretty impressive, no?" Dr. Nakano said. He took the scope from Victor and peered himself. He was quiet for a moment, then straight-ened up. "The disappointing thing is that it is getting progressively worse. The kid's brain is still swelling. I'm surprised it's not coming out his ears. Nothing has helped; not the decompression, not the shunt, not massive steroids, not mannitol. I'm afraid we've just about given up."

Victor had noticed there was no nurse in attendance. "Any hemor-rhage or signs of trauma?" he asked.

"Nope," Dr. Nakano said simply. "Other than the swelling, the kid's clean. No meningitis as I said earlier. We just don't understand. The man upstairs is in control." He pointed skyward.

As if responding to Dr. Nakano's morbid prediction, the cardiac monitor let out a brief alarm, indicating that Mark's heart had paused. Mark's heart rate was becoming irregular. The alarm sounded briefly again. Dr. Nakano didn't move. "This happened earlier," he said. "But at this point it's a 'no-code' status." Then, as an explanation, he added: "The parents see no sense in keeping him alive if his brain is gone."

Victor nodded, and as he did so, the cardiac monitor alarm came on and stayed on. Mark's heart went into fibrillation. Victor looked over his shoulder toward the unit desk. No one responded.

Within a short time the erratic tracing on the CRT screen flattened out to a straight line. "That's the ball game," Dr. Nakano said. It seemed like such a heartless comment, but Victor knew that it was born more of frustration than callousness. Victor remembered being a resident too well.

Dr. Nakano and Victor returned to the desk where Dr. Nakano informed the secretary that the Murray baby had died. Matter-of-factly the secretary lifted the phone and initiated the required paperwork. Victor understood you couldn't work here if you let yourself become upset by the frequent deaths.

"There was a similar case last night," Victor said. "The name was Hobbs. The child was about the same age, maybe a little older. Are you familiar with it?"

"I heard about it," Dr. Nakano said vaguely. "But it wasn't my case. I understand many of the symptoms were the same."

"Seems so," Victor said. Then he asked: "You'll get an autopsy?"

"Absolutely," Dr. Nakano said. "It will be a medical examiner's case, but they turn most over to us. They're too busy downtown, especially for this kind of esoteric stuff. Will you tell the parents or do you want me to do it?"

Dr. Nakano's rapid change of direction in his conversation jarred Victor. "I'll tell them," he said after a pause. "And thanks for your time."

"No problem," Dr. Nakano said, but he didn't look at Victor. He was already involved with another crisis.

Stunned, Victor walked out of the ICU, appreciating the quiet as the electronic doors closed behind him. He returned to the waiting room where the Murrays guessed the bad news before he could tell them. Gripping each other, they again thanked Victor for coming. Victor murmured a few words of condolence. But even as he spoke a frightful image gripped his heart. He saw VJ white and hooked up to a respirator in the bed where Mark had lain.

Cold with terror, Victor went to Pathology and introduced himself to the chief of the department, Dr. Warren Burghofen. The man assured

515

Victor that they would do everything in their power to get the two autopsies, and get them as soon as possible.

"We certainly want to know what's going on here," Burghofen said. "We don't want any epidemic of idiopathic cerebral edema ravaging this city."

Victor slowly returned to his car. He knew there was little likelihood of an epidemic. He was only too conscious of the number of children at risk. It was three.

As soon as Victor got back to his office he asked Colleen to contact Louis Kaspwicz, the head of Chimera's data processing, and have him come up immediately.

Louis was a short, stocky man with a shiny bald head, who had a habit of sudden unpredictable movements. He was extremely shy and rarely looked anyone in the eye, but despite his quirky personality, he was superb at what he did. Chimera depended upon his computer expertise for almost every area, from research to production to billing.

"I have a problem," Victor said, leaning back against his desk, his arms folded across his chest. "I can't find two of my personal files. Any idea how that could be?"

"Can be a number of reasons," Louis said. "Usually it's because the user forgets the assigned name."

"I checked my directory," Victor said. "They weren't there."

"Maybe they got in someone else's directory," Louis said.

"I never thought of that," Victor admitted. "But I can remember using them, and I never had to designate another path to call them up."

"Well, I can't say unless I look into it," Louis said. "What were the names you gave the files?"

"I want this to remain confidential," Victor emphasized.

"Of course."

Victor gave Louis the names and Louis sat down at the terminal himself.

"No luck?" asked Victor after a few minutes when the screen remained blank.

"Doesn't seem so. But back in my office I can look into it by using the computer to search through the logs. Are you sure these were the designated file names?"

"Quite sure," Victor said.

"I'll get right on it if it's important," Louis said.

"It's important."

After Louis left, Victor stayed by the computer terminal. He had an idea. Carefully he typed onto the screen the name of another file: BABY-FRANK. For a moment he hesitated, afraid of what might turn up—or what might not. Finally he pushed Execute and held his breath. Unfortunately his fears were answered: VJ's file was gone!

Sitting back in his chair, Victor began to sweat. Three related but uncrossreferenced files could not disappear by coincidence. Suddenly Victor saw Hurst's engorged face and remembered his threat: "You're not the white knight you want us to believe. . . . You're not immune."

Victor got up from the terminal and went to the window. Clouds were blowing in from the east. It was either going to rain or snow. He stood there for a few moments, wondering if Hurst had anything to do with the missing files. Could he possibly suspect? If he did, that might have been the basis for his vague threat. Victor shook his head. There was no way Hurst could have known about the files. No one knew about them. No one!

5

MONDAY EVENING

Marsha looked across the dinner table at her husband and son. VJ was absorbed in reading a book on black holes, barely looking up to eat. She would have told him to put the book away, but Victor had come home in such a bad mood she didn't want to say anything that would make it worse. And she herself was still troubled about VJ. She loved him so much she couldn't bear the thought that he might be disturbed, but she also knew she couldn't help him if she didn't face the truth. Apparently he'd spent the whole day at Chimera, seemingly by himself because Victor admitted, when she'd specifically asked, that he'd not seen VJ since morning.

As if sensing her gaze, VJ abruptly put down his book and took his plate over to the dishwasher. As he rose, his intense blue eyes caught Marsha's. There was no warmth, no feeling, just a brilliant turquoise light that made Marsha feel as if she were under a microscope. "Thank you for the dinner," VJ said mechanically.

Marsha listened to the sound of VJ's footsteps as he ran up the back stairs. Outside the wind suddenly whistled, and she looked out the window. In the beam of light from over the garage she could see that the rain had changed to snow. She shivered, but it wasn't from the wintry landscape.

"I guess I'm not too hungry tonight," Victor offered. As far as

Marsha remembered, it was the first time he'd initiated conversation since she'd gotten home from making her hospital rounds.

"Something troubling you?" Marsha asked. "Want to talk about it?"

"I don't need you to play psychiatrist," Victor said harshly.

Marsha knew that she could have taken offense. She wasn't playing psychiatrist. But she thought that she'd play the adult, and not push things. Victor would tell her soon enough what was on his mind.

"Well, something is troubling me," Marsha said. She decided that at least she'd be honest. Victor looked at her. Knowing him as well as she did, she imagined that he already felt guilty at having spoken so harshly.

"I read a series of articles today," Marsha continued. "They talked about some of the possible effects of parental deprivation on children being reared by nannies and or spending inordinate amounts of time in day care. Some of the findings may apply to VJ. I'm concerned that maybe I should have taken time off when VJ was an infant to spend more time with him."

Victor's face immediately reflected irritation. "Hold it," he said just as harshly, holding up both hands. "I don't think I want to hear the rest of this. As far as I'm concerned, VJ is just fine and I don't want to listen to a bunch of psychiatric nonsense to the contrary."

"Well, isn't that inappropriate," Marsha stated, losing some of her patience.

"Oh, save me!" Victor intoned, picking up his unfinished dinner and discarding it in the trash. "I'm in no mood for this."

"Well, what *are* you in the mood for?" Marsha questioned.

Victor took a deep breath, looking out the kitchen window. "I think I'll go for a walk."

"In this weather?" Marsha questioned. "Wet snow, soggy ground. I think something is troubling you and you're unable to talk about it."

Victor turned to his wife. "Am I that obvious?"

Marsha laughed. "It's painful to watch you struggle. Please tell me what's on your mind. I'm your wife."

Victor shrugged and came back to the table. He sat down and intertwined his fingers, resting his elbows on his place mat. "There is something on my mind," he admitted.

"I'm glad my patients don't have this much trouble talking," Marsha said. She reached across to lovingly touch Victor's arm.

Victor got up and went to the bottom of the back stairs. He listened for a moment, then closed the door and returned to the table. He sat down, and he leaned toward Marsha: "I want VJ to have a full neuro-medical work-up just like he did seven years ago when his intelligence fell."

Marsha didn't respond. Worrying about VJ's personality development was one thing, but worrying about his general health was something else entirely. The mere suggestion of such a work-up was a shock, as was the reference to VJ's change in intelligence.

"You remember when his IQ fell so dramatically around age three and a half?" Victor said.

"Of course I remember," Marsha said. She studied Victor intently. Why was he doing this to her? He had to know this would only make her concerns worse.

"I want the same kind of work-up as we did then," Victor repeated.

"You know something that you are keeping from me," Marsha said with alarm. "What is it? Is there something wrong with VJ?"

"No!" Victor said. "VJ is fine, like I said before. I just want to be sure and I'd feel sure if he had a repeat work-up. That's all there is to it."

"I want to know why you suddenly want a work-up now," Marsha demanded.

"I told you why," Victor said, his voice rising with anger.

"You want me to agree to allow our son to have a full neuro-medical work-up without telling me the indications?" Marsha questioned. "No way! I'm not going to let the boy have all those X-rays etcetera without some explanation."

"Damn it, Marsha!" Victor said gritting his teeth.

"Damn it yourself," Marsha returned. "You're keeping something from me, Victor, and I don't like it. You're trying to bulldoze right over my feelings. Unless you tell me what this is all about, VJ is not having any tests, and believe me, I have something to say about it. So either you tell me what's on your mind or we just drop it."

Marsha leaned back in her chair and inhaled deeply, holding her breath for a moment before letting it out. Victor, obviously irritated, stared at Marsha, but her strength began to wear him down. Her position was clear, and by experience he knew she'd not be apt to change her mind. After sixty seconds of silence, his stare began to waver. Finally he looked down at his hands. The grandfather clock in the living room chimed eight times.

"All right," he said finally as if exhausted. "I'll tell you the whole story." He sat back and ran his fingers through his hair. He established eye contact with Marsha for a second, then looked up at the ceiling like a young boy caught in a forbidden act.

Marsha felt a growing sense of impatience and concern about what she was about to hear.

"The trouble is I don't know where to begin," Victor said.

"How about at the beginning," Marsha suggested, her impatience showing again.

Victor's eyes met hers. He'd kept the secret surrounding VJ's conception for over ten years. Looking at Marsha's open, honest face, he wondered if she would ever forgive him when she learned the truth.

"Please," Marsha said. "Why can't you just tell me?"

Victor lowered his eyes. "Lots of reasons," he said. "One is you might not believe me. In fact, for me to tell you we have to go to my lab."

"Right now?" questioned Marsha. "Are you serious?"

"If you want to hear."

There was a pause. Kissa surprised Marsha by jumping up on her lap. She'd forgotten to feed her. "All right," she said. "Let me feed the cat and say something to VJ. I can be ready in fifteen minutes."

VJ heard footsteps coming down the hall toward his bedroom. Without hurrying, he closed the cover of his Scott stamp album and slipped it onto the shelf. His parents knew nothing about philately, so they wouldn't know what they were looking at. But there was no reason to take any chances. He didn't want them to discover just how large and valuable his collection had become. They had thought his request for a bank vault more childish conceit than anything else and VJ saw no reason to make them think otherwise.

"What are you doing, dear?" Marsha asked as she appeared in his doorway.

VJ pursed his lips. "Nothing really." He knew she was upset, but there was nothing he could do about it. Ever since he was a baby he realized there was something she wanted from him, something other mothers got from their children that he couldn't give her. Sometimes, like now, he felt sorry.

"Why don't you invite Richie over one night this week?" she was saying.

"Maybe I will."

521

"I think it would be nice," Marsha said. "I'd like to meet him."

VJ nodded.

Marsha smiled, shifted her weight. "Your father and I are going out for a little while. Is that okay with you?"

"Sure."

"We won't be gone long."

"I'll be fine."

Five minutes later VJ watched from his bedroom window as Victor's car descended the drive. VJ stood for a while looking out. He wondered if he should be concerned. After all, it was not usual for his parents to go out on a weekday night. He shrugged his shoulders. If there was something to worry about, he'd hear about it soon enough.

Turning back into his room, he took his stamp album from the shelf and went back to putting in the mint set of early American stamps he'd recently received.

The phone rang a long time before he heard it. Finally, remembering that his parents were out, he got up and went down the hall to the study. He picked up the receiver and said hello.

"Dr. Victor Frank, please," the caller said. The voice sounded muffled, as if it was far away from the receiver.

"Dr. Frank is not at home," VJ said politely. "Would you care to leave a message?"

"What time will Dr. Frank be back?"

"In about an hour," VJ answered.

"Are you his son?"

"That's right."

"Maybe it will be more effective if you give him the message. Tell your father that life will be getting progressively unpleasant unless he reconsiders and is reasonable. You got that?"

"Who is this?" VJ demanded.

"Just give your father the message. He'll know."

"Who is this?" VJ repeated, feeling the initial stirrings of fear. But the caller had hung up.

VJ slowly replaced the receiver. All at once he was acutely aware that he was all alone in the house. He stood for a moment listening. He'd never realized all the creaking sounds of an empty house. The radiator in the corner quietly hissed. From somewhere else a dull clunking sounded, probably a heating pipe. Outside the wind blew snow against the window.

Picking up the phone again, VJ made a call of his own. When a man answered he told the person that he was scared. After being reassured that everything would be taken care of, VJ put down the phone. He felt better, but to be on the safe side, he hurried downstairs and methodically checked every window and every door to make sure they were all securely locked. He didn't go down into the basement but bolted the door instead.

Back in his room he turned on the computer. He wished the cat would stay in his room, but he knew better than to bother looking for her. Kissa was afraid of him, though he tried to keep his mother from realizing the fact. There were so many things he had to keep his mother from noticing. It was a strain. But then he hadn't chosen to be what he was, either.

Booting up the computer, VJ loaded Pac-Man and tried to concentrate.

The fluorescent lights blinked, then filled the room with their rude light. Victor stepped aside and let Marsha precede him into the lab. She'd been there on a few occasions, but it had always been during the day. She was surprised how sinister the place looked at night with no people to relieve its sterile appearance. The room was about fifty feet by thirty with lab benches and hoods along each wall. In the center was a large island comprised of scientific equipment, each instrument more exotic than the next. There was a profusion of dials, cathode ray tubes, computers, glass tubing, and mazes of electronic connectors.

A number of doors led from the main room. Victor led Marsha through one to an L-shaped area filled with dissecting tables. Marsha glanced at the scalpels and other horrid instruments and shuddered. Beyond that room and through a glass door with embedded wire was the animal room, and from where Marsha was standing she could see dogs and apes pacing behind the bars of their cages. She looked away. That was a part of research that she preferred not to think about.

"This way," Victor said, guiding her to the very back of the L, where the wall was clear glass.

Flipping a switch, Victor turned on the light behind the glass. Marsha was surprised to see a series of large aquariums, each containing dozens of strange-looking sea creatures. They resembled snails but without their shells.

Victor pulled over a stepladder. After searching through a number of the tanks, he took a dissecting pan from one of the tables and climbed the ladder. With a net, he caught two creatures from separate tanks.

"Is this necessary?" asked Marsha, wondering what these hideous creatures had to do with Victor's concern about VJ's health.

Victor didn't answer. He came down the stepladder, balancing the tray. Marsha took a long look at the creatures. They were about ten inches long, brownish in color, with a slimy, gelatinous skin. She choked down a wave of nausea. She hated this sort of thing. It was one of the reasons she'd gone into psychiatry: therapy was clean, neat, and very human.

"Victor!" Marsha said as she watched him impale the creatures into the wax-bottomed dissecting pan, spreading out their fins, or whatever they were. "Why can't you just tell me?"

"Because you wouldn't believe me," Victor said. "Be patient for a few moments more." He took a scalpel and inserted a fresh, razor-sharp blade.

Marsha looked away as he quickly slit open each of the animals.

"These are Aplasia," Victor said, trying to cover his own nervousness with a strictly scientific approach. "They have been used widely for nerve cell research." He picked up a scissor and began snipping quickly and deliberately.

"There," he said. "I've removed the abdominal ganglion from each of the Aplasia."

Marsha looked. Victor was holding a small flat dish filled with clear fluid. Within, floating on the surface of the liquid, were two minute pieces of tissue.

"Now come over to the microscope," Victor said.

"What about those poor creatures?" Marsha asked, forcing herself to look into the dissecting pan. The animals seemed to be struggling against the pins that held them on the bottom of the tray.

"The techs will clean up in the morning," Victor said, missing her meaning. He turned on the light of the microscope.

With one last look at the Aplasia, Marsha went over to Victor, who was already busily peering down and adjusting the focus on the two-man dissecting scope.

She bent over and looked. The ganglia were in the shape of the letter H with the swollen crosspiece resembling a transparent bag of clear marbles. The arms of the H were undoubtedly transsected nerve fibers. Victor was moving a pointer, and he told Marsha to count the nerve cells or neurons as he indicated them.

Marsha did as she was told.

"Okay," Victor said. "Let's look at the other ganglion."

The visual field rushed by, then stopped. There was another H like the first. "Count again," Victor said.

"This one has more than twice as many neurons as the other."

"Precisely!" Victor said, straightening up and getting to his feet. He began to pace. His face had an odd, excited sheen, and Marsha began to feel the beginnings of fear. "I got very interested in the number of nerve cells of normal Aplasia about twelve years ago. At that time I knew, like everyone else, that nerve cells differentiated and proliferated during early embryological development. Since these Aplasia were relatively less complicated than higher animals, I was able to isolate the protein which was responsible for the process which I called nerve growth factor, or NGF. You follow me?" Victor stopped his pacing to look directly at Marsha.

"Yes," Marsha said, watching her husband. He seemed to be changing in front of her eyes. He'd developed a disturbing messianic appearance. She suddenly felt queasy, with the awful thought that she knew where this seemingly irrelevant lecture was heading.

Victor recommenced his pacing as his excitement grew. "I used genetic engineering to reproduce the protein and isolate the responsible gene. Then, for the brilliant part . . ." He stopped again in front of Marsha. His eyes sparkled. "I took a fertilized Aplasia egg or zygote and after causing a point mutation in its DNA, I inserted the new NGF gene along with a promoter. The result?"

"More ganglionic neurons," Marsha answered.

"Exactly," Victor said excitedly. "And, equally as important, the ability to pass the trait on to its offspring. Now, come back into the main room." He gave Marsha a hand, and pulled her to her feet.

Dumbly she followed him to a light box, where he displayed some large transparencies of microscopic sections of rat brains. Even without counting, Marsha was able to appreciate that there were many more nerve cells in one photograph than the other. Still speechless, she let him herd her into the animal room itself. Just inside the door he slipped on a pair of heavy leather gloves.

Marsha tried not to breathe. It smelled like a badly run zoo. There were hundreds of cages housing apes, dogs, cats, and rats. They stopped by the rats.

Marsha shuddered at the innumerable pink twitching noses and hairless pink tails.

Victor stopped by a specific cage and unhooked the door. Reaching in, he pulled out a large rat that responded by biting repeatedly at Victor's gloved fingers.

"Easy, Charlie!" Victor said. He carried the rat over to a table with a glass top, raised a portion of the glass, and dropped the rat into what appeared to be a miniature maze. The rat was trapped just in front of the starting gate.

"Watch!" Victor said, raising the gate.

After a moment's pause, the rat entered the maze. With only a few wrong turns the animal reached the exit and got its reward.

"Quick, huh?" Victor said with a satisfied smile. "This is one of my 'smart' rats. They are rats in which I inserted the NGF gene. Now watch this."

Victor adjusted the apparatus so that the rat was returned to the start position, but in a section that did not have access to the maze. Victor then went back to the cages and got a second rat. He dropped it inside the table so the two rats faced each other through a wire mesh.

After a moment or two he opened the gate and the second rat went through the maze without a single mistake.

"Do you know what you just witnessed?" Victor asked.

Marsha shook her head.

"Rat communication," Victor said. "I've been able to train these rats to explain the maze to each other. It's incredible."

"I'm certain it is," Marsha said with less enthusiasm than Victor.

"I've done this 'neuronal proliferation' study on hundreds of rats," Victor said.

Marsha nodded uncertainly.

"I did it on fifty dogs, six cows, and one sheep," Victor added. "I was afraid to try it on the monkeys. I was afraid of success. I kept seeing that old movie *Planet of the Apes* play in my mind." He laughed, and the sound of his laughter echoed hollowly off the animal-room walls.

Marsha didn't laugh. Instead she shivered. "Exactly what are you telling me?" she asked, although her imagination had already begun to provide disturbing answers.

Victor couldn't look her in the eye.

"Please!" Marsha cried, almost in tears.

"I'm only trying to give you the background so you'll understand," Victor said, knowing that she never would. "Believe me, I didn't plan what happened next. I'd just finished the successful trial with the sheep when you started talking of having another child. Remember when we decided to go to Fertility, Inc.?"

Marsha nodded, tears beginning to roll down her cheeks.

"Well, you gave them a very successful harvest of ova. We got eight."

Marsha felt herself swaying. She steadied herself, grabbing on to the edge of the maze.

"I personally did the in-vitro fertilization with my sperm," Victor continued. "You knew that. What I didn't tell you is that I brought the fertilized eggs back here to the lab."

Marsha let go of the table and staggered over to one of the benches. She wanted to faint. She sat down heavily. She didn't think she could stand hearing the rest of Victor's story. But now that he had begun she realized he was going to tell her whether she liked it or not. He seemed to feel he could minimize the enormity of his sin if he confined himself to a purely scientific description. Could this be the man she married?

"When I got the zygotes back here," he said, "I chose a nonsense sequence of DNA on chromosome 6 and did a point mutation. Then, with micro-injection techniques and a retro viral vector, I inserted the NGF gene along with several promoters, including one from a bacterial plasmid that coded for resistance to the cephalosporin antibiotic called cephaloclor."

Victor paused for a moment, but he didn't look up. "That's why I insisted that Mary Millman take the cephaloclor from the second to the eighth week of her pregnancy. It was the cephaloclor that kept the gene turned on, producing the nerve growth factor."

Victor finally looked up. "God help me, when I did it, it seemed like a good idea. But later I knew it was wrong. I lived in terror until VJ was born."

Marsha suddenly was overcome with rage. She leaped up and began striking Victor with her fists. He made no attempt to protect himself, waiting until she lowered her hands and stood before him, weeping silently. Then he tried to take her in his arms, but she wouldn't let him touch her. She went out to the main lab and sat down. Victor followed, but she refused to look at him.

"I'm sorry," Victor said again. "Believe me, I never would have done it unless I was certain it would work. There's never been a problem with any of the animals. And the idea of having a super-smart child was so seductive . . .'' His voice trailed off.

"I can't believe you did something so dreadful,'' she sobbed.

"Researchers have experimented on themselves in the past,'' he said, realizing it was no excuse.

"On themselves!'' cried Marsha. "Not on innocent children.'' She wept uncontrollably. But even in the depths of her emotion, fear reasserted itself. With difficulty, she struggled to control herself. Victor had done something terrible. But what was done, was done. She couldn't undo it. The problem now was to deal with reality, and her thoughts turned to VJ, someone she loved dearly. "All right,'' she managed, choking back additional tears. "Now you've told me. But what you haven't told me is why you want VJ to have another neuro-medical workup. What are you afraid of? Do you think his intelligence has dropped again?''

As she spoke, her mind took her back six and a half years. They were still living in the small farmhouse and both David and Janice were alive and well. It had been a happy time, filled with wonder at VJ's unbelievable mind. As a three-year-old, he could read anything and retain almost everything. As far as she could determine at the time, his IQ was somewhere around two hundred and fifty.

Then one day, everything changed. She'd gone by Chimera to pick VJ up from the day-care center, where he was taken after spending the morning at the Crocker Preschool. She knew something was wrong the moment she saw the director's face.

Pauline Spaulding was a wonderful woman, a forty-two-year-old ex-elementary-school teacher and ex-aerobics instructor who had found her calling in day-care management. She loved her job and loved the children, who in return adored her for her boundless enthusiasm. But today she seemed upset.

"Something is wrong with VJ,'' she said, not mincing any words.

"Is he sick? Where is he?''

"He's here,'' Pauline said. "He's not sick. His health is fine. It's something else.''

"Tell me!'' Marsha cried.

"It started just after lunch,'' Pauline explained. "When the other kids take their rest, VJ generally goes into the workroom and plays chess on the computer. He's been doing that for some time.''

528

"I know," Marsha said. She had given VJ permission to miss the rest period after he told her he did not need the rest and he hated to waste the time.

"No one was in the workroom at the time," Pauline said. "But suddenly there was a big crash. When I got in there VJ was smashing the computer with a chair."

"My word!" Marsha exclaimed. Temper tantrums were not part of VJ's behavioral repertoire. "Did he explain himself?" she asked.

"He was crying, Dr. Frank."

"VJ, crying?" Marsha was astounded. VJ never cried.

"He was crying like a normal three-and-a-half-year-old child," Pauline said.

"What are you trying to tell me?" Marsha asked.

"Apparently VJ smashed the computer because he suddenly didn't know how to use it."

"That's absurd," Marsha said. VJ had been using the computer at home since he'd been two and a half.

"Wait," Pauline said. "To calm him, I offered him a book that he'd been reading about dinosaurs. He tore it up."

Marsha ran into the workroom. There were only three children there. VJ was sitting at a table, coloring in a coloring book like any other preschooler. When he saw her, he dropped his crayon and ran into her arms. He started to cry, saying that his head hurt.

Marsha hugged him. "Did you tear your dinosaur book?" she asked.

He averted his eyes. "Yes."

"But why?" Marsha asked.

VJ looked back at Marsha and said: "Because I can't read anymore."

Over the next several days VJ had a neuro-medical work-up to rule out any acute neurological problems. The results came back negative, but when Marsha repeated a series of IQ tests the boy had taken the previous year, the results were shockingly different. VJ's IQ had dropped to 130. Still high, but certainly not in the genius range.

Victor brought Marsha back to the present by swearing that there was nothing wrong with VJ's intelligence.

"Then why the workup?" Marsha asked again.

"I . . . I just think it would be a good idea," Victor stammered.

"I've been married to you for sixteen years," Marsha said after a pause. "And I know you are not telling me the truth." It was hard for her to believe she had anything worse to discover than what Victor had already told her.

Victor ran a hand through his thick hair. "It's because of what has happened to the Hobbs' and the Murrays' babies."

"Who are they?"

"William Hobbs and Horace Murray work here," Victor answered.

"Don't tell me you created chimeras out of their children, too."

"Worse," Victor admitted. "Both of those couples had true infertility. They needed donor gametes. Since I'd frozen the other seven of our zygotes, and since they could provide uniquely qualified homes, I used two of ours."

"Are you saying that these babies are genetically mine?" Marsha asked with renewed disbelief.

"Ours," Victor corrected.

"My God!" Marsha said, staggered by this new revelation. For the moment she was beyond emotion.

"It's no different than donating sperm or eggs," Victor said. "It's just more efficient, since they have already united."

"Maybe it's no different to you," Marsha said. "Considering what you did to VJ. But it is to me. I can't even comprehend the idea of someone else bringing up my children. What about the other five zygotes? Where are they?"

Exhaustedly, Victor stood up and walked across the room to the central island. He stopped next to a circular metal appliance, about the size of a clothes washer. Rubber hoses connected the machine to a large cylinder of liquefied nitrogen.

"They're in here," Victor said. "Frozen in suspended animation. Want to see?"

Marsha shook her head. She was appalled. As a physician she knew that such technology existed, but the few times she even thought about it, she considered it in the abstract. She never thought that it would involve her personally.

"I wasn't planning on telling you all this at once," Victor said. "But now you have it: the whole story. I want VJ to have a neuro-medical work-up so that I can be sure that he has no remedial problems."

"Why?" said Marsha bitterly. "Has something happened to the other children?"

"They got sick," Victor said.

"How sick?" Marsha asked. "And sick with what?"

"Very sick," Victor answered. "They died of acute cerebral edema. No one knows why yet."

Marsha felt a wave of dizziness sweep over her. This time she had to put her head down to keep from passing out. Every time she got herself under control, Victor unveiled a further outrage.

"Was it sudden?" she asked, looking up. "Or had they been ill for a long time?"

"It was sudden," Victor admitted.

"How old were they?" Marsha asked.

"About three years old."

One of the computer print-out devices suddenly came to life and furiously printed out a mass of data. Then a refrigeration unit kicked in, emitting a low hum and vibration. It seemed to Marsha that the lab was running itself. It didn't need humans.

"Did the children who died have the same NGF gene as VJ?" Marsha asked.

Victor nodded.

"And they are about the same age as VJ when his intelligence fell," Marsha said.

"Close!" Victor said. "That's why I want to do the work-up, to make sure that VJ isn't brewing any further problem. But I'm sure he's fine. If it hadn't been for the Hobbs' and the Murrays' babies, I wouldn't have thought about having VJ examined. Trust me."

If Marsha could have laughed, she would have. Victor had just about destroyed her life, and he was asking her to trust him. How he could have experimented on his own baby was beyond her comprehension. But that couldn't be changed. Now she had to worry about the present. "Do you think the same thing that happened to the others could happen to VJ?" she asked hesitantly.

"I doubt it. Especially with the seven-year difference in ages. It would seem VJ already survived the critical point back when his IQ dropped. Perhaps what happened to the other children was a function of their being frozen in zygote form," he said, but then broke off, seeing the expression on his wife's face. She wasn't about to take a scientific interest in the tragedy.

"What about VJ's fall in intelligence?" Marsha asked. "Could that have been the same problem in some arrested form, since he was nearly the same age when it happened?"

"It's possible," Victor said, "but I don't know."

Marsha let her eyes slowly sweep around the lab, seeing all the futuristic equipment in a different light. Research could provide hope for the future by curing disease, but it had another far more disturbing potential.

"I want to get out of here!" Marsha said suddenly, getting to her feet. Her abrupt movement sent her chair spinning to the center of the room where it hit the freezer containing the frozen zygotes. Victor retrieved it and returned it to its place at the lab bench. By that time Marsha was already out the door, heading down the corridor. Victor quickly locked up, then hurried after her. The elevator doors had almost closed when he squeezed in beside her. She moved away from him, hurt, disgusted, and angry. But most of all she was worried. She wanted to get home to VJ.

They left the building in silence. Victor was smart enough not to try to make her talk. The snow had started to stick, and they had to walk carefully to keep from slipping. Marsha was aware Victor was watching her intently as they got into the car. Still she didn't say anything. It wasn't until they crossed the Merrimack River that she finally spoke.

"I thought that experimenting on human embryos was against the law." She knew Victor's real crime was a moral one, but for the moment she couldn't face the complete truth.

"Policy has never been clear," Victor said, pleased not to have to deal with the ethical issue. "There was a notice published in the Federal Register forbidding such experimentation, but it only covered institutions getting federal grant money. It didn't cover private institutions like Chimera." Victor didn't elaborate further. He knew his actions were indefensible. They drove in silence again until he said, "The reason I didn't tell you years ago was because I didn't want you to treat VJ any differently."

Marsha looked across at her husband, watching the play of light flickering on his face from the oncoming cars. "You didn't tell me because you knew what a terrible thing it was," Marsha said evenly.

As they turned on Windsor Street, he said, "Maybe you're right. I suppose I did feel guilty. Before VJ was born, I thought I'd have a nervous breakdown. Then, after his intelligence fell, I was again a basket case. It's only been during the last five years that I've been able to relax."

"Then why did you use the zygotes again?" Marsha asked.

"By that time the experiment seemed like a big success," Victor said. "And also because the families in question were uniquely qualified to have an exceptional child. But I shouldn't have done it. I know that now.''

"Do you mean that?" Marsha asked.

"Oh God, yes!"

As they pulled into their driveway, Marsha felt for the first time since he'd shown her the rats that she might someday be able to forgive him. Then maybe—if VJ was truly all right, if her concern about his development was groundless—maybe they might be able to continue as a family. A lot of ifs. Marsha closed her eyes and prayed. Having lost one child, she asked God to spare the other. She didn't think she could suffer such a loss again.

The light in VJ's room was still on. Every night he was up there reading or studying. For however aloof he seemed, he was essentially a good kid.

Victor used the automatic button to raise the garage door. As soon as the car came to a stop, Marsha dashed out, anxious to reassure herself VJ was fine. Without waiting for Victor, she used her own key on the door to the back hall. But when she tried to push it open, the door wouldn't budge. Victor came up behind her and tried it himself.

"The dead bolt's been thrown," Victor said.

"VJ must have locked it after we left." She raised a fist and pounded on the door. It sounded loud in the garage but there was no response from VJ. "Do you think he's all right?" she asked.

"I'm sure he's fine," Victor said. "There is no way he could hear you knocking out here unless he was in the family room. Come on! We'll go to the front."

Victor led the way out through the garage and around to the front of the house. He tried his key. But that door had been dead-bolted as well. He tried the bell. There was still no response. He rang again, beginning to feel a little of Marsha's anxiety. Just when they were about to try another door, they heard VJ's clear voice asking who was there.

As soon as the front door was opened, Marsha tried to hug VJ, but he eluded her grasp. "Where have you been?" he demanded.

Victor looked at his watch. It was a quarter to ten. They'd been gone about an hour and a half.

"Just been over to the lab," Marsha said. It wasn't like VJ to notice one way or the other when they weren't around. He was so self-sufficient.

VJ looked at Victor. "You got a phone call. I'm supposed to give you the message that things will be getting unpleasant unless you reconsider and are reasonable.''

"Who was it?'' Victor demanded.

"The caller didn't leave a name,'' VJ said.

"Was it male or female?'' Victor asked.

"I couldn't tell,'' VJ said. "Whoever it was didn't speak into the receiver, or at least that's what it sounded like.''

Looking from husband to son, Marsha said, "Victor, what is this all about?''

"Office politics,'' he said. "It's nothing to worry about.''

Marsha turned to VJ. "Did the caller frighten you? We noticed the doors were all bolted.''

"A little,'' VJ admitted. "Then I realized they wouldn't have called with that kind of message if they intended to come over.''

"I suppose you're right,'' Marsha said. VJ had an impressive way of intellectualizing situations. "Why don't we all go into the kitchen. I could use some herbal tea.''

"Not for me, thanks,'' VJ said. He turned to head up the stairs.

"Son!'' Victor called.

VJ hesitated on the first step.

"I just wanted to let you know that we will be going to Children's Hospital in Boston tomorrow morning. I want you to have a physical.''

"I don't need a physical,'' VJ complained. "I hate hospitals.''

"I understand your feelings,'' Victor said. "Nonetheless, you will have a physical, just like I do and your mother does.''

VJ looked toward Marsha. She wanted to hold him and make sure that he didn't have a headache or any symptoms whatsoever. But she didn't move, intimidated by her own son.

"Nothing is wrong with me,'' VJ persisted.

"The matter is closed,'' Victor said. "Discussion over.''

His cupid's mouth set, VJ glared at his father, then turned and disappeared upstairs.

Back in the kitchen, Marsha put on the kettle. She knew it would take days before she could sort out all her feelings about what she'd learned that evening. Sixteen years of marriage and she wondered if she knew her husband at all.

Wind whipped snow against the window, causing the sash to rattle against the frame. Rolling over, Marsha squinted at the face of the digital radio-alarm clock. It was half past midnight, and she was a long way from sleep. Next to her she could hear Victor's rhythmic breathing.

Swinging her feet from under the covers, Marsha searched for her slippers. Getting up, she picked up her robe from the chair in the corner, opened the door, and stepped into the hall.

A sudden gust of wind hit the house and the old timbers groaned. She thought of going down to her study on the floor below, but instead continued down the long corridor, to VJ's room. She pushed open the door. VJ had left his window open a crack and the lace curtains were snapping in the snowy breeze. Marsha slipped through the door and silently pushed the window shut.

Marsha looked down at her sleeping son. With his blond curls and high coloring, he looked perfectly angelic. She had to restrain herself from touching him. His aversion to affection was so strong; sometimes it was difficult to think of him and David as brothers. She wondered if his disinclination to hug or cuddle had anything to do with Victor's injection of foreign genes. She'd probably never know. But she realized her earlier concern about VJ had some basis in reality.

Moving the clothes from the chair next to VJ's bed, Marsha sat down. As an infant, he'd been almost too good to be true. He rarely cried, and he slept almost every night the whole night through. To her astonishment, he began to talk when he was only a few months old.

Marsha realized that her excitement and pride of VJ's accomplishments had been the reason she'd never questioned them. And she'd certainly never suspected any artificial enhancement. Now she realized she'd been naive. VJ's brilliance was more than genius. She remembered when a French scientist and his wife had come to Chimera for a six-month stay when VJ was just three. Their daughter, Michelle, had been brought to the day-care center. She was five, and within a week she could say a number of sentences in English. But what was more astounding was that during the same period of time, VJ had become fluent in French.

And then there was VJ's third birthday. To celebrate, Marsha had planned a surprise birthday party, inviting most of the children his age from the day-care center. When he came downstairs Saturday for lunch, he'd found a roomful of mothers and kids shouting "Happy Birthday." It was not a success. VJ pulled Marsha aside and said, "Why did you ask these kids? I have to put up with them every day. I hate them. They drive me crazy!"

535

Marsha was shocked, but at the time she told herself that he was so much brighter than the other children that being forced to socialize was a punishment. VJ much preferred the company of adults, even at age three.

VJ suddenly turned over, muttering in his sleep, bringing Marsha back to the present and all the problems she wanted to forget. He was such a beautiful boy. It was hard to reconcile his innocent face in slumber with the monstrous truth revealed at the lab. At least now she felt she had some understanding of why he was so cold and unaffectionate. Maybe that was why he shared so many of the personality disorders displayed by Jasper Lewis. Ruefully, she reflected that at least her absences from home in VJ's early years were not to blame.

Well, as long as Victor was insisting on a neuro-medical work-up, Marsha decided that she would give VJ a battery of psychological tests. It certainly wouldn't hurt.

6

TUESDAY MORNING

They took separate cars to drive to Boston since Victor wanted to return directly to Chimera. VJ chose to ride with Marsha.

The ride itself was uneventful. Marsha tried to get VJ to talk, but he answered all her questions with a curt yes or no. She gave up until they were a few minutes away from Children's Hospital.

"Have you been having any headaches?" she asked, breaking the long silence.

"No," VJ said. "I told you I'm fine. Why the sudden concern about my health?"

"It's your father's idea," Marsha said. She couldn't think of any reason not to tell the truth. "He calls it preventive medicine."

"I think it's a waste of time," VJ said.

"Have you had any change in your memory?" Marsha asked.

"I'm telling you," VJ snapped, "I'm entirely normal!"

"All right, VJ," Marsha said. "There is no reason to get angry. We're glad that you're healthy and we want you to stay that way." She wondered what the boy would think if he were told he was a chimera, and that he had animal genes fused into his chromosomes.

"Do you remember back when you were three and suddenly couldn't read?" Marsha asked.

"Of course," VJ said.

"We've never talked much about that period," Marsha said.

VJ turned away from Marsha and looked out the window.

"Were you very upset?" Marsha asked.

VJ turned to her and said, "Mother, please don't play psychiatrist with me. Of course it bothered me. It was frustrating not being able to do things that I'd been able to do. But I relearned them and I'm fine."

"If you ever want to talk about it, I'm available," Marsha said. "Just because I've never brought it up doesn't mean I don't care. You have to understand that it was a stressful time for me too. As a mother I was terrified that you were ill. Once it was clear you were all right, I guess I tried not to think about it."

VJ just nodded.

They all met in the waiting room of Dr. Clifford Ruddock, Chief of the Department of Neurology. Victor had beat them by fifteen minutes. As soon as VJ sat down with a magazine, Victor took Marsha aside. "I spoke with Dr. Ruddock as soon as I arrived. He's agreed to compare VJ's current neurological status with what he found at the time VJ's IQ dropped. But he is a little suspicious about why we brought him in today. Obviously, he knows nothing about the NGF gene, and I do not plan to tell him."

"Naturally," said Marsha.

Victor shot her a look. "I hope you are planning to be cooperative."

"I'm going to be more than cooperative," Marsha said. "As soon as VJ is finished here, I'm planning to take him to my office and have him go through a battery of psychological tests."

"What on earth for?" Victor asked.

"The fact that you have to ask means that I probably couldn't explain it to you."

Dr. Ruddock, a tall, slender man with salt and pepper hair, called all the Franks into his office for a few minutes before the examination. He asked if the boy remembered him. VJ told the man that he did, particularly his smell.

Victor and Marsha chuckled nervously.

"It was your cologne," VJ said. "You were wearing Hermès aftershave."

Somewhat taken aback by this personal reference, Dr. Ruddock introduced everyone to Dr. Chris Stevens, his current fellow in pediatric neurology.

It was Dr. Stevens who examined VJ. In deference to the fact that both parents were physicians, Dr. Stevens allowed Victor and Marsha to remain in the room. It was as complete a neurological exam as either had ever witnessed. After an hour just about every facet of VJ's nervous system had been evaluated and found to be entirely normal.

Then Stevens started the lab work. He drew blood for routine chemistries, and Victor had several tubes iced and put aside for him to take back to Chimera. Afterward, VJ was subjected to both PET and NMR scanning.

The PET scanning involved injecting harmless radioactive substances which emitted positrons into VJ's arm while his head was positioned inside a large doughnut-shaped apparatus. The positrons collided with electrons in VJ's brain, releasing a burst of energy with each collision in the form of two gamma rays. Crystals in the PET scanner recorded the gamma rays, and a computer tracked the course of the radiation, creating an image.

For the second test, the NMR scanning, VJ was placed inside a six-foot-long cylinder surrounded by huge magnets supercooled with liquid helium. The resultant magnetic field, which was sixty thousand times greater than the earth's magnetic field, aligned the nuclei of the hydrogen atoms in the water molecules of VJ's body. When a radio wave of a specific frequency knocked these nuclei out of alignment, they sprang back, emitting a faint radio signal of their own which was picked up in radio sensors in the scanner and transformed by computer into an image.

When all the tests were done, Dr. Ruddock summoned Victor and Marsha back to his office. VJ was left outside in the waiting room. Victor was plainly nervous, crossing and uncrossing his legs and running his hand through his hair. Throughout the testing neither Dr. Stevens nor the technician made any comment. By the end, Victor was almost paralyzed with tension.

"Well," Dr. Ruddock began, fingering some of the printouts and images from the tests, "not all the results are back, specifically the blood work, but we do have several positive findings here."

Marsha's heart sank.

"Both the PET and the NMR scans are abnormal," Dr. Ruddock explained. He held up one of the multicolored PET scan images with his left hand. In his right hand he held a Mont Blanc pen. Carefully pointing to different areas, he said, "There is a markedly elevated but diffuse uptake of glucose in the cerebral hemispheres." He dropped the paper and picked up another colored image. "In this NMR scan we can see the ventricles quite clearly."

With her heart pounding, Marsha leaned forward to get a better look.

"It's quite obvious," Dr. Ruddock continued, "that these ventricles are significantly smaller than normal."

"What does this mean?" Marsha asked hesitantly.

Dr. Ruddock shrugged. "Probably nothing. The child's neurological exam is entirely normal according to Dr. Stevens. And these findings, although interesting, most likely have no effect on function. The only thing I can think of is that if his brain is using that much glucose, maybe you should feed him candy whenever he's doing much thinking." Dr. Ruddock laughed heartily at his own attempt at humor.

For a moment both Victor and Marsha sat there numbly, trying to make the transition from the bad news they'd expected to the good news they'd received. Victor was the first to recover. "We'll certainly take your advice," he said with a chuckle. "Any candy in particular?"

Dr. Ruddock laughed anew, enjoying that his humor was so well received. "Peter Paul Mounds is the therapy I recommend!"

Marsha thanked the doctor and ran out the door. Catching VJ unaware, she had him in a bear hug before he could move away. "Everything is fine," she whispered in his ear. "You're okay."

VJ extracted himself from her grasp. "I knew I was fine before we came. Can we go now?"

Victor tapped Marsha on the shoulder. "I've got some other business here and then I'll go directly to work. I'll see you at home, okay?" Victor said.

"We'll have a special dinner," Marsha said, turning back to VJ. "We can leave but you, young man, are not finished. We are going to my office. I have a few more tests for you."

"Oh, Mom!" whined VJ.

Marsha smiled. He sounded just like any other ten-year-old.

"Humor your mother," Victor said. "I'll see you both later." He gave Marsha a peck on the cheek and tousled VJ's hair.

Victor crossed from the professional building to the hospital proper and took the elevator to Pathology. He found Dr. Burghofen's office. The man's secretary was nowhere to be seen so Victor looked inside. Burghofen was typing with his two index fingers. Victor knocked on the doorjamb.

"Come in, come in!" Burghofen said with a wave. He continued to peck at the typewriter for a few moments, then gave up. "I don't know why I'm doing this except my secretary calls in sick every other day, and I'm constrained from firing her. Administering this department is going to be the death of me."

Victor smiled, reminding himself to remember that academia had its own limitations the next time he got fed up with office problems at Chimera.

"I was wondering if you had finished the autopsies on the two children who died of cerebral edema," Victor said.

Dr. Burghofen scanned the surface of his cluttered desk. "Where's that clipboard?" he asked rhetorically. He spun around in his chair, finding what he was searching for on the shelf directly behind him. "Let's see," he said, flipping over the pages. "Here we are: Maurice Hobbs and Mark Murray. Are those the ones?"

"Yup," Victor said.

"They were assigned to Dr. Shryack. He's probably doing them now."

"All right if I go look?" asked Victor.

"Suit yourself," he said, checking the clipboard. "It's amphitheater three." Then as Victor was about to leave, he asked, "You did say you were a medical doctor, didn't you?"

Victor nodded.

"Enjoy yourself," Dr. Burghofen said, returning to the typewriter.

The pathology department, like the rest of the hospital, was new, with state-of-the-art equipment. Everything was steel, glass, or Formica.

The four autopsy rooms looked like operating rooms. Only one was in use and Victor went directly inside. The autopsy table was shining stainless steel, as were the other implements in sight. Two men standing on either side of the table looked up as Victor entered. In front of them was a young child whose body was splayed open like a gutted fish. Behind them on a gurney was the small, covered body of another.

Victor shuddered. It had been a long time since he'd seen an autopsy and he'd forgotten the impact. Particularly when viewing a child.

"Can we help you?" the doctor on the right asked. He was masked like a surgeon, but instead of a gown, he wore a rubberized apron.

"I'm Dr. Frank," Victor said, struggling to suppress nausea. Besides the visual assault, there was the fetid odor that even the room's

541

modern air conditioning could not handle. "I'm interested in the Hobbs baby and the Murray baby. Dr. Burghofen sent me down."

"You can watch over here if you like," the pathologist said, motioning Victor over with his scalpel.

Tentatively, Victor advanced into the room. He tried not to look at the tiny eviscerated body.

"Are you Dr. Shryack?" asked Victor.

"That's me." The pathologist had a pleasant, youthful voice and bright eyes. "And this is Samuel Harkinson," he said, introducing his assistant. "These children your patients?"

"Not really," Victor said. "But I'm terribly interested in the cause of their deaths."

"Join the group," Dr. Shryack said. "Strange story! Come over here and look at this brain."

Victor swallowed. The child's scalp had been cut and pulled down over the face. Then the skull had been sawed around the circumference of the head, and the crown lifted off. Victor found himself looking at the child's brain, which had risen out of its confinement, giving the child the appearance of some sort of alien being. Most of the gyri of the cerebral cortices had been flattened where they had pressed against the inside of the skull.

"This has to be the worst case of cerebral edema I've ever seen," Dr. Shryack said. "It makes getting the brain out a chore and a half. Took me half an hour with the other one." He pointed toward the shrouded body.

"Till you figured out how to do it," Harkinson said with a faint Cockney accent.

"Right you are, Samuel."

With Harkinson holding the head and pushing the swollen brain to the side, Dr. Shryack was able to get his knife between the brain and the base of the skull to cut the upper part of the spinal cord.

Then, with a dull, ripping sound, the brain pulled free. Harkinson cut the cranial nerves, and Dr. Shryack quickly hoisted the brain and placed it in the pan of the overhead scale. The pointer swung wildly back and forth, then settled on 3.2.

"It's a full pound more than normal," Dr. Shryack said, scooping the brain back up with his gloved hands and carrying it over to a sink that had continuous running water. He rinsed the clotted blood and other debris from the brain, then put it on a wooden chopping block.

With experienced hands, Dr. Shryack carefully examined the brain for gross pathology. "Other than its size, it looks normal."

He selected a carving knife from a group in a drawer, and began slicing off half-inch sections. "No hemorrhage, no tumors, no infection. The NMR scanner was right again."

"I was wondering if I could ask a favor," Victor said. "Would it be at all possible for me to take a sample back to my own lab to have it processed?"

Dr. Shryack shrugged. "I suppose, but I wouldn't want it to become common knowledge. It would be a great thing to get into the *Boston Globe* that we're giving out brain tissue. I wonder what that would do to our autopsy percentage?"

"I won't tell a soul."

"You want this case, which I think is the Hobbs kid, or do you want the other one?" Dr. Shryack asked.

"Both, if you wouldn't mind."

"I suppose giving you two specimens is no different from giving you one," said Dr. Shryack.

"Have you done the gross on the internal organs yet?" asked Victor.

"Not yet," Shryack said. "That's next on the agenda. Want to watch?"

Victor shrugged. "Why not. I'm here."

VJ was even less communicative on the ride back to Lawrence than he'd been on the ride into Boston that morning. He was obviously mad about the whole situation, and Marsha wondered if he would be cooperative enough to make psychological testing worthwhile.

She parked across from her office. They waited for the elevator even though they were going up only one floor because the stairwell door was locked from the inside. "I know you're angry," Marsha said. "But I do want you to take some psychological tests, yet it's not worth your time or Jean's unless you cooperate. Do I make myself clear?"

"Perfectly," VJ said crisply, fixing Marsha with his dazzlingly blue eyes.

"Well, will you cooperate?" she asked as the elevator doors opened.

VJ nodded coldly.

Jean was overjoyed to see them. She'd had a terrible time juggling Marsha's patients, but she'd managed in her usual efficient way.

As for VJ, she was really happy to see him, even though he greeted her without much enthusiasm, then excused himself to use the bathroom.

"He's a bit out of sorts," Marsha explained. She went on to tell Jean about the neuro work-up and her desire to have him take their basic battery of psychological tests.

"It will be hard for me to do it today," Jean said. "With you out all morning the phone has been ringing off the hook."

"Let the service handle the phone," Marsha advised. "It's important I get VJ tested."

Jean nodded and immediately began getting out the forms and preparing their computer to grade and correlate the results.

When VJ returned from the bathroom, Jean had him sit right down at the keyboard. Since he was familiar with some of the tests, she asked him which kind he wanted to take first.

"Let's start with the intelligence tests," VJ said agreeably.

For the next hour and a half, Jean administered the WAIS-R intelligence test, which included six verbal and five performance subtests. From her experience she knew that VJ was doing well, but nowhere near what he'd done seven years previously. She also noted that VJ tended to hesitate before he answered a question or performed a task. It was like he wanted to be doubly sure of his choice.

"Very good!" Jean said when they'd reached the completion. "Now how about the personality test?"

"Is that the MMPI?" VJ asked. "Or the MCMI?"

"I'm impressed," Jean said. "Sounds like you have been doing a little reading."

"It's easy when one of your parents is a psychiatrist," VJ said.

"We use both, but let's start with the MMPI," Jean said. "You don't need me for this. It's all multiple choice. If you have any problems, just yell."

Jean left VJ in the testing room, and went back to the reception desk. She called the service and got the pile of messages that had accumulated. She attended to the ones that she could and when Marsha's patient left, gave her the messages she had to handle herself.

"How's VJ doing?" Marsha asked.

"Couldn't be better," Jean reported.

"He's being cooperative?" Marsha asked.

"Like a lamb," Jean said. "In fact, he seems to be enjoying himself."

Marsha shook her head in amazement. "Must be you. He was in an awful mood with me."

Jean took it as a compliment. "He's had a WAIS-R and he's in the middle of an MMPI. What other tests do you want? A Rorschach and a Thematic Apperception Test or what?"

Marsha chewed on her thumbnail for a moment, thinking. "Why don't we do the TAT and let the Rorschach go for now. We can always do it later."

"I'll be happy to do both," Jean said.

"Let's just do the TAT," Marsha said as she picked up the next chart. "VJ's in a good mood but why push it? Besides, it might be interesting to cross check the TAT and the Rorschach if they are taken on different days." She called the patient whose chart she was holding and disappeared for another session.

After Jean finished as much paperwork as she could, she returned to the testing room. VJ was absorbed in the personality test.

"Any problems?" Jean asked.

"Some of these questions are too much," VJ said with a laugh. "A couple of them have no appropriate answers."

"The idea is to select the best one possible," Jean said.

"I know," VJ said. "That's what I'm doing."

At noon, they broke for lunch and walked to the hospital. They ate in the coffee shop. Marsha and Jean had tuna salad sandwiches while VJ had a hamburger and a shake. Marsha noted with contentment that VJ's attitude had indeed changed. She began to think she had worried for nothing; the tests he was taking would probably result in a healthy psychological portrait. She was dying to ask Jean about the results so far, but she knew she couldn't in front of VJ. Within thirty minutes they were all back at their respective tasks.

An hour later, Jean put the phone back on service and returned to the testing room. Just as she closed the door behind her, VJ spoke up: "There," he said, clicking the last question. "All done."

"Very good," Jean said, impressed. VJ had gone through the five hundred and fifty questions in half the usual time. "Would you like to rest before the next test?" she asked.

"Let's get it over with," VJ said.

For ninety minutes, Jean showed the TAT cards to VJ. Each contained a black and white picture of people in circumstances that elicited responses having psychological overtones. VJ was asked to describe what he thought was going on in each picture and how the people felt. The idea was for VJ to project his fantasies, feelings, patterns of relationships, needs, and conflicts.

With some patients the TAT was no easy test to administer. But with VJ, Jean found herself enjoying the process. The boy had no trouble coming up with interesting explanations and his responses were both logical and normal. By the end of the test Jean felt that VJ was emotionally stable, well adjusted, and mature for his age.

When Marsha was finished with her last patient, Jean went into the office and gave her the computer printouts. The MMPI would be sent off to be evaluated by a program with a larger data base, but their PC gave them an initial report.

Marsha glanced through the papers, as Jean gave her own positive clinical impression. "I think he is a model child. I truly can't see how you can be concerned about him."

"That's reassuring," Marsha said, studying the IQ test results. The overall score was 128. That was only a two-point variation from the last time that Marsha had had VJ tested several years previously. So VJ's IQ had not changed, and it was a good, solid, healthy score, certainly well above average. But there was one discrepancy that bothered Marsha: a fifteen-point difference between the verbal and the performance IQ, with the verbal lower than the performance, which suggested a cognitive problem relating to language disabilities. Given VJ's facility in French, it didn't seem to make sense.

"I noticed that," Jean said when Marsha queried it, "but since the overall score was so good I didn't give it much significance. Do you?"

"I don't know," Marsha said. "I don't think I've ever seen a result like this before. Oh well, let's go on to the MMPI."

Marsha put the personality inventory results in front of her. The first part was called the validity scales. Again something immediately aroused her attention. The F and K scales were mildly elevated and at the upper limit of what would be considered normal. Marsha pointed that out to Jean as well.

"But they are in the normal range," Jean insisted.

"True," Marsha said, "but you have to remember that all this is relative. Why would VJ's validity scales be nearly abnormal?"

"He did the test quickly," Jean said. "Maybe he got a little careless."

"VJ is never careless," Marsha said. "Well, I can't explain this, but let's go on."

The second part of the report was the clinical scales, and Marsha noted that none were in the abnormal range. She was particularly happy to see that scale four and scale eight were well within normal limits. Those two scales referred to psychopathic deviation and schizophrenic behavior respectively. Marsha breathed a sigh of relief because these scales had a high degree of correlation with clinical reality, and she'd been afraid they would be elevated, given VJ's history.

But then Marsha noted that scale three was "high normal." That would mean VJ tended toward hysteria, constantly seeking affection and attention. That certainly did not correlate with Marsha's experience.

"Was it your impression that VJ was cooperating when he took this test?" Marsha asked Jean.

"Absolutely," Jean said.

"I suppose I should be happy with these results," Marsha said, as she gathered the papers together, then stood them on end, tapping them against the desk until they were lined up.

"I think so," Jean said encouragingly.

Marsha stapled the papers together, then tossed them into her brief-case. "Yet both the Wechsler and the MMPI are a little abnormal. Well, maybe unexpected is a better word. I'd have preferred they be unqualifyingly normal. By the way, how did VJ respond to the TAT with the man standing over the child with his arm raised?"

"VJ said he was giving a lecture."

"The man or the child?" Marsha asked with a laugh.

"Definitely the man."

"Any hostility involved?" Marsha asked.

"None."

"Why was the man's arm raised?"

"Because the man was talking about tennis, and he was showing the boy how to serve," Jean said.

"Tennis? VJ has never played tennis."

As Victor drove onto the grounds of Chimera, he noted that none of the previous night's snow remained. It was still cloudy but the temperature had risen into the high forties.

He parked his car in the usual spot, but instead of heading directly into the administration building, he took the brown paper bag from the front seat of the car and went directly to his lab.

"Got some extra rush work for you," he said to his head technician, Robert Grimes.

547

Robert was a painfully thin, intense man, who wore shirts with necks much too large for him, emphasizing his thinness. His eyes had a bulging look of continual surprise.

Victor pulled out the iced vials of VJ's blood and sample bottles containing pieces of the dead children's brains. "I want chromosome studies done on these."

Robert picked up the blood vials, shook them, then examined the brain samples. "You want me to let other things go and do this?"

"That's right," Victor said. "I want it done as soon as possible. Plus I want some standard neural stains on the brain slices."

"I'll have to let the uterine implant work slide," Robert said.

"You have my permission."

Leaving the lab, Victor went to the next building, which housed the central computer. It was situated in the geometric center of the courtyard, an ideal location since the building had easy access to all other facilities. The main office was on the first floor, and Victor had no trouble locating Louis Kaspwicz. There was some problem with a piece of hardware, and Louis was supervising several technicians who had the massive machine open as if it were undergoing surgery.

"Have any information for me?" Victor asked.

Louis nodded, told the technicians to keep searching, and led Victor back to his office where he produced a loose-leaf notebook containing the computer logs. "I've figured out why you couldn't call up those files on your terminal," Louis said. He began to flip the pages of the computer log.

"Why?" Victor asked, as Louis kept searching through the book.

Not finding what he was looking for, he straightened up and glanced around his office. "Ah," he said, spying a loose sheet of paper and snatching it from the desk top.

"You couldn't call up the files on Baby Hobbs or Baby Murray because they'd been deleted on November 18," he said, waving the paper under Victor's nose.

"Deleted?"

"I'm afraid so," Louis said. "This is the computer log for November 18, and it clearly shows that the files were deleted."

"That's strange," Victor said. "I don't suppose you can determine who deleted them, can you?"

"Sure," Louis said. "By matching the password of the user."

"Did you do that?"

"Yes," Louis said.

"Well, who was it?" Victor asked irritably. It seemed like Louis was deliberately making this difficult.

Louis glanced at Victor, then looked away. "You, Dr. Frank."

"Me?" Victor said with surprise. That was the last thing he expected to hear. Yet he did remember thinking about deleting the files, maybe even planning on doing it at some time, but he could not remember actually having done it.

"Sorry," Louis said, shifting his weight. He was plainly uncomfortable.

"It's quite all right," Victor said, embarrassed himself. "Thank you for looking into it for me."

"Anytime," Louis said.

Victor left the computer center, perplexed at this new information. It was true that he'd become somewhat forgetful of late, but could he have actually deleted the files and forgotten about it? Could it have been an accident? He wondered what he'd been doing November 18. Victor went back to the administration building and slowly climbed the back stairs. As he walked down the second-floor corridor toward the rear entrance of his office, he decided to check back over his calendar. He took off his coat, hung it up, and then went to talk to Colleen.

"Dr. Frank, you frightened me!" she exclaimed when Victor tapped her on the shoulder. She'd been concentrating on typing with dictation headphones on. "I had no idea you were here."

Victor apologized, saying that he'd come in the back way.

"How was the visit to the hospital?" Colleen asked. Victor had called her early that morning to explain why he wouldn't be in until afternoon. "I hope to God VJ is okay."

"He's fine," Victor said with a smile. "The tests were normal. Of course, we are waiting on a group of blood tests. But I feel confident they'll be fine as well."

"Thank God!" Colleen said. "You scared me when you called this morning: a full neuro work-up sounded pretty serious."

"I was a little worried myself," Victor admitted.

"I suppose you want your phone messages," Colleen said as she peeked under some papers on her otherwise neat desk. "I've got a ton of them for you somewhere here."

"Hold the messages a minute," Victor said. "Would you haul out the calendar for 1988? I'm particularly interested in November 18."

549

"Certainly," Colleen said. She detached herself from her dictation machine and headed for the files.

Victor went back into his office. While he waited, he thought about the harassing phone call that VJ had unfortunately received, and he debated what to do about it. Reluctantly, he realized there was little he could do. If he asked any of the people he was having a problem with, they'd obviously deny it.

Colleen came into his office carrying the calendar already opened to November 18, and stuck it under Victor's nose. It had been a fairly busy day. But there was nothing that had anything even slightly to do with the missing files. The last entry noted that Victor had taken Marsha into Boston to eat at Another Season and go to the Boston Symphony.

Removing her robe, Marsha slid into the deliciously warm bed. She turned down the controls of the electric blanket from high to three. Victor had edged as far away from the heat as possible. His side of the electric blanket was never used. He'd been in bed for over a half hour and was busy reading from a stack of professional journals.

Marsha rolled on her side, studying Victor's profile. The sharp line of his nose, the slightly hollow cheeks, the thin lips were as familiar to Marsha as her own. Yet he seemed like a stranger. She still hadn't fully accepted what he'd done to VJ, vacillating between disbelief, anger, and fear, with fear being paramount.

"Do you think those tests mean VJ's really all right?" she asked.

"I'm reassured," Victor said without looking up from his magazine. "And you acted pretty happy in Dr. Ruddock's office."

Marsha rolled over on her back. "That was immediate relief that nothing obvious showed up, like a brain tumor." She looked back at Victor. "But there still is no explanation for his dramatic drop in intelligence."

"But that was six and a half years ago."

"I'm still worried that the process will start again."

"Suit yourself," Victor said.

"Victor!" Marsha said. "Can't you put whatever it is you're reading aside for a moment to talk with me?"

Letting the open journal drop, he said, "I am talking to you."

"Thank you," Marsha said. "Of course I'm glad VJ's physical exam was normal. But his psychological exams weren't. They were unexpected, and a little contradictory." Marsha then went on to explain

550

her findings, finishing with VJ's relatively high score on the hysteria scale.

"VJ's not emotional," Victor said.

"That's the point," Marsha said.

"Seems to me the result says more about psychological tests than anything else. They probably aren't accurate."

"On the contrary," Marsha said. "These tests are considered very reliable. But I don't know what to make of them. Unfortunately they just add to my uneasiness. I can't help feeling that something terrible is going to happen."

"Listen," Victor said. "I took some of VJ's blood back to the lab. I'm going to have chromosome six isolated. If it hasn't changed, I'll be perfectly satisfied. And you should be as well." He reached out as if to pat her thigh but she moved her leg away. Victor let his hand fall back to the bed. "If VJ has some mild psychological problems, well that's something else and we can get him some therapy, okay?" He wanted to reassure her further, but he didn't know what else to say. He certainly wasn't about to mention the missing files.

Marsha took a deep breath. "Okay," she said. "I'll try to relax. You'll tell me about the DNA study as soon as you look at it?"

"Absolutely," Victor said. He smiled at her. She managed to smile back weakly.

Victor raised his journal and tried to read. But he kept thinking about the missing files. Victor wondered again if he could have deleted them. It was a possibility. Since they weren't cross-referenced, it was unlikely someone else could have deleted all three.

"Did you find out what caused the death of those poor babies?" Marsha asked.

Victor let the journal drop once more. "Not yet. The autopsies aren't complete. The microscopic hasn't been done."

"Could it have been cancer?" Marsha asked nervously, remembering the day David got sick. That was another date that Marsha would never forget: June 17, 1984. David was ten, VJ five. School had been out for several weeks and Janice was planning to take the children to Castle Beach.

Marsha was in her study, getting her things ready to take to the office when David appeared in the doorway, his thin arms hanging limply at his sides.

"Mommy, something is wrong with me," he said.

Marsha didn't look up immediately. She was trying to find a folder she'd brought from the office the day before.

"What seems to be the trouble?" she asked, closing one drawer and opening another. David had gone to bed the night before complaining of some abdominal discomfort, but Pepto-Bismol had taken care of that.

"I look funny," David said.

"I think you are a handsome boy," Marsha said, turning to scan the built-in shelves behind her desk.

"I'm getting yellow," David said.

Marsha stopped what she was doing and turned to face her son, who ran to her and buried his face in her bosom. He was an affectionate child.

"What makes you think you're turning yellow?" she asked, feeling the first stirrings of fear. "Let me see your face," she said, gently trying to pull the boy away from her. She was hoping that he was wrong and there would be some silly explanation for his impression.

David would not let go. "It's my eyes," he said, his voice muffled against her. "And my tongue."

"Your tongue can get yellow from a lemon candy," Marsha said. "Come, now. Let me see."

The light in her study was poor, so she walked him into the hall where she looked at David's eyes in the light streaming through the window. Marsha caught her breath. There was no doubt. The boy was severely jaundiced.

Later that day a CAT scan showed a diffuse tumor of the liver. It was an enormously aggressive cancer that destroyed the child's liver within days of making the diagnosis.

"Neither baby seemed to have cancer," Victor was saying, rousing Marsha from her reverie. "The gross studies showed no signs of malignancy."

Marsha tried to shake away the haunting image of David's yellow eyes looking at her from his gaunt face. Even his skin had rapidly turned yellow. She cleared her throat. "What do you think the chances are that the babies' deaths were caused by the foreign genes you inserted?"

Victor didn't answer immediately. "I'd like to think the problem was unrelated. After all, none of the hundreds of animal experiments resulted in any health problems."

"But you can't be sure?" Marsha asked.

"I can't be sure," Victor agreed.

"What about the other five zygotes?" Marsha asked.

"What do you mean?" Victor asked. "They are stored in the freezer."

"Are they normal or did you mutate them too?" Marsha asked.

"All of them have the NGF gene," Victor said.

"I want you to destroy them," Marsha said.

"Why?" Victor asked.

"You said you were sorry for what you'd done," Marsha said angrily. "And now you are asking why you should destroy them?"

"I'm not going to implant them," Victor said. "I can promise you that. But I might need them to help figure out what went wrong with the Hobbs and Murray babies. Remember, their zygotes had both been frozen. That was the only difference between them and VJ."

Marsha studied Victor's face. It was a horrible feeling to realize that she didn't know if she believed him or not. She did not like the idea of those zygotes being potentially viable.

Before she could argue further, a crash shattered the night. Even before the sound of the broken glass faded, a high-pitched scream reverberated from VJ's room. Marsha and Victor leaped from the bed and ran headlong down the hall.

7

LATER TUESDAY NIGHT

VJ was curled up in a ball at the head of his bed, cradling his head in both hands. In the center of the room, resting on the rug, was a brick. A length of red ribbon was tied around it, securing a piece of paper, making the package appear like a gift. VJ's window had been smashed and shards of glass littered the room. Obviously the brick had been thrown from the driveway.

Victor put out his hand to restrain Marsha from coming into the room and rushing to VJ's side.

"Watch the glass!" Victor yelled.

"VJ, are you all right?" Marsha shouted.

VJ nodded.

Reaching around Marsha, Victor grabbed the Oriental runner that extended down the hall. Pulling it into VJ's room, he let it roll out toward the window. Then he ran across it to look down at the driveway. He saw no one.

"I'm going out," Victor said, running past Marsha.

"Don't be a hero," Marsha yelled, but Victor was already halfway down the stairs. "And don't you move," she said to VJ. "There's so much glass, you're sure to be cut. I'll be right back."

Marsha ran back to the master bedroom and hastily pulled on her slippers and her robe. Returning to VJ's room, she finally got to the

MUTATION

bed. VJ allowed her to hug him. "Hold on," she said, as she strained to lift him up. He was heavier than she'd anticipated. Staggering to the hallway, she was glad to set him down.

"A few months from now I won't be able to do that," she said with a groan. "You're getting too big for me."

"I'm going to find out who did that," VJ snarled, finding his voice.

"Did it frighten you, dear?" Marsha asked, stroking his head.

VJ parried Marsha's hand. "I'm going to find out who threw that brick and I'm going to kill him."

"You're safe now," Marsha said soothingly. "You can calm down. I know you're upset, but everything is all right. No one got hurt."

"I'll kill him," VJ persisted. "You'll see. I'll kill him."

"Okay," Marsha said. She tried to draw him to her but he resisted. For a moment she looked at him. His blazing eyes held a piercing, unchildlike intensity. "Let's go down to the study," she said. "I want to call the police."

Victor ran the length of the driveway and stood in the street, looking both ways. Two driveways down, he heard a car being started. Just as he was debating sprinting in that direction, he saw the headlights come on and the car accelerate away. He couldn't tell the make.

In frustration, he threw a rock after it, but there was no way he could have hit it. Turning around, he hurried back to the house. He found Marsha and VJ in the study. It was apparent they'd been talking, but as Victor arrived they stopped.

"Where's the brick?" Victor asked, out of breath.

"Still in VJ's room," Marsha said. "We've been too busy talking about how VJ is planning on killing whoever threw it."

"I will!" VJ promised.

Victor groaned, knowing how Marsha's mind would take this as further evidence that VJ was disturbed. He went back to his son's room. The brick was still where it had fallen after crashing through VJ's window. Bending down, he extracted the paper from beneath the ribbon. "Remember our deal" said the typed message. Victor made an expression of disgust. Who the hell had done this?

Bringing the brick and the note with him, Victor returned to the study. He showed both to Marsha, who took them in her hands. She was about to say something when the downstairs doorbell sounded.

"Now what?" Victor questioned.

"Must be the police," Marsha said, getting to her feet. "I called

555

them while you were outside running around." She left the room, heading down the stairs.

Victor looked at VJ. "Scared you, huh, Tiger?"

"I think that's obvious," VJ said. "It would have scared anyone."

"I know," Victor said. "I'm sorry you're getting the brunt of all this, what with the phone call last night and the brick tonight. I'm sure you don't understand, but I've some personnel problems at the lab. I'll try to do something to keep this kind of thing from happening."

"It doesn't matter," VJ said.

"I appreciate you being a good sport about it," Victor said. "Come on, let's talk to the police."

"The police won't do anything," VJ said. But he got up and started downstairs.

Victor followed. He agreed, but he was surprised that at age ten, VJ knew it too.

The North Andover police were polite and solicitous. A Sergeant Widdicomb and Patrolman O'Connor had responded to the call. Widdicomb was at least sixty-five, with florid skin and a huge beer belly. O'Connor was just the opposite: he was in his twenties and looked like an athlete. Widdicomb did all the talking.

When Victor and VJ arrived in the foyer, Widdicomb was reading the note while O'Connor fingered the brick. Widdicomb handed the note back to Marsha. "What a dadblasted awful thing," he said. "Used to be that this kinda stuff only happened in Boston, not out here." Widdicomb took out a pad, licked the end of a pencil and started taking notes. He asked the expected questions, like the time it happened, if they saw anyone, whether the lights had been on in the boy's room. VJ quickly lost interest and disappeared into the kitchen.

After he ran out of questions, Widdicomb asked if they could take a gander around the yard.

"Please," Marsha said, motioning toward the door.

After the police left, Marsha turned to Victor. "Last night you told me not to worry about the threatening call, that you would look into it."

"I know . . ." Victor said guiltily. She waited for Victor to continue. But he didn't.

"A threatening phone call is one thing," Marsha said. "A brick through our child's window is quite another. I told you I couldn't handle any more surprises. I think you better give me some idea of these office problems you mentioned."

"Fair enough," Victor said. "But let me get a drink. I think I could use one."

VJ had the Johnny Carson show on in the family room and was watching, his head propped up against his arm. His eyes had a glazed look.

"Are you okay?" Marsha called from the doorway to the kitchen.

"Fine," VJ said without turning his head.

"I think we should let him unwind," Marsha said, directing her attention to Victor, who was busy making them a hot rum drink.

Mugs in hand, they sat down at the kitchen table. In capsule form, Victor highlighted the controversy with Ronald, the negotiations with Gephardt's attorney, Sharon Carver's threats, and the unfortunate situation with Hurst. "So there you have it," he concluded. "A normal week at the office."

Marsha mulled over the four troublemakers. Aside from Ronald, she guessed any of the other three could be guilty of acting out.

"What about this note?" she asked. "What deal is it referring to?"

Victor took a drink, put the mug on the table, then reached across and took the note. He studied it for a moment, then said, "I haven't the slightest idea. I haven't made any deals with anyone." He tossed the paper onto the table.

"Somebody must have thought you had," Marsha said.

"Look, anyone capable of throwing a rock through our window is capable of fantasizing some mythical deal. But I'll get in touch with each of them and make sure they know that we are not going to sit idly by and allow them to throw bricks through our windows."

"What about hiring some security?" Marsha asked.

"It's an idea," Victor said. "But let me make these calls tomorrow. I have a feeling that it will solve this problem."

The doorbell sounded again.

"I'll get it," said Victor. He put his mug on the table and left the kitchen.

Marsha got up and went into the family room. The TV was still on but Johnny Carson had changed to *David Letterman*. It was that late. VJ was fast asleep. Turning off the TV, Marsha looked at her son. He looked so peaceful. There was no hint of the intense hostility that he'd displayed earlier. Oh God, she thought, what had Victor's experiment done to her darling baby?

The front door banged shut, and Victor came in saying, "The police didn't find anything. They just said they'd try to watch the house best

557

they could over the next week or so." Then he looked down at VJ. "I see he has recovered."

"I wish," Marsha said wistfully.

"Oh, come on now," Victor said. "I don't want a lecture about his hostility and all that bull."

"Maybe he was really upset when his IQ fell," she said, following her own train of thought. "Can you imagine what kind of self-esteem loss the boy probably suffered when his special abilities evaporated?"

"The kid was only three and a half," Victor pleaded.

"I know you don't agree with me," Marsha said, looking back at the sleeping boy. "But I'm terrified. I can't believe your genetic experiment didn't affect his future."

The following morning the temperature had climbed to nearly sixty degrees by nine o'clock. The sun was out and Victor had both front windows open in the car as well as the sunroof. The air was fragrant with the earthy aroma that presaged spring. Victor pressed the accelerator and let the car loose on the short straightaways.

He glanced over at VJ, who seemed fully recovered from the previous night. He had his arm out the window and was playing with the wind with his open hand. It was a simple gesture, but so normal. Victor could remember doing it many times when he was VJ's age.

Looking at his son, Victor couldn't rid himself of Marsha's fears. He seemed fine, but could the implant have affected his development? VJ was a loner. In that regard he certainly didn't take after anyone else in the family.

"What's your friend Richie like?" Victor asked suddenly.

VJ shot him a look that was midway between vexation and disbelief. "You sound like Mother," he said.

Victor laughed. "I suppose I do. But really, what kinda kid is this Richie? How come we haven't met him?"

"He's okay," VJ said. "I see him every day at school. I don't know, we have different interests when we're at home. He watches a lot of TV."

"If you two want to go into Boston this week, I'll have someone from the office drive you."

"Thanks, Dad," VJ said. "I'll see what Richie says."

Victor settled back into his seat. Obviously the kid had friends. He made a mental note to remind Marsha about Richie that evening.

The moment Victor pulled into his parking space, Philip's hulking form appeared in front of the car as if by magic. Seeing VJ, a smile broke across his face. He grabbed the front of the car and gave it a shake.

"Good gravy," Victor said.

VJ jumped out of the car and gave the man a punch on the arm. Philip pretended to fall, backing up a few steps, clutching his arm. VJ laughed and the two started off.

"Wait a second, VJ," Victor called. "Where are you going?"

VJ turned and shrugged. "I don't know. The cafeteria or the library. Why? You want me to do something?"

"No," Victor said. "I just want to be sure you stay away from the river. This warm weather is only going to make it rise higher."

In the background Victor could hear the roar of the water going over the spillway.

"Don't worry," VJ said. "See you later."

Victor watched as they rounded the building, heading in the direction of the cafeteria. They certainly made an improbable pair.

In the office, Victor got right to work. Colleen gave him an update on all the issues that had to be addressed that day. Victor delegated what he could, the things he had to do himself he put in an orderly stack in the center of his desk. That done, he took out the note that had been wrapped around the brick.

"Remember our deal," Victor repeated. "What the hell does that mean?" Suddenly furious, he picked up the phone and called Gephardt's attorney, William Hurst, and Sharon Carver. He didn't give any of them a chance to talk. As soon as they were on the phone he shouted that there were no deals and that he'd put the police onto anyone who'd harassed his family.

Afterward he felt a little silly, but he hoped the guilty party would think twice before trying again. He did not call Ronald because he couldn't imagine his old friend stooping to violence.

With that taken care of, Victor picked up the first of Colleen's notes and started on the day's administrative duties.

Marsha's day was a seemingly endless stream of difficult patients until a cancellation just before lunch gave her an hour to review VJ's tests. Taking them out, she remembered the intensity of his anger over the thrown brick. She looked at clinical scale four that was supposed to reflect such suppressed hostility. VJ had scored well below what she would have expected with such behavior.

Marsha got up, stretched and stared out her office window. Unfortunately she looked over a parking lot, but beyond that there were some fields and rolling hills. All the trees in view still had that midwinter look of death, their branches like skeletons against the pale blue sky.

So much for psychological testing, she thought. She wished that she could have talked with Janice Fay. The woman had lived with them until her death in 1985. If anyone would have had insight into VJ's change in intelligence, it would have been Janice. The only other adult who had been close to VJ during that period was Martha Gillespie at the preschool. VJ had started before his second birthday.

On impulse, Marsha called to Jean: ''I think I'll be skipping lunch; you go whenever you want. Just don't forget to put the phone on service.''

Busy with the typewriter, Jean waved understanding.

Five minutes later, Marsha was going sixty-five miles an hour on the interstate. She only had to go one exit and was soon back to small country roads.

The Crocker Preschool was a charming ensemble of yellow cottages with white trim and white shutters on the grounds of a much larger estate house. Marsha wondered how the school made ends meet, but rumor had it that it was more of a hobby for Martha Gillespie. Martha had been widowed at a young age and left a fortune.

''Of course I remember VJ,'' Martha said with feigned indignation. Marsha had found her in the administrative cottage. She was about sixty, with snow white hair and cheery, rosy cheeks. ''I remember him vividly right from his first day with us. He was a most extraordinary boy.''

Marsha recalled the first day also. She'd brought VJ in early, worried about his response since he had not been away from home except when accompanied by Janice or herself. This was to be his first brush with such independence. But the adaptation had proved to be harder for Marsha than for her son, who ran into the middle of a group of children without even one backward glance.

''In fact,'' Martha said, ''I remember that by the end of his first day he had all the other children doing exactly what he wanted. And he wasn't even two!''

''Then you remember when VJ's intelligence fell?'' Marsha asked.

Martha paused while she studied Marsha. ''Yes, I remember,'' she said.

560

"What do you remember about him after this occurred?" Marsha asked.

"How is the boy today?"

"He's fine, I hope," Marsha said.

"Is there some reason you want to upset yourself by going through this?" Martha asked. "I remember how devastated you were back then."

"To be honest," Marsha said, "I'm terrified the same problem might happen again. I thought that if I learned more about the first episode, I might be able to prevent another."

"I don't know if I can help that much," Martha said. "There certainly was a big change, and it occurred so quickly. VJ went from being a confident child whose mind seemed infinite in its capability, to a withdrawn child who had few friends. But it wasn't as if he was autistic. Even though he stayed by himself, he was always uncannily aware of everything going on around him."

"Did he continue to relate to children his own age?" Marsha asked.

"Not very much," Martha said. "When we made him participate, he was always willing to go along, but left to his own devices, he'd just watch. You know, there was one thing that was curious. Every time we insisted that VJ participate in some kind of game, like musical chairs, he would always let the other children win. That was strange because prior to this, VJ won most of the games no matter what the age of the children involved."

"That is curious," Marsha said.

Later, when Marsha was driving back to her office, she kept seeing a three-and-a-half-year-old VJ letting other children win. It brought back the episode in the pool Sunday evening. In all her experience with young children, Marsha had never come across such a trait.

"Perfect!" Victor said as he held one of the microscope slides up to the overhead light. He could see the paper-thin section of brain sealed with a cover slip.

"That's the Golgi stain," Robert said. "You also have Cajal's and Bielschowsky's. If you want any others you'll have to let me know."

"Fine," Victor said. As usual, Robert had accomplished in less than twenty-four hours what would have taken a lesser technician several days.

"And here are the chromosome preparations," Robert said, handing Victor a tray. "Everything is labeled."

"Fine," Victor repeated.

Taking the preparations in his hands, Victor headed across the main room of the lab to the light microscopes. Seating himself before one, he placed the first slide under the instrument. It was labeled *Hobbs, right frontal lobe*.

Victor ran the scope down so that the objective was just touching the cover slip. Then, looking through the eyepieces, he corrected the focus.

"Good God!" he exclaimed as the image became clear. There was no sign of malignancy, but the effect was the same as if a tumor had been present. The children didn't die of cerebral edema, or an accumulation of fluid. Instead, what Victor saw was evidence of diffuse mitotic activity. The nerve cells of the brain were multiplying just as they did in the first two months of fetal development.

Victor quickly scanned slides of other areas of the Hobbs brain and then studied the Murray child's tissue. All of them were the same. The nerve cells were actively reproducing themselves at a furious rate. Since the children's skulls were fused, the new cells had nowhere to go other than to push the brain down into the spinal canal, with fatal results.

Horrified yet astounded at the same time, Victor snatched up the tray of slides and left the light microscope. He hurried across the lab and entered the room which housed the scanning electron microscope. The place had the appearance of a command center of a modern electronic weapons system.

The instrument itself looked very different from a normal microscope. It was about the size of a standard refrigerator. Its business portion was a cylinder approximately a foot in diameter and about three feet tall. A large electrical trunk entered the top of this cylinder and served as the source of electrons. The electrons were then focused by magnets which acted like glass lenses in a light microscope. Next to the scope was a good-sized computer. It was the computer that analyzed multiple-plano images of the electron microscope and constructed the three-dimensional pictures.

Robert had made extremely thin preparations of the chromatin material from some of the brain cells that were in the initial process of dividing. Victor placed one of these preparations within the scope and searched for chromosome six. What he was looking for was the area of mutation where he'd inserted the foreign genes. It took him over an hour, but at last he found it.

"Jesus," Victor gulped. The histones that normally enveloped the DNA were either missing or attenuated in the area of the inserted gene. In addition, the DNA, which was usually tightly coiled, had unraveled, suggesting that active transcription was taking place. In other words, the inserted genes were turned on!

Victor tried a preparation from the other child with the same results. The inserted genes were turned on, producing NGF. There was no doubt about it.

Switching to preparations made from VJ's blood, which must have taken much more patience on Robert's part since appropriate cells would have been harder to find, Victor introduced one within the electron microscope. Within thirty minutes he located chromosome six. Then, with painstaking effort, he scanned up and down the chromosome several times. The genes were quiescent. The area of the inserted gene was covered with the histone protein in the usual fashion.

Victor rocked back in the chair. VJ was all right, but the other two children had died as the result of his experiment. How could he ever tell Marsha? She would leave him. In fact, he wasn't sure he could live with himself.

Abruptly he stood up and paced the small room. What could have turned the gene back on? The only thing Victor could imagine was the ingestion of cephaloclor, the same antibiotic that he had used during the early embryological development. But how could these children have gotten the drug? It was not a common prescription, and the parents had been specifically warned that both children were deathly allergic to it. Victor was sure neither the Hobbs nor the Murrays would have permitted anyone to administer cephaloclor to their sons.

With both children dying at once, there was no way it could have been an accident. With a sudden chill of fear, Victor wondered if the area of chromosome six that he'd chosen to insert the manufactured genes was not an area of nonsense DNA as most people thought. Maybe its location in respect to an indigenous promoter caused the gene to turn on by some unknown mechanism. If that were the case, then VJ would indeed be at risk too. Perhaps his gene had turned on for a short burst of activity back when his intelligence fell.

Victor tried to swallow, but his mouth was too dry. Picking up all the samples, he went to the water fountain and took a drink. There were a number of lab assistants working in the main room, but Victor was in no mood to talk. He hurried into his research office and closed the door behind him. He tried calming himself, but just as the pounding of his heart began to ease he remembered the photomicrographs he'd made of VJ's chromosomes six and a half years ago.

Jumping to his feet, he dashed to the files and frantically searched until he came up with the photos he'd taken when VJ's intelligence fell. Studying them, he let out a sigh of relief. VJ's had not changed at all. His chromosome six looked exactly the same six and a half years ago as it did today. There was not even the slightest uncovering or unraveling of the DNA.

Breathing more easily, Victor left his office to find Robert. The technician was in the animal room, supervising Sharon Carver's replacement. Victor took him aside. "I'm afraid I have some more special work for you."

"You're the boss," Robert answered.

"There is an area on chromosome six in the brain samples where the DNA is exposed and unraveled. I want the DNA sequenced just as soon as you can."

"That is going to take some time," Robert said.

"I know it's tedious," Victor said. "But I have some radioactive probes you can use."

"That's altogether different."

Robert followed Victor back to his office and collected the myriad small bottles. For a few moments after he'd left, Victor stayed in his office, trying to come up with another explanation besides the cephaloclor. Why else would the NGF gene turn on in the two infants? At age two and a half to three, growth was decelerating, and there were no monumental physiological changes such as those that occurred at puberty.

The other curious fact was that the NGF gene had apparently turned on in the two children at the exact same time. That didn't make sense. The only way the two children's lives intersected at all was that both attended the day-care center at Chimera. That was another reason Victor had selected the two couples. He'd wanted an opportunity to view the children during their development. He had also made sure that the Hobbses and the Murrays did not know each other before they became parents. He didn't want them comparing notes and getting suspicious.

Reaching across his desk for the phone, Victor called personnel and got the bereaved families' home addresses. He wrote them down, then went to tell Colleen that he'd be out for several hours.

Victor decided on the Hobbses first because it was closer. They lived in an attractive brick ranch in a town called Haverhill. Victor pulled up to the front of the house and rang the bell.

"Dr. Frank," William Hobbs said with surprise. He opened the door wider, and gestured for Victor to enter. "Sheila!" he called. "We have company!"

Victor stepped inside. Although the house was pleasantly decorated in a contemporary fashion, an oppressive silence hung over the rooms like a shroud.

"Come in, come in," William said, escorting Victor into the living room. "Coffee? Tea?" His voice echoed in the stillness.

Sheila Hobbs came into the room. She was a dynamic woman with bobbed hair. Victor had met her at several of the obligatory Chimera social occasions.

Victor agreed to some coffee, and soon all three were sitting in the living room, balancing tiny Wedgwood cups on their knees.

"I was just thinking about giving you a call," William said. "It's such a coincidence that you stopped by."

"Oh?" Victor said.

"Sheila and I have decided to get back to work," William said, directing his attention at his coffee cup. "At first we thought we'd get away for a while. But now we think we'll feel better with something to do."

"We'll be pleased to have you back, whenever you choose," said Victor.

"We appreciate that," William said.

Victor cleared his throat. "There is something I wanted to ask you," he began. "I believe you'd been warned that your son was allergic to an antibiotic called cephaloclor."

"That's right," Sheila said. "We'd been told that before we even picked him up." She lowered her coffee cup and it rattled against the saucer.

"Is there any chance that your son had been given cephaloclor?" Victor asked.

The couple looked at each other, then answered in unison: "No." Then Sheila continued: "Maurice hadn't been sick or anything. Besides, we'd made sure that his antibiotic allergy was part of his medical

565

record. I'm certain he'd not been given any antibiotic. Why do you ask?''

Victor stood up. "It was just a thought. I didn't think he would have, but I'd remembered about the allergy . . .''

Back in his car, Victor headed toward Boston. He was pretty certain the Murrays would tell him the same thing the Hobbses had, but he had to be sure.

Since it was the middle of the afternoon, he made excellent time. His major problem was what to do with his car when he got there. Eventually he found a spot on Beacon Hill. A sign said it was a tow zone, but Victor decided to take the chance.

The Murrays' house was on West Cedar, in the middle of the block. He rang the bell.

The door was opened by a man in his late twenties or early thirties, sporting a punk hair style.

"Are the Murrays in?'' Victor asked.

"They're both at work,'' the man said. "I work for their cleaning service.''

"I thought they'd taken some time off.''

The man laughed. "Those workaholics! They took one day after their son died and that was it.''

Victor returned to his car, irritated with himself for not having called before coming. It would have saved him a trip.

Back at Chimera, Victor went directly to the accounting department. He found Horace Murray at his desk, bent over computer printouts. When the man saw Victor he sprang to his feet saying, "Colette and I wanted to thank you again for coming to the hospital.''

"I only wish I could have done something to help,'' Victor said.

"It was in God's hands,'' Horace said resignedly.

When Victor asked him about the cephaloclor, the man swore that Mark had not been given an antibiotic, especially not cephaloclor.

Leaving the accounting department, Victor was struck by still another fear. What if there was a link between the deaths and the fact that the children's files were missing? That was the most disturbing thought of all because it implied that the genes had been turned on deliberately.

Heart pounding again, Victor ran back to his lab. One of his newer technicians tried to ask a question, but Victor waved the man away, telling him to talk to Grimes if he had a problem.

Inside his office Victor bent down in front of a cabinet at the bottom of his bookcase. He unlocked the heavy door and reached in to grasp the NGF data books that he'd written in code. But his hand met empty space. The entire shelf was empty.

Victor closed the cabinet and carefully locked it even though there was no longer anything to protect.

"Calm down," he told himself, trying to stem a rising tide of paranoia. "You're letting your imagination run away with itself. There has to be an explanation."

Getting up, he went out to find Robert. He tracked him down in the electrophoresis unit, working on the task that Victor had earlier assigned him. "Have you seen my NGF data books?" Victor asked.

"I don't know where they are," Robert said. "I haven't seen them for six months. I thought you'd moved them."

Mumbling his thanks, Victor walked away. This was no longer some fantasy. The evidence was mounting. Someone had interfered in his experiment, with lethal results. Deciding to face his worst apprehensions, Victor went over to the liquid nitrogen freezer. He put his hand on the latch and hesitated. Intuition told him what he would find, but he had to force himself to raise the hood. He kept hearing Marsha telling him that he had to destroy the other five zygotes right away.

Slowly he looked down. At first his view was blocked by the frozen mist as it floated out of the storage container and spilled silently to the floor. Then it cleared, and he saw the plate that contained the embryos. It was empty.

For a moment Victor supported himself by leaning against the freezer, staring at the empty tray, not wanting to believe what his eyes were clearly telling him. Then he let the lid fall shut. The cool nitrogen mist swirled about his legs as if it were alive. He staggered back to his office and fell into the chair. Someone else knew about his NGF work! But who could it be and why had they intentionally brought about the babies' deaths, or had that been an accident? Was someone so intent on destroying Victor that they didn't care who else was hurt? Suddenly Hurst's threats took on a new dimension.

With a wave of apprehension, Victor realized that he had to find out who was behind all these strange events. He rose from the chair and began to pace, remembering with a start that David had died soon after the battle for taking Chimera public. Could his death have been involved as well? Could Ronald be involved? No, that was ridiculous.

David had died of liver cancer, not poisoning or an accident that someone could have caused. Even the idea that the Hobbs and Murray children had been intentionally killed was preposterous. Their deaths had to be an intracellular phenomenon. Maybe there had been a second mutation caused by the freezing which he would see when Robert completed the DNA sequencing.

Telling himself to calm down and think logically, he headed over to the computer center to see Louis Kaspwicz. The piece of hardware Louis had been working on had been reduced to an empty metal shell. Surrounding it were hundreds of parts and pieces.

"I hate to bother you again," Victor said, "but I need to know the time of day when my files were deleted," Victor said. "I'm trying to figure out how I did it."

"If it's any consolation," Louis said, "lots of people accidentally delete their files. I wouldn't be too hard on yourself. As for the time, I think it was around nine or ten o'clock."

"Could I look at the log itself?" Victor asked. He thought that if he'd accessed the computer before or after the deletion, it might give him a clue about why he did it.

"Dr. Frank," Louis said with one of his distracting twitches, "this is your company. You can look at whatever you want."

They went back to Louis's office and he gave the November 18 log to Victor. Victor scanned through the print-out. He couldn't find any entry between eight-thirty and ten-thirty.

"I don't see it," Victor admitted.

Louis came around the desk to look over Victor's shoulder. "That's odd," he said, checking the date on the top of the page. "November 18, all right!" He looked back at the entries. "Oh, for God's sake!" he exclaimed. "No wonder you couldn't find it. You were looking in the A.M. section." Louis handed the printout back, pointing to the entry in question.

"P.M.?" Victor asked, looking at the correct place on the sheet. "That couldn't be. At 9:45 P.M. I was in Symphony Hall in Boston."

"What can I say?" Louis said with a twitch.

"Are you certain that this is correct?" Victor asked.

"Absolutely." Louis pointed to the entries before and after. "See how it's sequenced? It has to be the right time. Are you sure you were at the symphony?"

"Yes," Victor said.

"You didn't use the phone?"

"What are you talking about?" Victor asked.

"Just that this entry was made off-site. See this access number? That's for your PC at home."

"But I wasn't at home," Victor complained.

Louis's shoulders jerked spasmodically. "In that case, there's only one explanation," he said. "The entry had to have been made by someone who knows your password as well as the unpublished phone number of our computer. Have you ever given your password to anyone?"

"Never," Victor said without hesitation.

"How often do you access the computer from home?" Louis inquired.

"Almost never," Victor said. "I used to do it frequently, but that was years ago when the company was just starting."

"Good lord!" Louis said, staring at the print-out.

"What now?" asked Victor.

"I hate to tell you this, but there have been a lot of entries into the computer on a regular basis with your password. And that can only mean that some hacker has found our telephone number."

"Isn't that difficult?" Victor asked.

Louis shook his head. "The phone number is the easy part. Just like the kid did in *War Games*. You can program your computer to make endless calls using permutations. As soon as you stumble on a computer tone, that's when the fun begins."

"And this hacker used the computer frequently?"

"Sure did," Louis said. "I've noticed the entries, but I always thought it was you. Look!"

Louis flipped open the log and pointed to a series of entries using Victor's password. "It's usually Friday nights." He flipped the pages and showed other entries. "Must be when the kid is out of school. What a pain in the ass! Here's another one. Look, the hacker'd logged into Personnel and Purchasing. God, this makes me sick. We've been having some problem with files and I wonder if this kid is the source. I think we'd better change your password right away."

"But then we stand less chance of catching him. I don't use my password much anyway. Why don't we keep watch on Friday evenings and see if we can trace him. You can do that, can't you?"

"It's possible," Louis agreed, "if the kid stays on line long enough and the telephone people are standing by."

"See if you can arrange it," Victor said.

"I'll try. There's only one thing that's worse than a meddlesome hacker and that's a computer virus. But in this case I'll put my money on the hacker."

As Victor left the computer center, he thought he'd better check up on VJ. Given the day's developments he thought he better warn him to stay away from Hurst and even Ronald Beekman.

The first place Victor looked was the lab, but Robert had not seen him or Philip all day. Nor had any of the other technicians. This surprised Victor, since VJ spent most of his time trying out the various microscopes and other equipment. Victor decided to try the cafeteria. Since it was late afternoon there were only a few scattered people having coffee. Victor talked with the manager, who was busy closing out the cash registers. He'd seen VJ around lunchtime, but not since then.

Leaving the cafeteria, Victor stopped in the library, which was in the same building. The circular cement columns that had been added for structural support had been left in plain sight, giving the area a Gothic feeling. The stacks for books and periodicals were shoulder height, affording a view of the entire room. A comfortable reading area to the right looked out over the inner courtyard of the complex.

When Victor asked the librarian if she'd seen VJ or Philip, she shook her head no. With rising concern, Victor checked out the gym and day-care center. No VJ and no Philip.

Returning to his lab prepared to call security, Victor found a message from the manager of the cafeteria, saying VJ and Philip had come in for ice cream.

Victor went to the cafeteria. He found the two sitting at a table near the window.

"All right, you two," Victor said with mock anger. "Where the devil have you been?"

VJ turned to look at his father. He had his spoon in his mouth upside down. Philip, obviously thinking that Victor was angry, stood up, with his large, shovel-like hands not knowing what to do with themselves.

"We've been around," VJ said evasively.

"Where?" Victor challenged. "I've looked high and low for you."

"We were down by the river for a while," VJ admitted.

"I thought I told you to stay away from the river."

"Oh, come on, Dad," VJ said. "We weren't doing anything dangerous."

"I would never let anything bad happen to VJ," Philip said in his childlike voice.

"I don't imagine you would," Victor said, suddenly impressed by what a powerfully built man Philip was. He and VJ were an improbable pair, but Victor certainly appreciated Philip's loyalty to his son. "Sit down," Victor said more kindly. "Finish your ice cream."

Pulling up a chair himself, Victor turned to his son. "I want you to be especially careful around here for a while. After that brick last night, I'm sure you've guessed that there are some problems."

"I'll be all right," VJ said.

"I'm sure you will," Victor agreed. "But a little prudence won't hurt. Don't say anything to anybody, but keep your eyes open when Beekman or Hurst are around, okay?"

"Okay," VJ said.

"And you," Victor said to Philip. "You can act as VJ's unofficial bodyguard. Can you do that?"

"Oh, yes, Dr. Frank," Philip said with alacrity.

"In fact . . ." Victor said, knowing Marsha would appreciate the idea, "why don't you come and spend a few nights with us like you used to when VJ was little. Then you can be with VJ even in the evenings."

"Thank you, Dr. Frank," Philip said with a smile that exposed most of his large teeth. "I'd like that very much."

"Then it's settled," Victor said, getting to his feet. "I've got to get back to the office; I've been running around all day. We'll probably be leaving in a couple of hours. We can stop by Philip's to pick up his things on the way home."

Both VJ and Philip waved at Victor with their ice cream spoons.

Marsha was just taking the groceries out of the bag when she heard Victor's car come up the drive. As Victor waited for the automatic garage door to rise, Marsha noticed a third head in the back seat and groaned. She'd only bought six small lamb chops.

Two minutes later they came into the kitchen. "I've invited Philip to stay with us for a few days," Victor said. "I thought with all the excitement around here it would be good to have some muscle in the house."

"Sounds good," Marsha said, but then she added, "I hope that's not in lieu of professional security."

571

Victor laughed. "Not quite." Turning to VJ and Philip, he said, "Why don't you two hit the pool?"

VJ and Philip disappeared upstairs to change.

Victor moved as if to kiss Marsha, but she was back to digging in the grocery bag. Then she stepped around him to put some things in the pantry. He could tell she was still angry and, given the previous evening's events, he knew she had good reason to be.

"Sorry about Philip; it was a last-minute idea," he said. "But I don't think we'll have any more bricks or calls, anyway. I phoned the people who might have threatened us and laid it on the line."

"Then how come Philip?" asked Marsha, coming back from the pantry.

"Just an added precaution," Victor said. Then, to change the subject, he added: "What's for dinner?"

"Lamp chops—and we'll have to stretch them," Marsha said, looking at Victor out of the corner of her eye. "Why do I have the feeling that you're still keeping things from me?"

"Must be your suspicious nature," Victor said, even though he knew she was in no mood for teasing. "What else besides lamb chops?" he asked, trying to change the subject.

"Artichokes, rice, and salad." It was obvious that he was covering something, but she let it go.

"What can I do?" Victor asked, washing his hands at the kitchen sink. It was generally their habit to share the preparation of the evening meal since they both worked long hours. Marsha told him to rinse the salad greens.

"I talked with VJ this morning about his friend Richie," Victor said. "He's going to ask him to go to Boston for a day's outing this week so I don't think it's fair to say that VJ doesn't have any friends."

"I hope it happens," Marsha said noncommittally.

As she put the rice and artichokes on to cook, she continued to watch Victor out of the corner of her eye. She was hoping that he'd volunteer some information about the two unfortunate babies, but he fussed over the salad in silence. Exasperated, Marsha asked: "Any news about the cause of death of the children?"

Victor turned to face her. "I looked at the inserted gene in VJ as well as in the Hobbs and Murray kids. In the toddlers it appeared overtly abnormal, like it was actively transcribing, but in VJ it looked absolutely quiet. What's more," he added, "I got out some photos of

572

the same gene back when VJ's intelligence dropped. Even then it didn't look anything like these kids'. So whatever VJ had, it wasn't the same problem.''

Marsha gave a sigh of relief. ''That's good news. Why didn't you tell me right away?''

''I just got home,'' Victor said. ''And I'm telling you.''

''You could have called,'' Marsha said, convinced he was still hiding something. ''Or brought it up without my asking.''

''I'm having the dead kids' genes sequenced,'' Victor said, getting out the oil and vinegar. ''Then maybe I'll be able to tell you what turned the gene back on.''

Marsha went to the cupboard and got out the dishes to set the table. She tried to control the rage that was beginning to reassert itself. How could he remain so casual about all this? When Victor asked if there were anything else he could do for dinner, she told him he'd done enough. He took her literally and sat on one of the kitchen counter stools, watching her set the table.

''VJ's letting you win that swimming race wasn't a fluke,'' Marsha said, hoping to goad her husband. ''He started doing that when he was three.'' Marsha went on to tell him what Martha Gillespie had said about his behavior in nursery school.

''How can you be so sure he threw the race?'' Victor asked.

''My goodness, that still bothers you,'' said Marsha, turning down the burner under the rice. ''I was pretty sure he did when I was watching Sunday night. Now that I talked with Martha, I'm positive. It's as if VJ doesn't want to draw attention to himself.''

''Sometimes by throwing a race you attract more attention,'' Victor said.

''Maybe,'' Marsha added, but she wasn't convinced. ''The point is I wish to God I knew more about what went on in his mind when his intelligence changed so dramatically. It might give some explanation for his current behavior. Back then we were too concerned with his health to worry about his feelings.''

''I think he weathered the episode extremely well,'' Victor said. He went to the refrigerator and took out a bottle of white wine. ''I know you don't agree with me, but I think he's doing great. He's a happy kid. I'm proud of him. I think he's going to make one hell of a researcher one day. He really loves the lab.''

''Provided his intelligence doesn't fall again,'' Marsha snapped.

ROBIN COOK

"But I'm not worried about his ability to work. I'm worried your unspeakable experiment has interfered with his human qualities." She turned away to hide new tears as emotion welled up within her. When all this was over she didn't see how she could stay married to Victor. But would VJ ever be willing to leave his precious lab and live with her?

"You psychiatrists . . ." Victor muttered as he got out the corkscrew.

Marsha gave the rice a stir and checked the artichokes. She struggled to control herself. She didn't want more tears. She didn't speak for a few minutes. When she did, she said, "I wish I'd kept a diary of VJ's development. It would really be helpful."

"I kept one," Victor said, pulling out the cork with a resounding pop.

"You did?" Marsha asked. "Why didn't you ever tell me?"

"Because it was for the NGF project."

"Can I see it?" Marsha asked, again swallowing her anger at Victor's arrogance, using her baby as a guinea pig.

Victor tasted the wine. "It's in my study. I'll show it to you later after VJ is in bed."

Marsha was sitting in Victor's study. She'd insisted on reading the diary alone because she knew Victor's presence would only upset her more. Her eyes filled with tears as she relived VJ's birth. Even though much of the record was no more than a standard laboratory account, she was painfully moved by it. She'd forgotten how VJ's eyes had followed her from birth, long before an average baby's had even begun to track.

All the usual milestones had been reached at incredibly early ages, particularly the ability to speak. At seven months, when VJ was supposed to be pronouncing no more than "Mama" and "Dada," he was already composing sentences. By one year he had a whole vocabulary. By eighteen months, when he was supposed to be able to walk reasonably well, he could ride a small bicycle that Victor had had specially made.

Reading the history made Marsha remember how exciting it had been. Every day had been marked by a mastery of some different task and the uncovering of a new and unexpected ability. She realized she had been guilty too of reveling in VJ's unique accomplishments. At the time she had given very little thought to the impact of the child's precociousness on his personal development. As a psychologist, she should have known better.

Victor came in with some flimsy excuse about needing a book as she reached a section labeled "mathematics." Discomforted by her own shortcomings as a caring parent, she let him stay as she continued reading. Math had always been her *bete noire*. In college she'd had to be tutored to get through the required calculus course. When VJ began to demonstrate an exceptional facility with numbers, she had been astounded. At three VJ actually explained in terms she could understand the basis for calculus. For the first time in her life, Marsha properly comprehended the principles.

"What amazed me," Victor was saying, "was his ability to translate mathematical equations into music."

Marsha remembered, thinking they had another Beethoven on their hands. "And I never thought to worry if the burden of genius was more than a toddler could handle," she thought with regret. Sadly, she flipped the next few pages and was surprised to see the diary come to an end.

"I hope this isn't all," she said.

"I'm afraid so."

Marsha read the final pages. The last entry was for May 6, 1982. It described the experience in the day-care center at Chimera that Marsha remembered so vividly. It then dispassionately summarized VJ's sudden diminution in intelligence. The last sentence read: "VJ appears to have suffered an acute alteration in cerebral function that now appears stable."

"You never made any further entries?" asked Marsha.

"No," Victor admitted. "I thought the experiment was a failure despite its initial success. There didn't seem to be any reason to continue the narrative."

Marsha closed the book. She had hoped to find more clues to what she considered the deficiencies in VJ's personality. "I wish his history pointed to some psychosomatic illness or even a conversion reaction. Then he might be responsive to therapy. I just wish I'd been more sensitive back when all this happened."

"I think VJ's problem was the result of some sort of intracellular phenomenon," Victor offered. "I don't think the history would make much difference anyway."

"That's what terrifies me," said Marsha. "It makes me afraid that VJ is going to die like the Hobbs and Murray children, or of cancer like his brother, or Janice for that matter. I've read enough about your work to know that cancer is a big worry for the future of gene therapy. People are worried that inserted genes might cause proto-oncogenes to become oncogenes, turning the involved cell into a cancer."

She broke off. She could feel her emotions taking over. "How can I go on talking about this as if it were simply a scientific problem? It's our son—and for all I know you triggered something inside him that will make him die."

Marsha covered her face with her hands. Despite her attempts to control herself, tears returned. She let herself cry.

Victor tried to put his arm around her, but she leaned away. Frustrated, he stood up. He watched her for a moment, with her shoulders silently shaking. There was nothing he could say in defense. Instead, he left the room and started upstairs. The pain of his own grief was overwhelming. And after what he'd discovered today, he had more reason than his wife to fear for VJ's safety.

8

THURSDAY MORNING

Wondering how the other people put up with it on a daily basis, Victor suffered the congested traffic of a normal Boston rush hour.

Once he got on Storrow Drive heading west, traffic improved, only to slow down again near the Fenway. It was after nine when he finally entered the busy Children's Hospital. He went directly to Pathology.

"Dr. Shryack, please?" Victor asked. The secretary glanced up at him and, without removing her dictation headset, pointed down the corridor.

Victor looked at the nameplates as he walked.

"Excuse me. Dr. Shryack?" Victor called as he stepped through the open door. The extraordinarily young-looking man raised his head from a microscope.

"I'm Dr. Frank," Victor said. "Remember when I stopped in while you were autopsying the Hobbs baby?"

"Of course," said Dr. Shryack. He stood up and extended his hand. "Nice to meet you under more pleasant circumstances. The name is Stephen."

Victor shook his hand.

"I'm afraid we haven't any definitive diagnosis yet," Stephen said, "if that is what you've come for. The slides are still being processed."

"I'm interested, of course," Victor said. "But the reason I stopped

577

by was to ask another favor. I was curious if you routinely take fluid samples."

"Absolutely," Stephen answered. "We always do toxicology, at least a screen."

"I was hoping to get some of the fluid myself," Victor said.

"I'm impressed with your interest," Stephen said. "Most internists give us a rather wide berth. Come on, let's see what we have."

Stephen led Victor out of his office, down the hall, and into the extensive laboratory where he stopped to speak to a severely dressed middle-aged woman. The conversation lasted for a minute before she pointed toward the opposite end of the room. Stephen then led Victor down the length of the lab and into a side room.

"I think we're in luck." Stephen opened the doors to a large cooler on the far wall and began searching through the hundreds of stoppered Erlenmeyer flasks. He found one and handed it back to Victor. Soon he found three others.

Victor noticed he had two flasks of blood and two of urine.

"How much do you need?" Stephen asked.

"Just a tiny bit," Victor said.

Stephen carefully poured a little from each flask into test tubes that he got from a nearby counter top. He capped them, labeled each with a red grease pencil, and handed them to Victor.

"Anything else?" Stephen asked.

"Well, I hate to take advantage of your generosity," Victor said.

"It's quite all right," Stephen said.

"About five years ago, my son died of a very rare liver cancer," Victor began.

"I'm so sorry."

"He was treated here. At the time the doctors said there had only been a couple of similar cases in the literature. The thought was that the cancer had arisen from the Kupffer cells so that it really was a cancer of the reticuloendothelial system."

Stephen nodded. "I think I read about that case. In fact, I'm sure I did."

"Since the tumor was so rare," Victor said, "do you think that any gross material was saved?"

"There's a chance," Stephen said. "Let's go back to my office."

When Stephen was settled in front of his computer terminal, he asked Victor for David's full name and birth date. Entering that, he obtained David's hospital number and located the pathology record.

With his finger on the screen, he scanned the information. His finger stopped. "This looks encouraging. Here's a specimen number. Let's check it out."

This time he took Victor down to the subbasement. "We have a crypt where we put things for long-term storage," he explained.

They stepped off the elevator into a dimly lit hall that snaked off in myriad directions. There were pipes and ducts along the ceiling, the floor a bare, stained concrete.

"We don't get to come down here that often," Stephen said as he led the way through the maze. He finally stopped at a heavy metal door. When Victor helped pull it open, Stephen reached in and flipped on a light.

It was a large, poorly lit room with widely spaced bulbs in simple ceiling fixtures. The air was cold and humid. Numerous rows of metal shelves reached almost to the ceiling.

Checking a number that he had written on a scrap of paper, Stephen set off down one of the rows. Victor followed, glancing into the shelves. At one point he stopped, transfixed by the image of an entire head of a child contained in a large glass canister and soaking in some kind of preservative brine. The eyes stared out and the mouth was open as if in some perpetual scream. Victor looked at the other glass containers. Each contained some horrifying preserved testament to past suffering. He shuddered, then realized that Stephen had passed from sight.

Looking nervously around, he heard the resident call. "Over here."

Victor strode forward, no longer looking at the specimens. When he reached the corner, he saw the pathologist reaching into one of the shelves, noisily pushing around the glass containers. "Eureka!" he said, straightening up. He had a modest-sized glass jar in his hands that contained a bulbous liver suspended in clear fluid. "You're in luck," he said.

Later, on the way up in the elevator, he asked Victor why he wanted the tissue.

"Curiosity," Victor said. "When David died my grief was so overwhelming I didn't ask any questions. Now after all these years, I want to know more about why he died."

Marsha drove VJ and Philip through the Chimera gates. During the drive VJ had chatted about a new Pac-Man video just like any other ten-year-old.

"Thanks for the lift, Mom," he said, jumping out.

"Let Colleen know where you're playing," she said. "And I want you to stay away from the river. You saw what it looked like from the bridge."

Philip got out from the back seat. "Nothing's going to happen to VJ," he said.

"Are you sure you wouldn't rather go over to your friend Richie's?" Marsha questioned.

"I'm happy here," VJ said. "Don't worry about me, okay?"

Marsha watched VJ stride off with Philip rushing to catch up. "What a pair," she thought, trying to keep last night's revelation from panicking her.

She parked the car and headed for the day-care center. As she entered the building she could hear the thwack of a racquetball. The courts were on the floor above, in the fitness center.

Marsha found Pauline Spaulding kneeling on the floor, supervising a group of children who were finger-painting. She leaped up when she saw Marsha, her figure giving proof to all those years as an aerobics instructor.

When Marsha asked for a few minutes of her time, Pauline left the kids and went off to find another teacher. After she returned with a younger woman in tow, she led Marsha to another room filled with cribs and folding cots.

"We'll have some privacy here," Pauline said. Her large oval eyes looked nervously at Marsha, who she assumed had come on official business for her husband.

"I'm not here as the wife of one of the partners," Marsha said, trying to put Pauline at ease.

"I see." Pauline took a deep breath and smiled. "I thought you had some major complaint."

"Quite the contrary," Marsha said. "I wanted to talk to you about my son."

"Wonderful boy," Pauline said. "I suppose you know that he comes in here from time to time and helps out. In fact, he visited us just last weekend."

"I didn't know the center was open on weekends," Marsha said.

"Seven days a week," Pauline said with pride. "A lot of people here at Chimera work every day. I suppose that's called dedication."

Marsha wasn't sure she'd call it dedication, and she wondered what kind of stress such devotion would have on family life that was already suffering. But she didn't say any of this. Instead, she asked Pauline if she remembered the day VJ's IQ dropped.

"Of course I remember. The fact that it happened here has always made me feel responsible sómehow."

"Well, that's plainly absurd," Marsha said with a warm smile. "What I wanted to ask about was VJ's behavior afterwards."

Pauline looked down at her feet, thinking. After a minute or so, she raised her head. "I suppose the thing I noticed the most was that he'd changed from a leader of activities to an observer. Before, he was always eager to try anything. Later, he acted bored and had to be forced to participate. And he avoided all competition. It was as if he were a different person. We didn't push him; we were afraid to. Anyway, we saw much less of him after that episode."

"What do you mean?" Marsha asked. "Once he finished his medical work-up, he still came here every afternoon after preschool."

"No, he didn't," Pauline said. "He began to spend most of the time in his father's lab."

"Really? I didn't think that started until he began school. But what do I know, I'm just the mother!"

Pauline smiled.

"What about friends?" Marsha questioned.

"That was never one of VJ's strong points," Pauline said diplomatically. "He always got along better with the staff than the children. After his problem, he tended to stay by himself. Well, I take that back. He did seem to enjoy the company of the retarded employee."

"You mean Philip?" Marsha questioned.

"That's the fellow," Pauline said.

Marsha stood up, thanked Pauline, and together they walked to the entrance.

"VJ may not be quite as smart as he was," Pauline said at the door, "but he is a fine boy. We appreciate him here at the center."

Marsha hurried back to the car. She hadn't learned much, but it seemed VJ had always been even more of a loner than she had suspected.

Victor knew he should go to his office the moment he reached Chimera. Colleen was undoubtedly inundated by emergencies. But instead, carrying his latest samples from Children's Hospital, he headed for his lab. En route he stopped at the computer center.

Victor looked for Louis Kaspwicz around the malfunctioning hard-

ROBIN COOK

ware, but the problem had apparently been solved. The machine
was back on line with lights blinking and tape reels running. One
of the many white-coated technicians said Louis was in his office
trying to figure out a glitch that had occurred in one of the accounting
programs.

When Louis saw Victor, he pushed aside the thick program he was
working on and took out the log sheets that he was saving to show
Victor.

"I've checked over the last six months," Louis said, organizing the
papers for Victor to see, "and underlined the times the hacker has
logged on. It seems the kid checks in every Friday night around eight.
At least fifty percent of the time he stays on long enough to be traced."

"How come you say 'kid'?" Victor asked, straightening up from
glancing at the logs.

"It's just an expression," Louis answered. "Somebody who breaks
into a private computer system could be any age."

"Like one of our competitors?" Victor said.

"Exactly, but historically there's been a lot of teenagers that do it
just for the challenge. It's like some kind of computer game for them."

"When can we try to trace him?" Victor asked.

"As soon as possible," Louis said. "It terrifies me that this has
been going on for so long. I have no idea what kind of mischief this
guy has been up to. Anyway, I talked the phone company into sending
over some technicians to watch tomorrow night, if it's all right with
you."

"Fine," Victor said.

That settled, Victor continued on to his lab. He found Robert still
absorbed in sequencing the DNA of the inserted genes.

"I've got some more rush work," Victor said hurriedly. "If you
need to, pull one of the other techs off a project to help, but I want
you to be personally responsible for this work."

"I'll get Harry if it's necessary," Robert said. "What do you have?"

Victor opened the brown paper bag and removed a small jar. He
extended it toward Robert. His hand trembled.

"It's a piece of my son's liver."

"VJ's?" Robert's gaunt face looked shocked. His eyes seemed even
more prominent.

"No, no, David's. Remember we did DNA fingerprinting on everyone in my family?"

Robert nodded.

"I want that tumor fingerprinted, too," Victor said. "And I want some standard H and E stains and a chromosome study."

"Can I ask why you want all this?"

"Just do it," Victor said sharply.

"All right," Robert said, nervously looking down at his feet. "I wasn't questioning your motives. I just thought that if you were looking for something in particular, I could keep an eye out for it."

Victor ran his hand through his hair. "I'm sorry for snapping at you like that," he said. "I'm under a lot of pressure."

"No need to apologize," Robert said. "I'll start work on it right now."

"Wait, there's more," Victor said. He removed the four stoppered test tubes. "I've got some blood and urine samples I need assayed for a cephalosporin antibiotic called cephaloclor."

Robert took the samples, tilted them to see their consistency, then checked the grease-pencil labels. "I'll put Harry on this. It will be pretty straightforward."

"How is the sequencing coming?" Victor asked.

"Tedious, as usual," Robert said.

"Any mutations pop up?"

"Not a one," Robert said. "And the way the probes pick up the fragments, I'd guess at this point that the genes have been perfectly stable."

"That's unfortunate," Victor said.

"I thought you'd be pleased with that information," Robert said.

"Normally I would," Victor said. He didn't elaborate. It would have been too hard for him to explain that he was hoping to find concrete evidence that the dead children's NGF gene differed from VJ's.

"So here you are!" a voice called, startling both Victor and Robert. They turned to see Colleen standing at the door, legs apart and arms akimbo. "One of the secretaries told me she saw you creeping around," she said with a wink.

"I was just about to come over to the office," Victor said defensively.

"Sure, and I'm about to win the lottery," Colleen laughed.

"I suppose the office is bedlam?" Victor asked sheepishly.

"Now he thinks he's indispensable," Colleen joked to Robert. "Actually, things aren't too bad. I've handled most of what has come up. But there is something that you should know right away.''

"What is it?" said Victor, suddenly concerned.

"Perhaps I could talk to you in private?" Colleen said. She smiled at Robert to indicate she did not mean to be rude.

"Of course," Victor said awkwardly. He moved across the lab to one of the benches. Colleen followed.

"It's about Gephardt," Colleen said. "Darryl Webster, who's in charge of the investigation, has been trying to get you all day. He finally told me what it was all about. Seems that he has uncovered a slew of irregularities. While Gephardt was purchasing supervisor for Chimera a lot of laboratory equipment vanished.''

"Like what?" Victor questioned.

"Big-ticket items," Colleen said. "Fast protein liquid chromatography units, DNA sequencers, mass spectrometers, things like that.''

"Good God!"

"Darryl thought you should know," Colleen added.

"Did he find bogus orders?''

"No," Colleen said. "That's what makes it so weird. Receiving got the equipment. It just never went to the department that was supposed to have ordered it. And the department in question never said anything because they hadn't placed the order.''

"So Gephardt fenced it," Victor said, amazed. "No wonder his attorney was so hot to cut a deal. He knew what we would find.''

Angrily, Victor remembered that the note around the brick referred to a deal. In all likelihood, Gephardt had been behind the harassment.

"I assume we have the bastard's telephone number," Victor said with venom.

"I guess," Colleen said. "Should be in his employee record.''

"I want to give Gephardt a call. I'm tired of talking through that lawyer of his.''

On the way back to the administration building, Colleen had to run to keep up with Victor. She'd never seen him so angry.

He was still fuming as he dialed Gephardt's number, motioning for Colleen to stay in the room so she could be a witness to what was said. But the phone rang interminably. "Damn it!" Victor cursed. "The bastard either is out or he's not answering. What's his address?''

Colleen looked it up and found a street number in Lawrence, not far from Chimera.

"I think I'll stop and pay the man a visit on the way home," Victor said. "I have a feeling he's been to my house. It's time I return the call."

When one of her patients called in sick, Marsha decided to use the hour to visit Pendleton Academy, the private school that VJ had been attending since kindergarten.

The campus was beautiful even though the trees were still bare and the grass a wintry brown. The stone buildings were covered with ivy, giving the appearance of an old college or university.

Marsha pulled up to the administration building and got out. She wasn't as familiar with the school as she might have been. Although she and Victor had made regular Parents' Day visits, she'd met the headmaster, Perry Remington, on only two occasions. She hoped he would see her.

When she entered the building she was pleased to find a number of secretaries busy at their desks. At least it wasn't a vacation week for the staff. Mr. Remington was in his office and was kind enough to see Marsha within a few minutes.

He was a big man with a full, well-trimmed beard. His bushy brows poked over the top of his horn-rimmed glasses.

"We are always delighted to see parents," Mr. Remington said, offering her a chair. He sat down, crossed his legs, and balanced a manila folder on his knee. "What's on your mind?"

"I'm curious about my son, VJ," Marsha said. "I'm a psychiatrist and to be honest with you, I'm a bit worried about him. I know his grades are good, but I wondered how he was doing generally." Marsha paused. She didn't want to put words into Mr. Remington's mouth.

The headmaster cleared his throat. "When they told me you were outside, I quickly reviewed VJ's record," he said. He tapped the folder, then he shifted his position, crossing the other leg. "Actually, if you hadn't stopped I'd have probably given you a ring when school reopened. VJ's teachers are also concerned about him. Despite his excellent grades, your son seems to have an attention problem. His teachers say that he often appears to be daydreaming or off in his own world, though they admit if they call on him he always has the right answer."

"Then why are the teachers concerned?" asked Marsha.

"I guess it's because of the fights."

"Fights!" exclaimed Marsha. "I've never heard a word about fights."

"There have been four or five episodes this year alone."

"Why hasn't this been brought to my attention?" Marsha asked with some indignation.

"We didn't contact you because VJ specifically asked us not to do so."

"That's absurd!" Marsha said, raising her voice. "Why would you take orders from VJ?"

"Just a moment, Dr. Frank," Mr. Remington said. "In each incident it was apparent to the staff member present that your son was severely provoked and that he only used his fists as a last resort. Each incident involved a known bully apparently responding childishly to your son's . . . er, uniqueness. There was nothing equivocal about any of these incidents. VJ was never at fault and never the instigator. Consequently, we respected his wishes not to bother you."

"But he could have been hurt," Marsha said, settling back in her chair.

"That's the other surprising thing," Mr. Remington said. "For a boy who doesn't go out for athletics, VJ handled himself admirably. One of the other boys came away with a broken nose."

"I seem to be learning a lot about my son these days," Marsha said. "What about friends?"

"He's pretty much of a loner," Mr. Remington said. "In fact, he doesn't interact well with the other students. Generally, there is no hostility involved. He just does 'his own thing.' "

That was not what Marsha wanted to hear. She'd hoped her son was more social in school than at home. "Would you describe VJ as a happy child?" she asked.

"That's a tough question," Mr. Remington said. "I don't feel he is unhappy, but VJ doesn't display much emotion at any time."

Marsha frowned. The flat effect sounded schizoid. The picture was getting worse, not better.

"One of our math instructors, Raymond Cavendish," Mr. Remington offered, "took a particular interest in VJ. He made an enormous effort to penetrate what he called VJ's private world."

Marsha leaned forward. "Really? Was he successful?"

"Unfortunately, no," Mr. Remington said. "But the reason I mentioned it was because Raymond's goal was to get VJ involved in extracurricular activities like sports. VJ was not very interested even though he'd shown an innate talent for basketball and soccer. But I agree with Raymond's opinion: VJ needs to develop other interests."

"What initially interested Mr. Cavendish in my son?"

"Apparently he was impressed by VJ's aptitude for math. He put VJ in a gifted class that included kids from several grades. Each was allowed to proceed at his own pace. One day when he was helping some high school kids with their algebra, he noticed VJ daydreaming. He called his name to tell him to get back to work. VJ thought he was calling on him for an answer and, to everyone's amazement, VJ offered the solution to the high schooler's problem."

"That's incredible!" Marsha said. "Would it be possible for me to talk with Mr. Cavendish?"

Mr. Remington shook his head. "I'm afraid not. Mr. Cavendish died a couple of years ago."

"Oh, I'm sorry," Marsha said.

"It was a great loss to the school," Mr. Remington agreed.

There was a pause in the conversation. Marsha was about to excuse herself when Mr. Remington said, "If you want my opinion, I think it would be to VJ's benefit if he were to spend more time here in school."

"You mean summer session?" Marsha asked.

"No, no, the regular year. Your husband writes frequent notes for VJ to spend time in his research lab. Now, I am all for alternative educational environments, but VJ needs to participate more, particularly in the extracurricular area. I think—"

"Just a second," Marsha interrupted. "Are you telling me that VJ misses school to spend time at the lab?"

"Yes," Mr. Remington said. "Often."

"That's news to me," Marsha admitted. "I know VJ spends a lot of time at the lab, but I never knew he was missing school to do it."

"If I were to guess," Mr. Remington said, "I'd say that VJ spends more time at the lab than he does here."

"Good grief," Marsha said.

"If you feel as I do," Mr. Remington said, "then perhaps you should talk to your husband."

"I will," Marsha said, getting to her feet. "You can count on it."

"I want you to wait in the car," Victor said to VJ and Philip as he leaned forward and looked at Gephardt's house through the windshield. It was a nondescript two-story building with a brick façade and fake shutters.

"Turn the key so we can at least listen to the radio," VJ said from the passenger seat; Philip was in the back.

Victor flipped the ignition key. The radio came back on with the raucous rock music VJ had previously selected. It sounded louder with the car engine off.

"I won't be long," he said, getting out of the car. He was having second thoughts about the confrontation now that he was standing on Gephardt's property. The house was set on a fairly large lot, hidden from its neighbors by thick clusters of birches and maples. A bay window stuck out on the building's left, probably indicating the living room. There were no lights on even though daylight was fading, but a Ford van stood idle in the driveway so Victor figured somebody might be home.

Victor leaned back inside the car. "I won't be long."

"You already said that," VJ said, keeping time to the music on the dashboard with the flat of his palm.

Victor nodded, embarrassed. He straightened up and started for the house. As he walked, he wondered if he shouldn't go home and call. But then he remembered the missing laboratory equipment, the embezzlement of some poor dead employee's paychecks, and the brick through VJ's window. That raised Victor's anger and put determination in his step. As he got closer he glanced at the brick façade and wondered if the brick that had crashed into his house was a leftover from the construction of Gephardt's. Eyeing the bay window, Victor had the urge to throw one of the cobblestones lining the walk through it. Then he stopped.

Victor blinked as if he thought his eyes were not telling the truth. He was about twenty feet away from the bay window and he could see that many of the panes were already broken, with sharp shards of glass still in place. It was as if his retribution fantasy had become instant reality.

Glancing back to his car where he could see the silhouettes of VJ and Philip, Victor struggled with an urge to go back and drive away. There was something wrong. He could sense it. He looked back at the broken bay window, then up the front steps at the door. The place was too quiet, too dark. But then Victor wondered what he'd tell VJ: he was too scared? Having come that far, Victor forced himself to continue.

Going up the front steps, he saw that the door was not completely shut.

"Hello!" Victor called. "Anybody home?" He pushed the door open wider and stepped inside.

Victor's scream died on his lips. The bloody scene in Gephardt's living room was worse than anything he'd ever seen, even during his internship at Boston City Hospital. Seven corpses, including Gephardt's, were strewn grotesquely around the living room. The bodies were riddled with bullets and the smell of cordite hung heavily in the air.

The killer must have only just left because blood was still oozing from the wounds. Besides Gephardt, there was a woman about Gephardt's age, who Victor guessed was his wife, an older couple, and three children. The youngest looked about five. Gephardt had been shot so many times that the top part of his head was gone.

Victor straightened up from checking the last body for signs of life. Weak and dizzy, he walked to the phone wondering if he should be touching anything. He didn't bother with an ambulance, but dialed the police, who said a car would be there right away.

Victor decided to wait in the car. He was afraid if he stayed in the house any longer he'd be sick.

"We're going to be here for a little while," Victor shouted as he slid in behind the wheel. He turned the radio down. The image of all the dead people was etched in his mind. "There's a little trouble inside the house and the police are on their way."

"How long?" VJ asked.

"I'm not sure. Maybe an hour or so."

"Any fire trucks coming?" Philip asked eagerly.

The police arrived in force with four squad cars, probably the entire Lawrence PD fleet. Victor did not go back inside but hung around on the front steps. After about a half hour one of the plainclothesmen came out to talk to him.

"I'm Lieutenant Mark Scudder," he said. "They got your name and address, I presume."

Victor told him they had.

"Bad business," Scudder said. He lit a cigarette and tossed the match out onto the lawn. "Looks like some drug-related vendetta— the kind of scene you expect to see south of Boston, but not up here."

"Did you find drugs?" Victor asked.

"Not yet," Scudder said, taking a long drag on his cigarette. "But this sure wasn't any crime of passion. Not with the artillery they used. There must have been two or three people shooting in there."

"Are you people going to need me much longer?" Victor asked.

589

Scudder shook his head. ''If they got your name and number, you can go whenever you want.''

Upset as she was, Marsha could hardly focus on her afternoon patients and needed all her forbearance to appear interested in the last, a narcissistic twenty-year-old with a borderline personality disorder. The moment the girl left, Marsha picked up her purse and went out to her car, for once letting her correspondence go to the following day.

All the way home she kept going over her conversation with Remington. Either Victor had been lying about the amount of time VJ was spending at the lab or VJ had been forging his excuses. Both possibilities were equally upsetting, and Marsha realized that she couldn't even begin dealing with her feelings about Victor and his unconscionable experiment until she had found out how badly VJ had been harmed. The discovery of his truancy added to her worries; it was such a classic symptom of a conduct disorder that could lead to an antisocial personality.

Marsha turned into their driveway and accelerated up the slight incline. It was almost dark and she had on her headlights. She rounded the house and was reaching for the automatic garage opener when the headlights caught something on the garage door. She couldn't see what it was and as she pulled up to the door, the headlights reflected back off the white surface, creating a glare. Shielding her eyes, Marsha got out of the car and came around the front. Squinting, she looked up at the object, which looked like a ball of rags.

''Oh, my God!'' she cried when she saw what it was. Shaking off a wave of nausea, she ventured another look. The cat had been strangled and nailed against the door as if crucified.

Trying not to look at the bulging eyes and protruding tongue, she read the typed note secured to the tail: YOU'D BETTER MAKE THINGS RIGHT.

Leaving her car where it was but turning off the headlights and the engine, Marsha hurried inside the house and bolted the door. Trembling with a mixture of revulsion, anger, and fear, she took off her coat and went to find the maid, Ramona, who was tidying up in the living room. Marsha asked whether she'd heard any strange noises.

''I did hear some pounding around noon,'' Ramona said. ''I opened the front door but nobody was there.''

''Any cars or trucks?'' Marsha asked.

"No," said Ramona.

Marsha let her go back to her cleaning and went to phone Victor, but once she got through, the office said he'd already left. She debated calling the police, but decided Victor would be home any minute. She decided to pour herself a glass of white wine. As she took a sip she saw headlights play against the barn.

"God damn it!" Victor cursed as he found Marsha's car blocking the garage. "Why does your mother do that? She could at least keep her heap on her side."

Angling the car toward the back door of the house, Victor came to a stop and turned off the lights and the ignition. He was a bundle of nerves following the experience at Gephardt's. VJ and Philip were blithely unaware of what had happened there, and they didn't ask for an explanation despite the fact that they had had to wait in the car for so long.

Victor got out slowly and followed the other two inside. By the time he closed the door he could tell that Marsha was in one of her moods. It was all in her tone as she ordered VJ and Philip to take off their shoes, get upstairs, and wash for dinner.

Victor hung up his coat, then entered the kitchen.

"And you!" said Marsha. "I suppose you didn't see our little present on the garage door?"

"What are you talking about?" Victor said, matching Marsha's testy tone.

"How you could have missed it is beyond me," Marsha said, putting down her wineglass, flipping on the courtyard light and brushing past Victor. "Come with me!"

Victor hesitated for a moment, then followed. She marched him through the family room and out the back door.

"Marsha!" Victor called, hurrying to keep up with her.

She stopped by the front of her car. Victor came up beside her.

"What are you . . ." he began. His words trailed off as he found himself looking at the gruesome sight of Kissa, brutally nailed to the garage door.

Marsha was standing with her hands on her hips, looking at Victor, not at the cat. "I thought you'd be interested to see how well you 'laid it on the line' with the problem people."

Victor turned away. He couldn't bear to look at the dead, tortured animal, and he couldn't face his wife.

"I want to know what you're going to do to see that this is stopped. And don't think you'll get away with a simple 'I'll handle it.' I want you to tell me what steps you're going to take, and now. I just can't take any more of this . . ." Her voice broke.

Victor wasn't sure how much more of it he could take either. Marsha was treating him as if he was to blame, as though he'd brought this down on them. Maybe he had. But he'd be damned if he knew who was behind this. He was as baffled as Marsha was.

Victor slowly turned back to the garage door. It was only then he saw the note. He didn't know whether to be angry or sick. Who the hell was doing this? If it were Gephardt, at least he wouldn't be bothering them again.

"We've gone from a phone call to a broken window to a dead pet," said Marsha. "What's next?"

"We'll call the police," Victor said.

"They were a big help last time."

"I don't know what you expect from me," Victor said, regaining some composure. "I did call the three people I suspected of being behind this. By the way, the list of suspects has been reduced to two."

"What does that mean?" Marsha asked.

"Tonight on the way home I stopped at George Gephardt's," Victor said. "And the man was—"

"Yuck!" VJ voiced with a disgusted expression.

Both Victor and Marsha were startled by VJ's sudden appearance. Marsha had hoped to spare her son from this. She stepped between VJ and the garage door, trying to block the gruesome sight.

"Look at her tongue," VJ said, glancing around Marsha.

"Inside, young man!" Marsha said, trying to herd VJ back to the house. She really never would forgive Victor for this. But VJ would have none of it. He seemed determined to have a look. His interest struck Marsha as morbid; it was almost clinical. With a sinking feeling she realized there was no sorrow in his reaction—another schizoid symptom.

"VJ!" Marsha said sharply. "I want you in the house *now!*"

"Do you think Kissa was dead before she got nailed to the door?" VJ asked, still calmly, trying to look at the cat as Marsha pushed him toward the door.

Once they were inside, Victor went directly to the phone while Marsha tried to have a talk with VJ. Surely he had some feelings for their cat. Victor got through to the North Andover police station. The operator assured him they'd send a patrol car over right away.

Hanging up the phone, he turned into the room. VJ was going up the back stairs two steps at a time. Marsha was on the couch with arms folded angrily. It was clear she was even more upset now that VJ had seen the cat.

"I'll hire some temporary security until we get to the bottom of this," said Victor. "We'll have them watch the house at night."

"I think we should have done that from the start," Marsha said.

Victor shrugged. He sat down on the couch, suddenly feeling very tired.

"Do you know what VJ told me when I tried to ask him about his feelings?" Marsha asked. "He said we can get another cat."

"That sounds mature," Victor said. "At least VJ can be rational."

"Victor, it's been his cat for years. You'd think he would show a little emotion, grief at the loss." Marsha swallowed hard. "I think it is a cold and detached response." She hoped she could remain composed while they discussed VJ, but as much as she tried to hold them back, tears welled in her eyes.

Victor shrugged again. He really didn't want to get into another psychological chitchat. The boy was fine.

"Inappropriate emotion is not a good sign," Marsha managed, hoping at last Victor would agree. But Victor didn't say anything.

"What do you think?" Marsha asked.

"To tell you the truth," Victor said, "I am a little preoccupied at the moment. A little while ago before VJ appeared I was telling you about Gephardt. On the way home I went to visit the man, and I walked in on a scene—you just can't imagine. Gephardt and his entire family were murdered today. Machine-gunned in their living room in the middle of the afternoon. It was a massacre." He ran his fingers through his hair. "I was the one to call the police."

"How awful!" she cried. "My God, what's going on?" She looked at Victor. He was her husband, after all, the man she'd loved all these years. "Are you all right?" she asked him.

"Oh, I'm hanging in there," Victor said, but his tone lacked conviction.

"Was VJ with you?" she asked.

"He was in the car."

"So he didn't see anything?"

Victor shook his head.

"Thank God," Marsha said. "Do the police have any motive for the killings?"

"They think it's drug-related."

"What a terrible thing!" Marsha exclaimed, still stunned. "Can I get you something to drink? A glass of wine?"

"I think I'll take something a bit stronger, like a Scotch," Victor said.

"You stay put," said Marsha. She went to the wet bar and poured Victor a drink. Maybe she was being too hard on him, but she had to get him to focus on their son. She decided to bring the subject back to VJ. Handing the glass to Victor, she began.

"I had an upsetting experience myself today—not anything like yours. I went to VJ's school to visit the headmaster."

Victor took a sip.

Marsha then told Victor about her visit with Mr. Remington, ending with the question of why Victor hadn't discussed with her his decision to have VJ miss so much school.

"I never made a decision for VJ to miss school," Victor said.

"Haven't you written a number of notes for VJ to spend time at the lab rather than at school?"

"Of course not."

"I was afraid of that," Marsha said. "I think we have a real problem on our hands. Truancy like that is a serious symptom."

"It seemed like he was around a lot, but when I asked him, VJ told me that the school was sending him out to get more practical experience. As long as his grades were fine, I didn't think to question him further."

"Pauline Spaulding also told me that VJ spent most of his time in your lab," Marsha said. "At least after his intelligence dropped."

"VJ has always spent a lot of time in the lab," Victor admitted.

"What does he do?" Marsha asked.

"Lots of things," Victor said. "He started doing basic chemistry stuff, uses the microscopes, plays computer games which I loaded for him. I don't know. He just hangs out. Everybody knows him. He's well-liked. He's always been adept at entertaining himself."

The front door chimes sounded and both Marsha and Victor went to the front foyer and let in the North Andover police.

"Sergeant Cerullo," said a large, uniformed policeman. He had small features that were all bunched together in the center of a pudgy face. "And this here is Patrolman Hood. Sorry about your cat. We've been tryin' to watch your house better since Widdicomb's been here, but it's hard, settin' where it is so far from the road and all."

Sergeant Cerullo got out a pad and pencil as Widdicomb had Tuesday night. Victor led the two of them out the back to the garage. Hood took several photos of Kissa, then both policemen searched the area. Victor was gratified when Hood offered to take the cat down and even helped dig a grave at the edge of a stand of birch trees.

On the way into the house, Victor asked if they knew anybody he could call for the security duty he had in mind. They gave him the names of several local firms.

"As long as we're talkin' names," Sergeant Cerullo said, "do you have any idea of who would want to do this to your cat?"

"Two people come to mind," Victor said. "Sharon Carver and William Hurst."

Cerullo dutifully wrote down the names. Victor didn't mention Gephardt. Nor did he mention Ronald Beekman. There was no way Ronald would stoop to this.

After seeing the police out, Victor called both of the recommended firms. It was apparently after hours; all he got was recordings, so he left his name and number at work.

"I want us both to have a talk with VJ," Marsha said.

Victor knew by the tone of her voice there'd be no putting her off. He merely nodded and followed her up the back stairs. VJ's door was ajar and they entered without a knock.

VJ closed the cover of one of his stamp albums and slipped the heavy book onto the shelf above his desk.

Marsha studied her son. He was looking up at her and Victor expectantly, almost guiltily, as if they'd caught him doing something naughty. Working on a stamp album hardly qualified.

"We want to talk with you," began Marsha.

"Okay," VJ agreed. "About what?"

To Marsha he suddenly looked the ten-year-old child he was. He looked so vulnerable, she had to restrain herself from leaning down and drawing him to her. But it was time to be stern. "I visited Pendleton Academy today and spoke with the headmaster. He told me that you had been producing notes from your father to leave school and spend time at Chimera. Is this true?"

With her professional experience, Marsha expected VJ to deny the allegation initially, and then when denial proved to be impossible, to use some preadolescent externalization of responsibility. But VJ did neither.

"Yes, it is true," VJ said flatly. "I am sorry for the deceit. I apologize for any embarrassment it may have caused you. None was intended."

For a moment Marsha felt like someone had let the air out of her sails. How she would have preferred the standard, childish denial. But even in this instance, VJ varied from the norm. Looking up, she glanced at Victor. He raised his eyebrows but said nothing.

"My only excuse is that I am doing fine at school," VJ said. "I've considered that my main responsibility."

"School is supposed to challenge you," Victor said, suspecting Marsha was stumped by VJ's utter calm. "If school is too easy, you should be advanced. After all, there have been cases where children your age have matriculated into college, even graduated."

"Kids like that are treated like freaks," VJ replied. "Besides, I'm not interested in more structure. I've learned a lot at the lab, much more than at school. I want to be a researcher."

"Why didn't you come and talk to me about this?" Victor said.

"I just thought it would be the easiest way," VJ said. "I was afraid if I asked to spend more time at the lab, you'd say no."

"Thinking you know the outcome of a discussion shouldn't keep you from talking," Victor said.

VJ nodded.

Victor looked at Marsha to see if she was about to say anything else. She was thoughtfully chewing the inside of her cheek. Sensing that Victor was looking at her, she glanced at him. He shrugged. She did the same.

"Well, we'll talk about this again," said Victor. Then he and Marsha left VJ's room and retreated down the back stairs.

"Well," Victor said, "at least he didn't lie."

"I can't get over it," Marsha said. "I was sure he was going to deny it." She retrieved her glass of wine, freshened it, and sat down in one of the chairs around the kitchen table. "He's difficult to anticipate."

"Isn't it a good sign that he didn't lie?" Victor asked, leaning up against the kitchen counter.

"Frankly, no," said Marsha. "Under the circumstances, for a child his age, it's not normal at all. Okay, he didn't lie, but he didn't show the slightest sign of remorse. Did you notice that?"

Victor rolled his eyes. "You really are never satisfied, are you? Well, I'm not convinced this is so important. I skipped a bunch of days back in high school. I think the only real difference was that I was never caught."

"That's not the same thing," Marsha said. "That kind of behavior is typical of adolescent rebellion. That's why you didn't do it until you were in high school. VJ is only in fifth grade."

"I don't think forging a few notes, especially when he is doing okay in school, means the boy is going to grow up to a life of crime. He's a prodigy, for God's sake. He skips school to be in a lab. The way you're acting, you'd think we'd discovered he was on crack."

"I wouldn't be concerned if it were just this. But there's a whole complex of qualities that are just not right about our son. I can't believe you don't see—"

A crashing sound from outside froze Marsha in midsentence.

"Now what?" said Victor.

"It sounded like it came from near the garage," Marsha answered.

Victor ran into the family room and switched off the light. He got a battery-driven spotlight from the closet and went to the window that looked onto the courtyard. Marsha followed.

"Can you see anything?" Marsha asked.

"Not from in here," Victor said, starting for the door.

"You're not going outside?"

"I'm going to see who's out there," Victor said over his shoulder.

"Victor, I don't want you going out there by yourself."

Ignoring her, Victor tiptoed onto the stoop. He felt Marsha right behind him, holding on to his shirt back. There was a scraping sound coming from near the garage door. Victor pointed the spotlight in the direction and turned it on.

Within the bright beam of light, two ringed eyes looked back at Victor and Marsha, then scampered off into the night.

"A raccoon," said Victor with relief.

9

FRIDAY MORNING

By the time Victor got to work, he had himself worked up to a minor fury over the killing of the family cat. With Marsha's concern for VJ deepening, all they needed was the added problem of harassment. Victor knew that he had to act, and quickly, to prevent another attack, especially since they were progressively worsening. After killing the cat, what was next? Victor shuddered as he considered the possibilities.

He pulled into his parking place and killed the engine. VJ and Philip, who had been riding in the back seat, piled out of the car and took off toward the cafeteria. Victor watched them go, wondering if Marsha was right about VJ fitting a potentially dangerous psychiatric pattern. Last night after they'd gotten into bed, Marsha had told him that Mr. Remington said that VJ had been involved in a number of fights at school. Victor had been more shocked by that news than by anything else. It seemed so unlike VJ. He could not imagine it was true. And if it was, he didn't know how he felt about it. In some ways he was proud of VJ. Was it really so bad to defend yourself? Even Remington seemed to have some admiration for the way the boy handled himself.

"Who the hell knows?" Victor said aloud as he got out of the car and started for the front door. But he didn't get far. Out of nowhere a man dressed in a policeman's uniform appeared.

"Dr. Victor Frank?" the man questioned.

598

"Yes," Victor responded.

The man handed Victor a packet. "Something for you from the sheriff's office," he said. "Have a good day."

Victor opened up the envelope and saw that he was being summoned to respond to the attached complaint. The first page read: "Sharon Carver vs. Victor Frank and Chimera, Inc."

Victor didn't have to read any further. He knew what he was holding. So Sharon was moving ahead with her threatened sex-discrimination suit. He felt like throwing the papers to the wind. It just made him fume all the more as he climbed the front steps and entered the building.

The office was alive with an almost electric intensity. He noticed that people eyed him as he approached, then murmured among themselves after he passed. When he got into his office and as he was removing his coat, he asked Colleen what was going on.

"You've become a celebrity," she said. "It was on the news that you were the one to discover the Gephardt family murder."

"Just what I need," Victor said. He went over to his desk. Before he sat down he handed the Carver summons over to Colleen and told her to send it to the legal department. Then he sat down. "So what's the good word?"

"Lots of things," Colleen said. She handed a sheet of paper to Victor. "That's a preliminary report concerning Hurst's research. They just started and have already found serious irregularities. They thought you should know."

"You are ever a bearer of good news," Victor said. He fingered the report. Based on Hurst's reaction to his decision to look into the matter, he wasn't surprised, though he hadn't thought the irregularities would show up so quickly. He would have guessed Hurst to be a bit more subtle than that.

"What else?" Victor asked, putting the report aside.

"A board meeting has been scheduled for next Wednesday to vote on the stock offering," Colleen said, handing over a reminder slip for Victor to put in his calendar.

"That's like getting invited to play Russian roulette," Victor said, taking the paper. "What else?"

Colleen went down her list, ticking off myriad problems—mostly minor ones, but ones that had to be dealt with nonetheless. She made notes, depending on Victor's reaction. It took them about half an hour to get through.

"Now it's my turn," Victor said. "Have I gotten any calls from security firms?"

Colleen shook her head.

"All right, next I want you to get on the phone and use your considerable charms to find out where Ronald Beekman, William Hurst, and Sharon Carver were around noon yesterday."

Colleen made a note for herself and waited for more instructions. When she saw that was it, she nodded good-bye and slipped out of the office back to her desk.

Victor started to work through the pile of papers in his in-box.

Thirty minutes later, Colleen returned with her steno pad from which she read: "Both Dr. Beekman and Dr. Hurst were here at Chimera all day, although Dr. Hurst did disappear for lunch. No one saw him at the cafeteria. Heaven only knows where he went. As for Miss Carver, I couldn't find out a thing."

Victor nodded and thanked her. He picked up the phone and tried one of the numbers of the security firms, one called Able Protection. A woman answered. After he had been put briefly on hold, a deep-voiced man got on the line, and Victor made arrangements to have his home watched from 6 P.M. to 6 A.M.

Colleen returned with a sheet of paper which she slipped under Victor's nose. "Here's an update on the equipment that Gephardt managed to have disappear."

Victor ran down the list: polypeptide synthesizers, scintillation counters, centrifuges, electron microscope . . .

"Electron microscope!" Victor yelled. "How the hell did that vanish? How did this guy get the equipment off-site, much less fence it? I mean the market for a hot electron microscope has to be small." Victor looked at Colleen questioningly. In his mind's eye he saw the van parked in Gephardt's driveway.

"You've got me," was all she could offer.

"It's a disgrace that he was able to get away with it for so long. It certainly says something about our accounting methods and our security."

By eleven-thirty Victor was finally able to slip out the back of his office and walk over to his lab. The morning's administrative work had only agitated him to an even more exasperated state. But, stepping into his lab, he began to unwind. It was an immediate, almost reflexive response. Research was the reason he'd started Chimera, not fussy paperwork.

Victor was walking to his lab office door when one of the technicians spotted him and hurried over. "Robert was looking for you," she told him. "We were supposed to tell you as soon as we saw you."

Victor thanked her and began to look for Robert. He found him back at the gel electrophoresis unit.

"Dr. Frank!" Robert said happily. "We had a positive on two of your samples."

"You mean—" Victor asked.

"Both blood samples you gave me were positive for trace amounts of cephaloclor."

Victor froze. For a moment he couldn't even breathe. When he handed those samples over to Robert, he'd never expected a positive finding. He was just doing it to be complete, like a medical student doing a standard work-up.

"Are you sure?" Victor voiced with some difficulty.

"That's what Harry said," said Robert. "And Harry's pretty reliable. You didn't expect this?"

"Hardly," said Victor. He was already considering the implications if this were true. Turning to Robert he added, "I want it checked."

Without another word, Victor turned and and went back to his lab office. In one of his desk drawers he had a small bottle of cephaloclor capsules. He took one out and walked back through the main lab, through the dissecting room, and into the animal room. There he selected two compatible smart rats, put them in a cage by themselves, and added the contents of the capsule to their water. He watched as the white powder dissolved, then hooked the water bottle to the side of the cage.

Leaving his Department of Developmental Biology, Victor walked down the long hall and up one flight to the Department of Immunology. He went directly to Hobbs.

"How are you doing now that you're back to work?" Victor asked him.

"My concentration isn't one hundred percent," Hobbs admitted, "but it is much better for me to be here and busy. I was going crazy at home. So was Sheila."

"We're glad to have you back," Victor said. "I wanted to ask once more if there was any chance at all that your boy could have gotten some cephaloclor."

"Absolutely not," Hobbs said. "Why? Do you think that cephaloclor could have triggered the edema?"

"Not if he didn't get any," said Victor in a manner that conveyed case closed. Leaving a somewhat confused Hobbs in his wake, Victor set out for Accounting to question Murray. His response was the same. There was no way that either child had been given cephaloclor.

On the way back to his lab, Victor passed the computer center. Entering, he sought out Louis and inquired about the evening's plans.

"We'll be ready," Louis said. "The phone company representatives will be here around six to start setting up. It's just up to the hacker to log on and stay on. I'll keep my fingers crossed."

"Me too," Victor said. "I'll be in my lab. Have someone get in touch with me if he tries to tap in. I'll come right over."

"Sure thing, Dr. Frank."

Victor continued on to his lab, trying to keep his thoughts steady. It wasn't until he was sitting down at his desk that he allowed himself to consider the significance of cephaloclor in the two unfortunate toddlers' bloodstreams. Clearly the antibiotic had somehow been introduced. There was no doubt it had turned the NGF gene on, which, when activated, would effectively stimulate the brain cells to the point at which they'd begin dividing. With closed skulls unable to expand, the swelling brain could swell only to a certain limit. Unchecked, the swelling would herniate the brainstem down into the spinal canal, as discovered in the children at the autopsy.

Victor shuddered. Since neither child could have gotten the cephaloclor by accident, and since both got it at apparently the same time, Victor had to assume that they'd both received the antibiotic in a deliberate attempt to kill them.

Victor rubbed his face roughly, then ran his fingers through his hair. Why would someone want to kill two extraordinary, prodigiously intelligent babies? And who?

Victor could hardly contain himself. He rose to his feet and paced the length of the room. The only idea that came to mind was a long shot: some rapid, half-baked moralistic reactionary had stumbled onto the details of the NGF experiment. In a vengeful attempt to blot out Victor's efforts, the madman had murdered the Hobbs and Murray kids.

But if this scenario were the case, why hadn't the smart rats been disposed of? And what about VJ? Besides, so few people had access to the computer and the labs. Victor thought about the hacker who had deleted the files. But how would such a person gain access to the labs, or even the day-care center? All at once, Victor understood that it was only at the day-care center that the Hobbs and Murray babies' lives intersected. They had to have received the cephaloclor at the day-care center!

Victor angrily considered Hurst's threat: "You're not the white knight you want us to believe." Maybe Hurst knew all about the NGF project and this was his way of retaliating.

Victor started pacing again. Even the Hurst idea didn't fit well with the facts. If Hurst or anyone wanted to get back at him, why not old-fashioned blackmail, or just exposure to the newspapers? That made more sense than killing innocent children. No, there had to be another explanation, something more evil, less obvious.

Victor sat down at his desk and took out some results from recent laboratory experiments and tried to do some work. But he couldn't concentrate. His thoughts kept circling back to the NGF project. Considering what he was up against, it was too bad he couldn't go to the authorities with his suspicions. Doing so would require a full disclosure of the NGF project, and Victor understood that he could never do that. It would amount to professional suicide. To say nothing of his family life. If only he had never done this experiment in the first place.

Leaning back in his chair and putting his hands behind his head, Victor stared up at the ceiling. Back when VJ's intelligence had dropped, Victor had never even considered testing him for cephaloclor. Could the antibiotic have been sequestered in his body since birth, only to leach out when he was between two and four years old? "No," Victor voiced to the ceiling, answering his own question. There was no physiological process that could cause such a phenomenon.

Victor marveled at the storm of events whirling around him: Gephardt's murder, the possible purposeful elimination of two genetically engineered children, an escalating series of threats to himself and his family, fraud, and embezzlement. Could these disparate incidents be related in some fantastic, grisly plot?

Victor shook his head. The fact that all these things were happening at once had to be coincidence. But the thought they were related nagged. Victor thought again of VJ. Could he be at risk? How could Victor prevent him from receiving cephaloclor if there was some sinister hand trying to effect just that?

Victor stared blankly ahead. The idea of VJ's being at risk had disturbed him since Wednesday afternoon. He began to wonder if his warnings about Beekman and Hurst had been adequate. He got up from the desk and walked to the door. Suddenly he didn't like the idea of VJ wandering around Chimera on his own.

Starting out in the lab just as he had done on Wednesday, he began asking if anyone had seen VJ. But no one had seen either him or Philip for some time. Victor left the lab building and went to the cafeteria. It was just before lunchtime and the cafeteria staff was in the final countdown in preparation for the noontime rush. A few people who preferred to get a jump on the others were already eating their lunches. Victor went directly to the manager, Curt Tarkington, who was supervising the stocking of the steam table.

"I'm looking for my son again," Victor said.

"He hasn't been in yet," Curt said. "Maybe you should give him a beeper."

"Not a bad idea," Victor said. "When he shows up, would you ring my secretary?"

"No problem," Curt said.

Victor checked the library, which was in the same building, but there wasn't a soul there. Stepping outside, he debated going to the fitness and day-care centers. Instead, he headed for the security office at the main gate.

Wiping his feet on a straw mat, Victor entered the small office that was built between the entrance and the exit to the Chimera compound. One man was operating the gates, another sat at a small desk. Both wore official-looking brown uniforms with the Chimera insignia patch on the upper sleeves. The man at the desk jumped to his feet as Victor entered.

"Good morning, sir," the guard said. His name tag gave his name: Sheldon Farber.

"Sit down," Victor said in a friendly tone. Sheldon sat. "I have a question about protocol. When a truck or van leaves the compound, does someone take a look inside?"

"Oh, yes," Sheldon said. "Always."

"And if there is equipment on board you make sure it is supposed to be there?" Victor asked.

"Certainly," Sheldon said. "We check the work order or call electronic maintenance. We always check it out."

"What if it is being driven by one of the Chimera employees?"

"Doesn't matter," Sheldon said. "We always check."

"What if it is being driven by one of the management?"

Sheldon hesitated, then spoke. "Well, I suppose that would be different."

"So if a van is driven out of here by one of the executives, you let it go?"

"Well, I'm not sure," Sheldon said nervously.

"From now on I want all trucks, vans, and the like looked into no matter who is driving. Even me. Understand?"

"Oh, yes, sir," Sheldon said.

"One other question," Victor said. "Has anyone seen my son today?"

"I haven't," Sheldon said. Then to the man operating the gates he said, "George, did you see VJ today?"

"Only when he arrived with Dr. Frank."

Sheldon held up a hand for Victor to wait. Turning to a radio set up behind the desk, he put out a call for Hal.

"Hal's been cruising around this morning," Sheldon explained. Some crackles heralded Hal's voice. Sheldon asked if VJ was around.

"I saw him down near the dam earlier this morning," Hal said through a good deal of static.

Victor thanked the security men and left their office. He felt a minor amount of irritation, remembering how willful VJ was. Victor could remember telling him to stay away from the river at least four or five times.

Pulling his lab coat more closely around him, Victor started for the river. He thought about going back to the main building to get his regular coat, but didn't. Although the temperature had dropped from the previous day, it still was not that cold.

Although the day had started clear, it was now cloudy. The prevailing breeze, from the northeast, smelled of the ocean. High above, several sea gulls circled, squawking shrilly.

Directly ahead stood the clock tower building with its Big Ben replica stopped at 2:15. Victor reminded himself to bring up the issue of renovating the structure as well as the clock at next Wednesday's board meeting.

The closer he got to the river, the louder the roar from the waterfall over the spillway of the dam became.

"VJ!" Victor shouted as he approached the river's edge. But his voice was lost in the crash of the water. He continued past the eastern edge of the clock tower building, crossed over a wooden bridge that spanned the sluice exiting from the basement of the building, and arrived at the granite quay built along the river below the dam. He looked down at the white water as it swirled furiously eastward toward the ocean. Glancing left, he gazed at the expanse of the dam spanning the river and at the broad millpond upstream. Water poured over the center of the dam in an imposing arc of emerald green. The force was enough for Victor to feel through his feet, standing on the granite quay. It was an awesome testimony to the power of nature that had started earlier that year with gentle snowflakes.

Turning around, Victor shouted at the top of his lungs: ''VJ!'' But he bit off his shout with the shock that VJ was standing directly behind him. Philip was a little farther away.

''There you are,'' Victor said. ''I've been looking all over for you.''

''I guessed as much,'' VJ said. ''What do you want?''

''I want . . .'' Victor paused. He wasn't sure what he wanted. ''What have you been doing?''

''Just having fun.''

''I'm not sure I want you wandering around like this, especially down here by the river,'' Victor said sternly. ''In fact, I want you home today. I'll have a driver from the motor pool give you and Philip a lift.''

''But I don't want to go home,'' VJ complained.

''I'll explain more later,'' Victor said firmly. ''But I want you home for now. It's for your own good.''

Marsha opened the door to her office that gave out to the hall and Joyce Hendricks slipped out. She'd told Marsha that she was terrified of running into someone she knew while coming out of a psychiatrist's office, and for the time being Marsha indulged her. After a time, Marsha was certain that she could convince the woman that seeking psychiatric help was no longer a social stigma.

After updating the Hendricks file, Marsha poked her head into the office waiting room and told Jean that she was going off to lunch. Jean waved in acknowledgment. As usual, she was tied up on the phone.

Marsha was having lunch with Dr. Valerie Maddox, a fellow psychiatrist whom she admired and respected, whose office was in the same building complex as Marsha's. But more than colleagues, the two women were friends.

"Hungry?" Marsha asked after Valerie herself opened the door.

"Starved." Valerie was in her late fifties and looked every day of it. She'd smoked for many years and had a ring of deep creases that radiated away from her mouth like the lines a child would draw indicating the rays of the sun.

Together they went down in the elevator and crossed to the hospital, using the crossway. In the hospital shop they managed to get a small table in the corner that allowed them to talk. They both ordered tuna salads.

"I appreciate your willingness to have lunch," Marsha said. "I need to talk with you about VJ."

Valerie just smiled encouragement.

"You were such a help back when his intelligence dropped. I've been concerned about him lately, but what can I say? I'm his mother. I can't pretend to have any objectivity whatsoever, where he's concerned."

"What's the problem?" asked Valerie.

"I'm not even sure there is a problem. It certainly isn't one specific thing. Take a look at these psychological test results."

Marsha handed Valerie VJ's folder. Valerie scanned the various test reports with a careful eye. "Nothing appears out of the ordinary," she said. "Curious about that validity scale on the MMPI, but otherwise, there's nothing here to be concerned about."

Marsha had the feeling that Valerie was right. She went on to explain VJ's truancy, the forged notes, and the fights he'd been in in school.

"VJ sounds resourceful," said Valerie with a smile. "How old is he again?"

"Ten," Marsha said. "I'm also concerned that he only seems to have one friend his own age, a boy named Richie Blakemore, and I've never even met him."

"VJ never brings this boy to your home?" Valerie asked.

"Never."

"Maybe it might be worth chatting with Mrs. Blakemore," Valerie said. "Get an idea from her how close the boys are."

"I suppose."

"I'd be happy to see VJ if you think he would be willing," Valerie offered.

"I'd certainly appreciate it," Marsha said. "I really think I'm too close to the situation to evaluate him. At the same time, I'm terrified at the thought he's developing a serious personality disorder right under my nose.''

Marsha left Valerie in the elevator, thanking her profusely for taking the time to hear her out, and for offering to see VJ. She promised to call Valerie's secretary to set up an appointment.

"Your husband called," Jean said as Marsha came back in the door. "He wants you to be sure to call back."

"A problem?" Marsha asked.

"I don't think so," Jean said. "He didn't say one way or the other, but he didn't sound upset."

Marsha picked up her mail and went into the inner office, closing the door behind her. Flipping through her mail, she phoned Victor. Colleen patched the call through to the lab, and Victor came on the line.

"What's up?" asked Marsha. Victor didn't often call during the day.

"The usual," Victor said.

"You sound tired," Marsha said. She wanted to say he sounded strange. His voice was toneless, as if he'd just had an emotional outburst and was forcing himself to remain calm.

"There are always surprises these days," Victor said without explanation. "The reason I called was to say that VJ and Philip are at home."

"Something wrong?" asked Marsha.

"No," Victor said. "Nothing is wrong. But I'm going to be working late so you and the others go ahead and eat. Oh, by the way, there will be security watching the house from 6 P.M. until 6 A.M."

"Does the reason you're staying late have anything to do with the harassment?" Marsha asked.

"Maybe," Victor said. "I'll explain when I get home."

Marsha hung up the phone but her hand remained on the receiver. Once again she had that uncomfortable feeling that Victor was keeping something from her, something that she should know. Why couldn't he confide in her? More and more, she was feeling alone.

A particular stillness hung over the lab when Victor was there by himself. Various electronic instruments kicked on at times, but otherwise it was quiet. By eight-thirty Victor was the only person in the lab. Closed behind several doors, he couldn't even hear the sounds of the animals as they paced in their cages or used their exercise wheels.

Victor was bent over strips of film that bore darkened horizontal stripes. Each stripe represented a portion of DNA that had been cleaved at a specific point. Victor was comparing his son David's DNA fingerprint—one taken when David was still healthy—and one of his cancerous liver tumor. What amazed him was that the two did not entirely match. Victor's first hunch was that Dr. Shryack had given him the wrong sample—a piece of tumor from some other patient. But that did not explain the vast homology of the two strips; for whatever differences there were between the two fingerprints, much was the same.

After running the two in a computer that could numerically establish areas of homology versus the areas of heterogeneity, Victor realized that the two samples of DNA differed in only one area.

To make matters more confusing, the sample that Victor had given Robert contained some small areas of normal liver tissue in addition to the tumor. In his habitually compulsive fashion, Robert had carefully fingerprinted both areas of the sample. When Victor compared the normal liver DNA fingerprint with David's previous fingerprint, the match was perfect.

Discovering a cancer with a documented alteration in the DNA was not a usual finding. Victor did not know whether he should be excited about the possibility of an important scientific discovery or fearful that he was about to find something that he either couldn't explain or didn't want to know.

Victor then started the process of isolating the part of the DNA that was unique in the tumor. By initiating the protocol, it would be that much easier for Robert to complete the work in the morning.

Leaving the main lab room, Victor went through the dissecting room and entered the animal room. As he turned on the light there was a lot of sudden activity in each of the occupied cages.

Victor walked over to the cage which housed the two smart rats whose water contained the single capsule of cephaloclor. He was amazed to find one rat already dead and the other semicomatose.

Removing the dead rat, Victor took it back into the dissecting room and did an autopsy of sorts. When he opened the skull, the brain puffed out as if it was being inflated.

Carefully removing a piece of the brain, he prepared it to be sectioned in the morning. Just then, the telephone rang.

"Dr. Frank, this is Phil Moscone. Louis Kaspwicz asked me to call you to let you know that the hacker has logged onto the computer."

"I'll be right there," said Victor. He put away his rat brain sample, turned out the lights, and dashed out of the lab.

It was only a short jog to the computer center; Victor was there within a few minutes.

Louis came directly to him. "It's looking good for the trace. The guy has been logged on now for seven minutes. I just hope to hell he's not causing any mischief."

"Can you tell where he is in the system?" Victor asked.

"He's in Personnel right now," Louis said. "First he did some sizable number crunching, then he went into Purchasing. It's weird."

"Personnel?" Victor questioned. He'd been thinking the hacker was indeed no kid, but some competitor's hired gun. Biotechnology was an extremely competitive field, and almost everybody wanted to compete against the big boys like Chimera. But an industrial agent would want to get into the research files, not Personnel.

"We got a positive trace!" the man with the two-way radio announced with a big smile.

There was a general cheer among all those present.

"Okay," said Louis. "We've got the telephone number. Now we just need the name."

The man with the radio held up his hand, listened, then said, "It's an unpublished number."

Several of the other men who were already busy breaking down their equipment booed at this news.

"Does that mean they can't get the name?" asked Victor.

"Nah," Louis said. "It means it just takes them a little longer."

Victor leaned against one of the covered print-out devices and folded his arms.

"Who's got a piece of paper?" the man with the radio said suddenly, holding the radio up against his left ear. One of the other men handed him a legal-sized pad. He jotted down the name given him over the radio. "Thanks a lot, over and out." He switched off his radio unit, pushed in the antenna, then handed Louis the paper.

Louis read the name and address and turned pale. Without saying anything he handed it to Victor. Victor looked down and read it. Disbelieving, he read it again. What he saw on the paper was his name and address!

"Is this some kind of joke?" Victor said, raising his head and looking at Louis. Victor then glanced at the others. No one said a word.

"Did you program your PC to access the mainframe on a regular basis?" Louis asked, breaking the spell.

Victor looked back at his systems administrator and realized the man was trying to give him an out. After an awkward minute, Victor agreed. "Yeah, that must be it." Victor tried to remain composed. He thanked everyone for their effort and left.

Victor walked out of the computer center, got his coat from the administration building, and walked to his car in a kind of daze. The idea of someone using his computer to break into the Chimera mainframe was simply preposterous. It didn't make any sense. He knew that he had always left the computer telephone number and his password taped to the bottom of his keyboard, but who could have been using it? Marsha? VJ? The cleaning lady? There had to have been some mistake. Could the hacker have been so clever as to divert a trace? Victor hadn't thought of that, and he made a mental note to ask Louis if it were possible. That seemed to make the most sense.

Marsha heard Victor's car before she saw the lights swing into the driveway. She was in her study vainly trying to tackle the stack of professional periodicals that piled up on a regular basis on her desk. Getting to her feet, she saw the headlights silhouetting the leafless trees that lined the driveway. Victor's car came into view, then disappeared behind the house. The automatic garage door rumbled in the distance.

Marsha sat back down on her flower-print chintz couch and let her eyes roam around her study. She'd decorated it with pale pastel striped wallpaper, dusty rose carpet, and mostly white furniture. In the past it had always provided a comforting haven, but not lately. Nothing seemed to be able to relieve her ever-increasing anxiety about the future. The visit with Valerie had helped, but unfortunately even that mild relief had not lasted.

Marsha could hear the TV in the family room where VJ and Philip were watching a horror movie they'd rented. The intermittent screams that punctuated the soundtrack didn't help Marsha's mood either. She'd even closed her door but the screams still penetrated.

She heard the dull thud of the back door slam, then muffled voices from the family room, and finally a knock on her door.

Victor came in and gave her a perfunctory kiss. He looked as tired as his voice had sounded on the phone that afternoon. A constant crease was beginning to develop on his forehead between his eyebrows.

"Did you notice the security man outside?" Victor asked.

Marsha nodded. "Makes me feel much better. Did you eat?" she asked.

"No," Victor said. "But I'm not hungry."

"I'll scramble you some eggs. Maybe some toast," Marsha offered.

Victor restrained her. "Thanks, but I think I'll take a swim and then shower. Maybe that will revive me."

"Something wrong?" Marsha asked.

"No more than usual," Victor said evasively. He left, leaving her door ajar. Ominous music from the soundtrack of the movie crept back into the room. Marsha tried to ignore it as she went back to her reading, but a sharp scream made her jump. Giving up, she reached over and gave the door a shove. It slammed with a resounding click.

Thirty minutes later, Victor reappeared. He looked considerably better, dressed in more casual clothes.

"Maybe I'll take you up on those eggs," he said.

In the kitchen, Marsha went to work while Victor set the table. A series of bloodcurdling gurgles emanated from the family room. Marsha asked Victor to close the connecting door.

"What in heaven's name are they watching in there?" he asked.

"*Sheer Terror*," Marsha said.

Victor shook his head. "Kids and their horror movies," he said.

Marsha made herself a cup of tea and when Victor sat down to eat his omelet, she sat opposite him.

"There is something I wanted to discuss with you," Marsha said, waiting for her tea to cool.

"Oh?"

Marsha told Victor about her lunch with Valerie Maddox; she also told him about Valerie's offer to see VJ on a professional basis. "How do you feel about that?"

Wiping his mouth with his napkin, Victor said, "That kind of question involves your area of expertise. Anything that you think is appropriate is fine with me."

"Good," Marsha said. "I do think it is appropriate. Now I just have to convince VJ."

"Good luck," Victor said.

There was a short period of silence as Victor mopped up the last of the egg with a wedge of toast. Then he asked, "Did you use the computer upstairs tonight?"

"No, why do you ask?"

"The printer was hot when I went upstairs to swim and shower," Victor said. "How about VJ? Did he use it?"

"I couldn't say."

Victor rocked back in his chair in a way that made Marsha grit her teeth. She was always afraid he was about to go over backward and hit his head on the tile floor.

"I had an interesting evening at the Chimera computer center," Victor said, teetering on his chair. He went on to tell her everything that had happened, including the fact that the trace of the hacker ended up right there in their home.

In spite of herself, Marsha laughed. She quickly apologized. "I'm sorry, but I can just see it," she said. "All this tension and then your name suddenly appearing."

"It wasn't funny," Victor said. "And I'm going to have a serious talk with VJ about this. As ridiculous as it sounds, it must have been him breaking into the Chimera mainframe."

"Is this serious talk going to be something like the one you had with him when you learned he'd been forging notes from you in order to skip school?" Marsha taunted.

"We'll see," Victor said, obviously irritated.

Marsha leaned over and grasped Victor's arm before he could leave the table. "I'm teasing you," she said. "Actually I'd be more concerned about you cornering him or pushing him. I'm afraid there is a side to VJ's personality that we've not seen. That's really why I want him to see Valerie."

Victor nodded, then detached himself from Marsha's grasp. He opened the connecting door. "VJ, would you come in here a minute? I'd like to talk with you."

Marsha could hear VJ complaining, but Victor was insistent. Soon the sound of the movie soundtrack was off. VJ appeared at the door. He looked from Victor to Marsha. His sharp eyes had that glazed look that comes from watching too much television.

"Please sit at the table," Victor said.

With a bored expression, VJ dutifully sat at the table to Marsha's immediate left. Victor sat down across from both of them.

Victor got right to the point. "VJ, did you use the computer upstairs tonight?"

"Yeah," VJ said.

Marsha watched as VJ glared at Victor insolently. She saw Victor hesitate, then avert his eyes, probably to maintain his train of thought. For a moment there was a pause. Then Victor continued: "Did you use the PC to log on to the Chimera mainframe computer?"

"Yes," VJ said without a moment's hesitation.

"Why?" Victor asked. His voice had changed from accusatory to confused. Marsha remembered her own confusion when VJ had so quickly confessed to his truancy.

"The extra storage makes some of the computer games more challenging," VJ said.

Marsha saw Victor roll his eyes. "You mean you are using all that computer power of our giant unit to play Pac-Man and games like that?"

"It's the same as me doing it at the lab," VJ said.

"I suppose," Victor said uncertainly. "Who taught you to use the modem?"

"You did," VJ said.

"I don't remember . . ." Victor began, but then he did. "But that was over seven years ago!"

"Maybe," VJ said. "But the method hasn't changed."

"Do you access the Chimera computer every Friday night?" Victor asked.

"Usually," VJ answered. "I play a few games, then I range around in the files, mostly Personnel and Purchasing, sometimes the research files, but those are harder to crack."

"But why?" asked Victor.

"I just want to learn as much as I can about the company," VJ said. "Someday I want to run it like you. You've always encouraged me to use the computer. I won't do it anymore if you don't want me to."

"In future, I think it would be better if you don't," Victor said.

"Okay," VJ said simply. "Can I go back to my movie?"

"Sure," Victor said.

VJ pushed away from the table and disappeared through the door. Instantly, the soundtrack for *Sheer Terror* was back on.

Marsha looked at Victor. Victor shrugged. Then the doorbell sounded.

"Sorry to bother you folks so late," Sergeant Cerullo said after Victor had opened the door. "This is Sergeant Dempsey from the Lawrence police." The second officer stepped from behind Cerullo and touched the brim of his hat in greeting. He was a freckled fellow with bright red hair.

"We have some information for you and we wanted to ask a few questions," Cerullo said.

Victor invited the men inside. They stepped in and removed their hats.

"Would you like some coffee or anything?" Marsha asked.

"No, thank you, ma'am," Cerullo said. "We'll just say what we come to say and be off. You see, we at the North Andover police station are pretty friendly with the men over in Lawrence, both being neighbors and all. There's a lot of talk that goes back and forth. Anyway, they have been proceeding with the investigation of that mass murder over there involving the Gephardt family, the one Dr. Frank here discovered. Well, they found some rough drafts of the notes that you people got tied to your cat and around that brick. They were in the Gephardt house. We thought you'd like to know that."

"I should say," Victor said with some relief.

Dempsey coughed to clear his throat. "We also have ascertained by ballistics that the guns used to kill the Gephardts match those used in several battles between some rival South American drug gangs. We got that from Boston. Boston is very interested to find out what the connection is up here in Lawrence. They've some reason to believe something big is going down up here. What they want to know from you, since you employed Gephardt, is how the man was connected to the drug world. Do you people have any idea whatsoever?"

"Absolutely none," Victor said. "I suppose you know the man was under investigation for embezzlement?"

"Yeah, we got that," Dempsey said. "You're sure there's nothing else that you can give us? Boston is really eager to learn anything they can about this."

"We also think the man had been fencing laboratory equipment," Victor said. "That investigation had just started before he was killed. But for however much I suspected him of these sorts of crimes, it never occurred to me he was involved with drugs."

"If anything occurs to you, we'd appreciate it if you'd call us immediately. We sure don't want some drug war breaking out up here."

The policemen left. Victor closed the door and leaned his back on it and looked at Marsha.

"Well, that solves one problem," Victor said. "At least now we know where the harassment was coming from, and better still, that it isn't going to continue."

"I'm glad they came by to let us know we can stop worrying," Marsha added. "Maybe we should send that security man home."

"I'll cancel in the morning," Victor said. "I'm sure we'll be paying for it one way or another."

Victor sat bolt upright with such suddenness that he inadvertently pulled all the covers from Marsha. The sudden movement awakened her. It was pitch dark outside.

"What's the matter?" Marsha asked, alarmed.

"I'm not sure," Victor said. "I think it was the front doorbell."

They both listened for a moment. All Marsha heard was the wind under the eaves and the rat-a-tat of rain against the windows.

Marsha leaned over and turned the bedside clock so that she could see the face. "It's five-fifteen in the morning," she said. She fell back against the pillow and pulled the covers back over her. "Are you sure you weren't dreaming?"

But just then the doorbell rang. "It was the bell!" Victor said, leaping out of bed. "I knew I wasn't dreaming." He hastily pulled on his robe, but had the wrong arm in the wrong hole. Marsha turned on the light.

"Who on earth could it be?" Marsha asked. "The police again?"

Victor got the robe on properly and tied the belt. "We'll soon find out," he said, opening the door to the hall. He walked quickly to the head of the stairs and started down.

After a moment of indecision, Marsha put her feet out on the cold floor and donned her robe and put on her slippers as well. By the time she got downstairs, a man and woman were standing in the front hall facing Victor. Small pools of water had formed at their feet, and their faces were streaked with moisture. The woman was holding a spray can. The man was holding the woman.

"Marsha!" Victor called, not taking his eyes from the new arrivals. "I think you'd better call the police."

Marsha came up behind Victor, clutching her robe around her. She glanced at the people. The man was wearing an oilcloth hooded cape, although the hood had been pushed back, exposing his head. All in all, he looked dressed for the weather. The woman was dressed in a ski parka that had long since soaked through.

"This is Mr. Peter Norwell," Victor said. "He's from Able Protection."

"Evening, ma'am," Peter said.

MUTATION

"And this is Sharon Carver," Victor said, motioning toward the woman. "An ex-Chimera employee with a sexual-harassment suit lodged against us."

"She was set to paint your garage door," Peter elaborated. "I let her do one short burst so we'd have something on her besides trespassing."

Feeling somewhat embarrassed for the bedraggled woman, Marsha hurried to the nearest phone and called the North Andover police. The operator said they'd send a car right over.

Meanwhile, the whole group went into the kitchen where Marsha made tea for everyone. Before they'd had more than a few sips, the doorbell sounded again. Victor went to the door. It was Widdicomb and O'Connor.

"You folks are certainly keeping us busy," Sergeant Widdicomb said with a smile. They stepped through the door and took off their wet coats.

Peter Norwell brought Sharon Carver from the kitchen.

"So this is the young lady?" Widdicomb said. He took out a pair of handcuffs.

"You don't have to handcuff me, for Christ's sake!" Sharon snapped.

"Sorry, miss," Widdicomb said. "Standard procedure."

Within a few moments, all was ready. The police then left with their prisoner.

"You are welcome to finish your tea," Marsha said to Peter, who was standing in the foyer.

"Thank you, ma'am, but I already finished. Good night." The security man let himself out the door and pulled it shut behind him. Victor threw the deadbolt and turned into the room.

Marsha looked at him. She smiled and shook her head in disbelief. "If I read this in a book, I wouldn't believe it," she said.

"It's a good thing we kept that security," Victor said. Then, extending his hand, he said, "Come on. We can still get a few more hours of sleep."

But that was not as easy as Victor had thought. An hour later, he was still awake, listening to the howling storm outside. The rain beat against the windows in sudden gusts; he jumped with every buffet. He couldn't get the results of David's DNA fingerprinting out of his mind nor of the cephaloclor being in the blood samples.

"Marsha," he whispered, wondering if she were awake as well.

617

But she didn't answer. He whispered again, but still she didn't answer. Victor slid out of bed, put his robe back on, and went down the hall to the upstairs study.

Sitting down at the desk, he booted up the PC. He logged onto the main Chimera computer with the modem, rediscovering how easy it was. Absently, he wondered if he had ever transferred copies of the Hobbs and Murray files onto the PC's hard disk. To check, he called up the directory of the hard disk and searched. There were no Hobbs or Murray files. In fact, he was surprised to find so few files on the disk at all, other than the operating programs. But then, just before he was about to turn the machine off, he noticed that most of the storage space of the hard disk was used up.

Victor scratched his head. It didn't make sense, knowing the fantastic storage capacity of one hard disk. He tried to pry an explanation of this apparent discrepancy out of the machine, but the machine wouldn't cooperate. Finally, in irritation, he turned the blasted thing off.

He debated going back to bed, but, glancing at the clock, he realized that he might just as well stay up. It was already after seven. Instead of going back to the bedroom, he headed downstairs to make himself some coffee and breakfast.

As he padded down the stairs, he realized that when he'd had his talk with VJ about using the computer, he'd forgotten to quiz the boy about the deletion of the Hobbs and Murray files. He'd have to remember to do that. Nosing around in files was one thing, deleting them was quite another.

Reaching the kitchen, Victor realized the other thing that was bothering him: namely, the issue about VJ's safety, particularly at Chimera. Philip was fine for watching VJ, but obviously his help could only go so far. Victor decided that he'd call Able Protection, since they'd obviously done such a good job watching the house. He'd get an experienced companion for the boy. It would probably be expensive, but peace of mind was worth the price. Until he got to the bottom of the Hobbs and Murray deaths, he'd feel infinitely better knowing VJ was safe.

Getting out the coffee, Victor was struck by another realization. In the back of his mind the similarities between David's and Janice's cancers had been bothering him, especially in light of the results of DNA fingerprinting of David's tumor. Victor resolved to look into it as best he could.

10

SATURDAY MORNING

It was still windy and rainy when Victor went out to the garage and got in his car. He'd breakfasted, showered, shaved, and dressed, and still no one else had stirred. After leaving a note explaining that he would be at the lab most of the day, Victor had left.

But he didn't drive straight to the lab. Instead he headed west and got on Interstate 93 and drove south to Boston. In Boston he got off Storrow Drive at the Charles Street and Government Center exit. From there it was easy to drive onto the Massachusetts General Hospital grounds and park in the multistory parking garage. Ten minutes later he was in the pathology department.

Since it was early Saturday morning none of the staff pathologists were available. Victor had to be content with a second-year resident named Angela Cirone.

Victor explained his wish to get a tumor sample from a patient that had passed away four years previously.

"I'm afraid that is impossible," Angela said. "We don't keep—"

Victor politely interrupted her to tell her of the special nature of the tumor and its rarity.

"That might make things different," she said.

The hardest part was finding Janice Fay's hospital record, since Victor did not know Janice's birthday. Birth dates were the major

619

method of cross-referencing hospital records. But persistence paid off, and Angela was able to find both the hospital record number as well as the pathology record. She was also able to tell Victor that a gross specimen existed.

"But I can't give you any," Angela said after all the effort they'd expended to find it. "One of the staff members is up doing frozens this morning. When he gets through, we can see if he'll give authorization."

But Victor explained about his son David's death of the same rare cancer and his interest in examining Janice's cancerous cells. When he tried to, he could be charming in a winning way. Within the space of a few minutes, he'd persuaded the young resident to help.

"How much do you need?" she asked finally.

"A tiny slice," Victor said.

"I guess it can't hurt," Angela said.

Fifteen minutes later, Victor was on his way down on the elevator with another small jar within a paper bag. He knew he could have waited for the staff man, but this way he could get to work more quickly. Climbing into his car, he left the Massachusetts General Hospital grounds and headed north for Lawrence.

Arriving at Chimera, Victor called Able Protection. But he got a recording—it was Saturday, after all—and had to be content to leave his name and number. With that done, he searched for Robert, finding him already deeply involved with the project that Victor had started the night before, the separation of the section of David's tumor DNA that differed from his normal DNA.

"You are going to hate me," Victor said, "but I have another sample." He took out the sample he had just gotten at Mass. General. "I want this DNA fingerprinted as well."

"You don't have to worry about me," Robert said. "I like doing this stuff. You'll just have to realize that I'm letting my regular work slide."

"I understand," Victor said. "For the moment this project takes priority."

Taking the rat specimens that he'd prepared the night before, Victor made slides and stained them. While he was waiting for them to dry, a call came through from Able Protection. It was the same deep-voiced man whom Victor had dealt with earlier.

"First, I'd like to commend Mr. Norwell," Victor said. "He did a great job last night."

"We appreciate the compliment," the man said.

"Second," Victor said, "I need additional temporary security. But it's going to require a very special person. I want someone with my son, VJ, from 6 A.M. until 6 P.M. And when I say I want someone with him, I mean constantly."

"I don't think that will be a problem," the man said. "When do you want it to start?"

"As soon as you can send someone," Victor answered. "This morning, if possible. My son is at home."

"No problem. I have just the person. His name is Pedro Gonzales and I'll send him on his way."

Victor hung up and called Marsha at home.

"How did you sneak out without waking me this morning?" she asked.

"I never got to sleep last night after all the excitement," Victor said. "Is VJ there?"

"He and Philip are still sleeping," Marsha said.

"I've just made arrangements to have a security man stay with VJ all day. His name is Pedro Gonzales. He'll be over shortly."

"Why?" Marsha questioned, obviously surprised.

"Just to be one hundred percent sure he is safe," Victor said.

"You're not telling me something," Marsha warned. "I want to know what it is."

"It's just to be sure he's safe," Victor repeated. "We'll talk more about it later when I come home. I promise."

Victor hung up the phone. He wasn't about to confide in Marsha, at least not about his latest suspicions: that the Hobbs and Murray kids might have been deliberately killed. And that VJ could be killed the same way if anyone introduced cephaloclor to his system. With these thoughts in mind, he returned to the slides of the rat brains that he had drying and began to examine them in one of the light microscopes. As he expected, they appeared very similar to the slides of the children's brains. Now there was no doubt in his mind that the children had indeed died from the cephaloclor in their blood. It was how they got the cephaloclor that was the question.

Removing the slides from the microscope, Victor went back to where Robert was working. They'd worked together so long, Victor could join in and help without a single word of direction from Robert.

After making herself a second cup of coffee, Marsha sat down at the table and looked out at the rainy day with its heavy clouds. It felt

621

good not to have to go to the office, although she still had to make her inpatient rounds. She wondered if she should be more concerned than she was about Victor's arranging for a bodyguard for VJ. That certainly sounded ominous. At the same time, it sounded like a good idea. But she was still sure there were facts that Victor was keeping from her.

Footsteps on the stairs heralded the arrival of both VJ and Philip. They greeted Marsha but were much more interested in the refrigerator, getting out milk and blueberries for their cereal.

"What are you two planning on doing today?" Marsha asked when they'd sat down at the table with her.

"Heading in to the lab," VJ said. "Is Dad there?"

"He is," Marsha said. "What happened about the idea of going to Boston for the day with Richie Blakemore?"

"Didn't pan out," VJ said. He gave the blueberries a shove toward Philip.

"That's too bad," Marsha said.

"Doesn't matter," VJ said.

"There is something I want to talk to you about," Marsha said. "Yesterday I had a conversation with Valerie Maddox. Do you remember her?"

VJ rested his spoon in his dish. "I don't like the sound of this. I remember her. She's the psychiatrist whose office is on the floor above yours. She's the lady with the mouth that looks like she's always getting ready to kiss somebody."

Philip laughed explosively, spraying cereal in the process. He wiped his mouth self-consciously while trying to control his laughter. VJ laughed himself, watching Philip's antics.

"That's not very nice," Marsha said. "She is a wonderful woman, and very talented. We talked about you."

"This is starting to sound even worse," VJ said.

"She has offered to see you and I think it would be a good idea. Maybe twice a week after school."

"Oh, Mom!" VJ whined, his face contorting into an expression of extreme distaste.

"I want you to think about it," Marsha said. "We'll talk again. It is something that might help you as you get older."

"I'm too busy for that stuff," VJ complained, shaking his head.

Marsha had to laugh to herself at that comment. "You think about it anyway,'' she said. ''One other thing. I just spoke to your father. Has he said anything to you about being concerned about your safety, anything like that?''

''A little,'' VJ said. ''He wanted me to watch out for Beekman and Hurst. But I never see those guys.''

''Apparently he's still worried,'' Marsha said. ''He just told me that he has arranged for a man to be with you during the day. The man's name is Pedro and he's on his way over here.''

''Oh, no!'' VJ complained. ''That will drive me nuts.''

After finishing her inpatient rounds, Marsha got on Interstate 495 and headed west to Lowell. She got off after only three exits, and with the help of some directions she'd written on a prescription blank, she wound around on little country roads until she found 714 Mapleleaf Road, an ill-kept, Victorian-style house painted a drab gray with white trim. At some time in the past it had been converted into a duplex. The Fays lived on the first floor. Marsha rang the bell and waited.

Marsha had called from the hospital so the Fays knew to expect her. Despite the fact that their daughter had worked for her and Victor for eleven years, Marsha had only met the mother and father at Janice's funeral. Janice had been dead for four years. Marsha felt odd standing on her parents' porch, waiting for them to open the door. Knowing Janice so intimately for so many years, Marsha had come to the conclusion that there had been significantly disturbing emotional undercurrents in her family, but she had no idea what they could have been. On that issue, Janice had been completely noncommunicative.

''Please come in,'' Mrs. Fay said after she'd opened the door. She was a white-haired, pleasant-looking but frail woman who appeared to be in her early sixties. Marsha noted that the woman avoided eye contact.

The inside of the house was much worse than the outside. The furniture was old and threadbare. What made it particularly unpleasant was that the place was dirty. Wastepaper baskets were filled to overflowing with such things as beer cans and McDonald's wrappers. There were even cobwebs in one corner up near the ceiling.

''Let me tell Harry that you're here,'' Mrs. Fay said.

Marsha could hear the sounds of a televised sporting event somewhere in the background. She sat down, but kept to the very edge of the sofa. She didn't want to touch anything.

"Well, well," said a husky voice. "About time the fancy doctor paid us a visit is all I can say."

Marsha turned to see a large man with a huge belly and wearing a tank-top undershirt come into the room. He walked right up to her and stuck out a calloused hand for her to shake. His hair was cut severely in a military-style crew cut. His face was dominated by a large, swollen nose with red capillaries fanning the side of each nostril.

"Can I offer you a beer or something?" he asked.

"No, thank you," Marsha said.

Harry Fay sank into a La-Z-Boy armchair. "To what do we owe this visit?" he asked. He burped and excused himself.

"I wanted to talk about Janice," Marsha said.

"I hope to God she didn't tell you any lies about me," Harry said. "I've been a hardworking man all my life. Drove sixteen-wheelers back and forth across this country so many times I lost count."

"I'm sure that was hard work," Marsha said, wondering if she should have come.

"Bet your ass," Harry said.

"What I was wondering," Marsha began, "is whether Janice ever talked about my boys, David and VJ."

"Lots of times," Harry said. "Right, Mary?"

Mary nodded but didn't say anything.

"Did she ever remark on anything out of the ordinary about them?" There were specific questions she could have asked, but she preferred not to lead the conversation.

"She sure did," Harry said. "Even before she got nuts about all that religious bunk, she told us that VJ had killed his brother. She even told us that she tried to warn you but you wouldn't listen."

"Janice never tried to warn me," Marsha said, color rising in her cheeks. "And I should tell you that my son David died of cancer."

"Well, that's sure different than what Janice told us," Harry said. "She told us the kid was poisoned. Drugged and poisoned."

"That's patently preposterous," Marsha said.

"What the hell does that mean?" Harry said.

Marsha took a deep breath to calm herself down. She realized that she was trying to defend herself and her family before this offensive man. She knew that wasn't the reason that she was there. "I mean to say that there was no way that my son David could have been poisoned. He died of cancer just like your daughter."

"We only know what we've been told. Right, Mary?"

Mary nodded dutifully.

"In fact," Harry said, "Janice told us that she'd been drugged once too. She told us that she didn't tell anybody because she knew no one would believe her. She told us that she got mighty careful about what she ate from then on."

Marsha didn't say anything for a moment. She'd remembered the change in Janice. Overnight, she'd gotten extremely fastidious about what she ate. Marsha had always wondered what had caused the change. Apparently it had been this delusion of being drugged or poisoned.

"Actually, we didn't believe too much of what Janice was telling us," Harry admitted. "Something happened inside her head when she got so religious. She even went so far as to tell us that your boy, VJ, or whatever his name, was evil. Like he had something to do with the devil."

"I can assure you that is not the case," Marsha said. She stood up. She'd had enough.

"It is strange that your son David and our daughter died of the same cancer," Harry said. He rose to his feet, his face reddening with the considerable effort.

"It was a coincidence," Marsha agreed. "In fact, at the time it caused some concern. There was a worry that it had something to do with environment. Our home was studied extensively. I can assure you their both having it was nothing more than a tragic coincidence."

"Tough luck, I guess," Harry admitted.

"Very bad luck," Marsha said. "And we miss Janice as we miss our son."

"She was all right," Harry said. "She was a pretty good kid. But she lied a lot. She lied a lot about me."

"She never said anything to us about you," Marsha said. And after a curt handshake, she was gone.

"You sure you don't mind?" Victor asked Louis Kaspwicz. He'd called the man at home to ask him about the discrepancy regarding his hard disk on the personal computer.

"I don't mind in the slightest," Louis said. "If your hard disk has no storage space available, it means the existing storage is filled with data. There is no other explanation."

625

"But I looked at the file directory," Victor said. "All there is listed are the operating systems files."

"There have to be more files," Louis said. "Trust me."

"I'd hate to mess up your Saturday afternoon if it is some stupid thing," Victor said.

"Look, Dr. Frank," Louis said, "I don't mind. In fact, on a rainy day like this I'll enjoy the excuse to get out of the house."

"I'd appreciate it," Victor said.

"Just give me directions and I'll meet you there," Louis said.

Victor gave him directions, then went out into the main lab and told Robert that he was leaving but that he'd probably be back. He asked Robert about what time he'd be calling it a day. Robert said that his wife had told him dinner was to be at six so he'd be leaving about five-thirty.

Louis was already at the house by the time Victor got there.

"Sorry to make you wait," Victor said as he fumbled with his keys.

"No problem," Louis said cheerfully. "You certainly have a beautiful house," he added. He stomped the moisture off his shoes.

"Thank you." Victor led Louis upstairs to his Wang PC. "Here it is," he said. He reached behind the electronics unit and switched the system on.

Louis gave the computer a quick look, then lifted his narrow briefcase onto the counter top, snapping open the latches. Inside, encased in Styrofoam, was an impressive array of electronic tools.

Louis sat down in front of the unit and waited for the menu to come up. He quickly went through the same sequence that Victor had early that morning, getting the same result.

"You were right," Louis said. "There's not much space left on this Winchester." He reached over to his briefcase and unsnapped the accordion-like file area built under the lid, pulled out a floppy disk, and loaded it.

"Luckily, I happen to have a special utility for locating hidden files," Louis said.

"What do you mean by hidden files?" Victor asked.

Louis was busy with manipulating information on the screen. He spoke without looking "It is possible to store files so that they don't appear on any directory," he said.

Miraculously, data started to appear on the computer. "Here we are," Louis said. He leaned aside so Victor could have a better view of the screen. "Any of this make sense to you?"

Victor studied the information. "Yeah," he said. "These are contractions for the nucleotide bases of the DNA molecule." The screen was completely filled with vertical columns of the letters AT, TA, GC, and CG. "The A is the adenine, the T is for pyrimidine, the G is for guanine, and the C is for cytosine," Victor explained.

Louis advanced to the next page. The lists continued. He advanced a number of pages. The lists were interminable. "What do you make of this?" Louis asked, flipping through page after page.

"Must be a DNA molecule or gene sequence," Victor said, his eyes following the flashing lists as if he were watching a Ping-Pong game.

"Well, have you seen enough of this file?" Louis asked.

Victor nodded.

Louis punched some information into the keyboard. Another file appeared, but it was similar to the first. "The whole hard disk could be taken up with this stuff," Louis suggested. "You don't remember putting this material in here?"

"I didn't put it in," Victor said without elaborating. He knew that Louis was probably dying to ask where it could have come from and who was the person logging onto the Chimera mainframe last night. Victor was grateful that the man held his curiosity in check.

For the next half hour, Louis rapidly went from file to file. All looked essentially like the first. It was like a library of DNA molecules. Then suddenly it changed.

"Uh oh," Louis said. He had to hold up hitting the sequence of keys that scrolled through the hidden files. What appeared on the screen was a personnel file. Louis flipped through a couple of pages. "I recognize this because I formatted it. This is a personnel file from Chimera."

Louis looked up at Victor, who didn't say a word. Louis turned back to the computer and went to the next file. It was George Gephardt's. "This stuff was pulled directly out of the mainframe," Louis said. When Victor still did not respond, he went to the next file, then the next. There were eighteen personnel files. Then came a series of accounting files with spread sheets. "I don't recognize these," Louis said. He looked up at Victor again. "Do you?"

Victor shook his head in disbelief.

Louis redirected his attention to the computer screen. "Wherever it came from, it represents a lot of money. It is a clever way to present it, though. I wonder what kind of program was used. I wouldn't mind getting a copy of it."

After going through a number of pages of the accounting data, Louis went on to the next file. It was a stock portfolio of a number of small companies, all of which held Chimera stock. All in all, it represented a large portion of the Chimera stock not held by the three founders and their families.

"What do you think this is?" Louis asked.

"I haven't the slightest idea," Victor said. But there was one thing that he had a good idea about. He was going to have another talk with VJ about using the computer. If the information before him represented actual truths and wasn't part of some elaborate fantasy computer game, the ramifications were very grave. And on top of that was the question of the deleted Hobbs and Murray files.

"Now we're back to more of the DNA stuff," Louis said as the screen filled again with the lists of the nucleotide sequences. "Do you want me to go on?"

"I don't think that's necessary," said Victor. "I think I've seen enough. Would you mind leaving that floppy disk you've used to bring these files up? I'll bring it to Chimera on Monday."

"Not at all," Louis said. "In fact, this is just a copy. You can keep it if you want. I have the original at home."

Victor saw Louis off, holding the front door ajar until the man got in his van and drove off. Victor waved and then shut the door. Going upstairs, he made sure that VJ was not around. Back in the study, he called Marsha's office but got the service. They didn't know where she was, although she'd been at the hospital earlier.

Victor put the phone down. Then he got the idea of contacting Able Protection. Maybe they could get in touch with their operative. If so, then Victor could find out where VJ was.

But a call to Able Protection only yielded the recording. Victor was forced to leave his name and number with the request that he be called as soon as possible.

For the next half hour, Victor paced back and forth in the upstairs study. For the life of him, he could not understand what it was all about.

The phone rang and Victor grabbed it. It was the grating voice of the man from Able Protection. Victor asked if it were possible to contact the man accompanying VJ.

"All our people carry pagers," the man told him.

"I want to know where my son is," Victor said.

"I'll call you right back." With that, the man hung up. Five minutes later, the phone rang again. "Your son is at Chimera, Inc.," the man said. "Pedro is at the security gate this minute if you want to talk to him."

Victor thanked the man. He hung up the phone and went downstairs for his coat. A few minutes later he was cutting his wheels sharply to do a U-turn in front of the house.

After a quick drive, Victor made an acute turn into the entrance to the Chimera compound and came to an abrupt halt inches from the gatehouse barrier. He drummed his fingers expectantly on the steering wheel, waiting for the guard to raise the black and white striped gate. Instead, the man came out of the office in spite of the rain and bent down next to Victor's window. Without hiding his irritation at being detained, Victor lowered his window.

"Afternoon, Dr. Frank!" the guard said. He touched the brim of his hat in some kind of salute. "If you're looking for that special security man, he's here in the guardhouse."

"You mean the man from Able Protection?" Victor asked.

"That I don't know," the guard said. He straightened up. "Hey, Pedro, you from Able Protection?"

A handsome young man came to the door of the guardhouse. His hair was coal black and he sported a narrow mustache. He looked about twenty.

"Who wants to know?" he asked.

"Your boss here, Dr. Frank."

Pedro came out of the guardhouse and over to Victor's car. He stuck out his hand. "Nice to meet you, Dr. Frank. I'm Pedro Gonzales from Able Protection."

Victor shook hands with him. He wasn't happy. "Why aren't you with my boy?" Victor asked brusquely.

"I was," Pedro explained, "but when we got here, he said he was safe inside the compound at Chimera and that I was supposed to wait in the guardhouse."

"I think your orders were pretty clear to stay with the boy at all times," Victor said.

"Yes, sir," Pedro answered, realizing he'd made a mistake. "It won't happen again. Your son was quite convincing. He said you'd wanted it this way. I'm sorry."

"Where is he?" Victor asked.

"That I can't say," Pedro answered. "He and Philip are on the grounds here someplace. They haven't left if that is what you're concerned about.''

"That's not what I'm concerned about," Victor snapped. "I'm concerned that I hired Able Protection to watch over him and the job's not being done."

"I understand," Pedro said.

Victor looked up at the gate operator. "Is Sheldon working today?"

"Hey, Sheldon!" the guard yelled.

Sheldon appeared at the doorway. Victor asked if he had any idea where VJ was.

"Nope," Sheldon said, "but when he arrived this morning, he and Philip headed that way." He pointed west.

"Toward the river?" Victor asked.

"Could have been," Sheldon said. "But he could have gone to the cafeteria, too."

"Would you like me to come with you and help find him?" Pedro asked.

Victor shook his head no as he put his car in gear. "You wait here until I find him." Then, to the guard, who was blankly listening to the conversation, he said, "I'd appreciate it if you could raise this gate before I drive through it."

The guard jumped and ran back inside to activate the gate mechanism.

Victor floored the accelerator and sped onto the Chimera lot. Forsaking his reserved parking space, he drove to the building that housed his lab and parked in front of the entrance. It said no parking but he didn't care. He pulled his coat collar up and hunched over, running for the door.

Robert was the only one still there. He was as busy as usual, again working with the gel electrophoresis unit. That was where the bits and pieces of the cleaved DNA were separated.

"Have you seen VJ?" Victor asked, shaking off some of the rainwater.

"Haven't seen him," Robert said. He rubbed his eyes with the heels of his hands. "But I have something else to show you." He picked up two strips of film which had dark bands in exactly the same location and held them out for Victor to take. "That second tumor sample you gave me had the same extra piece of DNA as your son's. But the sample was from a different person."

"It was from our live-in nanny," Victor said. "Are you positive that the moiety was the same in both samples?"

"Quite sure," Robert said.

"That's astounding," Victor said, forgetting VJ for a moment.

"I thought you'd find it interesting," Robert said with pride. "It's the kind of finding that cancer researchers have been seeking. It could even be the breakthrough that medicine has been waiting for."

"You've got to sequence it," Victor said impatiently. "Immediately."

"That's what I've been doing," Robert said. "I've got a number of other runs with the electrophoresis unit and then I'll let the computer have a go at it."

"If it turns out to be a retro virus or something like that . . ." Victor said, letting his sentence trail off. It was just one more unexpected finding to be added to a growing list.

"If VJ shows up, tell him I'm looking for him," Victor said. Then he turned and left the lab.

In the cafeteria, Victor went straight to the manager. "Have you seen VJ?"

"He was in here for an early lunch. Philip was with him along with one of the guards."

"One of the guards?" Victor questioned. He wondered why Sheldon hadn't told him that. Victor asked the manager to call his lab if VJ showed up. The manager nodded.

There were a handful of people in the library. Most of them were reading, a few were asleep. The librarian told Victor that VJ had not been around.

Victor got the same response at the fitness center and the day-care center. Except at the cafeteria, no one had seen VJ all day.

Getting an umbrella from his car, Victor set off toward the river. He walked north and hit it at about the middle of the Chimera complex. He turned west, walking along the granite quay. None of the buildings lining the river had been renovated by Chimera as yet, but they'd make ideal sites for some of the intended expansion. Victor was considering moving his administrative office down there. After all, if he had to spend all his time doing administrative work, he might as well have a view.

As he walked, Victor gazed down at the river. In the rain the white water appeared even more turbulent than it had on the previous day.

Looking upriver toward the dam, he could barely see its outline through the mist rising from the base of the falls.

Passing the line of empty buildings, he realized there were hundreds of nooks here a boy could find entertaining. It could be a paradise for games like hide-and-seek or sardines. But those games required a group of kids. Except for Philip, VJ was always on his own.

Victor continued moving upstream until his path was blocked by the portion of the clock tower building that was cantilevered out over part of the dam and a portion of the millpond. To go beyond, Victor had to skirt the building, then approach the river on its west side. There, Victor's path was blocked by the ten-foot-wide sluice that separated from the millpond, then ran parallel to it before leading to a tunnel. Back in the days when waterpower ran the entire mill, the sluice carried the water into the basement of the clock tower building. There the rushing water turned a series of huge paddle wheels which effectively powered thousands of looms and sewing machines as well as the tower clock.

Standing at the tunnel's edge, Victor inspected the bottom of the sluice. Besides a trickle of water, there was debris mostly made up of broken bottles and empty beer cans. Victor eyed the junction of the sluice and the raging river. Two heavy steel doors had once regulated the water flow. Now the whole unit was horribly corroded with rust. Victor wondered how it could still hold back the horrendous force the water exerted on it. The river was practically at the level of the top of the doors.

Victor skirted the sluice and continued his walk westward. The rain stopped and he lowered his umbrella. Soon he came to the last building of the Chimera complex. It, too, was cantilevered out over the river. Beyond it was a city street. Victor turned around and started back.

He didn't call VJ as he'd done the last time. He just looked around and listened. When he got back to the clock tower building, he headed toward the occupied portion of the complex. Stopping in at his lab, he asked Robert if VJ had appeared, but he hadn't.

At a loss as to what to do, Victor returned to the cafeteria.

"Hasn't shown up yet," the manager said before Victor even asked him.

"I didn't expect so," Victor said. "I came over for some coffee."

Still damp from the rain, Victor had become quite chilled as he'd walked along the river. He could tell that the temperature was dropping again now that the storm was over.

Once he'd finished his coffee and felt sufficiently warm, Victor pulled on his damp coat. He again reminded the manager to call over to the lab if and when VJ showed up. Then he returned to the security office. The warmth in there was welcome even if it was heavy with cigarette smoke. Pedro had been playing solitaire on a small couch in the back of the office. He got up when Victor appeared. Sheldon stood up behind his small desk.

"Anybody seen my son?" Victor asked abruptly.

"I just spoke to Hal not two minutes ago," Sheldon said. "I specifically asked him, but he said he hadn't seen VJ all day."

"The manager at the cafeteria told me that VJ had lunch with one of you guys today," Victor said. "How come you didn't tell me?"

"I didn't eat with VJ!" Sheldon said, pressing his palm against his chest. "I know Hal didn't either. He ate with me. We both brown-bagged it. Hey, Fred!"

Fred stuck his head into the main part of the office from the spot where he operated the entrance and the exit gates. Sheldon asked him if he ate lunch with VJ.

"Sure didn't," he said. "I went off-site for lunch."

Sheldon shrugged. Then he said to Victor, "There's only three of us on duty today."

"But the manager said . . ." Victor started, but he stopped. There was no point getting into an argument over who ate with VJ and who didn't. The point was, where the hell was he now? Victor was getting curious and a little concerned. Marsha had wondered, and now he did too, just what did VJ do at Chimera to keep himself occupied. Up until that moment Victor had never given it much thought.

Leaving the security office, Victor went back to his lab. He was running out of ideas of where to search.

"The manager over at the cafeteria just called," Robert said as soon as Victor appeared. "VJ's turned up."

Victor went to the nearest phone and called the manager.

"He's here right now," the manager said.

"Is he alone?" Victor asked.

"Nope. Philip is with him."

"Did you tell him I was looking for him?" Victor asked.

"No, I didn't. You just told me to call. You didn't tell me to say anything to VJ."

"That's fine," Victor said. "Don't say anything. I'm on my way."

Crossing to the building that housed both the cafeteria and the library, Victor chose not to enter through the main cafeteria entrance. He went in a side entrance instead, climbed to the second floor, and only then entered the cafeteria on the balcony level. Going to the railing and looking down, he saw VJ and Philip eating ice cream.

Keeping back out of sight, Victor allowed VJ and Philip to finish their afternoon snack. Before long they got up and disposed of their trays. As they were leaving, Victor came down the stairs, staying out of sight close to the wall. He could hear the door close behind them as they left.

Quickening his step, he got to the door in time to see them turn west on the walkway.

"Something wrong?" the manager asked.

"No, nothing is wrong," Victor said, straightening up and trying to appear nonchalant. The last thing he wanted was office gossip. "Just curious about my son's whereabouts," he said. "I've told him time and time again not to go near the river when it's raging like it is now. But I'm afraid he's not minding me at all."

"Boys will be boys," said the manager.

Victor exited the cafeteria in time to see VJ and Philip in the distance, turning to the right beyond the building housing Victor's lab. Clearly they were heading toward the river. Moving to a slow jog, Victor followed as far as the point where VJ and Philip had turned right. About fifty yards ahead he could still see them. He waited until they veered left just before the river and disappeared from sight. Victor ran down the alleyway.

When he arrived at the point VJ and Philip had gone left, he caught sight of them nearing the clock tower building. As he watched, the two mounted the few steps in front of the deserted building and entered through the doorless entranceway.

"What on earth can they be doing in there?" Victor asked himself. Keeping out of sight as much as possible, he went as far as the entranceway, then paused to listen. But all he could hear was the sound of the falls.

Perplexed, Victor entered. He waited a moment until his eyes adjusted to the dim light. Once they had, he found just the kind of mess he'd expected to find in the abandoned building. The floor was littered with rubble and trash.

The first floor was dominated by a large room with window openings over the millpond. Any glass had long since been broken. Not even the sashes remained. In the center of the room was a pile of debris giving evidence of squatters who had probably occupied the place before Chimera purchased the complex and fenced it in. Over the whole scene hung a pervasive smell of rotting wood, fabric, and cardboard.

Stealthily moving toward the center of the room, Victor tried to listen again, but the noise of the falls was even more dominating inside than it had been outside. He could make out no other sounds.

Along the side opposite the river was a series of small rooms that opened onto the main room. Victor started at the first and worked his way down. Each was filled with trash, to varying degrees. At either end and in the center of the building were stairwells that led to the two floors above. Victor went to the center staircase and slowly climbed up. On each floor he searched the warren of little rooms on both sides of a long hallway. Each room had its complement of rubble, litter, and dirt.

Mystified, Victor returned to the first floor. He walked to one of the front window openings and gazed out at the river, the dam, the pond, and then at the empty sluice, closed from the river with its rusted doors.

It was then that Victor remembered that the clock tower building was connected to the other buildings by elaborate tunnel systems to distribute the rotary mechanical power of the paddle wheels. It was obvious VJ was not in the clock tower building now. Victor wondered if it was this system his son had stumbled onto.

Victor whirled about, his hair standing on edge. He thought he'd heard something over the roar of the falls, or felt something; he wasn't sure which. His eyes rapidly scanned the room but no one was there, and when he strained to listen, all he heard was the sound of the river.

Going from one stairwell to the other, Victor searched for the entrance to the basement. But he couldn't find it. He looked again, still to no avail. There were no steps leading down. Stepping over to a window opening on the south side of the building, he looked to see if there might be a basement entrance from the outside, but there wasn't. There seemed no way to get into the basement.

Victor left the building and walked back to the occupied section of the Chimera complex to visit the office of Buildings and Grounds. Using his master key, he let himself in and turned on the lights. He immediately went to the file room. From a huge metal cabinet he retrieved the architectural drawings of all the existing structures on the

Chimera property. Referencing the clock tower building on the master site plan, he found the drawings for it and pulled them out.

The first drawing was of the basement. It showed where the water tunnel entered the edifice. Within the basement the water flowed through a heavily planked trough where it turned a series of paddle wheels that were mounted both horizontally and vertically. The basement itself was divided into one central room with all the power wheels and a number of side rooms. The tunnel system emanated from one of the side rooms on the east end.

Victor then looked at the plan for the first floor. He found the stairway that led down to the basement easily enough. It was immediately to the right of the central stairwell. He could not imagine how he had missed it.

To be doubly sure, he made a copy of the basement and first-floor plans, using the special copy machine that Chimera had for that purpose. He reduced the copies to legal-paper size. With these in hand, he returned to the clock tower building, determined to explore below.

Victor made his way through the trash on the floor and approached the central stairwell. Standing in front of it, he looked to the immediate right. He even took the copy of the existing floor plan and held it up to make sure he'd read it right.

Victor couldn't understand what he was doing wrong. There were no basement stairs. He even walked around the other side of the stairwell just in case the blueprints were in error. But there were no stairs going down on that side either.

Walking back to the location where the plans said the stairway was supposed to be, Victor noticed that the area was devoid of the debris that was scattered over the rest of the floor. Finding that odd, he bent down and noticed something else: the floor planking was wider than it was in the rest of the building. And it was newer wood.

Victor started at a sound from behind. He turned, but it seemed there was nothing there. Still, he felt there was someone there in the semidarkness. Someone very near. Terrified, Victor tried to scan the surrounding cavernous room. Again from behind he heard or felt a second sound or vibration. No doubt about it: a footfall. Victor turned, but too late. He could just make out the shadowy silhouette of a figure raising some sort of object over his head. He tried to lift his hands to protect himself from the blow, but could not save himself from its power. His mind collapsed into a black abyss.

* * *

After leaving Lowell, Marsha stopped at a roadside concession and used the phone and called the Blakemores. She felt mildly awkward, but managed to get herself invited over for a short visit. It took her about half an hour to get to their home in West Boxford at 479 Plum Island Road.

As she pulled in, Marsha was glad it had stopped raining. But as she opened the door to her car, she wished she'd taken one of her down coats. The temperature was dropping rapidly.

The Blakemore house was a cozy structure reminiscent of the kind of houses seen on Cape Cod. The windows were mullioned and painted white. Arching over the entranceway was a latticed wood arbor. Marsha climbed the front steps and rang the bell.

Mrs. Blakemore opened the door. She was a stocky woman about Marsha's age, with short hair turned up at the ends. "Come in," she said, eyeing Marsha curiously. "I'm Edith Blakemore."

Marsha felt the woman's stare and wondered if there was something amiss with her appearance, like a dark spot between her front teeth from the fruit she'd just eaten. She ran her tongue over her teeth just to be sure.

Inside the house was every bit as charming as the exterior. The furniture was early American antique with chintz-covered couches and wing chairs. On the wide-planked pine floor were rag rugs.

"May I take your coat?" Edith asked. "How about some coffee or tea?"

"Tea would be nice," Marsha said. She followed Edith into the living room.

Mr. Blakemore, who had been sitting by the fire with the newspaper, got to his feet as Marsha entered. "I'm Carl Blakemore," he said, extending his hand. He was a big man with leathery skin and dark features.

Marsha shook his hand.

"Sit down, make yourself at home," Carl said, motioning to the couch. After Marsha sat down, he returned to his own seat, placing the paper on the floor next to his chair. He smiled pleasantly. Edith disappeared into the kitchen.

"Interesting weather," Carl said, attempting to make conversation.

Marsha could not rid herself of the uncomfortable feeling she'd gotten when Edith had first looked at her. There was something stiff

637

and unnatural about these people but Marsha couldn't put her finger on it.

A boy came down the stairs and into the room. He was just about VJ's age but larger and stockier, with sandy-colored hair and dark brown eyes. There was a tough look about him, and the resemblance to Mr. Blakemore was striking. "Hello," he said, extending his hand in a gentlemanly fashion.

"You must be Richie," Marsha said, shaking hands with the boy. "I'm VJ's mother. I've heard a lot about you." Marsha felt an exaggeration was in order.

"You have?" Richie asked uncertainly.

"Yes," Marsha said. "And the more I heard, the more I wanted to meet you. Why don't you come over to our house sometime? I suppose VJ has told you we have a swimming pool."

"VJ never told me you have a swimming pool," Richie said. He sat on the hearth and stared up at Marsha to the point that she felt even more uncomfortable.

"I don't know why he didn't," Marsha said. She looked at Carl. "You never know what's in these children's minds," she said with a smile.

"Guess not," Carl said.

There was an awkward silence. Marsha wondered what was going on.

"Milk or lemon?" Edith asked, coming into the room and breaking the silence. She carried a tray into the living room and put it on the coffee table.

"Lemon," Marsha said. She took the cup from Edith and held it while Edith poured. Then she squeezed in a little lemon. When she was finished, she settled back. Then she noticed that the other three people were not joining her. They were just staring.

"No one else is having any tea?" Marsha asked, feeling progressively self-conscious.

"You enjoy it," Edith said.

Marsha took a sip. It was hot, so she placed it on the coffee table. She cleared her throat nervously. "I'm sorry to have barged in on you like this."

"Not at all," Edith said. "Being a rainy day and all, we've just been relaxing around the house."

"I've wanted to meet you for some time," Marsha said. "You've been awfully nice to VJ, I'd like to return the favor."

638

"What exactly do you mean?" Edith asked.

"Well, for one thing," Marsha said, "I'd like to have Richie come over to our home and spend the night. If he'd like to, of course. Would you like to do that, Richie?"

Richie shrugged his shoulders.

"Why exactly would you like Richie to spend the night?" Carl asked.

"To return the favor, of course," Marsha said. "Since VJ has spent so many nights over here, I thought it only natural that Richie come to our house once in a while."

Carl and Edith exchanged glances. Edith spoke: "Your son has never spent the night here. I'm afraid I don't know what you're talking about."

Marsha looked from one person to the other, her confusion mounting. "VJ has never stayed here overnight?" she asked incredulously.

"Never," Carl said.

Looking down at Richie, Marsha asked, "What about last Sunday. Did you and VJ spend time together?"

"No," Richie said, shaking his head.

"Well, then, I suppose I have to apologize for taking your time," Marsha said, embarrassed. She stood up. Edith and Carl did the same.

"We thought you'd come to talk about the fight," Carl said.

"What fight?" Marsha asked.

"Apparently VJ and our boy had a little disagreement," Carl said. "Richie had to spend the night in the infirmary with a broken nose."

"Oh, I'm terribly sorry," Marsha said. "I'll have to have a talk with VJ."

As quickly and as gracefully as she could, Marsha left the Blakemore house. When she got into her car, she was furious. She sure would have a talk with VJ. He was even worse off than she'd thought. How could she have missed so much? It was as though her son had a separate life, one entirely different from the one he presented. Such cool, calm deceit was markedly abnormal! What was happening to her little boy?

11

SATURDAY AFTERNOON

Victor regained consciousness gradually. Through a haze, he heard muffled noises he couldn't make out. Then he realized the noises were voices. Finally he recognized VJ's voice, and the boy was angry, yelling at someone, telling them that Victor was his father.

"I'm sorry." The words carried a heavy Spanish accent. "How was I to know?"

Victor felt himself being shaken. The jostling made him aware that his head hurt. He felt dizzy. Reaching up, he felt a lump the size of a golf ball on the top of his forehead.

"Dad?" VJ called.

Victor opened his eyes groggily. For a moment the headache became intense, then waned. He was looking up into VJ's icy blue eyes. His son was holding his shoulders. Beyond VJ were other faces with swarthy complexions. Next to VJ was a particularly dark man with an almost sinister expression on his face, heightened by the effect of an eyelid that drooped over his left eye.

Closing his eyes again and gritting his teeth, Victor sat up. Dizziness made him totter for a moment, but VJ helped steady him. When the dizziness passed, Victor opened his eyes again. He also felt the bump again, only vaguely remembering how he'd gotten it.

"Are you all right, Dad?" VJ persisted.

640

"I think so," Victor said. He looked at the strangers. They were dressed in the typical Chimera security uniforms, but he didn't recognize any of them. Behind them stood Philip, looking sheepish and afraid.

Glancing around the room to orient himself, Victor first thought he was back in his lab because he was surrounded by the usual bevy of sophisticated scientific instrumentation. Right next to him he noticed one of the newest instruments available on the market: a fast protein liquid chromatography unit.

But he wasn't in his lab. The setting was an inappropriate combination of high-tech with a rustic background of exposed granite and hewn beams.

"Where am I?" Victor asked as he rubbed his eyes with the knuckles of his index fingers.

"You are where you aren't supposed to be," VJ said.

"What happened to me?" Victor asked as he tried to get his feet under him to stand.

"Why don't you just relax a minute," VJ said, restraining him. "You hit your head."

That's an understatement, Victor was tempted to say. He reached up and felt the impressive lump once more, then examined his fingers to see if there was any blood. He was still confused but his head was beginning to clear. "What do you mean, 'I'm where I'm not supposed to be'?" he asked as if suddenly hearing VJ's comment for the first time.

"You weren't supposed to see this hidden lab of mine for another month or so," VJ said. "At least not until we were in my new digs across the river."

Victor blinked. Suddenly his mind was clear. He remembered the dark figure who'd clobbered him. He looked at his son's smiling face, then let his eyes wander around the unlikely laboratory. It was as if he'd taken a step beyond reality where mass spectrometers competed with hand-chiseled granite. "Exactly where am I?" Victor asked.

"We are in the basement of the clock tower building," VJ said as he let go of Victor and stood up. VJ made a sweeping gesture with his hand and said, "But we've changed the decor to suit our needs. What do you think?"

Victor swallowed and licked his dry lips. He glanced at his son only to see him beaming proudly. He watched as Philip nervously wrung

641

his hands. Victor looked at the three men in Chimera security guard uniforms—swarthy Hispanics with tanned faces and shiny black hair. Then his eyes slowly swept around the high-ceilinged room. It was one of the most astounding sights he'd ever seen. Directly in front of him was the yawning maw of the opening into the sluice. A slime of green mold oozed out of the lower lip with a trickle of moisture. Most of the opening was covered with a makeshift hatch made of heavy old lumber. The huge wooden trough that used to carry the water through the room had been dismantled to serve as raw materials for the hatch, the lab benches, and bookshelves.

The room appeared to be about sixty feet across and about a hundred feet in length. The largest of the old paddle wheels still stood in its vertical position in the center of the room like a piece of modern sculpture. A number of the laboratory instruments were pushed up against its huge blades, forming a giant circle.

At both ends of the room were several heavy doors reinforced with metal rivets. The walls of the room on all four sides were constructed of the same gray granite. The ceiling consisted of open joists supporting heavy planking. In addition to the largest of the paddle wheels, most of the old mechanical apparatus of huge rods and gears that had transmitted the waterpower were still in their original places, supported from the ceiling joists by metal sheaths.

Just behind Victor was a flight of wooden stairs that rose up to the ceiling, dead-ending into wooden planks.

"Well, Dad?" VJ questioned with anticipation. "Come on! What do you think?"

Victor rose to his feet unsteadily. "This is your lab?" he asked.

"That's right," VJ said. "Pretty cool, wouldn't you say?"

Wobbling, Victor made his way over to a DNA synthesizer and ran his hand along its top edge. It was the newest model available, better than the unit Victor had in his own lab.

"Where did all this equipment come from?" Victor asked, spotting a magnetic electron microscope on the other side of the paddle wheel.

"You could say it's on loan," said VJ. He followed his father and gazed lovingly at the synthesizer.

Victor turned to VJ, studying the boy's face. "Is this the equipment that was stolen from Chimera?"

"It was never stolen," VJ said with an impish grin. "Let's say it was merely rerouted. It belongs to Chimera, and it's still on Chimera grounds. I don't think you could consider it stolen unless it left the Chimera complex.''

Walking on to the next laboratory appliance, an elaborate gas chromatography unit, Victor tried to pull himself together. His headache still bothered him, especially when he moved, and he felt quite dizzy. But he was starting to think the dizziness could be attributed as much to the revelation of this lab than the blow to his head. This was something out of a dream—a nightmare. Gently touching one of the chromatography columns, he assured himself it was real. Then he turned to VJ, who was right behind him.

"I think you had better explain this place from the beginning.''

"Sure,'' VJ said. "But why don't we go into the living quarters where we'll be more comfortable.''

VJ led the way around the large paddle wheel, passed the electron microscope, and headed for the end of the room. When he got there, he opened the door on the left. He pointed to the door on the right: "More lab spaces through there. We never seem to have enough.''

As Victor followed VJ, he noticed over his shoulder that Philip was coming but the security guards paid them no heed. Two of them had already sat down on a makeshift bench and started playing cards.

VJ led Victor to the room that indeed looked like living quarters. Rugs in various sizes and shapes had been hung over the granite walls to provide a warmer atmosphere. About ten rollaway cots with bed linens cluttered the floor. Near the entrance door was a round table with six captain's chairs. VJ motioned for his father to have a seat.

Victor pulled out a chair and sat down. Philip silently sat down several chairs away.

"Want something to drink? Hot chocolate or tea?'' VJ asked, playing host. "We have all the comforts of home here.''

"I think you'd better tell me what this is all about,'' Victor said.

VJ nodded, then quietly began. "You know I've been interested in what was going on in your lab from the first days you brought me to Chimera. The problem was nobody let me touch anything.''

"Of course not,'' Victor said. "You were an infant.''

"I didn't feel like an infant,'' VJ said. "Needless to say, I decided early on I needed a lab of my own if I were to do anything at all. It started out small, but it had to get bigger since I kept needing more equipment.''

"How old were you when you started?'' Victor asked.

"It was about seven years ago," VJ said. "I was three. It was surprisingly easy to set the lab up with Philip around to lend the needed muscles." Philip smiled proudly. VJ went on: "At first, I was in the building next to the cafeteria. But then there was talk about its being renovated, so we moved everything here to the clock tower. It's been my little secret ever since."

"For seven years?" Victor questioned.

VJ nodded. "About that."

"But why?" Victor asked.

"So I could do some serious work," VJ said. "Watching you and being around the lab I became fascinated with the potential of biology. It is the science of the future. I had some ideas of my own about how the research should have been conducted."

"But you could have worked in my lab," Victor said.

"Impossible," VJ said with a wave of his hand. "I'm too young. No one would have let me do what I've been doing. I needed freedom from restrictions, from rules, from helping hands. I needed my own space, and let me tell you, it has paid off beyond your wildest dreams. I've been dying to show you what I've been doing for at least a year. You're going to flip."

"You've had some successes?" Victor asked hesitantly, suddenly curious.

"Several astounding breakthroughs is a better description," VJ said. "Maybe you should try to guess."

"I couldn't," Victor said.

"I think you could," VJ said. "One of the projects is something that you yourself have been working on."

"I've been working on a lot of things," Victor said evasively.

"Listen," VJ said, "my idea is to let you have credit for the discoveries so that Chimera can patent them and prosper. We don't want anybody to know that I'm involved at all."

"Something like the swimming race?" Victor asked.

VJ laughed heartily. "Something like that, I suppose. I prefer not to draw attention to myself. I don't want anyone to pry, and people seem to get so curious when there's a prodigy in their midst. I'd prefer you to get the credit. Chimera will get the patent. We can say I'll offer you my results to compensate for space and equipment."

"Give me an idea of what you've turned up."

"For starters, I've solved the mystery of the implantation of a fertilized egg in a uterus,'' VJ said proudly. ''As long as the zygote is normal, I can guarantee one hundred percent implantation.''

''You're joking,'' said Victor.

''I'm not joking,'' VJ said somewhat crossly. ''The answer turned out to be both simple and more complicated than expected. It involves the juxtaposition of the zygote and the surface cells of the uterus, initiating a kind of chemical communication which most people would probably call an antibody-antigen reaction. It is this reaction that releases a polypeptide vessel proliferation factor which results in the implantation. I've isolated this factor and have produced it in quantity with recombinant DNA techniques. A shot of it guarantees one hundred percent implantation of a healthy fertilized egg.''

To emphasize his point, VJ pulled a vial out of his pocket and placed it on the table in front of his father. ''It's for you,'' he said. ''Who knows, maybe you'll win a Nobel Prize.'' VJ laughed and Philip joined in.

Victor picked up the vial and stared at the clear, viscous fluid within. ''Something like this has to be tested,'' he said.

''It's been tested,'' VJ said. ''Animals, humans, it's all the same. One hundred percent successful.''

Victor looked at his son, then at Philip. Philip smiled hesitantly, unsure of Victor's reaction. Victor glanced at the vial again. He could immediately appreciate the academic and economic impact of such a discovery. It would be monumental, revolutionizing in-vitro fertilization techniques. With a product like this, Fertility, Inc., would dominate the field. It would have worldwide impact.

Victor took a deep breath. ''Are you sure this works in humans?'' he asked.

''Absolutely,'' VJ said. ''As I said, it's been tested.''

''In whom?'' Victor asked.

''Volunteers, of course,'' VJ said. ''But there will be plenty of time to give you the details later.''

Volunteers? Victor's head reeled. Didn't VJ realize he couldn't blithely experiment with real people? There were laws to think of, ethics. But the possibilities were irresistible. And who was Victor to judge? Hadn't he engineered the conception of the extraordinary boy he had before him now?

''Let me look at your lab again,'' Victor said, pushing away from the table.

VJ ran ahead to open the door. Victor returned to the main room where the security men were still playing cards, talking loudly in Spanish.

Victor slowly walked around the circle, gazing at the instrumentation. Impressive was an understatement. He realized his headache seemed suddenly better. He felt a growing sense of elation. It was hard to believe that his ten-year-old son was responsible for all this.

"Who knows about this lab?" Victor asked, stopping to appreciate the electron microscope. He ran a hand over its curved surface.

"Philip and a handful of security people," said VJ. "And now you."

Victor shot VJ a quick glance. VJ smiled back.

All at once Victor laughed. "And to think this has been going on under our noses all this time!" Victor shook his head in disbelief, continuing around the circle of scientific appliances, tapping the tops of some of them with the tips of his fingers. "And are you sure about this implantation protein?" Victor asked, already considering likely trade names: Conceptol. Fertol.

"Completely," VJ said. "And that's just one of the discoveries that I've made. There are many more. I've made some advances in understanding the process of cellular differentiation and development I believe will herald a new era of biology."

Victor stopped his wandering and turned back to VJ. "Does Marsha know anything about this?" he asked.

"Nothing!" VJ said with emphasis.

"She is going to be one happy lady," Victor said with a smile. "She's been worrying herself sick that something is wrong with you since you don't have time for kids your own age."

"I've been a little too busy for Cub Scouts," said VJ.

Victor laughed. "God, I'll say. She's going to love this. We'll have to tell her and bring her here."

"I'm not convinced that's such a good idea," VJ said.

"It is, believe me," Victor said. "It will relieve her enormously and I won't have to listen to another lecture on your psychological development."

"I don't want people knowing about this lab," VJ said. "It was an unexpected accident that you discovered it. I wasn't planning on telling you any of this until I'd moved the lab to the new location."

"Where is that?" Victor asked.

"Nearby," VJ said. "I'll show it to you on another day."

"But we have to tell Marsha," Victor insisted. "You have no idea how worried she's been about you. I'll take care of her. She won't tell anyone."

"It's a risk," VJ said. "I don't think she'll be as impressed as you by my accomplishments. She's not as enthusiastic about science as we are."

"She'll be ecstatic that you are such a genius. And that you've put all this together. It's just extraordinary."

"Well, maybe . . ." VJ said, trying to decide.

"Trust me," Victor said enthusiastically.

"Perhaps on this one issue I'll have to bow to your better judgment," VJ said. "I guess you know her better than I do. All I can say is that I hope you're right. She could cause a lot of trouble."

"I'll get her right now," Victor said with obvious excitement.

"How will you get her over here to the building without people noticing?" VJ said.

"It's Saturday," Victor said. "Hardly anyone is around, especially so late in the day."

"Okay," VJ said with resignation.

Victor headed for the stairs, practically running. "I'll be back in thirty minutes. Forty-five, tops," he said. He charged up a half dozen steps, then came to a stop. As he noticed before, the stairs dead-ended into heavy planks.

"Is this the way out?" Victor asked.

"Just give it a shove," VJ said. "It's counterweighted."

Victor went up the rest of the stairs more slowly until his hand rested on the overhead planks. Tentatively, he pushed upward. To his surprise, a large trapdoor opened with amazing ease. Casting a last glance down at VJ, Victor winked, then climbed up the rest of the stairs. When he let go of the trapdoor, it sank silently into place, cutting off the light from below.

Victor ran from the building, his pulse up from sheer exhilaration. He hadn't felt so ecstatic in years.

Having returned from her two upsetting visits, Marsha made herself a real cup of tea. She'd taken it into her study to try to calm down when she heard Victor's car start up the drive.

It wasn't long before his head popped through the door. He still had his coat on. "Ah, there you are, sweet thing!"

Sweet thing? Marsha thought disdainfully. He hasn't called me that for years. "Come in here!" she called to him.

But Victor was already on his way into the room. He grabbed her hand, trying to pull her from her couch. Marsha resisted and got her hand free. "What are you doing?" she questioned.

"I've got something to show you." There was a distinct twinkle in his eye.

"What's come over you?"

"Come on!" Victor urged, pulling her to her feet. "I've got a surprise for you that you are going to love."

"I've got a surprise for you that you are not going to love," Marsha said. "Sit down. I have something important to tell you."

"Later," Victor said. "What I've got is more important."

"I doubt that," Marsha said. "I've learned some more disturbing things about VJ."

"Isn't that appropriate?" Victor said with a smile. "Because what I've discovered is going to make you forget all VJ's traits you've been agonizing over."

Victor tried to drag Marsha from the room. "Victor!" she called out sharply. She pulled her arm free again. "You're acting like a child!"

"I'm immune to your worst epithet," Victor said gaily. "Marsha, I'm not kidding—I have some great news for you."

Marsha put her hands on her hips and spread her legs for stability. "VJ has been lying to us about other things besides the school situation. I found out that he has never stayed at the Blakemore house. Never!"

"I'm not surprised," Victor said, thinking how much time VJ would need to spend in his lab to accomplish what he apparently had.

"You're not surprised?" Marsha said with exasperation, throwing her hands into the air. "Richie Blakemore and VJ are not even friends. In fact, they had a fight recently in which VJ broke the Blakemore boy's nose."

"Okay, okay!" Victor said, assuming a calm tone of voice. He gripped Marsha's upper arms and looked directly into her warm eyes. "Calm down and listen to me. What I have to show you will explain where VJ has been spending most of his time. Now will you just trust me and come?"

Marsha's eyes narrowed. At least he sounded sincere. "Where are you taking me?" she demanded suspiciously.

"Out to the car," Victor said enthusiastically. "Come on, get your coat."

"I hope you know what you're doing," Marsha said as she allowed herself to be led from her study. She got her coat and a few minutes later she was holding on to the dash to steady herself. "Do we have to drive this fast?" she asked.

"I can't wait for you to see this," Victor said. He banked sharply. "And to think I was proud of a secret tree house I built when I was twelve!"

Marsha wondered if he'd taken leave of his senses. He'd been behaving so oddly lately, but she'd never seen him like this.

Victor thundered over the Merrimack River and eventually pulled into Chimera. The security shift had changed in the guardhouse. Fred wasn't the one manning the gate.

In deference to VJ's concern for secrecy, Victor parked in his usual spot in front of the administration building. "We have a little walk," he said to Marsha as they alighted from the car.

It was late afternoon as they approached the river. Long shadows had begun to creep across the alleyways. It was also quite cold. Marsha guessed it was in the thirties. Victor walked slightly ahead of her, glancing back over his shoulder as if he expected someone might be following them. Marsha glanced behind them out of curiosity, but no one was there. She pulled her coat around her more closely, and decided what was chilling her was more than the weather.

Victor took hold of her hand as her gait began to slow. She'd noticed they had moved from the occupied section of the complex to the part that was unrenovated. On either side of her were the dark hulks of abandoned buildings. They loomed ominously in the gathering dusk.

"Victor, where are you taking me?" she asked, threatening to stop.

"We're almost there," Victor said, urging her onward.

When they got to the gaping entranceway of the derelict clock tower building, Marsha stopped.

"You don't expect me to go in there?" she asked, incredulous. She leaned back and looked up at the soaring tower. Rapidly moving clouds made her momentarily dizzy. She had to look away.

"Please," Victor said. "VJ is here. You'll be wonderfully surprised. Trust me."

Marsha looked from Victor's excited face to the interior gloom of the building and back. Victor's eyes were bright with anticipation.

649

"This is crazy," she said. Grudgingly, she moved forward. The gloom enveloped them.

Marsha let Victor lead as they stumbled over the rubble-strewn floor. "Just a little further," Victor said.

Marsha's eyes adjusted enough to see vague outlines on the floor. To her left were large window openings through which came the roar of the falls as well as reflected light from the surface of the millpond. Victor stopped in front of an empty corner. He let go of Marsha's hand and bent down. He knocked on the floor. To Marsha's surprise, a section of the floor lifted and incandescent light flooded up.

"Mother," VJ said. "Come in quickly."

Marsha gingerly climbed down the stairs. Victor followed and VJ let the trapdoor glide back into place.

Marsha looked around the room. To her, it looked like a scene out of a science fiction movie. The combination of the rusted gears, the huge paddle wheel, and the granite, along with the profusion of high-tech instrumentation, was disorienting. She nodded to Philip, who nodded back at her. She nodded to the Chimera security guards but they didn't return the gesture. She noticed the man with the droopy eyelid.

"Isn't it the most amazing thing you've ever seen?" Victor said as he came up alongside Marsha. She looked at him. He was beside himself with excitement.

"What is it?" Marsha questioned.

"It's VJ's lab." Victor said as he launched into a brief explanation of the setup, including how VJ had been able to build it without anyone having had the slightest suspicion. He even told Marsha about VJ's discovery of the implantation protein, and what that would mean to the infertility field.

"So now you have some idea why VJ hasn't been as social as you'd like," concluded Victor. "He's been here, working his butt off!" Victor chuckled as he let his own eyes roam around the room.

Marsha glanced at VJ, who was eyeing her cautiously, waiting for her reaction, no doubt. There was an enormous piece of equipment in front of her. She had no idea what it was. "Where did all this equipment come from?" she asked.

"That's the best part," Victor said. "It all belongs to Chimera."

"How did it get here?" Marsha asked.

"I guess . . ." Victor began, but then stopped. He looked at VJ. "How did you get this stuff here?"

"A number of people helped," VJ said vaguely. "Philip did most of the actual moving. Some of the things had to be disassembled, then put together again. We used the old tunnel system."

"Was Gephardt one of the people that helped?" Victor asked, suddenly suspicious.

"He helped," VJ admitted.

"Why was someone like Gephardt willing to help you get equipment?" Marsha asked.

"He decided it was the prudent thing to do," VJ said cryptically. "I'd spent some time with the Chimera computer, and I'd discovered a number of people who'd been embezzling the company. Once I had that information, I merely asked these people for help from their respective departments. Of course, no one knew that the others were involved, or what they were doing. So it all stayed nice and quiet. But the point is, all this equipment belongs to Chimera. Nothing has been stolen. It's all right here."

"I'd call it blackmail," Marsha said.

"I never once threatened anybody," VJ said. "I merely let them know what I knew, then asked for a favor."

"I'd say VJ was quite resourceful," Victor said. "But I'd like to have this list of embezzlers."

"Sorry," VJ said. "But I have an understanding with these people. Besides, the worst offender, Dr. Gephardt, was already exposed by the IRS. The ironic thing was that he thought that I'd been behind his exposure." VJ laughed.

Victor's face lit up with sudden comprehension. "I get it," he said. "Gephardt was directing the messages at you when he tossed the brick and killed poor Kissa."

VJ nodded. "The fool," he said.

"I want to get out of here!" Marsha said suddenly, surprising both Victor and VJ.

"But there's more to see," Victor said.

"I'm sure there is," Marsha said. "But for the moment I've seen enough. I want to leave." She looked from father to son, then glanced around the room. She felt distinctly uncomfortable. The place scared her.

"There are living quarters . . . ." Victor said, pointing toward the west end of the room.

Marsha ignored his gesture. She walked back to the stairs and started up.

"I told you we shouldn't have told her," VJ whispered.

Victor put a hand on his shoulder and whispered back, "Don't worry, I'll take care of her." Then to Marsha he called, "Just a second, I'll come along."

Marsha went directly up to the trapdoor and pushed. Once out of the basement, she stumbled blindly across the wide expanse of rubble-filled floor space. When she reached the door and the fresh air, she felt a flood of relief.

"Marsha, for goodness sake," said Victor, catching up with her and turning her around. "Where are you going?"

"Home!" She walked on with determination. But Victor caught up to her again.

"Why are you acting this way?" Victor asked.

Marsha didn't answer. Instead she increased her pace. They were practically running. When they got to Victor's car, she opened her door and got in.

Victor got in on his side. "You won't talk to me?" he questioned with some irritation.

Setting her jaw, Marsha stared ahead. They drove home in strained silence.

Once they were home, Marsha poured herself a glass of white wine.

"Marsha," Victor began, breaking the veil of silence, "why are you acting like this? I thought you'd be as thrilled as I am, especially after all your worry about whether VJ's intelligence would drop again. Obviously the boy's just fine. He's as bright as ever."

"That's just the point," Marsha said sharply. "VJ's intelligence is fine, and it terrifies me. By the looks of that lab, he must still be in the genius range, wouldn't you say?"

"Clearly," said Victor. "Isn't that wonderful?"

"No," Marsha snapped. She put her wineglass on the table. "If he is still a genius, then the whole episode of his intelligence drop had to be a charade. He's been pretending all this time. He's been smart enough to outwit my psychological tests, except for that validity scale. Victor, his whole life with us is a sham. Just one big lie."

"Maybe there's another explanation," Victor said. "Maybe his intelligence dropped, then rebounded."

"I just did an IQ test this week," Marsha said. "He's tested around 130 since he was three and a half."

"Okay," Victor said with some irritation of his own. "The point is that VJ is okay and we don't have to worry about him. In fact, he is more than okay. He's put that lab together all by himself. His IQ has to be much higher than 130. And that means my NGF project is an unqualified success.''.

Marsha shook her head. She couldn't believe he could be so myopic. ''What exactly do you think you have created with VJ and your mutations and gene manipulations?'' she asked.

''I've created an essentially normal child with superior intelligence,'' Victor said without hesitation.

''What else?''

''What do you mean, what else?''

''What about this person's personality?'' Marsha asked.

''This person?'' Victor questioned. ''You are talking about VJ, our son.''

''What about his personality?'' Marsha repeated.

''Oh, damn the personality,'' Victor snapped. ''The kid is a prodigy. He's already accomplished research breakthroughs. So what if he has a few hangups? We all do.''

''You've created a monster,'' Marsha said softly, her voice breaking. She bit her lip. Why couldn't she control her tears? ''You've created a monster and I'll never forgive you for it.''

''Give me a break,'' Victor said, exasperated.

''VJ is an oddity,'' Marsha snapped. ''His intelligence has set him apart, made him lonely. He apparently realized it when he was three. His intelligence is so far above everyone else's, he doesn't respond to the same social restraints. His intelligence has put him beyond everyone, everything.''

''Are you finished?'' Victor demanded.

''No, I'm not!'' Marsha shouted, suddenly angry though tears streamed down her face. ''What about the deaths of those children that had the same gene as VJ? Why did they die?''

''Why are you bringing that up again?''

''What about the deaths of David and Janice?'' Marsha asked, lowering her voice, ignoring Victor's question. ''I didn't have a chance to tell you before, but I visited the Fays today. They told me that Janice had been convinced that VJ had something to do with David's death. She told them he was evil.''

''We heard that nonsense before her death,'' Victor said. ''She became a religious psychotic. You said so yourself.''

"Visiting her parents made me rethink what happened back then," Marsha said. "Janice had been convinced she'd been drugged and poisoned."

"Marsha," Victor said sharply. He grabbed her by her shoulders. "Get ahold of yourself. You're talking nonsense. David died of liver cancer, remember? Janice went a little crazy before she died. Remember that? She had some paranoia in addition to her other troubles. She probably had a brain metastasis, the poor woman. Besides, people don't get liver cancer because they're poisoned." But even as he said the words, doubts of his own sprang up. He recalled the troublesome bit of DNA that he'd found in both David's and Janice's tumor cells. "And about those children's deaths," Victor said as he sat down across from her. "I'm sure they had something to do with the internal politics of Chimera. Somebody has found out about the NGF experiment and wants to discredit me. That's why I want someone with VJ."

"When did you decide this?" Marsha asked, lowering her glass.

Victor shrugged. "I don't remember exactly," he said. "Sometime this week."

"That means even you think the deaths were really murders; that somebody deliberately killed those children," Marsha said with renewed alarm.

Victor had forgotten that he'd purposefully kept the information about the cephaloclor from her. He swallowed uncomfortably.

"Victor!" Marsha said with resentment. "What haven't you told me?"

Stalling, Victor took a sip from his drink. He tried to think of some smoke screen to cover the truth, but couldn't think of a thing. The day's revelations had made him careless. With a sigh he explained about the cephaloclor in the children's blood.

"My God!" Marsha whispered. "Are you sure it was someone at Chimera who gave the children the cephaloclor?"

"Absolutely," Victor said. "The only place the children's lives intersected was at the Chimera day-care center. That had to be where they were given the cephaloclor."

"But who would do such a terrible thing?" Marsha asked. She wanted to be reassured that VJ could not be involved.

"It had to be either Hurst or Ronald. If I had to pick one, I'd pick Hurst. But until I get harder evidence, all I can do is keep the security man with VJ to be sure no one tries to give him any cephaloclor."

Just then the back door burst open and VJ, Philip, and Pedro Gonzales came into the family room. Marsha stayed in her seat, but Victor jumped up. "Hello, everybody," Victor said, trying to sound cheerful. He started to introduce Pedro to Marsha but she interrupted him and said that they'd already met that morning.

"That's good," Victor said, rubbing his hands together. He obviously didn't know what to do.

Marsha looked at VJ. VJ stared back at her with his penetrating blue eyes. She had to avert her gaze. It was a terrifying feeling for her to harbor the thoughts she had about him, especially since she'd come to realize that she was afraid of him.

"Why don't you guys hit the pool?" Victor said to VJ and Philip.

"Sounds good to me," VJ said. He and Philip went up the back stairs.

"You'll be back in the morning?" Victor asked Pedro.

"Yes, sir," he said. "Six A.M., I'll be out in the courtyard in my car."

Victor saw the man off, then came back into the kitchen.

"I'll go have a talk with VJ," Victor announced. "I'll ask him directly about this intelligence question. Maybe whatever he says will make you feel better."

"I think I already know what he'll say," said Marsha, "but suit yourself."

Victor went up the stairs quickly and turned into VJ's room. VJ looked expectantly at his father as he entered. Victor realized how awed he felt by his own creation. The boy was beautiful and had a mind that must be boundless. Victor didn't know whether to be jealous or proud.

"Mother isn't as excited about the lab as you are," VJ said. "I can tell."

"It was a little overwhelming for her," Victor explained.

"I wish I hadn't agreed to let her see it," VJ said.

"Don't worry," Victor assured him. "I'll take care of her. But there is something that has been bothering her for years. Did you fake your loss of intelligence back when you were three and a half?"

"Of course," VJ said, slipping on his robe over his hairless body. "I had to. If I hadn't, I'd never have been able to work as I have. I needed anonymity which I couldn't have had as some superintelligent freak. I wanted to be treated normally, and for that to happen, I had to appear normal. Or close to it."

"You didn't think you could have talked to me about it?" Victor asked.

"Are you kidding?" VJ said. "You and Mom constantly had me on show. There was no way you would have been willing to let me quit."

"You're probably right," Victor admitted. "For a while there your abilities were the focus of our lives."

"Are you going to swim with us?" VJ asked with a smile. "I'll let you win."

Victor laughed in spite of himself. "Thanks, but I'd better go back and talk with Marsha. Get her to calm down. You have fun." Victor went to the door, but turned back toward the room. "Tomorrow I'd like to hear the details about the implantation project."

"I'll be excited to show you," VJ said.

Victor nodded, smiled, then went back downstairs. As he neared the kitchen he could smell garlic, onions, and peppers sautéeing for spaghetti sauce. A good sign, Marsha working on dinner.

Marsha had thrown herself into preparing the meal as a form of instant therapy. Her mind was such a jumble from the day's numerous revelations. Busywork was a way of avoiding thinking about the implications. When Victor returned from talking to VJ, she studiously ignored him, instead focusing her attention on the tomato paste she was in the process of opening.

Victor didn't say anything for a time. Instead, he laid the table and opened a bottle of Chianti. When he ran out of things to do, he sat on one of the bar stools at the kitchen counter and said, "You were right about VJ feigning his loss of intelligence."

"I'm not surprised," Marsha said. She got out the lettuce, onions, and cucumbers for the salad.

"But he had a damn good reason." He gave her VJ's to-the-point explanation.

"I guess that's supposed to make me feel more comfortable," Marsha said when Victor was done.

Victor said nothing.

Marsha persisted. "Tell me, when you were upstairs talking with VJ, did you ask him about the deaths of those children, and about David's and Janice's?"

"Of course not!" Victor said, horrified at the suggestion. "Why should I do that?"

"Why shouldn't you?"

"Because it's preposterous."

"I think you haven't asked VJ anything about them because you're afraid to," Marsha said.

"Oh, come on," Victor snapped. "You're talking nonsense again."

"I'm afraid to ask him," Marsha said flatly. But she could feel the tug in her throat.

"You're letting your imagination run wild. Now I know it's been an upsetting day for you. I'm sorry. I really thought you'd be thrilled. But someday I think you're going to look back on this day and laugh at yourself. If this implantation work is anything like he says it is, the sky's the limit for VJ's career."

"I hope so," Marsha said without conviction.

"But you have to promise that you won't tell anyone about VJ's lab," Victor said.

"Who would I tell?"

"Let me handle VJ for the time being," Victor said. "I'm sure we are going to be very proud of him."

Marsha shuddered involuntarily as a chill passed down her spine. "Is it cold in here?" she asked.

Victor checked the thermostat. "Nope. If anything, it's too warm."

12

SUNDAY MORNING

At four-thirty in the morning Marsha woke up with a start. She had no idea what had awakened her, and for a few minutes she breathed shallowly, and listened to the nighttime noises of the house. She heard nothing out of the ordinary. She rolled over and tried to go back to sleep but it was impossible. In her mind's eye, she kept seeing VJ's eerie lab with its juxtaposition of the old and the very new. Then she'd see the strange appearance of the man with the lidded eye.

Swinging her feet from beneath the covers, Marsha sat on the edge of the bed. So as not to bother Victor, she stood up, wiggled into her slippers, and pulled on her robe. As quietly as possible she eased open the door to the bedroom and equally as quietly, pulled it shut.

She stood in the hall for a moment, thinking about where she should go. As if pulled by some unseen force, she found herself walking the length of the hall, heading toward VJ's room. When she got there, she noticed the door was slightly ajar.

Marsha quietly pushed the door open wider. A gentle light was coming through the window from the post lamps lining the driveway. To her relief, VJ was fast asleep. He was lying on his side facing her. Sleeping, he looked like an angel of a boy. Could her darling baby really have had a hand in the dark events at Chimera? She couldn't bring herself to think of Janice and David, her beloved first son. But with horror, a vision of David in his last days, his skin yellowed from the disease, flashed upon her.

Marsha stifled a cry. All of a sudden her mind conjured up a horrid image of her taking a pillow and pushing it down on VJ's peaceful face, smothering him. Horrified, she recoiled from the thought and shook herself. Then she fled silently down the hall, running from herself.

Marsha stopped at the guest room door, which had temporarily become Philip's room. Pushing the door open, she could make out Philip's massive head silhouetted against the stark white of the bed linens. After a moment's thought, Marsha slipped into the room and stood next to the bed. The man was snoring deeply, his breath softly whistling on exhale. Bending down, Marsha gave his shoulder a gentle nudge. "Philip," she called softly. "Philip!"

Philip's closely set eyes blinked open. Abruptly, he sat up. A look of momentary fear flashed across his face before he recognized Marsha. Then he smiled, revealing his square, widely spaced teeth.

"Sorry to awaken you," she whispered. "But I need to talk to you for a moment."

"Okay," Philip said groggily. He leaned back on an elbow.

Marsha pulled a chair over to the bed, turned on the light on the nightstand, and sat down. "I wanted to thank you for being such a good friend to VJ," she said.

Philip's face broke out in a wide smile as he squinted in the light. He nodded.

"You must have been a great help in setting up the lab," Marsha said.

Philip nodded again.

"Who else helped with the lab?"

Philip's smile waned. He looked around the room nervously. "I'm not supposed to say."

"I'm VJ's mother," Marsha reminded him. "It's all right to tell me."

Philip shifted his weight uneasily.

Marsha waited but Philip didn't say anything.

"Did Mr. Gephardt help?" Marsha asked.

Philip nodded.

"But then Mr. Gephardt got into trouble. Did he get angry at VJ?"

"Oh, yeah!" Philip said. "He got angry and then VJ got angry. But VJ talked with Mr. Martinez."

"What's Mr. Martinez's first name?"

"Orlando," Philip said.

"Does Mr. Martinez work at Chimera, too?"

Philip's agitation began to return. "No," he said. "He works in Mattapan."

"The town of Mattapan?" Marsha asked. "South of Boston?"

Philip nodded.

Marsha started to ask another question but she suddenly felt a presence that sent a shiver up her spine. She turned to the door. VJ was standing in the doorway with his hands on the jambs, his chin jutting forward.

"I think Philip needs his sleep," he said.

Marsha stood up abruptly. She started to say something but the words wouldn't come out. Instead she hurriedly brushed by VJ and ran down to her room.

For the next half hour, Marsha lay there, terrified that VJ would come into their bedroom. She jumped every time the wind blew the oak tree branches against the side of the house.

When he didn't appear, Marsha finally relaxed. She turned over and tried to sleep, but her mind would not stop. Her thoughts drifted to the mysterious Orlando Martinez. Then she began to think about Janice Fay. She thought about David, feeling the familiar sadness. She thought about Mr. Remington and the Pendleton Academy. Then she recalled the teacher who tried to befriend VJ and the fact that he died. She wondered what he'd died of.

The next thing she knew, Victor was waking her to tell her he was leaving with VJ.

"What time is it?" Marsha asked, looking at the clock herself. To her surprise, it was nine-thirty.

"You were sleeping so soundly I didn't have the heart to wake you," Victor said. "VJ and I are off to his lab. He's going to show me the details of the implantation work he's done. Why don't you come along? I have a feeling this is really going to be something."

Marsha shook her head. "I'll stay here," she said. "You can tell me about it."

"You sure?" Victor questioned. "If this is as good as I think it will be, maybe you'll feel better about the whole situation."

"I'm sure," Marsha said, but her tone was doubtful.

Victor planted a kiss on her forehead. "Try to relax, okay? Everything is going to work out for the best. I'm sure of it."

Victor went down the back stairs, literally shivering with excitement. If the implantation was real, he could surprise the other board members with the news at the Wednesday board meeting.

"Mom's not coming?" VJ asked. He was near the back door with his coat already on. Philip was standing next to him.

"No, but she's calmer this morning," Victor said. "I can tell."

"She was pumping Philip for information in the middle of the night," VJ said. "That's the kind of behavior that disturbs me."

After the car pulled out of the drive, Marsha went to the upstairs study and got out the Boston phone book. She sat on the couch and looked up Martinez. Unfortunately, there were hordes of Martinezes, even Orlando Martinezes. But she found one Orlando Martinez in Mattapan. Taking the phone in her lap, she called the number. The phone was answered, and Marsha was about to start talking when she realized she was connected to an answering machine.

The message on the machine told her that the office of Martinez Enterprises was open Monday through Friday. She didn't leave a message. From the phone book she copied down the address.

Marsha took a shower, dressed, made herself some coffee and a poached egg. Then she donned her down coat and went out to her car. Fifteen minutes later, she was on the grounds of Pendleton Academy.

It was a blustery but sunny day with the wind roughing the surface of the puddles left by the previous day's rain. Many of the students were in evidence, most of them going to and from the obligatory attendance at chapel. Marsha pulled up as close as she could to the tiny Gothic structure and waited. She was looking for Mr. Remington and was hoping to catch him out and about.

Soon the bells in the bell tower tolled the eleven o'clock hour. The doors to the chapel opened and rosy-cheeked kids spilled out into the fresh air and sunshine. Among them were a number of adult staff members, including Mr. Remington. His heavily bearded profile stood out among the crowds.

Marsha got out of the car and waited. Mr. Remington's path would take him right by her. He was walking with a deliberate step. When he got about ten feet away, Marsha called his name. He stopped and looked at her.

"Dr. Frank!" he said with some surprise.

"Good morning," Marsha said. "I hope I'm not intruding."

"Not at all," Remington said. "Something on your mind?"

"There is," Marsha said. "I wanted to ask you a question which might sound a little strange. I hope you will indulge me. You told me that the instructor who tried so hard to befriend VJ died. What did he die of?"

"The poor man died of cancer," Mr. Remington said.

"I was afraid of that," Marsha said.

"Excuse me?"

But Marsha didn't explain herself. "Do you know what kind of cancer?" she asked.

"I'm afraid I don't, but I believe I mentioned that his wife is still on staff here. Her name is Stephanie. Stephanie Cavendish."

"Do you think I might speak with her today?" Marsha asked.

"I don't see why not," Mr. Remington said. "She lives in the cottage on the grounds of my headmaster's house. We both share the same lawn. I was on my way home and the cottage is just a stone's throw away. I'd be happy to introduce you to her."

Marsha fell in step with Mr. Remington and they walked the length of the quad. While they were walking, Marsha asked, "Was any staff member close to my late son, David?"

"Most of the instructors were fond of David," Mr. Remington said. "He was a popular boy. If I had to pick one, I'd say Joe Arnold. He's a very popular history teacher who I believe was close to your David."

The cottage Mr. Remington had spoken of looked like some cottage out of the Cotswold section of England. With whitewashed walls and a roof that was made to look thatched, it appeared as if it belonged in a fairy tale. Mr. Remington rang the bell himself. He introduced Marsha to Mrs. Cavendish, a slim, attractive woman Marsha guessed was about her own age. Marsha learned that she was the head of the school's physical education department.

Mr. Remington excused himself after Mrs. Cavendish invited Marsha inside.

Mrs. Cavendish led Marsha into her kitchen and offered her a cup of tea. "Please, call me Stephanie," she said as they sat down. "So you're VJ's mother! My husband was a big fan of your boy. He was convinced VJ was extraordinarily bright. He really raved about him."

"That's what Mr. Remington said," Marsha said.

"He loved to relate the story of VJ solving an algebra problem to everyone who'd listen."

Marsha nodded and said that Mr. Remington had told the story to her.

"But Raymond thought your son was troubled," Stephanie said. That's why he tried so hard to get VJ to be less withdrawn. Ray really did try. He thought that VJ was alone too much and was afraid VJ might be suicidal. He worried about the boy—oh, never academically. But socially, I think."

Marsha nodded.

"How is he these days?" Stephanie asked. "I don't have much occasion to see him."

"I'm afraid he still doesn't have many friends. He's not very outgoing."

"I'm sorry to hear that," said Stephanie.

Marsha gathered her courage. "I hope you don't think me too forward, but I'd like to ask a personal question. Mr. Remington told me your late husband died of cancer. Would you mind if I asked what kind of cancer?"

"I don't mind," said Stephanie. There was a sudden tightening in her throat. "It was a while before I could talk about it," she allowed. "Ray died of a form of liver cancer. It was very rare. He was treated at Mass. General in Boston. The doctors there had only seen a couple of similar cases."

Although Marsha had expected as much, she still felt as though she'd been hit. This was exactly what she was afraid of hearing.

As tactfully as she could, Marsha ended the conversation, but not before enlisting Mrs. Cavendish's aid in getting an invitation over to Joe Arnold's house.

He wasn't the sort of stuffy history professor-type Marsha had expected. His warm brown eyes lit up when he opened the door to greet her. Like Stephanie Cavendish, he seemed about her own age. Between his swarthy good looks, empathic eyes, and somewhat disheveled clothing, Marsha could see he had a beguiling demeanor. He was no doubt an excellent teacher; he had the kind of enthusiasm students would find infectious. No wonder David had gravitated toward this man.

"It's a pleasure to meet you, Mrs. Frank. Come in, please come in." He held the door for her and led her into the book-lined study. She looked around the room admiringly. "David used to spend lots of afternoons right here."

Marsha felt unbidden tears threaten to appear. It saddened her a little to think how much of David's life she didn't know. She quickly composed herself.

After thanking Joe for seeing her on such short notice, Marsha got to the point of why she was interested in seeing him. She asked Joe if David had ever discussed his brother VJ.

"On a few occasions," Joe said. "David admitted to me that he'd had trouble with VJ from the first day that VJ had arrived home from the hospital. That's normal enough, but to tell you the truth, I got the feeling it went beyond the usual sibling rivalry. I tried to get him to talk about it, but David would never elaborate. We had a strong relationship, I think, but on this one subject he wouldn't open up."

"He never got more specific about his feelings or what the trouble was?"

"Well, David once told me that he was afraid of VJ."

"Did he say why?"

"I was under the impression that VJ threatened him," Joe said. "That was as much as he'd say. I know brothers' relationships can be tricky, especially at that age. But quite frankly, I had a funny feeling about David's trouble with VJ. David seemed genuinely spooked—almost too afraid to talk about it. In the end, I insisted he see the school psychologist."

"Did he?" Marsha questioned. She'd never heard about that, and it added to her guilt.

"You bet he did," Joe told her. "I wasn't about to let this thing drop. David was very special . . ." For a moment, Joe choked up. "Whew, sorry," he apologized after a pause. But Marsha was touched by such an obvious display of feeling. She nodded, moved herself.

"Is the psychologist still on staff?" Marsha asked.

"Madeline Zinnzer?" Joe asked. "Absolutely. She's an institution around here. She's been here longer than anybody else."

Marsha made use of Joe Arnold's hospitality to get herself invited over to Madeline Zinnzer's home. Marsha couldn't thank him enough.

"Anytime," said Joe, giving her hand an extra squeeze. "Really, anytime."

Madeline Zinnzer looked like an institution. She was a large woman, well over two hundred pounds. Her gray hair had been permed into tight curls. She took Marsha into a comfortable, spacious living room with a picture window looking out over the Pendleton Academy quad.

"One of the benefits of being on the staff so long," Madeline said, following Marsha's line of sight. "I finally got to move into the best of the faculty housing."

"I hope you don't mind my stopping by on a Sunday," Marsha began.

"Not at all," Madeline insisted.

"I have some questions about my children that maybe you can help me with."

"That's what Joe Arnold mentioned," Madeline said. "I'm afraid I don't have the memory he does of your boy, David. But I do have a file which I went over after Joe called. What's on your mind?"

"David told Joe that his younger brother, VJ, had threatened him, but he wouldn't tell Joe much more than that. Were you able to learn anything more?"

Madeline made a tent with her fingers and leaned back in her chair. Then she cleared her throat. "I saw David on a number of occasions," she began. "After talking with him at length, it was my opinion that David was using the defense mechanism of projection. It was my feeling that David projected his own feelings of competition and hostility onto VJ."

"Then the threat wasn't specific?" Marsha asked.

"I didn't say that," Madeline said. "Apparently there had been a specific threat."

"What was it about?"

"Boy stuff," Madeline said. "Something about a hiding place that VJ had that David found out about. Something innocuous like that."

"Could it have been a lab rather than a hiding place?" Marsha asked.

"Could have been," Madeline said. "David could have said lab, but I wrote hiding place in the file."

"Did you ever talk with VJ?" Marsha asked.

"Once," Madeline said. "I thought it would be helpful to get a feeling for the reality about the relationship. VJ was extremely straightforward. He told me that his brother David had been jealous of him from the day VJ had arrived home from the hospital." Then Madeline laughed. "VJ told me that he could remember arriving home after he was born. That tickled me at the time."

"Did David ever say what the threat was?" Marsha asked.

"Oh, yes," Madeline said. "David told me that VJ had threatened to kill him."

From the Pendleton Academy Marsha drove to Boston. Much as she resisted putting the pieces together, she felt utterly compelled to assemble them. She kept telling herself that everything she was learning

665

was either circumstantial, coincidental, or innocuous. She had already lost one child. But even so, she knew she couldn't rest until she found the truth.

Marsha had taken her psychiatric residency at the Massachusetts General Hospital. Visiting there was like going home. But she didn't go to the psych unit. Instead, she went directly to Pathology and found a senior resident, Dr. Preston Gordon.

"Sure I can do that," Preston said. "Since you don't know the birthday, it will take a little searching, but nothing else is happening right now."

Marsha followed Preston into the center of the pathology department where they sat at one of the hospital computers. There were several Raymond Cavendishes listed in the system, but by knowing the approximate year of death, they were able to find the Raymond Cavendish of Boxford, Massachusetts.

"All right," Preston said. "Here comes the record." The screen filled with the man's hospital record. Preston scrolled through. "Here's the biopsy," he said. "And here's the diagnosis: liver cancer of Kupffer cell of reticuloendothelial origin." Preston whistled. "Now that's a zebra. I've never even heard of that one."

"Can you tell me if there have been any similar cases treated at the hospital?" Marsha asked.

Preston returned to the keyboard and began a search. It took him only a few minutes to get the answer. A name flashed on the screen. "There has only been one other case at this hospital," he said. "The name was Janice Fay."

Victor tuned his car radio to a station that played oldies but goodies and sang along happily to a group of songs from the late fifties, a time when he'd been in high school. He was in a great mood on his drive home, having spent the day totally engrossed and spellbound by VJ's prodigious output from his hidden basement laboratory. It had turned out to be exactly as VJ had said it would be: beyond his wildest dreams.

As Victor turned into the driveway, the songs had changed to the late sixties, and he belted out "Sweet Caroline" along with Neil Diamond. He drove the car around the house and waited for the garage door to open. After he pulled the car into the garage, he sang until the song was over before turning off the ignition, getting out and skirting Marsha's car, heading into the house.

"Marsha!" Victor yelled as soon as he got inside. He knew she was home because her car was there, but the lights weren't on.

"Marsha!" he yelled again, but her name caught in his throat. She was sitting no more than ten feet from him in the relative darkness of the family room. "There you are," he said.

"Where's VJ?" she asked. She sounded tired.

"He insisted on going off on his bicycle," Victor said. "But have no fear. Pedro's with him."

"I'm not worried about VJ at this point," Marsha said. "Maybe we should worry about the security man."

Victor turned on a light. Marsha shielded her eyes. "Please," she said. "Keep it off for now."

Victor obliged. He'd hoped she'd be in a better mood by the time he got home, but it wasn't looking good. Undaunted, Victor sat down and launched into lavish praise of VJ's work and his astounding accomplishments. He told Marsha that the implantation protein really worked. The evidence was incontrovertible. Then he told her the *pièce de résistance:* solving the implantation problem unlocked the door to the mystery of the entire differentiation process.

"If VJ wasn't so intent on secrecy," Victor said, "he could be in contention for a Nobel Prize. I'm convinced of it. As it is, he wants me to take all the credit and Chimera to get all the economic benefit. What do you think? Does that sound like a personality disorder to you? To me it sounds pretty generous."

Without any response from Marsha, Victor ran out of things to say. After he was quiet for a moment, she said, "I hate to ruin your day, but I'm afraid I have learned more disturbing things about VJ."

Victor rolled his eyes as he ran his fingers through his hair. This was not the response he was hoping for.

"The one teacher at the Pendleton Academy who made a big effort to get close to VJ died a few years ago."

"I'm sorry to hear that."

"He died of cancer."

"Okay, he died of cancer," Victor said. He could feel his pulse quicken.

"Liver cancer."

"Oh," Victor said. He did not like the drift of this conversation.

"It was the same rare type that both David and Janice died of," Marsha said.

A heavy silence settled over the family room. The refrigerator compressor started. Victor did not want to hear these things. He wanted to talk about the implantation technology and what it would do for all those infertile couples when the zygotes refused to implant.

"For an extremely rare cancer, a lot of people seem to be contracting it. People who cross VJ. I had a talk with Mr. Cavendish's wife. His widow. She's a very kind woman. She teaches at Pendleton too. And I spoke to a Mr. Arnold. It turns out he was close to David. Do you know that VJ threatened David?"

"For God's sakes, Marsha! Kids always threaten each other. I did it myself when my older brother wrecked a snow house I'd built."

"VJ threatened to kill David, Victor. And not in the heat of an argument." Marsha was near tears. "Wake up, Victor!"

"I don't want to talk about it anymore," Victor said angrily, "at least not now." He was still high from the day's tour of VJ's lab. Was there a darker side to his son's genius? At times in the past, he'd had his suspicions, but they were all too easy to dismiss. VJ seemed such a perfect child. But now Marsha was expressing the same kind of doubts and backing them up so that they made a kind of evil sense. Could the little boy who gave him a tour of the lab, the genius behind the new implantation process, also be behind unspeakable acts? The murder of those children, of Janice Fay, of his own son David? Victor couldn't consider the horror of it all. He banished such thoughts. It was impossible. Someone at the lab killed the kids. The other deaths had to have been coincidental. Marsha was really pushing this too far. But then, she'd been on the hysterical side ever since the Hobbs and Murray kids had died. But if her fears were in any way justified, what would he do? How could he blithely support VJ in his many scientific endeavors? And if it was true, if VJ was half prodigy, half monster, what did it say of him, his creator?

Marsha might have insisted more, but just then VJ arrived home. He came in just as he had a week ago Sunday night, with his saddlebags over his shoulder. It was as though he'd known what they'd been talking about. VJ glared at Marsha, his blue eyes more chilling than ever. Marsha shuddered. She could not return his stare. Her fear of him was escalating.

Victor paced his study, absently chewing on the end of a pen. The door was closed and the house was quiet. As far as he knew, everybody was long since tucked into bed. It had been a strained evening with

Marsha closeting herself in the bedroom after Victor had refused to discuss VJ anymore.

Victor had planned to spend the night working on his presentation of the new implantation method for Wednesday's board meeting. But he just couldn't concentrate. Marsha's words nagged him. Try as he would, he couldn't put them out of his mind. So what if VJ threatened David? Boys would be boys.

But the idea of yet another case of the rare liver cancer ate at him, especially in light of the fact that both David's and Janice's tumors had that extra bit of DNA in them. That had yet to be explained. Victor had purposefully kept the discovery from Marsha. It was bad enough he had to think of it. If he couldn't spare her the pain of what might be the awful truth of the matter, at least he'd spare her each small revelation that pointed to it.

And then there was Marsha's question of what else VJ was doing behind his lab's closed doors. The boy was so resourceful, and he had all the equipment to do almost anything in experimental biology. Aside from the implantation method, just what was he up to? Even during the tour, extensive though it was, Victor couldn't help but feel VJ wasn't letting him in on everything.

"Maybe I ought to take a look," Victor said aloud as he tossed the pen onto his desk. It was quarter to two in the morning, but who cared!

Victor scribbled a short note in case Marsha or VJ came down to look for him. Then he got his coat and a flashlight, backed his car out of the garage, and lowered the door with his remote. When he got to the end of the driveway, he stopped and looked back at the house. No lights came on; no one had gotten up.

At Chimera, the security guard working the gate came out of the office and shined a light into Victor's face. "Excuse me, Dr. Frank," he said as he ran back inside to lift the gate.

Victor commended him for his diligence, then drove down to the building that housed his lab. He parked his car directly in front of it. When he was sure that he was not being observed, he jogged toward the river. He was tempted to use his flashlight, but he was afraid to do so. He didn't want others to know of the existence of VJ's lab.

As he approached the river, the roar of the falls seemed even more deafening at night. Gusts of wind whipped about the alleyways, kicking up dust and debris, forcing Victor to lower his head. At last he reached the entrance to the clock tower building.

Victor hesitated at the entranceway. He was not the type to be spooked, but the place was so desolate and dark that he felt a little bit afraid. Again, he would have liked to use the flashlight, but again it would have been a giveaway if anybody happened to see the glow.

Victor felt his way in the dark, tapping his foot ahead gingerly before taking a step. He was deep into the first-floor level, close to the trapdoor, when he felt the flutter of wings right at his face. He cried out in surprise, then realized he'd only disturbed a bevy of pigeons that had made the deserted clock tower building their roost.

Victor took a deep breath and moved on. With relief, he reached the trapdoor, only to realize he didn't know how to raise it. He tried in various locations to get a grip on the floorboards with his fingernails, but he couldn't get it to lift.

In frustration, Victor turned on the flashlight to survey the area. He had no choice. On the floor among the other trash was a short metal rod. He picked it up and returned to the trapdoor. Without much trouble, he was able to pry it open about an inch. As soon as he did, it rose effortlessly.

Victor quickly eased himself down the stairs far enough to allow the trapdoor to close above him. It was dark in the lab save for the beam of his flashlight. Victor searched for the panel that would turn on the lights. He found it under the stairs and flipped the switches. As the room filled with fluorescent light, Victor breathed a sigh of relief.

He decided to examine a lab area VJ hadn't shown him, a room he'd been fairly dismissive of even when Victor questioned him.

But he never made it to the door. He was about fifteen feet away when the door to the living quarters burst open and an attack dog came snarling at him. Victor leaped back, throwing his arms up to guard his face. He closed his eyes and braced for the contact.

But there wasn't any. Victor opened his eyes cautiously. The vicious dog had been brought up short by a chain held by a Chimera security guard.

"Thank God!" Victor cried. "Am I glad to see you!"

"Who are you?" the man demanded, his heavy accent clearly Spanish.

"Victor Frank," Frank said. "I'm one of the officers of Chimera. I'm surprised you don't recognize me. I'm also VJ's father."

"Okay," the guard said. The dog growled.

"And your name?" Victor asked.

"Ramirez," the guard said.

"I've never met you," Victor said. "But I'm glad you were on the other end of that chain." Victor started for the door. Ramirez grabbed his arm to restrain him.

Surprised by this, Victor stared at the man's hand wrapped around his arm. Then he looked him in the eye and said, "I just told you who I am. Would you please let go of me?" Victor tried to sound stern, but he already felt Ramirez had the best of the situation.

The dog growled. His bared teeth were inches away from Victor.

"I'm sorry," said Ramirez, not sounding sorry at all. "No one is allowed through that door unless VJ specifically says it is okay."

Victor examined Ramirez's expression. There was no doubt the man meant what he said. Victor wondered what to do in this ridiculous situation. "Maybe we should call your supervisor, Mr. Ramirez," Victor said evenly.

"This is the graveyard shift," Ramirez said. "I'm the supervisor."

They stared at each other for another minute. Victor was convinced of the man's intransigence and of the dog's power of persuasion. "Okay!" he said. Ramirez relaxed his grip and pulled the dog away.

"In that case I'll be leaving," Victor said, keeping an eye on the dog. Victor decided that he would see to Ramirez in the morning. He'd take the matter up with VJ.

Victor left the way he'd come in. Stopping at the gate to exit, he called the guard over to his car. "How long has a Ramirez been on the guard staff?" he asked.

"Ramirez?" the guard questioned. "There isn't any Ramirez on the force."

13

MONDAY MORNING

The atmosphere at breakfast was anything but normal. Marsha had promised herself as she took her morning shower that she would act as if everything was fine, but she found it impossible. When VJ appeared for breakfast about fifteen minutes behind schedule, she told him he'd better hurry since it was a school day. She knew she was baiting him, but she couldn't help herself.

"Now that the secret is out," VJ said, "I think it is rather ridiculous for me to go to school and pretend to be interested and absorbed in fifth-grade work."

"But I thought it was important to maintain your anonymity," Marsha persisted.

VJ glanced toward his father for support, but Victor calmly drank his coffee. He was staying out of it.

"At this point, going to school or not going to school will in no way affect my anonymity," VJ said coldly.

"The law says you must go to school," said Marsha.

"There are higher laws," VJ retorted.

Marsha wasn't going to make a stand alone. "Whatever you and Victor decide is fine with me," she told them. She left for work before learning Victor's decision.

"She is going to be trouble," VJ warned once she was gone.

"She needs a little more time," Victor said. "But you might have to come to some compromise on the school issue."

"I don't see why. It's not going to help my work. If anything, it will slow things down. Aren't results more important?"

"They're important," said Victor, "but they're not everything. Now, how do you want to get to Chimera today? You want to ride with me?"

"Nope," said VJ. "I want to take my bike. Is it all right for Philip to use yours?"

"Sure," Victor said. "I'll see you in your lab about midmorning. I'll need the details on the implantation protein for the legal department to start the patent application. I also want to see the rest of your lab as well as the new lab." Victor didn't mention the episode with Ramirez earlier that morning.

"Fine," VJ said. "Just be careful about coming. I don't want any other visitors."

Fifteen minutes later, VJ was plunging down Stanhope Street with the wind whistling past his head. Philip was right behind him on Victor's bike, and behind Philip was Pedro in his Ford Taurus.

VJ told Philip and Pedro to wait for him outside when he went into the bank with his saddlebags. Luckily Mr. Scott was occupied with another customer, and VJ was able to use his safe deposit box for another large deposit without getting a lecture.

Victor's ride to work was not as carefree. Although he tried to think of other things, his mind was haunted by Marsha's words: "For an extremely rare cancer, a lot of people seem to be contracting it. People who cross VJ." Victor was wondering just how he'd feel if Marsha contracted it. Just how was VJ prepared to handle trouble?

Despite his apprehensions, Victor was fueled by enthusiasm for the new implantation protein project. He tackled the laborious administrative details that had accumulated by Monday morning with a good deal more equanimity than usual. He welcomed the busywork; it kept his mind from wandering. Colleen came in with her usual stack of messages and situations needing attention. Victor had her go through them rapidly before making any decisions, half hoping for some kind of communication that would suggest blackmail about the NGF project, but there was nothing.

The most satisfying decision involved the question of whether Victor wanted to press charges against Sharon Carver. He told Colleen to let the parties know that he was willing to drop charges if the groundless sex-discrimination suit was also dropped.

The final item that Victor requested Colleen to do was to schedule a meeting with Ronald so that he could confront the man about the problems associated with the NGF work. If that didn't turn up anything, which he didn't expect it would, he would schedule a meeting with Hurst. Hurst had to be the culprit; in fact, Victor prayed as much. More than anything else he wanted to uncover some hard evidence that he could lay in front of Marsha and say: "VJ had nothing to do with this."

Marsha found work intolerable. As much as she tried, she couldn't maintain the degree of attention that was required for her therapy sessions. With no explanation, she suddenly told Jean to cancel the rest of the day's appointments. Jean agreed but was clearly not pleased.

As soon as Marsha finished with the patients already there, she slipped out the back entrance and went down to her car. She took 495 to 93 and turned toward Boston. But she didn't stop in Boston. She continued on the South East Expressway to Neponset, then on to Mattapan.

With the address slip unfolded on the seat next to her, Marsha searched for Martinez Enterprises. The neighborhood was not good. The buildings were mostly decaying wood-frame three-deckers with occasional burnt-out hulks.

The address for Martinez Enterprises turned out to be an old warehouse with no windows. Undaunted, Marsha pulled over to the curb and got out of her car. There was no bell of any kind. Marsha knocked, timidly at first, but when there was no response, she pounded harder. Still there was no response.

Marsha stepped back, eyeing the building's door, then the façade. She jumped when she realized that at the left-hand corner of the building a man in a dark suit and white tie was watching her. He was leaning against the building with a slightly amused expression. A cigarette was tucked between his first and second fingers. When he noticed that Marsha had spotted him, he spoke to her in Spanish.

"I don't speak Spanish," Marsha said.

"What do you want?" the man asked with a heavy accent.

"I want to talk with Orlando Martinez."

At first the man didn't respond. He smoked his cigarette, then tossed it into the gutter. "Come with me," he said and disappeared from sight.

Marsha walked to the edge of the building and glanced down a litter-filled alleyway. She hesitated while her better judgment told her to go back and get into her car, but she wanted to see this through. She followed the man. Halfway down the alley was another door. This one was ajar.

The inside of the building looked the same as the outside. The major difference was the interior had a damp, moldy smell. The walls were unpainted concrete. Bare light bulbs were held in ceramic ceiling fixtures. Near the back of the cavernous room was a desk surrounded by a group of mismatched, threadbare couches. There were about ten men in the room, all in various states of repose, all dressed in dark suits like the man who had brought Marsha inside. The only man dressed differently was the man at the desk. He had on a lacy white shirt that was worn outside his pants.

"What do you want?" asked the man at the desk. He also had a Spanish accent, but not nearly as heavy as the others'.

"I'm looking for Orlando Martinez," Marsha said. She walked directly up to the desk.

"What for?" the man asked.

"I'm concerned about my child," Marsha said. "His name is VJ, and I'd been told that he has some association with Orlando Martinez of Mattapan."

Marsha became aware of a stir of conversation among the men on the couches. She shot a look at them, then back to the man at the desk.

"Are you Orlando Martinez?" Marsha asked.

"I could be," the man said.

Marsha looked more closely at the man. He was in his forties, with dark skin, dark eyes, and almost black hair. He was festooned with all manner of gold jewelry and wore diamond cuff links. "I wanted to ask you what business you have with my son."

"Lady, I think I should give you some advice. If I were you, I'd go home and enjoy life. Don't interfere in what you don't understand. It will cause trouble for everyone." Then he raised his hand and pointed at one of the other men. "José, show this lady out before she gets herself hurt."

José came forward and gently pulled Marsha toward the door. She kept staring at Orlando, trying to think of what else she could say. But it seemed useless. Turning her head, she happened to catch a glimpse of a dark man on one of the couches with one eyelid drooping over his eye. Marsha recognized him. She'd seen him in VJ's lab when Victor took her there.

José didn't say anything. He accompanied Marsha to the door, then closed it in her face. Marsha stood facing the blank door, not sure if she should be thankful or irritated.

Returning to the street, she got into her car and started it up. She got halfway down the block when she saw a policeman. Pulling to the curb, Marsha rolled her window down.

"Excuse me," she said, then pointed back to the warehouse. "Do you have any idea what those people do in that building?"

The policeman stepped off the curb and bent down to see exactly where Marsha was pointing. "Oh, there," he said. He straightened. "I don't know for sure, but I was told a group of Colombians are setting up some kind of furniture business."

As soon as Victor had the opportunity, he phoned Chad Newhouse, the director of security and safety. Victor asked the man about Ramirez.

"Sure, he's a member of the force," Chad said. "He's been on the payroll for a number of years. Is there a problem?"

"Was he hired through normal channels?" Victor inquired.

Chad laughed. "Are you trying to pull my leg, Dr. Frank? You hired Ramirez along with the rest of that special industrial espionage team. He's responsible directly to you."

Victor hung up the phone. He would have to talk with VJ about Ramirez.

After the administrative work was done and the meeting with Ronald scheduled for eleven-fifteen, Victor left for VJ's lab. Before he got to the clock tower building, he stepped into the shadow of one of the other deserted buildings and made certain he was not being observed. Only then did he run across the street into the clock tower building.

One knock brought up the trapdoor. Victor scampered down. Several of the guards in the Chimera uniforms were sitting around, entertaining themselves with cards and magazines. VJ came into the room through the door that Victor had tried to enter on his last visit, wiping his hands on a towel. His eyes had a more intense look than usual.

"Did you come here to the lab last night?" VJ demanded.

"I did—" Victor said.

"I don't want you to do that," VJ interrupted sternly. "Not unless I authorize it. Understand? I need a little respect and privacy."

Victor regarded his son. For a moment he was speechless. Victor had planned on being angry about the episode, but suddenly he was on the defensive. "I'm sorry," he said. "I didn't mean any harm. I was curious about what other facilities you had down here."

"You'll see them soon enough," VJ said, his voice softening. "First I want you to see the new lab."

"Fine," Victor said, relieved to have the ill feelings dissipate so quickly.

They used Victor's car, left Chimera, and crossed the bridge over the Merrimack. While Victor was driving he brought up the question of Ramirez.

"I inserted a number of security people into the Chimera payroll," VJ said. "If you are concerned about the expense, just remember the enormous benefit Chimera is about to accrue from such a small investment."

"I wasn't concerned about the payroll," Victor said. It was the ease with which VJ was able to do whatever he wanted that bothered him.

With VJ's directions, they soon pulled up to one of the old mills across the river from Chimera. VJ was out of the car first, eager to show Victor his creation.

The building was set right on the river. The clock tower building was in clear view on the other bank. But unlike VJ's previous quarters, the new lab was modern in every respect, including its decor. It had three floors and was the most impressive setup Victor had ever seen. In the basement were animal rooms, operating theaters, huge stainless-steel fermenters, and a cyclotron for making radioactive substances. On the first floor was an NMR scanner, a PET scanner, and a whole microbiology laboratory. The second floor had most of the general laboratory space and most of the sophisticated equipment necessary for gene manipulation and fabrication. The third and top floor was devoted to computer space, library, and administrative offices.

"What do you think?" VJ asked proudly as they stood in the hall on the third floor. They had to move frequently as there were workmen everywhere, installing the most recently delivered equipment, doing last-minute painting and carpentry.

"Like everything you've done, I'm simply astounded," Victor said. "But this has cost a fortune. Where did the money come from?"

677

"One of my side projects was to develop a marketable product from recombinant DNA technology," VJ said. "Obviously it succeeded."

"What's the product?" Victor asked eagerly.

VJ grinned. "It's a trade secret!"

VJ then went to a closed door, opened it a crack, glanced inside, then turned back to Victor. "I've got one more surprise for you. There's someone I'd like you to meet."

VJ threw the door open and gestured for Victor to go inside. A young woman bent over a desk straightened up, saying, "Dr. Frank! What a surprise!"

For a moment Victor didn't know what to say. He was looking at someone he'd never expected to see again: Mary Millman, the surrogate who'd carried VJ.

VJ reveled in his father's shock. "I needed a good secretary," he explained, "so I brought her in from Detroit. I have to admit I was curious to meet the woman who gave birth to me."

Victor shook Mary's hand, which she'd put out to him. "Nice to see you again," he said, somewhat dazed.

"Likewise," Mary said.

"Well," VJ said with a laugh, "I really should get back to my lab."

Victor self-consciously looked at his watch. "I've got to go myself."

The meeting with Ronald Beekman was a waste of time. Victor had tried to be confrontational about the NGF project to find out whether Ronald knew anything about it. But Ronald had said neither yes nor no, cleverly sensing this was an issue that might provide him with some leverage. When Victor had reminded him that at their last meeting Ronald had threatened to get even and make Victor's life miserable, Ronald had just brushed it off as being a figure of speech. So Victor left the man's office not knowing any more than he had when he'd entered.

The only possible potential benefit of the meeting was that Ronald had indicated a sharp interest in the implantation project, and Victor had promised to put something together for him to read.

Leaving Ronald's office, Victor headed back to his own. He'd ask Colleen to arrange a meeting with Hurst. Victor wasn't looking forward to it.

"Robert Grimes called you from your lab," Colleen said as soon as Victor entered the office. "He said he has something very interesting for you. He wants you to call him immediately."

678

Victor sat down heavily at his desk. Under normal circumstances such a message from his head technician would have made him tingle with anticipation. It would have heralded some breakthrough on one of the experiments. But now it had to be something else. It had to involve the special work that Victor had given Robert, and Victor wasn't sure he wanted to hear "something very interesting."

Fortifying himself as best he could, Victor made the call and waited for Robert to be located. While Victor waited he thought about his own experiments and realized that they now held very little interest for him. After all, VJ had solved most of the questions involved. It was humbling for Victor to be so far behind his ten-year-old son. But the good side was what they would be able to accomplish together. That was thrilling indeed.

"Dr. Frank!" Robert said suddenly into the phone, waking Victor from his musings. "I'm glad I found you. I've pretty well sequenced the DNA fragment in the two tumors, and I wanted to make sure you wanted me to go ahead and reproduce the sequence with recombinant techniques. It will take me some time to do, but it is the only way we'll be able to ascertain exactly what it codes for."

"Do you have any idea what it codes for?" Victor asked hesitantly.

"Oh, yeah," Robert said. "It's undoubtedly some kind of unique polypeptide growth factor."

"So it's not some kind of retrovirus," Victor said with a ray of hope, thinking that a retrovirus could have been an infectious particle artificially disseminated.

"Nope, it's certainly not a retrovirus," Robert said. "In fact, it's some kind of artificially fabricated gene." Then with a laugh he added, "I'd have to call it a Chimera gene. Within the sequence is an internal promoter that I've used myself on a number of occasions—one taken from the SV40 simian virus. But the rest of the gene had to come from some other microorganism, either a bacterium or a virus."

There was a pause.

"Are you still there, Dr. Frank?" Robert asked, thinking the connection had broken.

"You're sure about all this?" Victor asked, his voice wavering. The implications were becoming all too clear.

"Absolutely," Robert said. "I was surprised myself. I've never heard of such a thing. My first guess was that these people picked up some kind of DNA vector and it got into their bloodstreams. That seemed so strange that I gave it a lot more thought. The only possible mechanism that I could come up with involves red-blood-cell bags filled with this infective gene. As soon as the Kupffer cells in the liver picked them up, the infective particles inserted themselves into the cell's genome. The new genes then turned proto-oncogenes into onco-genes, and bingo: liver cancer. But there's only one problem with this scenario. You know what it is?''

''No, what?''

''There's only one way that RBC membrane bags could get into some-body's bloodstream,'' Robert said, oblivious to the effect all this was having on Victor. ''They would have to be injected. I know that—''

Robert never had a chance to finish his sentence. Victor had hung up.

The mounting evidence was incontrovertible. There was no denying it: David and Janice had died of liver cancer caused by a piece of foreign DNA inserting itself into their chromosomes. And on top of that, there was the instructor from Pendleton Marsha had told him about. All these people were intimately related to VJ. And VJ was a scientific genius with an ultramodern, sophisticated laboratory at his disposal.

Colleen poked her head in. ''I was waiting for you to get off the phone,'' she said brightly. ''Your wife is here. Can I send her in?''

Victor nodded. Suddenly he felt extremely tired.

Marsha came into the room and closed the door forcibly. The wind rustled the papers on Victor's desk. She walked directly over to Victor and leaned forward over his blotter, looking him directly in the eye.

''I know you would rather not do anything,'' she said. ''I know you don't want to upset VJ, and I know you are excited about his accomplishments, but you are going to have to face the reality that the boy is not playing by the rules. Let me tell you about my latest discovery. VJ is involved with a group of Colombians who are suppos-edly opening a furniture import business in Mattapan. I met these men and let me tell you, they don't look like furniture merchants to me.''

Marsha stopped abruptly. Victor wasn't reacting. ''Victor?'' Marsha said questioningly. His eyes had a dazed, unfocused look.

''Marsha, sit down,'' Victor said, shaking his head with sad, slow deliberation. He cradled his head in his hands and leaned forward, resting his elbows on his desk. Then he ran his fingers through his hair, rubbed his neck, and straightened up. Marsha sat down, studying her husband intently. Her pulse began to race.

"I've just learned something worse," Victor said. "A few days ago I got samples of David's and Janice's tumors. Robert has been working on them. He just called to tell me that their cancers had been artificially induced. A foreign cancer-causing gene was put into their blood-streams."

Marsha cried out, bringing her hands to her mouth in dismay. Even though she had begun to suspect as much, the confirmation was as horrifying as if she'd been given the news cold. Coming from Victor, who'd fought her tooth and nail when it came to her fears and apprehensions, made it all the more damning. She bit her lower lip while she quivered with a combination of anger, sadness, and fear. "It had to be VJ!" she whispered.

Victor slammed his palm on top of his desk, sending papers flying. "We don't know that for sure!" he shouted.

"All these people knew VJ intimately," Marsha said, echoing Victor's own thoughts. "And he wanted them out of the way."

Victor shook his head in grim resignation. How much blame lay at his door, and how much lay at VJ's? He was the one who'd ensured the boy's brilliance. But did he stop for one second to think what might go hand in hand with that genius? If David and Janice and that teacher had died by VJ's hand, Victor wasn't sure he could live with his conscience.

Marsha began hesitantly, but her conviction made her strong. "I think we have to know exactly what VJ is doing in the rest of that lab of his."

Victor let his arms fall limply to his sides and stared out the window. He looked at the clock tower, knowing that VJ was working there right now. He turned to Marsha and said, "Let's go find out."

14

MONDAY AFTERNOON

Marsha had to run to keep up with Victor as he made his way toward the river. The two soon left the renovated part of the complex behind. In broad daylight the abandoned buildings did not look quite so sinister.

Entering the building, Victor went straight to the trapdoor, bent down, and rapped sharply on the floor several times.

In a minute or two the trapdoor came up. A man in a Chimera security uniform eyed Victor and Marsha warily, then motioned for them to descend.

Victor went first. By the time Marsha was down the stairs, Victor had rounded the paddle wheel and was heading toward the intimidating metal door barring the entrance to the unexplored portion of VJ's lab. For Marsha, the lab itself was as forbidding as it had been the last time she'd been there. She knew that the fruits of scientific research could be put to good or evil use, but something about the eerie basement quarters gave Marsha the feeling that the research conducted here was for a darker purpose.

"Hey!" yelled one of the guards, seeing Victor approach the restricted door. He jumped up and sprinted across the room diagonally, and grabbed Victor by the arm. He pulled him around roughly. "Nobody's allowed in there," he snarled in his strong Spanish accent.

To Marsha's surprise, Victor put his hand squarely on the man's face and pushed him back. The gesture took the man by surprise, and he fell to one knee, but he maintained a hold on Victor's jacket sleeve. With a forcible yank, Victor shook free of the man's grasp and reached around to the door.

The security guard pulled a knife from his boot and flicked it open. A flash of light glinted off its razor surface.

"Victor!" Marsha screamed. Victor turned when he heard her scream. The guard came at him, holding the knife out in front of his body like a miniature rapier. Victor parried the thrust but the man got hold of his arm. The knife rose menacingly.

"Stop it!" VJ yelled as he burst through the door toward which Victor had been heading. The two other security men who were in the room got between the two combatants, one restraining Victor, the other dealing with the knife-wielding guard.

"Let my father go!" VJ commanded.

"He was going into the back lab," the guard with the knife cried.

"Let him go," VJ ordered even more sternly than before.

Victor was released with a shove. He staggered forward, trying to maintain his balance. Doing so, he made another move for the door. VJ reached out and grasped his arm just as Victor was about to push through to the other side.

"Are you sure you're ready for this?" VJ asked.

"I want to see it all," Victor said flatly.

"Remember the Tree of Knowledge?"

"Of Good and Evil," countered Victor. "You can't talk me out of this."

VJ pulled his hand back. "Suit yourself, but you may not appreciate the consequences."

Victor looked to Marsha, who nodded for him to go. Turning again to the door, he pulled it open. Pale blue light flooded out. Victor stepped over the threshold with Marsha right behind him. VJ followed, then pulled the door closed.

The room was about fifty feet long and rather narrow. On a long bench built of rough-hewn lumber sat four fifty-gallon glass tanks. The sides were fused with silicone. The tanks were illuminated by heat lamps and gave off the eerie blue light as it refracted through the contained fluid.

Marsha's jaw dropped in horror when she realized what was in the tanks. Inside each one and enveloped in transparent membranes were four fetuses, each perhaps eight months old, who were swimming about in their artificial wombs. They watched Marsha as she walked down the aisle, their blue eyes fully open. They gestured, smiled, and even yawned.

Casually, but with an air of arrogant pride, VJ gave a cursory explanation of the system. In each tank the placentas were plastered onto a Plexiglas grid against a membrane bag connected to a sort of heart-lung machine. Each machine had its own computer, which was in turn attached to a protein synthesizer. The liquid surface of each tank was covered with plastic balls to retard evaporation.

Neither Marsha nor Victor could speak, so appalled were they by the sight of the gestating children. Although they had tried to prepare themselves for the unexpected, this was a shock too outrageous to behold.

"I'm sure you're wondering what this is all about," VJ said, moving up to one of the tanks and checking one of the many read-out devices. He hit it with his fist and a stuck needle indicator sprang into the green-painted normal zone. "My early work on implantation had me modeling wombs with tissue culture. Solving the implantation problem also solved the problems of why a uterus was needed at all."

"How old are these children?" Marsha asked.

"Eight and a half months," VJ said, confirming Marsha's impression. "I'll be keeping them gestating a lot longer than the usual nine months. They will be easier to raise the longer I keep them in their tanks."

"Where did you get the zygotes?" Victor asked, although he already knew the answer.

"I'm pleased to say that they are my brothers and sisters."

Marsha's incredulous gaze went from the fetuses in the tanks to VJ.

VJ laughed at her expression. "Come now, this can't be that much of a surprise. I got the zygotes from the freezer in Father's lab. No sense letting them go to waste or letting Dad implant them in other people."

"There were five," Victor said. "Where's the fifth?"

"Good memory," VJ said. "Unfortunately, I had to waste the fifth on an early test of the implantation protocol. But four is plenty for statistical extrapolation, at least for the first batch."

Marsha turned back to the gestating children. They were her own!

"Let's not be too surprised at all this," VJ said. "You knew this technology was on its way. I've just speeded it up."

Victor went up to one of the computers as it sprang to life and spewed out a half page of data. As soon as it was finished printing, the protein synthesizer turned on and began making a protein.

"The system is sensing the need for some kind of growth factor," VJ explained.

Victor looked at the print-out. It included the vital signs, chemistries, and blood count of the child. He was astounded at the sophistication of the setup. Victor knew that VJ had had to artificially duplicate the fantastically complicated interplay of forces necessary to take a fertilized egg to an entire organism. The feat represented a quantum leap in biotechnology. A radically new and successful implantation technology was one thing, but this was entirely another. Victor shuddered to consider the diabolic potential of what his creation had created.

Marsha timidly approached one of the tanks and peered in at a boy-child from closer range. The child looked back at her as if he wanted her; he put a tiny palm up against the glass. Marsha reached out with her own and laid her hand over the child's with just the thickness of the glass separating them. But then she drew her hand back, revolted. "Their heads!" she cried.

Victor came up beside her and leaned toward the child. "What's the matter with his head?"

"Look at the eyebrows. Their heads slant back without foreheads."

"They're mutated," VJ explained casually. "I removed Victor's added segment, then destroyed some of the normal NGF loci. I'm aiming at a level of intelligence similar to Philip's. Philip has been more helpful in aiding me in all my efforts than anyone else."

Marsha shuddered, gripping Victor's hand out of VJ's sight. Victor ignored her and pointed to the door at the end of the room. "What's beyond that door?"

"Haven't you seen enough?" VJ asked.

"I've got to see it all," Victor said. He left Marsha and walked down the length of the room. For a moment Marsha stared at the tiny boy-child with his prominent brow and flattened head. It was as if human evolution had stepped back five hundred thousand years. How could VJ deliberately make his own brothers and sisters—such as they were—retarded? His Machiavellian rationale made her shudder.

Marsha pulled herself away from the gestation tanks and followed Victor. She had to see everything too. Could there really be anything worse than what she had just seen?

The next room had huge stainless-steel containers lined in a row.

They looked like giant kettles she'd seen at a brewery when she was a teenager. It was warmer and more humid in this room. Several men without shirts labored over one of the vats, adding ingredients to it. They stopped working and looked back at Victor and Marsha.

"What are these tanks?" Marsha asked.

Victor could answer. "They're fermenters for growing microorganisms like bacteria or yeast." Then he asked VJ, "What's growing inside?"

"E. coli bacteria," VJ said. "The workhorse of recombinant DNA technology."

"What are they making?" Victor said.

"I'd rather not say," VJ answered. "Don't you think the gestational units are enough for one day?"

"I want to know everything," Victor said. "I want it all out on the table."

"They are making money," VJ said with a smile.

"I'm not in the mood for riddles," Victor said.

VJ sighed. "I had the short-term need for a major capital infusion for the new lab. Obviously, going public wasn't an alternative for me. Instead, I imported some coca plants from South America and extracted the appropriate genes. I then inserted these genes into a lac operon of E. coli, and using a plasmid that carried a resistance to tetracycline, I put the whole thing back into the bacteria. The product is marvelous. Even the E. coli love it."

"What is he saying?" Marsha asked Victor.

"He's saying that these fermenters are making cocaine," Victor said.

"That explains Martinez Enterprises," Marsha said with a gasp.

"But this production line is purely temporary," VJ explained. "It is an expedient means of providing immediate capital. Shortly the new lab will be running on its own merit without the need for contraband. And yes, Martinez Enterprises is a temporary partner. In fact, we can field a small army on a moment's notice. For now, a number of them are on the Chimera payroll."

Victor walked down the line of fermenters. The degree of sophistication of these units also amazed him. He could tell at a glance they were far superior to what Chimera was using. Victor pulled away from them with a heavy sigh and rejoined Marsha and VJ.

"Now you've seen it all," said VJ. "But now that you have, we have to have a serious talk."

VJ turned and walked back toward the main room with Victor and Marsha following. As they passed through the gestation room, the fetuses again moved to the glass. It seemed they longed for human company. If VJ noticed, he didn't show it.

Without a word, VJ led them through the main room, back into the living quarters. Victor realized then that even here there was space he had not seen. There was a smaller room off the main area. Judging from the decor and journals, Victor guessed this was where VJ stayed. There was one bed, a card table with folding chairs, a large bookcase filled with periodicals, and a reading chair. VJ motioned toward the card table and sat down.

Victor and Marsha sat down as well. VJ had his elbows on the table with his hands clasped. He looked from Victor to Marsha, his piercingly blue eyes sparkling like sapphires. "I have to know what you are planning to do about all this. I've been honest with you, it's time you were honest with me."

Victor and Marsha exchanged glances. When Victor didn't speak, Marsha did: "I have to know the truth about David, Janice, and Mr. Cavendish."

"At the moment, I'm not interested in peripheral issues," VJ said. "I'm interested in discussing the magnitude of my projects. I hope you can appreciate the enormity of these experiments. Their value transcends all other issues that otherwise might be pertinent."

"I'm afraid I have to know about these people before I can judge," Marsha said calmly.

VJ glanced at Victor. "Is this your opinion also?"

Slowly, Victor nodded.

"I was afraid of this," VJ murmured. He eyed them both severely, as though he was their parent and they were his erring children. Finally he spoke. "All right, I'll answer your questions. I'll tell you everything you want to know. The three people you mentioned were planning to expose me. At that point it would have been devastating for my work. I tried to keep them from finding out much about the lab and my experiments, but these three were relentless. I had to let nature handle it."

"What does that mean?" Victor asked.

"Through my extensive research on growth factors involved in solving the problem of the artificial womb, I discovered certain proteins that acted as powerful enhancers for proto-oncogenes. I packaged them in RBC sacs, then let nature take over."

"You mean you injected them," Victor said.

"Of course I injected them!" VJ snapped. "That's not the kind of thing you can take orally."

Marsha tried to remain calm. "You're telling me you killed your brother. And you felt nothing?"

"I was only an intermediary. David died of cancer. I pleaded with him to leave me alone. But instead he followed me, thinking he could bring me down. It was his jealousy that drove him."

"And what about the two babies?" Marsha asked.

"Can't we talk about the major issues?" VJ demanded, pounding the table with his fist.

"You asked what we were going to do about all this," Marsha said. "First we have to know all the facts. What about the children?"

VJ drummed his fingers on the surface of the card table. His patience was wearing thin. "They were getting too smart. They were beginning to realize their potential. I didn't want the competition. A little cephaloclor in the day-care center's milk was all it took. I'm sure it was good for most of the kids."

"And how did it make you feel when they died?" Marsha asked.

"Relieved," VJ said.

"Not sorry or sad in any way?" Marsha persisted.

"This isn't a therapy session, Mother," VJ snapped. "My feelings aren't at issue here. You now know all the dark secrets. It's your turn for some honesty. I need to know your intentions."

Marsha looked to Victor, hoping he would denounce VJ's demonic actions, but Victor only stared blankly at VJ, too stunned for speech.

Marsha interpreted his silence to mean acquiescence, possibly even approval. Could Victor be so caught up in VJ's achievements that he could dismiss five murders? The murder of their own little boy? Well, she wasn't going to take this silently. Victor be damned.

"Well?" VJ demanded.

Marsha turned to face him. His unblinking eyes looked to her in calm expectation. Their crystal blue color, so striking since birth, and his angelic blond hair, dissolved Marsha to tears. He was their baby, too, wasn't he? And if he had committed such horrors, was it really his fault? He was a freak of science. For whatever Victor had accomplished in terms of ensuring his brilliance, a conscience seemed to have been lost in the balance. If VJ were guilty, Victor was as culpable as he. Marsha felt a sudden wave of compassion for the boy. "VJ," she began. ''I don't believe that Victor realized all the repercussions of his NGF experiment—''

But VJ cut her off. ''Quite the contrary,'' he told her. ''Victor knew precisely what he wanted to achieve. And now he can look at me and at what I've accomplished and know that he has been ultimately successful. I am exactly what Victor wanted and hoped for; I'm what he'd like to be himself. I am what science can be. I am the future.'' VJ smiled. ''You'd better get used to me.''

''Maybe you are what Victor intended in scientific respects,'' Marsha continued, undaunted. ''But I don't think he foresaw the kind of personality he was creating. VJ, what I'm trying to say is, if you did commit those murders, if you are manufacturing cocaine . . . and can't see the moral objections to these actions, well, it's not all your fault.''

''Mother,'' said VJ, exasperated, ''you always get so sidetracked. Feelings, symptoms, personality. I reveal to you the greatest biological achievement of all time and you probably want me to take another Rorschach test. This is absurd.''

''Science is not supreme,'' Marsha said. ''Morality must be brought to bear. Can't you understand that?''

''That's where you're wrong,'' VJ said. ''And Victor proved that he holds science above morality by the act of creating me. By conventional morality's dictates, he should not have gone through with the NGF experiment, but he did anyway. He is a hero.''

''What Victor did in creating you was born out of unthinking arrogance. He didn't stop to consider the possible outcome; he was so obsessed with the means and his singular goal. Science runs amok when it shakes loose from the bonds of morality and consequence.''

VJ clucked his tongue in disagreement. Then he turned his fierce blue eyes on Marsha. ''Morality cannot rule science because morality is relative and therefore variable. Science is not. Morality is based on man and his society, which changes over the years, from culture to culture. What's taboo for some is sacred for others. Such vagaries should have no bearing here. The only thing that is immutable in this world are the laws of nature that govern the present universe. Reason is the ultimate arbiter, not moralistic whims.''

''VJ, it's not your fault,'' Marsha said softly, sadly shaking her head. There would be no reasoning with him. ''Your superior intelligence has isolated you and made you a person who is missing the human qualities of compassion, empathy, even love. You feel you have no limits. But you do. You never developed a conscience. But you can't see it. It's like trying to explain the concept of color to someone blind since birth.''

VJ leaped from his chair in disgust. ''With all due respect,'' he said, ''I don't have time for this sophistry. I've got work to do. I must know your intentions.''

''Your father and I will have a talk,'' Marsha said, avoiding VJ's gaze.

''Go ahead, talk,'' VJ said, putting his hands on his narrow hips.

''We'll have a talk without children present,'' Marsha said.

VJ set his mouth petulantly. His breath had quickened, his eyes were afire. Then he turned and left the room. The door slammed and clicked. VJ had locked them in.

Marsha turned to face Victor. Victor shook his head in helpless dismay.

''Is there any question in your mind at this point what we're dealing with?'' Marsha asked.

Victor shook his head lamely.

''Good,'' said Marsha. ''Now, what are you prepared to do about it?''

Victor only shook his head again. ''I never thought it would come to this.'' He looked at his wife. ''Marsha, you have to believe me. If I'd known . . .'' His voice broke off. He needed Marsha's support, her understanding. But even he had trouble comprehending the magnitude of his error. If they ever got through this, he wasn't sure he could live with himself. How could he expect Marsha to?

Victor put his face in his hands.

Marsha touched his shoulder. For as awful as the situation was, at least Victor had finally come to his senses. ''We have to decide what to do now,'' she said gently.

Victor pulled himself up out of his chair, suddenly emboldened. ''I'm the one responsible. You're perfectly right about VJ. He wouldn't be the way he is if it weren't for me and my scientific meddling.'' He turned again to his wife. ''First, we have to get out of here.''

Marsha looked at him gravely. ''You think VJ is about to let us waltz out of here? Be reasonable! Remember how he's handled trouble in the past? David, Janice, that poor teacher, those kids, and now his troublesome parents.''

''You think he'll just keep us here indefinitely?'' Victor asked.

''I haven't the slightest idea of what his intentions are. I just don't think it's going to be so easy to get out. He must have some feeling for us. Otherwise he wouldn't have even bothered explaining, and he wouldn't be interested in our opinions or plans. But he certainly isn't going to let us leave here until he's convinced we'll present no problem for him."

For a moment, the two were silent. Then Marsha said, "Maybe we could make some kind of bargain. Get him to let one of us go while the other stays here."

"So one of us becomes a hostage?"

Marsha nodded.

"If he'll agree, I think you should go," Victor told her.

"Uh-uh," Marsha said, shaking her head. "If it comes to that, then you go. You've got to figure out how to put a stop to him."

"I think you should go," Victor said. "I can handle VJ better than you can at this point."

"I don't think anybody can handle VJ," said Marsha. "He's in a world of his own, with no restraints and no conscience. But I'm confident he won't harm me, at least not until he's sure that I mean to cause him trouble. I do think he trusts you more than he trusts me. In that sense, you can deal with him better than I can. He seems to seek your approval. He wants to make you proud. In that respect he seems to be like any other child."

"But what to do?" said Victor, pacing. "I'm not sure the police would be a lot of help. The best route to go might be via the DEA. I suppose he's the most vulnerable with the drug stuff."

Marsha only nodded. Tears sprang to her eyes. She couldn't believe it had come to this. It was still hard to think of VJ as anything but her little boy. But there was no question: because of the nature of his genetic manipulation, he'd become a monster. There'd be no reining him in.

"Could we get him committed to a psychiatric hospital?" Victor asked.

"We'd be hard put to commit him without psychotic behavior, which he hasn't demonstrated, or without getting him acquitted of murder by reason of insanity. But I doubt we could even get him indicted. I'm sure he was careful not to leave any evidence, especially with such a high-tech crime. He has a personality disorder, but he's not crazy. You're going to have to come up with something better than that. I only wish I could say what."

"I'll think of something," Victor assured her. He smoothed out his coat and ran his fingers through his hair in an attempt to comb it. Taking a deep breath, he tried the door. It was locked. He banged on it with his fist four times.

After some delay the lock clicked and the door swung open. VJ appeared in the doorway with several of the South Americans backing him.

"I'm ready to talk," Victor said.

VJ looked from Victor to Marsha. She looked away to avoid his cold stare.

"Alone," Victor added.

VJ nodded and stepped aside while Victor crossed into the main living quarters. Victor walked directly out into the main lab as he heard VJ locking Marsha in. It was clear that he and Marsha really were prisoners, held by their own son.

"She's really upset," Victor said. "Killing David. That was inexcusable."

"I didn't have any choice," VJ said.

"A mother has a hard time dealing with that," Victor said. VJ's eyes didn't blink.

"I knew we shouldn't have told Marsha about the lab," said VJ. "She doesn't have the same regard for science as we do."

"You're right about that," Victor said. "She was appalled at the artificial wombs. I was astounded by them. I know what an achievement they represent scientifically. The impact they'll have on the scientific community will be stupendous. And their commercial potential is enormous."

"I'm counting on the commercial profits to enable me to dump the cocaine connection," VJ said.

"That's a good idea. You're putting your work in serious jeopardy dabbling in the drug business."

"I took that into consideration some time ago," VJ said. "I have several contingency plans if trouble starts."

"I bet you do."

VJ eyed Victor closely. "I think you'd better tell me what your intentions are about my lab and my work."

"My main goal is to deal with Marsha," Victor said. "But I think she'll come around, once the shock of everything wears off."

"How do you plan to deal with her?"

"I'll convince her of the importance of your work and your discoveries," Victor said. "She'll feel differently once she understands that you've done more than any other person in the history of biology, and you are only ten years old."

VJ seemed to swell with pride. Marsha had been right: like any other kid, he sought his father's praise. If only he really could be like any other kid, Victor thought ruefully. But he never will be, thanks to me.

Victor continued. "As soon as possible, I'd like to see a list of the protein growth factors that are involved with the artificial womb."

"There are over five hundred of them," VJ said. "I can give you a print-out, but of course it won't be for publication."

"I understand," Victor said. He glanced down at his son and smiled. "Well, I have to get back to work and I'm sure Marsha has patients to see. So I think we'll be leaving. We'll see you at home."

VJ shook his head. "I think it is too soon for you to leave. I think it will be better if you plan to stay for a few days. I have a phone hookup so you can do your business by phone. Mom will have to reschedule her patients. You'll find it quite comfortable here."

Victor laughed a hollow laugh at this suggestion. "But you're joking, of course. We can't stay here. Marsha may be able to reschedule her patients, but Chimera can't be put on hold. I have a lot of work to do. Besides, everyone knows I'm on the grounds. Sooner or later they'd start searching for me."

VJ considered the situation. "Okay," he said at last. "You can go. But Mom will have to stay here."

Victor was impressed that Marsha had been able to anticipate him so correctly. "I'd be with her every minute," Victor said, still trying to get them both out.

"One or the other," VJ said. "It's not up for discussion."

"All right, if you insist," said Victor. "I'll tell Marsha. Be right back."

Victor made his way back to the door to VJ's living quarters. One of the guards had to come and open it with a key. Victor went over to Marsha and whispered, "He's agreed to let one of us out. Are you sure you don't want to be the one to go?"

Marsha shook her head no. "Please just contact Jean and tell her I won't be available until further notice. Tell her to refer emergencies to Dr. Maddox."

Victor nodded. He kissed Marsha on the cheek, grateful she didn't recoil. Then he turned to go.

Back in the main lab room VJ was giving instructions to two of the guards.

"This is Jorge," VJ said, introducing Victor to a smiling South American. He was the same man who'd earlier tried to knife Victor. Apparently there were no hard feelings on his side, because along with the smile, he stuck out his hand for Victor to shake.

"Jorge has offered to accompany you," VJ said.

"I don't need a baby-sitter," Victor said, suppressing his anger.

With a grim smile, VJ said, "I don't think you understand. It's not your choice. Jorge is to stay with you to remind you not to be tempted to talk with anyone who might give me trouble. He will also remind you that Marsha is here with one of Jorge's friends." VJ let the threat hang unspoken.

"But I don't need a guard. And how will I explain him? Really, VJ, I didn't expect this of you."

"I have perfect confidence that you will think of a way to explain him," VJ said. "Jorge will make us all sleep just a little better. And let me warn you: trouble with the police or other authorities would only be a bother and slow the program, not stop it. Don't disappoint me, Father. Together we will revolutionize the biotechnology industry."

Victor swallowed with difficulty. His mouth had gone dry.

15

MONDAY AFTERNOON

The day had turned cloudy and blustery by the time Victor emerged from the clock tower building and set off for his office. A few steps behind him was Jorge, who'd made a show of displaying the knife he kept hidden in his right boot. But the gesture had had the desired effect. Victor knew that he was in the presence of a man accustomed to killing.

Despite telling Marsha he'd think of something, Victor had no idea what to do. He was in a dazed frenzy by the time he reached his office. He traversed the pool of secretaries unsteadily, with Jorge one step behind him.

"Excuse me!" Colleen said as Victor cruised by her desk. She jumped up, snatching a pile of messages. Victor had reached the door to his office. He turned to the South American. "You'll have to wait out here," he said.

Jorge brushed past Victor as if Victor had not said anything. Colleen, who had witnessed this exchange, was appalled, especially since the South American was wearing a Chimera security uniform. "Should I call security?" she whispered to Victor.

Victor said it wouldn't be necessary. Colleen shrugged and got down to business. "I have a lot of messages," she said. "I've been trying to call you. I need—"

Victor placed his hand on her arm and eased her back so he could swing the door shut. "Later," he told her.

695

"But—" Colleen intoned as the door was shut in her face.

Victor locked the door as an added precaution. Jorge had already made himself comfortable on the couch in the rear of the room. The man was casually attending to his fingernails.

Victor went behind his desk and sat down. The phone rang immediately but he didn't answer. He knew it was Colleen. He looked over at Jorge, who waved with his nail clipper and smiled a toothy grin.

Victor let his head sink into his hands. What he needed was a plan. Jorge was an unwanted distraction. The man exuded a reckless, haughty confidence that said, "I'm a killer and I'm sitting in your office and you can't do a thing about it." It was difficult for Victor to concentrate with Jorge watching over him.

"You don't look like you're doing much work to me," Jorge said suddenly. "VJ said that you needed to leave because you had a lot of work to do. I suggest you get busy unless you want me to call VJ and tell him that you are just sitting around holding your head."

"I was just gathering my thoughts," Victor said. He leaned over and pressed his intercom. When Colleen responded, he said, "Bring in my messages and let's get to work."

For the first hour, Marsha occupied herself by looking through some of the hundreds of periodicals in the bookcase. But they were over her head; all were highly technical, devoted to theories and experiments on the cutting edge of biology, physics, and chemistry. She got up and paced the room and even tried the door, but, as expected, it was locked.

She sat down at the table again, wondering what course of action Victor would take. He would have to be very resourceful. VJ was an exceptional adversary. He'd also have to have an enormous amount of moral courage, and in light of his NGF experiments, she had no idea if he had it in him.

Just then the bolt of the lock was thrown and VJ stepped in. "I thought maybe you could use a little company," he said cheerfully. "There's someone I'd like you to meet." He stepped aside and Mary Millman walked in smiling, her hand outstretched.

Marsha stood up, searching for words.

"Mrs. Frank!" Mary said, shaking her hand with enthusiasm. "I've been looking forward to seeing you. I thought I'd have to wait for at least another year. How are you?"

"Fine, I guess," Marsha said.

"I thought you ladies would enjoy chatting," said VJ. "I'll be leaving this door ajar; if you're hungry or thirsty, just let one of Martinez's people know."

"Thank you," Mary said. "Isn't he wonderful?" she said to Marsha after he was gone.

"He's unique," Marsha said. "How did you get here?"

"It's a surprise, isn't it?" Mary said. "Well, it surprised me too, at the time. I'll tell you how it happened."

"What next?" Victor asked. Colleen was sitting in her usual spot, directly across from him. Jorge was still back on the couch, lounging comfortably. Colleen shuffled through her papers and messages. "I think that does it for now. Anything you want me to do?" She rotated her eyes toward Jorge meaningfully.

"Nope," Victor said as he handed over the last document he had signed. "I'll be heading home. If there are any problems, call me there."

After a quick glance at her watch, Colleen looked back at Victor. "Is everything all right?" He'd been acting strangely ever since he'd returned with the Chimera security guard in tow.

"Everything is just hunky-dory," he said, slipping his pen inside his top drawer.

Colleen looked at her boss of seven years. He'd never used that term before. She stood up, gave Jorge a dirty look, and left the room.

"Time to go," Victor said to Jorge.

Jorge pulled himself up from the couch. "We going back to the lab?" he asked in his heavy accent.

"I'm going home," Victor said, getting his coat. "I don't know where you're going."

"I'm with you, friend."

Victor was curious if there would be any trouble as he tried to drive off the site. But the guard at the gate saluted as usual. The fact that a Chimera guard was accompanying him drew no comment from the man stationed at the gate.

As they were crossing the Merrimack, Jorge reached over and turned on the radio. He searched for and found a Spanish station. Then he turned up the sound to nearly deafening levels, snapping his fingers to the beat.

It was clear to Victor that Jorge was his first hurdle. As he drove up the drive and rounded the house he began to think of his alternatives.

There was a root cellar below the barn with a stout door Victor felt he could secure. The problem was luring the man into it.

As they got out of the car, Victor let the garage door down, wondering if he could sneak up on Jorge and bop him on the head just as he'd been hit when he'd first stumbled onto VJ's lab. Victor opened the door into the family room and left it open for Jorge, who insisted on walking behind.

Victor took off his coat and draped it over the couch. Being a realist, he decided he couldn't hit the man. He knew he'd hit him either too softly or too hard, and either would be a disaster. He'd have to try something else. But what?

Victor was at a loss until he used the downstairs bathroom. Spotting a bottle of aspirin in the medicine cabinet, he remembered the old doctor's bag he'd been given as a fourth-year medical student. He'd used it all the way through his training and, as far as he could remember, it was still filled with a variety of commonly prescribed drugs.

Emerging from the bathroom, Victor found Jorge in front of the family room TV, flipping the channels aimlessly. Victor went upstairs. Unfortunately, Jorge followed. But in the upstairs study, Victor again got him interested in the television. Victor went into the closet and found the black bag.

Taking a handful of Seconal, Valium, and Dalmane, Victor put the bag back, slipping the pills and capsules into his pocket. When he backed out into the room, he discovered that Jorge had found the Spanish cable station.

"I usually have a drink when I get home," Victor said. "Can I offer you anything?"

"What do you have?" Jorge asked without taking his eyes from the TV.

"Just about anything," Victor said. "How about I make up some margaritas?"

"What are margaritas?" Jorge asked.

The question surprised Victor; he had thought margaritas were a popular South American drink. Maybe they were more Mexican than South American. He told Jorge what was in them.

"I'll have whatever you have," Jorge said.

Victor went down to the kitchen. Jorge followed, going back to the TV in the family room. Victor got out all the ingredients, including the salt. He made the drinks in a small glass pitcher, and, making sure that Jorge wasn't paying attention, opened each of the capsules and poured the contents into the concoction. The Valium went in as is. There was still some sediment on the bottom even after Victor had vigorously stirred the mixture, so he put it in the blender for a moment. Then he held the pitcher up to the light. It looked fine. Victor estimated there was enough knockout power in the concoction to take someone through abdominal surgery without stirring.

Victor took a tiny sip. It had a bitter aftertaste, but if Jorge had never had a margarita, he wouldn't know the difference. Victor then put the salt around the rim of the glasses. He made his own drink out of pure lemon juice. When he was ready, he carried the two poured drinks and the pitcher over to the coffee table.

Jorge took his drink without taking his eyes from the TV. Victor sat back and watched it himself. Some kind of soap opera was on the tube. Victor didn't understand Spanish, but he got the drift quickly enough.

Out of the corner of his eye, he watched Jorge swallow his drink, then lean forward and pour himself some more. Victor was pleased he was enjoying it so much. The first sign of an effect came quickly enough: Jorge began to blink a lot. He couldn't focus on the TV. Finally he looked over at Victor, trying to focus as best he could. The alcohol must have carried the drugs into his system efficiently enough. Jorge had barely touched his second glass and he could barely keep his eyes open.

All of a sudden, Jorge tried to get to his feet. He must have realized what was happening because he threw his glass across the room. Victor put his own glass down and grabbed Jorge as he tried to dial the phone. Jorge even attempted to pull out his knife, but his movements were already too uncoordinated and slow. Victor easily disarmed him. In another minute, Jorge was out cold. Victor laid his limp body on the couch. He got some parenteral Valium he kept upstairs and administered the man ten milligrams intramuscularly as a backup. Then he dragged his body across the courtyard and down alongside the barn. He got him into the root cellar and covered him with old blankets and rags to keep his body temperature steady. Then he locked the door with an old padlock.

Returning to the house, Victor enjoyed his sense of accomplishment, and he thought he had the luxury of time to think of the next step. But as he came through the door, the phone rang. Its ringing scared him into wondering if someone were calling Jorge or if Jorge was supposed to check in now and then. Victor didn't answer the phone. Instead, he put on his coat and went out to the car. Without coming up with another idea, he decided to go to the police.

The police station was in the corner of the municipal green. It was a two-story brick structure with a pair of ornate brass post lamps topped with blue glass spheres. Victor pulled up to the front and parked in the visitor parking area. When he'd left the house, he'd felt good about having finally made a decision. He was looking forward to dumping the whole mess into somebody else's lap. But as he climbed the front steps between the two spheres, he became less certain about going to the police.

Victor hesitated just outside the front door. His biggest worry was Marsha, but there were other worries as well. Just as VJ had said, the police probably couldn't do a whole lot, and VJ would be out on the street. The legal system couldn't even handle simple punks, what would it do with a ten-year-old with the intelligence of two Einsteins put together?

Victor was still debating with himself whether to go in or not when the door to the police station opened and Sergeant Cerullo came barging out, bumping into Victor.

Cerullo juggled his hat, which had been jarred from his head, then excused himself vehemently before he recognized Victor. "Dr. Frank!" he said. He apologized again, then asked, "What brings you into town?"

Victor tried to think of something that sounded reasonable but he couldn't. The truth was too much in his mind. "I have a problem. Can I talk to you?"

"Geez, I'm sorry," Cerullo said. "I'm on dinner break. We gotta eat when we can. But Murphy is in at the desk. He'll help you. When I get back from supper, I'll make sure they treated you right. Take care."

Cerullo gave Victor's arm a friendly punch, then pulled the door open for him. Whether he wanted to or not, Victor found himself inside.

"Hey, Murphy!" Cerullo called. His foot held the door open. "This here is Dr. Frank. He's a friend of mine. You treat him good, understand?"

Murphy was a beefy, red-faced, freckled Irish cop whose father had been a cop and whose father's father had been a cop. He squinted at

Victor through heavy bifocals. "I'll be with you in a minute," he said. "Take a seat." He pointed with his pencil to a stained and scarred oak bench, then went back to a form he was laboriously filling out.

Sitting where he was advised, Victor's mind went over the conversation he was about to have with Officer Murphy. He could see himself telling the policeman that he has a son who is an utter genius and who is growing a race of retarded workers in glass jars and who has killed people to protect a secret lab he built by blackmailing embezzlers in his father's company. The mere fact of putting the situation into words convinced Victor that no one would believe him. And even if someone did, what would happen? There would be no way to associate VJ with any of the deaths. It was all circumstantial. As far as the lab equipment was concerned, it wasn't stolen, at least not by VJ. As far as the cocaine was concerned, the poor kid was coerced by a foreign drug lord.

Victor bit his lower lip. Murphy was still struggling with the form, holding the pencil in his meaty hand, his tongue slightly protruding from his mouth. He didn't look up, so Victor continued his daydream. He could see VJ shuffled through the legal system and out the back door. He'd have his fully modern lab up and running with a capability of almost anything. And VJ had already proven his willingness to eliminate those who dared to stand in his way. Victor wondered how long he and Marsha would live under those circumstances.

With a sense of depression that bordered on tears, Victor had to admit to himself that his experiment had been too successful. As Marsha had said, he hadn't considered the ramifications of success. He'd been too overwhelmed with the excitement of doing it to think of the result. VJ was more than he'd bargained for, and with the constitutional constraints of law enforcement, the social system was ill-equipped to deal with an alien like VJ. It was as if he were from another planet.

"Okay," Murphy said as he tossed his form into a wire mesh basket on the corner of his desk. "What can we do for you, Dr. Frank?" He cracked his knuckles after the strain of holding the pencil.

Without much confidence, Victor got up and walked over to the duty desk. Murphy regarded him with his blue eyes. His shirt collar appeared too tight and the skin of his neck hung over it.

"Well, watcha got, doc?" Murphy asked, leaning back in his chair. He had large heavy arms, and he looked like just the kind of guy you'd like to have arrive if kids were stealing your hubcaps or removing your tape deck.

"I have a problem with my son," Victor began. "We found out that he'd been skipping school to—"

"Excuse me, doc," Murphy said. "Shouldn't you be talking to a social worker, somebody like that?"

"I'm afraid the situation is beyond the ken of a social worker," Victor said. "My son has decided to associate with criminal elements and—"

"Excuse me for interrupting again, doc," Murphy said. "Maybe I should have said psychologist. How old is your boy?"

"He's ten," Victor said. "But he is—"

"I have to tell you that we have never gotten a call about him. What's his name?"

"VJ," Victor said. "I know that—"

"Before you go any further," Murphy said, "I have to tell you that we have a lot of trouble dealing with juveniles. I'm trying to be helpful. If your son had done something really bad, like expose himself in the park or break into one of the widows' houses, maybe it would be worth involving us. Otherwise I think a psychologist and maybe some old-fashioned discipline would be best. You get my drift?"

"Yeah," Victor said. "I think you are entirely right. Thanks for your time."

"Not at all, doc," Murphy said. "I'm being straight with you since you're a friend of Cerullo's."

"I appreciate it," Victor said as he backed away from the desk. Then he turned and fled to his car. Once inside his car, Victor felt a tremendous panic. All of a sudden he realized that he alone had to deal with VJ. It was to be father against son, creator against creature. The comprehension brought forth a feeling of nausea that rose up into Victor's throat. He opened the car door, but by shuddering he was able to dispel the nausea without vomiting. He closed the car door and leaned his forehead against the steering wheel. He was drenched in sudden sweat.

From Old Testament studies as a child, the plight of Abraham came to Victor. But he knew there were two huge differences. God wasn't about to intervene in this instance, and Victor knew that he could not kill his son with his hands. But it was becoming progressively clear that it would be VJ or Victor.

Then, of course, there was the problem of Marsha. How was he to get her out of the lab? Another wave of panic settled over Victor. He knew that he had to act quickly before VJ's intelligence could become a factor. Besides, Victor knew that if he didn't act quickly, he might lose his nerve and commitment.

Victor started the car and drove home by reflex as his mind struggled with coming up with some kind of plan. When he arrived at home, he first went to the root cellar and checked Jorge. He was sleeping like a baby, comfy and cozy beneath his mound of blankets and rags. Victor filled an empty wine bottle with water and left it by the man's head.

Coming into the house, the phone again frightened Victor. Victor looked at it and debated. What if it were Marsha? As it started its fourth ring, Victor snatched up the receiver. He said hello timidly, and for good reason. The voice on the other end was a man's voice with a heavy Spanish accent. He asked for Jorge.

Victor's mind momentarily went blank. The voice asked for Jorge again, a bit more insistently.

"He's in the john," Victor managed.

Without understanding the Spanish, Victor could tell there was no comprehension. "Toilet!" Victor shouted. "He is in the toilet!"

"Okay," the man said.

Victor hung up the phone. Another wave of panic spread through his body like a bolt of electricity. Time was pressing in on Victor like a runaway train approaching a precipice. Jorge could only be in the john for so long before an army would be sent out like the one that visited Gephardt's home.

Victor pounded his hand repeatedly on the counter top. He hoped that the violence of the act would shock him into getting hold of himself so that he could think. He had to come up with a plan.

Fire was Victor's first thought. After all, the clock tower building was ancient and the timber dry. He wanted to come up with some sort of cataclysmic event that would get rid of the entire mess in one fell swoop. But the problem with fire was that it could be extinguished. Half a job would be worse than nothing because then Victor would face VJ's wrath, backed up by Martinez's muscle.

An explosion was a much better idea, Victor decided upon reflection. But how to pull it off? Victor was certain he could rig a small explosive device, but certainly not one capable of demolishing the entire building.

He'd think of something, but first he had to get Marsha out. Going into his study, Victor took out the photocopies he'd made when he had been searching for a way into the building's basement. He hoped he

703

might get Marsha out through one of the tunnels. But from studying the floor plans, it immediately became clear that none of the tunnels entered the clock tower building anywhere near the living quarters where she was being held. He folded the plans and put them in his pocket.

The phone rang again, further jangling Victor's frayed nerves. Victor didn't answer a second time. He knew he had to get out of the house. VJ or the Martinez gang were sure to get suspicious if Jorge remained incommunicado for long. Who could tell when they might show up to check for themselves?

It was well past dark now, as Victor pulled out of the garage. He turned his lights on and headed for Chimera, praying to God he might come up with some sort of strategy for getting Marsha out and ridding the world of this Pandora's box of his own creation.

Victor suddenly jammed on his brakes, bringing his car to a screeching halt at the side of the road. Almost miraculously, a plan began to form in his mind. The details began to fall into place. "It might work," he said through clenched teeth. Taking his foot from the brake, he stomped on the accelerator and the car leaped ahead.

Victor could barely contain himself as he went through the rigmarole of gaining entry to Chimera. Once in, he drove directly to the building housing his lab and parked right in front of the door. Because of the late hour, the structure was deserted and locked. Victor fumbled with his keys and unlocked the door. When he got into his lab, he forced himself to stop for a moment to calm down. He sat down in a chair, closed his eyes, and tried to relax every muscle in his body. Gradually, his heart rate began to slow. Victor knew that to accomplish the first part of his plan he needed his wits about him. He needed a steady hand.

Victor had all the things he needed in the lab. He had plenty of glycerin and both sulfuric and nitric acids. He also had a closed vessel with cooling ports. For the first time in his life, all the hours he'd spent in chemistry lab in college paid off. With ease he set up a system for the nitrification of the glycerin. While that was in progress, he prepared the neutralization vat. By far the most critical stage was carried out with an electrical drying apparatus which he set up under a ventilation hood.

Before the drying was complete, Victor got one of the laboratory timing devices and a battery pack and hooked up a small ignition filament. The next step was the most trying. There was a very small amount of mercury fulminate in the lab. Victor carefully packed it gently into a small plastic container. Carefully, he pushed in the ignition filament and closed the cap.

By this time the nitroglycerin was dry enough to be packed into an empty soda can that he'd retrieved from the wastebasket. When it was about one quarter full, Victor gently lowered the container with the ignition filament into the can until it rested on the contents. He then added the rest of the nitroglycerin and sealed the can with paraffin wax.

Taking everything back to his lab office, Victor started a search for some appropriate container. Glancing into one of the technicians' offices, he spotted a vinyl briefcase. Victor opened the latches and unceremoniously dumped the contents onto the individual's desk. He carried the case back to his office.

With the empty briefcase on his desk, Victor wadded up paper towels to create a cushioned bed. Carefully he laid the soda can, the battery pack, and the timing device on the crumpled paper towels. He then wadded up additional paper towels to fill the briefcase to overflowing. With gentle pressure, he forcibly closed and latched the lid.

From the main part of the lab, Victor got a flashlight. He took out the plans that showed the tunnel network. He studied them carefully, noting that one of the main tunnels ran from the clock tower to the building housing the cafeteria. What was especially encouraging was that close to the clock tower, a tunnel led off in a westerly direction.

Carrying the briefcase as carefully as possible, Victor crossed to the cafeteria building. Access to the basement was in a central stairwell. Victor went down into the basement and opened the heavy door that sealed the tunnel to the clock tower.

Victor shined his flashlight into the tunnel. It was constructed of stone blocks. It reminded Victor of some ancient Egyptian tomb. He could only see about forty feet in front of him since the passageway turned sharply to the left after that. The floor was filled with rubble and trash. Water trickled in the direction of the river, forming black pools at intervals.

Taking a deep breath for courage, Victor stepped into the cold, damp tunnel and pulled the door shut behind him. The only light was the swath cut by his flashlight beam.

Victor set off, determined but cautious. Too much was at stake. He couldn't fail. In the distance he could hear the sound of water running. Within a few minutes he'd passed a half dozen tunnels that branched off the main alley he was in. As he got closer to the river he could feel the falls' throb as much as hear it.

Victor felt something brush by his legs. Forgetting himself, he leaped back in terror, flailing the briefcase precariously. Once he'd calmed himself, he flashed a beam of light behind him. A pair of eyes gleamed in the beam of the ray. Victor shuddered, realizing he was staring at a sewer rat the size of a small cat. Summoning his courage, he pressed on.

But only a few steps past the rat, Victor slid on the floor's suddenly slippery surface. Frantic to maintain his balance, he had the presence of mind to hug the briefcase tightly as he fell against the wall of the tunnel. Victor stayed on his feet; he did not fall to the ground. Luckily, his elbow had slammed into the stone, not the case. If the briefcase had hit instead, or if he had fallen, it would undoubtedly have detonated.

A second time, Victor began to make his nerve-racking way through the subterranean obstacle course. Finally, he came to the path that left the main tunnel at the proper angle; it had to be the tunnel that went west. With some confidence, Victor followed this tunnel until it entered the basement of the edifice immediately upriver from the clock tower building.

Victor turned his flashlight off after noting where the stairs were located. He could not take the risk of the glow from the beam being seen by someone in the clock tower.

The next forty feet were the worst of all. Victor moved a step at a time, advancing first his right foot, then bringing up his left. He skirted the debris as best he could, ever fearful of a fall.

Finally, he got to the stairs and started up. Once he reached the first floor, he went to the nearest window and glanced at the clock tower building. A sliver of moon had risen in the eastern sky almost directly in line with the Big Ben replica. Victor surveyed the darkened hulk for ten minutes, but saw no one.

He then looked toward the river. Lowering his gaze, he saw his goal. About forty feet from where he stood was the point where the old main sluice left the river, running toward the clock tower and into its tunnel.

After one last look at the clock tower building to make sure there were no guards about, Victor left the building he was in and hurried over to the sluice. He kept as low to the ground as possible, knowing he was at his most vulnerable.

When he got to the sluice he quickly went to the steep steps just behind the sluice gates. With no hesitation, he made his way down the steps, hugging the granite wall to stay as out of sight as possible. Reaching the floor, he was pleased to see that he could only make out a portion of the clock tower. That meant no one at the ground level could spot him.

Wasting no time, Victor walked directly to the two rusted metal gates that held back the water in the millpond. There was a slight amount of leakage; a small stream dribbled along the floor of the sluice. Otherwise, the old gates were watertight.

Bending down, Victor carefully laid the briefcase on the floor of the sluice. With equal care, he unsnapped the latches and raised the lid. The apparatus had survived the trip. Now he just had to set it to blow.

Too little time would be a disaster; but so would too much. Surprise was his main advantage. But there was no good way to guess how much time he'd need for his next task. Finally, and a bit arbitrarily, he settled on thirty minutes. As gently as possible, Victor opened the face of the laboratory timing device. On his hands and knees, he shielded the flashlight with his body and turned it on. In the spare light, he moved the minute hand of the timer.

Victor killed the light and carefully closed the briefcase. Taking a deep breath, he carried it to the sluice gate and wedged it between the gate on the left and the steel rod that supported it. A single rusty bolt kept the steel rod in place. Victor felt that this bolt was the Achilles' heel of the mechanism; he pushed the briefcase as close to the bolt as he could. Then he headed up the steep granite steps.

Peering over the lip of the sluice, Victor looked for signs of life in the darkened clock tower building, but all was quiet. Keeping his head down low, he scampered back to the nearby building and descended into the tunnel system. He groped back to the cafeteria, already wishing he had given himself more than thirty minutes.

Once out in the open air, Victor ran toward the river, slowing as the clock tower came into view. In case someone was on watch, he wanted to appear calm in his approach, not anxious or stealthy.

Completely winded, Victor arrived at the front steps. He hesitated for a moment to catch his breath, but a glance at his watch horrified him. He only had sixteen minutes left. "My God," he whispered as he rushed inside.

Victor ran to the trapdoor and rapped on it three times. When no one came to open it, he rapped again with more force. Still no answer. Bending down, he felt around the floor for the metal rod he'd used on his last nighttime visit, but before he could find it, the trapdoor opened and light flooded up from below. One of Martinez's people was there.

Victor hopped down the stairs.

"Where's VJ?" he asked, trying to sound as calm as possible.

The guard pointed to the gestation room. Victor started in that direction, but VJ pushed the door open before he got there.

"Father?" VJ said with surprise. "I didn't expect you until tomorrow."

"Couldn't stay away," Victor said with a laugh. "I finished up what I had to get done. Now it's your mother's turn. She has some patients who need her. She hasn't made her hospital rounds."

Victor's eyes wandered away from VJ and once again surveyed the room. What he needed to decide was where he should be at zero hour. He thought he'd have to be as close to the stairs as possible. The instrument that was the closest was the giant gas chromatography unit, and Victor decided that he'd allow it to occupy his attention when the time came.

Directly in the middle of the wall facing the river was the opening of the sluice with its makeshift hatch constructed of rough-hewn timbers. Victor made a mental calculation of the force that would hit that door when the sluice gate blew and the water rushed in. The preceding concussion wave would be like an explosion, and combined with the force of the water, it could loosen the foundation and topple the whole building. Victor figured there would be an approximate twenty-second delay from the explosion to the moment the tsunami struck.

"I think it might be too soon to let Marsha leave," VJ said. "And it would be awkward for Jorge to be constantly with her." VJ paused as his sharp eyes regarded his father. "Where is Jorge?"

"Topside," Victor said with a shiver of fear. VJ missed nothing. "He saw me down and stayed up there to smoke."

VJ glanced over at the two guards, who were reading magazines. "Juan! Go up and tell Jorge to come down here."

Victor swallowed uneasily. His throat was parched. "Marsha will not be a problem. I guarantee it."

"She hasn't changed her opinion," VJ said. "I've had Mary Millman try talking with her, but her obstinate moralistic stance is unshakable. I'm afraid she'll make trouble."

Victor sneaked a look at his watch. Nine minutes! He should have allowed himself more time. "But Marsha is a realist," he blurted. "She's stubborn. That's nothing new to either of us. And, you'll have me. She wouldn't try anything knowing you had me here. Besides, she wouldn't know what to do even if she was tempted to do something."

"You're nervous," VJ said.

"Of course I'm nervous," Victor snapped. "Anybody would be nervous under the circumstances." He tried to smile and appear more at ease. "Mainly, I'm excited—about your accomplishments. I'd like to see that list of growth factors for the artificial womb tonight."

"I'd be delighted to show it to you," VJ admitted.

Victor walked over and opened the door to the living quarters. "Well, that's encouraging," he said, looking at VJ. "You don't feel you have to lock her in anymore. I'd say that was progress."

VJ rolled his eyes.

Victor hurriedly went into the smaller room where Marsha and Mary were sitting.

"Victor, look who's here," Marsha said, gesturing toward Mary.

"We've already met," Victor said, nodding at Mary.

VJ was standing in the doorway with a grin on his face.

"Not every kid has three legitimate biological parents," Victor said, attempting to ease the tension. He glanced at his watch: only six minutes to go.

"Mary has told me some interesting things about the new lab," Marsha said with subtle sarcasm that only Victor could appreciate.

"Wonderful," said Victor, "That's wonderful. But, Marsha, it's your turn to leave. You have dozens of patients who are desperate for your attention. Jean is frantic. She's called me three times. Now that I've handled my pressing problems, it's your turn to go."

Marsha eyed VJ, then looked at Victor. "I thought that you were going to take care of things," she said with irritation. "Valerie Maddox can handle any emergencies. I think it's more important for you to do what you have to do."

Victor had to get her out of there. Why wouldn't she just leave? Did she really not trust him? Did she really think he was just going to let this go on? Sadly, Victor realized that for the past few years he hadn't given her much reason to expect better from him. Yet a solution was coming, and it was only a few frightening moments away.

"Marsha, I want you to go do your hospital rounds. Now!"

But Marsha wouldn't budge.

"I think she likes it here!" VJ joked. Then one of the security men called him from the main part of the lab and he left.

Half-crazed with mounting anxiety, Victor leaned over to Marsha and, forgetting Mary, hissed: "You have to get out of here this instant. Trust me."

Marsha looked in his eyes. Victor nodded. "Please!" he moaned. "Get out of here!"

"Is something going to happen?" Marsha asked him.

"Yes, for chrissake!" Victor forcibly whispered.

"What's going to happen?" Mary said nervously, looking back and forth between the Franks.

"What about you?" Marsha questioned, ignoring Mary.

"Don't worry about me," Victor snapped.

"You're not going to do something foolish?" Marsha asked.

Victor slapped his hands over his eyes. The tension was becoming unbearable. His watch said less than three minutes.

VJ reappeared at the doorway. "Jorge is not upstairs," he said to Victor.

Mary turned to VJ. "Something is going to happen!" she cried.

"What?" VJ demanded.

"He's doing something," Mary said anxiously. "He's got something planned."

Victor looked at his watch: two minutes.

VJ called over his shoulder for Security, then grabbed Victor's arm. Shaking him, he demanded, "What have you done?"

Victor lost control. The tension was too much and fear overflowed into emotion, bringing a sudden gush of tears. For a moment he couldn't talk. He knew that he had utterly failed. He'd not been up to the challenge.

"What have you done?" VJ repeated as he shouted into Victor's face, shaking him again. Victor did not resist.

"We all have to get out of the lab," Victor managed through his tears.

"Why?" VJ questioned.

"Because the sluice is going to open," Victor wailed.

There was a pause as VJ's mind processed this sudden information.

"When?" VJ demanded, shaking his father again.

Victor looked at his watch. There was less than a minute. "Now!" he said.

VJ's eyes blazed at his father. "I counted on you," he said with burning hatred. "I thought you were a true scientist. Well, now you are history."

Victor leaped up, knocking VJ to the side, where he tripped on the leg of a chair. Victor grabbed Marsha's wrist and yanked her to her feet. He ran her through the living quarters and out into the main lab.

VJ had regained his feet instantly and followed his parents, screaming for the security men to stop them.

From their bench it was easy for the two security men to catch Victor, grabbing him by both arms. Victor managed to give Marsha a push up the stairs. She ran partway up, then turned back to the room.

"Go!" Victor shouted at her. Then, to the two guards he urgently said, "This whole lab is about to disintegrate in seconds. Trust me."

Looking at Victor's face, the guards believed him. They let go of him and fled up the stairs, passing Marsha.

"Wait!" VJ cried from the middle of the lab floor. But the stampede had started. Even Mary brushed by him in her haste to get to the stairs.

Marsha got out, with Mary following on her heels.

VJ's eyes blazed at his father. "I counted on you," he raged. "I trusted you. I thought you were a man of science. I wanted to be like you. Guards!" he shouted. "Guards!" But the guards had fled along with the women.

VJ whirled around, looking at the main lab. Then he looked over at the gestational room.

Just then, the muffled roar of an explosion rocked the entire basement. A sound like thunder began to build and vibrate the room. VJ sensed what was coming and started to run for the stairs, but Victor reached out and grabbed him.

"What are you doing?" VJ cried. "Let me go. We've got to get out of here."

"No," Victor said over the din. "No, we don't."

VJ struggled, but Victor's hold was firm. Wryly, he realized for all his son's vast mental powers, he still had the body—and strength—of a ten-year-old.

VJ squirmed and tried to kick, but Victor hooked his free hand behind VJ's knees and swept the boy off his feet.

"Help!" VJ cried. "Security!" he cried, but his voice was lost in a low rumbling noise that steadily increased, rattling the laboratory glassware. It was like the beginnings of an earthquake.

Victor stepped over to the crude door covering the opening of the sluice tunnel. He stopped five feet from it. He looked down into his son's unblinking ice-blue eyes which stared back defiantly.

"I'm sorry, VJ." But the apology was not for what he was doing that minute. For that he was not sorry. But Victor felt he owed his son an apology for the experiment he'd carried out in a lab a little over ten years ago. The experiment that had yielded his brilliant but conscienceless son. "Good-bye, Isaac."

At that moment, one hundred tons of incompressible water burst through the sluice opening. The old paddle wheel in the center of the room turned madly, cranking the old rusted gears and rods for the first time in years and, for a brief moment, the giant clock in the top of the tower chimed haphazardly. But the undirected and uncontrolled water quickly pulverized everything in its path, undermining even the granite foundation blocks within minutes. Several of the larger blocks shifted, and the beams supporting the first floor began to fall through to the basement. Ten minutes after the explosion, the clock tower itself began to wobble and then, seemingly in slow motion, it crumbled. In the end, all that was left of the building and secret basement lab was a soggy mass of rubble.

EPILOGUE

ONE YEAR LATER

"You have one more patient," Jean said, poking her head through the door, "then you're free."

"It's an add-on?" Marsha asked, slightly perturbed. She had planned on being free by four. With another patient she wouldn't be out until five. Under normal circumstances she wouldn't have cared, but today she was supposed to meet Joe Arnold, David's old history teacher, at six o'clock. He was taking her to the pet shop in the mall to pick up that golden retriever puppy he'd persuaded her to get. "It'll do you good," he told her. "Pet therapy. I'm telling you, dogs could put you psychiatrists out of business."

A few days after he'd read of the tragedy in the papers, he'd called Marsha to say how sorry he was and that he'd always regretted not contacting her to express his condolences after David's death. Gradually, the two were becoming friends. Joe seemed determined to break her willful isolation.

"The woman was insistent," Jean said. "If I didn't squeeze her in today, we couldn't have seen her for a week. She says it's an emergency."

"Emergency!" Marsha grumbled. True psychiatric emergencies were luckily few and far between. "Okay," she said with a sigh.

"You're a dear," Jean said. She pulled the door shut.

Marsha went around her desk and sat down. She dictated her last session. When she was through, she whirled her chair around and gazed out the large picture window at the scenic landscape. Spring was coming. The grass had become a more vibrant green than its pale winter hue. The crocuses would be up soon. A few buds were already on the trees.

Marsha took a deep breath. She'd come a long way. It was just a little over a year now since that fateful night when she'd lost her husband and second son in what had been deemed a freak accident. The newspapers had even carried a picture of the rusty bolt that had apparently given way on an old sluice gate when the Merrimack had been at its spring thaw heights. Marsha had never tried to contradict the story, preferring the nightmare to end with a seemingly accidental tragedy. It was so much simpler than the truth.

Dealing with her grief had been exceedingly difficult. She'd sold the big house that she and Victor had shared, as well as her stock in Chimera. With some of the profits from these sales, she had bought herself a charming house on an ocean inlet in Ipswich. It was only a short walk to the beach with its glorious sand dunes. She'd spent many a weekend alone on the beach in pensive seclusion with no sounds to trouble her save the waves and an occasional squawk of a sea gull. Marsha had found solace in nature ever since she was a little girl.

Neither Victor's nor VJ's body had been recovered. Evidently the tremendous force of the rushing water had washed them God knows where. But the fact there were no bodies made Marsha's adjustment all the more difficult, though not for the reasons most psychiatrists would suspect. Jean had gently suggested to Marsha that she go in for some therapy herself, but Marsha resisted this encouragement. How could she explain that by not finding their remains, she was left with the uncomfortable sense that the horrid episode was not over yet. No remains of the four fetuses had been found either, not that anyone had known to look for them. But, for months after, Marsha had had disturbing nightmares in which she would come across a finger or a limb on the beach where she walked.

Marsha's biggest savior had been her work. After the initial shock and grief had abated, she'd really thrown herself into it, even volunteering for extra hours in various community organizations. And Valerie Maddox had also been of tremendous help, often staying with Marsha for weekends at Marsha's new beach house. Marsha knew she was indebted to the woman.

714

Marsha swung back to her desk. It was just about four o'clock. Time to see the last patient and then get to the pet store. Marsha buzzed Jean to indicate she was ready. Getting to her feet, she went to the door. Taking the new chart Jean handed her, Marsha caught sight of a woman who was about forty-five years old. She smiled at Marsha and Marsha smiled back. Marsha gestured for the woman to come into her office.

Turning around, Marsha left the door ajar and walked over to the chair she always used for her sessions. Next to it was a small table with a box of tissues for patients who couldn't contain their emotions. Two other chairs faced hers.

Hearing the woman enter the office, Marsha turned to greet her. The woman wasn't alone. A thin girl in her teens who looked sallow and drawn followed in behind her. The girl's sandy blond hair was stringy and badly in need of a wash. In her arms was a blond baby who looked to be about eighteen months old. The baby was clutching a magazine.

Marsha wondered who the patient was. Whichever one it was, she'd have to insist the other leave. For the moment, all she said was, "Please sit down." Marsha decided to let them present their reasons for coming. Over the years, she'd found that this technique yielded more information than any question-and-answer session could.

The woman held the child while the girl sat down in one of the chairs facing Marsha, then settled him in the girl's lap. He seemed quite preoccupied with the magazine's illustrations. Marsha casually wondered why they'd brought the child along. Surely it couldn't be that difficult to get a baby-sitter.

Marsha felt that the young girl was not in the best physical health. Her frail frame and extremely pale complexion indicated depression if not malnutrition.

"I'm Josephine Steinburger and this is my daughter, Judith," the woman began. "Thank you for seeing us. We're pretty desperate."

Marsha nodded encouragingly.

Mrs. Steinburger leaned forward confidentially, but spoke loudly enough for Judith to hear. "My daughter here is not too swift, if you know what I mean. She's been in a lot of trouble for a long time. Drugs, running away from home, fighting with her brother, no-good friends, those kinds of things."

Marsha nodded again. She looked at the daughter to see how she responded to this criticism, but the girl only stared blankly ahead.

"These kids are into everything these days," Josephine continued. "You know, sex and all that. What a difference when I was young. I didn't know what sex was until I was too old to enjoy it, you know what I mean?''

Marsha nodded again. She hoped the daughter would participate, but she remained silent. Marsha wondered if she might be on drugs right then.

"Anyway," Josephine continued, "Judith here tells me she never had sex, so obviously I was surprised when she delivered this little bundle of joy about a year and a half ago." She laughed sarcastically.

Marsha wasn't surprised. Of all the defense mechanisms, denial was the most common. A lot of teenagers initially tried to deny sexual contact even when the evidence was overwhelming.

"Judith says that the father was a young boy who gave her money to put his little tube in her," Josephine said, rolling her eyes for Marsha's benefit. "I've heard it called a lot of things but never a little tube. Anyway—"

Marsha rarely interrupted the people who came to see her, but in this case, the girl in question wasn't getting a word in. "Perhaps it would be better if the patient told me her story in her own words."

"What do you mean, her words?" Josephine asked, her brow furrowing in confusion.

"Exactly what I said," Marsha said. "I think the patient should tell the story, or at least participate."

Josephine laughed heartily, then got herself under control. "Sorry, it struck a funny bone. Judith is fine. She's even gotten a little more responsible now that she's a mother. It's the kid who's messed up. He's the patient."

"Oh, of course," said Marsha, somewhat baffled. She'd treated children before, but never so young.

"The kid is a terror," Josephine went on. "We can't control him."

Marsha had to get her to be more specific. Plenty of parents could call their toddlers terrors. She needed more specific symptoms. "In what way is he a problem?" she asked.

"Ah!" Josephine intoned. "You name it, he does it. I'm telling you, he's enough to drive you to drink." She turned to the child. "Look at the lady, Jason."

But Jason was absorbed in his magazine.

"Jason!" Josephine called. She reached across and yanked the magazine out of the infant's hands and tossed it on Marsha's desk. It was then that Marsha noticed it was the latest issue of the *Journal of Cell Biology*.

"The kid can already read better than his mother. Now he's asking for a chemistry set."

Marsha felt a jolt of fear as it grabbed her by the throat. Slowly she raised her eyes.

"Frankly, I'm afraid to get the kid a chemistry set at age one and a half," Josephine continued. "It ain't normal. He'll probably blow the whole house up."

Marsha looked at the boy in Judith's lap. The child returned her stare with his own piercing, ice-blue eyes. There was an air of intelligence about him that far outstripped his cherubic baby face. Marsha was taken back in time. This boy was the spitting image of VJ at the same age.

Marsha knew instantly what was before her: the final zygote. The one VJ said he'd wasted on the implantation study. A child created from her own sixth ovum.

Marsha couldn't move. A small cry escaped her as she realized the chilling truth: the nightmare wasn't over.

Josephine got to her feet and stepped over to Marsha. "Dr. Frank?" she asked with some alarm. "Are you all right?"

"I . . . I'm fine," Marsha said feebly. "I'm sorry. Really, I'm okay." She couldn't take her eyes off the child.

"So like I was saying," continued Josephine, "this kid's beyond all of us. Why, just the other day—"

Marsha cut her off. Doing her best to keep a quaver out of her voice, she said, "Mrs. Steinburger, we'll have to set up an appointment for Jason himself. I really think it would be best if I saw him privately. But it has to be another day."

"Well, whatever," sighed Josephine. "You're the doctor. You're the one to know. I suppose we can wait a few days. I just hope you can help us."

Once they had gone, Marsha closed the door behind them and leaned heavily against it. She sighed and said aloud, "I hope so too."

She knew she had to do something about this child, this prodigy whose villainy might match or even surpass her son's. But what to do?

She picked up the phone to call Joe Arnold to say she was running a little late. Just hearing his voice on the line helped calm her down.

"Well, I'm glad you're not trying to cancel on me, 'cause I'm not letting you off the hook." He laughed warmly. "I thought we might eat in tonight. Can't leave a dog alone his first night home. I hope

717

you're up to braving my cooking. I make a mean chili. I'm working on it right now.''

Marsha hoped she was up to braving quite a lot of things, starting with the truth. And of the people she felt closest to—Valerie, Joe, Jean—Joe might be the one to confide in, the one she could count on the most. ''Chili sounds great,'' she told him. ''And I'd just as soon eat in.'' It was on the tip of her tongue to tell him about Jason, but it would keep. She didn't want to say anything over the phone.

''Terrific. I was beginning to think I'd have to sign up as a patient to get to see you alone. Meet you at the pet shop at seven? I think they're open until eight.''

''Seven will be fine. And, Joe . . . thanks.''

She hung up the phone and got her coat.

Marsha drove to the mall, feeling better already just knowing she'd soon be telling someone the true story behind Victor's and VJ's deaths. She'd bottled the whole thing up for so long. It would be a relief to finally get it off her chest. She felt all the luckier for having Joe to talk to. Ever since he'd come into her life, he'd been a real godsend.

She drove into the mall parking lot and picked a spot near the entrance closest to the pet shop and turned the engine off. Gripping the steering wheel, she broke into soft sobs. Somehow, she would have to face this last demon-child, and with Joe's help, end forever the nightmare her husband had begun.